D1267897

S-4-94

FIC

——— A WORLD FOR JULIUS ———

The Texas Pan American Series

A WORLD
FOR JULIUS

A NOVEL

Alfredo Bryce Echenique

Translated from the Spanish by Dick Gerdes

UNIVERSITY OF TEXAS PRESS
AUSTIN

First edition, 1992

Requests for permission to reproduce material from this work should
be sent to Permissions, University of Texas Press, Box 7819, Austin,
TX 78713-7819.

∞ The paper used in this publication meets the minimum
requirements for American National Standard for Information
Sciences—Permanence of Paper for Printed Library Materials,
ANSI Z39.48-1984.

The Texas Pan American Series is published with the assistance of a
revolving publication fund established by the Pan American Sulphur
Company.

Library of Congress Cataloging-in-Publication Data

Bryce Echenique, Alfredo, 1939–
  [Mundo para Julius. English]
  A world for Julius : a novel / Alfredo Bryce Echenique ; translated
from the Spanish by Dick Gerdes. — 1st ed.
    p. cm. — (The Texas Pan American series)
  Translation of: Un mundo para Julius.
  ISBN 0-292-79046-5 (cloth : alk. paper). — ISBN 0-292-79071-6
(paper : alk. paper)
  I. Title. II. Series.
PQ8498.12.R94M813 1992
863—dc20   91-45310

For Maggie

RESOURCE CENTER OF THE AMERICAS
317 SEVENTEENTH AVENUE SE
MINNEAPOLIS, MN 55414-2077
612-627-9445

CONTENTS

TRANSLATOR'S PREFACE

WITH THE PUBLICATION of *Aunt Julia and the Scriptwriter* in English in 1982 and later with his presidential campaign in 1989, Mario Vargas Llosa has been the Peruvian writer most visible to the North American reading public. Peru's past and present literary tradition, of course, includes many accomplished writers. Among contemporary Peruvian novelists, Alfredo Bryce Echenique is the best known in the Hispanic world after Vargas Llosa.

The writing of *Un mundo para Julius* (*A World for Julius*) in 1969, and its subsequent publication in 1970, coincided with the 1969 coup d'etat that took credit for expropriating vast landholdings belonging to Peru's oligarchy; not surprisingly, here literature and history fuse to symbolize the destruction of Peru's long-established ruling classes. Despite this first, political reading of the novel, making it very much a novel of its time, *A World for Julius* won the Peruvian Premio Nacional de Literatura in 1972 and continues to generate lasting interest for contemporary readers. The novel is not only an engagingly corrosive portrayal of the pretentious, morally blind Peruvian oligarchy and its transition to the dominant nouveau riche class subsidized by an influx of North American capitalism in the 1950s; it is also an early postmodern urban novel in which the *bildungsroman* motif and its curious, questioning, sentimental protagonist Julius bring together elements of the drama of lost innocence, black comedy of manners, playful parody, and social satire.

Bryce Echenique's first novel, *A World for Julius* recreates the life of a child protagonist in upper-class Lima in the 1940s and 1950s whose discovery of the real world of Peru's poor through the family's servants ironically and humorously subverts the mythic world of Lima's well-to-do class. The novel does not pretend to provide an exact mirror image of classes in conflict, but a strictly literary image of conflict. The probable reality behind the novel, the author believes, resides in the tremendous amount of care and concern he had for the servants in his parents' house. The novel, hence, while not intending to reflect Peru and its problems directly, does become a microcosm reflecting the rich and the poor in Peru, which is handily accomplished by liberating the conventional technique of point of view to include a virtual kaleidoscope of narrative perspectives that weaves dozens of situations and characters into a singular fabric that could be called Peruvian society. In a nutshell, it is a felicitous blend of humor and sadness, criticism and nostalgia.

In Peru, *A World for Julius* has become an integral part of the nation's literary canon, and in other countries it has achieved prominence as well. Translated into many foreign languages other than English, it won first prize for the best foreign novel in translation in France in 1974. As we begin to review the importance of the so-called boom period of the sixties—the fictional works of Carlos Fuentes, Mario Vargas Llosa, Julio Cortázar, and Gabriel García Márquez, among others—this novel ranks among the first works to emphasize the art of storytelling in which the notably oral tone of the novel handily juxtaposes invention and representation, hyperbole and reality, multiple points of view and the free indirect style, in addition to interior monologue. The incorporation of these elements into the novel does not place *A World for Julius* among those in which the allusion to societal fragmentation is the goal, as in the narrative worlds of Vargas Llosa's and Fuentes' early novels; it creates instead an obvious hierarchy of class and ethnic differences in Peru.

Alfredo Marcelo Bryce Echenique was born into a distinguished aristocratic family in Lima, Peru, in 1939. He seemed destined to become a writer: his mother, who admired French culture, had baptized him with the second name Marcelo in honor of Marcel Proust. Much of *A World for Julius* is autobiographical, for references to Julius' childhood and schooling are similar to the author's experiences at his grandfather's mansion or at the grade school run by North American nuns and priests in Lima. In 1964 Bryce Echenique graduated from law school, but he also received a degree in literature, having written a thesis on the function of dialogue in the works of Ernest Hemingway. That same year he boarded a steamer for Europe in order to study and write. Since then Bryce Echenique has traveled extensively and written three volumes of short stories, six novels, and two books of essays. Today he lives in Spain and writes extensively for newspapers and magazines throughout the Hispanic world.

A note on the translation: this Peruvian writer uses numerous English words and phrases (e.g., "darling") in the Spanish text and, in many instances, the English references are italicized; hence, italicized text in the original—English words, words emphasized in Spanish, etc.— remains italicized in the translation. The overall effect of English in the original text is to establish a social milieu that documents not only the presence of genteel aristocratic families with British backgrounds from nineteenth-century Peru but also the influence of North American capitalism in the 1950s. The false imitation of foreign elements appears, for example, in the proper name Cynthia which in the Spanish version is spelled Cinthia (and remains that way in the translation). In general, proper names remain in Spanish, and the seemingly indiscriminate use by the narrator of certain names for the same character (i.e., Santiago and Santiaguito, the latter a diminutive of endearment) may be based on formal and less formal perspectives among certain characters. Nevertheless, several names—especially nicknames—are translated into English, for they are almost always humorous and ironical, such as La Selvática (Jungle Woman), La Zanahoria (Carrottop), Pericote (Mouse), and Gargajo (Goober Hocker). Other words, particularly *Señor* and *Señora,* are kept in the English version because they connote not only a fuller sense of class difference between the dominant classes and their servants, but also a stronger sense of respect on different social levels that goes far beyond the simple courtesy we might find in a literal translation to *Mr.* or *Mrs.* in English. In Peru, the word *Chola/Cholo* refers to a mestizo Indian.

The heavy use of regionalisms, Lima slang, and diminutives presented challenges to translation. Narrative style, shifting perspectives and tones, and humor also presented a variety of challenges. Freeform, run-on sentences contain switches in point of view, voice, time, and space within the strings of clauses and phrases that are mainly linked by association, often with not even a comma to announce a transition. At once oral and cinematic, the tone of the novel forces the reader to apprehend much of the text as a sequence of images and multiple, intercalated narrative voices. Bryce Echenique's dark humor often leads to parody of other narrative styles. In Spanish, the reader picks this up quickly and, while the narrative is not easy, it is relatively fluid. In the translation, many of these long strings have been broken up.

I am indebted to the following persons who assisted me to bring about this translation: Michael Doudoroff, Aída Alva Gerdes, and the author himself. In addition, I wish to express special thanks to my good colleague Alfred Rodríguez who spent many long hours with me refining the text. Finally, I wish to thank the University of New Mexico for granting me a sabbatical leave in order to work on the translation.

DICK GERDES
UNIVERSITY OF NEW MEXICO

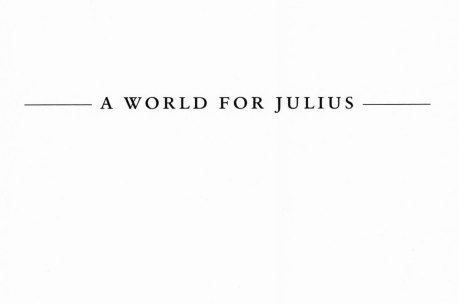
A WORLD FOR JULIUS

What little Johnny doesn't learn, John will never know.

— GERMAN SAYING

*Race of Abel, race of the just, race of the rich, how calmly you speak.
It is good, is it not, to have heaven all to yourself and the police on
your side as well. It is good to think like your father and like your
father's father . . .*

— JEAN ANOUILH, *MÉDÉE, NOUVELLES PIÈCES NOIRES*

THE ORIGINAL MANSION

I

*Remember how during those trips that our mother would take us on
when we were children, and we used to escape from the sleeper cars to
run through the third-class cars. We were fascinated by the men we
used to see sleeping against strangers' shoulders, or simply stretched
out on the floor, in the packed cars. They seemed more real than our
families' friends. At the Toulon station one night, during our return to
Paris from Cannes, we saw the third-class travelers drinking from the
water fountain on the platform; a worker offered you some water
from a soldier's canteen and you gulped it down, looking quickly at
me like the little girl who had just had her first adventure in life . . .
We were born to travel in first class but, in contrast to the rules of the
great ocean liners, it seemed to prohibit us from third class.*
— ROGER VAILLAND, *BEAU MASQUE*

JULIUS WAS BORN in a mansion on Salaverry Avenue, directly across
from the old San Felipe Hippodrome. The mansion had carriage houses,
gardens, a swimming pool, and a small orchard into which two-year-
old Julius would wander and then be found later, his back turned, perhaps bending over a flower. The mansion had servants' quarters that
were like a blemish on the most beautiful face. There was even a carriage that your great-grandfather used, Julius, when he was President of
the Republic, be careful, don't touch! it's covered with cobwebs, and
turning away from his mother, who was lovely, Julius tried to reach the
door handle. The carriage and the servants' quarters always held a
strange fascination for Julius, that fascination of "don't touch, honey,
don't go around there, darling." By then his father had already died.

Julius was a year and a half old at the time. For some months he just
walked about the mansion, wandering off by himself whenever possible.

Secretly he would head for the servants' quarters of the mansion that, as we've said, were like a blemish on a most beautiful face, a pity, really, but he still did not dare to go there. What is certain is that when his father was dying of cancer, everything in Versailles revolved around the dying man's bedroom: only his children were not supposed to see him. Julius was an exception because he was too young to comprehend fear but young enough to appear just when least expected, wearing silk pajamas, turning his back to the drowsy nurse and watching his father die, that is, he watched how an elegant, rich, handsome man dies. And Julius has never forgotten that night—three o'clock in the morning, a lit candle in offering to Santa Rosa, the nurse knitting to ward off sleep—when his father opened an eye and said to him poor thing, and by the time the nurse ran out to call for his mother, who was lovely and cried every night in an adjoining bedroom—if anything, to get a bit of rest—it was all over.

Daddy died when the last of Julius' siblings, who were always asking when he would return from his trip, stopped asking; when Mommy stopped crying and went out one night; when the visitors, who had entered quietly and walked straight to the darkest room of the mansion (the architect had thought of everything), stopped coming; when the servants recovered their normal tone of voice; and when someone turned on the radio one day, Daddy had died.

No one could keep Julius from practically living in the carriage that had belonged to his great-grandfather/president. He would spend the entire day in it, sitting on the worn blue velvet, once gold-trimmed seats, shooting at the butlers and maids who always tumbled down dead by the carriage, soiling their smocks that the Señora had ordered them to buy in pairs so that they would not appear worn when they fell dead each time Julius took to riddling them with bullets from the carriage. No one prevented him from spending all day long in the carriage, but when it would get dark at about six o'clock, a young maid would come looking for him, one that his mother, who was lovely, called the beautiful Chola, probably a descendant of some noble Indian, an Inca for all we know.

The Chola, who could well have been a descendant of an Inca, would lift Julius from the carriage, press him firmly against her probably marvelous breasts beneath her uniform, and not let go until they reached the bathroom in the mansion, the one that was reserved for the younger children and now belonged exclusively to Julius. Often the Chola stumbled over the butlers or the gardener who lay dead around the carriage so that Julius, Jesse James, or Gary Cooper, depending on the occasion, could depart happily for his bath.

And there in the bathroom, two years after his father's death, his mother had begun to say good-bye. She always found him with his back to her, standing naked in front of the tub, pee pee exposed, but she never saw it, as he contemplated the rising tide in that enormous, porcelainlike, baby-blue tub, which was full of swans, geese, and ducks. His mother would call him darling, but he never turned around, so she would kiss him on the nape of his neck and leave very lovely, while the beautiful Chola assumed the most uncomfortable postures in order to stick her elbow in the water and test the temperature without falling in what could have been a swimming pool in Beverly Hills.

And about six-thirty every afternoon, the beautiful Chola took hold of Julius by his underarms, raised him up and eased him little by little into the water. Seeming to genuflect, the swans, geese, and ducks bobbed up and down happily in the warm, clean water. He took them by the neck and gently pushed them along and away from his body, while the beautiful Chola, armed with soapy washcloths and perfumed baby soap, began to scrub gently—ever so gently and lovingly—his chest, shoulders, back, arms, and legs. Julius looked up smiling at her, always asking the same questions, such as: "And where are you from?" and he listened attentively as she would tell him about Puquio, a village of mud houses near Nasca, on the way up to the mountains. She would tell him stories about the mayor or sometimes about medicine men, but she always laughed as if she no longer believed in those things; besides, it had been a long time since she had been up there. Julius looked at her attentively and waited for her to finish talking so he could ask another question, and another, and another. And it was like that every afternoon while his two brothers and one sister finished their homework downstairs and got ready for dinner.

Those days, his brothers and sister already ate in the formal dining room of the mansion, which was an immense room replete with mirrors where the beautiful Chola would carry Julius, first, to give his father a sleepy kiss and then, after a long walk to the other end of the table, the last little kiss of the day to his mother, who always smelled heavenly. But that was when he was just a few months old, not now when he would go to the main dining room by himself and spend time contemplating a huge silver tea service, looking like a cathedral dome on an immense china cabinet that his great-grandfather/president had acquired in Brussels. Without luck, Julius tried over and over to reach that enticing polished teapot. One day, though, he did seize it; but he couldn't manage to stay on his tippy-toes nor let go of it in time, whereupon the teapot came crashing down with a big noise, denting its lovely shape and crushing his foot; it was, simply put, a complete catastrophe. From that point forward Julius never again wanted to have anything to do with silver tea sets in formal dining rooms in mansions. Along with the tea service and mirrors, the dining room had glass-paneled cabinets, Persian rugs, porcelain china, and the tea set that President Sánchez Cerro gave us the week before he was assassinated. That's where his brother and sister ate now.

Only Julius ate in the children's dining room, which was now referred to as Julius' dining room. It was like Disneyland: the four walls were covered with Donald Duck, Little Red Riding Hood, Mickey Mouse, Tarzan, Cheetah, Jane, properly dressed, naturally, Superman, probably beating up Dracula, Popeye, and a very, very skinny Olive Oil. The backs of the chairs were rabbits laughing raucously, the legs were carrots, and the tabletop where Julius ate was shouldered by four little Indians who were not related to the Indians that the beautiful Chola from Puquio would tell him about while she bathed him in Beverly Hills. Oh! and besides, there was a swing with a tiny seat when it was time for the bit about eat your soup little Julius (at times, even more endearingly, cutie pie Julie), a little spoonful for your Mommy, another for little Cindy, another for your brother Bobby and so on, but never one for your Daddy because he had died of cancer. Sometimes his mother would pass by the room while they swung Julius and fed his soup to him, and she would hear those horrendous nicknames the servants used that were ruining her children's real names. "Really, I don't know why we ever gave them such attractive names," she said. "To hear them say Cindy instead of Cinthia, Julito instead of Julius, what a crime!" she said to someone on the telephone, though Julius hardly ever heard her because, what with finishing his soup and that swinging motion embracing him like a somniferous plant, he would get drowsy, ready for the beautiful Chola to pick him up and carry him off to bed.

But now, unlike when his brothers and sister ate in Disneyland, all the servants hovered over Julius while he ate, even Nilda, alias Jungle Woman, who was also the cook, smelled of garlic, and terrorized everyone with a meat cleaver in her domain, that is, the pantry and the kitchen. She was always in their company too, but she never dared touch him. It was he who would have liked to have touched her, but then his mother's words were stronger than the smell of garlic. For Julius everything that smelled bad smelled like garlic, the way Nilda smelled. Since he didn't understand very well what garlic was, he asked Nilda about it one evening, and she began to cry. Julius remembers that day: it was the first saddest day of his life.

Julius was fascinated with Nilda's stories about the jungle and especially about the word Tambopata; the fact that it was located somewhere in Madre de Dios province made it special, something that really excited him, and he wanted to hear more and more stories about naked tribesmen, stories which led to intrigues and secret hatreds that Julius discovered when he was about four years old. Vilma, the name of the beautiful Chola from Puquio, attracted his attention while she bathed him, but then, when she took him down to the dining room, it was Nilda and her stories teeming with pumas and painted jungle savages that captivated his attention. Poor Nilda only tried to keep Julius entertained so that Vilma could feed him. But that's not true, no, because Vilma was consumed with jealousy and looked at Nilda with hatred. Amazingly, Julius quickly became aware of what was going on around him and figured out how to solve the problem astutely: he began to pump the butlers for information, then the laundress and her daughter who also washed clothes, then the gardener Anatolio, and even Carlos, the chauffeur, whenever he didn't have to take the Señora somewhere and happened to be around.

Celso and Daniel were the butlers. Celso would tell the story that he was the nephew of the mayor of the district of Huarocondo, province of Anta, in the department of Cuzco. Besides, he was the treasurer of the Friends of Huarocondo Club, located in the Lince neighborhood of Lima, where butlers, waiters, servants, cooks, and even a bus driver on the Descalzos–San Isidro line would meet. And if that wasn't all, Celso also said he was treasurer of the club, he was in charge of the cashbox and, moreover, since the lock on the club door was old, he kept the money upstairs in his room. Julius' imagination left him dumbfounded. He had forgotten all about Vilma and Nilda. "Show me the cashbox! Show me the cashbox!" he begged. And there, in Disneyland, the servants would delight in wondering why Julius, the owner of a big, plump piggy bank, which he found uninteresting, would insist on seeing, touching, and opening the cashbox belonging to the Friends of Huarocondo Club. That evening, Julius decided he would sneak out and enter, once and for all, the distant and mysterious servants' quarters that now also concealed a treasure. He would go there tomorrow, not tonight, no, because having polished off his soup, he felt the sway of the swing becoming more and more comfortable, the tiny flying seat would soon reach the moon, but it was the same as always: Vilma would surprise him with her chapped hands, frankly, they were like broomsticks, and carry him off to Fort Apache.

Fort Apache (that's what it said on the door) was Julius' bedroom. There all the known cowboys were affixed life-size to the walls; others, made of cardboard holding plastic pistols that shone like metal, stood in the middle of the room. All the Indians had been wiped out and now Julius could easily go to sleep without causing a ruckus; in fact, the battle was already over in Fort Apache and only Geronimo, for whom Julius showed a liking, perhaps he would become a friend of Burt Lancaster some day, for only Geronimo had survived and continued to stand pensive and proud at the back of the room.

Vilma adored Julius. His unlikely appearance, it must have been those huge floppy ears, had awakened in her an enormous affection and a sense of humor, which was almost as delicate as that of Señora Susan, Julius' mother, whom the servants had been reproaching a little recently because she was going out every evening and wouldn't return until all hours of the night.

She always woke him up, even though Julius would fall asleep long after Vilma thought she had left him fast asleep. In reality, he faked it and as soon as she would leave he would open his eyes wide and usually spend a couple of hours thinking about a thousand and one things. For instance, he would think about how much love Vilma had for him; after a while everything became utterly confusing because Vilma, though she was light-skinned, was also half-Indian and, besides, she never seemed to mind walking among the dead Indians in Fort Apache. In addition, she had never shown any liking for Geronimo, she always looked at Gary Cooper instead; of course, all that occurred in the United States, but Indians, and my bedroom, and Celso, for sure, he's an Indian . . . That's the way it would go until he fell asleep, perhaps waiting for Mommy's footsteps on the stairs to awaken him, there she is, she's coming up. He would listen for her footsteps and adored her, here she comes, now she's by my door, and then continues down the hallway toward her room at the end, where Daddy died, where tomorrow I'll go and wake her, lovely . . . He would fall asleep immediately so that the moment to wake her might come even sooner. He would always wake her up.

For Vilma, it was a temple; for Julius, a paradise; and for Susan, it was her bedroom, that's where she slept, a widow, thirty-three years old, and lovely. Vilma would take him there every day around eleven o'clock in the morning. It was always the same: Susan would be sleeping deeply and they would be reluctant to enter the room. They would just stand there spying on her from the half-open door until suddenly Vilma got up the courage to nudge him forward toward the dream bed replete with canopy, veils, carved bedposts, and tiny sculptured baroque angels high up on the four corners. Julius would turn to look toward the door where Vilma stood motioning for him to touch Susan, then he would extend his hand, pull back the veil and see his mother as she really was, without a trace of makeup, sleeping soundly, stunning, and lovely. Finally he would get up the courage to touch her, his hand barely grazing her arm, and she, who always woke up reliving the last moments of the previous night's outing, would respond with the same smile she gave the man who caressed her hand across the table at some nightclub. Julius would touch her again and Susan would turn over, facing away from him, burying her face in the pillow and trying to go back to sleep. For a second it was as if she had just returned tired from dancing and couldn't wait to fall into bed. "Mommy," he would say, daring to speak forcefully yet in a soft way, scolding her teasingly while being prodded all the while by Vilma who motioned from the door. When Julius touched her for a second time, Susan would start becoming aware of the new day but, having yet to open her eyes, would smile again across the table at the nightclub and turn over once more, sinking deeper into the bed on the other side to where she had turned when she finally went to bed feeling so tired; then, in a fraction of a second, she would sleep through the whole night all over again and then let the echo of "Mommy" coming from Julius initiate the arrival of another day and finally produce a sweet and lazy smile that this time was for Julius.

"Darling," she would yawn, lovely. "Who's getting my breakfast?"

"Me, Señora; I'll tell Celso to bring up the tray."

Susan was fully awake when she saw Vilma standing in the distant doorway. That was the moment when she truly thought that Vilma, even though she was fair-skinned, could be a descendant of a noble Indian: why not from some Inca king? After all, there were fourteen of them.

Julius and Vilma were always present for Susan's breakfast. It began with the arrival of the butler-treasurer who, without the slightest clinking, brought the demitasse of hot black coffee, the crystal glass of orange juice, the little sugar bowl and the dainty silver spoon, the silver coffeepot, just in case the Señora wished to make her coffee stronger, toast, Holland butter, and English marmalade. With the first little sounds of breakfast—knife spreading marmalade, spoon stirring sugar in the coffee, chinking cup returned to little saucer, crunching toast—as soon as these sounds were heard, the bedroom took on a warm and caring atmosphere, as if those first sounds of the morning had awakened infinite possibilities for affection in those who were present. It was hard for Julius to remain still, and Vilma and Celso would smile while Susan ate under their watchful eyes, admired and adored; she seemed to know what feelings her breakfast noises could bring forth. From time to time she raised her head and smiled at them as if to ask: "More little sounds? Do you want to play the game of the little sounds?"

When breakfast was over, Susan would begin making numerous phone calls and Vilma would leave with Julius for the orchard, the swimming pool, or the carriage. On this occasion, Julius didn't wait for Vilma to take him by the hand, for he ran after Celso who was taking out the tray. "Show me the cashbox! Show me the cashbox!" he blurted out while the butler was going down the stairs. At last Julius caught up with him in the kitchen and the butler-treasurer agreed to show it to him as soon as he had finished setting the table; Julius' brothers and sister would soon be arriving hungry from school. "Come back in fifteen minutes," he said.

"Cinthia!" Julius shouted, appearing in the big hall at the foot of the stairs.

As usual, Carlos, the family Negro-in-uniform-with-chauffeur-cap, had just brought them home from school and they were on their way upstairs to greet their mother.

"Dumbo!" Santiago shouted without stopping.

Bobby didn't turn around to look; Cinthia, however, had stopped at the landing.

"Cinthia, Celso is going to show me the cashbox that belongs to the Friends of Gua . . ."

"Huarocondo," she smiled, correcting him. "I'll be down for lunch in a minute."

Whereupon for the first time Julius ventured into the servants' quarters of the mansion. He looked all around: everything was smaller in comparison to the rest of the mansion, more common, plain, and ugly, too; in fact, everything there was smaller. All of a sudden he heard Celso's voice telling him to enter and just then he remembered that he had gone looking for him; but upon seeing the cold, dark-brown metal bed he realized that he was in a bedroom that really smelled bad.

The butler said: "There's the cashbox," pointing toward the little round table.

"Which one?" Julius asked, looking straight at the table.

"That one, of course."

Julius couldn't believe his eyes. "Which one?" he asked again, like when you look at something that's right in front of your nose waiting for someone to point it out to you. Don't you see it? That one! There! Right in front of your nose!

"Are you blind, Julius? Here, take it."

Celso reached over to pick up the cookie tin from the table and handed it to him. Julius grasped it the wrong way, by the lid, which came off spilling a wad of filthy paper money and coins onto his pants and all over the floor.

"What a child! Look what you've done . . . Help me."

". . ."

"Hurry up, I got to serve lunch to your brothers and sister . . ."

"I have to go eat with my sister."

JUST AS VILMA was Julius' nanny, Cinthia had hers too, but she wasn't beautiful, she was just fat and nice: fat, nice, decrepit, old, caring, and gray-haired. Julius would ask her the same question over and over again, and she never knew how to answer it.

"Mommy says that you are one of the only women in that village with gray hair. Why?"

A wonderful person, poor Bertha did everything humanly possible to find out and one day she had the answer:

"Poor people suffer the *mortal index* more than the well-to-do."

Julius didn't understand one iota, but he must have stored the phrase in his subconscious because one day, seven years later, it came back to him perfectly with all its errors as he rode his bicycle near the Polo Club. Then he understood.

But it also had been seven years since Bertha's death. She died on a hot summer afternoon; the swimming pool had been drained. She was waiting for Cinthia to return so she could comb out her hair and freshen her with cologne, always careful to shield her dear little eyes. Thirty years before, Bertha used the same care with little Susan, until she went away to study in England. And she continued when Susan returned, until she married Señor Santiago and they started having children. Cinthia came running, breathless, calling out, Here I am, Mammy Bertha! but the poor thing had just died from high blood pressure that had always plagued her. Before succumbing, she was careful to put the cologne bottle down securely so it wouldn't fall and break; she put it on the ground because it was closer to her and, barely able to hear Cinthia's voice, she placed the comb and brush next to the bottle.

Cinthia insisted on wearing mourning clothes and she kept begging her mother to buy a black tie for Julius.

"No! Not on your life!" Susan, lovely, blurted out. "You're going to ruin my poor Julius! I've had enough already, what with him goofing off all day long in the orchard. Besides, he spends the whole day with the servants. Not on your life!"

Later that day she would leave home smelling heavenly, not returning again until all hours of the night. And so it happened that not surprisingly Julius appeared feeling most uncomfortable with his neck rubbed red but determined not to shed that coarse black tie for anything. Which butler gave it to you? It was a secret that Mommy, as lovely as she was, never discovered. Julius, with his tie hanging down past the tiny fly on his pants, followed Cinthia around the mansion because with Cinthia he was better able to mourn Bertha's death. He found it difficult, however, when she would go to school and he wanted to go off and play in the orchard or in the carriage. One afternoon he removed his tie because he was sweating profusely after knocking off so many Indians. Fortunately, as soon as Julius saw Cinthia arrive home he remembered their mourning and, looking sad, put his tie back on while stepping down from the carriage.

Sadder than ever now because Cinthia had just found the photographs of Daddy's funeral and things began to make sense. Susan, lovely, complained; she couldn't believe how this poor child made her suffer, her fidgety nature tortured her. She's hypersensitive, Baby, she told a friend, she's driving me crazy with her questions . . . And Julius follows her everywhere, he just can't wait until she gets home from school. I told Vilma to keep them apart, but it's useless! Vilma worships the ground Julius walks on . . . everyone in this house does! Moreover, what Susan hadn't said was that Cinthia's obsession with her father's death was driving her crazy: Why, Mommy? Mommy, I escaped from my room and watched from the window. Why did they take Daddy away in a black Cadillac with a bunch of Negroes dressed the same way Daddy would dress when he would go to a banquet at the Government Palace? Why, Mommy? Huh, Mommy? Repeatedly, she would say, I know, Mommy, I saw them take Daddy away, they told me about it too. Back then she wasn't fully aware of what had happened, but now all of a sudden she remembered and compared it to the way they took Bertha away in an ambulance, Mommy, out the back door. At this point, she would stumble over her words and stutter because she couldn't find the right ones or the right accusation to express the evil deed, who's to blame for taking Bertha rapidly out the back door as if no one cared.

Julius was always present when Cinthia assailed her mother with these queries. While she asked questions, he would remain motionless, listening, jumbo ears looking like flying saucers, hands stuck to his sides, heels together, and toes pointing outward like a hapless soldier at attention. These assaults would take place in the bathroom that their father had used. Even his toiletries were still there. Nothing had been touched: lotions, shaving cream, razor blades, even a used bar of soap and his toothbrush were still there. Everything was half used up, forever. "It seems like he's coming back," Cinthia told Julius one day, but they didn't forget about Bertha because of that.

"Julius, clean up that black tie," she said the next day.

"Why?"

"Tomorrow afternoon is Bertha's funeral."

The next day, Cinthia was upset when she came home from school. No sooner did she greet her mother than she said she had no homework and ran off looking for Julius who was playing with Vilma in the orchard. The poor kid hadn't slept a wink all night. He'd been waiting for her all afternoon and, as soon as he saw her arrive, he ran to meet her. Cinthia took him by the hand and he followed along as was his habit those days. Vilma walked behind them. Cinthia took him to her bedroom and she asked him to wait outside the door while she changed out of her school uniform. She came out looking lovely but she was dressed all in black. Except for school, she had been wearing black ever since Bertha's death. Susan no longer tried to stop her. Cinthia took him by the hand to the bathroom and lovingly washed his face. Then she said to him she was going to comb him and moisten his hair. Julius let her sprinkle cologne all over him and fix his hair; he also let her tie the knot of his oversized black tie, despite the fact that Vilma might resent it because she was the one who would tie the knot in her own special way. A few drops of cologne trickled down his neck, how it stung! tears came to his eyes, so much so that Cinthia asked him if he wanted to change ties, but he said no and then felt like the one who blurts out you're welcome when he saw Cinthia smile, relieved, because without the black tie he wouldn't be able to go to the funeral. From the bathroom she led him again by the hand to her bedroom where she began to cry in front of Vilma, now frightened, who followed them around silently as if agreeing with everything, even with what she was witnessing. As she cried, Cinthia opened a drawer and took out a little box. Julius was terrified when he saw it: he knew they were going to bury Bertha, but

11

how? Cinthia opened it and showed them what was inside. Vilma and Julius began to cry when they saw the comb, brush, and cologne bottle that Bertha used every day to fix Cinthia's hair, and a little tuft of Cinthia's hair, *from your very first haircut*. They went downstairs sobbing. Cinthia had closed the box and carried it with both hands against her chest as they went by the pool toward the orchard. Julius was surprised to see that other servants had joined them on the way: Celso, Daniel, Carlos, Arminda, her daughter Dora, and Anatolio. Even Nilda, who at the time wasn't getting along at all with Vilma because of Julius, joined the group. They had been waiting for them to come. Cinthia had organized the whole thing, and it was also her idea for everyone to wear something that was at least dark in color. And there they were, asking her to hurry up, please, child, the Señora might catch us at this. The butlers were especially anxious. The chauffeur Carlos, who was fond of little Cinthia, was in attendance smiling but respectful. At last they found an appropriate spot where Anatolio could dig a hole in which the box with the comb, brush, and last bottle of cologne that Bertha had used would be buried. When the excavation was completed everyone, of course, started to weep. Now Julius' tie burned more than ever and his snot was hanging all the way to the ground. How heartbreaking it was! Surprisingly, though, no one was shocked; instead, they loved her all the more when Cinthia took the little platinum medal from her neck and buried it as well. Cinthia and Julius were first in line as they took turns filing by and throwing a little dirt into the hole, an idea that Nilda had suggested. Then everyone left hurriedly except Carlos, who walked back in a meditative mood for his six o'clock snack.

A week later, Susan tried to scold Cinthia for being so careless, for having lost the medal given to her by . . . , but precisely at that moment she completely forgot who had given it to her and instead remembered that Cinthia had become more demure recently and now, thinking about it a little more, it's been over a week that she hasn't worn a black dress either.

"And you?"

Almost pouncing on Julius, the little guy standing erect with toes pointing ever outward, she felt again the need to treat him like a baby and, instead of telling him that he's already five years old and that he should be starting school soon, gave him a kiss, smelling heavenly.

"Mommy's in a hurry, darling," she said, turning to look at herself in the mirror.

Then she bent down so they could reach her cheek and, as usual when she bent down for any reason, her straight, blond, marvelous hair came streaming down, engulfing them. Cinthia and Julius placed their kisses there, well-guarded, protected, making them last until her return.

———————————————— I I ————————————————

BERTHA'S FUNERAL BROUGHT Cinthia and Julius together more than ever. Sharing a secret now, they went everywhere together, even though Cinthia didn't show much interest in taking part in killing off Indians in the carriage that had belonged to their great-grandfather/president. But even that didn't create any differences between them, and Cinthia even took advantage of those moments to do her homework.

Why she didn't want to play in the carriage never became clear: was it because she was a girl and that kind of play was for boys, was it because she was ten years old, or was it because she never felt very well? Cinthia was terrible! She had made a pact with her mother: yes, she would agree to take all the medicine without a fuss, even the worst tasting one, no protesting, anything the doctor would order, anything they wanted her to take, only if Julius doesn't find out; if possible the doctor should come in secretly through the back door, Julius mustn't find out that she was sick, Mommy. No, none of that would ever be fully understood, nor why Julius—who did notice changes immediately—took so long this time in realizing that Cinthia wasn't well, not well at all. In reality, he only became fully aware of it the day his cousin, Raphaelito Lastarria, that shithead, had his birthday party.

Susan hung up the telephone and called to her children. Vilma brought them in by the hand, one on each side of the beautiful Chola, and they listened when their mother said:

"You have to go to the party, kids. Susana is my cousin and she just called to invite you. Santiaguito and Bobby used to go and now it's your turn."

And that Saturday afternoon they dressed them up all in white, shoes and everything; Julius even wore a small white silk tie, just like that ribbon that Cinthia used for tying up the outdated bun in her blond hair. They left in the Mercedes: in front, the chauffeur Carlos, Vilma, more beautiful and lighter-skinned than ever, and the gift which was a toy sailboat for their cousins' swimming pool; in back there were the two of them, silent, growing ever more terrified as they got closer to the Lastarria home, to their cousins' house, those shitheads. They knew what they were like: some years back their brothers Santiago and Bobby had been victimized by the same invitation. Cinthia, fragile and adored, sat pale and silent on the leather seat of the Mercedes. Julius, whose little legs couldn't reach the floor, sat beside her, hands clasped to his cold body and heels riveted together but trembling as they dangled in the air. That's the way they arrived. Vilma took them from the car and set them down on the sidewalk, while Carlos retrieved the sailboat whose mast was poking out of the package. Other children were arriving, some they knew, others not; and there, at the door of the Lastarria home, some children were handsome, others were not; some were confident, others were not; and the nursemaids who were wearing uniforms for taking children to birthday parties were there too. Everybody seemed to rival each other in beauty, in quality, in everything that they could possibly compete with, at the Lastarria front door, as if everyone were hating each other.

Vilma could hardly understand the strange house that belonged to the kids' cousins; she was used to living and working in a mansion, not a castle with massive stone walls, dark windows, and ceiling beams like tree trunks. It's not that she was really worried, but she calmed down while drinking her tea in the kitchen when the butler explained that the house was built to look like a castle and, what's yours like, honey, as he rinsed the cups.

The same butler, the respectable Lastarria family butler, opened the door and said come in and, checking out the nursemaids as they arrived, singled out Vilma. Julius understood immediately and elbowed Cinthia who, still frightened, was coughing. The children entered the castle and Señora Lastarria identified each one individually and kissed them all. "Good afternoon, Señora," Vilma said. She presented the gift with the little card attached and instantly became panicky because Julius had already disappeared. There he was, thank God, his back to her as he stared at the suit of armor that was standing like a sentinel at one of the doors to the castle. Cinthia walked over and took him by the hand. They were looking at it when all of a sudden an arm came crashing down, almost clubbing them: the work of Raphaelito—it was one of his favorite tricks—who bounded out to the garden without greeting anyone. Julius knew at that moment that his cousin's birthday had just begun. "Raphaelito, come here! Raphaelito, come and look at your presents!" his mother shouted, but Raphaelito had disappeared into the garden, and now everyone was obliged to follow him out to play.

"Everyone to the backyard!" Aunt Susana Lastarria yelled. "That's where Raphaelito and his brother are!" "Victor," she said, addressing the butler, "tell the other children who arrive to come to the garden."

The butler nodded, stood at the door, and waited for the other guests; but was reluctant because his eyes were on Vilma: she's hot stuff.

On their way to the garden, they passed through an immense hallway filled with suits of armor, swords, shields covered with objects made of coarse metal, huge tumblers as if for drinking blood like in the horror movies, and the black iron candlestick holders, weighing heavily on the tables, similar to the ones Robin Hood ate by when he was on good terms with the kings of England. The hallway was flanked by wide doors, protected by formidable armor that precious Cinthia noticed as she passed by and glanced into the dark rooms. One was for playing billiards, one for the piano, and others for the electric train, the study, the dining room, the library, and the other one, and then still another whose purpose Vilma couldn't figure out. "Here we are," Aunt Susana said at last.

The garden was teeming with children and nursemaids. The children were six, seven, or eight years old, but there wasn't one who was five like Julius. Many wore little white outfits with tiny vests without lapels and little poplin shirts from whose well-starched collars hung finely made minute ties, baby blue, red, or green like the ones bullfighters wear. Not one child showed signs of acne and they were happy, ready to start the games, don't get too close to the swimming pool, little boy, and don't throw rocks at the pretty fish in the fountain. Julius, Cinthia, and Vilma had become a trio holding hands and waiting apprehensively.

Raphaelito, who was celebrating his eighth birthday, was also waiting; he was waiting for them up in the tree, but they hadn't seen him and didn't know where to turn when they got bombarded with clumps of soggy dirt, hurled downward violently, well-aimed, hitting them everywhere. Screams, laughs, and cries ensued while Vilma covered them with her arms and tried to shield them with her legs, even using her uniform, calling out Señora! Señora! until she finally appeared on the scene and everything came to a halt while she dictated orders: Raphaelito, get down from there! Get down this instant! You are unbearable! You don't know how to act properly with your cousins! So why do you invite them, anyway? Next year there'll be no birthday party! . . . And so on, until Raphaelito, in dramatic fashion, began to climb down, slowly, smiling triumphantly, hands smeared with mud, wearing a Tarzan loincloth over his birthday suit.

Pipo, Raphaelito's brother, climbed down from another tree. Pipo was his mortal enemy except on those special days when guests came over; then they would revive some kind of weird bond between themselves, especially when it involved their cousins Julius, Cinthia, Bobby, etc. Pipo came down scowling because he hadn't had enough time to take aim and still shoot another arrow; he still had three more to go. And Cinthia was coughing but she wasn't crying, and she looked at Julius who looked at Vilma who, in turn, was looking at the Señora: "Come and let's brush you off! Thank God it didn't get in your eyes! (Vilma had been hit with a huge one in the mouth). I just don't know what to do with Raphaelito! Let's brush them off, Vilma, then I'll take them back outside myself."

They took them back to the garden, soiled clothes and all. Cinthia shivered from the cold and coughed; Julius' hands were glued to his sides and he was furious. Vilma, who was still spitting out dirt, was concerned about her uniform and thought about the butler, but she was also worried about Cinthia's cough, she could hear it right now and how many times have I told the Señora, she's coughing more and more, Señora, the medicine . . . but what did she know about those things? The Señora was busier and busier every day. Bertha and I are mothers to these children, especially since the Señor died . . . "Come here, Cinthia, rest for a minute. Come Julius, stay next to your sister" . . . He was watching her nearby.

And the Cholo was a handsome brute, light-skinned and all. Probably everyone who had been invited to the birthday party had already arrived and he didn't have to wait to open the door every time the doorbell chimed. By then everyone was in the garden and the party continued in typical fashion. Victor (the name of Vilma's suitor) crossed the garden and he knew that Vilma was watching him; he walked with the self-assurance that one acquires with years of service in a house like that and, with silver serving tray in hand, he provided everyone with little disposable cups filled with cold Coke or grape juice. The children would take their drinks or their nannies would take one for them. Several children, including Pipo and Raphaelito, of course, took drinking straws from their pockets and blew the cold liquid, for instance, right at their friends' eyes, those shitheads. The nannies would go to their aid and separate the rivals; Victor, on the other hand, who through the years had become immune to it all, didn't lose his poise but simply kept on serving, from one side of the garden to the other, without spilling a drop, always aloof, self-assured, arrogant, knowing full well that Vilma was watching him.

And, true enough, Vilma was watching him. She was sitting by a huge window, Cinthia, who was coughing, was next to her, and Julius, with his back turned, peered inside the window, looking toward the hallway with the suits of armor, swords, and shields. At that moment her Aunt Susana, horrible, came out and Cinthia said: "I like your house, Auntie, may I go in and look around?" She was surprised but said yes; after all, Susan's children were always a bit strange. Cinthia took Julius by the hand. "Come," she said, and in order to further vex her disgusting aunt she indicated she would be reading in the library. Julius picked up on something and followed after her. Vilma stood up to go with them but the aunt stopped her.

"You may go to the kitchen, Vilma," she said. "You're invited to have a cup of tea before the children go to the dining room. Stay together," she added, addressing the other nursemaids who were still there.

Cinthia and Julius spent a while examining the suits of armor; first they made sure no one was hiding behind or inside them, then they looked them over in detail. Cinthia explained what she had learned in school about suits of armor, swords, and shields; Julius, who was standing next to her, listened attentively and nodded his head as she talked. Soon they found themselves in the billiard room, and then in another, the study, better not go in there, and still another, the piano room. "Beethoven," Cinthia explained to Julius, pointing to the bronze bust that sat on a marble column scowling at the piano. "Did you know that our great-uncle who is in the study at home had another wife before he married our great aunt?" Julius nodded negatively, and mentally placed their great-uncle among the portraits of their forefathers that were hanging in the study of the mansion. "Yes," Cinthia added, and she told him a long story about their great-uncle, el romántico, that's what they called him; Mommy had told her the whole story.

And he was romantic (Julius was all ears) because he had loved a young woman, he really had, who was below his social class and played the piano marvelously. Mommy called her poor thing, for she was so humble, and finally it seemed like Julius was starting to understand, but he shouldn't always be asking so many questions, but rather he should listen and let her finish the story. They didn't allow him to visit her because she belonged to a different social class, but our great-uncle kept on seeing her and then they pressured him, that's what Mommy says, what do you want me to say? There was all this pressure and they put her in a convent; you see, in those days that's what they did with girls who acted improperly: they ended up becoming little nuns. But not this one, Julius, she had to leave because she was sick, though she continued to play the piano beautifully. And our great-uncle, el romántico, that's why he looks like that in the portrait, with that long beard and hair. Dad said he had ruined the family business, fortunately he had brothers, well, our great-uncle refused to marry anyone else, not even our great-aunt who was already in love with him. He waited and he waited, until she had to leave the convent because she had gotten so sick, and Mommy says she was already dying when he married her because he felt responsible and she said he was a gentleman despite it all. Don't you think he was a really good person? Julius nodded yes with his head and his eyes were telling her to go on with the story.

And Cinthia continued: she told him they got married and went to live in San Miguel, in a house that still exists today, a cute one, all white like a little dollhouse. And that's where they lived, but she was always in bed; she couldn't get up, she was always coughing, all the time, and she never stopped coughing. And our great-uncle let the business fall apart, for he was always at her side, begging her to play the piano, the one he had given to her as a wedding present. She only lived three months, Julius. One morning he asked her to play the piano, as he did every day, and she couldn't get up; but that one time she got up and began to play the piano magnificently. Then all of a sudden she started coughing and died while she was playing the piano. "And that's the end of the story," Cinthia told him, but Julius asked her more questions, and she explained that after he had married our great-aunt he died because he had caught a contagious disease from his first wife, the pianist. He was the president's oldest son and Daddy's uncle, but he died long before Daddy was born. That's why Daddy got worried every time one of us started coughing. They had become pensive as they sat down on the piano bench and discovered the piano keys. Their four little agile hands rested nervously on the ivory keys that belonged to the Lastarrias who, naturally, never even touched them.

In the kitchen, twenty-three nursemaids from all over Peru who had come to work in Lima managed to intimidate the second butler, Cirilo, but not Victor, who was the man in charge. He took control of the diverse electric utensils in order to impress the girls. He ran an air blower for drying the glasses; he sharpened knives by pushing a button that put a round, wheellike stone into motion; and he communicated with the Señora by intercom: "I'm bringing the Cokes now." At least ten nursemaids started to giggle as they watched him put two slices of bread in the toaster, wait a few minutes, then say listen, and just then a little bell went ding, ding and the toast popped up. At least five of them felt sinful shivers run down their backs when he offered the toast to Vilma. Why not? After all, she was the queen. The others watched the scene but they didn't catch on to what was going on: still too primitive, they had riveted their eyes to the bottom of their cups from where it seemed they might never look up again. But not Vilma, she accepted the challenge, or whatever it meant to give her the first piece of toast which, frankly, was quite a flirting pass. "Is there any butter?" she asked, coquettishly. At that point all the Cholas looked away, Vilma was really daring but she was beautiful and, actually, they all admired her. At that moment Victor almost blew his cool, but no, he pulled himself together and dashed for the butter dish. "This is for the Señorita," he said as he handed it to her. "Thank you," Vilma replied, and she began to spread the butter over the toast, smiling serenely, composed, but just then the Señora came in: time to go, the children were already in the dining room and she told Vilma that Julius and Cinthia had disappeared.

They looked high and low for them, first downstairs and then upstairs, for no one was in the garden either. "Victor," Aunt Susana commanded, "go look upstairs with Vilma and let me know if you find them." And that's why the two of them went upstairs together and quietly searched the austere bedrooms, the bathrooms with tubs big enough to live in, and the hallways, calling out Julius! Cinthia! They weren't in the study rooms nor were they on the back service stairs where Victor tried to flirt with her but no: no, because Vilma was teary-eyed, frightened, and distant, even though now she was less out of sorts, as if this part of the house seemed more familiar to her, even those cold floor tiles in the servants' quarters. She continued to call out to them until she heard Cinthia's tenuous voice—we're in here—coming from the servants' bathroom.

"How did you end up here?" Vilma exclaimed when she saw them.

"This bathroom doesn't have a tub, Vilma," noted Julius, which was the only answer she got, but what did it matter? They had found them and nothing had happened. Vilma began to smother them with kisses.

"Do you have a little one for me too?" Victor intervened brazenly.

Julius and Cinthia looked at him disconcertedly.

"Please tell the Señora that we found them," Vilma fixed the bun in her hair.

"But first won't you tell me when you've got your day off?" he asked, smiling, standing tall and waiting.

"Thursday, Thursday, now get going, let the Señora know! . . ."

Victor left in a hurry and Vilma let out a sigh. Slowly, kindly, and trembling, she led them by the hand toward the dining room while they continued to marvel at that part of the castle which was being left behind.

Raphaelito and Pipo had a friend, in fact he was their idol, and even though they didn't let it be known in front of the other guests, they had been waiting for him ever since the first guests began arriving. Martín.

Why wasn't he here? Will he come? It's true Mommy would have preferred that he not come. Hadn't she always told them not to play with him? But it was his birthday, Raphaelito's birthday, and there was nothing anyone could do to stop him from inviting Martín. "They invited him," she told her husband: no one knew him, he lived in one of those new apartment blocks and his mother, whom the Señora had seen at church, didn't fit in, the kid was a real devil, and he was older, it's just that he was small for his age, I hope he doesn't come, he had taught Raphaelito to say jackass, if you'll excuse the word, etc.

And Martín, who wasn't stunted but already eleven years old, arrived just in time for the afternoon snack. He came walking from home by himself, and as he entered he said he would bring a gift tomorrow when in reality his father had told him to stop this sissy stuff, he was too big for giving presents, but he shouldn't miss out on the big spread. And now, practically glued to the edge of the table, he ate his third sandwich while Raphaelito looked on, like a cat in heat. Victor was already attending to everyone, and the nannies were scrutinizing each morsel of food, taking the lettuce out of the sandwiches for fear of typhoid or the chocolates from the wrappers and keeping the verses by Campoamor that were printed on the inside. Julius and Cinthia were already eating their sandwiches; Vilma, beautiful, had calmed down again; Aunt Susana, horrible, was back in control; Pipo and Raphaelito were telling Martín that they were the ones, pointing at Cinthia and Julius. Everyone was eating, the fat kid too, naturally, look, how funny, he's almost choking, he's Augusto and Licia's child. Everyone ate the little candies made by the nuns who live in the earliest convents in the old part of Lima: Bajo el Puente, del Carmen, the old part of the city, it's the other end of the world, dear, the chauffeur got lost and he even grew up there, but no, he doesn't live there any more, now he lives in a slum, they're like that because they pretend to have land there, so they leave earlier in the morning, it's a real pain. Now everyone's eating bizcochitos, look at that, if fatty there isn't a little barbarian or what? And they're eating ice cream too, that one is Martín, the one over there. And they all ask for more Coke and Victor goes to get it, brings it out, and fills their cups, brushing Vilma as he passes by while she contemplates herself in the huge mirror that covers an entire wall: she's beautiful, that's why Victor likes her, hair is done up just right and her heels are just the right height, not too high for the uniform—the Señora wouldn't approve—nor too low either, it's almost impossible to see that they are a little high and yet they round out her legs, her breasts are well defined underneath the white dress, the cloth helps, they look good, and the belt helps define her waistline, wide hips, strong, they're fine . . . From the other side of the dining room the Señora is watching her; she talks about something else but she is watching her. Victor, he's too much: that Chola is beautiful, maybe a little plump but still beautiful, her hair isn't anything special but she's a knockout, got well-developed legs and she's sturdy, been taking care of Julius for some years now, ever since he was born, she's beautiful all right, a little cocky, see how she looks at herself: I'm ugly, isn't that Chola beautiful, poor thing . . . And that rascal Victor, trying to make her, probably trying to make her, winking now and communicating with her in the mirror.

Of course, birthday candles had to be blown out, even though Raphaelito would have preferred to dispense with all that because Martín, bullylike, was sitting next to him and watched with skepticism. But Victor wouldn't have missed this part for anything: there he was lighting all the little candles with only one match, Vilma thought he was burning his fingers but no, hurry up and light you damn little candle, but at last he was ready for his trick, for as he raised the match in the air and snuffed out the flame with his fingers, Vilma cringed.

"Cut the cake," Martín yelled.

"Didn't I tell you, he's the one."

Meanwhile Susana Lastarria was telling everyone about her sister Chela, who had come to help her watch over the little savages. And all these little monsters were eating their cake, *cake is the name,* and it was impossible to finish all that about the kid being the son of what's-his-name, the other one, the senator, such a good-looking man that he was, who has aged quite a bit recently, the same as his mother, like two peas in a pod. Susan? Poor Susan: don't think she's got it so bad, I've seen her with him, and why shouldn't she if she's already been a widow for three years . . .

And, in the midst of all this, it's a little like what one might call geographical determinism (man makes it antideterministic), Julius and Cinthia were there but never very far from Vilma. They had enjoyed a few moments of peace while the others ate, but it was coming to an end and soon it would be time to return to the garden to play.

Fortunately Martín had decided that they were going to form two teams for a soccer game. Everyone wanted to play on Martín's team. He was the new leader and the one who made the decisions: You're on this side! You're on that side! You're not playing! You, on this side! You too! Get that girl out of here! Raphael, you're on this side! He's too small! Then Raphaelito went over and pushed him away. Vilma and Cinthia went to get him: "Come, Julius," she said, "I'm going to teach you something, but you've got to learn it well, understand?" They started toward the castle but on the way, before going in, they came upon Aunt Susana.

"Don't get lost," she told them. "Stay around where we can find you. Vilma, don't let them out of your sight: the magician arrives in half an hour."

By the time the magician arrived, the soccer game was over. We all know that Martín's team won, 2–0. All it took was Pipo's corker in the goalie's stomach (he fell backward inside the net) and Martín's punt that shattered a window in the castle. It was getting dark already and the nannies were wiping their sweaty faces with warm, damp towels. Look how dirty you've gotten, child, my God! and with only their know-how they made them spiffy once again because the show was about to begin: this year, instead of a movie, a magician.

They were seated in tiny, neatly lined chairs in the great hall of the castle. Cinthia and Julius sat at the head of the third row, and Vilma stood to one side. From the back of the hall, Victor looked at her over the little heads of some fifty children and some fifteen stiff-necked maids who sought out seats wherever they could; those who were standing leaned against the walls. Seated in the first row were Raphaelito, Pipo, and Martín, the latter of whom was saying that everything was a fake (the magician still hadn't appeared in the hall), and at the other end were the two sisters, Chela and Susana, the latter hating Martín: "Oh no, no way! Sit down!" Martín was trying to organize a reception line: "Fake! Fake! Fake!" Insolent little snot.

Pollini the Magician, who had even performed on TV, couldn't have seemed more queer when he appeared running in from the side door of the great hall. Delighted to be in the castle, he quickly went up to the Señora and kissed her hand in a way that no hand had been kissed in Lima in a long time. "Se*n*-ñora," he said, "I am at your command," and it began to smell of perfume at that end of the hall. Then he presented himself to Aunt Chela, another little kiss on the hand, and he introduced his partner, who was also his wife and had traveled extensively throughout South America; but no, despite the admiration she had received she still wasn't like the Señora. The magician asked if he could proceed with the show and everyone approved; hence he turned to the table that had been set up for him in front of the children. The sisters sat down again and the magician took a look around the auditorium—there were several million sitting out there in front of him—and spotted Victor at the back. "May I have a glass of water?" That's what he said as if he really didn't want it. Victor pretended not to notice, who does he think he is? but the Señora turned to him and said, "Victor, get a glass of water for the magician . . . for the Señor," and the guy had no choice but to humiliate himself in front of Vilma. The magician had also cast a scrutinizing eye at her, but this wasn't the time for that: he was in a castle.

He raised up his arms as if he were going to be shot, but it was just to allow his partner to remove his cape. He had already donned his top hat and put the black leather bag on the table, which made him look a little less like Dracula and less frightening to Julius and several others who followed his every move with wide eyes and open mouths. Cinthia poked her brother with her elbow: "Don't forget how to do it, Julius, you won't forget, will you?" and it seemed like Vilma was also in on the secret. But at that moment Victor came in with the glass of water for the magician: just put it there on the table, he said, and Victor could see up close that the guy wasn't really that white, the prick used talcum powder and makeup. He set the glass down and gave the magician a dirty look. Now the performance could begin.

And it was going to begin but at that moment Raphaelito's father Señor Lastarria arrived and the magician came unglued. Mr. Lastarria, the Señor Juan Lastarria, entered the hall and went over to his wife to greet her once again, it's been going on seventeen years that he's been greeting her the same usual way. The magician watched him but also admired him, waiting for a signal which would allow him to rush over and greet him. He was the Señor Lastarria, deserving of his admiration and who looked at him now, signaling him to go over and greet him, happily ready to shake hands, the bootlicker, and naturally the Señor did not intend to kiss his partner, that is, his wife, on the hand.

On the other hand, he did plan on kissing Susan, yes, Susan, not Susana, for Juan Lastarria knew the difference: Susan, lovely, was Julius' mother and had just arrived. It was proper for a mother to pick up her children from a birthday party, it was maternal love, a sense of responsibility, etc., and she took advantage of the moment, killing two birds with one stone: she would pick up the children and at the same time make her horrible, irritating cousin Susana happy with a visit which, in passing, also made Juan happy as she let him kiss her hand, *my duchess*, which was like a wet sponge on that forever lovely hand.

Everyone was there. Susan and Susana greeted each other. Then Juan Lastarria and the magician. And his partner and Susana, and then Susan: impossible. Susan was a widow and Susana was ugly, simply horrible. Juan was just a working man on his way up, and he had ac-quired a castle through marriage, and now he was a simpleton. The magician was an artist. Señor Lastarria had triumphed. The magician's assistant looked like she was dead . . . well, it had been twenty years of a life full of tricks. The greetings were over. "Julius, Cinthia!" Susan called out, turning around to where she knew they were seated and then going over to kiss them, lovely. "A whiskey, *my duchess?*" which is what her cousin Juan called her. "Yes, darling, with just a little ice." Poor darling, he had married Susana, her cousin Susana, and then discovered there was more, *something called class, aristocracy*. It was like her, for example, and ever since then he went around with a stiff neck, as if trying to reach something, something you'll never be, darling.

For the magician, however, everything was something else; he wasn't aware of these subtle differences or about that fine line of distinction. He really admired Señor Lastarria and hence he cursed himself for having asked for that glass of water, why the hell had he asked for it, now for sure he won't be invited to drink a glass of whiskey with them. The butler was already serving the drinks and he counted each glass, he wasn't a magician for nothing: nope, there wasn't one for him, for each one took a glass from the tray, including Señor Lastarria, and now it was show time.

Juan Lastarria found a place for the duchess next to him, took a sip of whiskey, and looking at her out of the corner of his eye, nodded for the show to begin. Susan also looked at him: her cousin Juan, he was so happy! with his rounded little breasts poking out underneath his silk shirt, the paunch that he and his tailor tried to hide, the unbearable way he stood with his fingers inserted between the buttons of his sport coat, the straight little moustache, an idea picked up in who knows what cabaret (she wouldn't ever forget when Santiago, her husband, said that it was the shortest distance between two cheeks), the swept-back look of the Greek-Argentine magnates, for instance, the big, all-year-round dark glasses, her cousin really lacks taste. The image that he had created astonished her, what a silly cousin . . . The children's laughter brought her back to reality: the magician had already begun.

Not only had he begun but he had pulled a whopping number of eggs out of his hat, and he continued to pull out one after another and, finally, one more. In reality, he continued pulling out eggs just like some old gaudy made-up aunt of yours, one of those romantics who never married, who you believe will never have any more boyfriends and pam! one day they appear at your door with some candies, this one's for you, sonny, and another sweetheart, an Italian this time. Even Martín was dumbfounded with the number of eggs. Everyone applauded. The magician thanked the crowd, sought more applause, and pointed to his partner so everyone would clap for her as well. In reality, the applause for her fell short because the only thing the woman did was put away his tools of the trade, that is, the things he pulled from his hat, his shirt cuffs, his mouth, his lapel, or the inside pocket of his coat. The guy must have been possessed by the devil, he just pulled out three doves from inside a pocket where moments before there was nothing. Of course someone had to have a rubber band to make a slingshot; no one confessed to doing it, but the magician was not at all pleased when one of his doves was just about knocked down with a missile.

"Quiet down, children," Señora Susana commanded at the same moment Juan Lastarria added, "Go ahead, please, everything's all right." The magician obeyed and kept the show going, but no way he would leave his doves exposed; instead he started to stick things back into the bag himself: he swallowed a red-hot piece of steel, then a sword, and on and on. Then he played some card tricks. The magician was an expert, for he had even performed on TV, but his partner was tired of repeating it over and over: a spectacular, unique event for children from Peru and all over South America, a special event just for little Raphael Lastarria whose birthday we're celebrating today, let's give him a hand (Martín, of course, didn't join in), he's the son of Señor and Señora . . . Hey, that's enough, you clown.

But there comes that moment when magicians try to prove to children that nothing in life is impossible. That's when they call upon the audience to participate: come on up and do a trick. Then the children turn shy, get embarrassed, hush up, and look down at the floor, but the maids push them forward, go on! until finally one decides to venture forward, one, for example, who helps at mass and offers to assist the magician perform a trick, winning the eternal admiration of his companions. It's always like that, or rather almost like that, because something spectacular will happen on this birthday, a colossal scene.

The magician was already beginning his customary spiel, "Let's see, who wants to perform a little trick?" when without anyone noticing (except Vilma and Cinthia), the magician discovered a little person standing next to him near the table: a floppy-eared kid, heels riveted together, toes pointing outward, and hands straight down to his sides.

"I know a trick."

"Ah ha, ah ha, ah ha! What's your name, sonny?"

"Julius."

They were splitting with laughter. Susan, lovely, trembled, Vilma was frightened to death, and Cinthia coughed: "I hope he remembers how to do it."

"Fantastic! Marvelous! Extraordinary! And how old are you, sonny?"

"Five."

"Marvelous! Fantastic! Unbelievable! Julius, under my direction, will perform the most trickiest of all tricks!"

"No. I will do the trick."

"Ah ha, ah ha! Well, let's see, sonny."

The magician started to get nervous. He looked at the parents of the birthday child and they smiled.

"You know a trick?"

"Yes."

"Ah ha. Well, sonny, let's see, ah ha. Come over here. What's your little trick? Tell us . . ."

Julius looked at Cinthia and she motioned with her finger as if helping him to remember something. Vilma covered her face.

"I need another kid to help me," Julius said with a monotone voice, as if he knew exactly what he was doing. His hands were still glued to his sides and his ears seemed to flop even more, but he was looking straight at Raphaelito.

"Ah! So it's a complicated trick, two of you! Dynamite! Fantastic! What's your name, kid?"

"Julius."

"And now Julius is going to show us his greeeeeeeat intelligence! Don't miss out on this one, folks! Here comes the best one of all! And who's going to help you?"

"Raphael."

"Ah! Raphaelito! Sure, why not! Raphaelito, the birthday boy. Perfect! Excellent!"

The magician's partner pointed with both arms at Raphaelito, who watched with fear and trepidation. Martín was sitting next to him, smiling more skeptically than ever.

"C'mon, do it," he told him, jabbing him with his elbow.

The birthday boy stood up and walked distrustfully over to the table. Never had he hated his cousin more than right now; in fact, he was hating all the guests, and the noise they were making was incredible: Do it, Raphael! C'mon, do it! they yelled, getting stirred up in their seats.

"I need an ashtray and a small rock," Julius said as he removed an ashtray and a rock from his jacket pocket. "Here."

"Fantastic! Outstanding!" exclaimed the magician. "And what's the trick?"

Julius placed the ashtray and the small rock on the table and looked at his cousin Raphael.

"I'll place the rock here and cover it with the ashtray. Then I'll say some magic words and I bet you I can take the rock out without touching the ashtray."

Raphaelito turned green and would hate him forever. He looked out at the audience and noticed his father, mother, and Julius' mother among the infinite number of bobbing heads: they were watching him, waiting. Also, Martín, who was in the front row, seemed to be saying to him: "Go on, do it, make a fool of yourself. Get it over with."

Everyone in the room had forgotten that it was his birthday, and he didn't have any choice but to blurt out:

"That's a lie!"

"It's true," Julius said, and he covered the little rock with the ashtray.

"Do you see it? There it is, underneath."

"Yeah. Now what?"

"I . . . I say," Julius stuttered as he looked at Cinthia, "some magic words."

"Say them."

"Abracadabra," Julius proclaimed, putting his hands a few inches above the ashtray.

The magician and his partner, powdered up and dressed in gaudy fashion, respectively, looked at Julius beseechingly.

"And now what?" Raphaelito said angrily.

"Now I will remove the rock without touching the ashtray."

Vilma finished biting one nail and started on another. Cinthia sighed with relief.

"How?"

"Look, you'll see."

Raphaelito stood over the ashtray and lifted it up to see if the rock was still under the ashtray. Right then, Julius' shaky little hand mechanically snatched the rock.

"See?" he said, "I haven't touched the ashtray."

At first no one understood what had happened. Actually, the children were slow to break out in laughter, but Juan Lastarria had begun to pull on his moustache and Susana would forever hate Susan, who was lovely, while the magician rapidly sent doves flying throughout the castle, made millions of eggs appear everywhere, and almost swallowed his magic satchel. Julius looked at Cinthia and the children began to applaud when little Raphael turned green, went into a frenzy, and yelled:

"But you don't have a beach house in Ancón!" And he disappeared.

The magician was still cutting off an imaginary finger, pulling out an imaginary arm, sticking a sword right into his partner's heart, and performing several other tricks that finally calmed down the children, who were very noticeably excited. Julius returned to his seat next to Cinthia and Vilma, who had ruined three fingernails by then, and he watched the expression on Martín's face.

The children had already returned to the garden where they waited for their mothers or the chauffeurs to pick them up. Everything was all lit up with a thousand lights and the nannies' faces seemed pale, almost as white as their uniforms. All they cared about now was to keep the children from getting any dirtier, soon someone would be there to pick them up. And that's where they called out to them by first and last names, so-and-so, this one and that one, and they started to leave, receiving first a kiss from Señora Susana and then a look of scorn from Raphaelito, who was also at the door.

Things were much livelier in the castle bar, where Juan Lastarria, Susan, Chela, and other relatives and friends had accepted an invitation to have a whiskey and were smoking and talking in lively fashion.

Of course there was always some irritating person who insisted on talking about her son's school but, in general, the ambience was propitious for Juan Lastarria to carry on a conversation with Susan and address her over and over as my duchess, while feeling elated when she would say darling to him in front of just about everyone around. All that made life more pleasurable, yes, made it worth living, which is why one works so hard in life, like talking about our families' pasts, about your grandfather, Susan, so British about everything he did, such a gentleman, there's no one like him today, and such an interesting name—Patrick, didn't he attend Oxford?—what tradition! Anything that seemed English absolutely fascinated Lastarria; the castle was a good example and that's why it was so marvelous to have Susan in his bar where now no one was missing and nothing was lacking; after all, she's the granddaughter of English stock, the daughter of an Englishman, and she's even educated in London.

Except the magician: the poor wizard had already put his things away—doves, swords, silk handkerchiefs; in fact, he even wanted to stuff his partner into the bag; but now, some thirty feet from the bar, he was swinging the Dracula cape around and over his head and then his partner buttoned it for him, as is customary on important occasions. Juan Lastarria took notice of his presence and called him over; he called them both over and offered them a whiskey. He served the drinks himself, even putting the ice in each glass, after which they started to answer a few questions: "And the trick with the doves, how do you do it? Do you bleed when you cut yourself?" And there were questions about his life, his life as an artist, of course, which is when his partner—how daubed up she was!—became sentimental and all, until it was time to leave.

Things were also happening in the garden. The Raphael-Pipo-Martín threesome, with some new members of the mafia in tow, reappeared on the scene ready to play the dog-and-owner game that, frankly, meant getting revenge against Julius and beating him up. Cinthia was the last remaining young girl and complained of being cold and sweating, while Vilma hurried to cover her and then return to chat with Victor. The two, standing under a tree, were pretentious about everything, but Vilma made the children stay close by, and they could hear their conversation that went something like:

"I'll meet you at the corner, then?"

"But, listen, I don't even know you," smiling faintly.

"Thursday. I can take my day off then too."

"And how do you know that Thursday is my day off," another subtle smile and a quick glance at the children.

"You told me."

"And what if it's not true?"

"Are you one of those who always goes around telling lies?"

"I ain't ever fibbed to nobody."

"Then it's the truth?"

"And how do you know?"

"Are you mysterious, then?" Victor said. The poor guy was becoming impatient and his hands perspiring and all.

"Do you think so?" a giddy smile, three tiny giggles, and those big, shining black eyes: a true Chola and she's downright beautiful.

"I wonder if that magician has wooed you too?"

"Good Lord! The things you say! Don't you see the wizard has a wife?"

"I wonder how they live? . . . they sez they's artists . . ."

"Did you see how many doves he pulled out of his hat?"

"Just a trick."

"Maybe you're some kind of magician?" Vilma seemed to ask seriously.

"I never lie to a lady," recited Victor with the assurance that his little book wouldn't let him down, the one he had bought at the downtown market which was called *The Art of Courtship,* and it had already come in handy on several occasions.

"You're a real Ricardo Montalban," Vilma said, looking up flirtingly at the top of the tree where there was the platform from which little Raphael had let fly with a thousand dirt clods; she turned immediately to look at the children who were talking together at some distance from the other children but who were close enough to scrutinize her out the corner of their eyes.

"It's not difficult to be like him in front of a beautiful young lady."

"My Lord! How civilized!" Vilma exclaimed as she smiled. "You'll make me become conceited."

According to *The Art of Courtship,* this was the moment when he should ask her if she liked romantic movies; she would answer yes, and then he would tell her that he also was a romantic. But the famous little book didn't provide for scenes that took place under a tree, only at the movie theater. Logically Victor was a little perplexed for a moment without anything to say until he got started again on the matter of taking the day off on Thursday.

"How about if I meet you on Thursday?"

That remained to be seen, as well as what was going on in the middle of the yard where there was total disorder and lots of yelling going on. Vilma looked over to where she had just seen the children: Julius and Cinthia were gone. She took off running, calling out Julius! Julius! Amid the confusion several children were crawling on their knees, they were the dogs, and their owners, who were other children, the bigger ones, pulled them along with ropes and belts tied around their necks. And there were Julius and Cinthia in the middle of it all, Cinthia coughing and protesting no! and Raphaelito yes! they had to play like everyone else! Julius has to let them put the belt around his neck! Julius also screamed no, and Cinthia said yes, they wanted to play too, but she would be Julius' dog. Then Vilma, who was still upset, saw Cinthia fall to the ground, kneel on all fours, and slip the belt around her neck. "Let's go, Julius, grab it!" He did and Vilma was helping them get away from the group when at that moment they saw blood trickling down Cinthia's arm. Cinthia removed the belt from her neck as fast as she could and screamed as she took off running, it's nothing! it's nothing! stay with Julius! I'm going to find Mommy! As she ran off, she was coughing.

Julius never found out—he never really wanted to know—what happened in the bar. He only remembers that Aunt Susana came to the garden to look for him and to say it was time to go. They began to leave and his Uncle Juan said good-bye to him at the front door without forgetting to kiss his duchess on the hand. "It wasn't anything, Juan. Really it wasn't, darling. She must have gotten a bloody nose." Susan said good-bye to everyone, looking lovely but nervous.

When they reached the car, Carlos and Victor argued over who would open the door for them.

Cinthia! My adorable Cinthia! No, there weren't any stains. She was immaculate, revived, smiling, combed, and washed. It was nothing to frighten Julius about as he looked at your arm, adorable Cinthia, while they drove home: at last another one of their Lastarria cousins' birthdays was over and done with, those shitheads. And now they were going home, straight to the bathtub, and then off to bed. Mommy, lovely, would too, sitting up front and turning around from time to time to look back at them: how her children made her worry so much! They're always so nervous, always getting sick, tonight she would stay home, not go out, but call him on the phone because it's true, Cinthia had begun to worry her. Her older children had never given her so much to worry about, these children were growing up without a father, among nannies and butlers, it was unavoidable and they were so fragile, so intelligent but so fragile, different, difficult, should they attend a boarding school? No, Susan, you're not a bad person, you've never been bad, you're just that way, nothing more, you just can't go it alone, it's boring without your friends, giving orders in a mansion with children, your children, Susan . . . A butler opened the iron gate of the mansion and the Mercedes wound its way up the road to the big door. Everyone was there waiting, even Nilda Jungle Woman. They had been waiting the whole afternoon and now they welcomed them smiling and happy, ready to answer Julius' endless number of questions. But they must have noticed something—a sign from Vilma—for they all quickly disappeared. Susan didn't like the servants having the run of the house, going in all the rooms, which didn't happen when the older Santiago was growing up; of course, now they lived with the children and she was unable to prevent it, she just didn't have the time or the energy to stop it. It was barely possible to give a few simple orders, like now: give him a bath, put her to bed, bring a thermometer, it's too late to call the doctor, and make sure she takes her medicine. Vilma set to work immediately: she took them upstairs, brought them something to eat, put her to bed, bathed him, and told the Señora that it was time to say good night to the children. She sat with Julius for a while, talking, laughing, and joking, almost as if she wanted to bring up the subject and talk about it: would he understand that Victor, as he opened the car door, told her that he would be waiting for her at the corner at three on the dot on Thursday, which was her day off?

III

NO ONE, HOWEVER, left the mansion that Thursday, not a soul left because that evening the Señora and Cinthia were leaving for the United States. The doctor had decided it would be for the best, things had gotten worse, she wasn't well. He didn't want to be an alarmist, but it was better for her to seek help at a hospital in Boston, yes, yes, it was critical that they leave as soon as possible, there was no time to lose. They started to get ready for the trip immediately. They called the travel agency, put the passports in order, and went crazy packing the suitcases. Once the trip had been announced, everyone in the mansion spoke softly and Julius learned that the United States had nothing to do with the amusement park that had been built recently in Lima's new Campo de Marte that was replete with ferris wheels and a thousand other attractions in English. The United States was a lot farther away than this, ugh! a lot farther away from the airport, and through the dark sky, try to imagine some place far away, no, farther still, real far away . . . "No!" he cried out, but his sobbing only served to dampen his burning, angry face, turning it to sadness.

Cinthia remained in bed, coughing all the while, until a few hours before their departure. All bundled up, she came into the main dining room where today Julius had taken a seat along with the others. They ate in silence and acted friendly to each other, passing along the butter dish before anyone asked for it, filling their glasses with water before the butler did, never looking at each other, and quietly saying thank you. At last they finished supper and it was time to go to the piano room where they continued to wait. There Cinthia tried to conceal her malaise, sitting on the piano bench a little while, striking the keys disinterestedly, perhaps a little absent-mindedly, until she saw that Julius, who was terrified, just stared at her; she took her little twitching hands from the keyboard and ran over to sit next to him.

"When I come back I hope you'll be tired of playing in the carriage," she told him, coaxing him to smile, please, as she tickled him under his arm.

The piano room was sad. Just one lamp was on, the one that shed light onto the armchair where Susan was sitting. Cinthia, Julius, Santia-guito, and Bobby, all elegantly dressed, sat together on a couch in semi-darkness. Outside, in the hallway, the servants were whispering, which seemed to confirm their participation in the suffering. When they be-came quiet the absence of their voices would leave the children defense-less against a chill and Susan, who became mute, was covered with goose bumps. When the servants spoke again, their murmurs were like brief, fragile pauses from the accumulation of a resounding lull, a si-lence that screamed out her name, continuing forward and stopping for a time when some clock in another room, sad and tenebrous, chimed ten o'clock in the evening, for on the day that Cinthia departed and beginning with that evening, the rooms in the mansion became com-municating vessels of sadness and substance, vessels like lakes into which time dripped, tic-tac, tic-tac, tic-tac, second by second. It was still half an hour until departure time. Hushed and immobile like a sick person damp from fever who discovers sleep after respectfully accepting insomnia, they listened and counted with some precision the drops of water that dripped from a leaky faucet that seemed to say: "This is too much, I won't be able to sleep tonight."

No one was aware that outside in the night the suitcases were being loaded into the burgundy Mercedes. Susan sighed from deep down in-side. The sad news had surprised her, just as she was looking particu-larly lovely, extremely elegant, but now a wounded swan navigating at the mercy of the wind toward some distant shore that perhaps she had reached when all of a sudden the phone rang. "At least you've got some-thing to help you kill the time," Santiago thought as he watched her answer the phone. The servants took advantage of her absence and came in tiptoeing with Nilda at the front leading them and looking like she would speak on behalf of all of them: dear Cinthia, dear little Cin-thia, they didn't know what else to say.

"Follow us, Juan Lucas," Susan told the person driving the other sporty-looking Mercedes parked behind them. He had arrived about the same time they were leaving and they had opened the big iron gate so he could drive up to the massive front door of the mansion. He put the car in gear and started for the airport behind them. Cinthia turned around to look, but it was too dark to see who was driving. Juan Lucas was not a familiar name and she elbowed Julius, scaring him half to death: it was the first time he had ever gone out at night, the first time to an airport, and the first time he was going to be separated from his sister for such a long time. An endless number of thoughts ran through his sleepy little head, which excited him more and more. Cinthia's un-expected elbow in his side jolted him and, as soon as he was able to react, he made an effort to return her smile. It was too crowded in the Mercedes: his brothers Santiago and Bobby stretched out in the back seat, making it difficult for him as he got pushed further and further into the deep crevices of the back seat. Up front, Susan cried, but only Carlos and Vilma who were seated next to her were aware of it.

CACA, "Civilian Airport Corporation Authority," Cinthia explained to Julius who, during the last few minutes of the ride to the airport, had become conscious of what was happening and began to inundate her with questions. She began to cough and Vilma covered her up even more when she got out of the car. "Hurry, it's windy," she said. Carlos, on the other hand, announced that he would take care of the luggage, but a skycap appeared saying the same thing, after which they hated each other. In simultaneous fashion, a third man wearing a cap and an identification number on his lapel approached wanting to charge them to watch their car, but Carlos told him that's why he was there and those two despised each other as well. The guy insisted upon asking who would pay for the parking. Susan opened her purse and everything spilled out onto the ground: airline tickets, rouge, dark glasses, and her gold lipstick case. She picked up the dark glasses and the others stooped down to help her with the rest. Cinthia began to cough and Bobby said that Mom never has a red cent in her purse. Vilma searched through the pockets of her uniform and said she didn't have any money either. Bobby refused to loan any of his money. Finally Carlos paid for it and cursed the guy with a nasty look because the Señora and the children were present. Of course, he couldn't carry all her bags and he had to go looking for the guy with that damn cart, "Call one over here, please!" Julius yawned so wide that he just about fell backward into the street, but as soon as he caught his balance he asked which airplane were they taking, even when he still couldn't see any. "Please shut up," Susan barked at him, but then immediately kissed and hugged him, drenching his face with tears.

A man approached and said "Susan," but he said it in a way that they had never heard before, as if it was the only word that he could say, or as if he had ordered golden vocal cords for pronouncing it more stylishly. Susan put her dark glasses on and smiled as if to say: Juan Lucas, if you only knew what I'm going through; and he took her by the arm: calm down, calm down. Juan Lucas raised his left arm and snapped his fingers: "Over here," and everyone calmed down and skycaps appeared out of nowhere, all good-natured and ready to carry every last bag belonging to the Señores. Taking her by the arm, he directed her toward the immense, brightly lighted, thickly carpeted reception area of the airport. Now they could see him better: his evening was ruined but he had dropped everything in order to go to the airport. The children came next, followed by Vilma and Carlos, who made sure he got at least one small suitcase to carry. The four children, sad and sleepy, approached the Panagra Airways ticket counter; Santiago, however, felt a terrible anger well up inside him: who was this idiot taking his mother by the arm?

And now that he could see him from the side, leaning in distinguished fashion against the Panagra ticket counter, he felt as if he was going to explode with rage. But he didn't know where to sock it to him. How could Santiago smash this guy if his refined nature had already captivated him? For sure he's one of those smoothies straight from the Costa Azul who appears at the golf course, which is where Susan must have met him, that's where he must have seen her for the first time while taking a swing at a little white ball that disappears into a sea of green perfection, and walking on as the breeze tosses his hair elegantly, curling around his silver-tinted temples and refreshing his skin that would be forever tan. And later, why not? Together they would drink *gin and tonics* at poolside on silver serving trays held by invisible and obedient hands that disappeared silently, letting them talk in private, their words melting into the breeze and reaching their destination as soft whispers, with music in the background that soothed the Club members, their guests, and with colored fish . . . He was the one who had been taking her out every night! He was the one who danced with her! He was the one who drank with her! He was the one who had kept her out late! He was the reason they never got to see her anymore! He was sad now. Young Santiago had just discovered something really painful.

"They don't even make these guys in Hollywood," the Panagra ticket agent thought admiringly as he watched Juan Lucas say, "Sign these papers, Susan," handing her a gold fountain pen of the type that would never appear in newspaper ads. He handed it to her as if he were holding a cigarette between two fingers that were undoubtedly trained to hold gold fountain pens and crystal glassware a certain way. Poor Susan finished signing her three documents and discovered that she had signed her name differently each time. "I don't have a steady hand," she announced as she turned to Juan Lucas, frightened. "What should I do,

darling? What kind of trouble am I getting into now?" Juan Lucas retrieved his pen, put it back in the little pen pocket of the jacket you wear
for those occasions, looked straight at the Panagra agent—just in case
he was thinking about making a wisecrack at the Señora—and led her
away by the arm. The passports were in order and everything was ready.
Santiago wanted to stop looking at him that way, to stop staring at this
Juan Lucas guy, but once again Santiago found himself watching him
as he crossed the waiting area with his mother, seemingly on their way
to heaven. Susan turned to tell Vilma to keep Cinthia bundled up and
to bring the children to the bar. Of course, Julius had disappeared and
everyone began to swear up and down, but Juan Lucas had already
spotted him and he pointed to him with such a refined and long finger
that people could hardly get by: there he is, over there, at the window,
looking out at the runway. When Vilma almost scared him to death as
she grabbed him by the arm from behind, he told her that Cinthia was
leaving on that plane, the Air France one, that was his favorite.

Except for Cinthia, the children drank Coke in the bar. You'd better
not have anything, darling, but Julius gave her half of his glass, con-
tending that since his had no ice, he didn't think the drink would be
too cold for her. Susan wanted to scold him but Juan Lucas found the
scene amusing and leaned back, ha, ha, ha, that's great, just as if he
had scored eighteen straight holes-in-one, at which time Susan covered
her face with her hands as if to say this is too much for me, but then
the whiskeys arrived. "Why don't we let Santiago have one too?" the
golfer said. Looking at him with surprise, she would have said something to him, but just then Santiago stood up and shouted he would
pay for his own drinks and even have them over at the bar. Juan
Lucas made a face as if he had lost an easy round. "Take a package of
Chesterfield cigarettes to that young man," he responded quickly, "he'll
need them."

By the time they started announcing the flight, Santiaguito had already downed three whiskeys and was about to have another. He didn't
want to say good-bye, not even to Cinthia. Juan Lucas was the only one
who wasn't crying as they headed toward the gate, but that's when
Vilma began to wail in earnest which disturbed the golfer because he
was tired of this childish stuff. Cinthia was brief: she hugged and kissed
everybody and then told Julius that she would write him and that he
had to write her too. Susan began saying good-bye, kissing each one
and shaking hands with Vilma and Carlos, but then she almost had to
pounce on Bobby who was about to jump on another kid because he
had been making fun of him. At that moment it would have been better

if Santiaguito had not been there. They saw this Señor by the name of Juan Lucas hug their mother, kiss her tenderly, and tell her that if she had to stay on in the USA, he would join her there.

Afterward Juan Lucas, Vilma, and Carlos took the children up to the observation deck so they could wave good-bye to Mommy and Cinthia and watch the plane take off. "There they go!" Bobby yelled, who was the first one to spot them walking to the plane. They turned around to wave good-bye, Susan always with her dark glasses on and Cinthia coughing. But Julius had spotted something else: he watched them filling the gas tanks of the plane that he was sure Cinthia would take, but it turned out to be one that was leaving much later, the same one that he had chosen for her and was expecting them to board when he abruptly threw up all over the pants of a man standing next to him who naturally started fuming. However, Juan Lucas, very distinguished, took care of the problem with a few well-chosen words and a perfumed, silk handkerchief that he relinquished to the man as if he were distributing flyers, ready to hand out hundreds more.

"Don't forget about Santiago," he told them as he started to leave without becoming fully aware of the vomit that jerk was complaining about, at least not until it began to smell.

They waited in the car while Carlos went to get Santiago. He was in the bar and it took a long time to convince Santiago that he had to go home. His brothers were falling asleep. At last it seemed like he was going to give in and when it came time to pay for the drinks, the waiter said that the young lad's father had already paid the bill. Then all hell broke loose. Santiaguito screamed that pimp isn't my father, I'll show him, I'll kill him, my mother's sacred, and other such things until he began to cry and fell on the floor. Carlos carried him to the car, where he continued to kick and swear. Julius said he was crazy but Bobby said he wasn't, he was just drunk because of Mommy's friend.

A week later the first letter, which was addressed to Julius, arrived from Boston. Vilma had trouble reading it.

Dear Julius:

How are you? Do you miss me? I really miss you. Mommy and I are always thinking about you. She says that you should already be in school and as soon as she returns to Lima she'll put you in Immaculate Heart School where you'll be able to learn English. Mommy says it's important for you to learn English and, once and for all, how to read. She said you're behind in everything and she's going to write Aunt Susana who has Señorita Julia's address so she can tutor you at home. I told her that you already know how to read pretty good, but she doesn't believe me and says you spend all your time playing in the carriage and in the garden with the butlers or with Vilma. Be good until we get back because Mommy worries about you.

I'm really doing great. I'm happy. I'm practicing my English with the nurses and the doctor. There are three doctors who always come around to see me. I can really understand what they say to me and when I told them I was going to write you they said to say hello. I've already told them what you're like and they always ask about you when they come to see me. That's why you have to write and tell me what's going on so I can tell them more about what you're doing. Just tell Vilma to write down what you want to tell me, but you write something too so I can see what your writing is like. I'm really sorry we can't continue with our classes. You were really learning fast. When Señorita Julia starts giving you classes, show her what you've learned with me and Vilma because Mommy can't believe you've learned so much.

I'm really doing great. I just about slept the whole way on the plane and Mommy slept too. At first she cried a lot, probably because of the way Santiaguito was acting, but then she took a bunch of pills and fell asleep next to me. We had to change planes in New York, but we didn't leave the airport because Mommy said it was cold outside, and we didn't have time either. We slept on the second plane too and when we woke up we were in Boston. We went directly to a hotel and slept some more. The next day we came to this hospital. It's big, and when we were entering Mommy ran into a man from Lima who had cancer. Then they brought me to my room; it's real pretty. Mommy is staying at the hotel but she comes early and stays with me all day long, and at night she goes to the movies to take her mind off things. I'm trying hard to get this over with and get well soon so she won't be so nervous. Mommy is so pale and she doesn't put any makeup on. She's real sad too when she has to leave me and cries a lot at night. She misses everything and I feel like I'm to blame. That's why you've got to behave so that nothing will bother her right now. Be good, please. I hope that by the time I return you won't be playing in the carriage anymore because you spend too much time there.

Say hello to Vilma and Carlos and Arminda and to everyone else for me. I'm going to write them but I wanted to write to you first. Don't forget to write me back. Promise? Hugs and kisses,

CINTHIA

Fifteen days later, a second letter arrived for Julius. Once again, Vilma cried as she read it to him.

Dear Julius:

I didn't write last week because I wrote to Bobby, Santiaguito, and the servants. I'm a little worried because I think I forgot to include Carlos and the letter was for him also. Tell him, please. I'm really tired. I got your little letter. Mommy read what you wrote and was surprised. She didn't realize you knew so much and says if you work hard with Señorita Julia you're going to learn a lot and perhaps you can get into first grade and you won't have to go to kindergarten. I hope so, because kindergarten is really boring. I think it's for babies. I'm really tired. Your little letter is precious. I love you a lot, Julius, and be good. Señorita Julia isn't very nice and she's got black hair on her arms. She's always pinching and I don't know why Mommy always calls her ever since Aunt Susana recommended her. Put up with her for Mommy's sake; she's really feeling bad. I'll finish writing to you this afternoon because I have to rest now.

They said I shouldn't finish the letter today. I just woke up and it's already nighttime. It'll be better if I write again tomorrow, so I'll just send what I have. The oldest doctor just came in. Here he is. Bye, Julius. I love you,

CINTHIA

Then three letters came from Mommy and after that Juan Lucas stopped by the house looking refined and serious. Finally there was a phone call from the United States. It seems like Juan Lucas had been there waiting for it, because he sat for a long time next to the telephone and as soon as he finished talking he said he was going to Boston and taking Santiago with him. Santiago fell into his arms crying and Juan Lucas grimaced, seeming to grow old. Santiaguito kissed everyone at the mansion door and it was over. No one went with them to the airport to say good-bye. They would return when the miracle happened.

Meanwhile Julius was being tutored for hours on end by Señorita Julia, but she never pinched him. Something strange was happening because he was always waiting for the big pinch, despite his absentmindedness, but nothing happened; on the contrary, Señorita Julia seemed a little frightened and always looked at him with fear. Later she began to speak to him softly, and each time her voice got softer and softer. One day she barely murmured, pray, child, pray, after which Julius threw up and began to shake all over.

That night Aunt Susana and Uncle Juan came over to the house with a telegram. Bobby had gone to a friend's house and Julius had gone to bed. The servants went to the door to let them in, shrugging their shoulders on the way, expressing fear and despair, and then Nilda's scream offended the mansion. And she screamed again and again. Calm down, please calm down, you're going to frighten the children, go get Julius, you've probably woken him up, it's better for him not to know anything until his mother returns, poor thing. Then the Lastarrias became bored watching the servants cry and so they went into the study to sit for a while. She was praying. He remained silent until he couldn't stand it any longer and began to walk from painting to painting, jealous of so much family history and muttering there's nothing like tradition. Julius, kneeling in front of his bed upstairs, prayed by heart while the servants knelt around him: Vilma, attentive, held a chamber pot; Carlos, hiding his face in his large hand, cried; Nilda sobbed as quietly as possible. Julius looked at them, trembling, getting choked up, and understanding what had happened.

Then there was the scene at the airport. From there they went directly to the cemetery. Orders from the Señores: no one was to go, they didn't want to see anybody, only Bobby and Carlos, who would drive. Juan Lucas directed the whole affair with a grimace, as if he were suffering from a severe upset stomach, hair in slight disarray and wearing a sport coat that he probably preferred not to put on for such an occasion. Susan was drugged. She remembered clutching a handkerchief and a little box of different-colored pills, when was that? She opened her eyes and through her dark glasses she saw a brownish-looking airport and then Juan Lucas' brown chest, come this way, woman. Carlos took charge of Bobby who was clinging to Santiaguito.

My God! When will it all end! The Mercedes drove through old, poor, ugly neighborhoods. This is Lima? They were following the hearse through strange old hostile streets that were new to her when Santiago died. My God! My God! Susan, honey. People were staring at the two vehicles as they drove by, men and women were sitting on the curb, in the doorways of their houses, watching them go by; some children crossed the street and turned to look at them curiously, hatefully, wretchedly. Then a curve, now a straight, wide stretch, the people seemed farther away standing on the sidewalks. We're getting closer. The police let them through respectfully: go ahead, go ahead, motioning them on with their arms.

"You can park the car here, Carlos," Juan Lucas tells him, running his hand over his hair. Look out the window before you open the door, even here they want to be paid to watch your car. He opened the door, Go on, scoot, beat it! Open the back door, come this way Susan, with me, come on Bobby, you too Santiago. They know the way to the family crypt; their father, Santiago, is there. They walked among the tombs and row after row of stacked niches formed recesses in the walls which looked like huge white, frozen beehives that were shut forever. Other people like them were there, but they don't see them passing by silently, never touching, always apprehensive. There were women with little bottles of alcohol who were cleaning tombs, a priest, gardens and, of course, flowers. Here it is. A priest was waiting for them, and they descended into the cold depths of the tomb, a world of marble, and came upon the funeral home employees again who proceeded with technical virtuosity, the professionals of the irreparable, experts in sadness, working in an unbearable situation, and the priest working now for the hereafter. Cinthia, little angel, next to your father. Wet cement. Juan Lucas extends his hand and, trembling, scratches a few letters in the mixture, then a little cross, drops the trowel and embraces everyone. Slowly, he nudges them up the stairs, they don't look back but go up like the rest of the men, into the wind, through the gardens and among the dead. They reach the gate and continue forward while Juan Lucas, still in command, lets Bobby, Santiaguito, and Susan walk on ahead. Outside the cemetery, hoards of children had been watching the car, unaware and not taking heed that everything had ended.

They turned down the lights at the mansion. They didn't open a single venetian blind, a drape, nothing. Bobby and Santiaguito would go to mass with their mother every day before going to school. They had to study like crazy so they could take their final exams early and then travel to Europe. They were leaving at the end of the month with their mother and Uncle Juan Lucas. Julius, meanwhile, would continue studying with Señorita Julia and next year they would put him straight into first grade. Several decisions had been made quickly. The mansion remained dark, but inside everyone acted nervously in order to forget. Susan took too many sedatives and Uncle Juan Lucas recommended she dress in gray and play golf until the day they left. One day Julius asked Susan to take him with them to Europe and she noticed that he was squinting. The only thing to do was call the doctor and tell him that he's squinting the same way Cinthia did when her nanny Bertha died. The doctor told her of his extreme susceptibility and for no reason should they even consider taking him to Europe. However, he recommended taking him to Chosica's dry climate (outside of Lima, heading toward the mountains) and inundating him with vitamins. They considered taking him to Juan Lucas' house in the fancy Condor neighborhood, but where would they put the servants? He owned a bachelor's apartment. Something had to be decided quickly.

IV

JULIUS AND ALL the servants left for Chosica. The laundress Arminda took advantage of the situation and brought along her daughter, Dora, who had been causing problems recently; she had even run off with one of the D'Onofrio ice cream vendors. Nilda brought along her new baby and it's still unknown today how she had it, only that one day she began to look inflated under the cook's apron and one afternoon she asked for the day off to have her baby. She returned the following week, lugging that little monster around, ready for the trip to Chosica. But her aesthetic concerns were directed more toward Julius than toward her baby and, as soon as they moved in, she decided to take advantage of the Señora's absence in order to train Julius' ears to stay closer to his head. Bandages, adhesive tape . . . what she didn't use in order to put them in their place! It got to be so bad that Vilma began to gripe but Jungle Woman threatened her with an enormous butcher knife, recently purchased for their new abode.

Invisible from the street because it was surrounded by tall, white walls, the house was located in a pretty part of Chosica. The backyard butted up against the rocky hills where one lives in constant fear of the huge boulders up there; however, none ever came rolling down. No wonder the rent was so high: there was a swimming pool and a large garden full of trees, even a small cane thicket where Julius would find a toad on the trail and, sweating, return yelling, Nilda, I made it to Madre de Dios, all of which took place in front of Jungle Woman's and her little son's bedroom. It didn't seem necessary to leave the house at all, especially on Sundays and holidays when half of Lima would end up in Chosica to take in the sun and fill up the place with horrendous yellow cars and long-haired free and easy women who, by the end of the day, would eventually leave the entire place littered with fruit peels and paper wrappers. But the ones they simply had to visit some afternoon were the French nuns at the Belén de Chosica monastery. They just had to go because one of the nuns was Juan Lucas' aunt and she had given them a card of introduction.

Three times a week—Mondays, Wednesdays, and Fridays—that witch Miss Julia, whose arms were covered with black hair, would come to teach Julius a million different things. Once the lessons got going in Chosica she began to pinch him and Julius wanted to kill her. Nevertheless, there were times when she would awake his curiosity, which was mainly when she talked to him about Cinthia, when Cinthia was her student and how intelligent and sweet and tender the little child was. Julius always wanted to hear more about his sister, and he never tired of listening to her, even though they were the same anecdotes, the same adjectives: tender, sweet, adorable Cinthia.

Others who came were the two doctors; they came together on a weekly basis and would examine him while he stood there naked. Then they would consult each other for a long while, right there in front of him, but his mind was already on Cinthia. On their way out, they would leave a pile of prescriptions: one preferred syrups, the other shots. They would say Julius was just fine, that he was recuperating astoundingly well. Also, a young woman would come by to give him the shots. Getting them made Julius' rear tremble like jelly out of fear, so she would pay him a nickel to let her give him the shot; then she would charge a dollar afterward for having given him the shot.

Despite these annoying moments, life in Chosica was peaceful. Finally they went out for a walk one day and knocked on the green door of the Belén de Chosica school. A French-speaking nun opened the door but quickly resorted to Spanish when she saw they didn't understand one iota. Vilma handed her the little introduction card. The nun read it and immediately motioned for them to go inside. She loved having visitors and showing them how pretty their school was. She would take them from one place to another and then to the surrounding patios and gardens. From a window Julius could see a bunch of girls who were studying. He was told that they were in class now and he should wait because they would be out soon. In the meantime, they could visit the Mother Superior in her office. Come teesway, said the French nun, all in white, who led them to the principal's office.

The Mother Superior was an old lady and her Spanish was bad. Also she didn't seem to recall the nun who had given them the calling card. Nevertheless she offered them little chocolates and gave them miniature illustrated prayer cards. The one she gave Vilma was larger than the others and it looked more important too. The ones she gave Julius, on the other hand, were more angelical with a lot of white and blue, some big trees, and little, obedient lambs. It was a little bucolic, kind of pastoral-looking. There wasn't a second round of chocolate candy— that would have been gluttony—yet the visit never seemed to come to an end; then, all of a sudden, the nun sat down and began to ignore them completely. It was as if she had left the room, she didn't even see them. Four long minutes seemed to turn into four hours, a cold silence shrouded the room, and without a doubt the little nun had abandoned them in order to concentrate on someone else. And how could they possibly know? The Mother Superior had just drifted off into one of her brief but frequent celestial states of ecstasy and was about to complete a whole life of absolute goodness . . . it was just an instant: the poor thing would quickly realize that it was not her time to die and would become disappointed, just as if another had taken the exact little pastry that she wanted. Next time it'll be me. One thing for sure, she quickly fell silent and it seemed as if someone was softly fanning her. At last she tried to get the conversation going again, but she would drift off once more into the other world of celestial wonder and memories of trips. And the silence continued. And how were they to know? The silence, and the little old white lady, smiling, always somewhere else. They had goose bumps all over and were still there, above all, surrounded by all those Sacred Hearts. They started to tremble, wondering what was go- ing to happen next, and the fourth minute was just about up . . . when the Mother Superior spoke again in normal fashion, and Julius and Vilma let out a sigh. That strange moment came to an end and not one saint could make use of it: the situation, everything, was perfect for an apparition . . . the good kind . . . with three witnesses . . . all of differ- ent ages.

The Mother Superior stood up, temporarily abandoning the contem- plation of her celestial world. She approached Julius and made the sign of the cross over his head which sent him into a state of panic. She told him to run along and play with the boys et girls.

There was a large group of them who couldn't run and play at recess time because they had asthma and really looked pale. Julius talked to them and explained that his mother was in Europe with his brothers because his sister Cinthia had died. Then he told them that's why he squinted half the time and was going to get well in Chosica, that's why he had come here, and his story simply amazed the girls. Then bigger girls came over to where they were; they were in higher grades and babied him affectionately, hugging and kissing him until he started to frown. Then they began to ask him when he was going to start school and how old he was. He told them that he would be six that summer and that he was being tutored at home by Señorita Julia. He told them that he already knew how to read and write correctly, and with no spelling errors either. A pretty girl pulled out a pencil and a writing pad from her apron pocket and said, here, write something. He took the pen and began to write: "Miss Julia has black hair on her arms." He was about to add something else when the piece of tape holding back his floppy ear fell off and everyone broke out laughing. He took off running and Vilma followed after him but he didn't stop until he reached the street. He said he'd never go back there again.

In order to get home, they followed the school building to the right and up a steep street whose sidewalks were built like stairs. They were walking up the street quietly and pensively when Julius saw something that caught his attention. "They're beggars," Vilma told him, "don't go near them." But it was too late: Julius took off running and had already reached the place where they were sprawled out next to a side door of the school. He stopped nearby and began to look at them uninhibitedly. The beggars turned to look at him and some of them even smiled. He was about to ask them why they all had all those stewpots, but Vilma cut him off: "Let's go!" she ordered as she pulled hard on his arm. But it was useless. He stood firm, heels together, toes pointing in opposite directions, and hands straight down to his sides. Better let him be for a moment. The beggars began calling him sonny as they smiled at him inoffensively in all their wretchedness. They were a bunch of old, half-disabled Indians from the Andes. Just then the school door opened and a woman came out who was dressed almost like a nun, except for her hair done up in a bun. A man followed behind her calling out, the stew, the stew, as he pushed forward a rolling table upon which sat an enormous cauldron. An undoubtedly kind-hearted little nun stood behind them with her arms outstretched, blessing the whole operation.

IT WAS ABOUT this time that the first letters from Europe began arriving. The first one, postmarked Madrid, was addressed to Vilma with instructions to read certain parts to Julius. A letter indicating how Julius had recuperated reached Madrid from the doctors; hence, the family already knew that he was eating well, that he had gained back two pounds, and that he wasn't vomiting anymore. They knew as well that he didn't mention Cinthia anymore in any of his conversations and that he slept better now with new sedatives. Things were going well for them in Spain, but they were sad and missed Julius very much. It was a real pity they couldn't have brought him along, but it was better this way because, frankly, he wasn't old enough to enjoy all those museums and he would have had to walk everywhere. They still hadn't visited a museum yet but, for the children's sake, after all, they were behaving so well, they would sometime soon. Señor Juan Lucas has some really good friends in Madrid, and every day they would take him to play golf somewhere outside the city. No doubt about it, that really worked to calm down everyone's nerves. It was just what they needed. Find some kind of diversion, forget about things. Yet they were sad. It wasn't easy to cheer them up, but Señor Juan Lucas and his friends were doing everything they could to entertain them. No one knew them in Madrid as they were known in Lima, and they were freer to go out and eat at restaurants. Moreover, they didn't have to dress in black which was always so depressing. Vilma would understand how important it is to do something different, go out, change environments, try to forget. Señor Juan Lucas was teaching Santiaguito to play golf and he was learning quickly. He was getting along better with his uncle all the time. Bobby was swimming a lot now and he had met some friends his age. Frankly, they were doing fine in Madrid and they would like to stay a little longer than they had planned. Then they would go to Paris and London in order to buy clothes and presents for everyone. It was important to travel around and take your mind off things in order to forget. They were waiting to receive a little note from Julius. Please write. They wanted to know how he was getting along with Miss Julia. Señor Juan Lucas asked about him many times, so he should write him a little note too. She should write them about everything Julius is doing in Chosica. Take a picture of him and send it. Take him out for a drive in the car with Carlos, but be careful with all the traffic. And,

Julius, darling:

The doctor tells me that you are doing just fine. He says you are eating better every day and soon you'll be as strong as Tarzan. Do what he and Vilma say. Study hard so you can start grade school. Next time you'll come with us. Mommy promises you. Your Uncle Juan sends his love. He's just finished tying his tie. He's a very handsome guy, darling. That's the way you'll be when you grow up. He's asking me to hurry up. Your Mommy still isn't ready and it's already time to go. Hugs and kisses.

LOVE

46

Susan signed the letter English-school style, stuck it in an expensive envelope, quickly stood up, and went toward the mirror where Juan Lucas was looking at himself as he perfected the knot in his tie. A few minutes later they were in the hallway where Santiaguito and Bobby were waiting for them. The elevator took them smoothly to the first floor where Juan Lucas' friends were waiting, then effusive greetings and, where shall we dine tonight? First an appetizer in the bar and then we'll decide. The golfer knew all the restaurants: local fare, expensive local fare, and simply expensive. And some bullfighters came along so that Santiaguito would be even more impressed with Juan Lucas, so much so that after that night was there going to be anything Juan Lucas didn't know about? Was there anyone he didn't know? The drinks had barely arrived and he was already very ebullient, laughing gaily, doting on Susan more than ever as with no other woman and, in fact, there wasn't anyone else like her, olé! What's the verdict? Is Juan Lucas going to get married on us? Well, that's not easy to answer; his buddies had been speculating, and now they were all in the bar, happy, watching the drinks being served, looking at Juan Lucas look at Susan. Wow! This couple deserves a toast . . .

THINGS WERE GOING so well in Chosica that those who were in Europe could have remained there for years if they had wanted. Julius was feeling better all the time. He was squinting less; in fact he was hardly squinting at all, although he still looked thin, especially his face with those ears held back flat to the sides of his head with adhesive and scotch tape. He managed to tolerate Señorita Julia without protesting too much, but he found Jules Verne to be much more entertaining. He discovered him during one of his excursions to Chosica Baja while Vilma made eyes at the bookstore clerk. In Chosica Baja, Julius was overwhelmed with the fruit market and dead animals hanging from enormous hooks. Lately he had been accompanying Vilma and Nilda to buy food. People there began to recognize him and greet him with smiles: he was the Dumbo-eared little boy who came with the insolent cook and the good-looking nanny.

One day, while strolling through the market, he discovered a North American painter sporting a beard, smoking a pipe, and wearing tennis shoes. This guy captured his imagination immediately, sitting there in a funny way, painting pictures of the market sellers and learning Spanish.

The gringo stuttered but was super likable. "Draw me, Mister! Draw me!" the stallkeepers begged, and he would answer, li-little by little, because he couldn't paint them all at once. But as soon as he spotted Julius with an overflowing basket of food and Vilma at his side, he asked them to pl-please not leave, for he wanted to-to paint them. And within minutes he had finished the sketch, and later he would add color because Julius was getting tired of holding the basket with a huge fish flopping out. Also, everything that he was telling him while he posed seemed cute and worthy of attention. Vilma just about had a heart attack when he invited them to have a soft drink and talk a while. Julius said fine with him, but she said no, another time, they were in a hurry. Nevertheless, at that moment Nilda appeared with a basket full of garlic, cabbage, celery, onions, etc. and in order to go against whatever Vilma would say, she said yes. They went to a restaurant-bar, a kind of enormous terrace over the river, near the hanging bridge.

That's where Nilda drank a quart of beer and talked the Mister's head off, telling story after story about the jungle. Vilma, on the other hand, just listened and smiled. Julius was all eyes and ears because Peter, that was the painter's name, had already been to the jungle and knew Iquitos, Tarapoto, and Tingo María like the back of his hand. Besides, he had been down the Amazon River and to Brazil and Belem du Pará: he'd been just about everywhere. Now he was traveling all over Peru and he would earn his way by painting pictures. He had a beard because he was too lazy to shave and he hardly ever lit his pipe even though it never left his mouth. "It's his pacifier," said Nilda, letting out a wide laugh that displayed an abundance of cavities and gold teeth. Peter didn't understand the joke, so he just smiled and asked more questions about the jungle. That's when Nilda really opened up and told him everything she knew, even more. For her the most important thing to do was to keep talking, talk and more talk, and to flaunt herself in front of the Mister and to charm him, well, not just him and Julius but all of them, you know, leave them flabbergasted so that Vilma would seem inarticulate and dumb to them. Also, if she entertained him, he might paint her picture. That morning was a happy one for Julius. Never before had Jungle Woman told so many stories about the jungle, never had the snakes been so venomous, the baby tarantulas so terrible, nor the banana spider so small and annoying. Nilda had no idea as to history; basically her chronology of life in the Peruvian jungle was a pile of shit: her childhood, her adolescent years, her adult years in Tarapoto, she mixed everything up and, little by little, the jungle turned into a place where savage jungle Indians, totally naked at the time, came and went through the dangerous greenery, from the encampment of the foreign linguists to the ones run by the Evangelists, for example, and on the way they would run into millionaire rubber magnates who were a lot richer than Julius' father, may he rest in peace. Nilda even remembered the names of those who lit their cigarettes with paper money and built palaces in the middle of the jungle. The poor woman did everything she could to enrapture the Mister. But he didn't paint her; he preferred instead to listen to her talk, after which it became late, time to return home and give Julius his lunch. As it turned out, Peter and Julius hardly had a chance to talk, but they agreed to meet again, and the painter promised to get more done on the painting by the next day.

A LETTER FROM the Señora postmarked France was waiting at home for Vilma. They wrote that they had received Julius' little letter just before leaving Madrid. It was beautiful, exquisite, and they wanted him to write more. They were on the Cote d'Azure but the weather wasn't very nice. Santiaguito had met an Italian girl and didn't want to leave there for anything and he was even refusing to go to Paris. Señor Juan Lucas was going to take charge when the moment came to do something about the matter. The Señor's friends were taking good care of them. She felt a little more at ease. All the hustle and bustle and so many airplanes kept her mind off things. That morning they were invited to go out on a boat (Susan used the English word *yacht*) and she would be able to relax at sea. It always relaxed her a great deal. They were delighted with Julius' progress. The doctors had written again, indicating that things couldn't be better. Only Paris, London, Rome, and Venice were left, but they would be returning in time for Julius' sixth birthday and he should get ready for school. And,

Julius, darling:
   We're really in a hurry now because they are waiting to take us out on the yacht. Your little letter is simply a jewel. We all read it. Your uncle, too. Bobby and Santiaguito just adore your Uncle Juan Lucas. You are going to love him, too, darling. That's very important for all of us. Hugs and kisses.

MOMMY.

Twenty minutes later, Susan, Juan Lucas, Santiaguito, and Bobby were plying the waters in *La Mouette;* they had been invited by one of the golfer's friends who lived in that area where life is seen through rose-colored glasses. They sailed along looking constantly at the sky because at first it didn't look like the weather would get any better. They spoke English so the boys would understand, but later, when the sun came out and the hours, blue on the ocean, began to go by, and when the lobster with its salty tinge allowed them to enjoy the ocean through all five senses, Juan Lucas drank a sip of dry white wine and, rounding his Spanish mouth in order to eulogize the wine, began a long speech in French with the best of pronunciation.

THE YOUNG WOMAN who always gave Julius his shots was sick, so Palomino came. He showed up one afternoon riding a bicycle and carrying a black doctor's bag with gold initials and the works. He rang the bell acting like he was important, and when Celso opened the door he said he had come looking for the little boy Julius, as if he were a friend who had come to visit him. He even took a seat in the vestibule. Celso despised him immediately and then Palomino scorned Celso. The Mestizo backlander was a medical student and he earned money giving shots. He considered himself the Don Juan of Chosica, which required that he always show off a new, horrible but impeccable dark blue suit every Independence Day; in reality he was the king of the housemaids at the main plaza in the center of town. Moreover, he was an expert at giving shots, which made him proud (he himself would say it).

Around that time things were not going very smoothly between Vilma and Nilda, and they almost got into it precisely the day Palomino came for the first time. Julius was playing in Nilda's room, asking her when she thought she would baptize her baby. First Nilda frightened him by the way she said that she wasn't a Catholic but an Evangelist. Then she informed him as to what it meant to be an Evangelist, that there were many religions, and that Catholicism wasn't necessarily the single true religion. Whatever Julius understood from all this, perhaps it was very little or practically everything, he was dumbfounded. The poor little guy just stood there, his eyes bulging out, hands straight down at his sides, ecstatic, and still wanting to hear more. Right then Nilda's baby began to cry and she held him with one hand as if he were just a small package. With her other hand she unbuttoned her dress, withdrew an enormous fleshy breast with an incredible pink-pimpled nipple in the middle, and began to breast-feed her baby. She continued to talk about Evangelism and he became paralyzed, unable to leave. He was trembling, he couldn't hold it anymore, he felt a bitter taste in his mouth and by the time he looked over at the door, it was too late: he had already vomited. Even while he was throwing up he felt he didn't want to do it there. At that moment Vilma walked in looking for him and understood immediately what was going on, perhaps because she was so prejudiced against Nilda for the knife incident the other day. Moreover, the scene with Peter the painter at the marketplace had made their relationship even worse. Julius looked at Vilma as if seeking help but he couldn't help himself. He looked down at the dirty floor and then at Vilma and Nilda, who continued to feed her baby. And there was her bosom. Vilma accused Nilda of a million things and Jungle Woman told her to wait until she had finished with the baby, for she was going to kill her. Luckily, Celso came in to announce that a certain Palomino had arrived to give a shot.

Vilma checked carefully to make sure that Julius had not dirtied himself and she cleaned out his mouth with a perfumed washcloth. She knew that he was practically well now and that the vomiting was caused by something else and it would be best if no one found out about it, especially the doctors and even the guy who had come to give the injection. Palomino got to his feet when he saw them coming. He didn't even notice Julius but, on the other hand, he completely ogled Vilma. "Who gets the shot?" he asked, knowing full well that it was for the child, but he wanted her to say who should receive it in order to be able to respond, "What a pity," just as a few rays of light shone through the window conveniently reflecting off the initials on his doctor's bag. Vilma smiled coquettishly.

THE YOUNG WOMAN who had been giving shots up until then never came back. Her month of sick leave went by and that was it. Now it was Palomino who came regularly, even when nobody needed a shot. And he spent hours talking to Vilma, which really bored Julius. Everybody except Vilma felt an aversion toward him, his bicycle, his dark blue suit, and his black doctor's bag. That guy Palomino acted like he was God's gift to medicine, not knowing that Carlos, Celso, and Daniel wanted to pulverize him. As for Nilda, she let everyone know that Vilma was a tramp: just wait until the Señora returns to find out what was going on, now that Vilma was going around flirting with that nurse and forgetting about the child Julius. Palomino totally ignored everyone else, he didn't even bother to say hello anymore. Each day he spent more and more time with Vilma in the garden and one day, engrossed in conversation with her, he even forgot to give Julius his shot. Another time he brought his box camera and made her pose for the longest time. Carlos and the butlers had gone out, Nilda was tied up with her baby, and God only knows where Arminda and her daughter were. The only sure thing was that Julius, who was dying to see Peter the painter in the marketplace again, was going stir crazy. He had told the painter he would go that afternoon, but Vilma wouldn't pay any attention to him. And Palomino almost yelled at him to hold off a while, be patient, don't bother them. And then Vilma came out wearing a bathing suit that the Señora had given her, one that was ridiculously too tight on her and showed everything. Those stupid artistic poses made her look like she was aspiring to become a rumba dancer. One thing for sure, the Chola was ravishing and Palomino: that's it, yeah, just like that, and from all angles, in black and white, even in technicolor, he said, the hours flew by, and poor Julius just waited it out. Finally, he left.

It was easy to find his way to Chosica Baja: it was just a matter of taking the first street to the left and then finding the main plaza two blocks away. From there he would continue straight ahead until he reached one of those stairlike streets that would descend to the wide, main thoroughfare, 28 de Julio Avenue, with all its shops, bazaars, and grocery stores. The marketplace was at the end of one of the side streets near the river. It wasn't difficult to find. Of course, an adventure of this type would make any child who was Julius' age a little apprehensive, to say the least, but Julius, motivated to find Peter the painter at the marketplace, forgot about his fear and never felt lost for one single moment. And he had already found the hot dog stands, the vendor stalls, the peddlers, vegetables, large shiny fish, and huge hanging pieces of red beef and lamb. And there was Peter, too, with his palette and bag full of paints and all. He was talking to a vendor, surrounded by curious market people, some were pickpockets, others were sincere admirers. Upon seeing Julius, his pipe slipped slightly to the right as he smiled and called him over with one hand and pointed with the other to something at the back of a nearby stall. Julius went over to him and, for the first time in his life, took the initiative to shake hands without anyone towering over him and saying, shake his hand, child.

Peter the painter at the marketplace introduced him to the local vendors. Stuttering a great deal, he told him that the painting was finished and he was going to give it to him. Then he asked about Nilda and Vilma. Julius told him that they were busy at home, that's why he had to come alone, but he hadn't gotten lost or anything. Peter smiled and said he had been working on his Spanish classes (that's what he called talking to the people on the street). In reality, he learned a lot, but his accent was downright atrocious and there was always someone who made fun of him but, naturally, no real malice was intended. It was mainly kindness and respect because the Mister had become a kind of institution around there. He was always painting, always talking with the people, always talking about his country and his travels, always with his pipe in his mouth and, of course, always stuttering. It was difficult for him to communicate with the locals, but he never gave up trying.

After about ten minutes he said good-bye to everyone and went with Julius down to the kiosk where he had stashed the painting. Julius grasped it with both hands and stood there staring at it for a while before he said he liked it and thanked him. There they were—he and Vilma—identical to real life, and on one side was the big basket with the fish hanging out and the vegetable stand in the background. His friend was a good painter. Julius told him he was taking the painting home with him and going to hang it in his bedroom. His house in Chosica was new, he explained, and it needed some paintings. Peter the marketplace painter asked if he would like to have a soft drink at the restaurant overlooking the river. Sure he would.

They talked for a long time sitting in front of their bottles. Julius responded accurately to all his questions and covered the entire family history. Nothing was as moving for the gringo as the bit about the carriage at the house in Lima. The poor guy was dying to paint it, but by the time Julius would be going back to Lima, he'd probably be in Cuzco or Puno, places in Peru he hadn't visited yet. For Peter was taken by Julius' ingenious version of the family's splendor, his father, his mother's beauty, Bertha's funeral, his romantic great-uncle and the tuberculous pianist. Wanting to know more, he asked other questions, but he quickly realized that Julius became very agitated when he spoke about his sister Cinthia. He turned pale, unable to lift the glass from the table.

That's why he asked Julius if he had ever crossed a hanging bridge. The timing was perfect because the idea of crossing the river on one of those swinging bridges fascinated him. Vilma had refused to take him there. The gringo called to the waiter and paid for the soft drinks. "Let's go," he told him, and they left for the bridge. Before starting across, he showed him how much it rocked and then asked him if he was afraid. Julius responded that he wasn't and walked ahead serenely. At one point he was going across by himself, getting too close to the edge, and Peter got a little panicky but he didn't say a word; it wasn't because he didn't care but because he had modern ideas about educating children.

Because of Julius he was on the verge of conjuring up memories of his own childhood. The gringo was fascinated and, in fact, overcome with emotion. In reality he was a loner and lately . . . but once on the other side of the bridge he pointed to the Railway Hotel. The building was falling apart from old age, but it was a historical landmark and still had some charm to it. Julius seemed to understand its importance and began to listen attentively as Peter told him it was a very old hotel, made entirely of wood, look closely, hardly anyone stayed there anymore although in better times even pr-pre-presidents and government mi-ministers had stayed there. Finally Julius couldn't stand it any longer and asked him why he stuttered. Peter, who stopped stuttering imme-diately, told him that he wasn't born that way but it began when he was a child . . . and it was similar to what Julius had told him about Cinthia and about his crossed eyes. It was an emotional moment, right then and there in front of the Railway Hotel.

Then they talked for a time with a charming old man who was the hotel administrator. He knew the history of Chosica from prehistoric times. The old guy even invited them to have a soft drink. He was en-chanted with his North American guest, one at last after so many years, as if poor Peter were a rich tourist and his appearance that day signified the rebirth of that forgotten area of Chosica. That too was very sad. Julius felt he shouldn't accept the soft drink because he was feeling a little nauseous; besides, the gringo was looking forlorn and only the little old man was jubilant.

And he kept smiling as the others began to work their way down among the rocks toward the river. He stood there alone, smiling, im-mersed in his memories. After a moment he got up and moved to a point where he could continue watching them. There they were, down below, sitting on two rocks, sticking their feet in the river. He would have given anything to hear what they were talking about, but he was too far away and, moreover, they were hardly talking. They only exchanged photo-graphs. Julius said that's Cinthia and the gringo said that's me when I was young, about your age, when I was five. They had already been there a while when Peter began to show signs of fatigue and all of a sudden Julius saw that he had become very pale. In fact, he even looked worse—really tired and nervous—as they climbed up toward the hotel. By the time they reached the bridge, he was really bad off. But he asked Julius if he still dared to cross it and he assured him that he could; it hardly moves, he added, setting the other at ease. Peter smiled and patted Julius on the head as he started across. He stood watching him, there he goes, where'd he go? Be-be-be, he wanted to say be careful, but he got hung up on the first word, be-be-be . . . there wasn't anything left to talk about, tomorrow he was leaving for good, somebody at the market would say good-bye for him when Julius would go looking for him another day.

As Julius returned to Upper Chosica, he was invaded with feelings of doubt: Vilma's probably very worried and it was all his fault, but he just had to take full advantage of his adventure, maybe just a little longer. At that moment he remembered the vagabonds who must be waiting for their handout . . . Vilma would never take him there, they were probably looking for him, it was all his fault. Nevertheless he headed off for the Belén school. He arrived just as the woman appeared who looked like a nun except for the bun in her hair. The other two people were there also—the man pushing the portable table with the big pot and the nice little nun who blessed everyone with her smile. Poor Julius was disappointed: the beggars didn't even notice him because they went straight for the pot. He had been hoping to show them the painting and tell them he could bring his painter friend so he could paint them. He had been lugging that painting all over and had gotten tired out. Since it would take hours for them to finish eating, he decided to leave. Just then the little nun began asking those typical questions: Where's your Mommy? What are you doing here? Why are you all by yourself? Foolish child! And a thousand other things. The poor thing was becoming desperate, and she spoke with that luscious French accent. The beggars, who continued to make sure that their bowls were filled to the brim, didn't even notice the nun, Bendición, leading him away by the hand.

AT HOME World War III had started. It all began when Vilma finished posing for Palomino and went to her room to change back into her smock. Returning, she crossed paths with Nilda, who looked at her loathsomely. Jungle Woman asked her where little Julius was and she said he was in the garden. Where did she think he was? Suspecting something was up, she blurted out from habit, Juuuuuuuuuli-uuuuuuuuus!! but no response. He definitely was not in the garden. That's what you get for hanging around with that Casanova! Now where could that boy Julius be hiding? What if the Señora finds out! Vilma told her to quit bugging her. The poor girl was starting to get worried when Jungle Woman let out a second Juuuuuuuuli-uuuuuuuuus! Still no response. Maybe he's upstairs, but it would have been impossible for him not to hear them. The two women sensed simultaneously that something was wrong, and together they lunged toward the stairs, tripping several times on their way up. They ran from room to room. Julius was not to be found.

"You're to blame for goofing off, for whoring arou . . ."

She never got to finish because Vilma, nervous, pounced on her and they started to beat each other up, knocking themselves against the walls, falling over chairs, rolling on the floor, screaming, howling, and wailing.

In the garden, Palomino heard the noise but he really didn't know what to do. He wasn't even sure where the noise was coming from: Auuu! Ayyy! Let me go! Help! He even heard Palomiiiiiino! But the doors were locked and there was no way he could intervene. Minutes ticked away, but soon he was sure that the two women were fighting. The poor devil began to get worried. It frightened him to think that he might become involved in something serious; meanwhile the screaming continued and their howling made things as clear as a bell: they were trying to kill each other. Nilda had scratched Vilma's entire face and now Vilma was strangling her. Just then the men servants arrived. They entered with a bed that they had just unloaded from the Mercedes when they ran into Palomino, looking insolent, in the garden. They wanted to pulverize him but then they heard the screaming. Carlos dropped the bed and took off running, opened the front door, and ran upstairs. The first thing he saw were the two women, exhausted but still trying to inflict harm on each other. Their smocks were torn to shreds and Vilma sobbed in a corner of the room. Her little finger had been broken during one of the last falls, and when Carlos finally saw her she could only defend herself against Nilda's sporadic assaults with her legs.

"The boy has disappeared," Jungle Woman sobbed. "It's all her fault."

Carlos took off in a flash to alert the butlers. He found them in the garden thwarting Palomino's possible getaway and told them that Vilma had let Julius get away.

"Because she was fooling around with this jerk here."

It was the greatest opportunity of their lives. Palomino's smile expressed both insolence and fear, and he began to venture forth an explanation. He just wanted a brief word with them but by then there was no way to stop Celso and Daniel. The needle expert quickly put his camera away and began to back away when out of the clear blue both of them leaped on top of him and began to rip him apart right there in the garden among the trees by the little cane thicket. They really got him dirty, they messed up his hair, and they destroyed what they hated the most about him: his face, his satchel, and his dark blue suit. Lastly, they threw him bodily out the door and into the street.

Then they ran back upstairs to find out what had happened. Vilma and Nilda were standing up now, still crying and unable to explain things very clearly. Frankly no one really knew what had happened nor when Julius had disappeared, nor if he had been taken hostage, nor anything. Jungle Woman said that those beggars at Belén were gypsies and had most likely taken Julius, which meant that they'd probably never see him again.

"Perhaps he'll come back some day as a circus hand, but by then he would be a certified gypsy and wouldn't even remember his family."

Then she said that couldn't be right: more than likely, that degenerate, queer gringo painter had kidnapped, raped, and killed Julius. She was interrupted by Vilma's screaming, who was by then half out of her mind and throwing herself at the walls, sobbing loudly as she damned her luck and Palomino too, for she hadn't flirted with anyone! Please forgive her! She only wanted him to take a few pictures of her! Julito! Julito! Julito! My God! What's going to happen to me! Nilda became frightened by her own words and also weeped as the butlers were about to follow suit. Carlos began to think: he wouldn't dare call the police. And the Señores were in Europe!

At that very moment, the telephone rang and Carlos leaped at it. They were calling from the Belén school to say that Julius was there. The chauffeur said he would pick him up immediately and explained that the maid's carelessness had led to Julius' escape. He was on his way. Their hearts stopped pounding. They looked at each other, smiling sheepishly, trembling, worn out, relieved; they just stood there, smiling and embarrassed, while Carlos took off in the Mercedes.

Julius was waiting casually at the door of the school and when he saw him arrive in such a nervous state he hastened to explain that nothing had happened: only that nun, who was afraid of beggars, didn't want him to go home by himself. So why did she feed them if they were so bad? At that moment the nun approached and began to scold Carlos with her luscious French accent. Carlos lowered his bare head with respect and listened to the sermon, but as soon as he saw her smile and make the sign of the cross over Julius' head when she began to leave, he quickly put his cap back on fearing she might do the same to him: not all nuns are real Santa Rosas.

All of them came out to greet him. Vilma and Nilda were still sniveling, their smocks were in shreds; Celso and Daniel pushed their hair back into place, satisfaction. Those brief unfortunate moments were behind them now and they could only see the prodigal child, who still hadn't figured out what the hell had happened during his absence. The women didn't even allow him to think about it. They showered him with kisses and asked him where had he been. Why had he left the house? And why didn't he let someone know? Julius, who was astounded, just looked at them waiting for an explanation: who had beaten them up? A chair that had come crashing down the stairs during the scrap was lying there in accusatory fashion. Vilma couldn't hold it back any longer and began to cry and wail. She begged their forgiveness and said she wouldn't ever see Palomino again! And Julius, above all, meant everything to her! She would never shrug her responsibilities again! The pictures were to blame! She wasn't a bad person! She had never let anyone touch her! And Nilda was totally wrong about her! She couldn't live without her little Julius! In the end, Nilda became emotional and also started to cry. Julius witnessed one of the worst sob sessions ever to take place. The men tried to calm them down, saying that nothing had happened, that every cloud has a silver lining, that basically they had been lucky, and that they were rid of Palomino.

Right then Julius thought perhaps he should fetch the painting and show it to them. It was a mistake because as soon as Vilma saw it she started sobbing all over again when she remembered that her face was all scratched up. One eye was swollen and her body was burning up. She just moaned, exposing a fleshy leg, half undressed and scratched all over: what a beautiful Chola! Nilda also sobbed and the more she cried, the more she hurt because her upper lip had been smashed and split open; now it was swollen and covered with dirt. They quickly went to the medicine chest to disinfect the wounds. Then they had to find the first available doctor in Chosica to look at Vilma's little finger and to have Nilda examined; she was complaining she couldn't breathe very well. She said she had been half-strangled and was probably going to die from what Vilma did to her. She almost started at her again, but Julius' presence stopped her. It was time to quit this fighting and use their heads. What kind of story were they going to invent to cover this up? What would they tell the doctor?

That afternoon they put a cast on Vilma's finger. The poor thing was really hurting, but she did her best to show the contrary and to appear efficient in her work. She followed Julius around from room to room and tried to please him in everything. At dinnertime he told her about his adventures: he had spent most of his time with Peter the painter at the marketplace, later he had gone to see the beggars for a while, and if it hadn't been for that meddling nun he would have been back home much sooner; but she didn't want him coming home alone. At that point in his story Vilma noticed that he became quite nervous; in fact, the more he talked the more agitated he became. And he talked on and on, repeating the story, changing it around each time as if he needed to keep talking. She had never seen him act like that. She ran to look for Nilda who had just made peace with her. Like the Greek myth, the Cholas had been liberated: they achieved reconciliation through battle and pain. Jungle Woman came in acting unperturbed and ready to help her cohort, but Vilma noticed that when she walked into the dining room he began to talk more and more, even more rapidly than before, in fact a lot more rapidly, and things got worse, not better. Suddenly he wasn't hungry anymore and, as he retold the story about Peter and himself, he blurted out repeatedly, I don't want any more, take the plate away, his painter friend had taken him to the river, take it away Vilma, he had met the old man at the wooden Railway Hotel, I'm not hungry, it belonged to the Central Railroad. Vilma flew out of the room and cried in the kitchen. Nilda, who couldn't take it either, went to find the butlers. Julius was relieved when he saw them, smiling and happy, enter the room. Carlos came in immediately with a bottle of sedatives that the doctor said to use if it were necessary.

"Here, Julian . . ."

Carlos was right: the next day he woke up feeling more relaxed. He had slept well; in fact, he felt very good and was ready for his class with Miss Julia. He only told her that Vilma and Nilda had fought over something that involved the two of them; there wasn't any need for her to know any more than that. Once again peace had come to Chosica and everyone around Julius tried hard to make it seem like nothing had ever happened. So did he.

At first Vilma didn't dare show her face around Miss Julia, but then she got up the courage when Nilda appeared, looking more primitive than ever with a piece of raw meat over her right eye and a scowling look of what's-it-to-you jumping out at you from her good eye. In her own delicate way, Miss Julia indicated without saying so that she knew about the vulgar goings-on of servants and cooks. All that had nothing to do with her world of the eternal student in the College of Education at the Four-Hundred-Year-Old National Superior University of San Marcos, the Oldest in America, not to mention her world as teacher at the Supreme School of Education Constructed by the Government of General Manuel A. Odría Who Came Down to the Plains in 1948. Nor did that world have anything to do with hers of Spanish Classes and Grammar Rules. Would these unfortunate souls have any idea what Syntax and Prosody meant? Or who Rubén Darío was? Or who the Poet of America was? However, she was the most refined disciple of the Carreño grammar manual, for she knew to say bon appetit when she saw someone eating and, what's more, to say thank you when someone said bon appetit to her. And there she was sitting next to Julius, correcting his spelling lesson, arms and legs covered with long, straight, black hair, not one strand of which was close to another but all stood on end. She was so crass in her little homemade dress, carrying that small wallet stuffed with bus tickets she always bought for both ways and with the best curled permanent in all Jesús María. And it goes without saying she was delighted to be in a millionaire's house, even though the Señora wasn't there and with whom she would love to talk, although the Señora wouldn't ever say a word when Miss Julia mentioned the Poet of America or that it was time someone did an in-depth analysis of Vallejo's poetry, which still represented a big void in Peruvian Letters. Someday she'll write her thesis, but Vallejo was too profound to write a thesis on and too deep to fill that void. Nevertheless, she would get her degree in pedagogy and make a lot more money not having to tutor in homes, drinking her tea in the pantry with the servants who worked in the houses that she visited, always waiting for the rich Señoras, the ones she admired with devotion, and firing her when she least expected it, like Señora Susan with Cinthia: the same thing will happen the day Dumbo here goes to school . . . thinking, thinking, Señorita Julia became bitter, she had already adopted the psychological attitude of one holding a flyswatter waiting for the fly to land: Julius missed a word and she pinched him hard.

Julius screamed and Vilma came in but she didn't dare intervene, fearing the teacher would overpower her with her educated Spanish. Ill-humored, the tutor seized the moment to say, girl, you look terrible. Who battered and bruised you like that? But Nilda interrupted her as she entered, demanding defiantly to know why the child had screamed out loud. Julius said that she had pinched him. By then Jungle Woman was furious and yelled at her: did she want to make him vomit again or what? It got to the point that the poor child began feeling nauseous and he asked if they could continue with the class. He didn't want any more problems. Miss Julia became frightened and said they would continue with the lesson, but the cook stood guard until the class was over. And the session was kind of interesting because she enjoyed the little poem that the tutor was teaching Julius for Mother's Day. Even though it was still a long way off, he'd have more time to memorize it, he was going to like it, your mother too. What else was he to do? . . . The poor kid would struggle through one of those poems that everyone recites as they extend a bouquet of flowers to their mommies, in the bathroom, for instance: you surprise her there and it's terrible, you die of shame.

Arminda was the laundress and her daughter, Dora, had prevented things from going very smoothly in Chosica. However, the doctors really didn't need to make those house calls anymore because Julius couldn't have felt better. Someone came in Palomino's place a few more times after which additional shots were not necessary. Vilma's finger was fine after the cast was removed and she was behaving wonderfully. In the afternoons all of them would take a ride in the Mercedes and drive as far away as Palomar or watch soccer games played by twenty-two Cholos, who would wear twenty-two different uniforms and all types of shoes—some were even barefoot—on improvised fields next to the highway. Sometimes there were games in the central park, but each team had its own uniform and each player had his own pair of soccer shoes. Upon returning from one of those games one afternoon, they found Arminda feeling distraught: Dora had run away to Lima with the ice cream man.

When Dora returned, Arminda slapped her up one side and down the other. She even threatened her with a kitchen knife, but Nilda demanded it back immediately. No, I won't, she told her. Poor Arminda. And Dora with that look of insolence on her face. No way. Mocking. Arrogant. Where'd she learn that? She's insolent. Nilda said she should wash her mouth out . . . if she were her child . . . and poor Arminda was fit to be tied: such a good person, so noble. Hadn't I been telling you? My God, what horrible manners! Up yours! She was about to hit her. Yes, give it to her. There. Forty years! More than forty years with her head stuck inside the washtub and her feet frozen from scrubbing and scrubbing. No! She had no conscience! She was a monster like her father! Poor Arminda just kept screaming at her. She was going to have a heart attack. Julius was frightened out of his wits and now Nilda's baby was screaming. Dora was trying to protect herself from the punches, and Nilda was exposing her breast to feed her baby. By the next day Dora had disappeared. She left a note saying she was going to the mountains with the D'Onofrio ice cream man. Arminda would be ashamed for the rest of her life.

"THE SEÑORA IS getting married to Señor Juan Lucas!" Nilda shouted, holding the open letter in her hand. Julius had just arrived from the market, where they had told him for the sixth time that Peter the painter had gone away without leaving a forwarding address. He was imagining him sitting on the edge of Lake Titicaca, palette and brush in hand, when he heard Jungle Woman's scream. "Give me that letter," he told her, clicking his heels together, toes pointing outward. Nilda gave it to him and he began to read a few words but, wanting to know quickly what was going on, he passed the letter to Vilma, hands glued to his sides.

> *Julius, darling:*
> *I'm really excited. Your Uncle Juan and I just got married in a little church in London. Just a few of his friends were there, some of Daddy's and mine too. We're happy. Santiaguito and Bobby are with us. You'll see how much you'll love Uncle Juan Lucas. He's a treasure, like you. We've only been married two hours and now we're going out to lunch to a restaurant near Onslow Gardens. I would give anything if you could be with us!*
> *I'm happy you're well. Soon our trip will be over. Only Venice and Rome are left, I think, but you should be preparing for our return to Lima because we'll be back soon. Anyway, we'll have a great summer in Lima with Uncle Juan Lucas, don't you think, darling? And then, Julius, it's off to school. I must run now, Juan Lucas is waiting for me in the bar. Everyone sends hugs and kisses.*

That night she was still wearing the green dress that she had worn for the marriage ceremony. She felt like she was the most beautiful woman on earth, the happiest there could be. And she probably was that morning while she walked, lovely, toward the hotel bar. Juan Lucas was there watching her enter; Santiago and Bobby were next to him, looking truly handsome in their dark suits with that air of primitive elegance that Susan liked in young men. They chatted with people they had just met, with their father's friends, the incredible John and Julius, who were drunk and still as enchanting as the first time she had met them. It seemed like yesterday! Yesterday she had met a Peruvian in London and married him in Lima, now she was marrying a Peruvian in London whom she had met in Lima. And to think that Juan Lucas was in London when she was going out with Santiago . . . It seemed like yesterday when she had promised Julius that she would name one of her children after him and now, upon seeing him, she decided to dash off a few lines to Julius . . . She smiled as she joined the group at the bar, preferring not to remember. And Juan Lucas helped her: he welcomed her by gently placing his hand on the back of her neck and, as he continued talking, drew her toward him, happy. Susan felt a slight pressure of the warm squeezing sensation on her neck and, reacting with a gesture of the Metro-Goldwyn-Meyer lion, opened her mouth uneasily. But as she was drawn over to Juan Lucas' shoulder, she began to discover that her neck perfectly accommodated the tenaciously delicious curve of his hand. She accepted a drink, putting her other arm around Juan Lucas, lowering her head as if to hide under a fallen lock of her blond hair which beautifully contrasted with the dark perfection that Juan Lucas had dressed in for the occasion. She closed her mouth with a smile and no one noticed the brevity of her gesture. Feeling his hand slide away from her neck, she was about to repeat the gesture again, almost turning her neck away but was afraid of not encountering his hand, afraid to demand too much, to bite, and that it may be just a memory, not the moment, that was slipping away. Really? How was it possible? They were asking her something. She always came out of those tender states, that's why they always found her so lovely, that's why they always forgave her and loved her so much.

V

THE MANSION, NOW full of light, awaited their arrival. The summer's sun filtered in through the spacious windows illuminating even the darkest corners, making it bright and cheery. Together Celso and Daniel had made sure that everything was shining again. Even the floors were brought back to their original shiny condition. Bad memories were banished, everything was ready for a new life, and they themselves got prepared to serve their new master. So much work—cooking, ironing, waxing, sweeping, mopping, and polishing—had inured them to the point that they didn't notice Cinthia's absence anymore.

They were up early on the day they were to go to the airport. Nilda filled the pantry with food while Vilma fixed the boy's clothing and

Carlos cleaned the cars. They told Julius to stay away from the carriage and to wait patiently until it was time to go. They had practically dressed him up for First Communion, which included his little bull-fighter tie. He waited nervously, remembering and associating this second trip to the airport with the first one, and preferred not to wait in the piano room. They checked on him every so often, always finding him at ease: I'm okay, he told them, not knowing all the while that he was learning the art of faking it, as his hands would tremble.

Carlos talked to him incessantly on the way. He told him that Santiago would be a man now. Everyone at home had agreed: Santiago was turning sixteen, and now he was coming back a young man, Europe had to have changed him. They insisted on this idea, as if a few months of being away were sufficient for them to accept the boy's adulthood, making him grow up in their minds. Bobby, too, for he would be approaching thirteen, going into high school, and no more short pants, he'd be bigger now. They drew near to the airport and Carlos continued to talk his head off trying to keep Julius entertained, and he was happy: you've had a good time in Chosica, now in just a few more months you'll be off to school. That's life, everyone grows up, everyone comes back . . .

Everyone returns to the place where they were born, Carlos sang, large lips, excited by his happiness, pleased as he pointed out the plane to him. "Just so they don't end up crashing like the heroic Jorge Chávez," he said, as if trying to think of something to say. "Just so nothing goes wrong, look, get ready to wave to your Mommy." He couldn't keep silent or stand still, he just couldn't look: yes, yes, it was the plane he had chosen for Cinthia. For Cinthia. For Cinthia. And the loudspeakers confirmed it: Air France. Flight 207. Arriving from Paris, Lisbon, Point-á-Pitre, Caracas, Bogotá, Lima. He felt sick to his stomach but this wasn't the time . . .

The two of them held their breath. "Open Sesame," Carlos seemed to say as he stood there on the observation deck, waiting for the door of the plane to open and talking to that strange creature. Yes, it frightened him: the sky is for angels and buzzards shouldn't fly higher than the rooftops, but why didn't they open that door? The chauffeur started to get agitated, he even criticized himself: hey, what's wrong with you? Why are you getting so emotional? As if it were your Mommy who was arriving! Well, she's just your employer, that's all. But as soon as the door started to open, he took his cap off. The boss lady's here, and he began to hum a tune, getting nervous as he always did when he would fret over something for which he shouldn't have. "Señor Juan Lucas," he cried out, seeing him appear on the stairs. Julius postponed vomiting for another day and began waving excitedly. In effect, there was Juan Lucas, dressed for the occasion (on the day of an earthquake, for instance, Juan Lucas would turn up yelling, "Help! My golf clubs!" And he'd be dressed perfectly for the occasion). Next to him was an airline stewardess who would have died to go out with him; the young girl was in that experimental stage of life, flew for the airlines, and wasn't ready to get married yet. But she was eliminated anyway as soon as Susan appeared, even if she did seem terrified, seeming to say, where am I? She didn't recognize anything, who knows what she had been thinking about during those last few minutes. No matter what, she was lovely, much more beautiful now as she exerted herself to wave: Hi. Hi. Hi. And not even seeing him yet. She took off her sunglasses and the light almost blinded her. She put them back on immediately, asking: "Where's Julius?" "Over there, Mom, over there," Santiago shouted directly into her ear. "Over there! Don't you see him?" She could see Carlos but she couldn't see Julius. "Don't worry, Mom! Just go down the stairs! You're holding everybody up!" They had occupied the whole ramp. "Hurry up!"

Naturally, the excess baggage cost the equivalent of several employees' salaries but for them it still didn't amount to much. The bulk of their things was coming by ship: entire sets of golf clubs for the whole family; English, French, and Italian clothing; gifts for everyone, even the laundress. Everything was purchased in quantity without selection: rare, exquisite liquors; decorations; lamps; jewelry; and more Dunhill pipe collections with leather tobacco pouches, each with the famous little marble dot. The trip had been a happy one for them but also too short, especially now that they were back in Lima. It was impossible to sum it up in so few words. People would ask them and nothing would be enough. After all, according to Juan Lucas, the social pages would take care of that with their "unmatched mendacity." Despite their opposition to it, their trip will be the talk of the town . . . (I don't get involved in those things: all that malarky about something belonging to the inner self of the Lima character. No one will ever know if one wants to appear in the "social pages" or not, because they all swear they don't . . .)

How the mansion had changed! Who had purchased all that beautiful furniture? Who chose those paintings! Orders had come from Juan Lucas to hire an efficient person with good taste to make the purchases. Carlos continued to unload the pigskin suitcases and was wearing that I-was-with-them expression and feeling superior. Vilma noticed that Santiaguito had become a man: he was looking at her. She immediately turned to Juan Lucas, the Master, and accepted his elegant, nearly six-foot stature, but not really knowing why, not understanding why he was famous for being so handsome. Frankly, he didn't look like any Mexican movie star that she had ever seen. But he did to the Señora. She turned around again and there, still looking at her, was Santiago. Nilda had rinsed off her garlicky-smelling hands and was ready to let out a scream of joy, but Juan Lucas' grimace stopped her in her tracks. Why are these women so excited? Get out of here! Get everything put away right now! Fix a *gin and tonic* on some breezy terrace of the world. Susan, of course, cared about them, but she knew about Nilda always smelling like garlic and, besides, Arminda was crying and wouldn't be able to stop crossing herself and blurting out: "May God bless those who arrive at this abode." Poor Susan, she did her best and kissed the cook, but see what happens? Arminda broke down and spilled the story about her daughter, Dora, and the D'Onofrio ice cream man. Celso and Daniel had to stop unloading the bags in order to console her and, at the same time, pull her from the Señora's arms. Finally Juan Lucas decided to bring an end to all this fraternizing. Impatiently he extended his arms outward as if to say stop. It had been many years since such firm orders were heard in the mansion. Susan was impressed: Put the suitcases where they belong, please. Be careful not to scratch the leather. Go upstairs and get us unpacked. Woman, please stop crying. He didn't even know her name, nor Nilda's for that matter, who kept coming in to present her child, shouting that she was going to educate him properly upon which she showed them the little monster. Juan Lucas grew ever more impatient and those typical Duke of Windsor wrinkles appeared around his eyes. "Look, Mommy," said Julius, "Nilda's son," and then Juan Lucas disappeared while Susan, who was hugging the baby, decided to act lovingly with them a short while longer. Celso and Daniel ran after the Señor.

The next morning Susana Lastarria called. Susan felt an odd mixture of sorrow and boredom when she heard her voice on the phone. With a true sense of resignation, she put up with half an hour of her envy and, in turn, told her everything she wanted to know about the trip, especially about the wedding. Finally, when she thought they were about finished, Susana asked her if they were going to have a birthday party for Julius. Susan made a tremendous effort to remember, capture, and express in words the way her cousin would think: "No," she answered, "I think it's a little too soon to have parties in this house, even for a child."

"Of course! I understand perfectly. I think you're right. What would everyone say? . . ."

JULIUS' BIRTHDAY CAME but not the presents from Europe. So they had to run out and buy an electric train for him. A man came to the mansion to put it together, and Julius spent the whole afternoon asking too many questions. Finally around six o'clock the train was running; it had been set up in one of the living rooms and, taking advantage of the Señor's absence, all the servants came in to see it. Julius chose a spot for the Chosica train station, but he almost forgot about the train set that afternoon as he talked about Chosica with his mother. She was all his that afternoon, at least until seven o'clock, at which time she would have to get changed for a cocktail party. He told her about Peter the painter at the marketplace, the vagabonds and, when he was about to go into Palomino and the shots, Nilda suddenly announced that it was time to cook dinner and left. But so much fear on her part was unnecessary because Julius was so correct about everything and only told what could be told and, besides, he did it so well; so much so that Susan began to thank the servants for what they had done and told them that she would never forget how good they had been to him and that the Señor would compensate them for it. They immediately responded that they hadn't done it for personal interest, to which Susan responded by having ice cream and Coke brought in for everyone. Nilda reappeared with her little monster followed by Celso and Daniel who were carrying in serving trays.

"Let's give a toast to Julius on his sixth birthday with Coca-Cola!" Susan said, watching to see how they responded to her words.

Everything turned out perfectly for her. Everyone was moved, so much so that she ended up figuring out that Cinthia would have been eleven years old. Her eyes filled with tears that wouldn't do for the cocktail. "My eyes are going to be swollen." The servants quieted down. "Why?" she asked herself. "Do they notice?" At that moment Nilda, speaking on behalf of the others, said that they were with her in her memories. Susan remained pensive, they are capable of even . . . when it comes to . . . How deeply they care about others!

"The train can't remain in Chosica forever!" he said, reacting to the situation.

Everyone smiled. "For once a birthday without the Lastarrias,"

Julius thought happily as he knelt down to start the train. Everyone was all smiles while they ate ice cream and drank their Cokes. The train went round and round, always passing by Chosica, and it kept on going without stopping because he was caught up listening to her: Susan was telling them about Europe, omitting names in order not to confuse them. She only mentioned France, England, and Italy. She talked on and on and the train kept going round and round. They had finished their ice cream and she continued, not even noticing that the others had turned to look toward one end of the room, smiling nervously at the door where Juan Lucas, Santiago, and Bobby, who had just returned from playing golf, stood exuding irony and sarcasm, which embarrassed her.

IT WAS ALL DECIDED. For several days after their arrival they had gone to lots of parties and hadn't been able to attend to the matter. But now he had been able to get back to playing golf and could spend more time thinking about things. The first days back are always the worst: he had to read a thousand memos from executives and directors. And, believe me, some of them are really stupid! He had had to make many decisions concerning matters that had been neglected during his absence. Happily, everything was going smoothly. It only took a few decisions, some letters, and a round of meetings. Finally, everything was back on track. The construction that he had ordered done at the manor house in Huacho was going smoothly. Soon they would be able to invite guests to spend the weekend there. In fact, he was pleased with the way things had gone during his absence. He was bothered by two or three potential strikes. But, after all, that's Lima. The secret lay in displacing any problem or unpleasant event to the golf course, where they achieve their real and insignificant dimension: it's a wonder how it changes one's perspective. A good tee shot or a nice *swing* reflected the way things were really going for him. And then there are your affairs and those concerning the youngsters. It's all together now. It had been forseen . . . the reason for more meetings . . . meetings with the new North American business partners as well . . . for the matter of the factories . . . they were going to let them have three of them. As one could see, basically, there had been many meetings and they would still call while he was playing at the golf course, which really interrupted him. But that's the way it always is just after a trip. Only now was he getting back into his old routine which gave him more time to think.

"In fact, as I was leaving the Club yesterday, I came up with the idea. I said to myself: why not, Juan Lucas? And then I realized that it was all decided."

Susan was a little saddened to have to vacate the mansion, but she understood his enthusiasm and saw how well he explained that in a new house they could really begin a totally new life . . . And he was right. Also, it was great to see how happily the children had reacted to the idea. Yes, Santiaguito pronounced vociferously: Juan Lucas was right, and this house was too aristocratic for them, too dark, it was like a cemetery, and he almost let it slip that the place matched his father's temperament. He caught himself in time but was unable to prevent what he hadn't said from building up inside: Dad never played golf, nor anything, he was only interested in his real estate and the good name of his firm and winning law cases, he only thought about the family name, I'll never be a lawyer . . . Everyone present seemed to sense that something was coming to an end: perhaps those bygone days of a world of stuffy formalities, dark, serious, boring, respectable, antiquated, and sad. But one had only to look at Juan Lucas in order to see that he was giving them a new life, I don't know, one without so many paintings of ancestors, without those cabinets, without statues, busts, yes, yes, they want a house with lots of terraces, a house where one can always walk out onto a terrace and have Celso and Daniel serve cold drinks. It should be a place where old things are an acquired decoration, a memory, not anything that has been a part of the family. Instantly, Susan saw the mansion grow old. She pushed back a fallen lock of blond hair and discovered an ancient house, even down to the smells. Then she understood that the house had never suited her tastes. The house was him: I was nineteen years old then and I would have liked to live in that house, but only in a movie. She saw her husband Santiago when he approached her for the first time at a party in Sarrat, north of London, at John and Julius' house . . . that incredible duo . . . She adored him . . .

"Who will be the architect?" she asked in a triumphant attempt, happy, like the athlete who crosses the finish line first, being chased.

. . . It was marvelous for her to have remembered him that way, he had approached her with a smile, fell in love with her, and now his dream house had grown old . . .

One hot afternoon, that smart aleck Carlos took a nap in the carriage. He liked it and decided that from then on he would take his naps there. He would approach the carriage, remove his cap, throw it in the window, and climb in without realizing that his nap coincided with Julius' hour to play there. Hence, Julius' world was totally restructured after that. Normally, the Indians, if they dared, would reach the rear while, from the inside, he would extend his arm out through the window and blow them away with one shot. But suddenly he arrived one afternoon and found Carlos stretched out inside asleep on the old velvet seat. "What are you doing in there?" he asked him innocently, and all he got for an answer was a fart accompanied by a reference to asshole, because I'm one. He immediately began to snore and Julius took off to tell Vilma, who was finishing her lunch in the kitchen. Nilda answered back loudly that no one should accuse anyone else but he had every right to let them know what was going on. Vilma didn't react at all until Julius asked them what asshole meant. "Let's go," she told him.

"Carlos! Please get out of that carriage so that little Julius can play in it . . . It's his turn."

"And mine too."

Vilma and Julius just looked at each other. The beautiful Chola limited herself to say that he shouldn't teach swear words to the little boy, but Carlos had already covered his face with his cap and seemed to go back to sleep.

"He's just playing like he's snoring," Julius said.

But after some days he began to doubt it. Every afternoon he went to the carriage and found him snoring. And no matter how long he stayed, he snored the same way every time. The fact is that Celso, Daniel, and the gardener Anatolio didn't want to fall dead screaming or jump from the steps of the back of the carriage for fear of waking up Don Carlos, which is what they called him. Julius tried to change the rules of the game: now he was at the back of the stagecoach, saving the wounded passengers from the attack and facing the danger of falling headfirst onto the rocks and rolling down into the ravine . . . It didn't work. There was no way to attack with gunshots in a low voice or play without enraged, screaming Indians all around you.

And every day that summer Susan, Juan Lucas, and Julius' brothers played golf, so Carlos had nothing to do every afternoon. Julius would wait until he woke up, usually around five-thirty, climb into the carriage, and talk with him for a while.

"What does asshole mean?" he asked one afternoon.

"I'm one, for instance," Carlos was telling him as he got down from the carriage, looking enormous. "Let's go," he added, stretching. "Soon it's going to be bath time. Vilma must be looking for you now."

Half an hour later it was he who was looking for her; she hadn't gone to the carriage for him, she wasn't in the kitchen or upstairs. She had to be in her room. Julius headed toward the stairs leading up to the servants' quarters. As he started up he ran into Santiago who was coming down, looking nervous and agitated. He thought he must have returned early from golf, but since they hardly ever talked, he just let him go by and started up to Vilma's room. "Can I come in?" he asked. He loved to ask: "Can I come in?"

"No! Julius. Wait a second. Just a minute, please. I'll be out in a minute. This is horrible! And it's already late for your bath!"

GUESTS HAD ARRIVED at the mansion and Celso and Daniel, elegantly dressed, carried in trays of hors d'oeuvres and drinks. Susan, lovely, had triumphed. She had that marvelous way of throwing back a lock of golden hair that fell over her forehead. She would laugh, the lock of hair would tumble gently over her face, and everyone would stand still in awe while she threw her hair back, gently assisted with her fingertips. The men would raise their glasses to their lips when she returned the lock of hair to its proper place. The conversation would continue once again until her next laugh. Further away, Juan Lucas discussed his day at the golf course with three other men just like him. From time to time they laughed, as men do, and talked fashionably. Celso walked up to the group and said something in a low voice. It must have been something funny because Juan Lucas broke out laughing and went looking for Susan among the guests.

"Have you heard, dear?"

"No, darling. What is it?"

"The butler here tells me that our chauffeur is upset because Santiago has taken one of the cars."

Each word was pronounced with that perfectly virile intonation. Susan was ecstatic, looked at him and, not knowing if what Santiago had done was good or bad, thought it would have been bad during her husband's time, but now with Juan Lucas . . .

"Darling, what are we going to do?"

"Let's wait," Juan Lucas responded. "If he returns and the car doesn't smell like girl's perfume, we surely won't let him steal it again."

"He went out on a date!" Bobby tattled; he had been standing there the whole time.

One big guffaw, more laughter. They sipped from their glasses and Susan put her lock of hair back into place. She was happy with Juan Lucas and his friends, for they were the chosen ones, those who knew how to live without problems. The architect who was going to design the new house had arrived. "He's not a bad kid," thought Susan, "but he always follows me around. I wonder if he can hold his liquor like the others."

By then Julius was already in bed and the light was out. He tried to go to sleep just before the guests moved out into the garden. As usual, the guests would go out onto the terrace after dinner and drink until all hours of the night. And there was always music and dancing. Even though he might sleep some right now, the music and laughter would wake him up later. He would have to look out the window. For the moment, though, he could rest a while. They had barely started with the first round of drinks.

One of Juan Lucas' North American business partners had arrived and he enjoyed talking with him: a fine gentleman and an excellent golfer. He didn't have that disgusting North American accent either, and he had fit in well at the Golf Club. And in Lima in general. His wife was one of those typical little Anglo women, but after a while it became apparent that she was intelligent and experienced. Along with the others, she helped form an almost perfect group of suntanned, rich, athletic-looking people, none of whom were ugly or unpleasant. The only problem was that the Lastarrias wouldn't be long in arriving. What could they do? They had to invite them sometime!

Juan Lastarria almost had a heart attack waiting so long for his horrible wife to get ready. The stupid woman had to tuck their two children into bed before going out. Meanwhile he was downstairs, smoking more than he should and waiting for her to finish getting ready. For what? Who knows? And Susan and Juan Lucas had already been receiving and talking to guests for over an hour. At last they arrived. He would have preferred to take a last look at his moustache in the mirror and to assure himself that his suit really did conceal his paunch, for he was well aware of the fact that Juan Lucas was a great athlete. Daniel opened the door and Lastarria almost fell on his face in the mansion doorway. He gathered his composure and let his wife, horrible, go in first. And then Susan came over, lovely and leaving the lock of hair in its place while she kissed her cousin and he inflated his little chest enormously, with great pride, and bent over to kiss her hand, all of which Susan was barely able to endure. Upon entering the big hall of the mansion, Lastarria thought about these people's glorious pasts and all that tradition. But the call of the present was overwhelming: there was Juan Lucas. Lastarria felt like a dwarf around him but he was happy. Even more happy when the others would greet him. He was happier still when his wife would disappear among the guests later on. Ah no, there she was. Forget about her, Juan. Have some fun.

And that night before dinner was served, he announced to the others that he had decided to take up golf and that he was going to become a member of the Club. Juan Lucas, all the while, was signaling to one of his buddies that Lastarria was trying too hard that night. But, alas, the poor guy could hardly match up to them. Just before dinner was served (Nilda was very offended because whenever they had these parties they always catered the food from the Hotel Bolívar), Juan Lastarria began to pursue his duchess Susan all over the place. In reality, the poor guy found himself caught between Juan Lucas & Company and Susan. And now there were two of them because the architect of the new house was also following her around, adoring her. He was a brilliant young man and currently in vogue, but he was still lacking experience. Lastarria despised the brilliant young man. Lima must be getting big because the architect didn't even know who Lastarria was, even though he might have been interested . . .

As usual, the dinner at the mansion was sumptuous, and Aunt Susana, horrible, would have done anything in the world to ask for the recipes of such culinary wonders. She had read an entire library of cookbooks and had never prepared anything that could match it. No matter, at least she was taking better care of her children than Susan did of hers. Her husband, Juan, on the other hand, already knew that dinner had been catered, even from the Hotel Bolívar. From now on he was going to order from that hotel as well and his wife could go to hell with her recipes. "Delicious, *my duchess,*" and he tried to go to the head of one line while the architect started up the other. Juan Lucas and his look-alikes were talking about some great land not far from Lima where the possibility existed to build a new golf club. The North American was also interested in the deal and proposed a meeting for the next day in the Rosita Ríos Restaurant. The gringo was becoming more native every day and, in addition to being nice, he could tolerate spicy ethnic food from the coast. On his last trip to New York he took back several bottles of Pisco brandy and some ancient pottery; according to him, he astounded his business cohorts with the famous Pisco sour drink. At first everyone in New York wanted the recipe; then they wanted to invest money in Peru. If the gringo continued at that pace, being so nice and all, he would become one of the first North Americans to be invited to join the Club Nacional. And Susan had the opportunity not only to practice her exquisite English with Virginia, who was Lester Lang III's wife (the gringo was really too much), but also to escape momentarily from the architect's and Lastarria's pestering. Neither one could speak English and they wouldn't dare to make fools of themselves in front of the foreigner. They stood waiting while Susan talked with her and, if she took too long, Lastarria would make a dash over to Juan Lucas' group, that is, the other winners. He smiled as he approached, greeting the circle of drinkers with his glass, hoping they would pay attention to him, please, and swearing that he was going to become a member of the Club. The horrible part occurred when Susana would appear looking for him and then tell him, for instance, not to drink too much white wine and to be careful of the fish bones. He hated her because at mansions fish is not served with bones: she's revolting, my God! Any other road to get where he was today would have been better without her; however, there was no other road. That's what he was thinking and, for a few seconds, he even remembered their old dilapidated house in the center of Lima and his mother who had to work in order to pay for his education, but just then Susan became free again, so he inflated himself, sticking out his chest, his little chest, and took off in hot pursuit. He crossed paths with the architect. The golfers, feeling relieved, had been freed of a bad golfer.

Susan was thinking that the architect should have a girlfriend or at least someone to be with him, and it would be better if he came with her in the future. The young man was all wound up and perhaps he shouldn't keep drinking. She made an attempt to stop him by telling Celso and Daniel not to serve him any more wine, but it was useless. If the tray didn't pass by the architect, he went looking for it. And he would return posthaste with another glassful so as not to lose one instant with Susan, who was the passion of his life. And there were red French wines, desserts, and liqueurs. And the brilliant young man wanted more and more. And he adored Susan. And he would not let Lastarria get a word in edgewise. And he wanted to dance. And he asked them to turn up the music so it could be heard outside. The guests had moved out onto the terrace. Juan Lucas found out about these little intrigues without actually seeing them; it was as if he already knew about them since they happen anyway, or one learns about these things by osmosis or by whatever means. And he had his ways of finding out. So much experience had taught him that nothing in life was dangerous. Susan went over to tell him that the architect . . . but he took her by the arm, and she adored him and was completely reassured that once again Juan Lucas would take care of the matter in a friendly way at the right moment. In the meantime, he was talking about a golf club in Chile, about some cattle for fattening that were being shipped down from the Andes, and about some small planes for a fish meal factory in which Lester Lang III had become interested. Bobby took charge of turning up the volume of the record player, the architect danced with Susan, and Lastarria went into a tailspin. Susana, who was horrible, tried to hold back a yawn in front of a group of women, some of whom had children but all of whom had maintained slim waistlines. She knew all of them, their parents and their husbands, but she hadn't had much contact with some of them since their school days at Sacred Heart. The poor woman didn't know what to do because they didn't want to remember those school days nor talk about their children who should be in bed by now and not stealing the family car. In addition, she didn't know the Argentine golf pro who had arrived recently to replace the previous one and who seemed to know his place better than the last guy. But that's the way the previous guy began as well, and he ended up marrying the appropriate Club member. And people were already accepting him in places other than on the golf course. Those Argentine pros were amazing. Several of these women still used bikinis and swam at the Club swimming pool. Their pictures appeared in the social pages of the newspapers every Monday morning. Susana asked herself: Who would be taking care of their homes? Who would be taking care of their children? And then, heaven only knows why, she looked up and saw Julius standing at the window of his bedroom. It was her responsibility to let her cousin know.

The architect in vogue had already danced three straight with Susan and he was describing the house that he had dreamed of building some day. He wanted to make himself appear smart and to awaken in her a desire to live together in the dream house. "Can't you imagine it?" he was saying to her when Susan noticed that her cousin was motioning to her which, in turn, would make it possible for her to escape from him for a while.

"Susan, Julius is still awake and it's after eleven o'clock. He could get sick staying up so late."

"Darling, what are you doing up there?" Susan asked, looking up at the window out of which Julius had stuck his little head.

"I can't sleep, Mommy, there's too much noise."

Juan Lucas saw what was going on.

"Listen, young man," he said sarcastically, "what are you doing up so late?"

"I'm just watching, Uncle."

"Shall we send up a shot of whiskey?"

Julius didn't answer or, if he did say something, no one heard it. And Susana kept on insisting that he get into bed immediately.

"Darling . . ."

"Let him have some fun," Juan Lucas said. "What's one night going to hurt?"

Aunt Susana, horrible, thought that's probably the way it went every night around there. She felt like leaving, but Lester Lang III's delightful accent stopped her.

"How many Inca kings were there?" he asked as he looked up at Julius in the window.

"Fourteen."

"Well I'll be! Fantastic! *I don't know how many presidents there have been in the States. Must look at my history again.*" The gringo had forgotten the names of the presidents.

Those who could understand English broke out laughing. Even Lastarria started to show an interest in the American. He sidled up next to him and stuck out his chest. Lang III didn't know who he was and looked at Juan Lucas as if to ask, who is this guy with the moustache? Juan Lucas told him that he was a new Club member and part of the family. Lastarria almost melted, just so long as Susana doesn't show up . . . Luckily, she didn't and so he could rise to the occasion and feel that they were accepting him. After all, he was worth several million too . . . by marriage, of course.

By one o'clock in the morning the architect in vogue had moved the dream house to the beaches to the south and had built it on a hill overlooking the ocean.

"It's for you, Susan."

"The things you say, darling . . . Tomorrow you're going to feel rotten."

But he kept on dancing, reeling from side to side and before long he would cry over how much he loved this woman. Susan's friends watched the scene with laughter, even though they thought this guy was becoming a bore. They tried to invent any pretext to get her away from him but the architect, reeling and swaying back and forth, followed her around everywhere, even over to where they were, almost falling over them. How will they get him home?

It was getting late when Santiago returned. Then they remembered he had stolen the car.

"Over here, my friend," Juan Lucas said, motioning to him.

"What's up?" Santiago asked, smiling nervously.

"Let's go over there, buddy."

Santiago went over to him, cutting through the guests. Juan Lucas took him by the arm in a friendly way and bent over him slightly. Aunt Susana was all ears and about to die of suspense.

"What's the judge's sentence?" one of the golfers inquired, breaking out with laughter.

"*Tell us all about it, Santiegou.*" Lang III wanted to know the whole story.

"He reeks of whiskey but he's still in control. And he smells like perfume. This guy knows what he's doing!"

Susan adored Juan Lucas and motioned to him about the architect's antics while the others congratulated Santiago, telling him that he deserved a car of his own. Lester Lang III offered him a cigarette and promised he would bring his son down on his next trip to Lima, and maybe there would be a girl for his son too, unless Santiago, that is . . . the gringo is witty! Everyone praised his wit except Susana Lastarria. She was looking for her husband in order to leave and said tomorrow was the maid's day off, among other horrible things, right in front of the golfers. He would sacrifice the rest of the evening so long as she didn't get involved with the golfers or with Lester Lang III. He was fascinated with III.

Upstairs, Julius had just shut the window and was getting into bed, even though he knew the party would last until all hours of the night and the noise would keep him awake. He wondered why Santiago hadn't gone to bed yet. He disappeared from the patio before Julius had shut the window, but he hadn't come upstairs either. From his bed he could hear the men's guffawing and the women's delicate laughter. He recognized his mother's laugh, he enjoyed listening to her talk amid the music. Little by little sleep overtook him and he never found out how the party ended.

"Let's go . . . let's go, everybody," Juan Lucas directed.

Frankly, the architect had become a real problem. He had reached the point of wanting to swear on a Bible that by day after tomorrow he was going to have the house on the hill, overlooking the ocean, ready for occupancy. He was falling all over himself but he wouldn't stop dancing. Even though Susan felt sorry for the young guy, the moment had arrived to do something about him. Juan Lucas, sporting his champagne glass and smiling, approached and took him by the arm in a friendly way.

"My friend the artist . . ."

The architect in vogue heard something he liked and he turned to listen: he had to build him a house . . . that idea, . . . or whatever it was, became fused in his stupor with his dream house and he wanted to start dancing again.

"Yes, yes . . . let's dance but in a cabaret, someplace where we can really . . ."

He motioned to Susan to leave them alone while he took care of the artist. "We're all going, we'll meet you there," he said, pointing him toward the door of the mansion. A taxi that Daniel had called was waiting outside. The architect stumbled all the way out to the car and Juan Lucas helped him get in.

"Yes, we'll all meet there," he repeated, closing the door before he asked about Susan.

As the taxi drove off, the architect collapsed happily into the seat, positive that he was going to meet her somewhere.

THE LAST WEEK of summer vacation had already begun. Summer was just about over and the only thing left to do was to have their school uniforms fitted. As always at this time of year, Susan would realize at the last minute that she had lost the seamstress' address. They handed the phone to her and she dialed her cousin Susana's number.

"What time did Julius go to sleep the other night?"

Susan told her to please hurry, for Juan Lucas would be arriving soon and they had to go out with Lester and some friends. Susana knew the address by heart and gave it to her immediately.

"Before I forget," she added, "Juan wants to invite the Langs over one of these days. I'll let you know so you all can come too."

"Sure . . . Juan Lucas will be delighted."

Susan hung up and she called Santiago and Bobby to tell them to stick around the house until the seamstress arrived. Carlos was going to pick her up after lunch. Both of them objected vigorously.

"I know, I know, but you have to stay here," Susan said with a certain sweet, low tone in her voice that she would employ when she had to give orders that she wouldn't have obeyed herself when she was young.

She went downstairs to say good-bye to Julius; his class with Miss Julia had just ended and he was getting ready to eat lunch. It was his last week with that hairy Señorita, who was driving him crazy. No matter what, she wanted him to start school knowing everything. The poor kid was fed up. Susan told him to be patient, just a few more days. Then she gave him a kiss and disappeared because Juan Lucas had just arrived to take her to the Golf Club where they were to spend the day with the Langs. Julius ate lunch with the servants. Ever since the big blowup in Chosica, Nilda and Vilma were getting along as if nothing had ever happened; however, that morning he noticed something was not going well between them. Jungle Woman looked at her too intently and the Andean girl simply avoided her. When Celso came in carrying Nilda's child, Julius temporarily forgot about it. The baby was still too young to walk, but the butler-treasurer, holding him by the arms, made him take a few steps with his short little bowlegs dangling in the air; it was the first time the little monster did something other than scream and cry. Everyone celebrated the event and lunch quickly acquired its typical daily routine. Celso and Daniel started arguing about soccer, one of them wanted Julius to be a fan of the Municipal team while the other wanted him to root for Sporting Tabaco. Nilda intervened and complained that they shouldn't influence him. It was bad for the brain: let him decide on his own.

In the afternoon, Vilma and Julius sat in the driver's seat of the carriage while she read from *Tom Sawyer*. Today no one would require them to keep silent because Carlos had gone to fetch the seamstress and the carriage was empty. Nevertheless he was barely listening to her read; actually he was concerned about school, even trying to imagine it: what will it be like? Deep in thought, he was suddenly interrupted by Nilda's noisy announcement of the arrival of the seamstress, Mrs. Victoria.

Victoria Santa Paciencia, as she was called in the mansion, greeted the boys as usual, noting that they had grown enormously since last year. As usual, she also said that they had not called her soon enough in order for her to make two uniforms for each one in less than a week. Hence she would begin by letting out last year's uniforms so that Santiaguito and Bobby could use them in the meantime. Trembling, she asked them to try on their sport coats and there they were: furious, burning up, squirming from the itching while she, chalk in hand, marked the cloth as she measured it.

"Does that mean you start school this year?" she said, looking at Julius.

Not one pin fell from her mouth. Julius was dumbfounded, watching her talk incessantly while her mouth was full of pins. Not one fell from her mouth! It was as if they were stuck to her gums. She asked for a plain cup of coffee with two spoons of sugar and still nothing happened. A few minutes later Vilma, acting strangely, brought in a cup and Santiago bit his lip when he saw her and said Vil . . . Jungle Woman, who had been snooping around there, cleared her throat and left. Vilma spilled a little coffee.

About six o'clock Julius was making his way up the stairs to the servants' quarters when all of a sudden he ran into Santiago. One was as surprised as the other, and they just stood there staring at each other.

"What are you doing here, you little shit?"

". . ."

"Can't you play somewhere else?"

"I'm looking for Vilma, she has my *Tom Sawyer* book . . ."

"Vilma's not here. Get out of here! If you don't, I'll bust your little ass!"

"Julius! Julius! Up here! Come up, Julius!"

It was Vilma's voice. He was starting to go up when a slap and a push almost sent him flying back down the stairs. Crying, he took off running and didn't stop until he reached the kitchen.

He found Jungle Woman reading the newspaper: a small child had been kidnapped and she was cursing the gypsies. "What's the matter?" she asked when she saw that he was crying. Julius told her what had happened on the stairs and Nilda blurted out: enough was enough, this time it wasn't Vilma's fault, the child Santiago was awful, and the only thing to do now was to inform the Señores about it. He didn't really understand what was going on, only that his brother was doing something wrong.

That evening all hell broke loose. Celso and Daniel heard screaming coming from Vilma's room, they ran up to see what was going on, and they caught him in the act. And Vilma confessed saying that it wasn't the first time either; he had been going up to her room every day and she had been doing everything possible to keep it from getting out. But today the child Santiago had gone too far. First, the butlers stopped him from leaving the room; next, when he attacked them, they not only clobbered him but blindfolded him so he couldn't see, covered his mouth so he couldn't swear at them, and carried him to his room. He had three scratches on his face, one was near his eye, the result of the struggle with Vilma. She wouldn't be able to use that uniform anymore. That's what was happening when Susan and Juan Lucas arrived home after a long and tiring day with the Langs. Nilda confronted them directly, spilling the whole story. It took them a while to comprehend what had happened and they decided to put off the matter until the next day.

"Get some rest, everyone," Juan Lucas said. "We'll deal with this tomorrow."

WHAT THEY DEALT with the next morning was the way in which they got rid of Vilma without too much objection from the others, at least that's what Juan Lucas recommended as he sat up in his pavilion-sized bed finishing his breakfast. If it hadn't been ten o'clock in the morning, one would have thought that he was about ready to go to bed, not just getting up. His pajamas didn't show one crease in them and Susan, lovely, was at his side. She would have preferred to find a better solution, mainly because Julius was going to suffer so much. Stirring his coffee slightly more rapidly than usual, Juan Lucas, however, said that it was time for the kid to forget about servants and things like that. He was always hanging around the servants or talking to the gardener, he was always with someone of a lower class. Susan said he was right, it's true, darling, but she felt so sorry for Julius . . . Juan Lucas tried to be firm and make it final: call for Vilma, talk to her, he'll pay her a good sum, and that'll be the end of it. She kept insisting on her sorrow that morning, to the point that she blamed Santiaguito.

"Listen, Susan, the lad is starting to go out with girls and it's only natural that he would want to find some outlet for his . . . it's not easy in Lima at his age, you know . . . the Chola is attractive too . . . and there you have it . . . that's the way it is . . ."

"Yes, darling, but it's not her fault."

"And where did you get that idea, Susan?"

"Darling, but . . . she defended . . . herself."

"She's probably sorry she did, or do you think she's a saint?"

"Darling, I don't know, but . . ."

"Ring the bell for them to come get these trays, Susan."

"Darling, Santiago needs to . . ."

"What Santiago needs is a round of golf this morning . . . so he can clear his mind a little . . . that'll calm him down."

"And what about Vilma, darling?"

"Woman, I've already told you what to do. You speak to her and then I'll give her a nice bonus. Hey, my slippers . . . let's go, woman, get up . . . don't be lazy, *uuuup!*"

They went from the bedroom to the bathroom; they each had their own. Juan Lucas combed his hair a little before shaving because he couldn't resist perfection as he looked at himself in the mirror. Now, as he shaved, he was gearing up for the day, feeling the firmness of his manly arm move the razor up and down his face. He would wash away the foamy shaving cream from his tanned face and choose with a sense of class one of his colognes, Yardley's *For Men*. Three or four bottles for different occasions rested elegantly on the porcelain shelf, next to other men's toiletries: soaps, shampoos, things that smelled of well-bred men, *for men only,* that's the way they say it in *Esquire*. From time to time he would hum a tune, just to make sure his voice still performed well for those gatherings with whiskey-drinking men who talked business, for the gatherings at the Club, for the opportune phrases, the pertinent ones in order to gain the respect of wise-ass barmen who think they know everything. He finished shaving and his pajamas had become unbearable. A refreshing shower was in order, allowing him to sing a little before enveloping himself in vividly colored towels, also *for men only*. Then would come the Italian silk shirt and the rite of selecting a tie that only men knew how to do, it's a man's job that no woman knows how to do . . . and, little by little, he would find himself ready for another day in the world of rich men.

The other bathroom, the likes of which you'll never see, was Hollywoodesque—the colors, the size of the hygienic apparatus—but oriental in its perfume bottles and French in its Latin-inscribed apothecary jars. Susan relished her sensual shower. From time to time, Julius would hang around that part of the mansion listening for his mother to ask him to hand her a towel. He would fall over himself trying to get it to her and amid all the steam he would see his mother's arm reach out for it as she hummed. She was humming now too, even though from time to time she would think about Vilma and stop suddenly. She was washing her body just then with the finest soap to be had in the world and it gave her such pleasure to witness how she continued to remain so lovely. Later, as she dried off, she verified once more in front of the mirror that she could still do a nude scene from a movie. Vilma could too: what a pity, a nasty situation, poor Vilma! No doubt she could do well in a movie scene, imagine the Chola half-naked in a Mexican movie, their stars are fuller, like Vilma, poor thing, and Juan Lucas is going to get rid of her, poor Julius.

They were headed to a club south of Lima where they would have lunch with some friends. They gave the chauffeur the day off because they would go in the sports car themselves and they would leave the keys to the other car with Santiago. That's what Juan Lucas decided as they prepared to leave, but he hadn't mentioned a word about Vilma, as if only his wish to see her disappear was enough to make the Chola vanish into thin air.

But it didn't happen that way. That's why Juan Lucas was quite irritated and uncomfortable as he drove down the highway. The row with the servants had upset him a great deal. He wasn't accustomed to firing anyone, for whenever he had to get rid of someone or dozens of people at the same time, he did it by simply signing a document, one among many in a day's work and then others did the job of executing his orders. For once in his life he had lost control and Susan, still deeply pained about the mess, had been powerless to help him. She felt so sorry for Julius, how foolish of her, everything will get back to normal once we hire a new maid. And what's this about becoming so fond of these people? "You're so foolish, Susan," Juan Lucas thought as he drove south in his Mercedes, and out of the corner of his eye he watched her loving hair blow in the wind, free and loose, she was his love, wearing those big, black dark glasses. I don't want to have to discuss these things with you, but they bother me. What if we were to fire the whole lot? Get rid of all of them? Anyway, you've spoiled them too much. Do you really care about those people that much? What is she thinking about? Is she really concerned about that woman? Juan Lucas was on edge. And what is this about the other day when you went downstairs and asked them to get the car out and found the servants waiting for you at the bottom of the stairs? One goes downstairs ready to go out and enjoy a nice Sunday afternoon with friends only to find all the servants— arrogant and insolent—standing at the bottom of the stairs. No, Susan. Because you were present I didn't yell go to hell at them. That one woman, the cook, the one with the rotten teeth, was talking about sweat, it was running down all over her face, and about her child, showing him to you, almost throwing him in your face, and using absurd words which, coming from her, were meaningless: her legal rights, we're human beings, there are unions, grievances, all asinine things like that. And Susan, expressing sorrow and fear, telling them that you love them, telling them you are going to punish Santiago and, if that's not enough, that Chola, the cook, asking you how you are going to do it and you, Susan, not knowing how to answer her. They ask you to send him to a boarding school and you lower yourself to their level, you try to give them some explanations, and you tell them it's too late, the schools open in just a few days, would they forgive you? And you are frightened by Nilda's screaming, the one with the kid. Susan, you're so naive . . . they even give you the opportunity to do something: they tell you they're quitting together and you beg them, you're so sorry, you beg them to stay for Julius' sake, if anything for Julius' sake. Frankly, you've got a screwed up kid, Susan, you should see him there listening to everything that's going on, clinging to Vilma, looking at us as if we were the enemy. You're so naive, Susan . . . Juan Lucas wanted to talk about it, bring it out into the open once and for all, and then never have to bring it up again, totally forgetting about it before meeting with their friends; but Susan let the wind blow through her hair, lost behind her dark glasses, living in another world, ignoring it all, what was she thinking about?

"Susan, please light me a cigarette . . . they're in the glove compartment . . . Susan!"

"Yes, Juan."

"What do you make of all this, Susan?"

"Darling! This mess has been horrible. I'm so sad, Juan."

"Hey! You're so sentimental. Frankly, I think that woman took the best way out . . . if she hadn't left on her own accord, we'd still be listening to that cook lecture us."

"Now that she's gone, I feel worse than ever . . . she wasn't to blame, darling . . . why do you think all of them wanted to quit with her?"

"Circumstances . . . do you believe they're going to quit over this?"

"But, darling! . . . You know perfectly well that they were going to do it: if we had fired Vilma every last one of them would have left . . . what happened was she quit, she said she didn't want to continue working for us . . . she quit on her own. Didn't you see how it pained her so when she cried?"

"The winner here is Julius, Susan. Otherwise, he'd become a queer hanging around those women all the time . . ."

"Darling, please! That's not the problem. You're very clever and you've turned the situation around. First, Vilma tells them that she's quitting and, of course, the others don't know what to do, then you take advantage of the situation to say that Santiago himself will have to take a bonus to her and say he's sorry . . . that's very clever, darling . . . just like the other day when the architect . . . only that in this case Julius is going to die of sorrow . . . besides, Santiago won't say he's sorry."

"There'll be another way to send her money, Susan. Look for that cigarette lighter, it must be in the glove compartment . . . we're about to arrive . . . a good swim and some drinks, *voilà,* that'll make us feel better . . . the whole thing got out of hand but it's behind us now."

Susan handed him the cigarette lighter. She wanted to say something else, but just up the highway was the exit to the club, cutting a line into the desert, and she would have said something but all of a sudden she felt too weak.

"You're foolish, honey, to continue being sad."

SINCE EVERYONE WAS acting a little rebellious in the mansion, no one stopped Carlos from using the Mercedes to take Vilma to her house; in reality, it was a tenant room on a back street in Surquillo where one of her aunts lived. Celso and Daniel helped carry out her old pirate trunk, even though it was made of cardboard with metal flanges and caps on the corners. It looked ridiculous painted with bright vivid colors and, without a doubt, made in the mountain provinces. It was one of those trunks that you see on top of the interprovincial buses traveling between Oroya, Tarma, Cerro de Pasco, etc. Or to Puquio as well, or to any one of those places from which people flee in order to go down to Lima on the coast. Vilma kissed Julius. Julius kissed Vilma. Vilma shook hands with Celso, Daniel, and Anatolio and gently patted them on the shoulder. Then she hugged Nilda and held her baby for a moment. The baby began to scream. The scene took place in the kitchen. The girl from Puquio handed the baby back to Jungle Woman and hugged Arminda who had remained tragically quiet during it all. Covering her child's mouth, Nilda told her to beware of men: Vilma, make sure there ain't no young men where you go to work. Everyone lowered their heads and stood silent until Carlos said it was time to leave. They walked through the whole mansion, from the kitchen to the main door where there were more pats on the back, some good-byes, and addressing each other more formally than ever before. Julius participated in the ceremony without saying a word. As Vilma got into the Mercedes, Nilda said something worthy of Lope de Vega, but it was poorly expressed and totally anachronistic, something about the honor of the poor has remained untarnished in this house and, while Celso's and Daniel's eyes were riveted to the ground, Carlos started the car. Just seconds before it departed, Vilma stuck her head out the window and whispered into Julius' ear: "Your Mommy went to see me in my room and she promised to let Carlos take you to visit me sometime." The car started off and she began to sob loudly. She took out a wrinkled handkerchief from an ugly purse and held it up as if trying to hide her face. The car passed through the main gate of the mansion, drove out onto the street, and went down Salaverry Avenue. Vilma was bawling and she felt so ashamed. Carlos observed through the rearview mirror how her robust breasts were throbbing forcefully, how defiant they stood out! rising healthily and falling compact and firm, stimulating desire, as if they were going to burst out of her black blouse, the one that was way too small but that the Señora had given her. She couldn't stop sobbing. Poor Vilma. Still, that Chola was a knockout.

Three weeks later she called the Señora on the telephone.

"I'm going to Puquio, Señora. My mother's sick and I have to leave at once."

Susan repeated over and over how sorry she was that she had forgotten to send the money. She immediately sent it with Carlos, even though Julius was still in school and couldn't go with him. Six months later, Julius received a letter from her written with horrible green ink on a sheet of notebook paper. She took a lot of space to write just a few words. She told him to behave, to be good, to say hello to everyone for her. She asked how he was doing in school. Again, she said he should behave and she was going to work for a family in Nasca, but she didn't have the address yet. He might still be able to write her something in Puquio, though she was about to leave. Again she asked him to say hello to everyone at home and then she said good-bye. Julius answered her letter. He even put the letter in the mailbox himself, but he never received an answer. After all, he thought one day years later, a letter written by a little boy, with stamps purchased from his allowance and mailed one morning from San Isidro, didn't have much of a chance of reaching Puquio and then from there to a servant in Nasca.

THE SCHOOL YEARS

---------------------------------- I ----------------------------------

THE SCHOOL WAS called Immaculate Heart and it was comprised of two houses, the small one on Angamos Avenue and the big one on Arequipa Avenue. Well-scrubbed, impeccable little children, except for the Arenas kids, those filthy little brats, would begin to arrive about eight-thirty every morning.

Julius had already been attending school there for some months when the idea of his going in the station wagon had occurred to Juan Lucas. It was so neat to take the bus home in the afternoon and stare at Gumersindo Quiñones' huge black hand. He was a descendent of slaves of the Quiñones children at school and he was proud of it because he always smiled when he told you. Approaching the corner where those children would get off, Gumersindo's arm would reach across the width of the bus from the driver's seat and grab the door lever. Wait until the bus has come to a stop, he says, and he opens the door with his old black hand, wrinkled like a scab, you can get off now, see ya, Carlitos. He would close the door and pull his enormous arm back, and Julius would be sitting there behind him, wanting to be the best friend in the world of that very tall Negro's white-haired hand. There was, nevertheless, the matter of the station wagon.

They had a whole fleet of cars, for Juan Lucas bought a Jaguar sports car that went well with some sport coats he had purchased in London. He bought a new Mercedes for Susan and, while she didn't notice any difference from the old one, she did think it was beautiful. The children got a Mercury station wagon with enormous taillights that looked indecent when they came on and which later led to many jokes. One of Juan Lucas' friends said that when he saw the vehicle with those big round lights in the back, he thought it looked like a woman with hemorrhoids; in effect, the lights burned your eyes when someone stepped on the brakes. They also promised a car to Santiaguito if he graduated with good grades and went to college (to study agriculture in order to look after their vast landholdings).

The station wagon was for picking up the children from school, Bobby and Santiago from Markham and Julius from Immaculate Heart. Santiago wanted to drive and Bobby insisted on riding up front next to the passenger door. Consequently, Carlos always ended up sitting in the middle. This arrangement suited the two brothers because it would be embarrassing to be seen by classmates riding in the back seat, above all when the thing to do was to have the maid ride in the back. It used to be Vilma, now it's Imelda, and she wasn't too popular with the other servants, she simply didn't fit in, she wasn't friendly either, she showed no enthusiasm for her work, and it was just a matter of time before she'll quit her job, feeling no remorse, probably as soon as she finished her sewing course. Julius, sitting in the back seat next to her, was wearing his little blue school uniform, which was always clean and neat as he left for school in the morning and ended up filthy dirty, including that large, stiff overstarched shirt collar, in the afternoon, just like hundreds of other schoolmates.

The school was run by North American nuns who were really nice with the exception of Carrottop who always became furious and even turned red. Her dream was to build a new school, a huge one, and make it modern with a chapel and a meeting hall next to it. There would be lots of classrooms and play areas for Morales' soccer team. They had to train hard so that the bigger students at Immaculate Heart could beat the smaller ones at Saint Mary's, the school run by North American priests where you go after graduating from Immaculate Heart.

The nuns bought a large piece of land at the end of Angamos Avenue. They were happy but heavily in debt. Julius would always add one more Hail Mary to the twelve he would repeat at prayer time in the evenings before going to bed, so that the new school would become a reality some day. Morales would get his soccer field for training the team: Morales is quite a guy, always saying *yas* with his enormous loud mouth. The nuns, nevertheless, trusted him.

The construction began first with the little house on Angamos. The children entered from the side and would go directly to the back lawn where the lavatories were located. All the classrooms opened onto the back lawn, which is where Morales, holding a damp rag, was always waiting to wipe off the children's faces after recess or when they had stayed on for lunch at school. They always ended up sweating a lot because for thirty minutes they would hold hands, chant loudly, and run around Taboada in a circle: "Taboada, we're going to cook you alive, we're going to cook you alive." And poor Taboada would be screaming for his mother, whimpering as Morales would simply smile at him and continue to sincerely believe they were just growing up Peruvian. When the nun would come out to ring the bell, she would scold them for participating in such primitive dances and then she would look at the Cholo: "*Go ahead, Mourales.*" "*Yas,* Mother," he responded with a mouth that looked like an inner tube and began to grab them and wipe each one off with the rag. He would pull it out of the wash basin soaking with water and rub it roughly across their faces as water dripped onto their dry starched collars. Afterward he would give the more macho soccer players a swift kick in the butt and send them off to class. One would have always thought that working with so many Immaculate Heart kids he would have taken advantage of the situation and do a little blackmailing; for instance he could have said, "Hey, Santamaría, why don't you ask your old man to get me a job in the government? If you do, you're on the soccer team." But it never happened. Morales stayed on with the nuns, washing the kids' faces with that rag and watching them get out of station wagons that looked like women with hemorrhoids.

There were lots of those station wagons, hundreds of them: the Kings' blue station wagon (his father was a North American diplomat); the Otayzas' yellow one (they didn't have a maid but a German governess instead); the blue one belonging to Penti, who had an unbelievable number of sisters in Villa María, it was impossible to name them all. Julius' station wagon was brown.

After the children got older they went to school at the big adobe house on Arequipa Avenue. The first thing they learned there was that Pastor could get up late because he lived right next door. The big adobe house was really nice; in fact, it was even kind of mysterious in ways, but with so many children running all over the place, only the nuns' quarters were an enigma to them which, in turn, precipitated a thousand questions. By the time Julius started school there, La Pepa's gang had just been formed.

La Pepa was half mulatto and his dad was even more so, but they had a lot of money because he owned some mines. Since they had so many cars and such a big house, it wasn't difficult for him to become the gang leader. It all had something to do with horses. They would tie their school smocks around their waists, leaving part of them to hang out the back for the cowboy to hold on to like reins. The one with the smock tied around him would run around with the rider behind him screaming out: Faster! To the right! To the left! until they would catch up with you, and if you hadn't already been admitted to the gang they would wrestle you to the ground. That was when everyone went around with skinned knees. And that's when someone would become a hero or have an idol. La Pepa, however, was no hero to Julius who was always hiding from him, for he didn't want to hand over Cinthia's pen to him which was what he demanded from Julius in order to become a member of the gang. La Pepa's dominance must have ended about the time he had about 98 percent of the school in his gang. It got to be boring to punch out the same few who still didn't belong to the gang. Also, La Pepa stopped growing and one day Arzubiaga arrived on the scene and lifted an enormous rock. Everyone ran off to look for La Pepa so he could lift it too, but he responded that his chauffeur was waiting for him and he left. That must have been sad for him because from then on he never demanded any more pens and he started playing cops and robbers just like all the others.

The problem with Arzubiaga was that he never punched out anyone; in fact, once he even pulled two students apart who were going at each other on the ground. Everyone yelled at him to let them fight it out because the nun wasn't around, but Arzubiaga pulled them apart and carted one of them off. And besides, if you would ask him to knock the piss out of Gómez, a dumb Cholo with thick black hair, he always smiled and said some other time. That was the problem with Arzubiaga and one would even begin to forget that he had lifted the large rock and had even carried it on his head.

One afternoon Silva also hoisted up the big rock and put it on top of his head. Silva was a blond-haired guy with the face of a wildcat; he had green eyes and strong white legs. He lifted the rock and by the following week he had already punched out Ramírez, the one who was in the chorus. Then he beat up King, the North American, and then Rafaelito Lastarria, who was still in third grade and didn't even say hello or even look at his cousin Julius. Fortunately, Julius had already added one more Hail Mary to his evening prayers.

Arzubiaga was white but swarthy. He was very strong and talked with everyone; he didn't demand pens or kick you off his team when you wanted to play with him. That was the problem: he didn't have what it takes to be a bad guy, but he had already lifted that rock three more times. Moreover, he had already taken down Martinto who weighed three times more than the rock, even though they were just playing because Chubby was a good guy; in fact, he was Julius' best friend at the time.

One morning Silva came out to recess hopping mad, followed by his gang, which hadn't been formed yet because they never knew if Arzubiaga could beat him up. Chubby Martinto went looking for Arzubiaga and told him that Silva wanted to fight him, he had challenged him to a wrestling match out on the side lawn. Julius happened to be nearby because he had been looking for Chubby to challenge him to a duel with the wooden swords they had made. Martinto had seen a movie in which a musketeer had lopped off an ear of his adversary and he was dying to do the same to Julius, well, not really, for they had stuck corks on the tips of their swords. They spent a lot of time playing that way, Chubby trying to slice off his ear and Julius trying to deflate him. That morning he was waiting for him, but he showed up with the important news of Silva's challenge.

Arzubiaga said he was always around and he'd never run away from anyone. He was neat, man. Chubby Martinto took off running with the news and, naturally, he stumbled, fell, got his uniform dirty, and skinned his knee again. But he got up immediately, spit out the dirt, and continued running to make sure recess didn't end without a fight. "He's afraid," Silva said, and it seemed like he was baring his claws. He was all gringo that morning and really furious, it showed in his feline eyes and in his breathing. He couldn't stand it, so he crossed the lawn in search of his enemy, just like in the movies. The wary gang followed behind. Then came Martinto, looking grubby.

He put his hands on his waist, stuck out his chest, and squinted at him as no cat ever could, looking as mean as possible. "You're afraid of Silva," one of the gang members yelled. Of course, it was dumb to say that because Arzubiaga's unruffled nature wasn't out of fear. "Why do you want to fight," asked Arzubiaga, as Martinto, becoming desperate, felt the remaining minutes of the recess ticking away. "You're a queer," Silva responded, puffing out his chest even more. It wouldn't be long before he would probably collapse from the tension and fury that he was feeling at the moment. Arzubiaga heard the word queer and that didn't please him at all. He lifted his arm and pointed to the lawn where the fight was to take place, but Silva thought it was the first blow being struck at him and he went for Arzubiaga's neck. Entwined, they fell to the ground. Martinto began to tremble with emotion, simultaneously biting a finger, following every move, not missing one little detail of the fight, and watching out for the nuns who might show up at any moment. The gang got worried because Silva had become the underdog. His shoulders were pinned to the ground, and he was unable to get his adversary off of him. And things got worse, he no longer moved. It was obvious this wouldn't last long because Arzubiaga continued to sit on his enemy's chest, quietly choking him, each time squeezing a little more, waiting for that final yes. "Give up?" he would ask, waiting, but nothing. Then another little calculated squeeze, seemingly benign: "Give up?" And so it continued until an affirmative whimper was heard and the fight was over. Silva left crying, above all alone. More than anything, alone. And it was a sight to see the gang trying to carry Arzubiaga on their shoulders, celebrating his victory, pulling at him.

"Clean off your uniform! Clean off your uniform!" Chubby Martinto yelled, who was filthy and was trying to brush him off.

Arzubiaga was in third grade and one of the big boys, but since he would talk to everyone Julius considered him a friend and an idol. And he was always trying to get his mother to identify him by his name, the same with Chubby, for he wanted Susan to learn to identify all of his friends.

"No, Mommy, Chubby is Martinto and I want to invite him over. The one who beat up Silva is Arzubiaga, he's huge, next year he'll study with priests at Saint Mary's . . ."

"Yes, darling, so which one is your friend?"

"Both of them, Mommy . . ."

"Well, invite both of them . . ."

"No, Mommy, Arzubiaga is in third grade. I'll just invite Chubby . . ."

MARTINTO WASN'T MUCH of a problem for his family. He was always happy and his father had a huge ranch close to Lima that was ideal for Chubby to romp in. He wanted to invite his friends to the ranch, but his mother was opposed to inviting Arzubiaga because he was too big. What the hell did that matter to Chubby? Just so long as they had fun together. And to have fun only one other musketeer was necessary, and that was Julius. They would spend the whole day running all over the property, getting dirty, and in the evening they would return to the mansion that Chubby's parents had in San Isidro. Chubby would still have enough energy to jump over the tables and chase Julius from room to room, leaving an incredible trail of mud and dirt on the place mats and on the oriental rugs, or so they seemed because of what they had cost.

It was during that period in his life that Julius suffered a terrible embarrassment because of something he did. He was really sad afterward and he even told his mother about it. Juan Lucas, who was there, let out a tremendous laugh upon hearing the story and said finally the kid was coming around. Susan, lovely, gave him a kiss and admonished him to be careful and not go for other kids' eyes. Don't do it again, darling. She gave him another kiss when she noticed that he was still distraught and then she turned to Juan Lucas: Don't laugh, darling, Martinto was his friend . . .

"Was Martinto your friend, darling?" She could never remember all those names . . .

"That kid isn't dumb," Juan Lucas thought after he heard the story. After all, Martinto had already lopped off Julius' right ear nineteen times and he had managed to poke his gut only eleven times. He had seen the Cornel Wilde scene with the sand at the movies and he was tired of Chubby breaking the dueling rules. Here's what happened: they were in the middle of serious combat near the cliffs and the other one bore down on him with no style whatsoever, anybody could win like that, and all of a sudden Julius remembered the movie and while Chubby retreated, ready to charge forth once again like Atila, he grabbed a handful of sand and threw it in his face. "You stupid!" Martinto yelled, "I can't see anything." He rubbed and rubbed his eyes and Julius, just standing there not knowing what to do, wanted to see him laugh, make light of it, but Chubby became more and more agitated, his eyes kept watering more and more and the tears became mixed with the sand. He dropped the sword and started walking around in circles, blind and furious, searching for some water. Julius tried to approach him in order to help him clean off his face, but Martinto threatened him with waving arms and clenched fists. "You're gonna get it! You're gonna get it!" he yelled. And it was true, for no sooner had he recovered his sight than he chased Julius all over the place trying to beat him up. When he caught him, they had it out and he gave him a punch in the eye which turned black and then their mothers got into it as well.

Three days later Chubby was back to normal and there were attempts to become friends again; they glanced at each other in formation and in class, but it was never the same between the two of them again. Moreover, at the end of the school year, as was expected, Chubby failed the final exams. They failed him for being dirty and lazy, even though they accepted him back into school because his father had made a large donation to the construction of the new school. Martinto remained being as nice as he was unwashed, but the fact that they were in different classes kept them apart and, the following year, he became friends with a guy who had a large nose and with whom he would play all day long, sword in hand trying to lop off his nose.

However, in addition to the sand-in-the-eyes incident that year, something else left Julius quite concerned. That was the period in life when it was important to have your own soccer ball and take it to school. The bad thing about it was that in reality the school was a large house and there wasn't enough space to play so many soccer games at the same time. Arzubiaga managed to establish some order, he knew how to organize teams, eleven on eleven, even though as recess wore on, more and more players jumped in to play, usually on the team that had the best chance of winning. Hence, the games would finish with twenty players on one team and seven on the other (two players of the losing team just took off and two others went to the other side, unnoticed). Even Arzubiaga was unable to control such desertions, and about all he could do was see to it that the games began according to the rules. But that didn't bother him, he had the patience of a saint and he never pushed anybody around. No one ever called fouls on him, that's for sure. The gringo kid King was another problem. He never did learn to play soccer the way Peruvians do, not even up until the time his father was named ambassador to Nicaragua and he left. At the most crucial moment of the game he would grab the ball with his hands, take off running, and place himself and the ball inside the net, screaming "goaaaaaaal," thinking he was playing rugby. He was a nice guy, like his younger brother, but he was dumb when it came to playing the Peruvian way. And he always carried the ball over to Arzubiaga at the end of recess.

Arzubiaga was the owner of that soccer ball. In the afternoons he would store it in a white mesh bag and wait to be picked up. But one afternoon a group of students hung around the main gate and wanted to play. It was forbidden in the front yard because that's where Mother Superior grew her roses; besides, there were lots of windows in front. Nevertheless, Arzubiaga took the ball out and made a lateral pass to Martinto, who kicked it up into the air and used his head to pass it over to Julius, who then kicked it to Del Castillo, Del Castillo to Sánchez Concha, to Martinto, Chubby to Arzubiaga, and so on until Carrottop, speaking English, came out in a frenzy, ringing her bell and demanding the ball. They taught English very well at Immaculate Heart because everyone understood her when she screamed they were all a bunch of devils and she was going to give the ball to the poor kids at catechism. She stuck it under her arm and left in a huff, ringing her bell. Every year rumors circulated that Carrottop was going to be transferred, but she was always there to greet them on the first day of April, bell in hand, enveloped in her enormous rosary and ready to get mad. Like this afternoon, for instance. Del Castillo advised Arzubiaga to tell his mother. If not, they would keep it forever, and they hadn't even touched the Mother Superior's rosebushes. They will for sure but it was too late now. The nun wasn't going to come back outside, she had disappeared with his ball, and it wasn't fair, when all of a sudden he became frightened and started to scream, it was just too much for him and Arzubiaga started to cry . . . And he was in third grade to boot, he was big, and next year he would move up to Saint Mary's. Chubby Martinto told him that if his mother talked to Mother Superior, Carrottop would have to return his ball to him. Del Castillo asked who the poor kids at catechism were. No one seemed to know but they sort of feared them. Martinto explained that they were probably those kids you see on the little cards they pin on you when you give money to the missions. But Sánchez Concha interrupted him: "Don't be stupid, Chubby, those kids are in Africa." The discussion heated up a little and Arzubiaga stopped crying. The next day Carrottop yelled at him again and returned his soccer ball to him, but it was absolutely forbidden to buy chocolates at recess for a week: the money would go to the missions. For several days Julius continued to be concerned about Arzubiaga's sniveling and he was surprised that even big people cry.

THE CONSTRUCTION OF the new school was moving along smoothly. The nuns had built a high wall around the property. "Don't forget to look at it," the nuns would tell the children. "When you drive by the end of Angamos Avenue, be sure to take a look at it. That's where the new school is going to be built." One morning they laid the first brick, mass followed, for they had worn their white uniforms, and they got the day off. What happiness! They should lay the first brick every day. In addition, they were going to buy a new school bus, a huge one from North America with large letters on each side that read IMMACULATE HEART SCHOOL. Gumersindo Quiñones was pleased and very obsequious to the Mother Superior. And the chapel was going to be so beautiful! And the soccer field would be huge! Morales smiled and all the students looked at him beseechingly: me, Morales, choose me for the team. That school had to be paradise, what with all those windows, classrooms, hallways, special practice room for piano, and gardens and lawns that would produce roses for the chapel. Paradise had to be the new Immaculate Heart School. But they needed money. The Mother Superior would become demoralized when she told them that they were short of *the money.* She could make every last one of them really feel how demoralized she was. How they suffered with her! Happily, she would recover and say it was necessary for everyone to help out: every last one of them. And since the first brick had already been laid that morning, first there would be mass, then everyone would go into the hall where the architectural drawings were. So you'll see how beautiful it's going to be! And they're in color! From there they would go straight to the dining room for breakfast and hot chocolate. And finally . . . the Mother Superior became silent for a moment and they shivered . . . finally . . . No school today! The school anthem! Everyone! Let us sing! They sang with such enthusiasm . . .

WHAT WASN'T GOING so well was the construction of the new house, which was to be built on that enormous property adjacent to the Polo Club that belonged to Juan Lucas. No doubt everything was going to turn out all right, but for the moment no one could come to any agreement on the design. As it turned out, the architect was a practical person and he wanted to build a house that functioned well. He also wanted them to let him do whatever he pleased; after all, he was the artist. But Juan Lucas, for instance, wanted Spanish tile on the roof. The architect pointed out that they function well in countries where it rains a lot, but in Lima they would be absurd. Susan, tossing back a lock of hair captivatingly, said she wanted a Mexican ranch-style house with a stone patio where they would display the newly restored carriage. This seemed a little less absurd to the architect, and he even showed up one afternoon with large drawings of a Mexican ranch house with its special window and iron bars for serenades and all. Susan loved it and smiled happily, imagining the carriage on the patio, the stereo system playing music in the background, and a living room with thick white walls adorned with their colonial paintings from the Cuzco school and the others from the Quito school. Her paintings were so beautiful. She will take them herself to be restored. But Juan Lucas wanted modern things in the new house: big windows that would let in lots of light and allow him to see the Polo Club off in the distance. The architect would look at Susan and acknowledge the impossibility, but adored her through his drawings and willingness, giving in on everything and even forgetting about his functionalism. He would look at Susan, point to the Mexican ranch house that was expertly sketched on the drawing paper, and explain it to them. Juan Lucas interrupted him and insisted on the modern version, while Susan imagined herself walking carefree around the ranch house, so lovely, and wanting to get her own way. But at that moment Juan Lucas called for another round of drinks, looked at the drawings, and discovered that the house also had Spanish tiles on the roof and was, quite frankly, absurd. The three of them became a little impatient, but in a gracious way, and hardly got upset with each other. Because of that window, the one for serenades, Juan Lucas said, any cute Chola like Vilma will spend all her time there conversing with some cousin. Susan became emotional thinking about the enchanting serenades: the Hollywood Mexican pressing against the grating and saying to the American girl: "I am passionate for you." She tossed back that lock of blond hair, looked at Juan Lucas, and adored him immensely again, just as Daniel was returning with more bottles of tonic water and another bucket of ice and as the architect cocked his head to one side trying to imagine one last design, one that would please the three of them. Months and months went by without anyone ever mentioning a construction date.

ON THE OTHER hand, the construction at the nuns' school was moving forward. The foundation had been laid and there was mass and communion to ensure that the foundation would be strong and hence never allow the building to fall down. Poor Julius hardly had time to pray so many Hail Marys. In addition to the standard twelve that were required, there were the extras since he was a good boy: one for the Mother Superior's mother, who is sick in Missouri; another for the school foundation; one for which he never could remember the reason why; and another one for the souls in purgatory. The souls in purgatory obsessed him.

At the end of the school year the awards ceremony was held. It was nice because all the mothers would come, some fathers too, and younger and older sisters, even a grandmother. But Juan Lucas would never go. His checks were enough to make his presence felt among the nuns. They would send him the bill for the semester, he read it among a thousand other things at the office, and would write a check for the indicated amount. Susan, however, would always go, although she was never enthusiastic about it. The Lastarrias went every year until their last child had graduated from Immaculate Heart. Juan wouldn't dare kiss Susan's hand in front of the nuns and later he would return home feeling remorse. Susana, on the other hand, would enjoy herself and even knew the first names, last names, and family history of every child. She would spend the whole time putting her children, as if they were the king's valuable jewels, on display in front of her friends. She would go out of her way to say hello to each and every nun, greeting them with excitement as she presented her husband to them and proving to them she was in charge of an upright, decent home: she wasn't one of those who was always losing the seamstress' address like her cousin Susan. Susan, lovely, was bored out of her wits, and she couldn't wait for the ceremony to end. Julius adored her as he looked at her, watching admiringly from his seat, controlling her, using his will to make her pay attention to him, look for each one of his friends, and pay attention when their names were called. As soon as the new house is finished, I'm going to have a birthday party, a really big one, and I'm going to invite the whole class. Santiago and Bobby barely managed to pass each year; Julius, on the other hand, was always among the top students in his class. They didn't know it until the Mother Superior called him forth, patted his head, and hung a medal around his neck. He had finished preparatory school and he was third in his class. Aunt Susana turned green from envy but she managed to congratulate her cousin anyway. And poor Susan, who was going crazy by then, wanted to get out of there. Impossible: the recital was still to come.

The nun sitting at the piano was attractive, really lovely, and all those freckles! Her name was Mary Agnes. The piano room had a statue of Saint Joseph in the corner and a Cuzco rug in the middle of the room between two pianos. Julius would play the one on the left, the other one was for the nuns and it was always closed. At first he wasn't sure if it was something she wore or something the nun used to clean the keys because that perfume in the piano room was the first scent he ever needed in his life, for it really added so much to his musical sensitivity . . . The nun wore a kind of large, white starched bib that covered her bosom and made her seem even more saintly. Her long, chainlike rosary flowed down her sides. She was the nervous type and always bit her lips when you made a mistake; nevertheless she was a real saint and never got upset with Julius. No, never. Three times a week they seemed to spend hours sitting at that perfumed piano. She would bite her lip, smile immediately, and ask him to start over. Inundated with the scent of piano key cleaner, Julius would become inspired and worship her, looking at her and seeking out her smile; then she would show him the keys and smile. "Begin," she would tell him . . .

My Bonnie lies over the ocean
My Bonnie lies over the sea
My Bonnie lies over the ocean
Oh bring back my Bonnie to me! . . .

. . . And the perfume and how he adored her. Each time he would play more softly, with more feeling.

The freckled nun taught him well and he practiced arduously, all to the chagrin of Juan Lucas who was always complaining about the noise the little snot made with his practicing, until one day Susan gave him a kiss and led Juan Lucas slowly to the piano room. "Look at him," she said. His back was to them, ears still Dumbolike but so cute. His toes pointed outward so much that they slipped off the pedals. He played and sang simultaneously, ever so softly, as if he were also trying to discover a scent in that piano . . .

Oh bring back my Bonnie to me! . . .

. . . He adored Cinthia, Mother Mary Agnes, and the unknown Bonnie.

Julius had worked hard preparing "My Bonnie" for the recital at the end of the school year, and it occurred to Susan that he might make a mess of it. She didn't look around so that no one would realize he was her son who was playing. But she did listen affectionately while the poor kid did battle with an unexpected nervousness, for he played "My Bonnie" quite differently. But no one cared! They agreed he played the song with a great deal of feeling.

And that's the way those recitals went. The best students would play, for they had been chosen by the freckled nun who worked right up to the last minute to get them prepared. Once the prizes had been awarded, they would go up to the stage and, at times, make mistakes. The mothers would get nervous, ready to applaud, and almost die when their child got stuck in the middle of a piece, and then applaud loudly as if they had already finished in order to save them. It didn't matter, the final part would always be played with feeling. Even Rafaelito Lastarria managed to play in a recital. He cheated, of course, because he had been given private lessons at home. Still, he managed to finish "Apache Dance" and Susana felt very accomplished. Juan Lastarria was taken by it too and made a special donation to the new school.

When they finished the recital, bringing to a close the awards ceremony, Susan couldn't believe it was finally over. But it wasn't. A piano was heard once again, this time without any mistakes. The freckled nun was closing out the school year in grand style, filling them with emotion with one last little refrain from the school anthem, and all of them singing their hearts out while their parents stood up ready to go out onto the patio and say to one another Your child is also a treasure, or exchange vacation plans, We're going to Ancón, how about you? or something like that, all of which was executed with elegance, of course.

II

JULIUS SPENT THE summer between preparatory and grade school at the Golf Club. They would all go in the station wagon, except for Santiago who was preparing for entrance exams to study agriculture at the university. The poor guy had a lot of tutors; they were young and most of them were in their last years of college. They always came around in pickups, offering those strong Inca cigarettes. The university qualifying examination was like the garage door of the mansion: behind it was Juan Lucas' antique Mercedes sports car. If Santiago gets accepted, he'll have transportation to the university and wheels for picking up easy girls in Lince, for instance. "Poor Santiago, he sure studies a lot!" Susan commented, sitting at the edge of the Club swimming pool. Bobby, on the other hand, was taking life easy, springing a thousand times off the diving board in order to impress the Canadian ambassador's daughter, a thirteen-year-old gringa. Julius didn't have a nanny anymore, and when Juan Lucas finished a round of golf in the morning and came in for lunch, which was always prefaced with *gin and tonics,* he would take Julius with him to the table. Sometimes Carlos would take Santiago to the Club for lunch so he could get away from the books for a while.

That summer Juan Lastarria became a member of the Club. The family was in Ancón, but he spent most of his time in Lima taking care of the import and storage business and everything else; hence he took advantage of the situation to become a member of the Club and to go there without his wife. The poor guy almost went crazy hurrying all the time to finish his morning golf game so he could make a beeline to the pool and hover around his *duchess.* Still dressed in his golfing attire, he would kiss her hand ridiculously and sit there telling her he was a happy man, golfing had transformed him, it was rejuvenating him. Juan Lucas and his buddies named him Bulletproof because he would stick out his little chest when he appeared immaculate and pudgy in his bathing suit in order to take a dip in the pool. They made fun of him as he swam to keep fit. Susan felt sorry for him and begged them in English not to make her laugh anymore, and she told Julius not to listen to *those hor-*

rible things they were saying about his uncle. But Juan Lucas insisted on explaining what his aunt Susana looked like in a bathing suit which precipitated a lot of manly laughter, and then they ordered more *gin and tonics* brought out from the bar of the Club by waiters scurrying along statuelike among so many women in bathing suits, so many girls, so many gringas. No one in the group paid; they would gamble for the bill in the bar later in the afternoon; they would ask for the dice and, while the women waited out on the terrace, they rolled the dice, accompanied by a round of late afternoon drinks. As they threw the dice, they would comment on the day's round of golf, the final scores, who shot what, and the roll of the dice would determine the one among them who would blurt out Damn it! not showing any anger but just manly enough for the occasion, and then sign the check that sooner or later would reach his office. Lastarria always got sidetracked in the middle of the dice roll because he would be watching the Club professional. The Argentine had been giving lessons to him at a very expensive hourly rate. He was good-looking and seemed fairly sophisticated, but stood out nevertheless like a tango singer in his hair style, a good player and tanned; hence, Lastarria didn't know whether to treat him like an employee of the Club or as a Señor.

It may seem strange but Julius began to detest the headwaiter who waited on them at lunch. He was the one who brought them the menus and then treated the waiters like dirt whenever they made mistakes. And the amazing part is that the headwaiter began to dislike Julius, as if he were the son of some Club member whose financial ruin was already well known by everyone. Something odd would occur every time that headwaiter came to their table; undoubtedly, he must have felt superior to the other waiters because his jacket was finer. But what about those disparaging glances at Julius? . . . Maybe it's because the other day Julius bent down and picked up a piece of bread from the floor that the waiter should have done or maybe it's because he isn't forceful enough when he deals with the caddies and the other waiters. There wasn't a logical explanation. What could explain this incipient hatred between a fiddling, ass-kissing waiter and a young boy who was about to turn seven years old? Whatever the case, Julius was able to ignore it by the time the food had arrived: shrimp cocktails, stuffed avocados, sole in white sauce, or crêpes au cointreau, with flames leaping off the table that didn't even faze Juan Lucas.

The golfers and their wives would enter the dining room, looking tanned—in fact, elegantly tanned—and one could tell they were agile and in excellent economic shape. They would greet each other even if in the world of business they hated each other and there it wasn't a sin if someone had been divorced. Lovers, for instance, were accepted despite the gossip. And, of course, there were always those women whose names were more aristocratic, refined, and conservative than the others, but often these same people no longer had that much money and perhaps for that reason they didn't protest; in fact, many of them who came for lunch were merely invited: poor things, it was their proper social setting but there was the problem of the membership fee; frankly, they were in no position to judge vulgarities or immoralities. The drinks brought equality, the dining room became alive and, looking out the windows at the golf course, it was as if they were sailing over a sea of green, a pleasure trip on an ocean that unfortunately had it limits—the high walls enclosing the Club so that poor people couldn't get inside to steal the golf balls.

Lunchtime was always a problem for Lastarria. Even though he had spent a bunch of money outfitting himself to play golf, he had a hard time making friends at the Club. Everyone there, of course, knew who Juan Lastarria was, but that was precisely the problem: they knew what he was. They knew the same about others, but those were something: handsome, drunks, fun, friendly, or they simply managed to fit in easily. Lastarria, on the other hand, was still boorish and missed the point on just about everything. If Juan Lucas wouldn't invite him over to their table, the poor dummy would have to flee to another and, naturally, end up paying the bill; he would sign for it which is the one thing he had learned to do quickly. Susan became aware of the problem and many times she would be the one to invite him over to their table. She felt so sorry for him, dressed up like a golfer but not really looking like one. And that stupid sweater?

Once lunch was over there was lots of table talk. Then the men left to play another round of golf in order to complete the daily eighteen holes that they had begun in the morning. Susan also played, accompanied by several friends who were the wives of diplomats or people like Juan Lucas. There was always someone from England, a few Americans, and maybe a German woman as well. They would speak in English or Spanish, but no matter which language they used they always added delicious foreign words. Also they would occasionally speak French, whenever the ambassador's wife was along, but that's when many of the Peruvian women didn't say a word all afternoon. Needless to say, they all represented the latest in fashion: Aaaaahhhhh! and it's all very expensive. The men would walk on ahead in a group and blurt out Damn it! Bastard! or both, well said, appropriately timed, and manly. The caddies wouldn't dare to think that their refined ways were in any way queerish. If, for instance, you were on the outside looking in over the wall at the scene I'm describing, you'd be convinced that life couldn't be happier or more beautiful; moreover, you would have seen very good golfers. They were men who didn't show their age and had strong and sprightly arms; their women were lousy at hitting the ball but were beautiful. Spying over the wall a little longer and with keen sight, you could have also recognized Juan Lastarria and the Argentine professional, who knew how to deal with that kind of world, both walking after the little ball and all that it represented.

The children, meanwhile, would be in Ancón, at Herradura Beach, or in the pool at the Club. Julius played in the pool until the pressure of the water from diving started to hurt his eardrums. Bobby had nothing to do with him and he continued to jump off the diving board, always getting out of the pool near the Canadian ambassador's daughter. Naturally, rather than use the steps he would leap up onto the side of the pool in acrobatic fashion, adjust his bathing suit in order to let his belly button show, and trot over to the steps of the diving board to repeat the scene all over again. He would go up the steps, make sure she was watching, and take off running. Aunt Susana wouldn't have ever permitted her children to do this. When he got to the end of the board, he would fly off, transformed first into a gull, next into a plane nosediving into the sea, and then a round tire. But at the last moment he would straighten out gracefully and penetrate the water without a splash. A fantastic, daring jump. And he was ready to risk his life for the young Canadian girl. She was so pretty! . . . She, too, was attracted to him and, while she remained seated on her stool and watched, she soon smiled at him. Finally one day they met each other and started to swim together. Tarzan and Jane, that's the way he felt, and they dove down side by side from one side of the river to the other as if they were going to run into crocodiles on the way. Then one day a crocodile did appear: Julius. He approached them to ask the time and to tell Bobby that Mommy was about to call them to get ready to go home. For being a little brat and a crocodile, he received a tremendous swat from Tarzan, who was very embarrassed in front of the girl.

The golfers would return late in the afternoon. Some of the men took showers and others cooled off in the pool. Afterward they went to the locker rooms where, wrapped in a towel or naked depending on their masculinity or their stomachs, they would talk. The voices of Juan Lucas and his friends resounded throughout the numbered lockers of the Club while they got dressed and commented on that day's golf game. One day Lastarria undressed in front of everyone and his physique became the butt of a joke; everyone would laugh, he more than anyone else, and he finally started to feel like he had become a member of the Club. This was his favorite time. As soon as they were dressed they moved to the bar, this was their moment, the manly thing to do, roll the dice and there they accepted him and even commented on the progress he was making with the help of the Argentine golf pro. Little by little he became an insider and, if they kept on patting him on the back, soon he would feel right at home; in fact, he practically felt right at home, even though disagreeable things kept happening to him, like the other afternoon, for instance, when he thanked God for not being seen by anyone but feeling, just the same, so out of it. Poor guy. It was that ne'er-do-well count, that Peruvian Spaniard, the queer, so snobbish, a cretin, so broke but so elegant, so admired, and always getting himself invited everywhere. Well, that worthless count pushed him out of the way and beat him to the door, didn't even say hello, almost spit on him, the wise guy was drunk. And he, without even wanting to, blurted out excuse me, Count, and now that little incident didn't let him rest in peace; after all, I'm rich, important, a hard worker, a family man. What a stupid thing to say to the guy! and he would wake up in the middle of the night reliving the incident. Juan Lastarria had his dignity too, you know. Something else happened . . . Ah, if it wasn't for these incidents he would feel like a real Club member . . . they had introduced him to the Japanese consul—Juan, the Japanese consul—and immediately he didn't like him. He debated between using diplomacy or talking as if to any old Chinaman down at the corner grocery store. But he couldn't decide, he took too long, and he didn't know what to do when the other put out his silky, cold hand, the consul was very oriental, overflowing with reverence. They looked at him as if he were a total idiot, Chinese people can be very refined, too. Things like that happened to poor Juan and they almost gave him heart attacks. Then everyone will say he had one because of economic problems, too much work, too many worries, the standard heart attack because of the typical tensions of the well-minded *business man . . .*

They stayed in the bar until nightfall while the women waited outside on the terrace and the children, wanting to go home, began to get on people's nerves. The business deals came up in the bar also, but in general they simply used elegance to discuss the country's political situation or the current state of the fishing industry. Of course, they never forgot to crack the latest joke or to comment on the day's golf game. Once the "Damn it, today I have to pay" was heard, the golfers would begin to leave. Juan Lucas would go out to the terrace looking for Susan, kiss her, and they would adore each other. He would sit down next to her and they would remain there for a few minutes in silence, contemplating how the trees on the golf course would start to disappear as night came on, interrupting momentarily that enjoyable golden green summer. It produced a momentary imbalance in the organized equilibrium of their lives, but they didn't let it bother them. They would just round up the boys and point them to the station wagon in order to go home and, as they would leave, they said good-bye to a few Club members who were still there stretched out in lounge chairs: See you tomorrow, adiós! The caddies were leaving about that time as well and would pass by the station wagon. Juan Lucas was one who never missed the opportunity to make a sarcastic remark: "Well, they're letting the convicts out of jail," for instance, as he started the motor. "Good evening, Señor," said the headwaiter, opening the door to an old Oldsmobile that probably belonged to a Club member some ten or twelve years ago and was laden with chrome that squeaked. It was an obese Oldsmobile that took a while for its motor to warm up, just like a fat woman from Lima.

The new school got bigger and bigger but it wouldn't be ready for Julius' first communion. He had already started school at the large old converted house on Arequipa Avenue. It was huge too, and had a lookout up on top that was off limits because it belonged to the third graders, the big guys. Arzubiaga had gone on to Saint Mary's and Martinto was as fat as ever, a real slob, but he was back in preparatory once again. It was important to be very good in first grade because they would make first communion and also go through confirmation for which a godfather was required. And, above all, they shouldn't sin, nor hit anyone, much less steal a pen or think bad thoughts.

They had just arrived and they were talking in the courtyard when Carrottop appeared ringing the bell furiously in order for them to fall into formation. Everyone guessed that Carrottop had already seen him and it wouldn't be long before she got mad at him. She wanted the rows to be in twos and by height, which was quite difficult because no one wanted to admit that this guy, who was shorter last year, is taller this year. Flushed from aggravation and the heat, she stood them together and measured them instantly; a pinch and a bell in the ear for those who didn't obey ipso facto. She became enraged and each time she got worse. Fortunately, however, the Mother Superior came out to welcome them and say next year they would be moving to the new school. Then she introduced a new nun who had just arrived from the United States and she asked everyone to pray an extra Hail Mary tonight so that the climate in Lima wouldn't bother her. The new nun was Mary Trinity and she was pretty. This would create continual problems for those who study piano with Mary Agnes because now they won't know which one to dote on more; in fact, Mary Trinity was great and she would smile, rubbing her hands together, full of emotion, and it seemed as if she might start to cry in front of so many perfectly dressed little children. At last they heard her voice: she told them she was happy to be in Peru, she had always dreamed of coming, and now she was going to be their friend. She couldn't talk anymore and they became fidgety as they indicated their approval of her. But I think Carrottop was hating her for being so sweet and kind. One thing for sure, the bell shook all the harder in her hand and she rolled up her sleeves, which was a sure sign that she was about to begin to rant and rave. The nuns from the previous year came out with the same smile on their faces. Mary Agnes was also there, biting her lips and looking attractive. The terrace filled up with smiling nuns. Watching from the patio, the children were ready to break ranks, run up the stairs, and say hello to each one in person. Morales and Gumersindo Quiñones, who were standing on the third step below the nuns, also smiled. Gumersindo made a huge bow when the Mother Superior mentioned the new school bus and he would have liked to have said a few words. Morales, wearing his standard khaki uniform and sleeveless red sweater, silently chose the new team. A towel hung from his shoulder and his mouth was dry from the sun. Another happy school year had begun, and there was still some summer sun left.

The first weeks of that school year were great for Julius. Santiago had been admitted to Agriculture and Juan Lucas, who kept his promise, handed over his old Mercedes to him. But the old car wasn't enough, the sly fox demanded a new one. Finally the matter was resolved by the golfer's flat-out no which was accompanied by a large sum of money for re-upholstering the Mercedes with black leather and for painting it red. Take it or leave it. He took it. While the car was being renovated in the shop, they had to give him the Mercury station wagon because the university was out by La Molina, which was impossible to reach without a car; one had to be brave to take the bus from Grau Plaza, which was a bus line for poor people. Bobby swore up and down that this year it was his turn to be behind the wheel and he had already studied the curve in front of the Canadian girl's house which he wanted to take at high speed, leaving deep black tire marks on the pavement and putting Julius, Carlos, and Imelda's lives on the line. But he resigned himself to a raise in his allowance which was important because of his new expense: cigarettes. Julius, on the other hand, was pleased to learn that he would have to ride the school bus home every afternoon.

He became a close friend of Gumersindo Quiñones. When the bell would ring, those who rode the bus would run to get a seat next to the window. Then the nun whose turn it was would get on and someone would have to give up his seat, but that's when brownnosers were useful. With the nun's permission, Gumersindo would close the door, making sure that only he could open it again. The new school bus was huge, a lot wider than the old one, but Gumersindo could still reach across to the door from his seat. And Julius would watch the enormous black hand and the white ivory-colored palm reach out for it. How strange it was! And the white hair. It was so white that it made the Negro seem like a Señor. Julius told the family about it and Susan said it's true that the driver was courteous, for she had seen him once: that's the way those Negroes are, the ones who are descendants of slaves, they are very loyal, very noble, and they are happy to have the names of their previous owners. Julius listened with pleasure and he wanted to hear more about Gumersindo Quiñones, more about Negroes . . . yes, they could talk some more, but Juan Lucas was just arriving. For sure he knows a lot about it . . . but don't listen to him, darling, Uncle Juan Lucas is always joking: A lady was patting the head of a Negro, cute little Negro, cute little Negro, she said to him, and do you know what the little Negro said to her? Negro cute when little, ain't but shit when big. Don't pay any attention to him, darling.

Since he was one of the last ones to get off the bus, he could talk with him a little longer. The nun who rode the bus didn't really understand Spanish, that is, she didn't participate in the conversations, she just spent the time gazing out the window. Gumersindo told him stories about his family being slaves of the ancestors of the Quiñones children. He, too, had worked for that family, not as a slave, of course, but as a chauffeur. Now he just visits them from time to time because he's old and prefers to work for the nuns. It's easier working for them because he only had to make four trips a day and by six o'clock in the afternoon he was finished. Working for the Quiñones family, on the other hand, he didn't stop day or night, why they had him driving until nine at night and sometimes even later. The Chevrolet station wagon was for taking the nuns to the doctor, to go shopping, or to visit the other nuns at Villa María . . .

"Your mommy was probably educated there."

"No, she was educated in London."

"Ah, that's different."

... and the nuns at Villa María are Americans as well, they're from the same congregation as those at Immaculate Heart. The thing is that they started sooner and that's why they have already established their own school, as it should be. Many Señoras whose children study at Immaculate Heart were educated at Villa María ...

"Your mommy was probably educated there."

"No, Gumersindo, my mommy was educated in London."

"Das true, das true."

Sometimes the driver didn't follow the conversation too well, perhaps he had to pay a lot of attention to the traffic, so he never turned around once to distract himself, that could cause an accident what with all those kids on board; Julius, on the other hand, never missed a word. Unfortunately they were getting close to his stop, now it was his turn to get off, and Gumersindo would continue talking to the other two or three who were still left on the bus. Can you believe it? He was the one asking the questions and now they get to hear the whole story. As he got off, he scrutinized that huge hand on the door lever and just had to seal their friendship with a handshake. One day, finally, he did.

It happened on the last day. Santiago's refurbished Mercedes was ready to go; hence, starting tomorrow, they would have him driven and picked up from school in the station wagon. Once the bus approached his stop at the corner of Salaverry Avenue, he knew the moment had arrived and it was now or never. Gumersindo stopped the bus and Julius turned to say good-bye to the nun and then looked at him: "Tomorrow I won't be riding the bus," he told him, grabbing the hand that was on the lever. Gumersindo responded with a big smile: "Good-bye, kid," he answered, turning to look at the nun who watched the scene somewhat bewildered. Julius watched the bus leave and as always he let Imelda walk him home. He preferred not to talk about it because she only thought about her sewing classes anyway.

THE ARCHITECT HAD finally come up with an elegant yet conciliatory idea and came to dinner one night along with the drawings and the builder: the house would be ultramodern, just as Juan Lucas had wanted, and, in addition to those extravagant details, the house would be totally functional; nothing in it except for those extravagant details would be superfluous. Susan would be able to take her Cuzco and Quito paintings for restoration because they would help decorate more than just one room. Of course, there wasn't room for all of them, but four would soon disappear: she had already given them as presents to Lester Lang III to take back to the United States. Lester had fallen in love with our Peru and there wasn't any alternative but to give them to him. They were already getting the land ready and soon they would start digging the trenches to lay the foundation. The builder explained that the house was going to be earthquake-proof, making it unnecessary to go anywhere in case of an earthquake; in fact, they wouldn't feel anything. Juan Lucas thought this was great and said when one occurs they'll just go to the window and watch the people running around crazily and from here it'll look like a procession. They laughed out loud and drank another round to celebrate the occasion after which they sat down to dinner.

Julius was there too, for about that time in his life they agreed to allow him to sit at the table with the adults. The servants became confused: Julius never returned to eat in Disneyland. Something in his life had come to an end. Other things were changing as well, and not everything they wrote in the textbooks was the way Nilda, Vilma, or the butlers had described it to him. The worst part was that it wasn't easy to match up Jungle Woman's descriptions, for instance, with the ones in some of his books. Nilda was a poor reader and she clammed up at the sight of books; besides, she only wanted to look at the pictures and, to make things worse, a good number of those books were written in English, so that when he read them out loud and provided a translation, they looked at him distrustfully, half-fearful, half-ashamed, showing almost infantile attitudes toward things. They didn't understand a thing about the Greeks and the Romans. It was no longer like before. Nilda would bite her nails when he talked about Mochicas and Chimu Indians.

And now they were taking him to dine with the adults, who were practically yanking little Julius away from them. Imelda might have been of some help, for she was responsible for taking care of him and his things; however, she was very unpopular. She had not been present for any of the children's births in the mansion and she wasn't a part of anything that went on there, she didn't even chat with them in the kitchen. She was from Lima, part white, a little testy, and somewhat uppity. She would go to her sewing classes several afternoons every week and, as soon as she graduates, she'll quit. You watch, you'll see, she'll abandon the family and won't care a bit. Celso and Daniel hardly ever talked to her, only when it was strictly necessary. And Arminda grew old because she missed her daughter. She had heard that she was living in Cerro de Pasco with the D'Onofrio ice cream man, but she had never heard from her directly. She spent hours leaning over the tub washing everyone's clothes to perfection. When Juan Lucas found out that she was the one who washed and ironed his shirts so well, he gave her a raise. But she didn't even notice; she would just keep washing, imagining her daughter as nothing more than another victim of domestic violence, that man will never marry her, he'll just abandon her. Long, shiny, ordinary gray locks of hair fell down both sides of her face and, in the late afternoon when her feet and arms were cold, her daughter's affair grew more and more in her mind and became confused with her own youth, the time when her first child was born, the first one that died on her, yes, two times she escaped with two different men, she was fifteen years old at the time, that's why she knew her daughter wasn't bad, that's also why she knew life was like that: hard as a rock. And that it's better to find security, work for a family in a house where a child, someone like Julius, would bring happiness. I was in a bad way when I started with this family, and I only wanted to save this last daughter, but we're hot-blooded when we're young, and when you're poor like us history repeats itself just like the newspaper stories that Nilda reads . . .

And Nilda's stories about the jungle were over . . . and Celso had been the treasurer of the Friends of Huarocondo Club for so long . . . and except for Imelda everyone had worked in that house for many years and they all knew each other, maybe too well. What could have made them uneasy now? With nothing new to talk about, everything seemed to turn to memories. Even young Cinthia was nothing but a yearly visit to the cemetery and a man who came to collect for taking care of the grave site. Celso and Daniel remained bachelors but they had their women and a plot of land in a slum area. They were always looking for some pretext to leave because their presence on their land was necessary so the women could go for food; in the slums, someone always had to be on the property occupying the hut made of straw mats and sheets of tin; if they were to abandon it for an instant, someone could move in and take over. They were always worried about it. But then they only had time to play with Julius in his little eating area, but now it wasn't used for anything. Everything seemed better before and little Julius' move to the adult dining room had made them aware of it. They suddenly realized that things had been better when Vilma was there. For some time little Julius had been talking about a Morales and a Gumersindo and only recently had they become aware of it. And he spent more and more time on the telephone talking to his school friends and less and less time in the kitchen talking to them. Before, the little Disneyland dining room was the last happy spot in the mansion and now, all of a sudden, they had done away with it. It was of no use anymore, only for remembering. That's why Nilda, while she was in her room by herself one night, even wanted to cry for Vilma to come back. Later she did cry out: Why should Vilma return? The same thing would only happen to her again. Anyway, what was happening to them? Nothing, really, only that little Julius was going to first communion and he had to learn his lessons well. Besides, now he ate at the table with the adults, like his brothers . . .

Father Brown talked to them half in English and half in horrible Spanish, but he left them filled with goodness, except for poor Sánchez Concha who was terrified by all that stuff about hell because he had just stolen an eraser from Del Castillo. The others, on the other hand, were waiting for God to appear anytime, even though it was most likely going to happen at night as they were praying on their knees next to their beds in the dark. They had waited for him and even thought it would be great if he appeared in front of me and not the Arenas brothers, for instance. For the first time they had been left alone in the classroom without making any noise. They were in some kind of trance. At last Carrottop came in and was a little taken aback because there was no one at whom she could yell. They were all hushed with clasped hands on their desks. That's the way Father Brown would leave them when he came to prepare them for their first communion every year. Carrottop put the bell on the desk and walked over to them: "Now you have to study your catechism book backward and forward. You have to learn everything it says by heart and never forget it throughout your whole life. Whoever forgets his catechism will always be in danger of sinning. Sin! And don't forget it, don't ever forget it! Never!" Now she was getting upset and she was doing it all by herself without anyone saying boo to her. "And when that day arrives, that great day of peace and happiness, we'll see if you can act like you are supposed to without making foolish mistakes. That's why we are going to practice every day, first here at school and when the big day gets closer, we'll go to the church so that you can get accustomed to it and everyone will know where they're supposed to go. You are going in by height! Don't forget! And I don't want to see anyone chewing the communion wafer! The communion wafer is not to be chewed! You swallow it softly! With your eyes closed! Without looking at the person next to you! Don't let me catch you looking at the person next to you! Understand? Do you understand?" Everyone answered affirmatively, but then they got frightened thinking that they might choke, so they were going to practice at home with a cracker, or whatever.

Father Brown came three times a week in order to prepare them; he came in the afternoons and would stay for an hour, or more if needed, talking about the profound transformation they were going to experience in their lives. He made them feel a little more at ease when he told them God always forgives, that it was enough to have a firm commitment never to sin again. First, they should avoid—at all costs—thinking bad thoughts; however, they should love God above all else. Well, they should love all men, too, because they were their brothers, and the poor ones as well, the little children in the missions in the Peruvian and Brazilian jungles, and in Africa and Asia too. All of them were their brothers and sisters and God loved each and every one of them equally. They learned the Ten Commandments without really understanding some that the priest preferred not to explain just yet. First, he said, learn them by heart, later on they would see how life explains to them who is their neighbor's wife and what fornication means. The talk left several of them quite perplexed, not that it was a problem for those who picked up on things faster, maybe it was more a problem of semantics but, whatever the case, de los Heros looked at Lastres apprehensively. Some weeks later they began to take them to the largest hall in the school. One by one they knelt down in front of a bench and Father Brown would give them a little slap, make a sign for them to leave, and tell the next one to come forward; then they would go back again and the priest would touch their mouths, which is the way it would be when he gave them the communion wafer. But they had to be more serious, more solemn, for on that day they were going to receive God through the consecrated wafer. They practiced several times which they enjoyed because they got out of Carrottop's classes. Also, when the school day was over, they would go to the patio and play confirmation, giving each other tremendous slaps; that's what they were doing one day when all of a sudden Carrottop appeared on the scene and discovered their game (every year she would discover the same game). She went into a frenzy, couldn't stop yelling at them, and threatened to beat them up if they continued to sin that way.

Finally confession day arrived. They were frightened out of their wits and each one trembled when it was his turn. They had learned their lists of sins by heart and someone had even numbered his, fearing he would miss one, and then what would happen? They made decisive, definitive resolutions for correction: no one would call the butler a stupid Cholo ever again; no one would hit his sister nor steal pens from her ever again; no one would hope for San Martín, the egghead of the class, to get sick or make a mistake in a lesson; no one again would pray for Carrottop to go back to the United States or to slip on the stairs so he would get a chance to see her underwear; no one would leave his dinner plate unfinished because there are little kids dying of starvation and cold in the mountains. Father Brown absolved them one by one, and they retreated fearing the worst, avoiding evil thoughts and walking daintily like little girls.

They had never been so obedient and so studious; only four days were left before the big day. They had gone twice to the church in the central park of Miraflores for the final rehearsals. Even Carrottop had changed. It seemed as though she too was going through her first communion like them, she treated them nicely and didn't get mad or anything. She practically gave them no homework. The only bad part was that the students in second and third grades, who had already received first communion, came around to make fun of them. The others laughed at them and at times they were about to think bad thoughts, fall into temptation, or get mad. But they remained undaunted and never answered back. They simply continued to be strong in their convictions. They would arrive like angels, like the ones who didn't rebel, and they would receive their first communion, be blessed, and then take communion the first Friday of each month. Sundays too, and why not? Each one worked hard trying not to commit a sin, and it wasn't always easy. You had to be on your toes. Susan laughed when Julius told her what had happened one afternoon three days before the solemn day. As always, he went upstairs to say hello and plead with her to get Juan Lucas to go to the ceremony. He had already agreed to let Juan Lastarria be his godfather for confirmation (for to say what he really thought about the Lastarrias would be a sin). Susan saw that he was quite distressed and asked him to tell her what was wrong. At first Julius was a little restrained but he couldn't hold it back, so he let loose. As it turns out, Aliaga, one of the big guys in second grade, had fouled him; he had pushed him just as he was about to score a goal, right in front of Morales too. Then things got worse when he called him a queer. Tears came to his eyes out of frustration. What should he have done? Hitting him would have been a sin. "Poor Julius," intervened Susan, improvising concern. "And what did you do?" "Nothing. I told him that I couldn't hit him because I'm going to first communion, so I talked to Bosco instead; he's a friend of mine in the third grade and he pounded the heck out of him."

Sánchez Concha had dreamed that the floor of the church fell out from under his feet and he couldn't make it to the communion altar while Carrottop, who was enveloped in flames and wearing horns, was pursuing him. He woke up terrified, thinking that the last part of the dream was a sin and broke into tears. His mother had to call an old friend of the family, Father Maquiavelo, who talked to him over the phone and convinced him that he could still go to communion. Fuentes stuck his toothbrush in his mouth and almost died thinking he could have swallowed one of the bristles. Del Castillo's mother bought him a special wafer dessert so that he wouldn't be afraid of the communion wafer. He showed up self-assured: he had already tried it, it didn't taste like anything special, and it dissolved all by itself in his mouth. That had been a bad night for all of them, but now they were all lined up, in rows of two, standing at the side of the church in the Miraflores park dressed in white uniforms and baby-blue ties, with the initials IH embroidered in light blue on the upper pocket of the jackets, a little silk ribbon pinned to the right arm, and a candle in the left hand which I hope doesn't blow out. Even Arenas, a classmate, the dirtiest of the Arenas kids, looked like he had just taken a bath that morning. His father, however, was the one who looked dirty; he's the one with the moustache getting out of that Ford. They watched their fathers arrive and were pleased, especially if one's father, for instance, turned out to be taller than Fuentes' father. The mothers arrived dressed up very elegantly, some wore hats, others shawls. Juan Lastarria showed up looking like the Prince of Wales, and he almost fell over when he saw the other men dressed in dark suits. At first he was perturbed, but then he remembered that he was a golfer and he felt reassured once more. He had come with his wife, who was happy to be able to attend another first communion. Her children had already been through it, my how time flies, yes, life goes on, now my children are attending Saint Mary's. But, of course, the nuns should remember who she was and afterward she would go around to greet them. Her husband knew that he would have to make a donation, for it was important that the new school be finished, nothing but the best for the nuns, for Lima was growing and it deserved first-class—that is, North American—schools, where their children could learn English well and play with other children like themselves, a school where they know that little Johnny is son of so-and-so and that we belong to a privileged class. We need schools that are deserving of our children . . . Aunt Susana was horrible and happy with her lace shawl, happy as well because Susan had finally remembered them, it was really their place to be god-parents of those children at baptism time, now finally they remembered . . .

. . . Thinking about all that didn't stop her from noticing everyone who arrived. She frowned at those who raised their voices too much, shh, we're in church now, this isn't a social event. Her roving eyes stopped when she saw her cousin enter the church and a pleasing smile came over her face when she saw that Juan Lucas was at her side. Half-asleep but still lovely, Susan looked for a seat near the door so that in case the ceremony went on too long they could go outside and rest a while. Inside, Juan Lucas seemed little more than an abandoned surf board leaning against the wall on the patio on a rainy day, for the stained glass windows of the old church filtered out the light and, consequently, the temple's dark, tomblike nature made it difficult to see the fine shading that differentiated his suit from any other good dark suit there; moreover, his tanned skin lost its color and that healthy athletic look had faded, and his dark glasses, which looked good on him, turned black for lack of sun, making him look like a blind man. He covered his mouth, expertly shielding a yawn and making sure not to look around to the sides so that no one could wave at him. "No businessman waves at another businessman in the Miraflores church at eight-thirty in the morning," he decided, feeling a surge of virility. "If my golfing friends would see me now, they'd crap in their pants laughing at me. They'd say that poor jerk has lost his marbles. Sure, he's a good family man and all that: well, Daddy, tell us how you insert those suppositories up your son's ass." He nodded his head in order to ward off such stupid thoughts. Susan couldn't help but feel sorry for him as she looked at him standing there so early in the morning and she jokingly, but discreetly, stuck out her tongue at him. "Just for bringing me here you're going to get a swift whack on your ass with one of my golf clubs," he told her smilingly. They were doting on each other when heaven only knows how their eyes met up with Susana's. Juan Lucas nodded as if to say hello and then turned away, exactly like a little child who doesn't want to admit that it's time to eat dinner. Susan acted as if she were coughing and searched for her missal that she had forgotten; then both of them turned to look back at her but she wasn't paying any attention to them anymore. The ceremony had just begun.

The children walked in saintly fashion toward the communion altar, moving forward up the middle between the church pews and looking out the corner of their eyes at their parents. Then came the godfathers. Susan, spotting Julius, was surprised to see how well his hair was combed and she jabbed Juan Lucas with her elbow so he wouldn't miss him. Juan Lucas also spotted him and winked when Julius turned as he passed by them. Juan Lucas continued to watch Julius as the children approached the altar: "Your son is going to be a bishop." "Pum!" she mimicked with her pistollike hand. The organ began to play above them and the members of the chorus with their red altar-boy suits remembered their first communion and adopted solemn postures, ready to sing, as Susan knelt and Juan Lucas, at her side, remained standing like the other men.

Once the ceremony was over, the parents went looking for their children to hug and kiss them near the door of the church. They had just taken communion for the first time in their lives and their stomachs were fluttering. The Lastarrias, who were elated to be able to stand next to Susan and Juan Lucas, remembered with tenderness their own Pipo and Rafaelito's first communion. Of course they gave Julius all kinds of advice. Then Carrottop approached them, ready to walk the children to the bus. Some city gardeners watched them cross the park and, though they really didn't understand what was going on, they didn't make any wisecracks. The nun directed them as they climbed into the bus; Gumersindo Quiñones was in the driver's seat, waiting to pat each one on the head as they filed past. Julius felt his huge hand on his head and became teary-eyed. That's the way saints must feel, some day he'll put his hand on the heads of all the little Negroes in Africa and all the Indians in Peru. How nice it would be to put your hand on the heads of poor people and make them good.

Another head needing a hand belonged to Juan Lucas: he was fuming, for he had just been told that the communion ceremony would continue at the school. It turned out that it was time to say hello to the nuns and to thank them for everything they had done for their children . . . and then wait for breakfast to finish . . . and take more pictures . . . as if they hadn't taken enough already . . . Susana, horrible, explained everything, asking for patience, and Susan told her that yes, she was informed of everything that was going on because she had read the newsletter the nuns had sent. But she enjoyed this part, making him suffer, for last night he had spent hours talking with the Chilean ambassador's wife. Time for sweet revenge.

"Darling, I want you to meet the Mother Superior. Tell her that you have an aunt who is a Sacred Heart nun . . . you'll be a hit, darling . . ."

A long table with a white tablecloth had been set up. Resting gently against the orange juice glasses were religious prayer cards, in color, representing scenes from the life of Christ or other saints. The Virgin appeared on some of the cards, floating amid the clouds, hands in prayer position and rosary hanging from her extra long fingers. Name cards had been placed at each seat. It was quite a sight: all were now

116

seated, they were waiting patiently for breakfast to be served. And they were behaving very well. Now that the wafer had reached there, they repeatedly touched their quivering stomachs searching for some kind of transformation. The photographers continued to blind them with their flashbulbs and the nuns constantly scurried back and forth, patting them with love on their heads. It wouldn't be long now before they left for heaven, hand in hand. But the presence of Morales, who was bringing in an immense pot of hot chocolate, transported them back to earth. Besides, their parents began to enter the dining room and other common sounds could be heard. But the real clincher came when Juan Lucas lit up a cigarette and Julius immediately thought of hell. No one else was smoking, only him. His smoke filled up that part of the room: No, Uncle Juan Lucas, please, no. It was useless because by then other Señores were starting to light up, then there were others and, finally, even more. Soon everyone was smoking, and the nuns were accomplices, traitors, for they brought out ashtrays. The whole dining room filled up with smoke. Good for you! For neither Mary Agnes nor Mary Trinity went for ashtrays. The children didn't want to be around smoke, they didn't want to have anything to do with smoke, they just wanted clouds, but the Señores had ruined it all. It was enough to see them talking, but the whole thing had been converted into a social gathering, a cocktail. At last the Mother Superior came forward to give her talk.

They set their hot chocolates down on the table and watched her through that darn smoke. The nun was brief: she told them that a new stage in their lives had begun. As Catholics it would be a long struggle in order to get to heaven . . . Julius felt he could have easily gone to heaven minutes earlier, but it was ruined when Morales appeared with the boiling hot chocolate; then it got worse when his Uncle Juan Lucas and the other Señores began to smoke. Now his stomach wasn't even quivering, the chocolate was too hot to drink, and he burned himself the way he did every day at breakfast. There was nothing to do but wait, perhaps another day in church . . . The Mother Superior ended her presentation by referring to the importance of finishing the new school and took advantage of the warm applause in order to get their money out of them. Now it was Father Brown's turn.

Susan almost died when she heard his horrible accent: "A cowboy with a robe," she commented. Julius had always found something wrong with Father Brown: maybe he smiled too much, he wasn't sure what it was and, just as he was looking at him, he heard his mother's voice very clearly. He turned around unable to see her among the people, yet he had heard her say something: "There's a big difference between this one and the others at the church, he doesn't have any class." He turned around to listen to Father Brown and saw that she was right: he had just called them little soldiers of Christ, he was winking now, and then he shot with his pistol hand, pum! pum! pum! He was probably alluding to the devils that they would have to kill in order to go to heaven. The Señores applauded and the priest went over to shake hands with everyone. They invited him to smoke a cigarette, which he did.

All that smoke, hot chocolate, and talking sent the children plummeting back to earth. But they landed on their feet, for as soon as they were allowed to leave the table they began to exchange their commemorative prayer cards and, of course, there was always someone who would say mine is nicer than yours or I'll trade you one of mine for two of yours. Susan motioned to Julius for him to give a card to his aunt and uncle; it was time to leave. But just then Father Brown came over and they got into a conversation in English, which left Juan Lastarria in a state of desperation because he didn't understand a word. On the other hand, Susana was able to remember her English from school and she put in her two cents' worth which, of course, was horrendous. "Translate, translate," her husband demanded nervously, sticking out his chest a little more. The two of them wanted to talk to Father Brown. Susan looked at Juan's moustache and Susana's little one too, thinking it must be at least eleven o'clock or later and she didn't have any of her pills. She tried to imagine herself at the golf course in order not to collapse. What an accent that priest has! His English is as bad as his Spanish! Only Juan Lucas' supportive arm could save her, but he had just been told that the priest-cowboy was a golfer and, according to him, a good one. When Lastarria heard the word golf, he pinched his wife saying, "Translate, translate." She told him that they were inviting the priest to play golf because he was a good player. "Tell him I'm going too, tell him, tell him . . ." Julius wanted to go too, so he stuck his hand into his godfather's jacket pocket in order to remove the gift that stuck out like a sore thumb, thinking that if he opens the gift perhaps they'll talk about something else or maybe they'll stop all together.

"Oh, my godson! I'm sorry! I forgot! . . ."

"Is it a pistol, Uncle?"

"No, child, it's a gold Parker pen set. Did you want a pistol?"

"A real pistol? . . . To kill the devil? . . . Pum, pum, pum? . . ."

Julius stood there looking at him ready with answers but without much of anything to say.

Gumersindo Quiñones bowed reverently to them and opened the gate. Juan Lucas didn't see him. He never paid any attention to those who opened the gates, it was a part of his sophistication. On the other hand, the Lastarrias' good-bye was limited to a grimace: better to have done nothing. But it was Susan whom Julius was observing and he almost said Mommy, don't forget. And she didn't forget. Lovely, she smiled at Gumersindo and the old, tall, white-haired, uniformed Negro bowed elegantly once again, but even lower this time. Julius was happy. "Goodbye, Gumersindo," he said proudly to his friend, shaking hands with him in front of his parents, aunt, and uncle. But, more than anything, he was so happy that Susan was aware not only of who the man was but also of how much Julius liked him. The Lastarrias said goodbye and started walking up Arequipa Avenue in search of their car which was parked on a side street. The others walked in the opposite direction toward the Jaguar sports car. They squeezed Julius in between them and, while Juan Lucas started the motor, Julius felt his mother put her arm around his neck. He looked up at her: she's always so lovely! She was even more so right then as she held her hair from blowing in the wind. Juan Lucas quickly sped off, leaving everyone else behind on the street. The Jaguar was like a bullet and, hence, with the top down they enjoyed the air blowing into their faces. They closed their eyes, which made it even more enjoyable. Then they would open and close them to notice the difference; closing them was exciting and, as they repeated the game, something strong came to him. Julius opened his eyes toward the sun, closed them again, and then heard his mother's voice as she hugged him as the wind blew all around: Gumersindo is very nice, darling. Eyes closed, he felt good waiting for a kiss in the wind and for the inevitable; that love, right there next to him, made his world perfect.

Juan Lucas hummed a tune that announced their arrival at the mansion. What a beautiful, sunny day! It's almost like summer! Got to get out of these unbearable clothes! He was already visualizing the Panama shirt waiting for him in the closet that he would wear to the Golf Club. As he made the last turn and approached the mansion, he noticed his arm covered with the dark cloth of his suit. Feeling completely out of season, he accelerated all the more. Susan laid her head back and felt happiness. The playful wind had carried off any residue of the presence of so many mothers at eleven o'clock in the morning and she, grateful, offered her hair to the wind as well. It all disappeared at the moment she lazily removed her arm from Julius' neck and placed it on his shoulders, just where his uniform's rough, hot wool next to his skin became unbearable.

Carlos opened the gate to the mansion and barely got out of the way in time as Juan Lucas came barreling through.

"Clean her up a bit while I change!" he yelled to him, turning off the ignition. He looked at Susan: "Let's hurry, honey, we're eating lunch at the Golf Club . . . and this little whipper-snapper here who's dressed like an angel is going too."

He was about to get out of the Jaguar when they all came outside. He saw them with big smiles on their faces as they filed out through a side door. Right then he hated them: Nilda, Arminda, Celso, Daniel and the gardener whose name he didn't even know. Carlos also joined them. They were anxious to see the little boy who was all decked out for his first communion. Susan looked at Juan Lucas begging him to be patient. Celso had an old camera, one of those black boxes for taking pictures of himself with the child. Julius, who was just getting out of the car, thought the whole thing was perfectly normal. He immediately got involved in the picture-taking event, but he didn't realize that Juan Lucas, for instance, could very well have been planning for a divorce. Just then Nilda took over: she wanted pictures, lots of them, all together, at the front door, and with the Señor and Señora too. The golfer lit a cigarette and ordered a bottle of mineral water to get him through the ordeal. Celso took off running to get it, leaving the group without a photographer. Susan, who was nervous, couldn't stop giggling. Juan Lucas removed his suit coat, maybe things would be a little more tolerable that way, but just then Celso returned with the mineral water. But then Jungle Woman said, Señor, please put your coat back on for the picture, and Susan was caught between feeling sorry for him and breaking into laughter. Naturally, Juan Lucas didn't want the mineral water anymore. At last they were all together in front of the main door, and he was a little nonplussed because the cook's black pig hair was too close to him. Susan stopped laughing and realized deep down inside that Carlos and Daniel were the two men posing next to her. Out of respect for the Señores, there was no "Look at the birdie." The camera had barely clicked when Nilda said just one more picture, just one more: Don't move anybody, now let's get one with Julius holding the lit candle. Besides, it was time to change photographers so that Celso could be in a picture too. Juan Lucas lit the candle and Carlos took the picture. "That's it," said the golfer, but just then Imelda appeared and, although she wasn't very popular, Nilda insisted on a third and last picture. Juan

Lucas took that one so that later on Susan wouldn't be able to accuse him of mistreating the servants. He looked at them through the lens, exaggerating his suffering in taking the picture: only Susan didn't make him suffer, Julius was standing there stupidly with his little candle, it's about time his voice started to change, what's that gardener's name? and there's Nilda's club feet, the witch laundress, the butlers, there's nothing worse than a dignified Indian. He pretended it was a revolver and he pulled the trigger. "Done!" he blurted out, looking at Susan and nodding for her to go inside. Let's get going, he seemed to be saying. But the poor devil couldn't get going because Jungle Woman had prepared a cake in Julius' honor and she insisted on bringing it out right then. Susan said she would try a teeny-weeny piece, the Señor was in a hurry, and she went over to him asking him in English to be patient. They gave him a piece of cake and he had to try it while Nilda, horrible, was at his side trying to talk to him, well, not so much with him but with the Señora. Juan Lucas began to entertain himself admiring how hypocritical Susan could be: she really knew how to talk to them, she even asked them about their problems, she was good at discussing important topics and feeling nothing but the heat of the day. "Ah, woman!" he exclaimed, taking off his coat once again and embracing her. She looked at him ironically and pointed to something that moved next to him. Juan Lucas turned around and it was none other than the gardener. What's your name, boy? He offered him a soggy, bent, nasty-looking cigarette, do you care? For a moment, Juan Lucas felt as if golf courses didn't exist anymore, that he had never played golf, and that he would never get to play golf again. He hoped the sensation of the elevator going up would stop at his stomach, then he spoke: No more cake. He lit their cigarettes and thanked them for everything as he patted them on the back. He especially thanked Arminda because she was the best laundress in the world, a true artist, he told her. He was going to say something to Carlos, but he stopped himself; this guy wasn't quite so innocent and he wouldn't have kept silent, he wouldn't play the game, those Mestizo chauffeurs are sly foxes, real wise guys. Susan had been observing him ironically and admiringly. "Let's go, darling," she said, and whispered thank you to him in English. They just needed to get Julius, who was downing his cake as fast as he could and who, between bites, examined his conscience to determine whether he had sinned or not, everything had changed so much since leaving the church . . . "Come, darling!" Susan called from inside. "You can't stay in that hot uniform!" And then Juan Lucas spoke: "Hurry up! . . . Let's get changed! . . ." He didn't quite hear the rest . . . something about an overgrown angel.

The day of the awards ceremony Julius played *Indian Love Song* with feeling, but Juan Lucas didn't go to hear him, even though he had placed second in his class. Bobby narrowly passed at Markham that year, but the one who did badly was Santiago: too much Mercedes sports car, too much love, too many dates, too many nocturnal American bars and they flunked him; naturally, only by one point because of some professor who was frustrated because of his social class. One thing for sure: he had to work hard on his English because it had been decided that he was going to continue his famous agricultural studies in the United States. They were sending him early, moreover, so he could become accustomed to living there. The kid insisted on staying a few more weeks in Lima in order to enjoy the summer at Herradura Beach, but Juan Lucas convinced him that it was better to get there early and learn the ropes; if not, those gringos would eat him alive. Money and other things like that weren't a problem. Juan Lucas would send him a small fortune every month so he could rent an apartment near the university in the event he didn't like living on campus. He advised him to get a gringa girlfriend as soon as possible but to be careful about having babies and getting ideas about marriage. He shouldn't get married right now, just spend four or five years studying and getting ready to take over the ranches. Of course Juan Lucas had been a university student in the United States, then in London and in Paris, and when he got started telling his anecdotes and memories, Santiago was sure that this was exactly the kind of change he needed. He promised to work during vacation periods and Juan Lucas said it would be nice and broke out laughing.

They got along well together and it was sad to see them say good-bye to each other at the airport. Susan hugged her big, handsome son and told him to take care of himself and to write, although she was sure he would write only when he needed to ask for more money. As she watched him leave, she thought about the strange yet good feeling she was experiencing and smiled when she remembered those women who never grew old and whose children were much older than Santiago. They were called the immortals, and she remembered Marlene Dietrich, laughing to herself: what did that have to do with all this? She waved good-bye from the observation deck, smiling as the tears welled up in her eyes, I wish you could see me, darling. Bobby was in tears, his idol was leaving. Julius, on the other hand, seemed more worried than sad; he frowned, his hands stuck to his sides, trembling: there goes his loving brother, the one who got Vilma fired, Vilma who brought me to the airport when Cinthia went away . . .

III

THERE WASN'T MUCH construction going on in that neighborhood yet, and the new school stuck out like a sore thumb among the empty lots. The school was barely inaugurated in April. Julius had already had his eighth birthday and he would be entering second grade. It would be his next to last year at Immaculate Heart School. He wouldn't go on to Saint Mary's, which was the way it was done normally; he would go to Markham instead, perhaps because of his English grandparents on his mother's side, but most likely because she couldn't stand that North American accent while trying to digest her lunch that afternoon. Her opinion was somewhat pretentious but nevertheless true. When she made her declaration, she looked so lovely and refined that no one there dared disagree with her. Not even a cognac stopped her from bringing up the North American accent after lunch. Julius was sad, for it was almost like treason to break the logical course of things that meant going from North American nuns to North American priests.

But that was still a long way off. For now, he should make the best of the new Immaculate Heart School. And now it was his turn to stomp on any other kid in a uniform because my school is bigger than yours. With that idea and other similar ones in mind, they entered the school through the big gate at the back where the school bus always stops, or through the side door where the Pirate rattled a can full of stones and tried to poison them with his candies. They put up a wire fence and planted cypress trees so he couldn't reach in, but he would stick his hand through the wire fence and sell poisoned chocolates and caramel candy plagued with microorganisms that caused typhoid. "Can't you see old one-eye there has dirty hands and swears? What an attraction for sin and filth these children have! Don't they realize that we sell clean products at school and the profits go to the missions?" From the very first day, Carrottop would repeat similar statements over and over just before declaring war against her business rival. The Pirate would take off running and then return at recess. And it was always the same: he would act as though he was afraid but come back later rattling his can. He's probably standing there near the side entrance, even today.

Gumersindo Quiñones had enough parking space for two school

buses, and Morales had a huge field where he could train the school team even better. The children could see that the two men were proud and happy, as if finally they had been afforded the importance they deserved. The bad part was that the new school wasn't completely finished: bags of cement were still lying around here and there, and there were little piles of construction material spread about, all of which was just perfect for the Arenas kids, who had already arrived dirty on the first day of school and would get even dirtier from now on, which was their duty. Another one who was already filthy on the first day was Chubby Martinto. Since he had passed into a higher grade, they had given him a fountain pen and heaven only knows how the pen had exploded inside his jacket pocket which left a large stain on his shirt. But he was happy, standing on a mound of sand with his wooden sword, challenging anyone who passed by, even though he didn't know their names. Carefree, he would make and lose friends as quickly as he dirtied the rugs with mud or said three times four is a hundred. And there he was standing on a hill of sand and looking for rivals when Del Castillo, whom he didn't see, poked him from behind with a branch. "Traitor," screamed Chubby, and he fell down the hill, rolling in the dirt, and stopped at Mary Charity's feet. She was the cross-eyed nun who had just arrived from the United States. She didn't get too upset but ordered him to brush off his uniform immediately because the bell was about to ring and the Mother Superior would soon come out to give her welcoming talk.

Some newly arrived, funny little kids were bawling out loud; they weren't about to let go of their mothers who pointed to other small kids who were acting bravely and quickly integrating themselves. The little weeping kids just looked at them and, acquiring their first inferiority complex, turned back around and clung to their mothers' dresses, digging their nails into their thighs in desperation and not wanting to ever let go. But right then Mary Trinity and Mary Charity, bathed and friendly, gave them hugs and understood their predicament. They told the children that the school was nice and new and that they were going to be very happy there; also, they assured them that their mothers would be back for them in the afternoon. Some of them kept bawling despite their efforts, and the nuns, friendly and patient, showed them their enormous rosaries and gave them religious prayer cards that the kids found interesting. They calmed down, finally, and allowed themselves to be separated for a few hours from their mothers who would then depart in some big cars driven by chauffeurs or in station wagons also driven by chauffeurs.

Morales was greeted not only by potential soccer team members but also by those who didn't have any ulterior motives: they simply liked him because he was a Cholo who cussed a lot. Gumersindo Quiñones was also there to be greeted by all those kids wearing uniforms; he had just finished his first morning pickup and he was bowing to the Señoras who brought their children to be placed in the hands of the nuns. The patio kept filling up, the one with colored bricks that made it easier to line up straight at formation time. The bell was about to ring.

The children realized that now they had more space to run and play. This year they could kick the ball hard without worrying about breaking windows; nevertheless, they still weren't fully aware of how large, complete, and magnificent the new school was, and the Mother Superior was about to take care of that detail.

Filled with emotion, she told them that there was an infinite number of classrooms. Then she talked about the chapel and the balcony for the chorus. Only some benches were lacking, but all that would come in due time through the generous donations from their parents. She talked about the dining room for those who would be eating lunch at school and for the breakfasts after communion every first Friday. Also, she told them about the field where they could play soccer under Morales' supervision without getting caked with dirt like before. "Be careful in the bathrooms!" she ordered, "No writing on the walls! And don't forget to flush the toilet when you finish your business." They laughed jovially when she made the reference to their business. Gumersindo bowed happily and Morales, who was partially hidden between some bushes, chuckled heartily. Mother Superior introduced them to the new nuns, but since there were so many new ones this year there wasn't time for them to say anything. Welcome to the new nuns and welcome to all the students! Study hard! Yes, study hard so you can become the men of tomorrow, so you can become intelligent young Christians that Peru needs. And now the school anthem! Sing, everyone! The students who were standing next to the new ones would sing louder in order to frustrate them since they didn't know the words. Finally the Spanish teacher, who was quite crass and had been seen with her boyfriend walking along Wilson Avenue, raised her hand which signaled the Peruvian National Anthem.

SOME WEEKS LATER, Martinto had written LONG LIVE MARTINTO on a wall. He was punished immediately: no buying candy at recess for one week. But the worst came when Sánchez Concha broke a third grade classroom window with a slingshot. The nuns really got upset that time and called a meeting on the patio: Carrottop pinched them, trying to make them line up perfectly to receive their scolding. The Mother Superior shouted at them saying they were terrible and made them understand to what extent they were in debt to the new school. There was still much left to do before it would be finished, and here they were already getting it dirty and tearing it up. From now on the bad ones, those who were determined to destroy the new school, would be severely punished. The Mother Superior almost started to cry and they had never felt so much remorse, they felt it in their souls; hence, they all decided to mend their ways: they wouldn't ever scribble on the walls again and when they ate chocolates they would always throw the silver wrappers into the garbage. They made promises, gave their word of honor, and said they were really sorry. However, while they were singing the school hymn, which made them even more emotional and feel the Immaculate Heart in their souls, Chubby Martinto slapped a sticky caramel wrapper on the back of one of the Arenas kids. Since Arenas couldn't reach around to pull it off, he went around for the rest of the day with the wrapper stuck to his jacket. The next day he came to school with a white spot on the jacket; after a week it had turned brown. The Arenas kids really smelled bad too.

At recess time large groups of soccer fans representing Alianza Lima and the U would mobilize. There were others who supported Municipal too, but the majority were for either Alianza or U. Each group formed a chain at opposite ends of the patio and then advanced forward, insulting each other. The ones representing U were the queers and would say oh, oh, oh, and other things, while those representing Alianza were the flat-nosed Negresses: Hey, Panama Blackie, say hi to your mother and, of course, they would say oh, oh, oh too. They would crash into each other in the middle of the patio and begin to scream and yell. Anyone could be a fan of the Alianza team; after all, none of the kids were Negroes and it was just a feeling of passion for soccer that they had. To be a fan of the U was quite natural, since there were white players on the team as well. And even Municipal was accepted as a recognized team from Lima. But one morning Cano came up and declared himself a Sport Boys fan. It was a team from Callao. He tried to organize a group of fans, but no one wanted to join. Somebody explained that the Sport Boys fans were knife-wielding thugs who worked on the docks. Then everyone turned to Cano and suddenly realized his tie was old and something seemed different about him. Not knowing how to defend himself, he put on a sad face and clammed up. Then someone said there were lots of thieves in Callao and it was dangerous there, for that's where they kill everyone. Cano tried to defend himself, or at least his team, but he wasn't very successful at it. About then the Alianza and U fans, including the Muni fans, began to notice that in addition to the old tie, which was wrinkled and faded, Cano's uniform was old and shiny from use and his shorts fell down below his knees; they were too long. He was always partially bent over, sullen, pale, and thin. And he was always scratching his head as if he had fleas. Then someone said he walked to school; he had been seen crossing an open field, and it was on that morning they discovered that Cano was different. One day he asked someone to lend him a nickle and everybody just looked at each other because he had stuck out his sad hand like a beggar and they noticed that his shirt cuffs were ragged. Cano was different and never again did he say he was a Boys fan, for he talked less and less and everyone became aware of it. At recess one day, someone called him Caño instead of Cano and everyone laughed. Even Julius: he thought the name Drainpipe was funny, especially since Cano was thin like a pipe. But when Julius noticed Cano's long, sad pale face, his hands froze at his sides and, worried, he marched off to the other side of the patio, from there to the bathroom, then to the hallway, the chapel, back to the bathroom, always trying to separate himself from the merry scene that went awry, always looking for a place where his sorrow didn't exist but that now was growing into a feeling of remorse.

THE NEW SCHOOL had arched passageways surrounding a beautiful garden in the center of which they had plans to place a statue of the Virgin. The chapel was off to the right in one corner and nearby were the stairs leading to the upper part of the cloister where the piano room was located. Julius climbed the stairs three times a week for his classes. Quivering, head over heels in love, he went up in search of the nun and would pass finally from the desire-filled shadows of the cloister to the maddening fragrance of the piano: his love had overwhelmed him. Mary Agnes had brought all her bottles of perfume to the new school just for the piano keys, and the marvelous fragrance was too much for him. He had dreamed of the nun bathing the keys with the liquid before his class began, after which she would put a drop on each freckle. He almost caught her red-handed because she was just finishing up as he opened the door. Furthermore, since he was the one who was dreaming and was deeply in love, he believed he had really caught her in the act. He had taken her by surprise and he told her about it night after night in his dreams when he would save her from a fire in the school kitchen or from lion's claws because that day the nun had decided to become a missionary in the bad part of Africa. That part of Africa led him to think about Gumersindo Quiñones and then about the Negroes who play for Alianza Lima, and then Cano, who looked dumb when they called him Drainpipe. At night, Julius' life would become extremely complicated; he would climb the stairs to the cloister remembering his dreams, or dreaming about his memories. Whatever the case, they all seemed real to him, but he didn't let them get to him because he had come that day to play a perfect rendition of a Chopin prelude. The nun and her freckles and all were seated at the piano waiting for him, and she smiled when he entered, totally consumed with love, nerves on edge, and the serious and important Chopin prelude at hand. Julius allowed himself to be adored a while and waited to be begged to begin playing. He would open his music book and put his feet next to each other pressing the piano pedals which would add tenderness and emotion to his music. Then, when she moved, the enormous rosary made beautiful sounds, which was like a prelude to the prelude. Moving a little more, she extended her arm and utilized her seductive fingers that she must have just washed in holy water to put his hands in the correct position. When she touched him amid the perfume, the music book with all its notes evaporated before his eyes. The poor kid made mistakes, well, he always made mistakes when he began to play, and she was so patient but nervous and would lament one more mistake during her afternoon as piano teacher, looking up to the ceiling and searching for a small corner in which to hide her little sigh. This time she didn't sigh but smiled at her student, telling him how and why he had made the mistake. Don't worry, he was getting better, it wasn't important, each time was better, let's begin again. But Julius had been distracted, and the nun was not aware that her skin was to blame, it was all those freckles . . .

When the lesson was over, the nun would open the door for him and watch him leave through the darkness of the cloister. He went down the stairs and headed toward the patio where there were always some students, usually the filthy Arenas kids talking among themselves or offhandedly with some gardener. They lived in Chorrillos and were always picked up late in the afternoon, maybe that's why they never had time to take a bath or clean their uniforms. Martinto always hung around there too. He would probably miss the bus on purpose just so he could stick around and sword-fight until he had finished off his last rival.

Julius would pass nearby frequently, but Chubby never paid any attention, for he probably had gone through three million friends since the time they had been friends. Nevertheless, he seemed crazy to be continually daring the Arenas kids, but they never paid any attention to him. The Arenas kids were loners, and someone had said that in Chorrillos the houses were old and ugly and that someone had seen the Arenas' car parked in front of a large, old adobe house where a servant who wasn't wearing a uniform worked. One could live in San Isidro, in Santa Cruz, or in several areas of Miraflores (but not on the street with the tram, unless it was one of those mansions or large houses). But the Arenas family lived in Chorrillos. They were never invited to birthday parties; however, since there were two of them and they were close brothers, they never had it as bad as Cano, who the other day asked Carrottop to give him a chocolate candy and the whole class broke out laughing. Cano didn't have much tact and he made his poverty stand out in much the same way he would stick his foot in his mouth. He could have gotten away with being poor, after all he wasn't that poor, not real poor, he was just poor at school. But the things he did, for example, like crossing the street between trucks after school and then heading for the open fields all by himself . . . it was a shortcut home.

JULIUS HAD HIS prelude and Susan had her antiques. She spent all of her time looking for old but valuable objects. The timing was just right because about that time Juan Lucas had become involved in a thousand new business deals, he was investing like crazy, it had something to do with the North Americans who were going to take care of everything which, among other things, would give him more free time for golf. He spent night after night inviting boring people out to dinner, and Susan preferred to stay at the mansion with some friend who was also attractive, intelligent, or witty, and who knew a lot about Cuzco painting or Ayacucho arts and crafts. An elegant English woman had been at the mansion all afternoon and, when Julius arrived home from school, they smothered him with praises in English and idolized him while they drank cups of tea and ate toast with marmalade. Susan had bought such expensive tea sets! How can I describe them? She definitely had a preference for old things . . . and meticulously chosen as well . . . one by one she knew the names of the antiques, and she pronounced the names so well. One day she showed up alone in her Mercedes, bringing an old door that she had purchased from a convent that was being demolished.

Frightened to death, she still had managed to drive out to the boonies and even a policeman had thought she was crazy: a woman of her class . . . Finally she made it to the place where the door was being sold and some workmen at the site made some gross remarks, whistled at her, did the usual, and even said Little Momma to her. But Susan pretended not to notice. Lovely, with her yellow skirt and white blouse, she went looking for the foreman. She spoke with him briefly and bought the door for a song. According to the foreman it was worthless but, for her it was a real find and she was going to have it refinished for her new house. The foreman called over two workmen to place the door on top of the Mercedes and tie it down. The two filthy dirty workers were ecstatic and then about ten of them scrambled over to carry the door for the Little Momma; of course, they said Señora to her and afterward they were in seventh heaven when she tipped each one of them.

As she drove up Salaverry Avenue, she was thinking about that little man from the Andes who was so adept at refinishing antiques. The guy was a real darling and quite a conversationalist too. Juan Lucas was going to fall in love with the door, he always approved of everything. And now he was looking at it with a drink in his hand and telling his friends about it, motioning them over to look at my wife's latest acquisition, he really enjoyed her last purchase: "It's useless but revered," he had exclaimed when she unpacked the violin signed by one of the country's founding fathers. Susan was elated when she arrived home and ordered Celso and Daniel to take the door down from the top of the car. She was going to supervise so they would be sure to take the utmost care with it. She almost choked from the dusty, termite-ridden filthy door but she insisted on helping to carry it too, let me hold it here . . . but just then she felt a terrible pain in her arm and, before she fainted, barely caught a glimpse of that scorpion.

Bobby and Carlos took off in the station wagon to get the doctor. Julius, who was at her side, saw her revive quickly, but she complained that her arm was hurting terribly and the butlers had to take her to her room. Nilda came in shouting instructions for curing scorpion bites: Señora, do you remember what it looked like? Susan almost fainted again. No, no, she couldn't remember. Then Nilda said it was important to act fast and she offered to suck the wound; she also wanted to bring some herbs from the garden that she used to stop toothaches. Meanwhile, Celso went to call the Señor. Juan Lucas said he would be there immediately.

Since the Señora had refused to allow herself to be sucked on and continued to moan, Nilda thought that bringing in her own son might help alleviate things. Being with her son, maybe she might forget about the pain a little. The fact is that she brought in the horrible little creature, cuchi, cuchi, cuchi, say hello to the Señora. Susan, poor thing, surrounded by all the servants and the little baby who was about to start bellowing, suddenly felt completely abandoned; before long, her arm had become puffy, it already looked dreadful and, to top it off, when she saw her arm start to turn purple, she remembered a cocktail party for tomorrow. She told everyone to leave, they could at least let her die in peace, but at that moment Bobby came in waving his arms as if he were pushing his way through a crowd. He was heroically and frantically forcing everyone aside, almost as if he were really enjoying it and just about stepping on Nilda's son: he was bringing in the doctor to save his mother. Under Nilda's scrutiny, the doctor whom she considered a thief examined the bite and asked for a thermometer. If they just would have let me suck on it, nothing would have happened. Julius brought the thermometer and Bobby jerked it out of his hand and turned to give it to the doctor, who had just decided to give her some shots. "It's going to swell a bit, Susan," he told her, "but don't worry, these shots will bring down the swelling considerably." It was easy to tell from his neck tie and the fancy car parked outside that he was the family doctor, one of those doctors who never mentions the bill or to whom you never ask how much for the visit, Doctor, nothing like how much do I owe you, Doctor? or any other reference to such crass matters; instead, he was one of those who unexpectedly sends a large bill later or one who is never around when your aunt dies, poor thing.

A few minutes after the first shot Juan Lucas arrived, looking almost like he was dressed for the occasion, at least he made a face to fit. He greeted his doctor buddy and entered the bedroom displaying concern, although deep down inside he was convinced that a scorpion would never dare to interrupt the confluence of tremendous business deals and rounds of golf that made up his life; besides, it couldn't be a serious bite. And, moreover, when has anyone ever heard of a woman like Susan dying tragically, that's asinine, man, it only happens to other people. We've got a happy life, he seemed to tell her, while he held her in his arms and she snuggled into his chest like a spoiled child, acting like I'll have this swollen arm forever. "It'll last a couple of days," the famous doctor explained, while Juan Lucas added sarcastically: "Susan and her doors." Then she begged him to tell her the truth: Wasn't it true that she looked horrible with that swollen arm? And wasn't he probably going to divorce this monster? . . . "Ha! My pretty poisoned one! Hey, Celso, bring two glasses . . ." All the servants disappeared immediately

without a word, one by one, and they left the room as if they were returning to their army post in the evening after their day off on Sunday.

The whole scene made quite an impact on Julius. Only now did he
dare approach the huge bed and break that barrier that had kept him at
a distance, since he had watched everything from the doorway. He also
wanted to make Susan feel better, something like what Nilda tried to
do when she brought in her baby, and he began by talking about his
piano classes. He tried to impress upon her how important Mother
Mary Agnes was to him—the one with the freckles and the rosary beads
that clinked, she was so nervous—but his story became more and more
complicated, it was beginning to fuse with his dreams and with what he
had hoped to dream that night. In any event, it was difficult to explain,
it was better simply to say he was the best student of the pianist-nun
and he was learning a prelude by Chopin . . . "Too many nuns, too
many nannies," Juan Lucas interrupted, growing impatient because
they hadn't brought the glasses for drinks, and that Julius could interpret the abetting smile with which the doctor praised the cutting statement. He was choking and the two of them were as alike as their ties,
hundreds of them were against him, a knot in his throat was overcoming
him and, happily, Susan pulled him over to her in order to protect him,
trying to shield him next to her chest from another joke: "Your Uncle
Juan Lucas is never in agreement with you, darling . . . Oh! This horrible arm, Juan . . ."

The Nicaraguan ambassador visited her the next day. She had come
straight from the beauty salon and was aghast. How tragic! she said, as
she gave Susan a kiss and then told her how everyone at the Golf Club
was totally *abasourdies* when they learned about the poisonous bite.
Smiling but suffering from the pain, Susan welcomed her. You should
have seen her wearing her little bed jacket made by some nuns in
Oviedo, Spain! Her skin was perfect, she wasn't wearing a drop of
makeup, she was so well preserved, and her blond hair was purposely
unkempt to capture the appearance of the bed-ridden patient. And
everything had the fragrance of cologne which nicely embraced the
morning that cheerfully filtered in through the windows. The Nicaraguan ambassador sat at the foot of the bed and said the bedroom was
real paradise. Then she told the story of how she was bitten by a scorpion once: "Scorpion, scurry, scurry, scorpion, scurry, scurry," she sang,
trying to remember a song from somewhere in Central America. She
seemed to stay for hours intermingling stories about golf and about
insects and scorpions in Cairo and Guanajuato; the Señora had traveled
quite a bit. Susan listened to her from memory and the woman exagger-

ated everything, bla-bla-bla, inappropriately interpolating little French words. Susan couldn't wait for her to leave in order to consult a dictionary about three words that sounded strange.

Baby Richardson, whose brother had helped them out in London, came to visit in the afternoon. Baby arrived exactly at teatime and Susan rang the bell for Celso to bring up the tray and bed table. The butler-treasurer appeared instantly with everything that was needed to make an exquisite visit. The poor servant bowed humiliatingly every time he entered the Señora's bedroom, tiptoeing and looking dumb. Baby Richardson thought he was a *competent butler* and asked if he was pure *Indian*. Then she went on to proclaim that the toast was perfect and she giggled delectably but oh so idiotically when she discovered the little plate with the orange marmalade. Susan told her the story behind the purchase, how she had acquired it, etc. And that was the departure point for a long conversation about antiques. Once they had finished their tea, Baby got onto the topic of bug bites and, half serious, half joking, she got into an elaborate explanation about the effects of insect bites on certain types of blood: the finer the blood, the worse the bite, according to her. "That can't be scientifically true," Susan mocked, but just to make sure, she would have to examine her swollen arm, secretly, underneath her silk bed sheets. She uncovered her deformed arm in order to offer Baby a cigarette. At that moment Julius came in from school. Baby Richardson confessed that she simply melted when she saw him, so cute, and then on to things like he's getting bigger every day . . . Rigid, Julius endured the scene with his hands glued to his sides and his toes pointing outward, hating Baby Richardson. She insisted that she wanted to marry his ears and things like that, which really didn't sound that bad in English. Susan interrupted her to ask Julius about the friends he didn't have which started to look bad in front of her friend, but who cares? Besides, he didn't bother to correct her anymore, he already knew his mother well and he idolized her for the way she was: always lovely and totally out of it. Finally, Baby Richardson decided to go and she almost killed herself as she tried to stand up. While she was saying in distinguished fashion how much she had enjoyed the visit, she didn't realize that one of her legs had gone to sleep. She left saying that the little porcelain plate was so . . .

"BAD TIME TO BE bitten by a scorpion," Juan Lucas thought, seated in the dining room at the Golf Club, impatient because Susan asked him to hurry up so they wouldn't be late to the parish. Also, he had to be back early to the office; otherwise he would have scoffed at her piety and tried to blame Julius.

Lately Susan had become heavily involved in the parish charities and such things, especially helping families living at the racetrack. It's as if that scorpion had injected her with holy germs, for Susan abandoned the folly of the antiques, there wasn't much more she could buy anyway, and she dedicated all of her time to a much more intense religious life. She spurned her afternoon naps and would take off in the Mercedes, preceded by a cold Coke and a green-colored pill, feeling she could easily fall asleep on the way. But she always managed to arrive in fine shape and assist in catechism and the distribution of clothes, food, and medicine to the needy families at the racetrack.

This all started with Julius' first communion, and that's why Juan Lucas blamed the little snot for getting his mother involved in such nonsense. He was wrong. Susan would go to the parish of her own free will: she took the whole thing very seriously and dedicated lots of love to the project. She even learned how to give simple injections and neither the poor people nor the beggars seemed repugnant to her. Believe it or not! It's true! She would go to church because Julius begged her to take him, and she did that because there was no one to take him before school every morning. This other stuff happened later when that severe priest not only convinced her of it but also confessed her one morning. His German accent and the low voice behind the little curtain enchanted her. While fulfilling a penance that was, frankly, generous, she discovered that the statues in the church were really marvelous; they seemed to possess a certain Prussian austerity. Afterward, walking back to the Mercedes where Julius waited impatiently because he was going to be late for school, she noticed how pleasant it was to be out in the early morning when certain words made her feel good: sunrise, dawn, matins, they are playing the sunrise serenade, daybreak . . . daybreak . . . of course, it wasn't that early but they had attended the seven o'clock mass and the streets in the area were still empty. She felt refreshed, but there are some saltwater baths that produce the same effect . . . "Not always," she thought, three hours later as she was still enjoying that feeling of freshness. "Not always and, above all, the effect never lasts more than an hour in Lima because it's so humid. Today, however . . ."

Three days later she contacted some ladies who were even more gracious and who carried their own gushing refreshed spirit to the slums. They would spend entire afternoons there and then return covered in sweat, ready to tell incredible stories. One of them said she had cured a drunk who had been hurt in a recent fight. The man almost assaulted her but she acted like it was nothing: calmly and valiantly, she disinfected the wound and applied a bandage with two assistants holding him down so he wouldn't attack her. Susan, somewhat muddled and feeling the effects of the green pill, looked at the parish priest and made a decision: yes, she would go and work in a slum too. "Is there one near the golf course?" she asked, quickly explaining that this would allow her to save a lot of time and thus be with her husband as well. The fattest Señora of the "We-are-going-to-the-slums" group told her that slums existed everywhere. We're not lacking in poverty, Señora. Susan agreed to go the following week.

That night she told Juan Lucas all about it. Julius intervened saying he would go with her on Saturday afternoons, but the golfer interrupted the devilish little snot and sent him off for his bath and to bed. He immediately told Susan not to get worked up over this, they would talk about it: how about if we go out for a while? He asked her to get dressed and they went out dancing until four o'clock in the morning. They idolized each other while they danced. And they talked.

And he must have done some fancy talking, because the next day Susan had no desire to visit a slum. After seeing her so lovely, sophisticated, and so in love, the women on the committee were totally convinced with her reasoning not to abandon her husband in the afternoons. The parish priest intervened and told her that she could go out and distribute food whenever her husband was busy. She could also take charge of a group of families at the racetrack and go with a social worker; hence she would always be safe in the company of someone else. Susan was pleased and Juan Lucas had no choice but to accept it begrudgingly. After running her fingers through his hair and hugging him, she explained she would be close to home and the people at the racetrack had to be less dangerous than the real slum people. "Fine, fine," Juan Lucas said. He despised Celso when he told him to fetch a cognac.

That's the way Susan's new intense life had begun. She got up early to take Julius to mass and to receive Holy Communion herself. Then she returned home to eat breakfast with Juan Lucas and to read the newspaper out loud to him. In reality she read to herself because there were just a few things that interested him; for instance, a friend of his was named a new cabinet minister. Was Eisenhower still playing golf? And there was the news from the Spanish bullfighting world. The real news came from his assistants, advisers, and friends at the office. Susan didn't mention the headlines—the death of some important person in

Lima—because he couldn't tolerate any distasteful news while he drank his orange juice in the morning. Of course, he would never admit it, he was too virile, but she knew very well that you don't talk about people who suffer and die in front of such an elegant man. However, one day she tried to talk about one of the poor people at the racetrack. Immediately Juan Lucas motioned *stop* with his hand, and she felt his refined fingers buried in her throat. Unexpectedly a tear rolled instantly down her cheek: it was time to kiss her eyes but Juan Lucas couldn't stand amorous moves at nine o'clock in the morning in front of dry toast and delicious melted butter. Anyway, he didn't see it, solitary, falling, splat! on the social page.

Julius hadn't been there, but he came running into the dining room at the same time Juan Lucas' hand, which had just motioned *stop,* was returning to its original position and picking up a piece of toast. While he gulped down his breakfast in order to scurry off to school, that teardrop had initiated a sudden and unexpected sadness in Susan. He only noticed it when he gave her a kiss and started off to school. He abruptly noticed the taste of salt on his lips. Is Mommy crying? He didn't pay any attention to Bobby's reckless driving that always put everyone's life in danger, including Carlos' and Imelda's lives. Like every day, the chauffeur would say to Julius' brother: This is the last time you're gonna drive. Today, however, Julius wasn't listening, he just continued smacking his lips as he tried to taste that tear in order to prove it was true: Mommy was crying. That morning, standing near the big gate, Gumersindo Quiñones' big white smile also convinced him that sadness had been left behind.

His piano class was in the afternoon and he reenacted his adoration of the nun until about six o'clock. Carlos arrived very late because it occurred to Bobby to visit with Peggy, the Canadian girl, and he had secretly taken her out for a ride in the station wagon. Julius waited impatiently thinking about his mother. He had missed her at lunchtime and he was anxious to see her. When he arrived at the mansion he saw that happiness had returned to Susan and Juan Lucas: they had just returned from the Golf Club and were having a drink with the architect and the builder who had come to discuss some matters concerning the new house. The project was moving along nicely, for soon they would put the roof on the second floor. Hanging on to Juan Lucas' arm, Susan listened to the architect's explanations and enchantingly pretended to pay close attention. This guy wasn't ever going to finish; in fact, he would have loved to continue standing there for the rest of his life explaining this and that in order to watch her toss back a lock of hair each time he insisted on some detail. The builder, on the other hand, didn't catch on to what was happening; he was an experienced builder but he didn't realize how marvelous she was. For that reason the architect scorned the builder while Juan Lucas offered them another stupendous sherry.

That night Susan and Juan Lucas went to meet some Panamanian friends at the Hotel Bolívar. As for Bobby, he had dinner sent up to his room where he had been talking to Peggy on the telephone for hours on end and was getting worse: today they dined together over the telephone. Hence Julius ate alone which gave the servants the opportunity to join him in the big dining room. The only one missing was Imelda who had just about graduated from her sewing classes and was becoming even less popular every day. Nilda became worried when Julius told her that if her son should die one of these days without being baptized, he would end up in limbo. Celso and Daniel nodded their heads in agreement and Arminda stared harshly at her: "Stop all this Evangelical stuff," she told her. "Baptize him a Catholic." Julius would forget momentarily about their presence at the table and look at his mother's empty chair, trying to reconstruct the scene at the breakfast table that morning: it must have been Juan Lucas . . . but what does it matter now? They're probably eating in some very fancy restaurant . . . Suddenly he felt as if his mother had gone back to her old ways.

The next day he confirmed it: he went looking for her in her bedroom to go to mass and she was still asleep. He wouldn't be able to take communion. She wasn't there for lunch either because she was playing golf with the Panamanians. At last he had an interview with her that evening. A thousand times she said she was sorry for not having taken him. She kissed him repeatedly and promised she wouldn't let him down in the morning.

She didn't break her promise, for at six forty-five in the morning the two of them were in the Mercedes headed toward the church. Susan yawned while she talked to him and he responded freezing to death on the cold leather seats. It was too early to dedicate herself to love and affection, whereas Julius was wide awake and chose very carefully what he said to his mother, making sure his words were clear to him, Yes, Mommy, the door is closed tightly, while at the same time showing loving care. Anyone would have felt the same way upon seeing Susan at that moment. She had taken the matter of the church more seriously than anyone could imagine. She had invented a certain early morning style for going to mass. It was simple, almost austere, but deep down, exquisite. She yawned, patting the yawn with three fingers that, minutes later, she would be introducing into the fountain of holy water. The Mercedes veered to one side and she had to abandon the yawn in order to put her hands on the wheel which didn't stop the car from swaying because she had completely forgotten to change to third gear. Then she wouldn't change gears because she couldn't make the decision: all of her energy went to looking out the windshield, as if completely engrossed in the condition of the street. Then she would make a hard turn and discover Julius at her side while outside the same old lady in black that she always sees, when was it? who was in the same place on the sidewalk. She would let up on the gas pedal apprehensively, not paying attention to the heavy swerving of the Mercedes, and would give herself over to a yawn again and the old lady, behind her now, was someone pulling time together from all corners until it completely crashed down into instant-long pieces that with effort and patience she would manage to pull together into a puzzle of a little old lady walking to seven o'clock mass every day along the same street and at the same hour, of course. As Susan regained the present moment, she would even rediscover Julius, but now it was the agonizing lurch of the Mercedes with which she had to do battle; it shook her, she thought about the accelerator, they struggled, she accelerated again, and just then they came to a corner, it isn't fair: another car might come along, she would have to brake and start all over again; she almost gave up but at that moment she discovered Julius again, the bells were ringing for early mass, and the austere church towers enchanted her.

She wouldn't have been able to endure an old dark colonial church and the complicated baroque altars with beggars at the door and beyond. And a sign DO NOT SPIT ON THE FLOOR OF THE TEMPLE would have devastated her at that hour, but in her parish there weren't any beggars, for they had an organized parish relief. There was, however, a little kid who was the child of one of the poor people at the racetrack. He waited every day to watch the car for her. His name was Mañuco and he said Señorita to her as he opened the door and waited for her to put the white scarf on her head. Remember his name and smile at him. On the other side of the car, Julius closed his door well and told her to hurry because mass had to be starting.

The only sounds of pum, pum, pum were heard in the empty church: it was somebody tripping over a pew, pum, or the sexton, running late, slamming the door behind him, pum. They were sounds that seemed to come from far away, making the church seem even bigger. When Julius would hear pum at the rear, he would look back and see the old woman dressed in black arriving. The only thing that sounded different was the nervous, hurried footsteps of Señor Aurelio Lovett scurrying up to the front row, a real pious old maid as Juan Lucas would call him. He would clear his throat, then open his enormous missal that was full of religious prayer cards and multicolored ribbons indicating each day of the ecclesiastical calendar. Susan handed her missal to Julius so he could find the right page, then she would forget to use it and limit herself to feeling very pious and exchanging intelligent glances with Saint Matthew, her favorite among the twelve apostles carved in cold stone that surrounded them austerely. From time to time one could hear the priest speaking Latin lickety-split or the deacon's bell, and Julius would motion to Susan to follow the mass properly. He prayed from his missal which was embellished with mother-of-pearl covers and a gold clasp, a gift from Aunt Susana for his first communion, along with the pens that Juan Lastarria had given him. One morning after Julius had returned from church, Juan Lucas caught him with his missal and decided right on the spot that there was absolutely nothing else for them to talk about. He was on edge when he told Susan about it, but she only managed to say darling, it's too soon for us to have problems, and ordered grapefruit juice instead of the usual orange juice. Julius hadn't been present and he continued to use his missal every day. It was marvelous to be standing silently next to his mother at seven o'clock mass where, notwithstanding the pum-pums from time to time and the sprint of the rich pious Señor to the front, the only thing one could hear was the shuffle of some priest who had been praying since daybreak in the garden next to a rosebush who, at that moment, was crossing through the church to the sacristy hardly making a sound and seemingly elevated above the floor, with only the chaffing of his robe like angels' wings must sound when they go to heaven. And Mommy was next to me wearing her white scarf, a lock of her hair was peering through, how pretty it hides her forehead! She's forgotten to put it back because now she's listening to mass, her white blouse without any jewelry, no makeup, eyes fixed on the altar: the poor people at the racetrack! Is her mind wandering? What is she thinking about? You're at mass, Mommy, do you know the priest who just went by? Did you hear the swishing sound of his robe? Do you hear it? Look at me, now Mommy, like yesterday, so that I can feel that again. Do you feel it? Only here, Mommy, not at home, Juan Lucas, Uncle Juan Lucas Juan Lucas, Mommy, don't forget to turn around like you did yesterday, do you feel it? It starts when we go down the stairs and I open the garage door for you, when the seats of the Mercedes are freezing cold every morning, and when you put the key in the ignition and I'm at your side, the car won't go and I let you be, I don't say the hand brake's on nor do I say use third gear on the curve at the corner. And then you acted like what you would touch was repugnant, the holy water, you laughed when I saw you. Are you going to turn around today, do you feel it? I told you they put fresh water in it every day; if we arrive first, you can touch it. "Darling, that's not necessary," and you saw my face, you touched the water, do you feel it . . . "Julius, darling, what page are we on now?" "Here, Mommy, we're here . . ." They smiled at each other.

Outside the church Mañuco called her Señorita and was grateful for the coin, but he had to hurry, yeah, because soon Don Aurelio would be coming out, that faggot, and did this guy know how to be a cheapskate, the queer is repulsed by dirty coins and lets them fall directly into my hand from his coin purse, thank you, Señor. Don Aurelio was impeccable as he left, while Susan sat at the steering wheel of the Mercedes imagining her house somewhere, anxious to get there, almost hugging the wheel. Julius, who was idolizing her, took the car keys out of her purse and handed them to her. "Ah!" she said, removing the silk scarf and shaking her blond hair until she began to imagine a glass of orange juice at the mansion with Juan Lucas sitting in front of her. "So long as he doesn't want to take me to the Golf Club today," she thought. "Today I have to go to the racetrack."

"She's very practical. My wife is almost a veteran in these battles," he told the journalist, handing him a gin and tonic that he had fixed for him. "I don't know anything about it. She's the one who will have to talk to you . . . You'll see how well she responds."

"But I really don't know where to begin . . ."

"Don't worry about that, Señora, just tell it as it comes to you. Later I'll put it into proper form. You'll like how well you appear in our newspaper column. Besides, a priest has taken charge of this new column and he'll make the final approval. Just tell the story the way you see it, Señora."

"I'll try . . . I met some poor people through my parish. Then I took my son Julius to mass one day, a priest called me over, and he told me that my help could be important, any type of help would be appreciated. I was assigned to the racetrack. But we don't go alone, a paid social worker who has taken courses in order to have that degree accompanies us. We don't have degrees but I've learned to give shots. My first attempt was with Zoila, we call her Big Zoila . . . Darling, please don't laugh. This is incredible . . . Big Zoila was a cook but she was out of work because she had too many children. You know who they are, darling. Don't you remember seeing that cute little boy who comes to see me from time to time? He's marvelous. I call him Pepone and if you only knew how sweet he is. Also, there's little Zoila and all the others. It was a typical situation: an unwed mother with a lot of kids. Well, they needed a mattress and their level of poverty in those horse stalls was so heartbreaking that I ran out to buy a mattress. They only had one for the whole family and they didn't have any blankets either.

"Here's to you! A little more ice? . . ." Susan had even managed to learn the lingo of the social worker: "Big Zoila needed shelter."

"Don't pay any attention to him . . . Juan Lucas also helps with money."

"Please don't stop, Señora, continue . . ."

"Zoila started living with a man on a piece of vacant land and I went looking for her. It really bothered me to have to abandon Pepone, that little guy was so adorable . . . he's got those big, black, sad eyes . . . I'll never forget that place: people were piled on top of each other, drinking water from a nearby construction project. They lived in huts, the best ones were made of adobe, others with straw, pieces of wood, tin, cardboard, etc. When they were thrown out, they took possession of a lot and some stables and made a home where they used to keep horses. The place was full of flies."

"Susan, why don't you tell him about how Big Zoila sold the mattress that you gave her? Explain how she preferred to stay with the old man . . ."

"Darling, let me tell it, please . . . I'm the one telling the story, aren't I?"

"And I'm all ears, honey. Wait, I'm going to fill up these glasses . . . Now, go ahead."

"I also visited them when they worked knocking fruit off the trees with sticks . . . I love that word, fruitpicker. They lived in hovels that were even worse than the stables."

"Susan, excuse me, but I think you're exaggerating . . ."

"Juan Lucas, honey, you don't know what it's like. According to you, the only poor people in this world are your caddies, but they're really shrewd, darling, they're more scamps than poor people. Believe me, darling, you really don't know what you're talking about . . ."

"Bobby! Julius! Come here for a minute! Listen to your mother while she talks to the press! Anyone need ice? Don't stop writing, young man . . . Are you a Christian Democrat?"

"Continue, Señora. Please, continue . . ."

"The parish would make monthly donations: a pound of sugar, two pounds of rice, two pounds of noodles . . ."

"For Big Zoila . . ."

"Juan! Stop drinking! You're ruining everything this afternoon! Where have you spent the day? May I go on with the story? . . . Excuse me . . . he's acting like a child . . . They would give them cooking oil and other things, an article of clothing . . ."

"An article of clothing: a perfect social worker . . . Oops, don't stop, Susan."

"Señores, I'm sorry . . ."

"Continue, Susan!"

"Sometimes we gave them money, but only in extreme cases and only after we had consulted with the parish priest. It's hard not to give them money because they're always asking for it and they manage to convince you how badly they need it. Over the long haul, however, the parish priest is probably right: he doesn't want to support beggars. That's why his parish is so charming: there are no beggars at the door and you can go to mass without being assaulted by them, it's not like downtown, in the . . . no, I don't think I should say it."

"Say it, Susan! Point a finger! Have courage, honey!"

"Juan! Darling! That's enough! . . . They help them find work and resolve their marriage problems; there are litigations . . ."

"Litigations! Perfect! Look at Julius: his eyes are about to pop out. Litigations!"

"I'm not even listening to you, darling . . ."

"Don't look at me that way, Susan . . ."

"Perhaps we can continue another day . . ."

"No! Now! young man."

"Yes. Let's continue, sir . . . We have a clinic that's open twice a week. It has two doctors, a nurse, and several ladies who help distribute medicine, give shots, and wrap wounds. It's well organized with medical files, records, etc. There are families with seven or eight children . . . they always have more children. Sometimes there's an abnormal child and it's difficult to find a place in a hospital or a home for him. Thanks to Juan Lucas, I was able to place one in the Larco Herrera Hospital . . ."

"That's a lie! I've never placed anyone anywhere."

"Darling! My God! And stop drinking! . . ."

"Don't tell me not to drink! Let me drink my wine. Perhaps some day I'll want to drink and I won't be able to, because I won't be happy . . ."

"Why can't you accept this, honey? Why does it bother you that I work at the racetrack?"

"Susan, honey! Yesterday it was the old doors! Then mass with this little kid! Now you discover poor people at the racetrack. Frankly, you're something else! Cheers! Go ahead, continue . . ."

"Cheers, Señor, continue, Señora . . ."

"Don't look at me, Susan . . . continue . . . don't look at me . . ."

"By the way, the promiscuity in which they live breeds rape, quarrels, and drunken binges . . ."

"Don't look at me, woman . . ."

". . . At times I've been called after eleven o'clock at night to give shots and I've had to dodge potholes all over the place, in total darkness . . . I'll never forget this beautiful child . . ."

"Pepone, Señora?"

"No. His surname was Santos. Now that he's better, I remember the night when he was delirious with fever and I managed to make him better with a shot; in fact, maybe it saved his life."

"Saint Susana! Just like her cousin!"

"Whatever you want, darling! Whatever you want. But just accept it: my way of life is different from yours. Accept it, Juan Lucas . . . once and for all, darling. Your way of life is not mine, darling. You and your intimidating Jaguar. You go from here to the golf course and you're happy. But not me, darling, just accept it . . ."

"You look quite happy when you arrive at the Golf Club in your immense Mercedes, deeeeear . . ."

"Well, I'll tell you right now: you can give the Mercedes to Bobby and buy me a Mini-Minor . . ."

"Mini-rubbish is what I'm having to endure here! Well . . . finish this tirade."

"First you finish drinking, darling . . . Excuse me, Señor, I'm going to finish right now. These people are different than what everyone thinks about them. Now I think differently. These people are eternally grateful for the smallest thing that you do for them . . . Julius, darling, don't bite your nails . . . They are not envious nor are they insolent to me. Just treat them kindly and don't make them feel like they are charity cases . . . that's the help you give them. It's important to treat them kindly, to give them affection. With me, they went overboard with their appreciation. Now, every time I go there . . ."

"Isn't it true she's Saint Susana? . . . She even looks like her . . . here, give me some more ice . . ."

"*They love me, darling!* Excuse me, Señor, but it's true: they do care for me. The social worker jokes with me and says they're going to erect a monument in my name . . . And I never take money to them. They come to the house for medicine or shots. They are always welcome and I help them in every way possible . . ."

"And they dirty the railing with their hands . . ."

"*So funny!* . . . They're so sweet . . . Sometimes I give them shots and they ask how much do I owe you, Señorita?"

"And she doesn't charge them, that's why they're going to build a monument to her in the middle of the stables, surrounded by flies."

"Darling! *Are we having a fight?*"

"Yes, Susan! Bobby! Get the Jaguar out of the garage . . ."

"*PANDO VERY DRY SHERRY. Shipped and Bottled by Williams and Humbert Ltd. Jerez and London. Produce of Spain.*" Juan Lucas stroked the bottle while he showed it to Bobby and told him to learn the better brands. At that moment Carlos brought in the boxes of Havana cigars. "Put them next to the bottles of sherry," Juan Lucas told him and watched how it all came together to make him feel like he was in Madrid during the October bullfights. The sherry and cigars became a small altar dedicated to the bullfights. Stacked together there were boxes of cigars and bottles of sherry along with red wine like the blood of the bulls at the end of the afternoon, amid the bullfighting music that in the evenings transformed into guitars playing throughout the tavern because the year was eighteen hundred, Señores, so the song goes, three more whiskeys, and long live October, month of miracles! Those superstitious bullfighters are already in Lima, and they don't mind riding in that son of a bitch promoter's Cadillac. He still can't decide whether to bring in Briceño, the one who has driven everyone wild in Spain and who should be here in Lima with us now. The Gypsy consented to be photographed at the international airport, revealing his little piece of wood, the one he always takes with him because up in the superconstellations there isn't any wood and he has to be able to knock on wood. And Juan Lucas cannot stand waiting for Susan to come downstairs. He waits for her in front of the bottles of sherry that will be consumed by his guests during the coming weeks, and he still feels the pleasure of spending hours in a cold shower, when the water bounces off his tanned, strong shoulders, preparing his skin for those Oxford shirts which arrived recently from London, and for that silk ascot that was now perfect around his neck and that once someone in a tavern, precisely at three o'clock in the morning, said was sensuous. He hears some steps on the stairs and Susan descends, lovely and ready to accompany him captivatingly until the October bullfights were over. Like the sherry, Susan is rich and creamy-looking. And she's a bullfighting fan, she's always talking about bullfighters in the diminutive, giving them nicknames as if she were in love with them. She lets them surround her in the taverns after the bullfights which is when they overcome their fear and they deserve her voice and words as they look imploringly at her to say darling to them. And she gives them what they want as they become even more Andalusian, even more gypsy, and they begin to whirl handsomely around her, reciting in drunk exasperation verses that García Lorca never retrieved from the people, until the moment when, only from the middle of October until late November, she finally introduces them to young blonds, Ava Gardner types, who have special bulls for bullfighting on their haciendas. Susan embraces Juan Lucas and calls Julius over because everyone is going to eleven o'clock mass and from there to a typical Peruvian lunch. From there they'll hurry on to the bullfights where everyone greets and waves to everyone else as the bullfights start. Celso hands Juan Lucas his sport coat for the day and while he's putting it on he asks everyone to leave their missals at home because they ruin the atmosphere. Susan fixes his silk ascot but not his hair, it's already perfect with his interesting fortyish gray strands, sporting an elegant profile that will be photographed this afternoon while The Gypsy performs in the ring, that profile of an expert aficionado that some lady with season tickets sitting nearby will find sensational. Susan doesn't touch his hair, and while it will take on a desired slightly unkempt look due to the breeze and the sun, it will always look good, because that son of a bitch even knows how to make his hair look uncombed but elegant and manly looking, which is why Susan continues to prefer him over the bullfighters who, after all, always possess a history of poverty and can even be brutes. Susan continues to prefer him and more than ever now that he tips her Pepone wherever he sees him and lets him into the yard to wash the Jaguar. Of course she doesn't go to the racetrack that much anymore, there's no time in October what with the bullfights and all, but "I'll return," Susan thinks. And Juan Lucas always uses that metallic virile voice of men who are forever right and she'll never be able to do without the way he lives, she'll never be able to do without it, never miss seeing him triumph, or leave a tavern sober where Negroes sing songs about slavery, for even they know and admire him, for he's the real aristocratic gentleman whether he's in London or at a local blowout. "Let's go, Julius. Hurry up, Bobby," Susan says, asking how many bottles of sherry there are in all while she reads the words *Sherry* and *London* on the labels and feels something intimate with them, as if they were a symbol of her noble origins.

When he gets to church, Juan Lucas looks like a lion trapped in a monkey's cage. The children and Susan file in first, then he takes his place in the pew. It's impossible to know what he's thinking, but at least he's already recovering and displaying a definitive posture for Sunday mass, not that he works on it, perhaps it comes from his distant aristocratic ranching past. Whatever it is, he doesn't invent it because now he goes to church, he takes Susan to Sunday mass, the later one, of course, and the parish priest looks at them benevolently: the Señora's goodness is winning out. Juan Lucas hears murmuring at his side and, as he turns, he discovers that Susan is praying. Mass has begun and there's a priest walking down the middle aisle handing out songbooks and he gives one to Juan Lucas looking as if he had just given him the secret of salvation. He doesn't thank him because you don't do that in church and, besides, what the hell is he going to do with this book that looks like Julius' notebook? He hands it to Julius but he's already got one; he hands it to Bobby but he says he already has one too. "Here, take it, Susan," and she shows him her copy. So he lays it down on the pew and tries to forget about it. He looks at his shirt cuffs and wants to drink a *gin and tonic*. "Señor," says someone who wasn't there a minute ago: it's Arminda, the laundress, proud to be next to the Señor, with the family. Juan Lucas hands her the book, but she already has one too. "Let us sing the song on page 27," says the priest who handed out the books as he begins to sing, partly in tune, strolling through the aisles, going forward, backing up, encouraging everyone to sing out: louder, louder, please. Juan Lucas hears Arminda's horrendous squeaking voice as she sings at the top of her lungs unaware of how ridiculous she sounds but then there's something marvelous on his other side: it's Susan's voice, unhurried, no doubt about that, and lovely, as if she truly believed that God was really listening to her. "My adorable hypocrite," he thought, "now she's turned pious and just her looks are enough to achieve it." But at that moment someone touched him on the arm. It was Arminda again: "We're on page 27. Sing, Señor." He picked up the book acting as if he were looking for the page and then would find it just as the song ended but, just at that moment, the singing priest came up to his pew, don't make things difficult, Father, and smiling with love at humanity and because he had been tortured in China, well, that's what Julius said, the priest repeated let's sing everyone, with his arms outspread like an orchestra conductor, coordinating the event, getting everyone to sing except Juan Lucas. All he wanted to do was shout olé!

But the singing priest, whose rounded lips matched the tonsure on his head, sang with love and didn't lose hope in getting something good out of that Señor. He approached the pew again, this time next to the side where Julius stood and signaled to Juan Lucas. He was sure he was a good person. "Come with me, Señor," he told him, "you can help us with the Sunday collection." Juan Lucas would have preferred to say I'll pass on this one, Father, like with drinks, but Susan, Bobby, and Julius, who acted surprised and pleased or made fun of him, stood back against the bench seat letting him leave the pew. And the singing priest rounded his mouth like his tonsured head and smiled showing gratitude, motioning to Juan Lucas to follow him to the little table with the collection baskets. He explained to him that he should begin with the first pew, go down each row until he reaches the last one and then return coming up the other side until he reaches the first pew again, after which he would have to kneel down in front of the altar and then do the pews to the left, going down one side and then up the other because they were very wide and one could only reach halfway across. "Yes, Doctor," Juan Lucas responded to the singing priest, remembering, who knows why, a black Creole who had talked with a priest cussing up one side and down the other, saying afterward, "Pardon me, Doctor," and the poor priest turned green. But this priest was immutable, perhaps he liked people to recognize that he was a doctor of theology; and besides, since the Señor was elegant, it was manly to say Doctor which was more appropriate than to say Father like everyone else. Juan Lucas thought that the next time he was in the company of a priest and Julius was present too, he would say Doctor just to pester the little snot who probably didn't understand why priests are called doctors and who is probably thinking right now that I'm turning into a pious hypocrite. "Now it's time," the singing priest told him and Juan Lucas approached the first pew on the right, coughing to let people know he was there and that it was time to drop their money into the basket. In the first rows there were a lot of acquaintances, businessmen wearing ascots or fitted lightweight suits who pulled out new, crisp bills as if they were trying to get rid of them; others not only gave money but also were good fathers and made sure their children and wives had something to contribute, ready for Juan Lucas. And as he drew closer, those important Señores in the front rows, who insisted on going to mass despite the tiresome priest, the one who happily latches on to you and every year,

God only knows which Sunday, says that it's more difficult to get to heaven than for a camel to pass through the eye of a needle. One would like to take note and make sure not to hear that sermon next year but at the same time what happens is that during the year one forgets. When Juan Lucas approached them, they smiled sarcastically as if to say they finally got you too, Mr. Golfer, or that's the way I'd like to see you at a business meeting, or do you know, Juan, if the Pratolinis have decided to invest? And they nodded to him while their wives not only admired him but also hated Susan, or they might be her friends. He continued down the rows and further back he could see others whom he knew, one of his employees perhaps, contributing the crispest $5 bill ever and pointing him out to his wife . . . while one of the daughters would comment that he looked like the husband of some princess she saw in *Paris Match* whose name I've forgotten, and feeling bad that her father wasn't as rich or good-looking as him. Sitting at the back, Carlos tossed in a few coins and a group of Cholas, the ones who were probably singing horribly, contributed filthy little coins, dropping them to one side of the basket without daring to touch his shirt cuff. One of them had to put her baby down on the bench in order to untie a grimy little handkerchief of money that she had taken out of her pocket. What the hell is this? as he stared at the little improvised pouch. "Thank you, thank you," he repeated, hurrying a little because the baby began to cry, probably wanting to be held again by his mother who hadn't finished retying the disgusting handkerchief into a pouch again. Now he had to return to the first row from the other side. Everything was the same at the back: there were three more with their handkerchief pouches and the singing priest said let us turn to page 33, and one could hear those women screech, "Let us sing the love of loves," which are songs the cooks sing in the kitchen when one goes there to get ice for a drink and hears something horrible emerging from that area; it's the cooks but not Nilda however, she's an Evangelist according to Julius . . . "We're getting there," Juan Lucas said to himself, while he approached the first pew; the basket was heavy now because of all those dirty coins the ones at the back of the church had tossed in. Once again some faces seemed more familiar and he went to the altar, genuflecting without even coming close to touching the floor which must have been pretty dirty, and began all over again on the left side where there were several of those camel-and-needle types. And his family was also there: Susan, lovely, was desperately asking Julius for money for the collection basket, but he only had his own; and then Bobby, who was just lending it, of course, and nothing more. But it wasn't enough: Bobby, please,

please, Juan Lucas is coming, and Arminda was already handing him a bill! At last they were all happy because when Juan Lucas got to them each one had something to give while he, on the other hand, displayed a nasty face because he had to be there with that basket. Really, this is idiotic! Susan, don't make things worse, got it? This is the last time I'll say it, while she barely sticks out the tip of her tongue at him and Bobby acts outwardly respectful, though they'd never get him to do it, and Julius was surprised but happy.

The singing priest approached and continued to sing, urging everyone in the pews to continue singing while Juan Lucas, standing right in front of him, stuffs the largest amount of money into the basket wishing instead he could ram it down the priest's throat. The priest just looked at him in appreciation as he continued with his music and doting on the faithful, rich and poor alike. Three girls smiled at Juan Lucas and he responded with a look that left them on the verge of fainting and hoping to see him the following Sunday during the same mass: He's really handsome, don't you think? A Golf Club member asked him where he was sitting for the afternoon bullfights and he said he would be in his usual seat; they agreed to look for each other. He continued forward and a gorgeous blond adolescent girl, who was probably in a state of affliction or not getting along with her parents, sang "Let us sing to the love of loves" to him in a loud voice and looking at him straight in the eye. Then she showed him three fingers and he never understood that she had been in love with him for three Sundays running. He continued moving forward until he reached the area of the coin givers, and dirty coins to boot, an area of the church that he moved through quickly in order to return to more familiar surroundings over on the other side. Finally, done! He was already back at the altar. He remained standing there with the basket and asked himself jokingly: So, Moe, where do we put the dough? At that moment the priest with the rounded mouth, still singing and smiling, made his way forward and told him to give it to him: Thank you very much, you may return to your seat now. "Get ready to sing," he added. "We still need to sing the song on page 55. And don't forget, Señor, he who sings, prays twice." "Ah, yes, Doctor, you're right," Juan Lucas responded, returning to his pew while being admired by many women of all ages and by Susan who adored him and needed him at her side once again.

After mass Carlos drove them to see Luis Martín Romero, the one who signed his bullfighting articles in the newspaper with an alias: Pepe Botellas. Romero wrote about bullfights all year long and everyone in Lima read him like crazy but only during the weeks before and during the bullfighting season. The whole city wanted to be up on what was going on so they could argue and defend themselves during October and part of November. After that no one gives a damn, at least not until next year. But this wasn't the situation at lunch today; everyone there knew a lot about bulls and some even had complete libraries on the art of bullfighting with books covered in fine leather and gold lettering. Carlos stopped the car in front of the building where the journalist lived, and Juan Lucas told him to take the children home and get them fed quickly.

"You need to hurry, too," he added while he helped Susan get out of the car. "As soon as you're all ready, come back to get us so we can go to the bullfights."

The elevator door opened at the fourth floor and flamenco guitar music could be heard perfectly coming from a stereo they would fully appreciate upon entering Fats Luis Martín's apartment. A butler waited for them at the door, and then strong virile voices with Spanish accents could be heard more clearly, expressions like Balls! or Who gives a shit! those phrases worldly men had learned in Spanish bullfighting circles and now repeated in Lima today without fear of seeming trite because in reality they were like blood transfusions at some point in their lives demanded by their biographies as the years passed by. They embraced and gave each other slaps on the back as they arrived. Luis Martín Romero shouted, "Damn, it's been a hundred years!" when he saw Juan Lucas and went over to him for the fraternal virile hug. Then he kissed Susan and told her that even though he was fat and ugly, he never lost hope of being her lover. Susan, lovely, kissed him, took his arm, and told him as soon as he would stop smoking those offensive cigars that always hung from his lips, she'd come running to him. "My cigars never!" Fats bellowed and everyone laughed. Then someone turned up the music and the room started to vibrate with the sound of the flamenco guitars while Fats, cigar plugged in, returned to the bar to pour more Pisco sour drinks based on his magic formula, a secret that he would carry with him to the grave unless, that is, Susan asked for it . . . Another round of laughs while Susan and Juan Lucas greeted more people. The room started to fill up. Soon the typical Creole dishes would be served, which had been prepared by the Negress Concepción de los Reyes. She's been working as a cook in Malambito for seventy years and a Spaniard, me, Luis Martín Romero, found and convinced her to expand her business, to set up a decent restaurant for tourists who always go crazy over our food. Long live dual citizenship! You'll be tasting her food very soon ... The woman, who came in a taxi, prepared the food herself. She didn't even know where she was until they put all the ingredients in front of her on a table in the kitchen. Then the veteran Negress made herself at home, and began ... a true artist, my good friends, to prepare ... and where did I put that huge container for making my Pisco sours? Where is it? "Ah, here it is in my hands," responded Romero. "Allow me to reassure you that in all my twenty years in Peru I've never tasted anything like it!" And he shook it like crazy, sweating profusely, giving it his all. He shook it by hand because he detested electric utensils and he enjoyed being bartender, it's like shaking the maracas, ice cubes rattling inside the silver shaker, while the fat, knowledgeable epicurean host is carried off to the Bahamas.

But that euphoria didn't last long because the flamenco guitars, the high fidelity voices of the singers coming from the stereo, the decorations in the bar, the living room and den, even the keepsakes from that bullfight you lost, bring Fats Romero back to the congenial present: proud, he opens the shaker, wraps it in a white towel, pampering it in his pink hands like a baby in diapers, and proudly pours the white froth into cocktail glasses and happily announces another round of Pisco sours. "Susan! Juan Lucas!" he yells amid the flamenco guitars, "try this nectar of the gods!" and he hands them the drinks himself, he himself presents them with glasses, cold to the fingers and to the lips. They took a sip and congratulated him, each one in his or her own way: Susan, lovely, pushing her lock of hair back each time Fats appears, looks out the window half-distractedly, half-lovingly, catching a glimpse of that area of Lima before her eyes, and then turns to look at everyone, accepting the glass with a smile. She tastes it and a lock of hair falls over her face, saying finally, "delicious, darling, delicious," and kisses both of his cheeks. Fats is overjoyed with his prize, turns around with a glass for Juan Lucas and looks for him. He crosses the living room in a festive mood and people admire him; he has lots of friends. He looks pink, strutting around with a big butt and protruding nipples. But it's October and he can wear his white Panamanian shirts, which are one of his characteristics, one that his buddies like about him, and just because he's fat it doesn't mean he's a little dumb, effeminate, or queer, but because he resoundingly voices his views among his buddies, and the fat man's lack of pride but sense of faithfulness brings him respect among his virile-voiced buddies who always invite him to go out. He prepares those Pisco sours for them without losing that movement, the natural pon-pon pon-pon rhythm of Creoles. The fat guy seems to achieve the rhythm of manly corpulence and carries a cuss word on the tip of his tongue after so many long, secret daily endeavors. Then, once he's got it back and none of that pink plumpness falls out of place, that is to say, it's not excessive or queer-looking necessarily, once he's got that Creole pon-pon pon-pon way of walking down pat, he goes to the coffeeshop in front of the newspaper office where he encounters his friends for the first time of the day; from there it's back to the news desk and later, around noon, off to the Italian bar on the corner of some main street downtown in search of important people like Juan Lucas, his big buddies with whom he enjoys delicious appetizers and turnovers, or the special ones, the Chilean empanadas, they're the best.

Later Fats has lunch at someone's house or in a restaurant of recent renown the quality of which he himself always discovers, and then returns to his apartment for a long but constantly interrupted nap in which he reads for fifteen minutes, goes back to sleep, wakes up again, and so on until he breathes easier and digests well what he's eaten that day, and then leaves again like new to go downtown where friends and drinks await him once again: drinks that go way into the night in bars where you've never eaten better fried pork rinds, or in La Victoria or Bajo el Puente either, but it doesn't matter, it's not dangerous because Fats is well known down there. They are places where he can knock on a door and be received immediately by friends and, also, because he's got that rhythmic, Creole gait and overweight profile that's a part of our culture, the way we are; hence he can walk down many avenues and streets that are prohibited to refined people without anyone ever whistling at him, calling him queer, or yelling nervously at him, Hey, fairy!

"Superb!" Juan Lucas exclaimed as he sipped the Pisco sour. "You've found the right formula, my dear professor."

"I'll be right back with another! . . . I'll be right back! . . ."

Fats said, as he served the rest of the glasses from the silver tray to the other guests. Discussions about the bulls were already under way. Susan was surrounded by her friends and other people whom she had just met and explained more or less what her new house was going to be like, but she became terribly bored each time she realized that Juan Lucas was not next to her. At that moment Fats Romero, who had been in the kitchen, appeared hugging Concepción de los Reyes next to his impeccable white Panamanian shirt, so that they would see and admire her and then applaud. "Hey, Carlos, put on some Peruvian waltzes!" he yelled at one of his guests. "We've got to create the right atmosphere for what's coming! And here's the culinary artist." And Concepción de los Reyes? What did she see? She limited herself to her ancient smile and acted as if she didn't understand the instantaneous enthusiasm that a world of masters manifested toward her. Were they aware of it? Or did she simply feel touched, smiled at, and applauded by incredible and, above all, very mutable beings. Luis Martín tired of flattering her, there were some olés, and he finally stored his pampered jewel once again in the kitchen so that she would put her energy into fixing that marvelous Creole Ocopa dish made with potatoes and hot sauce. And she had to get a move on because it was getting late: he has to be at the right place and at the right time in order to explain the bullfights in his know-it-all way, judging each move and the attitude of the bullfighters.

Half an hour later Susan was burning up from so many hot spicy dishes. Juan Lucas called her my valiant gringa and offered her some bread, explaining that it was more effective than water or wine. The guests finished eating and asked for coffee and cognacs before leaving. More flamenco music came from the stereo and someone who was up on contemporary music said that the singer was popular in Spain when, all of a sudden, Susan, who had three Pisco sours before lunch and quite a bit of wine during lunch, exclaimed that the kid was a darling! . . . "But how do you know? . . . You don't even know him," interrupted Juan Lucas sarcastically as he doted on her, having downed seven of Fats's Piscos to top it off. Somebody arrived while Susan, embarrassed but lovely, found harbor in his Oxford shirt and kissed him where he had shaved with Yardley shaving cream; his skin, pink from a rush, was extremely masculine.

"Goober Hocker López of Peru!" yelled Fats Romero, greeting a tiny, half-deformed, horrible little man who arrived at that moment wearing an old suit and a shirt with a filthy collar. It was true, they were brutal with each other, but that's the way it was and Goober Hocker, who was nervous, began greeting everyone saying he had already eaten lunch with one of his girlfriends. He was a journalist and a good one too. Despite his hideous appearance that the flamenco guitars, wine and cognac, ambience, and beauty of some women accentuated to an extreme, Goober Hocker was respected by several men who liked him and shouted at him this bullfight season was the worst ever, as he turned his back on the women he didn't know and looked for a group of people he knew before their looks of nausea banished him forever. And they served him drinks which would eliminate his inhibitions and give way to his terrible outbursts, his incredible cursing, and his sharp, sarcastic jokes. Despite his monstrosity and grubbiness, those antics had given him an identity throughout years of encounters with that group of friends in those city bars. "Why?" Susan asked herself, as she even saw Juan Lucas embrace the group in which this man's ugliness reigned supreme and, now, cognac in hand and cigar in mouth, Juan Lucas listened to Goober Hocker's comments, blasting Fats Romero, giving explanations about Fats's body, and telling about the one time he discovered him, dying of thirst and heat, writing an article about bullfighting as he sat naked in a straw chair on the terrace of his apartment. Susan couldn't resist and drew closer to hear more about it. Using that same name, Juan Lucas introduced her to Goober Hocker and when she shook his hand, she felt a moist rag and then he looked away. She stood there in the middle of the group listening to that witty monster's jokes and stories, and she also began to laugh out loud like the rest of them. In her effort to enjoy what Juan Lucas was enjoying, she went to extremes saying darling to Goober Hocker to see if she would feel anything for him and perhaps save him. Three times in a row she said darling to him, but he didn't respond. This Goober Hocker guy was as horrible as ever, and hypersensitive, he caught on to what was happening, felt abominable and despised, and then lowered his eyes. He grew silent and remained grimy and deformed for the rest of the afternoon.

"If you can't appreciate my darky's potatoes, you've got no taste," Fats Romero exclaimed while everyone hurried out to their cars. Carlos, Bobby, and Julius had already been waiting a while in the Mercedes. Juan Lucas told Bobby to get in the back seat while he got up front next to the chauffeur in order to indicate the quickest way to get there and avoid all the traffic. Susan sat in the back. She immediately opened her purse, took out a mirror, and shrieked. She said she looked terrible and asked them to stop at the house for a few minutes while she fixed herself up a bit. Juan Lucas told her nicely to go to hell because there was no time and when she tried to protest he stuck his watch in her face. Susan felt bad that she had drunk so much and began thinking about an ice-cold Coke at the bullring. Juan Lucas made Carlos run three red lights and they were about to go through the fourth one when a row of cars made them screech to a halt. "What shitty luck," he bellowed, without paying any attention to the string of insults he was receiving from the other drivers. A few minutes later the Mercedes was shooting down Abancay Avenue. It was the first time Julius had been in the old downtown neighborhoods of Lima. They were fascinating. Susan sat next to him and put on her dark glasses which darkened everything because she didn't even want to think about poverty after the heavy meal with so much wine and, above all, just before the bullfights. "It's going to be a nice day," commented Juan Lucas, while at the same time indicating to Carlos all the spaces where he could inch forward and beat out the car next to them. "It's going to be a mess to park the car," he added. "Get as close as you can to the bullring. I'll tell you which tier of seats we're in so you can be waiting for us after it's over. And don't try to park too close so you can leave easily afterward." Poor Carlos didn't take his eyes off the car in front of them, the Señor's vehemence was going to make them crash. And so the Mercedes managed to get close to Bajo el Puente and poor Carlos had to dodge pedestrians who were playing like bullfighters with the car or were just trying to make it difficult for them to get through. Others who didn't manage to make it across the street before they came barreling through fired off tremendous insults that filtered into the car through the windows of the Mercedes along with the smoke from the street vendors' portable cooking stoves. It was an incredible mixture of people of all ages and colors, a kind of free-for-all that advanced toward the bullring. Julius watched with trepidation, sticking his floppy ears out the window. But he suddenly pulled his head back inside when a Negro teenager stuck his head inside the window with his flat nose almost reaching Susan and popping a huge bubble he had made with his gum or when a maimed lottery seller thrust his stump arm with tickets pinned to it inside the window announcing millions for tomorrow. Susan felt sorry for someone whose car collided with the one in front of them: "Ugh! By the time they pull them apart, they'll miss the start of the bullfight." "They won't make it at all if they keep arguing like that," Juan Lucas assured them, looking at the drivers of the smashed cars. "They're just starting to swear at each other." Bobby who never swore in front of Peggy, the Canadian, was a little disconcerted with the words Juan Lucas used in front of his mother. Julius was also disconcerted, thinking it was a sin as well, but what caught his attention at that moment was the bizarre spectacle in front of the Plaza de Acho bullring on that sunny Sunday afternoon. The poor kid was a little frightened and Susan must have noticed it from behind her dark glasses, even with that desire for the cold Coke to top it off, because she hugged him and sang in a low voice in his ear: "To the bullfight, what a sight!" and they were coconspirators for a moment. Together they became a part of the spectacle going on outside the bullring: the immortal French and/or North American Marines who would arrive drunk-looking for tickets to get in to see Manolete or El Cordobés; the hoards of street urchins who followed them around screaming Mister at them, asking for anything or trying to sell them something or steal their wallets; young guys who arrive with their San Isidro or Miraflores girlfriends, protecting them with their bodies so that no asshole Cholo will try to grab them, while at the same time smoking cigars, getting dizzy, and looking for their places with tickets in hand, waving at a schoolmate who is arriving with another girl, pretty and liberal because they're going to sit in the sun, not any of this pansy sitting-in-the-shade stuff: I'll do that when I graduate, make some money, and can pay for seats in the shade, even first row in the shade because I'll triumph in life, all of us will triumph in life, she won't be just a pansy in the shade but my wife and I've got a right to take her wherever I like! I'm somebody, man. People exactly like Juan Lucas are also arriving and telling their drivers to get as close to the bullring as possible and then to look for a place to park. And the chauffeurs sweat and inch forward like Carlos until a policeman yells Stop! Don't go any further! Go to the right!

He blew his whistle like crazy and redirected traffic because the President of the Republic was arriving with an accompanying entourage of enormous black cars that were so shiny the reflection of the sun blinded the crowd of people that had put their faces up against the windows wanting to see the President up close after which, tonight, they'll get drunk in some bar and end up screaming and crying, Long live Peru, screw it! They wouldn't let us play in the '36 World Olympics because we were Negroes! Long live Lolo Fernández, damn it! And Manguera Villanueva! Long live Peru, damn it! The President waves to them, smiling at their faces that press against the windows, clouding them with their breath and tarnishing the black body of the superlong Cadillac with their filthy, sweaty hands. They are people who won't go to the bullfight, only a few will crash gates and some are ticket scalpers waiting for someone to drop something or until the President reappears later, just before the bullfight is over, waving to him once again, Hey, don't push, and then they run over to someone like Juan Lucas, who is more noticeable because of his car: Señor, I watched your car for you! I watched your car for you, Señor! They wait until its all over, about dusk, when there's only trash and cigarette butts scattered around, the hour of the day when they start to drink away their tips.

A Mulatto with a red cap looking appropriate for the occasion took Susan, Juan Lucas, Bobby, and Julius to their seats and placed their little cushions on the numbered seats in the front row of the shady section. An incredible number of people waved at Susan while she went down the aisle to her seat, but she couldn't see who they were because of the bright sun and she couldn't get that cold Coke out of her mind either. Susan looked lovely, and she was anxious to know the names of the bullfighters who had come to Lima this year. Juan Lucas began to explain patiently that the organizer was a son of a bitch because he hadn't contracted Briceño who was the current star. Then, one by one he began naming the bullfighters who had come to Lima, explaining who The Gypsy was and reminding her that they had seen him in Madrid. Susan said she did remember, so as not to upset him. Also, he was really handsome but she simply could not remember The Gypsy. Juan Lucas pointed to the afternoon's three bullfighters who were waiting for the group to make its appearance. The couple was still standing and looked up behind them and to the sides, waving to many people who were dressed for the occasion. Bobby was in seventh heaven with all the pretty girls around him. He would bring Peggy someday, although she said this bullfighting stuff was inhumane. At that moment Miss Universe arrived. She was a very blond Swede who had won that year and all the playboys lit their cigars and, once again, experienced the feeling of youth, handsomeness, and self-confidence.

In the open air sections, the marines who had managed to buy tickets to the event without someone snatching their cameras were getting ready to watch the bullfight through their lenses. They also ordered beer and the waiters in the stands would charge them on the spot and never return with their change, but only say I'll be right back, Señor, when they take off with your money. Groups of young men discussed the bulls and past bullfight spectacles, gave opinions about the prospects for this one while cursing their cigars that would go out right after they would light them. They were in their seats waving exaggeratedly and wearing red handkerchiefs like in Pamplona; they felt like real experts. They consumed vast amounts of beer when they were without their girlfriends, and they felt exhilarated and free to get drunk, yell, sing, and throw their seat cushions in the air in jubilation or protest just at the moment when that girl next to me is watching. She's watching right now, so I'll drink from the leather wineskin, like they do at Pamplona, like Hemingway . . . manly, macho, balls.

But, as fans go, there's no one like Mazamorra Quintana, the popular engineering student who is walking down the aisle while friends and acquaintances alike, even others who aren't friends, applaud his arrival. He's a real fanatic when it comes to bullfighting: he'll even walk in front of a woman, introduce his hand into his pants pocket and move it to one side, making it protrude to look like the sex organs of the bullfighters who always wear tight pants. Moreover, he has fought some heifers on his cousin's ranch and imitated a bullfighter, with Peruvian music and all, at parties. They make room for him to dance and he moves across the floor not toward the prettiest girl necessarily, but toward the one who is farthest away, so that his trajectory is greater, and always with his hand bulging in his pocket, simulated sex organs protruding, and leaving no doubt whatsoever: it's Sammy Stud of Peru. He's great everywhere, he's popular, and people envy his red and yellow car. He greets everyone seated in his row with a hug and waves at others nearby with a raised arm and looks for a drink. Everyone in the first few rows is drinking beer, or wine from wineskins, which they swap around with each other and invite everyone for a swig. Then they start to get drunk and shout bullfighting style when they think the right moment has arrived. People of all colors and ages sitting in the cheap seats to the back also drink and watch the young men down below, waiting for the bullfight to begin so they'll quiet down a little and stop being so rowdy.

And the bullfight begins because the President of the Nation has arrived. Some will say that he received too much applause, while others say not enough. The military band commences with the special bullfighting music that really creates the right atmosphere, while the bullfighters emerge from a large door underneath row 11 and proceed straight to the shady side of the ring near the judges' box. The spectators applaud those who did well in the last bullfight at the same time someone is telling Miss Universe what she has to say when the bullfight is over, just so the Swede won't foul it up. While the bullfighters move in disorderly fashion toward the shade and The Gypsy knocks on wood in front of Susan because he has to go first that afternoon; while Bobby decides he likes the women who are there more than the bulls and concludes Miss Universe would be all skin and bones in bed yet she'd be a great chick to invite out to dinner; while some veteran Hollywood stars are arriving, Hey, the gringa is still in great shape; while a Peruvian cattle breeder is about to faint: what if his bulls don't perform well?; while poor Susan finally gets her Coke and Juan Lucas lights a cigar; while Julius begins to side more with the sad black bull that had just come out into the ring than with the bullfighters; while the hackneyed millionaire Pepita Román arrives late with her boyfriend, a distinguished but broke Englishman, so that everyone would notice her; while an amateur Peruvian bullfighter arrives with his North American lover who is only interested in the bullfighters; while the spectators yell at the soft drink vendors to quit blocking their view; while a newspaper photographer for the social page tries to get Susan straight on; while

Juan Lucas asks Julius if he's feeling weak because this is a spectacle for men; while Susan dotes on Julius and senses his anger at Juan Lucas; while a peon shoots across the ring like a bullet with the bull on his tail; while The Gypsy moves forward ready to do battle with the bull; while Juan Lucas during the afternoon of bullfighting presents a profile that's slightly flushed from the sun, adorned with gray hair that curls over his neck and, like an expert, observes and dominates this expensive art that he likes so much; while Aránzazu Marticorena, who had been his lover, looks at him and continues to love him as she sits next to her husband; while Fats Luis Martín Romero, sitting in the press box with his cigar plugged in, finishes narrating the first bullfight of the afternoon and observes The Gypsy's movements, thus continuing his description of what will probably be read the next morning on the page dedicated to bullfighting in one of Lima's daily newspapers.

And the bullfights continue after the bullfights are over, well beyond the real bullfights, somewhat metafrivolously. The setting, at least for many present, past, and future Juan Lucas look-alikes, is transported to many bars in fancy hotels where the bullfighters are staying. Take Santillana, for instance: this afternoon he came down grinning and, following the Andalusian custom, taps on Juan Lucas' table to which he had been invited as he tries to get away from Lester Lang III's wife who had just arrived for the October bullfights. Like Juan Lucas, Lang III knows how to combine business and pleasure, letting his wife's North American curiosity dance to the sway of an I'm-tragic-and-interesting Santillana rhythm and, at the same time, ask for an explanation of his art. It was the same explanation that weeks later he would repeat in a round of whiskeys after a stockholders' meeting in New York, which was the source of this Peruvianized American's stockpile of money, but in terms of culinary and investment matters, he was still a gringo. Later on that night the entire group, who would appear in the next day's social page of the newspaper, would move on to the bars that are like old taverns or small jewels of colonial Peru embedded in modern buildings in Lima, the City of the Viceroys and the Little Villages. Photographers would also arrive and, amid the music, take pictures of bullfighters who were intermingling among the tables and dancing with young girls wearing clothes purchased in Paris. Susan and Juan Lucas arrive sans the children and then Lester Lang III and other friends arrive. Playboys arrive and are escorted to the tables by waiters. Finally the right atmosphere begins to emerge from the Peruvian marinera dance that eventually turns it all into a binge. The girls' Peruvian fiancés are there as well, jealous and barely managing to tolerate The Gypsy,

Santillana, and Lazarillo's autographs on pictures in which their sexual organs stick out even more than in the case of Sammy Stud, who is also just arriving.

THE ROOF OF THE second floor caved in on Saturday and the architect in vogue, keeping a promise that he had made to Julius one night after several glasses of sherry, picked him up early in order to go look at it. Lately the architect in vogue hadn't missed out on one of Juan Lucas' October parties celebrating the bullfights in Lima. He wasn't dumb: the mansion filled up with important Señores who might want to build a house. Also, it was pleasant to talk to them amid the virile smell of cigars and glasses of sherry and other drinks that Juan Lucas had purchased in order for his bar to correspond to his acquired level of prestige. The food was always catered from hotels or from Creole, Chinese, or international restaurants; meanwhile, in her kitchen Nilda the Jungle Woman felt rebuffed and reacted insolently, so Susan preferred not to talk to her for a few days afterward. On the other hand, Susan could easily face the architect, he had learned how to drink without blurting out what he felt and now he would bring his fiancée. They even announced the wedding date. Of course, he was still head over heels for Susan, but he learned to accept life the way it was and, moreover, he was making good money. Also, he was trying to make his fiancée, who was even smaller than Susan, learn everything about her, even how to remain exquisite and lovely beyond thirty-five. "Just shut up and watch her," he seemed to be telling her as they entered the mansion, because the poor thing would go from party to party without saying a word, always smiling and agreeing with everything, so that in reality the architect's fiancée didn't stand out very much. On the other hand, he had flourished significantly: you could notice the change by the big signs in front of the construction projects. He was in vogue now, and he was something to see surrounded by Juan Lucas' guests, explaining architecture up one side and down the other, to the point that the older Señores became bored and started talking about the bullfights again. Even though there wasn't much more to add after "It's a gorgeous house," praising his designs, he became so enthused that he would blurt out "Plasticity!" as he reflected on the drawing that he held stretched out between his arms. "What's gotten into this guy?" some businessmen seemed to smirk, beginning to withdraw and forget about him after which he folded up his architectural plans and drawings in order to return to his fiancée and steer her toward Susan for more lessons.

"They start work very early and never stop," the architect had told him. "When it's time to put the roof on they can't just stop, they keep working and drink beer to keep up the pace and their spirits. When they get to drinking they don't stop going up and down and some get a little soused." That's why Julius arrived smiling and ready to see something new, interesting, and lively. And that's why now, as he got out of the architect's car, he became a little apprehensive; besides the fact the whole group of workers would probably go to hell because of all the cussing, going around half-naked and all covered with cement; they looked like clowns who had been fighting, their clothing was ripped off, and, now, as laborers, they continued with their carnivalesque jokes as they scurried up and down the scaffolding, with no railings, from which they were about to fall. The architect forgot about Julius and went over to talk to the builder and the foreman. Julius tried to approach the cement mixer, but they yelled at least three times, "Get away from there, kid." Seized with fear, he backed away. No one had invited him to stick his nose into their work. He had no choice but to stand on the sidewalk in front and observe the curious ceremony from there: he watched them ferry large buckets full of cement on their shoulders, balancing themselves on the two scaffolds, as one worker advanced to the right toward the roof of the first floor and took a short rest against a railing just in case any overexertion from the climb might make him lose his balance and fall. After the short rest, he would scurry up the second scaffolding to the left reaching the point where they would dump out the cement from their buckets. Julius stood there alone not talking to anyone for some twenty minutes; finally the architect approached him to say he was going to another construction site with the builder. "Do you want to stay here?" he asked. "I'll come back for you a little later." Julius said he wanted to stay, so the architect told the foreman to watch out for him.

"So, he's the owner's son? . . . leave him with me . . . we'll put him to work . . . What's your name?" he asked as he watched the builder and the architect leave.

"Julius . . ."

The foreman smiled at him as if he didn't understand that kind of name, and he began to explain some of the details of the work they were performing that day in order to build the roof. He pointed to the cases of beer that would be consumed while they worked and explained once again they couldn't stop working, even though in a little while they would take turns eating lunch. Meanwhile the workers continued to strain while they climbed the scaffoldings, resting halfway up, readjusting the buckets on their shoulders, and pushing themselves up to the second part of the scaffolding. They would run into others coming down with empty buckets, making way for them to pass by, but since some of them liked to horse around they would elbow each other or grab the other guy's rear end, making the one coming up totter, all of which occasioned loud cussing, some of which Julius was learning without blaming them for it. He watched them strain, half-naked, scream out incredible names, nicknames he had never heard at school: Stable Hand, a skin-and-bones Negro; Cockroach, a guy with thick red hair; Whitey, a guy who was as fair-skinned as Julius but for some reason was just a laborer; Saw Blade; Turtledove; Fat Humphrey, a really fat guy; and Holy Water, one who was excessively puny and coughed all the time as he went up and down the scaffolding. All of them were going up and down and, while the person mixing the cement would fill their buckets, they took advantage of the moment to take some swigs of beer and from time to time, although they wore little pointed caps made of newspaper, they would stick their filthy heads into a huge barrel of dirty water. Then they would return to pick up their buckets and start all over again, sometimes wobbling too close to the edge, and Julius imagined seeing them, preceded by some cuss words, lying dead on the ground. Suddenly Cockroach pointed at him and said he must be the owner's son. "Why don't you guys talk to him so he'll get us a little more money," adding that "beer isn't enough." Julius heard them saying things like that as he stood on the sidewalk. From time to time he noticed they would look at him and smile as if he were some joke: after all, what could a snotty little shit like him do to help them get paid better? "They want better wages," the foreman told him, and Julius looked at him as if to ask for an explanation.

"Today, you see, they can't stop and they want to be paid a little extra . . . your dad bought beer for them but he's forgotten about the extra money."

Julius remained silent. He remembered that Juan Lucas complained the house was costing him a mint. "The architect and the builder are getting rich at my expense," he said once. "A lot of whiskey at home and bla bla bla; but when it comes time to collect they don't miss a lick." Juan Lucas was experienced in talking like that and he did so frequently.

"Good morning, Señora," said the foreman, and Julius turned around to look at the woman who was arriving. She was bringing Fat Humphrey's lunch and others started to arrive with the same kind of lunch containers and the workers began to take turns eating. They went over to the women, greeted them coldly, and waited for them to open their sacks. A collection of chipped enamel bowls emerged, half-full of a greasy mixture that had noodles and meat but was mainly potatoes. Silently the laborers took out their tin spoons and bread from little cloth bundles, formed a circle as they sat down on some rocks, and thrust their spoons into the mass of food, extracting a first enormous greasy spoonful that they stuck into their mouths. They lowered their face into the bowl rather than bring the spoon up to their mouths, the way Julius had learned as a child. They tore the bread apart with their yellow teeth, forming a huge mouthful that they chewed while they talked, laughed, and yelled at the others who hadn't stopped to eat but kept on carrying their buckets to the roof. As they chewed away, they got to know Julius. He was dying to become a good friend of theirs; in fact, he wanted to be a true friend, one who would even tell them that's not the way to eat. And he began to answer their questions.

"Do you have a sister, little gringo? . . . she's probably a real bombshell, right? . . ." asked Cockroach.

"I had a sister, but she died."

Cockroach lowered his head and seemed to stick his empty spoon halfway down his throat, licking it as he pulled it out. Julius drew closer to the circle of laborers, all of whom were silent for a moment, and he could see how much they were covered in cement, spotted all over, their hands with which they ate so covered with it they would never get it out from under their fingernails. The women took more beer over to them, and after the men had finished scraping the bottom of their bowls they took them over to a faucet to rinse them out.

"And do you have any brothers?" asked Turtledove.

"I have two, but one of them is in the United States."

"Turtledove's queer, he don't ask about nobody but men."

"Do you like beer?"

"Sure he does! Give 'im some!"

"Let 'im learn, man! Shit!"

"Let the little white kid have a swig of your beer, man!"

"Do you know how to drink beer?"

". . . Ha . . ."

"Sure he does. Give 'im some!"

Cockroach wiped off the mouth of his bottle with the palm of his filthy hand and handed it to Julius, but the foreman told Julius not to pay any attention to him.

"They're already half-drunk," he added.

"Shit, boss! Let 'im learn."

"Just a little bit," said the foreman. "And you guys get going so the others can eat."

Julius was holding the bottle with both hands and felt loath to put the bottle to his mouth, but he managed to down two or three sips of the bitter liquid as it splashed down his neck. Then he smiled because now he felt like he was everyone's friend. Cockroach swore and asked him if he liked it: Julius said he did, took another sip, they all broke out laughing as the liquid ran down all over him, then he wiped off the mouth of the bottle and passed it to Whitey who was approaching the group just then. Everyone laughed because the little snot was acting the way he was supposed to and maybe the kid was a little macho. That remained to be seen, and Stable Hand picked up a huge cement penis with testicles they had made. They handed it to him, it was very heavy, and they asked him what he would do with a real one, eh?

"That's enough," said the foreman, grasping the enormous penis that Julius was holding.

"Tell us where you're going to stick it," blurted out Stable Hand.

Everyone broke out laughing again and sprinkled the conversation with new cuss words that Julius tried to interpret. He also laughed, and hard too, so they would think he was following the rapid dialogue and because he had become their friend. If the parish priest would only see them now . . . what would he say? More women were arriving with containers of that rotten food and the ones who had arrived earlier were leaving without any good-byes. The men who had finished eating were resting and didn't pay any attention to the foreman when he told them the cement mixer was full and they had to get a move on.

"That shitty roof," griped one worker who hadn't been officially nicknamed.

"Give Julius a bucket so he can carry some," said Holy Water, coughing.

"You skinny shit! Don't cough up your lunch on me!"

"Hospital! Hospital!"

But Holy Water was already used to it and he kept on coughing, standing next to the group eating in a circle. When his coughing fit was over he pelted the side of the house with a big wad of spit. Then he picked up his bucket and handed it to Julius.

"No! That's enough joking!" ordered the foreman, who was fairly important and conversed with engineers and even architects.

"Don't ruin it, boss!"

"Let 'im learn."

Whitey, who was unbelievably white yet only a laborer and a U fan, stood up and left his bowl on a rock, picked up Holy Water's bucket, and told Julius to follow him. He took Julius over to the noisy cement mixer which made them yell and cuss at the top of their lungs and also let everyone know they were half-drunk. He told him he was going to pour in just a little bit so it wouldn't be too heavy. "Let me know if it's too much for you." He dumped some of the mixture into the bucket and put it aside. He grabbed another and filled it up to the brim because it was for him. "Ready?" "Yes." He put his bucket on the ground and lifted up the other bucket for Julius, placing it on his shoulder and asking him if he could carry it. Julius said yes. It was almost empty and, even though he was frightened to death, Julius was happy this was really happening and Whitey had placed his bucket on his shoulder, spilling cement all over himself and then making his way toward the scaffolding. He sent him first and told him not to be afraid, for he would be right behind him in case he lost his balance. Everyone stopped what they were doing and watched. The ones who were eating stood up. Holy Water began to cough and someone yelled at him, "Shut up, asshole!" Everyone on the roof also stopped. They set their buckets down on the edge of the roof and began to observe the ascent. Someone began to sing "The water jug's on the ground/Mommy can't lift it," but someone else told him to shut up and go to hell. Julius could have cried at first and he might have said I don't want to continue, but he didn't cry or want to say anything and now, caught in a panic at seeing he was about to fall, only heard Whitey's masculine voice pushing him forward, telling him he was right behind him and not to be afraid: "Keep going, Julio! Keep going, Julio!" he yelled at him, and Julius could feel how the edge of the bucket painfully cut into his shoulder; he might have to let it fall and grab the railing in order to rest. "First stage," rasped Whitey. "Do you want to rest a while? Do you want me to take your bucket?" Yes, he wanted to rest; in fact, he wanted to quit right then and there but, paradoxically, he said no, and from down below came a roar of laughter and more congratulatory cuss words, even a round of applause that was hardly audible because of the cement mixer. "Get him down from there," the foreman yelled, "the builder's coming back." But Whitey had already said, "Let's go, Julio!" and Julius wasn't going to listen to any kind of noise that came from down below, his world had been reduced to that steep and slippery part of the scaffolding where he struggled without the assistance of the railing and looked down and suddenly felt like he was going to fall, but he didn't because he could hear Whitey's breathing behind him which kept him going. He was halfway up the second part and he understood with Whitey behind him it would be impossible to fall. And he continued struggling just like the laborers who do it all day long, feeling the beer he had drunk which stimulated him to make it to the top, finally, and now on top he was an intimate friend of everyone there and he emptied his bucket which unfortunately didn't help much because there was just a small amount in the bottom. He turned around triumphantly and saw Cockroach, Holy Water, Turtledove, and the others down below grabbing their testicles, moving their torsos in all directions, and splitting with laughter. "Come on down and drink a beer," they yelled at him. Julius looked down and he saw the route he had taken in order to get up there and the one he would have to take in order to get down: he got panicky again. The descent seemed much more dangerous. The abyss below drew him toward it and when he wanted to take a small step he went too far and got too close to the edge. "Julio is a champ!" Whitey bellowed, grabbing both buckets and throwing them in the air in a sign of triumph. "We have to carry him down on our shoulders!" he added, and without saying anything to him, he lifted him up enthusiastically, put him on his shoulders and yelled at him to hold on to my head and they started down. Julius wasn't even aware of the scaffolding, he felt like he was flying and he almost asked him to go slower, please! But why should he if he was laughing hard and wasn't about to fall?

Down on the ground it was celebration time. It pleased the laborers when Julius asked them to pass the bottle to him again because he had already finished what they had given him when he came down on Whitey's shoulders and joined the group. Now the beer was really being consumed. It's your turn! Don't screw me around! Get going, asshole! Gulp it down fast! The foreman ordered them to get back to work, but only two or three of them paid any attention to him and the rest joined those who hadn't eaten lunch yet. The others wanted to continue talking to Julius. They got a kick out of the way he talked. As a prize for having carried the bucket to the roof, they taught him a bunch of new cuss words. Now they weren't babying him; they even began to talk about their problems in front of him.

"You know, your dad should pay us extra for working today," said Whitey.

"The builder knows that we're working our asses off but it doesn't seem to matter . . ."

"It's really up to your dad . . . he's the one who has the dough."

"We always get beer; what we don't get is money . . ."

"But my dad says the house is costing a lot of money . . . he says it's costing him an arm and a leg."

"Bullshit . . ."

"It's true . . . that's what he told my mother."

"Your dad has a lot of money . . . he's rich."

"It wouldn't hurt him to pay us a little extra."

"He comes to look at the construction and doesn't even say hello."

"Why don't you ask him to pay us a little more?"

" . . ."

"You'll probably say he doesn't have it."

"Did he say it costs a lot to build a new house?"

"So why build a new one? Doesn't he already own a mansion on Salaverry Avenue?"

" . . ."

"Here comes the builder!"

When they saw him and the architect get out of the car, they took off running for their buckets. The cement mixer was now full of cement and waiting for them; once again the laborers began their dangerous march. The short rest, somewhat extended because of Julius' presence, caused them to lose their rhythm and they tottered back and forth, especially on the first part. "Let's go, Julius," said the architect, who saw him go up and shake hands with the builder and the foreman after which he said good-bye effusively to the laborers.

As the car was pulling away, Julius saw the laborers through the window for the last time. They were splattered with cement, scurrying up and down the dangerous scaffolding that led them up to the new roof. Yep, they still looked like crazy clowns who had been thrown out of some cheap circus for trying to make the audience laugh at dirty jokes. To him, they still looked like they had been fighting, tearing up their clothes and, for some odd reason, had decided to drink at a construction site. Or they looked like they were drunk and crazy, trying to get into some house without ever finding out how, but never giving up either. And that's why now they continued to go up and down like ants, lugging buckets of cement in order to seal off an enormous hole and stop the winter rain from getting in, so that finally, once they were finished, someone else would find that damn door. Julius asked the architect four questions which the latter thought were ridiculous for a boy who is Susan's son. "Kid's stuff, of course," he thought. But his answers did not convince Julius. He asked questions because he wanted to find out something. He didn't know the answers but, in any case, he felt the architect's answers weren't the ones he wanted to hear: actually, they seemed a lot like answers that Juan Lucas would give . . . "Why don't you tell him to pay us a little more?"

That's why he waited impatiently for his parents to return from the Golf Club; that's why he hoped there would be a family dinner at home and not somewhere else, maybe they would stay at home and then he could tell them about it; that's why it was difficult for him to finish his homework for the weekend; that's why he rejoiced when he heard Susan returning and say they would be eating dinner at home and early, too, because they were tired and tomorrow was going to be another long day at the bullfights; that's why he smiled when he kissed her and ran to tell Nilda to hurry up and serve dinner; that's why he narrated, for the third time that afternoon, his adventure with the laborers and the buckets, his and Whitey's, and she accused him of being mischievous although she felt he was acting the same as always, and that's why Jungle Woman helped him get his ideas straight and told him what he should say first and when exactly to bring up the bit about paying the laborers a little more; that's why he waited impatiently for Daniel, who was also a partial coconspirator, to finish passing around the immense silver soup server with Andalusian gazpacho that Juan Lucas liked to eat during the bullfighting season; and that's why, finally, he blurted out his story that Nilda overheard while she stood behind the kitchen door.

Susan, lovely, opened her eyes wide and then smiled at him, putting forth her best to show how much she adored her last child. Juan Lucas began interrupting him with something about Jungle Woman will never learn how to make Andalusian gazpacho, this is nothing but plain tomato soup! And Susan, lovely, who knew Julius' stories would upset Juan Lucas sometimes, tried to stop him from continuing his story and told him to hurry up and eat his soup, it's going to get cold, darling. Juan Lucas snickered loudly, for there's no one like him to celebrate Susan's enchanting ways of distracting Julius: "Honey," he told her, "the soup you are eating is supposed to be cold." He adored her even more as she exquisitely rested her elbow on the dinner table, buried her chin in the palm of her hand, and opened wide her bewildered eyes in an effort to return to reality and comprehend gazpacho is a kind of soup that Juan Lucas likes in October and is served cold. That marvelous lock of hair came tumbling down, hiding her face for a moment. While he watched her take it between her fingers and toss it back over her head, Julius took a deep breath, exhaled, and let go with the rest of his story. He looked at Susan, but he was really talking to Juan Lucas: would he understand that the laborers worked like dogs today? Would he listen when he tells him that they should be paid a little more? Would he understand they are good people and had made his afternoon unforgettable? Are you listening, Uncle? Why don't you look at me? Why don't you put your spoon down and look at me? Why do you start eating faster as if you don't want to listen to me? Why don't you look at me in the eyes for a moment like Mommy does? Well, she looks at me but she's on the moon. Why don't you find out Whitey taught me how to carry cement buckets? And he helped me to make it to the top? And I wasn't about to fall while I was with him? When are you going to pay attention to me? . . . are you going to call me something I don't like? . . . always something new . . . because you always win . . . you always come up with some new word. Why do you wipe your mouth now but don't look at me? Why do you ring for Daniel, ask for the main dish and more wine, and then tell him to hurry? Listen, they need a little more. Money. And if I could . . . let me finish . . . you never let me finish . . .

"In other words this young man here thinks he can climb scaffoldings and traipse around on top of roofs? Susan, did you know about this?"

"Darling, you could have killed yourself . . ."

"And, get this: the boy is Whitey's friend who brings me this guy's demands . . ."

"Uncle, but . . ."

"Look! I don't know who your friend Whitey is and I don't want to know either."

"He's one of the men at the construction site," said Susan, well-informed. "You could have been killed because of that guy, darling."

"Nothing happened to me. It was easy to climb up there . . ."

"And even easier to kill yourself. That's enough of your laborer friends. No more going to construction sites! . . . I'll tell the architect this is the last time! You can't let this little kid out of your sight for a moment because he'll do whatever he wants! . . . Do you want to go back to having a nanny?"

"But, Uncle, they're only asking . . ."

"Why don't you shut up once and for all!" intervened Bobby suddenly.

"You have to learn, my little friend, that's why I have an architect, a foreman, and a whole bunch of sponges living off of me. And on top of everything else you come and tell me what to do! Finish your dinner and go to bed immediately . . . or I'll personally see to it this Whitey and his buddies are fired!"

"Darling, I believe Whitey could be a dangerous person . . ."

THE ARCHITECT IN VOGUE promised to have everything ready by fall. Susan spent her time those days reading magazines about houses and gardens, mainly interior decorating magazines. Just about anywhere throughout the mansion one could find issues of *Spanish Furniture, House and Garden, Eighteenth-Century French Furniture, Gardening,* and many more she would leaf through every day while she waited for Juan Lucas to come home and have a drink together. Each day they came up with new ideas. The truth is that they came up with so many new ideas that they didn't even consult with the architect anymore, not because their ideas weren't functional, for he had evolved somewhat, in fact he was more mature now, but because it was impossible to have in just one house seven bathrooms or twenty-seven little terraces for tea, especially when it came to that many different styles. They wouldn't say anything to the architect, but when they were alone they embraced amid *gin and tonics* and constructed dozens of houses in each of which they would throw in two or three bars he would dream up or four or five terraces she would want to include. Those were the days! The bullfighting season had ended but those sunny days that accompanied the best bullfights lingered on.

One afternoon Juan Lucas showed up ebullient because he had just sold the mansion, with all the furniture to boot, for the price he wanted. He was elated: there was nothing he liked more than to finish a project and begin anew again; it made him feel like he was being reborn, so he would get the urge to change clothes, have a drink, go out and eat at some new restaurant, and it should be summer already. Susan, on the other hand, was not happy about getting rid of all the furniture; she had wanted to save some of it for the new house; for instance, this piece and that piece were irreplaceable. "Irreplaceable?" exclaimed Juan Lucas, picking up a new magazine full of pictures of furniture. Bring out the ice for a drink! I'm going to show you myself if those old pieces are irreplaceable! Seeing that he was agitated, Susan went for ice herself. She knew the matter would end up in jokes: let's see who can make the other look more ridiculous. It was going to be a sarcastic duel of love and irony, in which a sharp comment or a precise comparison would destroy the other's preferred piece of furniture. It would be a duel without a winner or a loser, now they would begin by sitting down with their drinks, clinking them as they toasted each other and, as he put his arm over her shoulder, opening a magazine.

Those were the days when everything came together nicely to create a unified mental equilibrium in which your only secret desire might be to go to the beach, which was completely within your capabilities. Springtime in Lima insisted on being benevolent and the sun pleasantly reappeared every morning. One day Susan came out of her bedroom so enchanted that upon reaching the stairs she was taken aback by seeing herself leave, nineteen years ago, to enjoy the sun in a London public park when she was a single woman and the weather had suddenly turned nice: nineteen years later, again she was about to go out, married now, to sit in the sun in a private garden . . . "You've been sleeping like a log?" Juan Lucas surprised her, grasping her by the waist and helping her down the stairs on one of those days in which everything came together nicely, creating a unified mental equilibrium.

"I'm off to the office . . . if it gets any warmer and you're in the mood, call me and we'll go to the beach."

Susan didn't dress according to the styles found in the latest magazines in order to be able to take walks among the trees and climbing vines of the mansion. Her clothes didn't match the flowers but, of course, they didn't clash with them either. She was simply the best company they could hope for. If you were as inquisitive as a professor or an old aunt and had asked the flowers something like, "Tell me who your friends are and I'll tell you who you are," and surely all the flowers would have looked toward Susan. On the other hand, not even a wilted red carnation would have looked at Celso, as they all followed her around in single file and waited to hand her the Toledan scissors: Yes, that rose is perfect for the vase on the piano. Not everything consisted of lovely walks among the trees and vines: Susan had to concentrate on the vase on the piano. As soon as she decided on a flower, she would point at it without touching it because there might be a bee and hand Celso the scissors. Then he would cut the flower and return the scissors to her. The servants would line up in single file and proceed toward other plants where she would select another excellent carnation and return the scissors to him. That was the procedure until the vase was mentally full and then both would go to the washbasin in the service area where Susan would supervise the flower arrangement, indicating to the butler-treasurer which leaves were unnecessary. "This one we can get rid of," she would say and hand him the scissors, after which he would always return them to her because they would need to repeat it for the next flower.

"Divine!" exclaimed Susan, contemplating the vase of gardenias, roses, or carnations; "That's done," she would say immediately and look for Celso's approval who, frankly, would have preferred to adorn the piano room with native gooseberries from the mountains. It was eleven o'clock in the morning, the hour when Susan would take her place on the sofa with oriental pillows and wait for Daniel to bring her usual cup of hot coffee, take two or three sips in order to prevent the usual eleven o'clock weakness that she had read about in an ad while on the run one morning in Paris. Now, seated there, she leafed through magazines about houses and furniture, killing time while Juan Lucas was at the office, the golf course, or some bar where he had agreed to meet Luis Martín Romero; that's why she always had some new idea to present to him when he arrived home, but she would never tell him about it until he was seated next to her with a drink and a bowl of nuts in front of them; then, of course, she would explain her idea to him and they would become involved in some kind of architectural mysticism, contemplating imaginary terraces or possible gardens where the flowers were always blooming like the ones in the pictures in the magazines she was holding in her hands or held in her lap. There were gardens and terraces inhabited by people who always smiled and were happy, because perhaps they had blond hair like Susan or they had just arrived from the golf course wearing silk shirts like Juan Lucas. They would spend hours looking out the window toward the garden, imagining terraces and dining rooms of Andalusian country homes, dormitories like the ones built by Metro Goldwin Meyer for some movie, the Brazilian jungle drama of love-luxury-ants-and-Grace Kelly, or bars where waiters wore stripes like the ones on transatlantic ocean liners that Hitchcock required for his recent movie that was more suspenseful than the previous one. No sooner would they enter one of those bars than Luis Martín Romero would show up, shaking a cocktail mixer and telling incredible stories that Juan Lucas, laughing, would then retell to Susan while he added ice to his glass and remembered the prize joke Fats had just told him, after which he would drop him off at his apartment on his way home. The poor guy was sweating up a storm after eating so much spicy food at Cúneo's Bar. The thought of sweating led them to talk about bathtubs whose shapes looked like anything but bathtubs and the tiles for which turned the water pale blue, making you feel like you're in a swimming pool, darling. Suddenly, on page 123 of a magazine they saw a carriage in perfect condition and Juan Lucas decided to restore the carriage. He knew of a person who lived on a ranch on the road to Chosica who could do it for him: he would make the call tomorrow because right now he was more interested in lunch and a swim at the Golf Club.

Nilda blurted out that they also had a swimming pool at the mansion and protested furiously because she had already fixed lunch: this was starting to happen too many times, it's not right! She bared her rotten teeth at Susan. Jungle Woman complained bitterly: they didn't pay her to work in vain! How many people are dying from hunger in Peru and every day food from this house is thrown away! Susan, who became alarmed, recommended they take what was left over to the racetrack and turned to look at Daniel, but the Cholo turned around and marched off to the pantry. It was just a simple show of solidarity with Nilda because, in fact, he preferred they leave: two less to serve at the table. What is certain is that Susan left hurriedly to tell Juan Lucas that the cook was delirious: "More than ever, darling, and her poor kid seems sick and he doesn't let her sleep at night; it's as though she's going crazy because of no sleep . . ." Juan Lucas displayed a *stop* with his hand and declared solemnly that it was time to let this woman go. He would take care of it himself because Amazonians are prone to drugs and then they go stark raving mad. This explanation left Susan worried, mainly because of Julius. They had already been telling him horrendous stories and it was Nilda who clipped them out of those crude sensationalist newspapers. She didn't tell Juan Lucas, but she was worried when she left for the golf course.

JULIUS SPENT THE last few weeks of that school year studying for exams and preparing the Chopin prelude for Awards Day. The kid went around worried he might take first place in his class which meant he would be labeled a bookworm, an apple-polisher, a fairy. In addition, if he took first place, Lange, who was half-German and a good student, was going to hate him forever. Perhaps that's why he preferred to spend more time practicing the piano lately. The nun with the freckles, nerves, and piano key fragrances was pleased with his work and she would go past the hour just to watch him play the prelude a while longer. The bad thing was that Juan Lucas wouldn't be able to make it to the awards ceremony this year either. Susan asked him to take her but he coughed three times, straightened the knot of his tie, and made it clear these things were not for him; moreover, golfers from all over the world had just arrived for an international tournament, and he would have to take care of everything and practice because he was going to play as well. In other words, just leave him alone and no more first communions.

But Susan went to the awards ceremony and she wasn't sure what to say, much less how to respond, when she learned Julius was tops in his class, which explained why they called him every other second in order to pin more medals on his little white uniform. The nuns patted him on the head every time he went for another medal. Susan thought one person perhaps, one who looked at her with hatred, could be Lange's mother. Then she wished Aunt Susana was at her side to get her through this difficult moment, but she was alone and everyone there knew she was Julius' mother and they smiled at her, expecting to see in her a proud woman. And, naturally, there had to be someone who thought, it was even whispered in a low voice, she didn't deserve a son like Julius. She was capricious and had married twice, the second time to a Don Juan who, as likely as not, cheated on her. But the truth is that many who were there would have loved to have been Juan Lucas' wife. Susan looked around her and took in the whole scene. It was Julius' awards ceremony, complete with well-dressed mothers and fathers who suffered from the December heat. She was relieved when she remembered Juan Lucas wasn't there beside her; she would never have been able to love such a man: the one who knew the exact day and hour of an awards ceremony or goes to such events and gives up his siesta in the afternoon or the lazy moments of afternoon cognacs at the Golf Club just to hear a child play Chopin's prelude on the piano. A man isn't a man if he knows who Carrottop is and worries that she's pinching his son. Susan, lovely, thought deeply about those things and she was better than the rest because she really spoke Spanish and just added words in English. She thought a lot about those things during the few moments they were not hanging another medal around his neck, while Julius pointed out to her the boy who didn't have a mother but who lived with his grandmother in a filthy house. She thought it must have been Cano, the one about whom he had talked so much. "Look what you missed out on, Juan Lucas," she mused ironically and nodded yes with her head to Julius every time he pointed out his friends or enemies. She couldn't wait to get back to the mansion to drink a cold Coke, which was the only way to combat the afternoon nightmare without a nap or lazy conversation at the edge of the pool at the Golf Club. At last the piano professor—nun stood up and started calling forward her students. She led them to the piano and stood over them as they played marvelously well and with so much feeling but, according to Susan, sounding horrible. One by one these bright Immaculate Heart students paraded by, one by one they made mistakes, and one by one they were applauded which saved them when they got bogged down halfway through the piece and looked at Mary Agnes who was biting her rosary nervously. When Julius went up to play his prelude, the nun stopped him with her arm, turned him around toward the audience, and told him to stand there a moment for all to see that he was not only Number One but also a pianist. Then she led him over to the piano and motioned to begin. But Julius could not move. He looked at her as if something were missing which prevented him from beginning his song. "Go ahead, get started," the nun seemed to be saying to him, and he began but immediately got hung up as soon as he noticed that the piano wasn't the same one as always. Terrified, he looked at the nun. The fragrance! The fragrance was missing! He felt lost and the people behind him began to murmur. The fragrance was missing, this wasn't the usual piano, and she wasn't seated next to him either. He remembered the song in the music book but he could not continue; everything else had disappeared from his memory. Nevertheless, he began to play and made terrible mistakes . . . but it was no big deal, Susan didn't suffer, it was all due to his excessive feeling.

Two weeks later they abandoned the mansion and went to live at the Country Club until the new mansion was ready. Juan Lucas pointed out to Susan the advantages of living at the hotel: she wouldn't have to worry about a thing, she'd have dozens of servants at her beck and call, and she could forget about domestic chores for a while. In that way she could dedicate all her time to the selection and acquisition of the furniture that was still lacking (the major part of it was coming from Europe) and to everything that was going to be necessary to begin living next fall in the new mansion; hence the four of them were going to move to the hotel. Carlos was the only servant who would go with them so they wouldn't be without a chauffeur. The rest of them could take a few months of vacation time and Jungle Woman could get lost. Susan almost fainted when Juan Lucas told her about Nilda, thinking it was going to be impossible to get her to quit. She had been a part of the kitchen crew for centuries, always carrying that meat cleaver around, and she couldn't figure out how to fire her. She even felt sorry for her. Someone else came to mind and she wanted to explain to Juan Lucas that Zoilón was an unemployed cook who was dying of starvation at the racetrack, but he wouldn't hear of it. She also remembered what the parish priest would tell them about servants when she attended those boring meetings: they're human beings and they must be treated accordingly. She had been reminded that Juan Lucas was in the middle of a golf tournament, surrounded by Argentines married to Miss Something-or-Other and North Americans who had played in Calcutta and London . . . besides, he had promised to take care of the matter himself.

And one afternoon Nilda cried as she hugged all the Cholos who worked at the mansion, speaking in a formal tone to them and about things concerning the way poor people must act on this earth. She maintained her dignity by making believe that she wouldn't be cooking in the new house because the food would be sent daily from the Hotel Bolívar and that's why, Señora, you understand, she has to leave, she'd find a way somehow, money won't be a problem, and to find work with a three-year-old child, the Señora will give her some names for possible contacts, and if she does find work then she'll have to adapt to strangers, that's the least of my worries, what if they don't like her son, Señora? it's just a question of being friendly and not mentioning that the kid is sick, I'm telling you we won't be lacking for money, and then comes humiliation because she'll come back to visit, whenever you want, woman, because in this house we're friends, that's the way it is here, woman, all these years . . . Her friends also pretend they'll never need to cook at the new house. They share her pain, hug her, offer help, like calling a taxi and taking her suitcases to the curb, and calling Julius to come outside and say good-bye to Nilda.

It was sunny outside as they waited for the taxi on the sidewalk in front of the mansion. Nilda wasn't crying anymore but she was whimpering. Once again Julius participated in a conversation among servants in which they spoke formally and said strange things to each other, a mixture of Cantinflas and Lope de Vega, their imitation of the Señores is lousy and grotesque for its ridiculous seriousness, absurd philosophy, false actions, but terribly sincere in their desire to be someone better than just a name that waits on tables and cleans houses. Nilda was leaving, just like that, flushed and whimpering. The sun reflected off her gold teeth and you could see the tooth decay and knew her kid was horrible, always bawling, and she was always resentful because they despised her food, always reading sensationalist newspapers with the meat cleaver next to her, and one who had exhausted her stories about naked savages and incorporated stories from the newspapers into her childhood in Tambopata and told them as if they had happened to her; and she knew all about poor people's rights and a man whom she beat, and there in the mansion, in the kitchen, she wasn't as discreet or as bowlegged or ugly as she was right now as she stood on the sidewalk waiting for her *tasi* and preparing what she'll say when she opens the taxi door, because she'll feel important leaving in a *tasi* and associate all this, as only she knows how, with the rights of poor people, but she'll leave anyway, appearing to believe herself and, not like Vilma a long time ago, crying her heart out and pretty; but, yes, also like Vilma, for those horrible, gaudy trunks are just like her and, moreover, she smeared lipstick all over her lips as she got ready and what was left she rubbed on her cheeks; amid sobbing and gold teeth to top it off, she gives Julius a kiss and he smells her perfume which is like the Cholas when they get all spruced up. Then he hears the painful whimpering of servants who love you.

THE COUNTRY CLUB

I

"THAT WAS THE longest summer in my whole life," Julius might have said if someone would have asked him about the months he spent at the Country Club. And it was also sad without Nilda, forever. Celso and Daniel weren't around either, and he missed their complicated stories concerning their new house, that is, their house in that slum area where if you don't build on your lot, they'll take over, as opposed to what Juan Lucas owns: when he doesn't build, the land appreciates in value. And Julius was without Arminda, who came around once a week, now old and, frankly, ugly. A mixture of saint and witch, she headed out on foot today from the bus stop toward the Country Club, bringing the Señor's washed and ironed silk shirts; she got close to the hotel situated among the white houses with big gardens, houses that she can't see and from which she isn't seen, God only knows where she's coming from; besides, she's that woman in black who walks through San Isidro because perhaps the color matches her life or because her daughter never came back. Hers is a weeping, moaning face, along with those long locks of black hair, damp from continuous sweat, dripping down both sides of her face. She's unmistakable even from several blocks away, which is when Carlos sees her and realizes the Doña, or that's what he calls her, is arriving. Arminda has grown old with that family, never asks for anything, has been mute for several years, loves them as she irons their clothes or sits in silence on a bench in the kitchen, sometimes seeing the Señor, never judging the Señora, kids will be kids, Julius was the nicest of the lot, and someday she's going to die but God, in all his mercy, will protect her. Carlos sees her coming and identifies her from a ways off. He normally spends hours waiting at the hotel door, impeccably dressed in his summer uniform and cap, seated at the driver's seat of the Mercedes, next to the Jaguar that he also cleaned up in the morn-

178

ing, reading all the newspapers while he waits for the Señora, elegantly dressed and always very nice in every way, at least according to him, as she comes out begging him to take her to a street that doesn't exist or that exists but has the same name in Barrios Altos, Magdalena, and San Isidro. He turns off the motor, asks the Señora for the piece of paper with the address that, of course, doesn't indicate the neighborhood. He looks at it flippantly and returns it to her, telling her with his eyes he's smiling. But his moustache—two thin idiotic pencil lines that barely move— shows contempt. Susan, lovely, who has opened the car window an inch or so because she's suffocating from the heat even though the wind might mess up her hair, retrieves the piece of paper dying from embarrassment but smelling great. There's a slight moment when her voice, the look about her, the marvelous lock of hair that like the day's activities doesn't take long to come tumbling down, indicate to him the nice, rich Señora, rich and nice in every possible way, according to him, wants to find that unknown street and he must take her there. And quickly too. Carlos understands perfectly, he is the family chauffeur, better paid than the others but not their servant, and since the Señora is a woman in every sense of the word and knows how to ask him (that's the way he tells it to other drivers), and since he's from the mountains and only has one family in-law who is a Mestizo and whom he doesn't visit, he asks the Señora with a face, it's the moustache frankly, that indicates he's confident of solving the problem: "Señora, whose house is it?" And when she tells him she's going to pick up an antique, it must be the Barrios Altos neighborhood, Señora, and when she tells him it's a woman who makes the best curtains around, it could be Magdalena, Señora, because when she says it's a friend or an embassy, that has to be San Isidro, Señora. Then she shows admiration for the driver and discovers that his face is as dark as his hair. He sticks the key into the ignition again and starts the motor as he puts forth a face like Your chauffeur, Madam, I'm almost your darky driver and, as they pull away, he winks with a testy eye at the other drivers, that is, he winks at several other moustaches and caps waxing cars during the morning trying to earn more but work less as they all wait for their Señoras, the old man, or a client when they're working as hotel taxi drivers. They're all avid newspaper readers, right there in front of the Country Club, like Carlos, her darky.

BOBBY HAD BEEN given permission to drive the station wagon by himself. He would go looking for Peggy every day. Also, he loaded it up with friends from Markham, Saint Mary's, and San Isidro and dozens of them got together with girls from Villa María, San Silvestre, Sophianum, or Chalet. They would take off carefree and happy towards Ancón where many of their parents had houses or apartments, or wherever there's a party like tonight at the Casino or at Bunny Marticorena's house (she's Aranzazu's daughter and her mother was Juan Lucas' lover and had attended the bullfights) or at Chubby Lamadrid's house. He is Grimanesita Torres Humbolt's son. She seems older now as time passes. Ancón is really wild. Bobby spent all of his time there that summer. At first he would return to Lima at all hours of the night, but ever since Peggy was invited to stay for a while at a friend's house, he only came to see them at the Country Club when he was low on money.

The other who was festive that summer was Juan Lucas. Perhaps he looked somewhat ridiculous wearing the little checkered cap that gave him the look of a pimp when he drove the Jaguar to the Golf Club, but the truth was that Susan wanted to remarry him every time she looked at him sitting at the wheel with his little cap on and watching her approach, Hurry up, honey, they're waiting for us, looking at her through his dark glasses, the color of which was a perfect match for his tanned face, covering a few wrinkles when he smiled, those typical wrinkles of the Duke of Windsor. The guy was going on fifty although he looked as young as ever with a face that could defy death, where a heart attack had no place and where crab, *frutta di mare*, was the typical restaurant fare and the bill could have easily been your salary but never appears on those posters warning you about cancer.

No one was happier than Juan Lucas, but he was always happy. He was always about to go to the golf course or to one of his ranches because he liked to take care of his show horses or his polo ponies himself, but only as a hobby, mind you. Or he'd be off to a cocktail party because he had just gotten first, second, or third in an international golf tournament, and this afternoon there was a big good-bye cocktail for the Argentines and Chileans with their wives who are descendants of some president or who are very rich and very beautiful, or who recently joined the high social circles because they had just triumphed in some beauty contest in Palm Beach, Miami, or Long Beach. The fact of the matter is that either life begins at forty or an overabundance of opportunities in life turns to overindulgence and now pleasures were fewer in his easy-going life or, simply because he was a bastard, Juan Lucas had discovered a new game or, perhaps, rediscovered a game that he had almost forgotten: it's been centuries since he's done any traveling and now, living in the hotel, he wanted to feel once again like the perpetual traveler. His pleasure in coming and going was something to see: he continually tipped the bellboys dressed in green who followed him around waiting for his instructions and ready to take out his suitcases. And he really got into the suitcase bit. He enjoyed keeping a half-packed suitcase on his bed at the hotel. He left them there all the time, waiting in repose. He would empty them and send them out to be cleaned. He never wanted to stop being in transit. He reveled in leaving the hotel surrounded by dumb, uniformed bellboys, who would set his pig-leather suitcases, like Rolls Royce seat covers, on the curb momentarily, waiting for his command to load them into the car: this one goes next to that one, don't scrape the edges. Of course, sonny, they go in the trunk of that Mercedes. Or that Jaguar. First, he was satisfied that he had forgotten some things in his apartment in Los Cóndores which gave him the pretext to come and go with his suitcases. In fact, he would leave things there because he had nothing else to take to the hotel. Next he would suddenly decide to spend a weekend in Los Cóndores with Susan but not the boys. Once again he would pack the suitcases, make calls from his room, and invite buddies to go to his apartment (for instance, Luis Martín Romero one day and Lastarria the next because they're going to make some investments together and Ol' Big Chest is going to have to do some work). Then he would leave in festive fashion, tipping the bellboys who thought he was great. On other days he would have to travel to one of his ranches and, amid a big hubbub, he'd open his suitcases on the bed and begin filling them with silk shirts for whatever occasion, along with his riding poncho, the same one he's wearing in the picture at the ranch house in Chiclayo and also in the one taken at Huacho. He never forgot to take his suede we're-going-buffalo-hunting coat and, of course, his leather Buffalo Bill hat. Only Lastarria would have thought of purchasing this outfit in New York, not him, no, never. He rode horseback in perfect fashion among the cotton fields on one of his ranches, silver spurs, suede coat, and Susan's favorite horse, Azabache. She watched him come and go around the ranch house, thinking heaven knows why, perhaps because the coffee at breakfast was a little strong, that if someday she got sick or old, she would sneak away on a boat disappearing somewhere into the orient, so that during your life, darling, everything will always be perfect, like now as you ride, not because you run the ranch, that's for the others, but only because you like to ride, darling, and your coat, the hotel, Azabache, the pig-leather suitcases, golf, and all that we have, is coherently delightful, darling. You are coherently a millionaire, not me, darling, not me, I only think about Nilda. Come back Juan, come back, darling, some peasants are going by: Señorita, Señorita, Señorita, Señorita, peasants invading lands in Cerro de Pasco, a police detachment. Come back, ah, here you come, talking for two minutes without stopping: Yes, darling, yes, darling, *and I will be coherent once more,* even though the other day Polo Rivadeneyra's wife, Miss Argentina, was dying to have you at the Golf Club while her husband, the champion from Buenos Aires, played a round. She didn't stop looking at you, they say you are a one-woman man, darling, we're so happy, I'll play your game with you and I'll be at your side at the Golf Club . . . where, of course, Juan Lucas also had a pigskin locker bag and a beautiful set of golf clubs with a pigskin golf bag. He changed clothes a thousand times a day; in fact, his day was broken up into moments when he had to dress differently according to different areas and diverse environments in the immense hotel: sporting—hair slightly disarranged after playing golf in the afternoon, when Julius entered the bar to eat dinner; princely—when he went downstairs alone with Susan, the boy can eat in his room, toward the Aquarium, greeting men who were red due to the subdued lighting and sat like corpses in front of a plate of asparagus or some ridiculous diet because they are dying from their delicate, sophisticated aristocratic decline in life; or impeccably dressed in a white cotton suit—when he approached the small table in front of the windows, where Susan was drinking tea with an ugly large-nosed friend, the one who has the most gorgeous dalmatians in the world and lives in a house that would be suitable for a school, one of the newest houses that hangs over the ocean in the Barranco area. Or they were playing like they were drinking tea at five o'clock in the afternoon in front of the sun that was about to go down. Juan Lucas approached them and he was the king of this marvelous chess game, idea, or sham of a contest they played against life's passing, against everything that wasn't what they were. Juan Lucas approached, kissed Susan's forehead under her lock of hair, she was a queen sipping her tea, and said hello to his wife's ugliest friend. Well, when do we get to see those famous dogs, just to say something, for whenever there was a fly at the Country Club it invariably landed on her, she's a pawn who was happy one minute and sad the next because all her dogs, all the dogs she's had in her life didn't add up to a Juan Lucas, who also played around at her house in Barranco, the easy game of carpeted chess in which king, rooks, bishops, knights, and pawns intermingle out of necessity and pleasure, so that nothing stops, so that everything continues to be like Juan Lucas now, who, dressed all in white and having just said goodbye, lucidly crosses the reception area of the hotel, goes out to his

Mercedes, and heads in the direction of downtown Lima, the office, and the directors' meeting: checkmate.

Sometimes around that hour of the day, Bobby would turn up momentarily back in Lima with that eternal Mom-I-need-money look. Susan became worried because Bobby was spending more and more money every day; she, on the other hand, had never learned the value of money; in fact, everything just seemed to revolve around her and, now with Juan Lucas running things, go ahead, darling, ask for some money at the hotel office, tell them to give you what you need . . . and don't drive too fast on the highway, darling, I think what's-her-name's son was drunk . . . Mom, he just got banged up pretty bad, bye, Mom . . . And Bobby disappeared, taking off toward the hotel office and then back to Ancón. Every day he's more tanned and good-looking. "Susan, my dalmatians . . . Susan." "Excuse me, darling, I was thinking about Julius. It seems like years since he's eaten dinner with us. He detests the Golf Club . . . spends all his time at the hotel in the swimming pool."

But in the young kids' pool, because at the Country Club there was a wading pool for the small kiddies and their nannies who didn't get into the pool but pulled them by their arms along the edge of the pool which the kids enjoyed immensely; in the meantime, at the grown-ups' pool, their mothers—young women working on getting a tan—await the arrival of their husbands who leave the office at one o'clock in order to meet their wives and swim with them. That one wasn't Julius' pool either. His pool is the one in between, the one in which a gringo is going for his thirtieth high dive this afternoon; climbing up the side of the pool, he sticks a finger in his ear almost to his eardrum in order to get the water out and, amazingly without ever slipping, gets up on the diving board again and runs forward, completing dive number thirty-one of the afternoon, right in front of the skeptical and hateful eye of the guys from the nearby Marconi neighborhood who have decided to send their girlfriends home this afternoon because they're going to wait for the gringo at the gate: the other day he winked at Elena, Pedro's girlfriend, and Enrique is going to beat the hell out of him. The rest of us are going along because we're from the same neighborhood and just in case . . . Have a smoke, guys, smoke another one and let's wait, you guys, and you, just fly, man, you asshole, the dive you're gonna take outside will be your last. Go ahead, have a smoke, guys, smoke up, put away the strong ones because here comes Fatso Busto who smokes Virginias and if he hangs around too long just kiss your girls, guys, Fatso gets embarrassed easily and will leave. We never go swimming because we're not little twerps like them. When we're eighteen and we look like we're twenty-one, and smoking, too, we'll swim in the pool for members. But the girls swim, they're something else in those bathing suits: Hey, man, your girlfriend is really good-looking. Back off Enrique, back off. They're only women, Manolo, you gotta kiss 'em all the time so they don't lose their tempers. Back off, Juan, back off, wimp . . . Hey, Fatso, tell that Cholo to get the gringo out of the pool, tell him now, Fatso, the girls can't swim when he's there; if not we'll remove him . . . "Leave the poor guy alone, we can swim on the other side." She's going to make Pepe jealous, another chubby kid, me too, go on, I'll get jealous too, tell the Cholo . . . The gringo got out of the pool to rest a while and no one said a word to him. The girls dove into the pool, taking advantage of his absence. Hey, they're nice and firm, no bikinis though, and look over there man, that *flight hostess* is just about naked, they say she goes to bed with everybody. Which one? Anyone dare to give her a try? When our little women leave, the gringo is going to get it. Don't forget, smoke up, guys, smoke another one. Let's see, Fatso, pass 'em around, and look at that beauty, man! Which one? Which one? Over there, the one with that little brat . . .

It was Susan, lovely, and she wasn't with her friend who owns the dalmatians in Barranco. She had come to the pool to visit with Julius and to find out what was going on in his life. She found him without much difficulty among the dozens of kids who swam there all day long. It was past five-thirty in the afternoon and the sun was going down. Julius, who stood next to her, was shivering like crazy and felt even colder every time a drop of water dripped down from his shoulder to his waist, or ran from his nose down to his belly button. Susan must have been thinking about children with pneumonia or about little Eskimos, or something like that, for at that moment she began to love him immensely, mainly because right then only Julius was on her mind, not Juan Lucas, nor Bobby, nor anyone else. She decided, hence, to participate in her son's semiaquatic life, just for a little while anyway, because the pool closes at six o'clock and it was almost time to go to the dressing rooms to get changed. But there was still a while left and what if she offered him a sandwich in the bar, next to the members' kidney-shaped pool? Julius accepted immediately, the poor kid was always hungry because he usually ate alone when Juan Lucas would decide to go down to the bar or when Susan remembered that he should eat something and would ring the bell to order food for him up to the suite—ah, yes, that French word that meant sadness for Julius because it not only meant bedroom but also a living room for receiving guests who never came unless, that is, it was Arminda bringing the shirts. They went to the bar and Susan recognized him: it was Mouse Siles. What a nightmare! He had asked her to marry him when she was about to marry Santiago, he asked her again when she was widowed, and then a third time just a few months before marrying Juan Lucas. Even now he still tries to dance with her every time he sees her at some party. But it was the same story with every woman in Lima: no one took him seriously. Still, he was a lawyer, respected, a hard worker, and had saved his pennies like everyone else. Thanks to his money, he could take afternoons off and there he was, displaying a face like let's dance, drinking his orange juice, great vitamins for staying young. At forty-eight years of age, he looked quite stupid.

Mouse belonged to a social class that Juan Lucas knew existed but would never recognize. Mouse, with his white Panama shirt, gray slacks, and white and black loafers, was a mouse; nevertheless, he was always optimistic, that's for sure, well, he possessed a great capacity for optimism—it was almost like high-class amnesia—as he tried to forget the thousands of times a thousand women in Lima had told him to go to hell ever since he went to his first party thirty years ago, those times when he would invite everyone to smoke cigarettes and say hello to people he didn't even know. He hadn't changed a bit, and no sooner had Susan gone to the bar with Julius than he took a bow so low that he had to grab the bar in order to keep from falling over and looking like the gringo who was about to initiate dive number forty-two just as a group of guys from the Marconi neighborhood stood up and, smoking, moved to the bar to examine that lady who must have been a real hunk of meat but who was still pretty good. What the hell was she doing talking to that mouse?

"This is Julius, my youngest son."

"Well, my distinguished little gentleman . . ."

Distinguished little gentleman! He was furious, and he noted that Mouse's hand was about to pat his soaking head. Foreseeing what was going to happen, Julius stuck a finger in his ear, jumped on one foot and shook his head in order to get the water out of his ear that had reached his brain from so much diving, splattering water on Mouse's Panama shirt. At that instant, Mouse pulled his hand away without having touched anything or anybody. The plate of sandwiches arrived and Julius tore into them. Susan smiled at the three waiters all of whom awaited her command. She ordered two sandwiches on two plates, please, from the nicest of the three, without letting Mouse place an order using that same intonation he had learned during his first year of law school which was about when he began to think about dancing with someone. The whole Marconi gang was there, positioned perfectly with excellent vistas. They were without the girls, of course, but if they had been there, then the guys would only look out the corner of the eyes, smoking and watching the Señora's movements, who looked just as good up close as she did far away. Mouse ordered another orange drink for himself and two Cokes, or whatever you want, for his guests. Julius accepted the Coke and Susan, who noticed the sun was going down, ordered a brandy because the moment seemed like some earlier moment in her life, like just before leaving for the theater in London, for instance. Then Mouse almost screams out brandy for him, too, but they were already serving him his orange drink and he had no option but to accept the fact that he was quite inferior to Susan. "He's giving her booze," commented one of the neighborhood gang when he saw Susan with a glass of brandy. Another one was about to say maybe she's just like the *flight hostess* . . . but at that moment their girlfriends showed up. The guys acted indifferent, they took drags from their cigarettes and pretended they were up to something else, remembering just then the matter with the gringo as well: it won't be long before he goes to change, have a smoke, guys, take another drag. Mouse continued to think about finishing his orange drink quickly and having a brandy at this hour for the first time in his life, but at that moment Susan pushed the brandy away an inch or two and asked for a glass of water. He didn't know what to do, Susan hadn't even tried the brandy. The poor guy was so dumb he didn't realize that the darkening sky was just momentary, a cloud had blocked the sun for a few minutes, and now it was daytime again and the moment didn't seem like another in Susan's life, just before the opening of the theater in London, for instance. Hence, no brandy. Julius was downing the second sandwich and Susan thought that Aunt Susana would have told her children, *awful creatures,* not one more bite because when it's dinnertime you won't be hungry to even try your dinner. She looked at Julius imagining Aunt Susana, so horrible, and Mouse, so gray and drab, to the point that she almost felt like screaming at Julius to continue eating until he's stuffed. She couldn't stand it anymore: Mouse hadn't changed one iota since the days when he was the most perfect kid in Lima and the most irritating too; and now, twenty years later, he was as dim-witted as ever but at least he possessed something over the waiters, something, which was the only thing he had learned by dint of imitating playboys and interesting bachelors, by dint of signing checks that had the logo of Mouse's firm on them. He scribbled "Siles" with slanted letters.

"And your husband, Susan? . . . is he still a golf champion? I read somewhere in a newspaper that he started playing again . . ."

"He took third place. Julius, darling, eat my sandwich if you want."

"And are you going to be a future champion?"

Julius looked at him angrily with a huge bite of sandwich in his mouth and a piece of lettuce that was somewhere between entering his mouth and falling to the floor.

"Susan, do you remember that time in Ancón? . . . the Carnival party at Ana María's . . ."

"No . . . that must have been a thousand years ago, I imagine . . ."

"How can you forget the squirting . . . ?"

"You've got quite a memory . . ."

"Don't you remember . . . Alicita Dumont was engaged to Bingo León, later they had a fight and she met . . ."

"Julius, darling, get changed; you're shivering . . . I'll see you at the suite in a few minutes."

Julius took a last bite of Susan's sandwich, left the rest on the plate, and took off in the direction of the lockers. Mouse sensed that Susan was about to leave as well and he felt profound sorrow: now he would have to wait until the next time they ran into each other. Susan opened her purse and, of course, discovered she didn't have a dime to her name, while Mouse towered over her and said don't even think about paying, he was going to stay a few more minutes, and he would pay the bill. Susan didn't listen and asked for the tab so they could put it on her account. I'll take care of it, Mouse hastened to repeat but at that moment the Marconi girls passed by his right side in the direction of the women's lockers, the bikini-clad *flight hostess* passed on his left going to change also, and he didn't know where to look, for he was dying to meet the *flight hostess*, to get his wallet out to pay, and to wink at those young girls, but he didn't do anything, he just evinced a stupid expression on his face, and when he took out his fat wallet Susan had not only written her name on the bill but she had remembered the suite number as well. Susan, lovely, left unaware of anything, thinking that those little rooms over there were for changing and that Julius hadn't told her anything about how he spent his days at the swimming pool. And, now, when Juan Lucas returns, everything will be different, he'll probably have to change in a hurry in order to leave quickly for someplace he liked and she would discover; she was enchanted by it all.

The Marconi guys had ordered beer and seemed to growl at him. Mouse was still bewildered: he hadn't managed to get a good look at the girls in their bathing suits and, by trying to look at them, he missed the *flight hostess,* and by trying to look at her, this is the bad part, he missed paying Susan's bill. What will she think? He just stood there, poor Mouse, looking and feeling gray, reliving his fiasco, one more day in his life in which he'd go to the Club in the evening, relate his adventures, well, they're really not adventures like the time he was a law student and he fought with bullies and slept with beauties, now they were just stories about what he would like to do, what he yearned for deep down inside, always smiling. They listened to him because he was a forthright lawyer, but dumb, and an accommodating friend, reasons for which people would greet him, listen to his stories about the things he was going to do but never about what he had done, those stories he would narrate to himself in the dark recesses of his bedroom as he would lay his head down on his pillow. Then and there they became stories about things he had never done, the image of the glass of sherry/water/orange drink appeared and, with these, Susan scoffed at his third attempt to declare his love for her, or those moments when Alicia, Rosa María, and Mary Ann said "I don't want to dance," while they played *All day, all night Mary Ann,* and he would join in too. And Grimanesa, Elena, and Susan said "I don't want to dance," and then the image of the Marconi gang paying for their beers . . . Mouse yawned in his playboy pajamas and went to sleep depressed over everything that he hadn't done, which was just about nothing, in reality, like that same afternoon when Susan was impatient, wanting to leave, and he didn't pay her bill. He didn't even manage to see the *flight hostess* up close, nor get a glimpse of those young girls and, to top it off, those guys were looking at him insolently. Later the next day, he would get up half-smiling and partially suffering from loss of memory. He would eat breakfast on the run, and once again play the game of arriving at the office amid optimism and lots of work to accomplish, greeting the secretaries, asking them to make telephone calls which impressed them, telling them he's going to dictate a letter, smoking a cigarette. Then he began to believe once again in his power as an important lawyer, in his image as an interesting bachelor, a playboy, the future meeting with the *flight hostess,* an adventure at the Club, that's the way Mouse was.

SWIMMING AT THE pool every day made the summer go by quickly for Julius. A few weeks had already gone by and things were going well for him because he had made some friends. They ran all over the place together, sometimes on the lawns nearby which is where they would meet up with one of the Marconi guys kissing his girlfriend. Perplexed, they would return to the pool. The water was crystalline clear, like this glass of water, and they would dive in like Tarzans with knives, hurry, because the crocodile is getting closer, he was the fattest of them all until he got mad and they would even let him be a bad Tarzan, right down to the scream and all. Jane would be any one of the little girls swimming at the moment, always under the vigilance of nursemaids who would crochet sitting on green benches. The girls, looking like Cinthia at times, were nine, ten, and eleven years old and with whom they really didn't have anything in common, but Julius always looked at them out the corner of his eye which is why the crocodile would often grab him. But none of them talked to the girls, only the Marconi guys would look at them sometimes and calculate, who knows how, that sometime in the future, probably within two, three, or four summers, the girls would be theirs, or they might be for their eleven-year-old brothers who were diving stupidly. Now, as they were leaving, they said one of their little brothers needs to grow up, so they would make him fight with a street urchin outside who wanted to take care of the cars parked at the door and who had probably stolen a bicycle that belonged to Pedro's brother. The guys from the neighborhood smoked calculatedly and, between cigarettes, they talked about how many times the gringo had jumped from the highest diving board. I hope the next time he jumps he hits his head on the edge of the pool and kills himself. No matter, they were going to pulverize him as he leaves this afternoon. In the meantime, have a cig, guys, go ahead, as they watched their girls and don't forget to kiss them nicely, that's the most important thing to do.

On one of those afternoons after the sun had gone down, not momentarily because of some cloud, but had really gone down until the next day, perhaps because it was a Thursday, the day when Arminda usually brought the clean shirts, Julius decided to go back to the suite early. It must have been half past four when he went to change clothes. Also, there was the matter of tomorrow, which was his birthday, and he had spent the last three days looking at his mother from every possible angle in the mirrors—even at the reflection in the windows—searching for eye contact to determine if you remember, Mommy, it's almost my birthday. But Susan, lovely, who up until then hadn't managed to convince that person to sell her a small wicker table that had belonged to Bolívar, wasn't really obliged to remember that tomorrow she would have to say happy birthday to Julius, which would be accompanied by a leather-bound Encyclopedia Britannica, for instance. She could hardly remember that in the United States there was a blond kid, Santiago, who was just like her and who always asked for money whenever he wrote. They always began with references to maternal love and ended on financial matters, and love to Juan Lucas. But, for some unexplainable reason, it was Juan Lucas who had remembered Julius' birthday (yesterday, while he got a shave in the hotel barbershop, he grimaced and the barber apologized, thinking he had cut him), but he decided to keep his mouth shut. He wouldn't say anything like "And whose birthday is the day after tomorrow?" No, he wasn't like that, let's see if the kid grows up a bit more, maybe his voice will change once and for all and, besides, look at all the stupid things he does. What Julius didn't know was that Arminda wouldn't show up that afternoon and Susan was at the golf course with Juan Lucas. He didn't even know—well, was there a way of knowing?—that he was going to encounter his first great love in all its glory as he entered the hallway leading to the door of his suite.

They didn't see him, even though while they kissed each other they also watched for someone coming. They faced the imminent danger of going cross-eyed out of such efforts or even falling under some evil spell. Julius didn't know what to do: he had taken the first step backward out of fear and embarrassment, hiding behind the door at the end of the corridor. They were only thirty feet away and continued to kiss each other. Who would have thought right here? True, but perhaps Manolo and Cecilia believed this was the safest place to kiss, especially since a gardener had caught them smooching among the cypress trees that surrounded the swimming pool. Also, you'd think it was a whorehouse around there, all that kissing while at the same time the rest of the Marconi neighborhood was hiding behind the other cypress trees. Enrique was there too, always puffing on cigarettes and telling everyone that as he kisses a girl he exhales the smoke into her mouth and, oh yeah, they do the rest too. Bah!

Like the others, they make a dash toward the cypress trees, manage to get away, and hide from the waiters, the headwaiter, and that Señor who must be the hotel administrator. Then they go up some stairs they discovered one afternoon which took them down a long, dark, silent corridor where they thought, God only knows why, no one lived. And perhaps they had begun to lose their terrible but attractive fear of those initial days, the alluring panic provoked by the single idea of separating their quivering lips to find themselves in front of the administrator or some old pious millionaire who lived in the hotel and who wouldn't have understood what they were doing. They even thought they might get slapped if someone found them even though, at the age of fifteen, one is a man and smokes a lot, but when an administrator appears and one is kissing Cecilia in secret, one retreats, and not everything they say in the neighborhood is true: it only happens when we're all together. One thing for sure, they relished that first secret love, always hiding, and even if no one had followed them, even if no one had bothered them, they would have hidden themselves anyway in order to love each other even more, because it was fear that stimulated them to make promises and to say things that really weren't necessary but were so beautiful anyway. Marconi neighborhood, down below, among the cypresses, and us up here, alone, not having to fight with that gringo, amid the silence of this long corridor and with this marvelous fear at five o'clock in the afternoon . . . And there was Manolo kissing Cecilia who, rosy-cheeked, was hugging him. He counted how long their ardent kiss had lasted, then their lips disengaged so they could breathe, and he found himself drowning in Cecilia's moistened eyes that had opened wide with emotion and tears, like placid dark wells into which Manolo tried desperately to peer. He almost saw more but, clunk, he accidentally banged into her with another inexperienced kiss, their teeth had collided, the poor things, it even hurt them. They pulled apart and their eyes were still closed as they waited for a new, brief, cold feeling of disillusionment . . . But they still loved each other no matter what might have happened, and no sooner did they open their eyes than they saw the other in love once again, forgetting the sad reaction caused by the dental obstacle that had brought their love to a careening halt. They stared at each other frenetically and threw themselves at each other, not failing this time with just a kiss but enveloping each other desperately, eliminating their nervousness and the tension that had always been there but which insisted on accumulating in love affairs at fifteen years of age. Exhausted, they returned to reality without realizing how long they had been there. He looked toward the end of the corridor that led out to the cypresses and she toward the door. All of a sudden she jumped back and pushed him. Julius hid quickly but they had already seen him and he heard them say: "A little kid has been spying on us, Manolo." Julius was near the only door and they didn't know which way to run, but right then Manolo remembered that he was supposed to act like a macho and clout the kid. Just one problem: the kid wasn't the gringo and when Cecilia repeated that the kid was spying on them, he felt like they were the little kids and the little kid here was the grown-up. Then they heard someone whistling and a little brat with big ears came walking proudly down the hall, carrying his bathing suit and sporting an I-haven't-seen-anything expression on his face. But when he was about fifteen feet away everything went afoul because Julius couldn't find his key, even though he had stuck his hand into his pocket to pull it out and because Manolo, convinced there was no one around to punch out and the kid was a kid and not the administrator, went for Cecilia, kissing her again and proving to her that he hadn't ever been afraid. Cecilia, a little surprised and still not very stable after her first two weeks of wearing high heels, lost her balance from fright and Manolo fell back against the door that Julius couldn't open because he didn't have the key; he hadn't put it in his bathing suit. Now all three of them were terrified but Cecilia reacted quickly: she pulled out a package of Chesterfield cigarettes from her skirt pocket—a gift from Manolo—and told him to have a cigarette, honey, keep cool, and she won over Julius with a smile. "Hey, kid, do you live here?" Julius responded that he did and she got choked up with laughter. Manolo wanted to kill her because she had conquered her fear while he still fumbled with the package of cigarettes, unable to open them. His stupid hand just kept trembling! Julius started searching for his key once again and then found it where it had always been. Meanwhile Cecilia leaned against the wall next to the door of the suite and continued to laugh as she covered her mouth with one of her hands. Manolo and Julius just looked at her while she stood there coquettishly, about the same age as Cinthia, unable to stop laughing. She seemed exhausted from the exertion and looked like a schoolgirl, cute, with a turned-up nose, who had just played a trick on someone or won a volleyball game. Julius opened the door looking back at her and listening to Manolo's anger, who threatened to break up with her forever if she didn't stop laughing. A little uneasy, he closed the door behind him because he couldn't hear her laughter anymore, or maybe they did break up like he said they would . . . Fortunately, however, he saw them together at the swimming pool: she was laughing while he calmly lit a cigarette; at least that was the impression he gave.

II

THE DAY ARRIVED when Susan told everyone they would have paid vacation until the new mansion was ready. Imelda had finished her sewing classes and quit just like that. She had been so insensitive, so different from Nilda. The Señora informed everyone that they would get several months of paid vacation. Celso and Daniel were extremely happy because now they could begin to erect their house. Erect. That was the word they used and why bother with builders or architects? We'll do it ourselves. The dictionary must include a lot about the word erect: it's etimology and, of course, its Latin roots and all, but what the hell, they were actually going to create an erection themselves and they grinned showing all their teeth and you finally picked up on the associations with the word erect. For instance, there were big ones, that is, apartments, hotels, suites, and they continued to smile with pieces of bread stuck between their enormous teeth. And now a long paid vacation; hence, they were going to erect. As they dipped bread into their coffee at the table in the pantry, the association of words continued to grow and the color of the coffee and milk slammed you directly against the brown wall of the mud hut and all that about building lost its edifying purpose and, as they dipped their bread, their faces no longer made you think that the dictionary lacked the sorrowful effort involved, the caricature of the word, the insignificance of the word . . . If you could have seen them building in the sense of bread crumbs stuck between their smiling teeth, sitting in front of their coffee cups, just a few moments before abandoning the old mansion in order to begin to . . . on their lot in the slum.

Hence, the day had arrived when the Señora informed them about several months of paid vacation. Arminda stopped ironing and came to the pantry to listen, but she didn't say anything. As the Señora, Susan wasn't obliged to ask her where she would go during her vacation. And the men didn't ask her either because they had already initiated their building plans, right there on the kitchen table, so they'd never know either. She was horrified when she realized she would be out on the street, but she remained silent and still didn't make a move when the idea came to her that her friend who lives in La Florida could put her up for a while. The Señora left and no one had asked her about her plans. Without saying a word, she returned to the ironing room, continued her daily task, and once again the coal-black locks fell over part of her face and, once again, she became that witch who irons Juan Lucas' shirts so well. And since Juan Lucas himself had fired Nilda, there wasn't anyone else in the kitchen with whom she could talk about the situation. Now there was no one to represent them, not even to ask where they thought they were going. Old Arminda was already back to creating miracles with the Señor's silk shirts, converted once again into all that she is, the ironing woman with the face hidden by long, black locks of hair, nothing more. If only Nilda had been there she would have asked Arminda who, sweating, would have mentioned the words La Florida and my friend, among a few other inaudible words, and Nilda would have understood. But Nilda's not here now, so she'll just continue working on the Señor's shirts, growing old, suffering from the heat in front of the ironing table, and it's only logical in those big houses with all those rooms: many times no one's aware if anything happens in the ironing room, for instance, now she's more than sixty years old and at times her chest hurts, here on the left. My God, no! My God, no! She desperately needed to rest in order to make it to La Florida tomorrow.

My God! The things people think about when they feel bad! But I was really afraid. I'm always afraid even though right now it doesn't hurt, for some days now it hasn't been bothering me, but that day, the fear, and the Señor's shirts that never seemed to end and Nilda wasn't there anymore, she's not here now, and I thought I was going to die on top of the ironing table without seeing her again. She never came back and that damn ice cream man, no, no, you can't even feel hatred when it hurts and now you're afraid. No feeling of hatred but Nilda wasn't there, her anger would have brought them back next to the same bed in which I was dying. They would have brought them back from the mountains for her but, no, not that either because Nilda isn't here to help us anymore, and if they're not going to cook in the new house, where are we going to eat? At the hotel too? And what if it happened before she left? It hurt so bad here on the left side of my chest. No one would know about my friend in La Florida. Without Nilda there to inquire about things, who would ever find out? They didn't ask me where I was going. To my friend's house in La Florida. Nilda would have seen to it that Celso, Daniel, Carlos, Anatolio, all of them, knew where I was going. Nilda would talk, serve the coffee, and everyone would cry; but Nilda wasn't there anymore and they hadn't asked me. And what if it happens in the new house? It's not even possible to imagine the side door through which the black procession would pass like in Bertha's case and the Señor Juan Lucas taking care of things with a check like with Nilda and me disappearing through the side door like Bertha, little Cinthia died, poor thing, who was going to bury the box with the comb, the brush, and the electric iron? My God, no! My God, please, no! Thanks to God it stopped hurting that day and she could finish the shirts and rest until the next day in order to go to La Florida. My God! The things people can dream up when they feel bad! . . . Even though, just think, perhaps one of these afternoons, one of these nights, the Señora doesn't have to go out and she doesn't need Carlos, perhaps little Julius is bored and it occurs to the Señora to take a ride, perhaps she sees that I'm tired, perhaps she realizes that the pile of clothes is enormous, perhaps she tells little Julius he can go with Carlos to take me to La Florida and they find out where I live.

"Today it's little Julius' birthday," Arminda told her friend Guadalupe who had been cooking all day long while she watched Arminda iron. Sometimes the two old women managed to communicate with each other; for instance, Guadalupe had already understood that Arminda would stay for just a few months and then she would return to work for the family that was moving to a new house. Guadalupe was half-deaf and she would leave the house early for mass and shop for food to feed her ungrateful sons who only came around to eat while their women live somewhere else. She was half-deaf and Arminda had been feeling a little better. She still tried to save her strength for ironing the Señor's shirts. It must have been five o'clock when she finished the last of the weekly batch and began to prepare the white package that she would take to the family for whom she worked. It must have been yesterday, Guadalupe seemed to understand, thinking it was Friday and yesterday was Thursday. "It's the boy's birth . . . ," Arminda had said to her friend, watching her cook. "You usually go on Thursdays," Guadalupe said about ten minutes later, thinking today was Friday which had ended the Novena. "It's little Julius' birthday," Arminda was going to say to her, but she saved her energy for the shirts and her friend began to stir something in the pot. The package was ready. A chicken ran toward the bedroom.

A few minutes later Arminda was climbing onto an old, rundown bus which initiated her stressful efforts to keep the package of shirts from getting crushed. As always, every last seat was taken. And her long black hair didn't generate any respect or compassion as the gray hairs do. Even though she was old and the left side of her chest hurt, no one would stand up and give his or her seat to her because she didn't have much gray hair. But today she had to watch her purse as well because it contained a small present she had bought yesterday for little Julius' birthday. My friend must be thinking that I forgot to take the shirts yesterday and she looked at me when I came back so fast, but I only went out to buy the gift for little Julius. On the curves, Arminda held on to the back of the seat in front of her, trying not to fall sideways. At those moments, she protected the package the best she could, but on the straightaways she used hands, arms, and her whole body and mind to shield the Señor's shirts. He had refused to have them washed at the hotel. He said only she knew how to wash them. She wasn't being arrogant but it was all she had left in life. Then she thought about death again, it could be due to the gases Nilda would have explained . . . The

bus would take her to the Ministry of Finance Building, where she
would take the Descalzos–San Isidro bus and then get off at the intersection of Javier Prado and Pershing. Then she would walk to the Country Club: that was the easy part. But right now this part of the trip on
the bus was very hard and poor Arminda had to fight to keep the shirts
from getting crushed and wrinkled. With each passing minute it got
harder and harder to protect her package and, moreover, people would
look at her as if to say why don't you take a taxi with such a big bundle.
Today she was going later than usual because she wanted to see little
Julius; that's why she had waited until late afternoon in order to arrive
after he would have finished swimming. Finally a man gave her his seat,
but it was time to get off and she could only thank him with a grimace
that was her way of smiling. Now she would give anything to be able to
sit down for a few minutes. Raising her package the best she could over
the heads of the passengers who were standing, she managed to get to
the back door and get off just as the bus started up again. The Ministry
building was over there in front of her. As usual, Arminda looked up at
the high windows. Nilda occasionally read in the newspapers that
people frequently would jump from them. All of a sudden she felt really
fatigued. She wanted to sit down, but she felt it was best to cross the
street and wait at the bus stop. The bus always took a long time to
come, but maybe today she'd be lucky and Look, here it comes, run,
get across the street because it's here, but as the full bus passed right on
by without stopping, some young boys cursed vociferously at it, the
driver, the passengers, and humanity in general, making her feel like she
wasn't going to be lucky today either. So, dressed in black with her coal-
black hair hanging down loosely, she just stood there and looked at the
city around her; she felt something was really wrong because there were
no benches anywhere and she was desperate to sit down. Huh! What a
city, eh? Full of enormous buildings, really high ones from which people
kill themselves, yellow ones, dirty ones, lower ones, more modern ones,
old houses. Then there's the cement streets like Abancay Avenue, so
wide, and the sidewalks, all cement too but no benches. Now she really
needed to sit down. A Ministry building that's so big and not one bench
in front. How her feet hurt! The dirt floor at my friend's house is so
humid that now my kidneys hurt too. Pure cement and no benches,
what a city, eh! How can it be, then? Everyone walks and they never
take rests? They need benches, and it won't be long before she plops
down on the ground. Maybe I could set the package down on the hood
of that parked car and lean a little bit against the fender. But here comes
another bus and she went over to see if it was going to stop. Nope.

Maybe she could sit down on the ground and place the package on her outstretched legs, but there's a tramp lying down on the ground over there and people were going by. And how she desperately wanted to sit down, but not one bench anywhere, those bus drivers are crazy, sometimes two buses come one on the heels of the other, one is full, doesn't stop, and the other is empty.

Arminda saw a little half-gray head with curly hair, a Mulatta. There was an empty seat next to her, and she let herself fall into it and closed her eyes for a few moments: her blood pressure must have gone down to zero. When she opened them, the money collector was at her side with a bus ticket and she took out the coins from the bottom of her purse that were wrapped in a handkerchief and handed them to him. She closed her eyes again, feeling to make sure the package sat safely protected on her lap, to confirm that she had been lucky, and to make sure the small package for little Julius was still in her purse. She began to feel a little better and thought she could even continue ironing, when she heard a little voice at her side which sounded like whistling. She opened her eyes again in order to look at the old dark lady next to her. It's true, she was singing, but that wasn't the strange part: she had a baby's face and she smiled simple-mindedly while she sang and her stomach was bulging as if she was pregnant. When she saw that Arminda was looking at her like someone who wakes up and finds Little Red Riding Hood at the foot of her bed, she told her that she was a bird. Then she smiled directly at her new little friend and began to break out laughing. Birdie was ecstatic and, in effect, she began to warble. Everyone on the bus looked at her and she couldn't have been any happier until she finally stood up for a few minutes and warbled at other passengers who were for the most part well-behaved little children. Thank God it occurred to her to look out the window from time to time. She would see a tree or a bush and, thank God, that's when she would forget about Arminda and, as if she were flying through the clouds, she would even forget to warble for a while. But as soon as the tree or its image disappeared from her mind she began to sing those lullabies that were probably improvised. She grabbed her stomach and, all of a sudden, the package of shirts too that Arminda was so jealously protecting. Who knows what Birdie was thinking? Whatever the case, so long as it didn't go any further than a few caresses, she wouldn't say anything because, as like as not, if she protested the woman might change into an eagle. Who knows? poor Arminda thought, and now and then she even grimaced at her which is the way she smiled, as if to say life wasn't as rosy as she thought, in fact it was more like the color of an ant rather than a tree, an angel, a nice child, or any of those words for that matter, or any of the words the little Mulatta was saying while she stroked the Señor's shirts with growing insistence. The bus stopped at a light and Birdie turned to look out the window. This time she spotted another one of her favorite people: a policeman. The Cholo was huge and not bad-looking either. Then she stood on the seat in order to get closer to the window. Birdie was tiny and she wanted to make sure the policeman heard her song very very clearly. All the passengers on the bus watched because what she was doing was and wasn't in defiance of authority, and the policeman didn't know what to do. He looked like he was going to get mad, then he seemed as if he were going to laugh, but about then the passengers began to make fun of him. In any event, he wouldn't do anything to show that he was giving in to offensive remarks from a crazy woman. Nevertheless, the problem of his authority was at stake and the traffic light remained red, the bus didn't move, and by then the passengers were laughing their heads off. Finally, the poor guy gave in and had to turn away, spotting a car that perhaps had crossed the intersection on a yellow light. Whatever was going to happen, the light turned yellow and, showing anger but not blowing his cool, he blew his whistle, the pistol was in its case, he carried a nightstick, and he turned away to issue a ticket. This act would restore his authority, but as luck would have it the light turned green, the bus started off and, like Superman, he had to jump out of the way in order to avoid being run down, all of which was going on while Birdie sang her heart out to her beloved right in his face: "Good-bye child, good-bye child," she said to him as they passed by, but a shrill whistle drowned out her song of love for her childhood.

Birdie was awarded several candies for her successful defiance of authority. She smilingly savored the sweet image of the policeman who played whistling games with her. Meanwhile she had already forgotten, at least momentarily, the other little child, the one Arminda was carrying on her white stomach. The unfortunate thing about it all was that the closer the bus got to San Isidro, the prettier the area became. There were more and more trees and the houses became nicer and nicer until they gradually turned into mansions and castles. By the time they reached Javier Prado, everything had turned into flowers, vines, and trees along the sides of the avenue and Birdie, of course, as if awakening on a branch, started warbling that tune of a bird announcing springtime. She climbed up so close to the window of the bus that Arminda got worried she might go flying out; hence, she began to feel a certain responsibility to watch over Birdie. The Mulatta didn't stop warbling and when the bus let on new passengers she welcomed them aboard with the goodwill of Saint Francis of Assisi, frightening them to death because after all we're in the middle of the twentieth century and wars of liberation. Suddenly the money collector approached and yelled loudly at her not to put her head out the window. He frightened her into sitting down and he closed the window amid threats. Birdie started to cry with laughter and at that point she remembered the other little boy and put her hands on the package of shirts once again. She went as far as wanting to kiss it and Arminda was afraid she would stain it. She was about to scold her when the bus stopped and a blond man got on who looked somewhat Hungarian; he was strong with regular hair, his mother was probably Peruvian, and he looked like something between a minor league soccer player and a car mechanic's apprentice. Whatever the case, you could tell he was low class, but that blondness . . . he was something between a European Cholo, a white person from the mountains, and a decent Cholo. For Birdie, however, he was the child Jesus or the President of the Nation because she pushed Arminda aside violently, made a beeline to him, and began to lavish him with her warbling and caresses. The poor guy remained standing in the middle of the bus, trying to convince everyone that he still wasn't aware of what was going on. He turned his back on Birdie and acted as if he didn't feel her touching his head, which was a lie because he became very nervous and the passengers started laughing again as they had with the policeman. This guy doesn't know how to respond because now Birdie was sticking her head between his stomach and the seat against which he was leaning and she would appear from down below with a little smile for her big friend, he was the prettiest guy ever, the one most deserving of her caresses. Even the bus driver was watching through his rearview mirror and couldn't stop laughing. He almost forgot to turn at the corner as he listened to Birdie's cradle songs. Suddenly Arminda went up to him and stared at him with sad eyes that hadn't laughed the whole way and she not only let him know this was her stop but also he was the captain of the ship, it was his job to maintain order among the passengers, Birdie represented human wretchedness, and God knows what else.

It was getting dark when Carlos, who was driving the Mercedes, turned off Javier Prado onto the street leading to the Country Club and saw her coming. "The Doña is arriving," he said to himself, stopping the car so she could get in and thus avoid walking the last little bit. Arminda approached the Mercedes silently and he opened the door for her without getting out as he would have done for the Señora, but he joked with her as he could have done with the Señora too. Arminda tried to close the door two times but then he had to help her, giving her first a sharp look that she didn't even try to interpret. He asked about her health and she murmured that she was a little better. A little better than what? Carlos didn't even suspect that the Doña had been thinking about death recently, the wake, the funeral and all of those things that left one with the taste of marble. Arminda let herself sink into the padded seats of the Mercedes, taking advantage of the short ride to the hotel to rest her closed eyes, perhaps in darkness she could manage to forget that the package next to her on the seat was the Señor's shirts and not the handsome little child belonging to Birdie who, in reality, was the only happy person in existence.

One thing for sure, the bellboys weren't happy. At least not now anyway. Carlos, with his little moustache and other dumb characteristics, stopped the car in front of the main entrance to the hotel and three of those guys in green swooped down politely on the door of the Mercedes, thinking it was the Señora with their monthly tips. His daily sarcastic verbal duel with the hotel personnel led to another scrabble. He had pulled a good one on all three of them: sitting at the wheel, he couldn't contain his laughter at seeing the bellboys receive the package of shirts and, confused, look at the poor woman they were helping to get out of the car.

The night before they had returned at all hours of the night and, typically, Julius had eaten dinner alone in the suite and waited a while longer until, finally, sleep overcame him without his Mommy ever knowing that tomorrow is my birthday. That's why he practically jumped out of his skin and then, upon realizing what was happening, became overjoyed because it was his Mommy who had gotten into his bed to wake him up. She almost crushed him in her robe and asphyxiated him with kisses while she talked about the presents she was going to buy him this very afternoon. She asked him for a list of things he wanted and she needed it urgently so she could shower him with gifts, not with just kisses and love. She wanted to make him happy, instantly. She wanted him to know that I love you. And she wanted to be remembered like that forever: supple, happy, disheveled, a mother, smothering him with maternal love, saturating him with it, inundating him so that the feeling would last a long time. It was similar to Santiago's situation; they would send him money to the United States and tell him it's got to last a while. Susan was stretched out on her stomach across the bed, her head hung off the other side and her blond hair fell down to the carpeting, while her right hand, in an awkward position—*Mommy is getting old,* darling—managed to press the bell next to the nightstand which alerted the servants to bring breakfast so that the three of us could adore each other around the table. Juan Lucas was already humming in masculine fashion as he shaved in the bathroom. Once again, she began to perceive the existence of this other great love for one more day, the love she pursued with her eyes hidden behind big dark glasses at endless golf courses throughout the whole world. Blood had rushed to her head and Julius helped her to sit up; flushed, she sat up next to him and then stretched out again beside him. Susan put her hands behind her head and stretched out, slinking her body and yawning for the last time of the morning, and then feigned falling asleep next to Julius, for over there, in the bathroom, Juan Lucas was not only humming but singing under the gushing water of the morning shower, and she was listening to him.

Forty-five minutes later, the loving breakfast for three of them at the little table had come to an end: half a grapefruit, the empty, coffee-stained cups, the leftover buttered toast which was a little greasy now, and the marmalade awaiting its fly, even though it was very unlikely there would ever be any flies around there since they are in a suite at the Country Club; it was also Juan Lucas dressed impeccably in white, announcing an important meeting with other fishing industry personnel and the Minister of Finance; it was also his announcement he would come by at midday to pick them up and take them to lunch at the Golf Club; it was also Susan yelling from the shower that she couldn't hear him; it was Julius thinking the list of presents would be forgotten because they were going to spend the afternoon at the Golf Club anyway; and it was Julius, submerged in a sofa wearing an expensive robe that was definitely too big for him, following Juan Lucas around with his eyes, watching him take his things from the top of the dresser, gold key chain, gold cigarette case, gold cigarette lighter, gold pens, billfold with initials set in gold, fat checkbook—in all, a pickpocket's golden dream. Unfortunately, he never went to places where they hung out or, logically, vice versa. "Do you have an elegant suit, young man?" Julius was about to respond but, as usual, Juan Lucas beat him to it: "Tonight, sir, we're taking you out to dinner to the Aquarium. Don't you want to celebrate your birthday?" Julius thought about some school friends and the ones at the pool, and also about his cousins, the Lastarrias, those shitheads. And he thought about Susan's fantasies, like when she imagined she had already drunk a Coke. It's better not to think about anything; moreover, Juan Lucas was already saying good-bye to them,

201

abandoning the opulent suite and leaving Susan and Julius like million-aires, with the whole summer morning in front of them or at least until he comes back at midday to take them to the Golf Club.

There everything was always the same—Juan Lucas played golf al-most all afternoon, Susan would play for a while and then follow him around the course with some friends, while Julius would spend the day in the pool. He didn't really talk to any of the other children because it had been a while since he had gone there and he didn't know anyone. Around six o'clock, Juan Lucas returned to change clothes, take a quick shower, and have a couple of hurried drinks in the bar because that evening they had to go to a cocktail party and later we have to take the kid out to eat. Susan, happy, sent a waiter to tell Julius to get ready and to meet them in the bar because she wanted to give him a surprise. "Hurry, darling, get in the car," she told him when he came out. "We have to go to a cocktail party but afterward we're going to take you to eat at the Aquarium." She was ecstatic to be able to give him the big surprise—we're going out to dinner—but that morning when she was in the shower, she didn't hear Juan Lucas tell him as he was leaving.

On the other hand, this time she did hear the three little knocks on the door of the suite. It had only been minutes since they had returned from the golf course and they were already drinking a glass of sherry before changing to go to the cocktail party. "Who could it be?" Susan thought. She was too tired to get up. Julius had gone downstairs for a while but he usually opens the door himself without knocking. More little knocks. Juan Lucas got up and opened the door so as to be done with it.

"Hello there, woman," he said, using the right tone for the occasion. "Have you come with my shirts? Come in, come in . . . Hey, Susan, take care of this."

Arminda took three timid steps and she was inside the suite; but she was out of place. Susan observed that it was starting to get sorrowfully dark, which could depress her, and she went over to close the drapes, trying to make the night come sooner and with it the cocktail party. Then she turned on a floor lamp in the corner and another on a table to the right of the sofa. It created a perfect environment for having a sherry, in fact the goblets sparkled with a light brown tinge on the silver serving tray. Arminda remained standing there, three steps inside, and suddenly looked dirty and then murmured something. But Juan Lucas wasn't around anymore and Susan wasn't quite tuned in, because for her everything functioned somewhere in the subconscious, just a little behind everything else until, that is, she took a sip of sherry, returned the goblet to the table and now, finally, she could deal with Arminda. There must be some money somewhere, someone has to get it, give it to her, pay her and then take the shirts. Yes, let's do it right now, Arminda, just a second. Darling, *can you give me some money, please?* Juan Lucas, who was sitting down again and pretending to be deeply engrossed in a *Time* magazine, pulled out his billfold and, without taking his eyes off the magazine, extended his arm and gave it to Susan. The article had become even more interesting. Susan reached for the billfold, opened it, and took out any bill while she approached Arminda who stood motionless, dutifully holding the package, decrepit-looking. "Is that enough?" she asked, apprehensive and lovely. Arminda imparted her grimace which was her way of smiling and told the Señora that she didn't have change for that kind of money. She was going to say that they could pay her next week, but Susan, who still remembered her poor people at the racetrack and who would send them things they needed, couldn't have shown more kindness: her lovely Saxon composure was something to see as she received the package from Arminda, put it on a chair, gave her a large bill and told her to keep the change. Arminda was very embarrassed and her underarms smelled. The scene continued to the point that it looked like a repetition of the queen's trip to the colonies and there was nothing more to say, and the goblet of sherry, illuminated, waited. I have to get changed now for a cocktail party, but Arminda wanted to see little Julius and so she asked for him. "He must be at the swimming pool," Susan told her, thinking that Julius couldn't be in the pool because it had closed over an hour ago. She immediately went over to the goblet of sherry and took a sip: now let's see if she does something. No, she just stood there motionless in the middle of the suite. What were they going to do with her? Julius might take hours to come back. To talk or not to talk, Susan must have been thinking, because Arminda's presence grew ever larger, she didn't step forward, nor backward, nor start to leave, nor anything, and soon the sherry would be all gone. She neither sat down nor went to get changed, and Juan Lucas might ask her to fetch his glasses that he's never had, now that he's so interested in the *Time* article. All that was lacking was for him to have been reading the magazine upside down in order for the suite to explode, and considering what it cost to build and decorate it, just like in the great North American movies . . . but someone came to save them. There was a knock at the door. It had to be someone who was coming to save them; at least that's the way she felt when she lunged for the door and flew past Arminda who was looking without seeing and seeing without looking. She smiled at her but the lock of her hair had fallen down covering her mouth and Arminda didn't see it. She only saw that the Señora was in a hurry to open the door: it was the bellboy bringing the Señor's suitcases that he had cleaned and polished. He was loaded down with them, and wore a big smile hoping for an equally big tip. When Susan told him to enter, in fact, she was almost begging him to come in, the green uniform did so with pleasure, thinking that maybe the Señora was getting personal, but then he saw the other woman, completely out of place there and behind her, to top it off, the Señor was reading. Hence, he erased any crazy illusions from his mind and didn't even dare to show an expression as if to say "And where did she come from?" Moreover, she blocked his way and he had no choice but to drop his load right there and leave, leaving poor Arminda stranded there like an island, better yet, a big island, completely surrounded by a sea of suitcases. The bellboy disappeared and Susan went back to finish her sherry and ask herself what's going to happen now? She became terribly nervous watching Juan Lucas buried in his magazine without actually reading it. But that last little bit of sherry gave her the solution: lovely, she put the goblet down on the table, sat down on the sofa, and nervously displayed the best of her smiles. Arminda stepped back, answering her with a grimace that was her way of smiling, which returned the situation to square one and the scene started over again, only this time with a slight variation: Juan Lucas detected a voice that was saying something about Julius and a gift. Looking out the corner of his eye, he glimpsed Arminda, seeing her as some recently arrived traveler, but looking straight at her he saw a beggar who had won the lottery but who still hadn't found the time to buy a new dress, while at the same time was about to take a room in an expensive hotel accompanied by some incredible pigskin suitcases. Susan, on the other hand, continued to stare at Arminda and searched for another solution. Finally, she found it: light a cigarette. She picked up the package of cigarettes from the table in front of her, took one out, and lit it. She took a first drag, exhaled the smoke, looked at Arminda, and once again it was back to square one, but this time she anticipated another move and lunged for the service bell.

"I'm going to call someone to look for Julius," she said. "We have to get changed to go out."

It wasn't necessary because at that instant Julius opened the door, and as he entered the dimly lit suite he noticed that something was strange, like sad and absurd at the same time. "Hi, Arminda," he said, tripping over one of the suitcases. Juan Lucas strategically put down the magazine and stood up to say, "From time to time they write good stuff." Susan looked at him and actually believed it. Then she also stood up. They were about to leave the room when all of a sudden Arminda's personality seemed to change and she began to make her way forward amid the suitcases, telling Julius he was nine years old and this year he would be with the older students at Immaculate Heart. "I brought a little gift for the child," she announced, interrupting the Señores' exit. She opened her black purse and took out the little gift for Julius. Juan Lucas lit a cigarette, he'd do anything but remain standing there silently, so like a millionaire and quite uncomfortable, he prepared himself to observe the scene; the first drag on his cigarette convinced him that Arminda wasn't important and the second drag told him that Julius was a born imbecile. Susan, on the other hand, was very interested in it all and found herself transported once again back to the racetrack as she watched the package being opened with energetic yet false enthusiasm. What she wasn't sure about was whether she could maintain that enthusiasm because the truth was the tiny package was loosing the status of I've-brought-you-a-gift and was becoming what it really was: a gift from a poor woman to a rich kid soaked in sorrow . . .

. . . sorrow that you'll never forget, Julius. Because when one is like that . . . when on the day of your birthday or New Year's or Christmas or any other day; when it's important to love or to be loved; when on a day like today you are disheartened; when you come back from the Golf Club and you walk alone around the empty dark pool; when one's like that, when anticipated happiness turns to immense sorrow, worse yet, to a constantly threatening and indefinite, immense pain of a sorrow that has to come at any moment; when you've seen the pool devoid of people, devoid of girls who remind you of Cinthia, devoid of Bertha who combed her hair, devoid of Celso or Daniel who haven't come to see you all summer and who, by themselves, are building those houses that you can't even imagine, devoid of the young guy you caught kissing his girlfriend; when at last there's an afternoon, night almost, that the Marconi boys aren't going to beat up anybody, but they weren't there now; when in the bottom of the pool that made you so cold, you saw the rocks and Tarzan's knives down there, also looking sad, immobile under the crystalline blue sorrowful water; when the pool was devoid of the friends you made this summer . . . it was strange how the feeling of loneliness and the cold made you want to go to the bathroom and you felt your body, you felt yourself creating these strange moments, and you thought that in the suite the situation would be better but you stayed on, you remained there, and you could see off in the distance, on the counter in the bar, the sandwiches of another time, like this morning, when she came and gave you a few minutes of happiness that always threaten to turn to sorrow later on, at any time, at any time, Julius, and it can be right now. Now that it's your birthday Vilma appears seated on a bench and you look at her, but there's no one there, nothing, just the threat of sorrow that is your sadness, and you don't know why it doesn't become worse even though nothing happens, even though now it's Nilda who speaks loudly at the edge of the pool and the people look at her and it's horrible, embarrassing, embarrassing for you, when you feel more than the cold and the need to go to the bathroom is even greater. You spend some time with her until you remember that Arminda didn't come yesterday and she might come today because it's your birthday, and you see yourself climbing out of the carriage because Cinthia has come home from school and you continue being Julius, and you know your life is full of those moments, full of that threat of sorrow that is sadness that will always remind you: when the benches that surround the swimming pool turn into holes that swallow up the people and then turn green; when the bellboys surround Juan Lucas who's taking you to the Aquarium tonight; when the moment is definitely full of sorrow that you'll never forget, Julius, then you leave all the threats in the pool devoid of loved ones or interesting people and return to the suite, go in, say hello, and discover there something strange and sad. They've turned on the lights that throw off a low glow and who knows why they've placed Juan Lucas' suitcases around Arminda. How sad the suite is when you open it and see that Arminda's back. How strange everything seems as you go to the table with Arminda where they're standing impatiently, taking in the scene which shouldn't have been sad but occurred so you could hear what Nilda might have said: it's my wish, this is what I wanted to do, little one. She finishes opening the package for you and there was a moment in which we were all silent and felt a sense of black vertigo, the moment in which they thanked her so she would leave, that's what I wanted, Julius. Those are your words and no one will ever appreciate your meaning of those words in a suite at the Hotel Country Club on your birthday, and the lights turned low, as if pushed out by the dark sorrow that was building up in the corners and extended out toward you people, and it grew when you heard Susan's silk dress descend over her skin over there in the bathroom, while Arminda handed the gift to you, and you didn't know what to say because it was a pair of yellow and black checkered socks, which you'd never be able to use because they were so ugly; when she handed you the little bottle of blue water, which Arminda surely thought was cologne because of its color and bottle which was when that damn Juan

Lucas pronounced the cutting word from the bathroom: Isn't this a little too soon? and the letters on the bottle that you didn't want to understand, for you've done all right by yourself up to this point, the letters were words and they meant something to you, it's what I wanted to do, child, the words meant it's what I wanted to do, child, it's what I wanted to do, child, it's what I wanted to do, child, it's what I wanted to do, child, the label on the bottle said it's what I wanted to do, it's what I wanted to do, it's what I wanted to do, it's what I wanted to do, it's what I wanted to do, AFTERSHAVE LOTION, it's what I wanted to do, child, it's what I wanted to do, child . . . "She's several years too soon," Juan Lucas said. "*Poor thing,* perhaps Carlos could . . . ," Susan began to say, but it was better for her to go out and tell them herself: "Darling, we're not going to use the Mercedes . . . Arminda is probably tired, why don't you go with Carlos to take her home?"

CARLOS DIDN'T LIKE the idea very much but he gave in finally, only because it's the child's birthday . . . whereas Julius got into the car raring to go. He was eager to be with Arminda a little longer; maybe talking to her and Carlos would also help him forget about the scene with the gift. In any event, the best part was the drive: it would help him to kill time that he would have had to spend alone in the suite waiting for Susan and Juan Lucas to return from the cocktail party in order to take him out to dinner at the Aquarium. He was sitting in front, next to Carlos, paying serious attention to the route that they took from San Isidro to La Florida. Arminda sat in the back. She had been silent for several minutes, assaulted by her memories of Birdie. After they got onto Javier Prado Avenue, she began to remember Birdie's excitement and the melancholy created by all those trees and the two rows of bushes bordering the parkway that advanced like a long green strip, dividing the avenue. She looked at Julius for an instant and thought she could tell him the story, but it had been several minutes since anyone had said anything and several years since she had even told a story. It was better to remain silent and take advantage of the trip in order to rest in an automobile and not in an overpacked bus; it was better to close her eyes, not to imagine Birdie but to rest. She leaned her head back against the seat and tried to go to sleep. Carlos had turned on the radio without asking anyone because the one in the back was a Señora but not the Señora and, as for the child, Carlos couldn't give a damn what kind of music he liked. Julius didn't even realize that the radio was on and for a long while he observed how Lima changed as they drove from San Isidro to La Florida. The contrasts were less noticeable at night, but it was still possible to see the different areas of Lima that the Mercedes was traveling through: today's Lima, yesterday's Lima, the Lima that had disappeared, the Lima that should have disappeared, it was high time it disappeared, in sum: Lima. It doesn't matter whether it's day or night, the houses that were at first mansions or castles began to lose their large yards, and everything started to get smaller. Now there were fewer trees and the houses became less attractive, they were even ugly, because they had just left the we-have-the-prettiest-neighborhoods-in-the-world neighborhood, just ask any foreigner who has been in Lima. And then you begin to see more of those ugly square buildings that always seem to be lacking a coat of paint; those buildings with the perennial FOR RENT or APARTMENTS FOR SALE ads in the windows; buildings that seemed to say we-moved-from-a-large-old-colonial-adobe-house-in-Chorrillos-to-Lince; smaller buildings, apartment blocks with a store, bar, or small restaurant on the ground floor and free and easy girls living above them, or that's the impression one gets anyway; a converted, old colonial house, now a boardinghouse for a recently contracted Argentine soccer player who is a little fat now but who was good once, or for the radio soap opera actor of the same nationality who came to Peru to check things out and in order to feel nostalgia for Buenos Aires, even though at times the Peruvians remember their xenophobic laws and there's talk of the national artists and all that, and my house, your house, his house, no comment, for we're so used to seeing them and because they're there; another house like Villa Carmela, year 1925; then the tacky little abodes of downward mobile society; the Rospigliosi castle, a mixture of ugliness and patriotism: Long live Peru!; small houses owned by the seamstress or the professor; houses of the newly rich, a mixture of the Government Palace and Beverly Hills; boat-style houses with no style at all and the Chola who can't reach the peephole is afraid to open the door; tudor houses with native accents; stupidly designed pistachio cake houses, in front of which the owner happily gets into a five-year-old pink Cadillac; a building where an established Argentine actor lives, with an apartment *decorated with a feminine touch;* then a new building, nicely done, expensive single apartments on each floor, all for sale, which is now in style; a tall high-rise, our national pride, but I'd never live there because of the earth tremors in Lima! with a lot of offices for rent and, on the top floor, a penthouse where Juan Lucas' bachelor friend lives. Then they'd go through the center of the city, which is a real architectural potpourri, tremendous buildings, efficiently modern, that crush the old ones, even the ones with the famous colonial balconies. But now they're leaving that area and the Mercedes travels through another zone where the buildings had seemed as if for centuries they were about to fall down. They ended up in a strange place that looked like the moon: there were huge buildings, like pale mountains, then all of a sudden open areas with huts and chicken pens. There's a strange light creating an atmosphere that was like traveling across a dry lake in which the road becomes a *"path that time has erased,"* while the Mercedes suffers nostalgically for the big freeways. Arminda wakes up in the back and at first Julius is bewildered, he can't believe it, he can't imagine what they are. Of course! Huts! Of course! And the area became replete with do-it-yourselfers, even though occasionally a little house is repeated where perhaps a humble seamstress lives, and then, pam! the huts, so that you'll see one, Julius, look, it seems like they're on fire but they're cooking inside. Not too far away is where the school's physical education director may live and there are those buildings covered with dust, a military barracks, or an open field. Carlos feels like he's a little lost, even though his native instincts help him find his way. Who said he's afraid? Let's see, Señora, tell me where to go. Arminda is somewhat confused because she's in a car and not on the bus, so she doesn't know what to tell him. The Mercedes pushes on, lost, enabling Julius to see more of this strange area, which seems as remote as the moon from the Country Club.

The Mercedes was becoming covered with dust and it wouldn't be long before someone ripped off all the hubcaps and the chrome from the car, while Guadalupe stirred something in a pot that looked like a cauldron. She looked at Arminda, not understanding the two guests, especially the child. Julius remained standing near the door. A draft of cold air filtered through the cracks, chilling his back and making him sneeze, but he didn't dare move any closer. Also, this was the first time he had been in a house where, in the middle of the dining room in which no living room was to be seen, a chicken was looking at him distrustfully, nervous, under a dim light bulb that hung from a humid ceiling. Frankly the whole place was ready to short-circuit and cause a fire. Then the family would be out on the street. He didn't know what to look at, so he looked this way so as not to look that way and he felt like he was insulting Guadalupe, Arminda, and even Carlos. Why? Because the dirt floor is cold, the stove is made of bricks and, unlike the enormous glass cabinet in the dining room at the mansion, in this primitive cupboard there were three metal saltshakers turning green because they're not made of silver, a cracked cup, an orange, and three fly-ridden bananas. Besides, the four table chairs are all different and the stove, which was made of bricks, is really in the dining room and because it's an insult to look anywhere, over there, over here, and the chicken, yes, the chicken, and now her baby chicks. Julius takes a step and he would have stooped down to pet them, but the chicken and her babies bolted out of the room—another insult. He wanted to pet them and then smile at Guadalupe but he frightened the little animals. They cackled as well and, once again, he's insulted Guadalupe who doesn't understand and is deaf, and that's why he believes she hates him. To look at Carlos doesn't necessarily mean he's insulting him, but Carlos has forgotten about him. Carlos, self-assured, rubs his hands and smiles as if to say, "And that cup of tea, Señora?" Arminda asks them to sit down and she sets the boiling teapot next to them. She leaves it on the table and goes to get cups. She asks Guadalupe if she wants some and Julius thinks that Guadalupe completely despises him because she doesn't even answer. Arminda doesn't insist: My friend doesn't drink tea at night, Guadalupe is becoming more deaf every day.

"Let's see how good this tea is for our trip back," Carlos says, exhaling smoke while Arminda places the three large, chipped porcelain cups on the table, and Julius insults them again; he feels bad and he knows he's insulting her but he reacts cleverly and smiles happily although he's nervous. He lifts up the cup with both hands when she's about to serve, he just couldn't wait another second without any coffee or tea, his hands tremble but he manages to control them while she serves him. He places the cup on the table without spilling very much, and he lifts it up again, burns himself, and learns to endure, it tastes very good, but Carlos, experienced and confident, doesn't pay any attention to Julius when he looks at him, slurping and using bad manners, acting boisterous when he sees Arminda bring out three rolls and some butter. What bad manners the way he grabs that roll, but Julius wants to be able to drink his tea like that and just now, amid the silence of Arminda who is sitting down at last to drink her tea like a corpse, Carlos makes slurping sounds, lets the bread that he has dipped into the tea drip into the cup, bites off a huge piece and soaks his moustache, chews noisily. That's all you hear, slurping that sharply pierces the silence beneath the sickly light bulb and repeated over and over thanks to Carlos' voracious yet exuberant appetite, over and over, acquiring a rhythm and ending in a commentary, we're about to smile, I'm going to be Julius here, we're going to laugh, Guadalupe also, but Guadalupe looks at them indifferently, she must believe that she's continuing to stir something in the cauldron, peacefully, and perhaps for that reason the light bulb darkens each sound a second before the next one and the humidity of the decrepit place corrodes them. It's night in La Florida and Carlos' little tea-soaked moustache stopped exuding the carefree and happy attitude of before and acquired a seemingly sarcastic and depressed state, just at the moment when Julius looked to him for moral support, for right then something black hung down next to him on the right: it was Arminda's hair falling down both sides of her face when she lowered her head and pressed her lips to the cup without raising it up, Arminda's hair folding itself around the bread that she had forgotten to give him, "Eat, child," she told you, with a grimace that was her way of smiling. She insisted that it was for you and she was pushing it closer and closer to you with her hand when Carlos had already finished and was ready to go. Her hand kept pushing the little plate with the bread and butter closer and closer and, all of a sudden, you saw the huge dark purple fingernail and a little white dot. Keep eating child, she said, and you imagined those white gloves that Celso and Daniel wore when they served dinner in the mansion but they didn't help you get through this one: You vomited, Julius. You vomited right when Carlos wanted to leave, so he had to smoke another cigarette while Arminda ascertained that the tea didn't set well with you, did it? She cleaned your neck with a damp cloth and you didn't move, you only saw how Guadalupe took three steps toward you, looked at you closely, but kept her distance. She was deaf.

DOWN THE WAY from the slum area but still on the dirt road, Carlos saw a sign that read PRIVATE PROPERTY which was annoying because it would have been neat to drive in there with your chick. But this time you've got to continue straight ahead on the highway. On the roadside, the architect in vogue had put up a sign in huge black letters with his name on it, and that's how he got started. They were in Monterrico now, which is more like San Isidro than San Isidro itself. Later, they say, the family left their children in boarding schools and went to Europe. They wanted to return when it was all finished and not have to lift a finger. They gave the architect in vogue carte blanche and a large sum of money. Well, it's true, they did say they wanted lots of windows and, revising his functionalist ideas and the check they left him, he opted for a happy eclectic mixture: It's that glass house on the hill in Monterrico. What? You haven't seen it yet? But there were pictures in all the magazines!

The owners of the crystal house on the hill in Monterrico were decent people, and some say that Juan Lastarria screamed "I'm in!" when he received his invitation to the inaugural cocktail party. Whatever he might have said, he thought of Juan Lucas: they had been partners for some time now and more and more people were saying hello to him. And the twelve suits he had made for himself in London still fit well. But he always wanted to be more than just a Lastarria. At night, half-asleep and half-awake, he imagined some Italian count in Siena, for instance, who had lost his fortune and would secretly sell his title. The difficult part would be how to present the title in Lima. How do you do that? Juan Lucas was going to split his sides from laughing and in front of that secretary: After one more building purchase, I'll make her my mistress. But that's what he would think about when he was half-awake, between dream and reality, not now when he was wide awake getting into his Cadillac which was like a torpedo. The street leading to the crystal house was still a dirt road. "Damn, I screwed up," poor Lastarria said to himself, turning into the driveway in front of the illuminated house. There wasn't one single car there: he was the first one to arrive. "Juan Lastarria is a crass little fat guy who always arrives first and is the last to leave," someone had said once and he knew it. He turned the steering wheel hard and almost ran over an effeminate waiter, one who should be run down, one of those who hires out and becomes stylish at parties to the point that they get to know Lastarria and they greet him with something in between "Buenas noches, Señor. Good evening, Sir" and "You don't fool me," despite his torpedolike Cadillac.

Unfortunately, it was a torpedo only in the way it looked because now that he was driving slowly around Monterrico trying to kill time and to let someone else arrive first and become the target instead of him, he saw a car through his rearview mirror coming like crazy from behind, the nut was going to kill himself, he probably wanted to fly right over the top of him but that was obviously impossible and now, suddenly, there was this Cadillac in the way, then screeching brakes right in front of another car, most likely a sports car although one could hardly see anything through the dust and the glaring lights. This looked like a freeway scene with all those Pass me! Pass me! I'm letting you pass, damn it! And then a thousand obscene gestures and a lot of cussing. Lastarria decided not to get out for anything because his car was bigger and much more expensive. He decided to act as if he were in a meeting with millionaires who were negotiating monopolies: if they've got sixty, we've got a hundred. Someone was yelling "You bastard" with a strange accent and he jumped out of the car, almost on the run, got his shoes dirty, who knows why because he wasn't going to slug that huge blond who had hopped out of her MG sports car and who, with even a more strange accent, wearing pants, screamed at him: "Hey, man, move it!" Lastarria felt like he was returning to that time in life when he courted his wife with just one suit to his name, although the time was already here when she would get sick before any social engagement. He was returning to the Cadillac and, as he started to open the door, he wanted to be Juan Lucas and began to say Señori . . . "Are you gonna move it or not?" the tall blond shrieked, wearing pants, and he thought she might know judo like the ones in the North American spy movies, one never knows, so he hopped back in, sank into the red sofa of the Cadillac, started the motor, felt like it was a coal plane and wanted to intimidate the fearless Russian spy. But one of the fins or wings, who knows which one of the chrome pieces of the Cadillac, was scraping against the side of the hill and Lastarria, bullheaded, pressed the button to close the window in order not to listen to the ridiculous scraping sound. He moved forward rasping the car and the blond who was driving the MG with the top down heard the entire crunching sound while he started out again, thinking as she laughed to herself that all those going to the cocktail party would be like him and that she would never change her marvelous dirty pants.

All of the rooms opened out onto an enormous patio with a lagoon in the middle, and no one could figure out where the lights came from that illuminated it so marvelously well. The glass house was shaped like a U which enclosed the patio on three sides. One side was open and, in the distance, became a garden where one could see a swimming pool, also mysteriously lighted, and from there a thicket that extended along one side of the hill in the middle of which people said there was a lagoon with wild ducks. Some one hundred guests passed through the enormous open glass entryway that was the front door and shook hands with Ernesto Pedro de Altamira, who was suffering from a nervous prostration, looked pale but was very elegant, maybe a little like Dracula, and who read in German everything he could get his hands on. But he wasn't altogether incongruous with the ultramodern vestibule of his house whose very library was also made of glass. Many greeted his wife, Finita, calling her Countess which, in fact, everyone thought she was; whatever the case, many men bowed to kiss her hand, being diplomatic above all. The women, on the other hand, called her by her name and they would barely graze her cheek with their lips. Poor Finita was getting dizzy from everyone's heavenly perfumes in her new house that night, hoping they wouldn't destroy it, since it was made entirely of glass. She was panicked, and she had always been so sweet, but there were always jealous people in the world. Finita was admiring everyone who greeted her, but her arm was already tired: "Ernesto Pedro, Ernesto Pedro, how many more guests are coming?" she thought beseechingly, smiling, while another kissed her hand, but even if she would have screamed it out loud, Ernesto Pedro wouldn't have answered because he was a Germanophile in the worst sense of the word and he hadn't married for love but to have refined, beautiful children. Juan Lastarria arrived, for he had gone back to his castle to switch the Cadillac for his wife's Mercedes, and now he was arriving a second time in a different car, just in case someone besides the waiters might have seen him; probably not, though. He entered the mansion and kissed Finita's hand: Countess. He had practiced it and he didn't do it too badly, for they gave him a passing grade. Upon seeing him, Ernesto Pedro de Altamira felt the left side of his face grow tense. Now he really did look like Dracula, watching Lastarria join a group that was walking by the masturbatory looks of several waiters who were smiling before melting into subservience, without really knowing what they were looking at, except the one who had the face of a traitor. One hundred guests paraded by, including the architect and his wife, the diminished Susan. He beamed with pleasure when he heard them ask who the artist of the crystal house was. He counted the sheets of glass: it looked like he was going to run short of glass to build such a unique house. What was the College of Architecture? A pile of shit. What was it to be a professional? And those principles? His wife knew how to handle herself and hence he was ready to explain whatever they asked. The architect managed to join the group with Susan, lovely, and Juan Lucas, always in perfect shape. He greeted them radiantly and together they crossed the immense living room and went out through the gigantic, twentieth-century open glass door to the enchanting patio with the lagoon.

It was perfect outside. Men and women were served glasses of whiskey and appetizers from silver serving trays that always seemed to be there waiting. Everyone became deeply involved in conversation; but there was a large Swedish woman seated at the edge of the lagoon, wearing pants that were probably dirty. They couldn't explain very well who she was when everyone saw her and she didn't seem to know what the devil was going on around there either. Susana Lastarria would have said she was the governess, clearly, in that get-up . . . But Susana Lastarria hadn't come and the guests thought differently: because Ernesto Pedro de Altamira was very European and refined, or because his oldest son was studying in Europe, maybe the kid brought her with him for a vacation. That possibility went against everyone's morals, of course, but the Altamiras, you know, they're very cultured. Of course. In any case, the Swede didn't seem to pay any attention, smoking serenely and surrounded by Altamira's sons when others looked at her as if to say: "And where did you come from?" But she continued smoking, surrounded by Altamira's boys. One of them was also smoking, choking, laughing, and blowing smoke in her face, while the Swede protected herself by letting her blond hair fall over her face. She remained that way for a long time and no one seemed to catch on when she would part the locks of her hair and look over at Juan Lucas who hadn't seen her yet, but Lastarria had and he quickly turned his back to her, careful that his group didn't move toward the lagoon. Everyone was ebullient and their conversations were lost into the night, pulverized by the music that emerged from the stereo room that had already cost the jobs of two butlers due to a kick with the foot or a blow given with a broom in who knows what part of the basic system in which the famous musicians, so clearly could they be heard, seemed to live imprisoned and shrunken; one thing for sure, you're fired, etc., and Finita, so refined, took care of the rest while Ernesto Pedro brought out the stereo technician to fix it once again and install seven new speakers, even one in the Swede's bedroom, for instance. And the Swede, who had been a swimming champion and even looked like she had participated in decathlon competitions, was telling the Altamira boys why her breasts were so firm and her arms so perfect. She explained to them that rigorous exercise had formed each muscle perfectly. And a lot of swimming makes your breasts firm. The thirteen-year-old Altamira boy asked for a cigarette from the fourteen-year-old. Then he told the Swede that he'd like to feel her breasts. The stupid or maybe quite healthy woman, of course we'd call her a whore, no, the stupid woman unbuttoned her shirt that belonged to the older Altamira son, the one who had brought her from London and wasn't there because he went to a party at a cousin's house in Villa María, and don't even think of bringing the Swede, in Europe yes but in Lima no way; moreover, in Europe Swedes and Negroes are fine but not here: the other day they took her to an hacienda and her behavior was scandalous; neither Finita nor Hitler found out, of course, but it seems the stupid girl got bored and took off with José María, the Negro who fixes the tractors. Ever since then the Altamira boys have followed her around everywhere and now she's discussing sports, free love, prostitution, in Sweden they're socialists, and she bared them, clear as day, those marvelous breasts, and she's never used a bra. One of the guests alerted the others, saying the Nordic was ready for action and so the elegantly dressed men who had common interests, the prophesiers of your desire, grabbed glasses of whiskey from the trays and left to see what was going on, aroused, ready to buy, shameless, even to the point that the Swede was repulsed and she stopped talking about swimming and athletics. She turned around full circle at the edge of the lagoon, turning her back to them; however, she was great from that angle too. She didn't want to talk to that gang of cretins or with those women who were like parrots in mourning, so she started to play with the fish. The Swede was really stupid: she didn't understand that the Señoras were very elegant and wore makeup. Incredible, the only strange person there was her. How could she? What nerve! Come dressed like that to a cocktail party! Don't you see? The girl lives here in this house and she's just a girl. Well, even if she lives on the North Pole she's obliged to take off those filthy pants, and that shirt must smell to high heaven! . . . "A beautiful obligation," Juan Lucas exclaimed. Susan said something like "Ooooh, darling," and someone else became uneasy and embarrassed, but Juan Lucas' own laugh was contagious and forced them all to laugh. But it was Lastarria who wanted to splatter a star with his whiskey as he just about flung his glass into the clouds and exploded ipso facto into a belly laugh, just like everyone else there who, between laughs, would explain to others the golfer's brilliant joke which spread quickly. "You're terrible, Juan Lucas," someone said over there, while Lastarria went around ready to launch another round of laughs. The architect in vogue was caught between laughing and watching how Susan, lovely, had marched off to some mysterious place like Japan. The Swede turned around to see what was happening, for she didn't have a clue, and then she looked at Juan Lucas: it was the first time they had looked at each other, he out the corner of his eye while taking a sip of his whiskey. He set the glass down on a layer of air that immediately transformed itself into a serving tray as he riveted his eyes on her in that special way without anyone else noticing. Only Susan was watching him from a distance, as if understanding him. She observed him without looking at him among the people who came up to talk about anything and seconds later she turned to look toward the door of the living room: Ernesto Pedro de Altamira. He was feeling very very tense, and he barely touched the Prime Minister's arm with his three fingertips. "Be careful on the steps," he told him and they walked onto the patio. The Swede had no idea who he was.

But the Swede was an exception and so were the Altamira boys: they were at that age when the only important part of the newspaper was the movie page, that's all. Not the other guests; conversely, it was a sight to see how they approached him, some little by little as if they didn't want to, others the way Lastarria does as if they really want to, and there were others who didn't greet him at all, probably because of some aversion toward the Prime Minister. And he must have been aware of it because most of the time he was trembling slightly, nothing more or less than if he was dying of fright. The enchanted twentieth-century patio was constructed without corners, but he acted as if he were looking for one, one could almost say he was creating them himself, as if he were always looking for a corner in which to hide; moreover he took care, in fact meticulous care, of his hand because he would extend to you a kind of rag and before you felt any bones you felt nothing. Ernesto Pedro de Altamira protected his guest at important moments, helping him to avoid certain conversations with questions that got to be too long, or assaults by certain enthusiasts, or the faces of some who approached with an expression of you-know-who-you're-going-to-screw-with-your-new-law. Finita, extra fine, came over with a glass of grapefruit juice and put it in the Prime Minister's hand who felt elated and then saw Susan, lovely, and asked if he could please say hello to her: he adored her, he had been a schoolmate of her first husband, it's been years since he's seen her, he liked her a great deal, he had always, always liked her a great deal, he had to go over and say hello. "Susan, lovely, my lovely Susan, Susan, lovely," the Prime Minister was saying while he went over carrying his glass of grapefruit juice. The guests were becoming accustomed to his presence and, after all, his latest law wasn't really going to hurt anyone. They watched him cross the patio, Lastarria pumped up his chest with pride, and the architect in vogue would have liked to have designed a house for the Prime Minister for free.

"Here is the Prime Minister," Ernesto Pedro de Altamira said, adding tensely, "I didn't know he was one of your great admirers." "From way back, from way back," the Prime Minister repeated while Altamira excused himself, feeling a strained muscle in his shoulder that forced him to close his left eye. What Susan saw was a young man wearing an outdated suit, but who was still very elegant and was always talking politics. He had wanted to dance with me, she also saw Santiago, her boyfriend, dancing with me . . . "From way back, from way back," the Prime Minister kept repeating, and she saw a yellow glass on a white table and then the Minister in a bunch of photographs in all the newspapers, dressed elegantly this time but looking horrible in those deformed caricatures. Then she visualized him again talking about politics just before feeling his two cold hands, minus the bones, as he extended his arms to her saying: Susan, Susan. "Darling," she said, a little distracted, throwing her lock of hair back in order to return to the patio. Even Juan Lucas came into view nearby as he conversed with the Swede who had stood up and looked beautiful. "Darling," she repeated, making an effort: "And now what am I supposed to call you?" She kissed him affectionately on both cheeks, while he repeated "Dodó, call me Dodó, like always . . ." "Such an important man, darling . . ." "Dodó, Dodó, like always." The Prime Minister, clutching his grapefruit juice, wanted to move away a bit from the din of the other conversations. He took Susan by the arm and slowly led her over to a place in the garden where they could see the entire city of Lima, a galaxy of stars that fell to earth. He would never forget Lima but in an instant he was already talking politics. This time she feigned deep seriousness and listened to him: she loved him very much and at no time was she going to cry.

With one foot resting on the edge of the lagoon, Juan Lucas took another glass of whiskey and continued telling stories about the Peruvian jungle to the Swede. "Ah, that's something no one should miss," he told her while, who knows how, she forced one hand into the back pocket of those tight jeans and with the other hand received her fifth whiskey, bursting all of a sudden into a tremendous laugh and spilling half the glass: Juan Lucas had just shrunk her head with a secret jungle potion and he too laughed loudly when she extended her arm holding her little shrunken head by its hair, looking at it and then dangling it in the Altamira boys' faces. They didn't find anything funny about it at all and the poor kids came to realize that they wouldn't get anything from the Swede that night; hence they left for the pantry to hide from their parents and have a few whiskeys.

Some of the guests didn't like the fact that the Swede was whoring around in the middle of the cocktail party, but the majority of them had drank enough by then so that the incident didn't seem that important anymore, and it became less so as the night wore on. Only Lastarria kept bringing up the joke about Juan Lucas and the Swede. He wanted to go over to Juan Lucas and talk with him and the others for a while, but he was deathly afraid of another string of those rare cuss words, especially in the middle of the cocktail party. If that happens, make me disappear. The poor guy didn't really know what to do and Susan was nowhere to be found. On the other hand, he saw the architect in vogue everywhere: he was a young guy and his wife was young, elegant, and even pretty; moreover, she didn't seem to say stupid things when she talked to the other wives. Lastarria looked at him and debated between having him build a house for him or not even saying hello to him: look how he smiles, calculating, pleasant, see how he doesn't even have a stomach, me neither (and he sticks out his chest), in reality, he's husky and undoubtedly owns a surfboard . . . Lastarria changed positions, his whiskey too, and then spotted Finita over there at the back: he still hadn't talked to her. That's where he was going now, and between quick short steps and nodding to others, it probably wouldn't be long before he would trip and smash face down on the floor, but since he had recently become a partner with Juan Lucas, he didn't seem as ridiculous and he made it safe and sound. He stuck his whiskey into the middle of the circle, announcing his arrival and waiting for Finita to smile: "And where's Susana, Juan?" Finita asked, and he set off on an interminable story that everyone in the group listened to with great patience until, all of a sudden, a blast of hot air made him say: "Well, and you, Finita? I imagine everyone has congratulated you on this beautiful glass palace . . ." With the second hot blast Finita thought perhaps she should introduce them: "Juan," she said, "This is Lalo Bello, our great historian, the person who knows more about Peruvian history than anyone around." Lastarria switched the whiskey to the other hand, extended his right hand, pleased with himself and thinking about the war with Ecuador, because that's where history ended for him and his smile like do-you-want-to-be-my-friend? evaporated when he shook the hot, humid rag that belonged to the immense fat man, who didn't even pay any attention to him as they met and only turned to look at him when he withdrew his nauseating hand. Lastarria thought he was going to speak because he became inflated, ready to . . . but all he expelled was another breath of hot air, right in his face, carrying with it a charge of scorn that undoubtedly went all the way back to the viceroyalty.

And in fact the fat guy lived in an old, aristocratic house in the center of Lima, which came complete with an interior patio and all. His aunt was the one with a little money and she gave him a weekly allowance with a little extra for books. Lalo Bello didn't have a car, or anything for that matter, but he used taxis to go to any number of parties like the one at the Altamiras, after which he would get himself invited out to dinner. At some moment tonight he would narrate to the owner of the house the story of who in 1827, for instance, owned the hacienda that today is Monterrico where the house is located. His wide hips were always hurting him and he had flat feet, asthma, corns, and bunions, and a face that could outdo Frankenstein. Today, at any rate, this face signifies a botched effort. Nevertheless, Lastarria didn't lose hope with the fat slob, so he pulled out his gold cigarette case and offered him an Egyptian cigarette, but just then Lalo Bello barely contained an attack of hysteria, introduced a homosexual finger between his neck and his shirt collar, did a complete roundabout as if he couldn't tolerate the heat, his tie, or anything else for another second, and finally, with another gust of hot air, he said Nooooooooo to poor Lastarria who just stood there, waiting forever with the open gold cigarette case in his hand. And there wasn't anyone else to whom he could offer a cigarette because Lizandro Albañiles and Cocoter Tellagorri had just left the group, the doctor had prohibited Finita from smoking and, moreover, Ernesto Pedro was calling her over because the Prime Minister had finished his glass of grapefruit juice and was getting ready to leave. The truth is that Lastarria decided to accept a cigarette from himself and he was putting it in his mouth when he noticed that the historian took out a crumpled pack of the worst Peruvian cigarettes that were also half-yellowed and crushed. When he put a cigarette in his mouth, he began to get fidgety because the tobacco strands stuck to his lips. Lalo Bello was out of control, and what the hell was he doing spitting out little bits of tobacco that could have easily landed on the lapel of Juan Lastarria's custom-made English suit? In order to defend himself, he came up with the brilliant idea of lighting this guy's cigarette with a gold lighter exactly like Juan Lucas'. Pleased with the idea, Lastarria extended his arm at the end of which the following was visible: the perfect cuff of a pure silk shirt, a gold cuff link bearing his false family coat-of-arms and, finally, the flame of the wick that gave a yellowish tinge to Lalo Bello's greasy and poorly shaved double chin. Also, he had a drooping shoulder and his backside was completely flat. But Lastarria didn't give in and was ready to pardon him for everything that had happened; it looked like he had arrived at the stadium with the Olympic torch. He was so happy because the historian held his hand and assisted him . . . And he continued to assist him and wouldn't let go; it seems Lalo was obsessed with rotating the cigarette in his mouth and completely lighting the whole end of it because the tobacco was always loose at the end, almost falling out, and it was hard to smoke it. One thing for sure: he had taken poor Lastarria's hand and enveloped it in what seemed like warm damp towels, that is, Bello's own hands. Lastarria was slightly bent over, almost hanging there in between smiling and Hey, let go, because over there the Prime Minister gave Susan a kiss, saying good-bye, and he would soon be coming this way. Now the Prime Minister was walking by and it would have been so natural to say good-bye, unpremeditatedly, among friends, because even though Lalo Bello might have the dirtiest shirt cuffs around he was definitely important. Just then Lalo Bello let go of his hand but too late, the Prime

Minister didn't see him. But he did see Fatso Bello and now for sure those two were going to greet each other and then he could get in on the action. However, the Prime Minister, who was being directed to the door by Ernesto Pedro de Altamira's three Aryan fingers and was still thinking about Susan, perceived those wide hips, the drooping shoulder, and imagined himself in his office where his secretary had read to him from the newspaper column "Old Documents," in which Lalo Bello wrote about the origin of certain fortunes and political hatreds . . . the Prime Minister passed by the historian and his satanic left eye almost pierced his ear, it was a sideward glance that became frontal, loaded with hatred, and Lastarria became extremely worried. Just then Lalo Bello deflated amid the hot smoke from his first, immense puff which he hid behind, furious because his aunt had scolded him for writing the petty article. Poor Lastarria disappeared amid the asphyxiating air and Lalo Bello's horrible coughing attack.

When Lastarria began to hear music and the guests went to the patio again, the fat historian had backed off a few yards from where they were and was looking for a chair and a waiter to give him a whiskey. Lastarria understood that it was his opportunity to escape, perhaps Susan is by herself somewhere over there or Juan Lucas has abandoned the Swede . . . But he noticed something strange and looked for a column to hide behind that didn't exist on that patio: Lalo Bello, sitting down now, was wiping his face with a grimy handkerchief and calling to a waiter, then to another, and to that one also, but none of them would pay any attention to him. They saw him but did nothing. They not only hovered around groups of guests where someone had just thought I need another whiskey, but also treated Fatso Bello as if he didn't even exist. They even gave him secret looks of scorn because one waiter diagnosed the quality of the cloth of his suit and said he had at least two suits that were better. What Lastarria didn't understand is that Fatso wasn't even aware what was going on. He was oblivious to anything that had to do with acknowledging that the waiters despised him. He simply kept asking, wiping his face, and saying whiskey over and over again. He was so thirsty that he began to think about his little aunt, hoping she would bring him a glass and put it to his lips. Again he said whiskey, this time in a louder voice, and Lastarria continued to hide behind the column that didn't exist. Finally, the architect in vogue, who was a nice but calculating person and was wearing a suit that he bought in Nassau on his honeymoon, told the headwaiter: "Hey, get a whiskey for this gentleman." His loud voice was even heard at some distance away. In any case, the person in charge who had been around enough to know who Señor Bello was and who also knew to show him the respect he deserves, ran off to find the nearest waiter and that's how Lalo Bello managed to get a whiskey and forget about his aunt. Seconds later, feeling alleviated, the historian looked up and saw the architect turn and face his group. But the architect in vogue had shown his face. Lalo Bello had observed that smiling profile and, a little to the right, he had seen Lastarria leave his hiding place, ready to build a house with the young artist. Immediately the historian threw his head back as if he didn't want to see them anymore, but both of them continued floating in the air and, exhaling an enormous, hot viceregal puff of satisfaction, he began to think about Plutarch and parallel lives in which, as always, someone would offer him a ride and tonight he would ask to be dropped off at the Aquarium because he wanted to eat a lobster and drink some good wine in order to continue imagining things about which, perhaps, he might write.

Everyone looked perfect on the enchanted twentieth-century patio. They had finished off several rounds of drinks, the conversations were in full swing, and the groups were completely formed. The enchanted twentieth-century patio witnessed the presence of elegance and festivity, offering the guests the protection of glass walls with which the marvelous house was made, enveloping them in light and secluding them from the night in which Lima was lost, out there, forgotten somewhere. Olé! was heard above the music and probably came from the Swede, because the architect in vogue turned to look and saw her stick her finger, curved like a bull's horn, into her chest and Juan Lucas was laughing loudly and leaned back slightly, always maintaining one foot on the edge of the lagoon, and the whiskey glass suspended between his very long fingers and resting lightly on his flexed knee. Finita and Ernesto Pedro had accompanied the Prime Minister to the door, where they waited for his car to pull away and drive off down the road that descended toward the dark streets of Monterrico and, further on, the highway to Lima. Now both returned to the patio. "How long will this go on?" Finita asked herself when she saw that several guests were still talking merrily. "Only the Prime Minister showed enough consideration to leave early, these people don't even look at their watches, and they throw their cigarette butts all over the ground, my flagstones, good heavens! they're trampling the butts, it'll take months, good heavens! before my house is clean again and the butlers . . ." Seemingly invisible, Finita heard some of them calling her over to their group and she panicked because she didn't have any recourse but to join them. "It's Beba Marinas," she said to herself, transforming her psychosis into a smile as she went over to where an enormous diamond bracelet was waiting for her smiling: "Finita, you still haven't explained where that little rock-and-roller talking with Juan Lucas came from." "A friend of the boys, Beba, a friend of the boys," she began, being careful that the air didn't get to her exposed, narrow back and thinking that she really didn't know where she came from: "The boys, the boys, they're absolutely wild these days." She was in agony because Beba was capable of asking more questions. She twitched when she smiled, but insisted on being affable with her guests who were also calling her over from everywhere and were forcing her to put everything she had into the cocktail party, even though it was highly probable that soon she would faint. Meanwhile, Ernesto Pedro, with both eyes open momentarily, managed to escape from the diverse groups that were also calling to him as he passed by; he smiled at them, of course, and calculated the type of smile according to the person to whom he was smiling: three-quarters of a smile for his partner in the consortium; a kind of half-grin, half-smile for the fishing-business owner; a combination of bow, smile, and grin for the rancher/consortium member/fishing-business owner; a light touch on the architect's arm; close one eye for Lastarria; communicate nervous prostration for Lalo Bello who was drowning in a chair; and, finally, a full smile with both eyes open because he was coming upon Susan who, between being distracted and mischievous, and no one would ever know if she was also very sad, balanced herself on the edge of the patio steps going down to the garden. "One, two, three," Susan counted mentally, but she slipped slightly and stepped onto the grass, abandoning her game; she walked several feet over to the edge of the illuminated swimming pool. She stopped there with her back turned and waited for Ernesto Pedro Altamira: "Don't move," she heard him say as he grabbed her by her elbows: "Stay right where you are for a moment, Susan . . . it's pure pleasure to look at Lima over your pretty white shoulder . . . don't move . . . let me contemplate it a while longer, reduced to those flickering lights . . . of course, I could place a statue on this spot but what about your hair, dear." Susan felt his hands drop away and she turned around smiling, throwing back her blond lock of hair and presenting the beauty of her breasts, daringly free at the neckline of her shiny blue dress. Even though she had the words and warmth of a perfect phrase in English on her lips, "Darling" was all she said. Her voice trembled because, looking over Altamira's shoulder, she could see Juan Lucas talking enthusiastically with the jovial Swede, probably telling her about Jeep excursions through Brazil. She knew him all too well, it was the expression he used when he was about to go on a fling. Susan had seen that expression on his face many times before but only with her. "Juan Lucas is behaving terribly, Ernesto: I don't know how long he's going to keep talking to that girl." Altamira, apart from his nervous prostration, had a thousand phobias, aged instantly, his left cheek turned into a sea of wrinkles, and he began to hate Juan Lucas and all the other guests because at ten o'clock on the dot he had to remove his false teeth. "He'll come back, Susan, he'll come," he told her, trying to restrain himself. He took her by the arm and led her over to an overlook from where they could almost see the entire city of Lima. "You're trembling, Ernesto," she told him. She was going to say something else, but he asked her to wait a minute: "I'm going to get a glass of water, Su-Susan," he stuttered, and scurried inside to look for water for the nine-thirty electric blue pill. And because that emptiness out there in front of them, that immense black hole that was the night on this side of the hill, had propelled him with unbridled impetuousness to want to throw his false teeth on top of Lima or at least on top of Monterrico, well, it was closer, for he was at the end of his rope. The image of his chalk-white hands, all wrinkled with blue veins like the color of the eleven o'clock pill, didn't offer any solace. There was almost nothing that would calm him down: "Only Susan, only Susan," he said to himself as he raced in for water, almost moved to tears with one eye completely shut. Fortunately he didn't run into Lastarria on his way in, because he would have knifed him. And fortunate as well that Finita had remembered the Señor's pill and had sent a waiter with a glass of water to look for him. They crossed paths and now Ernesto Pedro was going back to Susan, thinking that to take the electric blue pill in front of her would calm him down, although there's still the false teeth at ten o'clock and the guests . . . "I've been depressed lately," he told her when he was next to her side again. "Sunday afternoons especially are terrible," and he was about to say that he was going to return to Europe in order to see a neurologist in Germany, when all of a sudden he felt that the electric blue color of the nine-thirty pill was having its effect and his faith in God hadn't dissipated as much as he feared: always on Sundays, especially after lunch. He also felt strong enough to wait with Susan while the guests began to leave and Juan Lucas finished pestering the little savage. He calculated that for one day he could withstand his false teeth until ten-thirty. Susan, who was still at the lookout, welcomed him back with a smile and took the glass from his hand, waiting for him to speak.

"The Swede is very wild," he told her, feeling a bit better. "She's really wild, but at least she livens up things around here."

"How did she end up here, darling?"

"My son Ernesto met her in London and decided to invite her to visit Peru. The things kids do these days. One thing for sure: he doesn't pay much attention to her anymore . . . instead, it's the young boys who are all aroused . . ."

Susan turned to look at Juan Lucas. He was over there with another glass of whiskey and still talking to that Swede. She didn't have to open her mouth for Ernesto Pedro to understand that Juan Lucas also was aroused and it's been a long time since he was a young boy. God only knows why Altamira decided to enunciate a long phrase in perfect German, but he couldn't finish it because a muscle in his shoulder twitched, forcing him to shut his left eye completely as he looked at Susan, who in turn didn't understand one iota but nevertheless even expressed certain irritation in her face, for she imagined that Ernesto Pedro was trying to utilize some literary text to capture the destiny of women who marry guys like Juan Lucas. It annoyed her terribly and she looked at Altamira whose eye was still half-shut and, remembering Nilda, was about to say to him I hope you're struck by lightning and blinded forever! But she was too tired to bother.

"Darling, even though you won't believe it, Juan and I are very . . ."

Ernesto Pedro felt that the word happy was orange-colored, which mixed horribly with the electric blue pill, and the whole world was going to hell on him, including Monterrico. It occurred to him that he might have to say good-bye to his guests without his false teeth; they'll see him with a shrunken face, more wrinkled than usual, and the day after tomorrow is Sunday after lunch. He almost threw himself off the lookout, false teeth and all, but he stopped himself because men are stronger than women and, in the name of the white race, he turned around to observe his great house and its mysteriously illuminated patio. Perhaps that scene would manage to save him from his terrible languor. Some of the men were wearing white jackets and seemed perfect as they went around like flies that never light anywhere; other men were wearing dark suits and silver ties over a perfect background of white or ivory silk shirts. These men didn't see the flies, for the flies were tacit and necessary, a part of the environment, like the electric blue color or the patio itself, so beautifully illuminated, where Juan Lucas, the Señor, played with a blond. In Monterrico, everything was elevated above Lima and it was possible to travel to Europe at any moment or be cured of nervous prostration and fill up the country house with guests on a day when neither Indians nor orange-looking peons appeared, not even the orange but blue administrator: look for me at the office which is beautiful and where I'm fine, of course, of course, of course, and turning now toward Susan and feeling better, finding her next to me . . . A look around Ernesto Pedro's patio did some good. He felt better, and then a whole lot better when the first group of guests came up to him to say good-bye: "I'll take you to the door, Señores, I'll go with you," Altamira told them as he put his Aryan fingers on the blue elbows of the guests, directing them forward through the enchanted patio, the incredible living room, the glorious vestibule, etc. Others came up to say good-bye as he continued walking forward, and he wanted to tell them, smilingly: "Señores, others are leaving too and, if the exodus continues at this rate, I'll be able to remove my false teeth before ten-thirty, and then there's the blue sleeping pill at eleven o'clock and my children, my house, my everything, and Germany . . ."

"Susana, woman," Juan Lucas called out, addressing her very Spanishlike.

He almost startled her to death. Susan, lovely, turned around, but she left the lock of hair covering her face when she saw the Swede.

"Hello, Ramón del Valle Inclán," she said. Juan Lucas had already gained impetus and he took the sarcastic remark as a flattering compliment, becoming even more Spanish.

"There's a young boy by the name of Julius who is waiting for us." All that was missing was Niño de Triana and his flamenco guitars.

"There's a young boy by the name of Julius who is waiting for us," she imitated, almost dancing the flamenco mockingly, but the Swede, God only knows how, squeezed both of her hands into the rear pockets of her tight pants while her breasts swelled arrogantly underneath the white shirt, forcing Susan to close her eyes, as if someone had turned on two headlights in your eyes. She wanted to escape immediately to the mysterious Orient but she missed that plane too. It got worse because she mumbled something; frankly, she hardly managed to say anything and realized that she was probably capable of turning red.

"My name's Dita," the Swede said, taking her crushed hand out of her pocket and extending it to Susan.

Juan Lucas, who was ready to dance flamenco, felt like a real bastard and he limited himself to one heel click just at the moment when Susan felt as if she had just had her ice cold Coke, and extended her arm in order to put the lock of hair back into place, making the Swede wait and then, just now, shaking hands and converting her into what she really was: an adolescent with dirty pants.

"Would you like to have dinner with us?" she asked, looking like a combination of the Queen of England and Greta Garbo. "We're going to the Aquarium."

"I'm not sure, I don't think I can," the Swede answered, looking like something between Little Cinderella and a shorthand stenographer.

Susan confirmed the invitation with a smile, while Juan Lucas, holding his glass, scratched the back of his head like a jerk and decided that the best thing to do was to leave the girl with the Altamiras and go get Julius because he must be starving. The three of them left the overlook and walked smilingly past the few groups of guests who were still talking on the patio. The architect in vogue fell in love with Susan again when he saw her pass by talking in English with the Swede who walked along, diminished and twenty years less beautiful than Susan. The poor thing acted like she didn't know how to swim, and would have loved for Susan to show her, and she would have preferred even more not to have that enormous scab on her elbow. "I have to go," she said as a way of saying good-bye and then ran up to her room. Perhaps the scab was dry now and she could peel it off, clean it up for Juan Lucas, but where was she going to get a dress that wasn't one of young Ernesto Pedro de Altamira's shirts? "I hate him," the swimmer screamed.

Meanwhile Susan, lovely, and Juan Lucas, a combination of playboy and prodigal son, kissed Finita's immaculate left cheek in appreciation and asked for Ernesto Pedro in order to say good-bye to him as well. "Here he comes," said Finita, always about to faint, and Juan Lucas saw that Ernesto Pedro approached with one eye completely shut and looking at his wristwatch, three minutes to ten. He had grown old so fast that as Susan embraced him, she implored him not to bother to accompany them to the door.

A few minutes later the Jaguar was speeding down the abandoned hill that was Ernesto Pedro de Altamira's private property. The Swede, standing naked in her bedroom, had opened slightly an enormous curtain and, through an illuminated glass wall of that marvelous house, she watched the automobile disappear into the night. Out on the patio, some thirty-five dark blue people continued their animated conversations without managing to figure out the source of the mysterious light that somehow enchanted that ultramodern patio. They simply accepted it in the same way that they, and only they, accepted the fact that they could leave a glass suspended in thin air which would immediately materialize into an engraved silver platter that received the glass as they put it down. They talked happily, protected by the glass house and its transparent walls. Their words were swallowed up by the music and by the elegant evening among the stars. The smoke from their cigarettes curled upward, forming arabesque shapes through the mysterious rays of the hidden reflectors, while they drank whiskey and truly felt like they were floating on a solitary island alone in the world, traveling God only knows where, but nevertheless exhilarated, orangely happy.

THE LAST CURVE convinced him that there was nothing tonight that would frighten Susan. For some time now he had been wanting to speed crazily in the Jaguar, but he never imagined that tonight would be ideal. And that she would be at his side, feeling the wind, letting her hair fly around freely. The Jaguar quickly devoured the distances, and the curves always appeared just before he was able to achieve top speed, for he always saw them at the last moment. Juan Lucas had penetrated the very dark undeveloped areas of Monterrico, and Susan must have closed her eyes because she remained still and quiet, letting her hair fly out the back with the wind.

"We're lost," Juan Lucas told her suddenly.

"You ought to get lost, darling."

As she said that, she turned to look at Juan Lucas. He also wanted to look at her and get a glimpse of her facial expression, but at that moment the wind enveloped her face with hair, completely covering it.

"You ought to get lost," Susan repeated.

He would have liked to have seen her face, he wanted to accuse her of talking a long time to Ernesto Pedro.

"Darling of Altamira," he said, testing her, half-worried and half-bantering, but the image of the Swede, ultramodernly savage with her dirty tight pants invaded his thoughts, destroying his sentence, and his words lost their force as he pronounced them and they disappeared unintelligibly amid the roar of the motor.

"Darling of Altamira," he insisted, fawning and feigning jealousy that neither one of them felt. Once again his words were consumed by the nocturnal roar of the Jaguar.

"Darling of Neanderthal," Susan struck back with a dynamite allusion to the adolescent Swede; then she turned and looked straight ahead calmly, abandoning herself to the vertigo of the high speed and letting the wind once again blow her hair back, for now her mind was flying too. Juan Lucas floored it and the Jaguar went crazy, but everything in Monterrico had disappeared for Susan . . . Cinthia had said it to me: you are the most attractive girl in school, Susan. I don't want to leave London, Cinthia. I have to return to Buenos Aires, when will I see you again, Susan? I'll name my first girl after you, Cinthia, I promise. Mine will have your name, too, Susan. We've been at boarding school for seven years, Cinthia. What's your real name, Susana or Susan? I never did know which. Well, Daddy calls me Susan and Mommy calls me Susana. I would sign my name Susana but no one in London has ever called me by that name, only Mommy in her letters, and it got to the point that it sounded strange to me, Cinthia. It's going to be terrible to have to leave you, Susan. Don't cry, Cinthia. I always cry, I'm silly. I've never seen you cry Susan. It's strange, but it's true, Cinthia. You're the only one who didn't shed a tear at graduation, Susan. Good-bye. Good-bye. Yes, I'm waiting at the airport because his plane arrives in half an hour, he should have arrived in time for graduation but the plane was late. It's been three years since I've seen him. Don't cry. Good-bye, Cinthia. What a pity I couldn't see him this time, Susan. Daddy! Daddy! Daddy! You're so handsome, Daddy. My little daughter! You're all grown up, Susan! I'm finished with boarding school, Daddy. My lonely little Peruvian, my poor Susan. I never suffered, they never noticed, my English is perfect, better than my Spanish. Mommy is always complaining, how is she? Excuse my spelling mistakes, Mommy. Susan, your letters get worse each time, you're forgetting your Spanish, what are you going to do when you return home, Susan? I don't want to go back, Daddy. But Susan. Just a few more months, Daddy. Our flight stops off in New York, we leave at eight o'clock tonight, Susan. Don't make faces, it's only a few more months, Daddy. Miss Stone will take care of everything, Susan. Nice to meet you, Miss Stone. I have an apartment ready for you next to my house, in Stanhope Gardens, Miss. Mine! Mine! Mine! I'm ecstatic, no one's going to bug me, Cinthia. Write me always, tell me everything, Susan. I'm on my own, Cinthia, no teacher to stop me from doing this or that, and I've cut my hair short short, everything would be perfect if I just wasn't living next to Miss Stone, she's so irritating. Do not ever come home late, Miss. Don't worry, Miss Stone. Do not smoke so much, Miss. Get off my back, Miss Stone. Who do you think you are, Miss? Go to hell, Miss Stone. I will write to him and tell him everything. He is going to hear all about it, Miss. Don't believe her, Daddy. Susan, how could you be so disrespectful to Miss Stone? She's lesbian. Well, all she's responsible for now is to give you your monthly allowance. Don't let her into your apartment. I'll come to see you as soon as I can, Susan. Thanks, many thanks, your letter is precious, you are so sweet, Daddy. I must postpone my trip because of business, Susan. And I cut my hair even shorter. I'm sending you five pictures, *I love you*, Daddy. Your mother wants you to write, Susan. I don't feel like writing and anyway, I'm not doing anything wrong. I don't have time for it. I'm happy, David. Let me hug you, Susan. I don't want to get involved, I just want to feel free, forever free, David. Are all you Peruvian girls alike, so good-looking? Do you think so, David? You're the prettiest sixteen-year-old I've ever seen, good-looking. Nineteen, David. Liar. You are a good-looking, lying Peruvian, Susan. Put my passport down, idiot. Are you coming to the party, good-looking? My passport, dummy. At the party, I'll give it to you at the party, Susan. Let go of me, stupid. What's going on? Hey, listen! Let her go, dimwit! Prick-teaser! Crazy bitch! Let him go, Paul! Let's get out of here, we need some fresh air. Hold on to my waist, Sue. Sure, Paul. Have you ever ridden a motorcycle, Sue? Faster, faster, Paul. The pubs are closed, Sue. Stanhope Gardens then. Faster, Paul. Another whiskey, Sue? I don't want to get involved with anyone, I always want to feel free, Paul. Bye, baby! Paul! Paul! Come back, Paul! You crazy girl, Sue. I'm going to get some more ice. I didn't cry then either. I didn't cry that night either. Yes, it was that night, Elizabeth. How long have you been going out with him, Susan? Almost a year, Elizabeth. What are you going to do about your daddy, Susan? Miss Stone, that idiot: Your daughter has disappeared from London, she left without telling me, sir. She wrote from France, says she's happy, Miss Stone. I'm obliged to inform you that your daughter left with an unknown person on a motorcycle, sir. She wrote from Sweden, swears that she's with a friend, someone named Elizabeth. You're lucky to have found me here, Susan. I got tired of Paul. If you flirt once more with that damned Swede I'll kill you, Susan. They almost killed each other, Elizabeth. I have enough money for the two of us, Susan. I'll pay you back in London, Daddy's checks are waiting for me there. That witch Miss Stone probably has them. He is coming, yes, he is coming to get you, your father communicated that to me, Miss. I'm doing great. I'm sending you seven pictures, my hair has grown out, I want to study, don't deny me this opportunity, I beg you, with all my love, Susan. I convinced him! Here's your money, Liz. And you've still got pants on, they'll be by any minute and you look tacky, Susan. Can't I go like this? I'm too lazy to change. Who are they, anyway, Liz? The JJs, two guys from Oxford: John and Julius. A party at our house in Sarrat. You don't know where it is? In northern London. Now there's no time for you to change; anyway, your pants look better on you than a party dress, let's go, Susan. Let's go faster! Faster! Faster, John! You've had too much to drink, don't go so fast, Julius. You're Peruvian Susahhna? Yes, and I won't show you my passport either, you drunk. Peruvian like Santiago, John, classmates at the university, your big buddy, right, Julius? From Lima, owner of half of Peru: when he becomes president he'll send us a plane and we'll have an orgy in the Presidential

Palace! John, slow down. Julius, last time I broke the door down, ha-
hahaha. How old are you, Susahhna? How many whiskeys have you
had, Julius? I'd love to kiss you, but before I can do that I need another
drink, let's go in to see if with another drink I'll get up the courage to
tell you I love you, Susahhna. I like him, Liz. Oh, he'll invite you out,
he'll get drunk, he'll forget about you, you'll have to go home in a taxi,
it's always the same, Susan. Everyone's getting drunk, Carol, just like
always at Julius' parties. When will your damn compatriot Susahhna
arrive? I hadn't thought anymore about him, Liz. You were lucky he
didn't find you drunk, Susan. I had gone over to sit on the edge of the
lagoon and I hadn't heard anyone speak Spanish in centuries. The
Swede had turned her back toward us, sitting on the edge, playing in
the water. Juan Lucas went over to her. It's been years since I've heard
Spanish and it had to be Santiago: Julius sent me over to meet you,
Susan. Santiago? Wait, don't move, stay just like you are, Susan. My
hair had begun to grow, darling. Long like it is now, Mommy? Yes,
Cinthia. Daddy said that? He said you should always let the lock of hair
fall down over your face? And you should repeat it? And then reach up
and put it back in place? Daddy fell in love with you because of that,
Mommy? I really hadn't thought about it, Santiago; in any case, I had
imagined you would be different, Santiago. Disillusioned? Julius told
me you owned half of Peru, Santiago. They said the same thing about
you, Susan. I imagined you to be brown-skinned and bigger, Santiago.
Disillusioned, Susana? It's been years since anyone has called me by that
name. He was short, blond, and he repeated the word disillusioned.
He's so ironic and he has a thick beard, but I couldn't stand the way he
looked at me. He's shorter than me, I noticed it when we danced, I'm
enchanted, he left me sitting on the edge of the lagoon and went for
another whiskey. The Swede watched him while I pushed my lock of
hair aside with my finger, and suddenly I said darling to him, he looked
at me ironically, I felt like a savage, dirty, with pants on, from the caves
of Altamira or from the caves, darling, of Neanderthal. I couldn't stand
the way he looked at me, but I almost cried because I was in love.
Daddy, he's from a prominent family, his name is the same as your
father's. A great friend, Susan. September 27, 1937: I love you, Santiago. Let's celebrate. My car is waiting impatiently. Where do you live,
Susana? Stanhope Gardens, Santiago. I was going to stay at Sarrat. My
things are in the trunk of the car, Susan. And he's got a bright red silk
robe! He's a dandy! And some marvelous blue slippers with his name
engraved on them in silk! And he looks at you and you have to look
away, Liz. Your time has arrived. No longer the free Peruvian anymore,

Susan. I love you, Santiago. You're going to be nineteen. We'll return to Lima and get married, Susan. Let's stay in London a little longer, please, Santiago. Impossible, I've got to start work. We have to return to Lima right away, Susana. Dear Julius: Santiago is very busy. He doesn't have time to write you. I'm going to have my second child and he has to be named Roberto, or Bobby, after an uncle who is going to be his godfather. If it's a girl, she'll be named Cinthia after an Argentine friend (I never saw her again). The way things are going, it looks like I'll have a lot more kids, and we'll keep our promise: the next one will be named after you. All my love, Susan. Let's get married here and then stay a little longer, Santiago. Impossible, Susana. Good-bye, Miss Stone. I hope you have made a good choice, Mr. Santiago. What do you think, Susan? Go to hell, Miss Stone. I am pleased you are taking her with you, Mr. Santiago. You know you won't be able to behave like that in Lima, Susana. The Swede. I prefer you call me Susan, Santiago. Dear Julius: our fourth child was just born, and now it's time for us to keep our promise. We'll name him Julius, after you. That's nice. I hope I can stop working soon, I don't feel well at all. I would like to go to London to see a doctor. Don't worry, we'll see each other again, Julius. My dear Susan: life is terrible. What I would give to see you again! I never thought that I wouldn't see you again. Please write me, Susan. Darling: just a few lines to describe Julius. He's got big ears but he's cute. Julius must be dying of hunger at the hotel. We'll be back no later than ten o'clock, Julius. Who's that man, Mommy? I'm not going to cry over the Swede . . . just needle him, Darling of Neanderthal. He'll take you for a ride in his race car. This is Julius, Juan Lucas . . .

"Susan, Susan!"

"You almost frightened me to death, Juan Lucas."

"I stopped the car five minutes ago. You didn't even see that we almost got killed on that last curve! How many drinks have you had?"

"Less than John and Julius," Susan blurted out, staring at him in a delightful way, a little lost and terribly sad.

Juan Tenorio started the motor, then turned it off, took the key out of the ignition, inserted it again, and stopped himself when he was about to take it out again; the golfer was just about out of it. Susan looked at him, holding back a laugh and a tear. Juan Lucas lit a cigarette, took a drag, and exhaled three perfectly round white circles in homage to peace, then he coughed twice in manly fashion, started the motor, let it idle for a moment in order to say once again "Darling of Altamira" which he said quite well this time and then started off again . . .

"Darling of Neanderthal," she responded accusingly, believing that he had understood the allusion but, just in case, she let the lock of hair fall over her face and parted the lock in order to make that famous opening through which she looked at this imbecile. Juan Lucas turned off the motor for good and crossed his arms, ready to listen to whatever and see if he had missed something else.

"Where were you September 27, 1937?" she asked him strangely, holding back a laugh because she might start to weep.

"Susan, excuse me but I don't understand anything you're saying."

"Who approached whom, and who was sitting on the edge of a lagoon on September 27, 1937?"

"Not a clue, Susan! But tell me something: is the Swedish girl the Darling of Neanderthal?"

"I would say rather that the Darling of Neanderthal was sitting on the edge of the lagoon in Sarrat on September 27, 1937," Susan said, continuing to play the game.

"Then you are the Darling of Neanderthal?"

"And who, then, is the Darling of Altamira?" Susan felt like vomiting.

"Calm down, Susan; let's get Julius . . ."

"Julius was completely drunk that night . . . Where were you, Juan Lucas?"

"I've told you a thousand times, Susan; I was also in London at that time . . ."

"And the Swede, darling?"

"That's enough, Susan! We're going. It's almost eleven o'clock and Julius must be starving."

"Or drunk."

"No, Susan. Julius your son! That pious little church mouse that neither of us wants to see tonight!"

"The other one, Juan Lucas, the one who was always drunk . . ."

"I don't know him!"

"But you just said you were in London at that time; he even went to our wedding . . ."

"Let's get out of here!"

The Jaguar pulled away, slowly advancing along the dark streets of Monterrico.

"Did you find the way, Juan Lucas?" Susan asked a few moments later.

"Yes, we're going the right way."

"But I can't see at all . . . There's a road that leads from Darling of

Neanderthal to Darling of Altamira, but you can't take it unless you find a lagoon in Sarrat in northern London . . . and a Peruvian, darling. But what happens if the lagoon is in Sweden? . . . it doesn't matter, it's not important because Lima is to blame, the longest part of the road passes through Lima . . ."

"What are you talking about, Susan?"

"The road between Darling of Neanderthal and Darling of Altamira: it goes through Lima, Juan. Tonight, when you leave, remind me to tell you something."

"What, Susan?"

"It's for me, Juan."

She begged him to hurry up. She was frightened: for the first time in many years she was afraid that she might cry . . . I don't feel like changing. Who are they, Liz? The JJs: John and Julius. A party at our house in Sarrat in northern London, your pants look better on you than a party dress, Swede, just needling him . . ."

" . . . THE SEÑORES WOULD like . . . ," the waiter started to finish saying, alienated, handing them the list of wines. He was under the watchful eye of the headwaiter who had approached the table as if he were skating on ice.

"Champagne," Susan said, speaking from deep down inside to Julius . . . the one in London. "We've got to celebrate this young man's birthday," she explained, jesting, almost to the point of exaggerating.

"That's fine: champagne," Juan Lucas agreed, ready to continue the game or whatever it was they were playing. Nevertheless, he couldn't conceal a feeling of annoyance that the waiter failed to grasp but that the sensitive headwaiter did notice. Now it was the headwaiter's turn to make known that he hadn't noticed anything. He removed the wine glasses with a certain French flair and a good salary and left skating off among the tables. He met up with another waiter a little further away, and together they formed an arabesque design, skating on one foot and sliding along, smiling, slightly bent over with the left leg extended to the back until they reached the table where the Prime Minister had finished his jello dessert and was getting ready to leave. All Juan Lucas needed at that moment was a golf ball to shove into the mouth of Julius who, yawning out loud, was being initiated into la dolce vita. They found him asleep on the sofa in the suite, and Susan couldn't help but feel touched when she noticed that his tie was hanging from one ear, an old joke that years before Vilma had taught him: she would hang the tie from his ear while she buttoned his collar. "Hurry up, young man," Juan Lucas said, waking him up. Julius had washed his face, not quite sure for a moment whether it was yesterday or today. He put on his sport coat and followed them half-asleep down to the famous restaurant. Nothing provoked his desire to be there, he would have preferred to eat some crackers in the room and then go to bed. But there he was at the table, vaguely hearing something about champagne. In some way he had associated the odd presence of the headwaiter in the low light of the Aquarium with one of his little old clowns that much as he would try to make it stand up straight, always ended up bowing at him. Then he yawned out loud and Juan Lucas looked at him with eyes that said something between *Happy Birthday,* because it's your birthday, and you boorish little turd. That woke him up a bit and he began to look at the other tables. He finally woke up completely when he saw that the person at the table a little to the right, almost in front of theirs, was sucking his huge fat fingers without noticing that he had dripped food all over his lapel. Then he joyfully attacked the lobster but little meat fibers got stuck between his teeth and, nervously, he had to put down the lobster in order to extract them. The fat guy was exhausted, he couldn't breathe or something like that; in fact, he sighed loudly, seeming to inflate his whole body and, as he expelled the air, he held a filthy handkerchief over his mouth that was probably wet when he put it down on the doubly white tablecloth.

It was Lalo Bello, and he could care less about anything. He had come to spend his allowance and, what the hell, if it's not enough I'll sign for it. They knew Señor Bello very well at the Aquarium. "The strange thing is that he's alone," the waiters gossiped when they went into the kitchen. "Fatso here always knows how to get himself invited." But not tonight, and Lalo Bello continued eating as Julius, astonished, looked on. Susan wanted to laugh and let Juan Lucas think she was laughing at Lalo Bello because, even though they hardly ever said hello to each other, they were relatives: Lalo belonged to the branch that had become impoverished; it was the oldest branch too. Juan Lucas detested meeting him anywhere. He always had a dirty collar. He had even gone to the Golf Club one afternoon and appeared among a bunch of people with that extravagant, ridiculous white shirt; now he was even shorter from behind because he wasn't wearing a jacket. Fortunately he left quickly: "Too many Yanquis, too many Yanquis," he said on that occasion. He was so bad-mannered that those who had invited him to the Club had to get him out of there. Juan Lucas waved to him as if to say don't come near me and Fatso answered him with much more contempt and despising money. But he nodded hello at Susan, then he looked at Julius, a little surprised, and he jammed a leg of lobster into his mouth. "Darling, don't stare at him," Susan said to Julius. But he was astonished, now more than ever, when he saw a friendly waiter furnish a wine list for Lalo Bello and immediately began with What would the Señor like? and provided a wine list indicating the year of harvest and all the rest. Lalo, however, didn't pay any attention to him whatsoever and simply stabbed the wine list with his large dirty fingernail, "Naah," he said, "I want this one, this one, this one," and then turned to look at Julius with hatred. Julius had to look away and Susan was frightened, wanting them to bring the champagne soon because the kid was looking at everyone insolently and someone might get upset.

But not the Prime Minister: "So nice seeing you again, so nice seeing you again, so nice . . ." Juan Lucas, Susan, and Julius turned slightly in order to confirm that the Prime Minister was approaching, he just wanted to say hello again, for he couldn't stay. "No, no, no, don't get up, please don't bother," he told them, standing next to their table. Juan Lucas made like he was going to get up . . . "No, no, don't bother," he insisted, smiling. "Darling," Susan pronounced, extending her hand, letting him hold it in his and communicate his trembling to her. They remained like that until Juan Lucas intervened as respectfully as he was able: "So, Your Excellency is leaving now." "The life of a Minister, the life of a Minister, the life of . . . ," he began repeating, and Susan felt a slight tingling in her arm, it wouldn't be long before she breaks out laughing, God only knows how long this was going to last, but Juan Lucas, as always, found the solution: He made everyone in the Aquarium think that he was going to stand up . . . "Don't bother young man, don't bother young man," the Prime Minister stopped him. In fact, he wasn't that much older for him to be able to say young man. He looked at Julius, just then noticing him, and began trying to figure out whether he was from this marriage or the other one. He didn't want to stick his foot in his mouth when he said hello to him. "Is he the younger one?" he asked, because his math wasn't working: he had forgotten the date of Santiago's death and he was unable to calculate the child's age. Susan answered that he was, Julius was the youngest, and the Prime Minister tried once again to figure it out but it was impossible: the numbers got all balled up in his head, deeply confusing him, even for a Prime Minister. Juan Lucas stood up finally, bruskly interrupting the old man. "The youngest one, the youngest one, the youngest one," the Prime

Minister said, quickly saying good-bye and discovering that he was still holding Susan's hand. Outside in the car, he continued calculating and the two men who were with him for dinner tried to help him. They were two guys who waited in the shadows while he said hello to his friends. The Prime Minister had left, accompanied by the two unidentified men.

"Julius, please!" Susan said when she noticed he was staring at Lalo Bello again.

"Don't bite your fingernails and quit staring like a jerk," Juan Lucas intervened.

"Don't pay any attention to him, darling," Susan said, going against the grain and adding: "It's your birthday and you should be having fun."

"But it doesn't mean that . . ."

"Can I get the list, Señores?" intruded a waiter, who was a real dolt: Señores are not to be interrupted.

Juan Lucas expressed a very delicate go-to-hell with a slight movement of his hand, accompanied by a new wrinkle in his face, for which the waiter thanked him and left.

"What is an Aquarium?"

"A place where there are lots of fish, darling," Susan explained, extremely interested in her son's education and wanting to needle Juan Lucas some more.

"I don't see them, Mommy; may I see the fish?"

"This is an Aquarium without fish," concluded Juan Lucas, seeing that the headwaiter was skating toward their table with the bottle of champagne; another waiter came as well, carrying the little valise with the champagne glasses.

The cork popped within the limits of the best possible elegance as the headwaiter orchestrated the event, which stimulated Julius' admiration, not allowing one bit of foam to drip onto the tablecloth, as he feared would happen, but instead into the silver ice bucket for keeping the champagne at the right temperature. The headwaiter's eyes indicated that he was satisfied with his work: he had captured the attention of the son of the Señores, but Juan Lucas' eyes doused his feeling of ebullience. He had opened a thousand bottles himself in his lifetime and had seen forty thousand opened by someone else, so quit the pimping, just hurry up with the rest, he said with a single facial expression. After filling the glasses bubbly full, the headwaiter skated away with his back turned at which time Juan Lucas looked down at his watch.

"Well, Julius, cheers!" noticing that it was starting to get late.

"Go slowly, darling," Susan added, "there's time."

"Cheers," Juan Lucas repeated, riveting his eyes first on Susan, then on Julius.

Julius put the glass to his mouth and took a small sip. He wasn't interested in drinking; he would rather look over at Fatso Bello. The historian had turned to one side because he didn't want to look at the four elegant young men who, seated at another table, had already laughed at him more than once which pissed him off. On the other hand, they were only students who had been drinking and were in a festive mood. Two of them were studying to be like Juan Lucas, another to become a cabinet minister, and it was hard to interpret what the fourth was studying; besides, he didn't look too happy.

"It's been years since we've been together. Not since high school," a neo–Juan Lucas said.

"Why in the hell did it occur to you to attend San Marcos?" the other asked.

"It was easier to get in. I didn't have any pull to get into the Catholic University."

"You can still switch universities, there's still time," said the one who was going to be a cabinet minister.

"That's the way we should do it," a neo–Juan Lucas said. "Switch schools and the four of us will be together like in high school."

"Maybe in fourth year of law school, no, better yet, in fifth. Fuck them all, switch to San Marcos," said the other.

"It's easier to graduate there," neo–Juan Lucas.

"There's the problem of reputation," the future cabinet minister intervened.

"And those asinine strikes. They go on strike and you're likely as not to lose the whole academic year," neo–Juan Lucas.

"Let's go back to the Catholic U.," the other. "Cheers," they all laughed, except one of them.

"Don't talk so loud," the future cabinet minister said. "And hold down the cussing too."

"Waiter, another whiskey."

"Four more."

"I don't have enough money," the fourth one.

"Forget it, tonight we'll pay," a neo–Juan Lucas.

"Damn it, Carlos . . ." the other.

"Shhhssss . . . Don't be an ass," the future cabinet minister.

"Screw it."

"And the bill my old man's gonna get, too."

"You guys sign for all this?" said the fourth one.

"And where do you think we'd get the money to drink like this? Yep, it's up to the parents: if they want us to study, then they have to give us an allowance."

"You work your butt off clerking at the law office and they don't give you one red cent for your studies."

"Do you clerk, Carlos?"

"No, but you know what? I'm getting sick and tired of law.

"But what the hell! . . . the thing is to get the degree."

"Look! Over there! It's my Uncle Juan Lucas . . ."

"Hey, that guy is a real wheeler-dealer!"

"Hi, Uncle! . . . Listen, we've got to hold it down. We don't want him to think we're drinking too much . . . my uncle's wife gets lovelier every day."

"You're right! Do you know what happened to me the other day at the Golf Club? Unbelievable! She almost didn't realize what had happened: I saw this young chick wearing a bikini, so I got closer to get a better look. And what a looker, man! . . . it was your Aunt Susan . . . She looks like a young girl in a bikini."

"Don't stare, dummy; they might think we're talking about them."

A waiter approached with a tray of four whiskeys.

"Compliments of your uncle, Señor."

"Thanks."

"Thanks, Uncle."

"Thanks."

Juan Lucas was eating dinner serenely and he winked at them. They discovered a piece of paper with a message on it: "Nephew, even though you won't believe it, the fat guy in front of you is your cousin. Make a wad with this paper and throw it at him." They broke out laughing. The nephew looked at him and Juan Lucas winked again.

"I'll throw it if it's all the same to you," the fourth one.

"No! Don't be stupid," the one who studied to be a minister. "It's Bello, the historian."

Too late: the headwaiter, who was keeping a close eye on the four young men—they'd better not act up just because they're drinking a lot—saw the piece of paper sail through the air converted into a butterfly. He transformed his serving tray into a butterfly net, jumped up smiling, placatingly, but failed, then turned around despairingly toward Bello, and watched it hit him in the forehead. Bello acted like he didn't notice and turned around smiling: the gentlemen may continue now, that was real cute. Juan Lucas sent them another round of whiskeys.

"Thanks, Uncle."

"Your uncle's great."

"I hate to say it, but I would like to be like him . . . When bullfighters come to Lima, he puts them up or takes them out to dinner. Whenever any famous people hit town, my uncle goes with them everywhere, and they even autographed books for him. He's always in the newspapers, with a whiskey in his hand, attending to everyone and enjoying himself. Do you remember when that movie star from Hollywood came? What was that gringa's name? . . . I can't remember but my uncle took her around to meet everyone and no joking, I'm sure he laid her.

"Don't talk so loud," the one who studied to be a minister.

"My uncle's a real expert, and not because I've had a lot to drink, but who cares, deep down I would like to be like him . . . what's deep down inside is the only thing that matters to me."

"First you've got to get that degree," the other one.

"Do you think my uncle has degrees? He doesn't need degrees for what he does. What do you think, Carlos? Wouldn't you like to be like him?"

"I don't know . . . in any case I congratulate you for being the only sincere one among us."

The Juan Lucas types and the future prime minister opened their eyes wide and looked at Carlos with surprise and distrust. And they didn't like the bit about sincerity. Something had filtered through the conversation, "San Marcos," thought Carlos, something that prevented them from being the high school gang again, the four of them together again like in their last year at Villa María, they were going to marry the richest girls there were, and all of that stuff. Carlos felt like he had put his foot in it once and for all, but he had drunk enough in order to be able to put up with a few more hours of the abyss that existed between them. The future, moreover, was an even greater abyss: he would be with them for the evening, all this luxury would help him maintain the smile with which he was looking at them now.

"Your aunt is really lovely," he said, turning insolently toward Susan's table.

"They're probably Santiago's friends," Juan Lucas commented, referring to the four students. "I didn't know my nephew was old enough to go out on binges."

Julius couldn't find one bone in his corvina, whereas Juan Lucas' mackerel even included the spine, which required him to work with a smaller knife specially made for eating fish, an activity that Juan Lucas performed without equal and with pleasure as well.

"Uncle," Julius said, "one day you got mad at Nilda when you found a bone . . . now you're really going to be mad."

Susan wasn't up to laughing but she did anyway, it was a good opportunity to do so.

"Mackerel is one thing and corvina another. Have you found any bones in your fish? . . . Your plate's clean."

"Ha, ha, perhaps I swallowed one . . ."

Susan covered her face.

"Waiter!" Juan Lucas called out. A headwaiter and a waiter came over. "You can bring the meat for this boy now."

"How would you like the meat? Well done? How would the young gentleman like his meat?"

"With fish bones," Susan uttered.

The waiter didn't have a clue, whereas the headwaiter's face turned red: he hadn't understood anything, Señora, the joke was great, Señora, please understand, Señora, trying to find some French influence, but nothing.

"Weeeeell . . . ha, ha . . ."

"Listen, medium, for the kid," Juan Lucas said, squinting. The head-waiter and the other waiter turned and left, skating away on ice.

"Cheers," Susan said, raising her glass of champagne.

"Bravo, woman! Cheers!"

"Thank you, darling. Julius, they're going to do their best to bring you a chateaubriand with fish bones."

"As you can see, young man, your mother is really happy tonight."

"Juan, ask for dessert. I'm not hungry."

"Thanks for speeding things up, but let's wait until this young man finishes his meat."

"I can stay with him, if you want . . ."

"Susan . . ."

"Why don't you sing *Happy Birthday,* Juan?"

Julius knocked over his glass of champagne and, terrified, looked at Juan.

"Waiter, wipe this up," Juan Lucas said to the absent waiter.

But then one appeared out of nowhere.

"Immediately, Señor," occupying himself with the task.

When they finished wiping up, they brought out the chateaubriand for Julius.

"I don't want it, Mommy . . ."

"May we have dessert now?" Susan asked.

"Wouldn't the Señores like . . . ?"

"Nothing. Dessert. The kid's falling asleep."

"And the Señor is in a hurry . . ."

Julius raised his eyes to look at Juan Lucas: in a hurry?

Two waiters had labored a long time to convert the filthy table that
Lalo Bello left behind into a typical table belonging to the Aquarium.
They had just finished when a man came in, the one whom Julius was
watching now, a man without his wife but accompanied by two others
just like him, they were younger and undoubtedly his sons, and two
young women who didn't quite fit in and who must have been their
girlfriends. The five of them sat down, lit five cigarettes, smiled com-
plaisantly as they puffed away and covered each other in smoke,
changed postures, rehearsed it once more, and eluded getting smoke in
their faces. They smiled. The man looked at Julius and winked at him.
Julius looked at Susan, Susan at Juan Lucas, and Juan Lucas realized
right then that it was someone whom he knew: it was that rich guy. The
Señor, with two sons and their girlfriends, greeted him with a lot of
fanfare, then stretched, smiled at his sons and their girls, and waited
while they chanted: One, two, three, you look so young, Dad! You look
younger every day. It's incredible how you manage to stay so young.
And the girls: Isn't that the truth! The less timid girl said he was a young
lad in reality, and the other one agreed with her eyes. Then the sons
again: You look younger every day, Dad. Then he would swell with
pride again and hide his stomach in his chest. Really? he asked. Really?
Yes, Dad, young and firm like your two gold cuff links, just like your
brand new Lincoln. You are young, Dad. Ha, ha, everyone must think
we're your brothers, not your sons, they probably think . . . the dumbest one stopped talking, and the timid girl lowered her head, lest they
think she was his girlfriend or lover. People in Lima tend to gossip a lot,
and the boys told her the other day her father-in-law, well, he's not her
father-in-law yet, daughter, was seen following the Villa María girls'
bus, the dirty old man, in a car replete with wings, mirrors, antennas,
tons of chrome and buttons. Push one and the seat converts into a bed.
Your father-in-law is terrible. The headwaiter and the waiter arrived
and stood next to the group that continued to smile. One of the sons,
who worked in his dad's office, asked the headwaiter if they looked like
father and sons or simply three brothers, one without a girlfriend . . .
The headwaiter, in his best French, stepped on the waiter's foot and
blurted out, Brothers, what else could they be? He looked at the waiter,
who finally understood and got the idea: They were brothers, of course,
what else could they be? They smiled. They couldn't stop smiling. The
father was radiant, wearing his brown-striped suit and a cream-colored

silk shirt with a big collar, the lapel sporting a handkerchief matching the tie. Ah, how young my mistress is and people notice it, but then suddenly he turned a little sad because there in front of him is Juan Lucas who is without a doubt much younger looking. I can count my age by the number of stripes on my suit: a zebra. His sons noticed his sudden perplexity, looked at the headwaiter, and once again, together, they said in chorus: You're looking younger every day, Dad. No doubt about it, with every passing day you look younger, Dad, raising their voices and all. The younger son, the one who was going to work in his father's office, couldn't hold it back any longer: I wouldn't ever leave you alone with Martita, Dad. No sir, you're a tiger. Martita lowered her eyes, Dad looked at his suit, brown without zebra stripes, dark-green Lincoln, wife with a good last name who takes care of the house, a young and beautiful mistress and I spend a fortune on her, as a Señor should, beautiful secretaries, purchase an hacienda, own those beautiful Peruvian horses, every day I'm making more money. Shouldn't give the boys too much; hope they don't make me, ay! a grandfather yet. Long live my reputation, power, life, and my boys: Getting younger every day, Dad. With every hour that passes, you're making me more jealous of you, Dad . . . And Dad taking it all in, providing a new smile, what do you think?

You were the headwaiter and didn't have an opinion because you were terrified. Instead he begged them, having lost momentarily his French training, he implored them with the expression on his face to place their orders, he beseeched them with his good salary to choose, to lower their voices, to comprehend, please: he had looked at them, he who never looks, he had moved, he who never moves, he had just bowed, he who never bows, he who was looking at them furiously. They understood something from the headwaiter's strange behavior, intuiting something between smiles, and turned to look: coldness, fear, and terror was what they felt when their eyes met with José Antonio Bravano's bloodshot, alcohol-glazed eyes. The world of the father of his brothers fell apart, his sons saw him old and frightened to death. José Antonio Bravano bent over slightly, his blue, green, or red face appearing bright next to his third wife, who sat motionless next to him. His eyes glistened with sickness, he was hating them, he was fed up with so much joking at the table to his left. Those who were aware of the situation expected something nasty to happen. The father of his brothers realized he had blown his only chance: Great, now I've really done it, right here in front of Rockefeller. He bent over as if to kiss the table, closed his eyes, and then opened them as he straightened up, no longer looking at Bravano but waiting—pallid and old—for just about anything, even a shot. But nothing happened. Endless silence and fear. He ventured a look at his sons and they looked at him. Martita talked naively, preferring sole with tartar sauce, and the dumbest son said that the guy's wife had stuck something into his mouth. The headwaiter began once again to take their orders and someone said he goes well with his third wife. At his table, meanwhile, Juan Lucas was explaining the situation to Susan: "World War III almost began," he told her. Julius looked again at that odd gentleman who seemed dead.

The dessert didn't appeal to Juan Lucas because he detested everything that wasn't French pastry, that is to say, pastry in Paris at six o'clock in the evening. The golfer was getting bored and he made his impatience felt as he tapped the empty champagne glass with his long finger. They brought Susan one small scoop of vanilla ice cream in an exquisite chalicelike silver cup. Perhaps she might taste a bit of it. In any case, she would entertain herself by sticking the silver spoon into the top of the white ball of ice cream and then watch for a while how the ice cream melted: how pretty everything was on the extrawhite padded tablecloth, and the game with the spoon had taken on a ridiculous meaning: it was a little sword now stabbing the scoop of vanilla, getting closer and closer to the bottom of the cup, an occurrence that she began to fear, half-serious, half-jesting, and thinking that her game was strange or dumb. Still, she wanted to see what would happen in the end, that is, when the little spoon touched the bottom of the cup and Juan Lucas asked for the bill because it was time to leave and get on with things, now that she was starting to get sleepy, feeling lazy, and didn't want to suffer. Perhaps Julius' bonfire would speed things up, perhaps it was better that way.

The headwaiter had suggested the bonfire for Julius: crepes suzette. The young gentleman would enjoy them. Susan agreed thinking this would delay their departure. How strange I am! To think the fire will make the ice cream melt faster and precipitate the inevitable collision of the little sword and the bottom of the cup. "Yes, yes, you'll love crepes, darling," she said. Julius, who was even yawning right in Juan Lucas' face, didn't have any option but to wake up again upon seeing the headwaiter and the waiter, both pleased, place the apparatus on the table—the shiny silver burner, the small skillet, and all. They watched him do his soft soap and he wanted Julius to ask them something: How do you do it, eh? What's next? Then the moment arrived: take out the elegant matches and light the fire for the young gentleman, the Señores' son, so he would marvel at the sight of it and his mommy would be happy because Don Juan Lucas was annoyed tonight. We had better simply light it and leave as soon as it's done. And the two of them stood there fixing the crepes, swabbing them in Grand Marnier and curacao, transferring to them a sweetened orange and lemon flavor and sticking their hands in the fire to see if the child gets excited at last, but no reaction. The child yawned out loud again. The Aquarium seemed to be getting darker, and he had forgotten all about the Country Club, school, the golf course, and the map of Peru. But immediately the black hole of sleep lit up with flying sparks and a distorted aquarium began to take shape: it was a warm restaurant with an enormous fire at his table and crazy flames that were going to set fire to everything and leap over to José Antonio Bravano's table. He and his wife were already red but neither seemed to burn or sweat, but the flames lost their force and became smaller around his table, enabling them to continue sitting there because they had always been there, forever. The flames brought back the Aquarium and put everything in its place, they brought back the Country Club and put it back in place, they brought back all the head-waiters and waiters in the world and put them all around him. It was as if they had never entered the Aquarium or as if they had never left it: they had always been sitting there and they didn't fear the flames, the fire, the devil, the young gentleman. The young gentleman would like . . . Julius held back another yawn with the palm of his hand and they told him to wait because the dessert was still hot; they were happy, the little gentleman's crepes were ready, the fire was going out, he grimaced, shook his head as if to shoo away a fly and felt sleep coming on again . . . then the heat, and he still had to eat those crepes . . .

The headwaiter and the waiter stood guard at the table and waited until they started to get up. When they started to do so, the headwaiter and the waiter rushed over and gently pulled out their chairs from the table. Now the three of them were standing up. Julius looked over once more, the last time: José Antonio Bravano, lifeless, lit a cigar. His wife was also lifeless, or asleep, or the smoke was bothering her. They had to pass by their table in order to get to the door that connected the restaurant to the hotel. He began walking when he heard Juan Lucas calling to him and pointing to the door that led to the outside garden and onto the street. "Why go that way if this way is shorter," he thought, but the waiter lunged educatedly at the other door, forcing him to change direction and to follow them. Susan lingered a moment at the table and used her hand to push down the little spoon that was still sticking into the deformed, half-melted ball of ice cream: the little sword sank into the cream but found no support and fell over. She moved quickly toward the door, there was still someone there, sitting toward the back of the restaurant, who knew her and watched her leave in her enchanted way.

Now they were silent. Julius was too tired to ask why they left through the door that led to the street or why didn't they take the shortcut along the little path through the garden to the main door of the hotel. Juan Lucas walked ahead and Susan followed behind. Julius, who was about six feet behind, saw her extend a rigid arm with an open hand, as if to say come here, grab my hand, we'll walk together. No one said anything and Julius was falling asleep: it couldn't be, but something was happening because suddenly his uncle stopped walking, leaned up against the Jaguar, and waited for them to catch up.

"Well, young man, the night's over for you," he said, almost defiantly. He was wearing enough Yardley perfume to keep him going for a few more hours.

"We're going to sleep, Julius."

"I thought Uncle Juan Lucas wanted to take us for a drive . . ."

"Darling, if there's something your Uncle Juan Lucas doesn't want to do tonight it's take us for a drive."

"I'm going to have a drink. Come with me, Susan . . . I don't think you're so sleepy."

"You're wrong, darling. I'm also falling asleep."

"Well, whatever you want. But I'm going."

"Good-bye, darling."

Juan Lucas got into the car and started the motor while Susan and Julius went toward the hotel garden. Susan stopped and turned around: the Jaguar was backing up. Juan Lucas was trying to maneuver it straight back and he stopped the car when he saw that she was watching him.

"What's wrong?" he yelled.

Susan put her arm over Julius' shoulder and started walking again. Nothing was wrong. The Jaguar remained stopped in the middle of the street.

"What are you trying to tell me, Susan?"

They entered the garden and took the sidewalk leading up to the main revolving door of the hotel. What was she trying to tell him? Susan didn't hear the motor of the Jaguar anymore. It remained stopped there, and probably another speeding car was going to enter the curve on that street, hit the car, and kill Juan Lucas. What are you trying to tell me? . . . They reached the door at the top of the stone steps.

"You first, darling."

The enormous revolving door was massively done in glass and wood with four small compartments for four persons. Julius stepped in, made it turn, Susan followed in another compartment, he pushed it hard, a joke he had played on her before; she couldn't stop the door, starts to totter, but can't stop it, and appears once again on the steps looking out to the street: the Jaguar had just started off, the motor rumbled, and she couldn't see Juan Lucas who had looked the other way in order to turn onto Golf Avenue, in the direction of Freddy Solo's Bar, where so many times they had . . . tell her, tell her to die, tell him to stay in Lima, he'll see, you'll see that tomorrow you'll have been here twenty years now, not that you're unhappy, but twenty years ago you stopped being happy, or young, or free, or single, or a motorcyclist: from motorcyclist to wife; from free to whore; from single to housewife; from whatever you want to whatever you discover you are one day; from Serrat, in London, to a humid mansion in Lima. Stay here. Lima will give you back everything, right down to your virginity, the wedding dress, the church, your respectability, everything is returned to you if you want to play around with it . . . Susan lunged at the door and kicked it so it would turn. Julius pushed it from the inside and then he waited for her. This time she hadn't liked the joke, and they started walking silently toward the elevator, then wait for her to light a cigarette, look toward the bar that's already closed, come back, wait for her with the elevator door open. Susan felt like something was swallowing her up, the elevator door closed behind her, something had ended.

THE SWEDE SAT waiting in the MG that was parked in front of Freddy Solo's Bar. The poor thing was getting tired of waiting, but she couldn't wait for Juan Lucas to show up either. First she sat with her legs stretched out, smoking. Three playboys walked up to her: two of them were drunk, one a Chilean purser on an airline, another said he was a ship magnate, and one who presented himself as Mouse Siles had just stepped on dog crap and walked away, embarrassed. The Swede told them they were all sons of bitches, which was the latest phrase she had learned and she loved it. Feeling brave and self-assured, she remained sitting there until someone came up to her who wanted to watch her car for her. This guy almost frightened her to death and the Swede just about screamed for help. She still hadn't even dared to do it and the guy just stood there with his filthy sailor cap on. Everything he was wearing was filthy. He had appeared out of the dark recesses of the night and the neon sign from Freddy Solo's Bar made him look green. He moved closer, surely he was a thief, a Peruvian assassin, a crazy man, or directly from the slums. The fact is that he repeated his offer to watch your car, Señorita. Naturally, she didn't understand him because she was frightened to death. He thought the blond was an American and, in order to translate for her, he couldn't think of anything better than to wipe the windshield with his dirty rag, leaving it completely blurry and dirtier than before. Now she was sure that this was the beginning of some horrible crime in this land of savages. The Swede leaped up and fell on the sidewalk on the other side of the car. Get out of here! Get out of here! she begged, but the guy just kept repeating his offer to watch her car. He even offered to bring a bucket of water to wash the tires. By then the Swede was putting the top up on the sports car and tightening it down on all sides; then she got inside. Disconcerted, the watchman just stood there but now he insistently pointed to his Coca-Cola bottle cap that he had stuck to his lapel which, according to him, gave him jurisdiction over all the cars parked on the street in front of that bar; besides, he's been doing it for seven years now. The bottle cap badge calmed down the Swede somewhat, and the fact that he never did commit the crime led her to believe that he was nothing but a harmless crazy man. Just in case, though, she closed the windows and locked both doors and she wouldn't make a move until Juan Lucas arrived. That shit, he's late. But Juan Lucas had taken even longer, and the Swede could see that the men who arrived alone or accompanied with women of all types and sizes weren't afraid of him. Nor did they show any disgust toward the eccentric guy. And no one had thought of calling the police or taking him to an insane asylum either. On the contrary, the men told him to take charge of their cars: "You can watch it for me but don't get it dirty," they told him, jokingly. Some of them even patted him on the shoulder, but he must have leprosy or something that dogs get. And the guy was even popular too, and he could tell if someone wasn't Peruvian from their blond hair or from the "tongue" the foreigner would speak, because those who didn't speak Peruvian spoke "tongue" and he knew the words: "Me, Mister, Me, Mister," he would say, after which they would give him a few coins and assign him to watch their cars. "I'm going to ask Juan Lucas about this," the Swede thought, who was still afraid.

She forgot what she was going to ask him. She forgot what she was going to ask him about the guy with the filthy sailor cap. She also forgot about her fear. She forgot about everything when she saw the aerodynamic nose of the powerful Jaguar appear on her right, filling precisely the space that a Cadillac had just vacated. Juan Lucas parked the car, took the key out of the ignition, and leaned over slightly, at which time the Swede took advantage of the flashing light of the neon sign at the bar to delight in contemplating the back of his head down which a few perfect gray hairs glided, which was very appropriate for her, the symbol of an interesting man and masculinity. She extinguished her last cigarette, got out of the MG to wait for him and go in together. She wanted to order a whiskey so she could look at him through the glass in the dim light amid the music and the smoke. She wanted him to say little but to say it well, while she would turn to him from time to time, taking pleasure in the back of his tanned neck, adorned with silver and silk. Juan Lucas opened the door to Freddy Solo's Bar for her.

SUSAN LOOKED AT him sitting on the bed, almost falling asleep. His tie hung from an ear while he unbuttoned his shirt with difficulty. She would have preferred to throw her blue dress off the balcony of the suite but you don't do those things, she wasn't the Swede, oh to hell with it! Why had she come into Julius' room? Oh, yes. It wasn't to tell him that Mommy was going to sleep alone tonight and that he could get into her huge bed with her if he wanted. There's space for twenty more people in this big thing, do you want to, darling? The idea terrified him and he just stared at her. What's wrong? Anything wrong with Uncle Juan? There's never anything wrong, they're always laughing when they're together but . . . what the devil was she doing in here? It wasn't to tell him that tonight I'm going to sleep . . . the robe asphyxiated her, she could take a shower, no, maybe a sleeping pill . . . Susan raced out of the room looking for a whiskey but on her way out everything became so unimportant. It's just that Julius must have noticed she was acting strange . . . What's going on tonight? Now Mommy has closed her door and she's coughing. Or maybe she's crying.

III

THE GIRLS FROM the Marconi neighborhood put on their bathing caps and together jumped into the shallow end of the pool. It was a good moment to get in the water because the gringo, looking tired after high dive number fourteen of the afternoon, had left and disappeared into the nearby garden area. He was a shitty faggot, always disappearing just when they were going to pulverize him. He escaped the other afternoon as well. But it wasn't important, the moment to beat the crap out of him would come soon: any one of them could take care of the matter. The problem was that all of them wanted to punch him out; in the end it's a matter of my girl will love me more if I do it. Now that we french-kiss, just imagine what she'll do if I punch out the puny gringo. The other day Carmincha asked Pepe why he didn't do dives like the gringo. Stupid bitch, of course she's a little whore and even her mother's divorced. Poor Pepe, one of these days they're going to make a cuckold of him. They didn't want any cuckolds in the neighborhood. Our reputation is at stake, guys. And Pepe needs some advice: he should go for Norma, she'll accept him for sure, anything, because they didn't want cuckolds in the neighborhood.

The guys from the Marconi neighborhood who always show up well combed after lunch were smoking while they took account of every unknown swimmer who would jump into the pool. They were at their usual place, the bench nearby. Some were sitting on it, others were standing next to it, and the rest were behind it, leaning on the back and flicking cigarette ashes from time to time on the ones sitting on the bench in front of them. "Shit," the victim would yell, standing up to take vengeance by spitting a small, compact ball of liquid that would hit the culprit's shirt. "You slimeball," the other would holler, cleaning himself off with a handkerchief, while the other would reach into the back pocket of his khaki or blue pants and take out a wide-toothed comb, the best instrument for fixing the little greased mountain that would give you an extra one, two, sometimes two and a half inches of height. They smoked the cigarettes down to where they burned their fingers, then they flicked the lighted butts toward the end of the pool hoping someone barefoot would come by and burn his feet. When they had been seen flicking the butts, the administrator talked to them about it, but they flat out denied it: We are accused of everything and, hey, don't screw us around, man. They continued to enjoy themselves every time someone would burn the bottom of his foot and jump desperately into the pool. They filled the gringo's route from the pool to the diving board with smoldering butts, but when he got out of the pool soaking wet, he would drench everything in his way, so he never got burned. The butts stuck to his feet and he kept running as if nothing had happened. He would climb up onto the diving board, fly off—God only knows how many dives he's done today—get out of the pool at the side and, for the nth time, run toward the diving board with cigarette butts stuck to his feet that had gone out before they could burn him. "Poor gringo," Carmincha had said, but everyone knew who Carmincha was: she got the cold shoulder. Hey, Pepe, take some medicine for your mental weakness, they had to apply the law of the neighborhood.

But the Marconi girls said no, absolutely not: he couldn't break up with Carmincha. Who did they think they were? They smoked some more and the guys fought with the girls and said they were going to some other neighborhoods to look for chicks, a lover in every port, and all that stuff. That night Luque stole his brother-in-law's car and the whole neighborhood, packed in like sardines, took off drinking and landed up drunk in a whorehouse on Colonial Avenue. Three of them took on girls while others neither tried nor had money to try, they just had enough to drink a few more beers. Two others deserted them, falling in love with their girlfriends after the third bottle, and one wanted to commit suicide. The next day all of them were feeling rotten when they showed up at the Country Club pool. The girls hadn't gone swimming in the morning. The guys were smoking like chimneys and spent hours on end glued to the counter at the bar, asking for cold water to put out the fire that consumed them. From time to time they would glance over at the entrance to the pool, but still no girls. They knew that they had gone to try on their school's uniforms. Summer was coming to an end.

The girls came that afternoon, but the guys said to hell with them and didn't even say hello. The poor girls were really sad. Carmincha wanted to talk to them and explain that she was the way she was, that there was nothing bad about the way she was. She wanted to ask them to forgive her, hoping that they would do it quickly because her friends had convinced her: You have to say you're sorry, do it for us, and then she started to lose interest. She would do it for Cecilia who was the only one who understood her, poor thing, she liked the gringo more than Pepe. Cecilia understood her when she cried. Yes, she would do it for her. She would wait until the gringo finished his great exhibition diving and only then would she swim with everyone, it was the only way in which they would realize that her girlfriends were in love with them, that's the most she would do. They put on their bathing caps, jumped into the water together, swam around slowly, looked at the guys, swish, they dove down under the water where they loved them intensely.

The guys continued to smoke. The gringo had disappeared and his route from the pool to the diving board was full of smoldering cigarette butts. But all of a sudden he came running full speed out of the garden toward the diving board, climbed out like a madman, and jumped from the diving board imitating the whistle of an airplane in a nosedive and then pierced the water. What squealing, eh? . . . Geez, the gringo was a fairy besides. The boys smoked more and more when they saw the girls leaving the pool together. The girls called out to Carmincha, asking her, pleading with her, to get out of the pool, but Carmincha completely ignored them and didn't even look at them.

"Fucking whore," Luque said, standing up and fixing his hair on the sides with the palms of his hands. "Fucking whore," Carlos said, standing up and rearranging his testicles in front of the whole Country Club. The entire Marconi neighborhood looked up at the same time when the gringo walked in front of them heading toward the diving board, but those gringos never learn and, besides, this gringo hadn't even seen them. "Fucking whore," Enrique said, rubbing his wrists. "Yeah, fucking whore," Pepe murmured, forlorn. Manolo, who was next to him, offered him a lit match with a shaky hand when the other already had his cigarette well lit. Cecilia took Manolo's arm and blew out the match with a new and marvelous smile. She's a young woman, that's what she is. A large drop of water fell from her wet hair down to her turned-up nose and followed the curve that made her profile look so cute. From there it fell finally onto her upper lip, quenching her smile and giving her face a serious expression that was appropriate for important occasions like the one that was about to happen: "Leave Carmincha alone," she blurted out nervously, unable to control herself, falling into Pepe's arms and giving him a poorly aimed kiss on the cheek after which she took off running. Manolo took off after her, still holding the match in his hand. Pepe also wanted to follow and the others tried to stop him. "Leave me alone," he yelled. He managed suddenly to pull away from Luque and Carlos who were holding him by his arms. He got away from them, and they debated whether to help the fallen one or attack the enemy, but then the girls decided to follow Cecilia's example and they went up and kissed their guys on their cheeks. Some of the girls even stuck their hands underneath the guys' shirts in order to caress those virile chests. Carlos was going to yell something at the gringo who was coming back from another high dive, but at that moment he felt his girl's warm hand where each day more and more hair was growing. He couldn't hold back his urge to smoke and dropped down onto the bench, opening a new pack of Chesterfield . . . Little by little, the Marconi neighborhood began to calm down.

But Chino, who was a perfect wise guy and didn't have a girlfriend, thought the matter couldn't end just like that; in fact, he was furious. Moments earlier he had yelled be quiet, you old bitch! at a woman who went by saying that today was the last day for swimming, tomorrow back to school, and bla, bla, bla. Of course he was going to punch out the gringo but the matter involving Carmincha . . . "We've got to do something to that whore." Chino was really crude because he had said whore in front of the girls. They turned to him: Be careful, guy, keep it to yourself, show some respect. Between acting like little dolls and showing indignation, they said that if you guys defend him, we'll defend Carmincha. The row was about to begin all over again, but Chino himself defused it saying we're not going to fight over this and create more problems while this whor . . . oops, sorry, while Carmincha goes swimming like nothing's happened. Why don't we do something to her . . . play a joke on her? Look, I've got a can of shoe polish left over from Carnival. How about it? What do you think, guys? . . . and if the gringo gets involved, I'll take care of him. It wasn't a bad idea after all, because that Carmincha was acting so stuck up. She didn't even look at them. She just stayed in the water, holding onto the side of the pool and admiring the gringo. What's she gonna do next? Clap for him when he jumps? Screw this! Hey, guys, let's do it for the neighborhood. Hand me a Chester, buddy, now give me the shoe polish, man, but what can we do to make her come over here?

That's when it occurred to Manolo, the imbecile, to send Julius over to get him a cigarette from the neighborhood gang. For some time lately Cecilia had been talking to Julius when she saw him at the pool. At first Manolo didn't like the idea but after a while he got used to their conversations and now he even liked to talk to him. Cecilia was so cute when she talked to the kid; she was so happy and really put on a show. It was great to sit down together, just the three of them and talk, away from the gang. And they listened to him talk about Cinthia, a little sister he once had, and about a thousand other things. Some of them seemed strange, but the little guy was a millionaire and anything was possible; in fact, very possible because the kid, Cecilia would say, was always very nervous and he would shake all over from the cold because he would spend the whole day in his bathing suit and he was skinny, but he also shivered because he was nervous. He was cute and she would take her towel from her shoulders and put it around him so he wouldn't shake so much. The three of them just talked together, thinking what it would be like when they get married. My first child has to be a boy, a little Manolo. Of course, they talked about other things in front of Julius, less intimate topics, but in their eyes you could see they were thinking about the future, like when you become an engineer or something, they would talk about when it started to get dark and they were

253

alone . . . "Go ask the gang to lend me a cigarette," Manolo told him. He was an imbecile, not thinking about what those guys—that Marconi riffraff—were capable of doing to Julius, who had been going about for the first time in his life idolizing a girl who wasn't Cinthia's age nor his mother's. He didn't understand Manolo at first and waited for Cecilia to say something, but she was an idiot as well and sent him off: "Go ahead but come right back, kid." In truth, she was dying to give Manolo a kiss and at the same time make him understand once and for all that Carmincha wasn't a bad girl or anything, simply that she was drooling over the gringo. It was time for the gringo to stop diving and discover that there are women in this world. Julius had approached them at that moment and it was good he left for a while: getting the cigarette was a good pretext and, besides, it was true.

The famous Chino saw Julius and thought he was perfect. Sure they would give Manolo a cigarette, but first Julius had to do them a favor. The girls protested: sure it was a joke, but it was a bad joke. They had refused to call Carmincha over to them and now they refused to let the little guy get her for them. "Well, why don't you just get into the water with her? Are you on her side?" Luque asked. No, no, but the joke was too cruel and Carmincha was going to believe that they were the ones who sent him over to get her and they didn't want to have anything to do with their plan. "So . . . ?" Luque said. No, no, no, they had just made peace and they didn't want to start fighting again. "It's only a joke," Chino told them. But they didn't want to fight either, and what else could they do? They gave in, finally, and Chino explained the plan to Julius: they only wanted her to get out of the pool for a moment so they could grab her and toss her back into the water. If she didn't come, it was going to be worse: they'd throw all of her things into the pool. Go ahead, kid, tell her to come over here, tell her that we only want to shake hands and be friends. When she goes to shake hands, we'll grab her, we'll lift her up a little and throw her into the water, that's all . . . Julius left, had reached the edge of the pool, and was about to get in when a bloodcurdling scream was heard all over the Country Club and even in nearby San Isidro. Everyone looked toward the diving board where the gringo was screaming and whirling his arms like propellers: he's gone craaaaaaaaaaaaaaaaaazy! Running like never before, he flew like never beeeeeeeeeeeeeeefore! The gringo flew hiiiiiiiiiiiiiiiiiiiigh into the air! And then hit the water. Seconds later Cecilia and Manolo ran over to the neighborhood bench. There was absolute silence: the gringo didn't come up, he had disappeared into the deep part of the pool.

"He must have drowned," several began to think, and even the guys from the Marconi neighborhood began to feel sorry for him. Maybe the gringo would have been a nice guy, too. But he wasn't coming up, the people around the pool were holding their breath, panicked to death, and didn't dare look over the edge. Only Julius stood there next to the edge and he could see that the gringo hadn't hit the bottom of the pool or broke his head open or anything. At first he was a little afraid when he saw him go to the deepest part and sit down as if he were meditating, until it seemed like he had made the decision to swim under the water to the shallow end, where Carmincha was probably waiting for him as if the whole thing had been a preconceived plan. That's what was happening under the water, not around the pool where Luque was already taking his shirt off in order to dive in and look for the poor gringo who, putting all the asinine behavior aside, seemed like a decent enough guy. A lady prayed nearby: "Do something, for heaven's sake!" and Luque had already forgotten about the law of the neighborhood and all the rest, when all of a sudden a hysterical but fake shriek was heard coming from Carmincha and everyone saw her rise out of the water about three feet: it was the gringo who had swum between her legs and raised her up on his shoulders out of the water—a happy rebirth for the king of the great high divers. Carmincha was laughing now, poised perfectly on his shoulders, and that's the way love would be for her in the future: a jump and a dive. She wouldn't have to ask this guy to stop smoking like she had asked Pepe. The only thing she would ask him not to do was kill himself on the diving board. Everyone was still stunned from what had happened, and then they got furious later when the gringo who had made them suffer let out another infuriating scream. Then he would lift Carmincha onto the edge of the pool, jump up, run over the smoldering cigarette butts but never get burned, pull up poor Carmincha from the edge, she's dumb but likes the gringo, and carry her any way he could over to the diving board, there he goes with her, that gringo is quite a guy! The Marconi gang watched him pick her up between her legs—not trying to be fresh with her nor grab her inner thighs, her cunt, or anything—and carry her off to his kingdom, up there, on the diving board. He only wanted her to jump off the diving board with him. Poor Carmincha, a new life had begun for her. "She always liked what was forbidden," Luque thought, but his thoughts didn't seem to bear out the truth. That gringo's a brute: now he was screaming savagely again and throwing poor Carmincha into the water; she fell on her stomach, a belly flop, and the gringo landed right next to her, happy. Carmincha came to the surface feeling brave but crying, the gringo screamed again, Cecilia waved good-bye to them, and Chino, who hadn't forgotten the law of the neighborhood, pushed a servant into the pool, grabbed another on her rear end, daubed shoe polish all over a third one, the Cholo porter came over to quiet them down and they got polish all over him too, Luque threw Chino into the water and wiped shoe polish all over Carlos, Manolo got it in his eye, and Cecilia broke out laughing on seeing Manolo half-blind and furious. At that moment the gringo noticed that crazy group of guys for the first time, but the hotel manager came over just then: tomorrow everyone's going back to school! The pool would be closing. The gringo closed the place with another happy shriek and poor Carmincha belly-flopped again. She'd never learn and her chest and stomach hurt. She tried to tell him but all he wanted to do was go on jumping, and she would have to study her English more because the gringo didn't even understand pain in Spanish.

THE BIG GUYS

THE ARENAS BROTHERS were already dirty by the time they arrived at school. They looked like they had been trying on their uniforms the day before and, since no one was careful to make sure they didn't get dirty, they left them on and in half an hour they were filthy. Someone said they had even slept in their uniforms which were, in fact, wrinkled and dirty. Still, the Arenas kids would show up happy, and the fact is as a pair they were never picked on. Naturally, Cano was the one who showed up really sad. He had stopped feeling sad off and on some time ago, but now he was sad all the time and, besides, he had dandruff. Chubby Martinto had come back but he had failed again. It was difficult for him to remember Julius had been his friend once. Everyone was returning now and the annual scene was being repeated next to the door that opened onto the big patio: it was the group of new kids who were arriving for the first time and who absolutely refused to stay. "I want my Mommy! I want my Mommy!" they screamed. The poor things, it was heartbreaking, wearing their impeccable blue uniforms and large white, stiffly starched collars that were so bothersome at first, for the madder they got and moved their little necks, the more irritated their necks became. The job of receiving them at the school fell to Mary Agnes, who had already been waiting for them patiently, smiling, so enchanting that some mothers suffered more than their children upon seeing they were leaving little Ricardo, for example, in the hands of such a pretty nun who smelled so good. The nuns at Immaculate Heart School were American and they always smelled so clean. For breakfast they probably ate cornflakes that you find in boxes containing the best corn and a great deal of California sun. Mother Mary Agnes didn't suffer because of the new kids: sometimes she felt like she was going to lose her patience, but then she would touch the beads of her rosary and

257

from down there a smile would rise to her lips again. Sánchez Concha
had grown up, man, he had really stretched out during the summer, but
he wasn't dumb and, before taking on the role of bully, he preferred to
spend the first day checking things out, just in case there was some other
third grader who had grown taller than him and who just might belt
me. Del Castillo had turned blond but he hadn't grown much. Julius
had grown taller but he was getting skinnier every day and would only
punch out someone if they challenged him to it and he had no alternative. He came to school in a brand new Mercury station wagon, the
same one that Juan Lucas said he had insured against all hazards except
Bobby who, before arriving at Markham School, had planned on hitting
at least twelve curves at full speed in front of the car belonging to a girl
from Villa María. He met her in Ancón one day when Peggy, the Canadian, had a cold. Bobby had dropped off Julius at Immaculate Heart:
Hurry, get out, shithead, and he sped off to look for the new girl's car.
He had already figured out the route between the house and Villa
María. Carlos sat next to him and ate calmly. He had lost any fear of
death and he didn't mind Bobby driving the car; hence, he could continue eating his bread and roast pork, for that was the hour he preferred
to eat breakfast, and he even brought along his thermos with hot tea.

Upon entering the school, Julius felt like his feet were sinking down
into the ground as he walked. At first he thought he was going to faint
but, once he knew that he wasn't, he began to realize that he had grown
taller. He was in third grade now, and he was one of the older ones at
the school; hence the cement floors seemed further away and the school
smaller: I'm one of the older guys. It was always a big place but now
everything seemed within his reach, everything was easier this year and
even though the windows were still massive, perhaps the largest he had
ever seen, at least they couldn't swallow him up now, they'd never be as
large as they used to be. It was a strange sensation, even more strange
now because he was looking at all the boys, those whom he knew and
those little kiddies who are arriving for the first time. He wouldn't even
try to learn their names and none of them would ever manage to
frighten him. He didn't know why, no matter how much he thought
about it, he didn't know why he felt he could let out a scream and
silence everyone. He also felt that it would be easy to be one of the bad
guys too. Of course, Del Castillo, the Arenas brothers, Sánchez Concha
and the others in third year could also be bad guys this year. So what
does one do? . . . You can be bad among all of those who aren't in third
grade but you can also be bad among the bad ones, and he looks down
at the ground for an answer: Who is going to answer you, Julius? . . .

The piano teacher/nun approached him nervously. Why Julius? Why did your mother decide to do such a thing? Julius looked at her without understanding why she was so nervous. Just when he was starting to be a bad guy she approaches with the fragrance of those piano keys. What had Mommy decided to do? She had already made the decision and had informed the nun by letter. Now the nun, smelling luscious, was informing him: your mother says you must take your piano lessons seriously and you are going to practice several hours every week with a German lady, who is a prominent piano teacher. Her cousin Susana Lastarria, whose little kids studied here, had convinced Susan to do it; frankly, Julius was talented. You are talented, Julius, and this year you'll work with another teacher, an excellent German teacher . . . That's when she must have offered up her humility to God upon relinquishing her student to the great German professor, it must have been that way because the piano teacher/nun with that fragrance became nervous and bit her lip. "I had planned on teaching you the United States national anthem," she managed to say, leaving in a hurry under the pretext that they were going to ring the bell, and I still have to talk to several more students who want to continue their classes with me. Trembling, the piano teacher/nun left and Julius froze in his tracks, searching for reasons: why wouldn't Mommy have said something to me? He postponed being bad at school for a more appropriate time. After all, what did it matter to be older if the important decisions still came from above, without even consulting him. He imagined the aromatic piano, the squeaky clean keys, and he ran off to join Del Castillo and Sánchez Concha, next to whom he might grow some more perhaps. Look, there's Chubby Martinto. Get a load of the Arenas brothers. Hey, look at Chávez, and there's Cano.

Poor Cano. He only had a few cents he had stolen from his grandmother and was buying some candy from the Pirate who had stuck his wares through the wire fence. He was about to transact some business when right then Carrottop saw what was going on and rushed over to them, ringing her bell furiously and turning red as she ran. How many times do I have to tell you? Listen, Mister, it is absolutely forbidden to sell poisoned candies to the children, all this in English. Meanwhile, the Pirate worked desperately to pull his hand back through the fence and, at the same time, tried to hand over the candies and get the money. Cano, who was tall now, also froze on the spot. "I'm going, Mother, I'm going," the Pirate kept saying. Undoubtedly worms were growing under that black patch covering his left eye, "I'm going," he repeated. True, he was going but only because it was class time and the kids were going to leave the patio area. As always, he would return at recess time; for years he had competed with the clean, pasteurized North American candy that the nuns were selling to collect money for the missions and to promote the religious calling. The Pirate was something of a businessman; he would manage to get the money but wouldn't let go of the candy. Carrottop led Cano away. He was sad again. "I'll get 'em to you later," the Pirate called out, but heaven only knows if Cano heard him because his grandmother had told him one day that a thief who robs a thief will be freed of a hundred years of grief and that's exactly what had happened to him.

Out of breath, Carrottop had taken her place on the platform along with the other nuns. She had just aligned the classes by rows in perfect formation, two by two and by height. And now they were going to sing the Peruvian National Anthem and the school song. The piano teacher/nun raised her arm to begin, and it was still up in the air when Chubby Martinto let out "We're free," words directly from the national anthem, completely out of tune, and Carrottop, furious, ran over to pinch him soundly. She was unable to do it, fortunately, because the Mother Superior decided that it was the first day of school and he had only been joking. They would be practicing every day, nevertheless, and soon we'll be singing this country's anthem the way it should be sung, including the school song and the anthem of my country. It's a very pretty and very big country, and one day you'll be able to visit it because here we are going to teach you the best English, and you'll be able to take a plane and fly zooooooooooooom and land rrrrrrrrrrrrrrrrr in the United States, and when you start to miss your own country, which is also pretty, you'll take another plane and rrrrrrrrrrrrrr you'll come flying back to Lima, what do you think, eh? And everyone yelled yeeeeeeeeeees and laughed. Carrottop returned to join the other nuns and some of the kindergarten kids had been frightened by the roar of the airplane engines: rrrrrrrrrrr. Showing loving care, Mary Trinity ran over to the crying children, while the piano teacher/nun raised and lowered her arm rapidly in order to prevent Martinto from making another mistake. Everyone sang the Peruvian National Anthem and the Immaculate Heart school song. Then the Mother Superior spoke again; she was more serious this time and Carrottop nodded approvingly. The new nuns were presented to the children and they each nodded upon hearing their name called out. Smelling of cleanliness, they smiled. When the Mother Superior alluded to the immense sacrifice that they had made to leave their country and to come here to educate the best little children of Peru, the nuns turned serious and grasped their rosaries, for their lives centered around their enormous rosaries at the end of which hung beautiful black, gold-edged crosses with gold Christ figures.

Entering their classrooms signified that another school year had begun. The first day the third year students spent the whole morning staring at each other, studying each other, and calculating the inches that one was taller than the other. Little by little they calmed down, but Sánchez Concha spent several days making everyone realize that he could barely fit into his school desk; and he had to make a big deal out of it. In addition, Sánchez Concha was an agile soccer player, Morales had said it himself. He'll probably be appointed captain of the school team, which frustrated Del Castillo.

Two weeks later, Sánchez Concha had become the captain of the soccer team, and Del Castillo's black eye was disappearing after he was punched out when he fouled the team captain. Julius was also on the team, but he wasn't the goalie as he had asked to be, but rather an outside forward. "You'll do better at the wing position," Morales told him, snapping a towel on his ass. "You're so skinny, you've got to be an end. They have to be tall and thin so they can do the running, forget about being goalie and the other cra . . ." He was going to say crap but he saw Mother Mary Joan approaching. She was one of the nuns who had come this year but who had been in Mexico before and understood the rules of soccer. Mother Mary Joan went to all the practices. In the afternoons, as soon as Morales blew his whistle as referee, trainer, and technical director, the nun would show up, always smiling and blessing the game with her kindness and, of course, preventing Morales from using foul language. Then she would roll up her sleeves because she was the athletic nun and she loved soccer.

Three weeks later Sánchez Concha punched out Del Castillo again, and had added to his list of stompings those given to Zapatero, Espinosa, de los Heros, and Julius who had just been pulverized by Sánchez Concha in a fight that morning. Julius was telling the incredible story about his German music teacher, who was the granddaughter of Beethoven, etc., when all of a sudden the other guy showed up yelling Liar! at him. No one even believes what you eat! and then he said his sister was going to have a party but she wasn't going to invite his brother, Bobby, because he didn't have a father but a stepfather. Julius wasn't opposed to anyone calling Juan Lucas a stepfather, but what he couldn't stand was that this guy had screwed up his story about Beethoven's granddaughter. They challenged each other to a fight after school, and Julius went to his piano classes that afternoon with a huge scratch on his face.

261

"ACTUALLY, DARLING, it was your Aunt Susana's idea," Susan explained to him when Julius, upon returning from his first day of classes, practically accused her of high treason, of having put him in an extremely delicate situation in front of the nun who went off in a huff. Mommy, she was a very good teacher and I want to continue taking lessons from her. Please say yes, Mommy. Please, Mommy. But Mommy was a little tired that day. It seemed like it was the last sunny day, fall was on its way, and the garden at the Country Club, out in front, would soon fill up with *autumn leaves* and *feuilles mortes*. Moreover, Mommy had just returned from the beauty shop and she had her hair covered with a white silk handkerchief. There was no way she could toss back her marvelous lock of hair because there wasn't any this time. Also, if she continued trying to think of an explanation for Julius, who was standing there waiting for one, her tea that a waiter had just brought her in a delicate silver tea service would get cold. She picked up a piece of toast, put some English orange marmalade on it, and offered it to Julius. You're really skinny, darling.

"Mommy, I don't want to take lessons from the German teacher, I like the nun better."

"And, little man, how do you know you like the nun better?"

It was a bad moment to initiate that dialogue-protest, because the one who responded was none other than Juan Lucas. Elegantly dressed, he had just appeared crossing the lobby of the hotel before the interested stare of an exiled Bolivian woman who was drinking tea at a table a little further away from Susan.

"Let's see, here, prove to me that the nun is a better teacher. And tell me, young man, are you really interested in playing the piano or do you want to become an organ player in some church? They castrate those guys, don't they? Ah, no, they do that to those who sing . . ."

"Darling," Susan intervened, "your aunt Susana is right: she says the sooner you change teachers, the better. You will have to change teachers next year anyway, when you go to another school . . . My tea is getting cold, and we should start thinking about getting you enrolled in another school for next year . . ."

A waiter crossed the immense lobby of the hotel and Susan called him over to order the child's tea, right away, please.

"It's getting late, darling. Drink your tea and tomorrow when you go to your first piano class you'll see how much you like your new teacher."

"You know, young man, that Germany is a country of musicians," said Juan Lucas, adopting the role of educator that he bungled miserably. "Do you know who Beethoven is? Do you? Well, your uncle Juan Lucas is paying for you to take classes with none other than Beethoven's granddaughter."

Susan loved the bit about Beethoven's granddaughter. Julius, on the other hand, remembered that Beethoven was the bust with an embittered face sitting on the piano at the Lastarria castle. If Cinthia only knew I was going to take lessons from Beethoven's granddaughter . . . but it probably wasn't true.

"Mommy, Uncle Juan is lying."

Uncle Juan was in excellent humor and he didn't have to go anywhere, so he had all the time in the world for his family, his children, their education, etc.

"What do you mean lying? . . . about such an important matter? . . . lying about a person's genealogy?"

They really got Julius with that word. It sounded important. It sounded like the truth. One doesn't lie about matters of genealogy. What was genealogy? Juan Lucas noticed that he was impressed and impressionable. The penal code severely punishes those who lie about genealogy.

Susan's tea had become delicious as she noticed that Juan Lucas was happily spending some time with Julius. Ah, Juan darling.

"Come over here, young man. Sit down here between your mother and me. Let's see, they're already bringing your tea . . . put it here, there you are, thanks . . . bring me a mineral water, please . . . the duck and rice dish we had at Romero's for lunch was a little strong . . . let's see, you know about Beethoven, right? Good. And you know that when he died he was as deaf as that wall? And do you know why he became deaf? You don't know? . . . ah, then you don't know anything about the family relationships of geniuses, my good friend.

Susan felt like her tea had just arrived from India. An English colony?

"*What about them?*" she asked, delighted. She wanted to know everything about geniuses.

"Geniuses," said Juan Lucas. "Geniuses," he repeated, but couldn't remember anything from high school or university. He had read *Time* once, something about Einstein. "Geniuses! Sure! Beethoven! of course . . ."

Julius didn't waste any time insisting again on the piano teacher/nun and he was going to say . . .

"A problem of genealogy. Look here, young man, geniuses are difficult types, the strangest creatures there are, always wearing huge wigs and fuming all the time. I know, it sounds exaggerated. Look, Julius, Beethoven had three children all of whom were real turkeys at the keyboard. They played so badly that their father threw them out of the house and never again did he want to be affiliated with them. Ah, now there's a problem of genealogy . . . Remind me that I have to call one of my lawyers, Susan. Where's that dunce waiter with my mineral water . . . Here he comes, here he comes."

"Lawyers are always involved in matters of genealogy," Susan intervened, wishfully hoping that Juan Lucas would say his lawyers only occupied themselves with other matters because maybe he was involved in problems of genealogy with that Swede . . . I didn't think he was dumb enough to get himself so involved . . .

"That depends on their specialty," explained Juan Lucas. "Mine only handle business matters."

Susan was joyous that the affair involving the Swede didn't amount to anything. Basically, they're darling's little adventures and nothing more. It would have been so clumsy for all of us if one day she would have gone to Juan's office with a sad, stupid face, wearing a dress and explaining in poor Spanish that she had missed her period and was expecting . . .

Juan Lucas drank his mineral water in moderation, Susan dedicated herself to her tea from colonial India, Julius ate a snack and, at the table a little further away, the exiled Bolivian was talking to the Chilean ambassador, a very elegant woman. Julius began to feel sorry for the piano teacher/nun again, he could still smell those piano keys, Mommy . . .

"The genealogy of geniuses!" Juan Lucas exclaimed again, inventing something else, for he was in a good mood. "Papa Beethoven threw his three kids out of the house. Forever. Now you know what's waiting for you if you bamboozle us as a pianist."

"Our little Beethoven," Susan called him, pleased, Indian tea garden and gypsy violins, with a stereo and no gypsies, fresh air and a setting sun. Juan Lucas appeared to be wearing a wig, he was disgusted, but Susan's joke triumphed and she removed the silk scarf from her hair, discovering that marvelous lock of hair, clean, recently done up at the beauty shop. Juan Lucas thought that if they hurried they could catch the sun setting over the ocean. Why don't we have an aperitif at the Yacht Club in Callao? And you, son, don't worry about it, I'll tell you all you'll need to know. Now you're going to find out who geniuses are, and above all about your teacher's grandfather. You start classes with her tomorrow, right? . . . but now you're coming with us to the Yacht Club.

"And you, what do you know about genius genealogy? Julius yelled at Sánchez Concha. He had already gone to nine classes with the German teacher and now he was positive that she was Beethoven's granddaughter. Sánchez Concha didn't know anything about genius genealogy and he left burning mad. The rest stayed there: Del Castillo, de los Heros, Broken Mirror (his last name was Espejo or Mirror and he had a scar on his forehead), the stinking Arenas brothers, Zapatero, Espinosa, Cano, who was still sad, and Winston Churchill, yes, that was his name and he was from Nicaragua. Julius was also surrounded by other boys in second grade and even some first graders. The story of genius genealogy sparked their interest.

"But one of the three children got married and had a daughter whom he taught to play the piano. She was the one who turned out to be the genius," Julius said remembering the story that Juan Lucas had told him at the Yacht Club. Those were his words: At the age of five the little girl played the piano perfectly and her father taught her every day because one day he was going to take her to Beethoven and say: Here, listen to your granddaughter. You denied me genealogy but you can't with her because she too is a genius, like you, Father, and for sure Beethoven was going to break down and cry and pardon them all.

Martinto showed up armed with a huge sword made out of a piece of wood and challenged the whole group to a duel but no one even turned around to look at him. Chubby didn't feel at all rebuffed by those cowards, and so in furious fashion he continued forward and joined in a deadly battle with a cypress tree at the back of the patio.

"And one afternoon he took her to see Beethoven. He didn't want to see them but the other wouldn't give up until he had no choice but to let them in."

"I'll bet the little girl was afraid and peed her pants," Del Castillo said.

"You think so! The girl began to play the piano and even played better than Beethoven who turned green with envy. Since he was a genius he used his superpowers to tune her out, he was dying of envy, he tried really hard not to listen to her and he went deaf forever."

"And then?"

"Then she grew up and the Nazis in Germany were really mean and began to blame her that she had struck her grandfather in the ear. They began to harass her, so she escaped to America and changed her name. No one knows she's Beethoven's granddaughter, no one is supposed to know. She changed her name and doesn't want to have anything to do with the genealogy of geniuses. I've been taking lessons from her for three weeks and now she's called Frau Proserpina."

"Have you asked her about it?"

"Don't be stupid."

"Liar! No one believes what you say!" No one noticed that Sánchez Concha was back to attack Julius again. "My sister is going to have a party for her friends at Villa María and she's not going to invite your brother Bobby because he doesn't have a father, only a stepfather, and I'll see you after school!"

It was going to have to be after school because Carrottop, who was happy, rang her bell announcing that recess was over.

BOBBY WAS INVOLVED in cutting up with the car in front of the new girl's house, she was the one who attended Villa María. He would get the station wagon every afternoon and Susan had to give the Mercedes to Carlos, three times a week, to take Julius to the middle of Lima for his classes with Frau Proserpina. It would be getting dark at the golf course at that hour and Juan Lucas would be showering after his afternoon golf game; Susan would wait for him as she talked with some of her friends whom she would see in the winter months, the Marquis, for instance, or ambassadors, wives of Juan Lucas types, or other golfers' wives. It was getting dark in Lima when Carlos crossed Colmena Avenue and headed up Tacna in order to turn onto Arequipa Avenue where Beethoven's granddaughter had her academy. He couldn't help but laugh upon seeing the unfortunate condition of Julius' cheek and his inability to hide his anger after the fight. Fortunately his anger was dissipating somewhat and, as they approached the academy, Julius began to feel a different sensation was consuming him; it was fear perhaps, but not the fear of a poorly prepared piano student, but rather because once again he would have to penetrate that old, large broken-down house where everything looked like it was about to come tumbling down any day now. "He got punched out and the one who did it is Sánchez Concha. He also has a station wagon and a chauffeur . . ." The idea hit Carlos suddenly: he began imagining how he would like to clobber Sánchez Concha's chauffeur a couple of times tomorrow. "Who gives a damn, after all," he thought, while he drove the Mercedes. "Who gives a damn, but they did punch out little Julius. Well, maybe he deserved it; in any case it's not my problem. Christ! Change lights will you!" He looked at Julius: "Look what they've done to him. Change lights, damn it!" "Hey, Julius," he said suddenly. "What did you say to the guy who punched you out? Did you tell him off? Do you know how to cuss someone out? . . . Well, listen, because I'm going to teach you a few words so you can tell the next one who gives it to you where to go, listen . . . And you've got to learn to use your head to hit someone when you fight. The problem is that you little white kids don't know how to use your heads, I'm going to show you how to shell it out with your head. Nope, you white kids don't use your heads when you play soccer. Or do you just assume that your head is only for thinking? You can spend your whole life thinking and along comes someone and they give it to you. Well, here we are at your teacher's house, hop out fast and I'll look for a place to park, then I'll meet you at the door . . . they've beaten you up because you don't know how to use your head, go on, hop out . . ." Tomorrow he was going to cut Sánchez Concha's driver off and if he says anything I'll crown him, all because of that stupid Julius, the little wise guy.

It was like a carriage entrance, an entryway or whatever the name was they gave to the horrible patio that he had to cross through. Julius just stood there, examining the immense rotten vestibule doors at the entrance, no one closed them anymore because the hinges were completely rusted and the doors would just stay that way, open forever. A little further away, he saw a broken electric light switch. It was probably the same one that electrocuted those kids Nilda had read about in the newspapers. They would stick their fingers in broken light switches. And then the story about the little baby, poor little creature, the one who was peeing on the ground, to pee is to urinate, Julius, the one who was peeing next to a switch which was broken and all. Well, because of the urine, the electricity went up his pee pee and his mother became an orphan. No, Nilda: orphan is the one whose mother electrocutes herself. Whatever the case, it was safer for him to go through the patio in the dark, being careful not to twist his ankle where a brick was missing, most of them were missing anyway, or in one of the holes where the bricks used to be, cross the entryway looking at the people hiding behind those filthy windows, or sitting under single light bulbs hanging from way up high. They're all so strange, I've never seen people like them before. A schoolgirl entered the patio, even though most girls who go to school don't live here. But this schoolgirl opened the door and Julius stopped, dying of curiosity: a friend was waiting for her. He was half-hidden: I hope they don't see me watching them. The schoolgirl let the other in and they sat down with their books to study under that single dim light bulb that hung from way up high, how can they study without good light? One of the schoolgirls looked up and Julius continued walking slowly and crossed the middle of the patio. So many doors and big windows, they can't be houses but then he saw a bed and a white woman all dressed in white who closed her door defiantly. What are you looking at, kid? Then the curtain was drawn, she'll probably get undressed. Now Julius continued forward rapidly and he stumbled on a step. He came upon a dark area and then another patio with more windows and another schoolgirl: pretty, pretty, pretty. But Julius started to get cold. At the stairs, he looked back, she was pretty, real pretty, and she smiled at him. There were innumerable windows with light bulbs hanging down from high ceilings. That's an office, but what does that man do with so many newspapers? He's got thousands of them, no, millions, and I've been coming for three weeks and he's still reading them. He's probably going to read all of them, I've got to ask Mommy what a court clerk is, yeah, that's what I think it says, should I get a closer look or not? COURT CLE . . . Now the white schoolgirl is smiling at me but she's not like the ones who go to Villa María. Cinthia: she has a friendly smile and she's pretty pretty pretty. Julius barged up the stairs that led to the second balcony where there were a lot more windows, just like downstairs: rows of windows on the four sides of the courtyard, all with light bulbs, too. While he walked along the corridor, he could see another bed, no, there were four beds in that room and he kept walking. There's the little man who always smiles at me and his old bald noggin is still shining. The little old man is always reading the newspaper, his bald head always shining, and he's got to be an intelligent person: his round little glasses look like the ends of soft drink bottles. He must be real intelligent. Today, he greeted me. It's time for class. I had better hurry. I'm not prepared for this lesson. I didn't have time to go over it after school. Carlos has taught me how to cuss out Sánchez Concha, to use my head to land hard blows, and I'm going to cuss him out, but don't say anything using Mother, Julius, Nilda would always warn. Gotta hurry, she must be waiting, Frau Proserpina is really strange, she's so old. Uncle Juan says not to talk to her about Beethoven, it might be too painful for her but she probably doesn't remember anymore because now she's so old. Turn to the left. Julius continued down a long corridor where he could also electrocute himself if he decided to turn on the light that probably doesn't exist. He kept walking and there was another row of windows along there, too, but the people were never white and they had hung their clothes out, so the place always smelled of soap and dampness. Poor Frau Proserpina, she only speaks German and has to live there besides, but she's also hard as nails, and I don't want her to rap my hands anymore when I make mistakes. Julius continued along the corridor, passing by the windows of those shabby rooms, smaller than those facing out onto the patio. Are these houses, homes, apartments, rooms, a building? It's all so strange . . . the last door, the lion's den, the Academy. Three weeks he's been going to this immense auditorium with its four benches pushed up against the back wall, all dark inside, the raised platform on the other side which was also dark with only two well-lighted pianos. Three times a week, Frau Proserpina was waiting at the piano on the left with all of her shawls spread over a shredded stuffed chair: Good afternoon, Frau Proserpina.

"Three minutes late, three minutes less class time," was the way Beethoven's granddaughter greeted him. She surely had inherited the character of geniuses, but it was better not to think about that in the event he might let something slip in front of her. "Take a seat, young man." Julius sat down and tried to explain that he had fought with Sánchez Concha; hence he was unable to go over his lesson one last time. But Frau Proserpina didn't show any interest in his scratched cheek, much less in his attempt to explain what had happened: Julius didn't have any option but to stop in the middle. That was his tenth class and Beethoven's granddaughter still didn't show any affection. The first day she asked who had been his previous teacher and, delighted, he even tried to tell her about the perfumed piano, but she interrupted him: "I'm only interested in the method. What kind of exercises did you use with that young lady?" He wanted to explain that she wasn't a young lady, and, with a smile on his lips, he began with the fact that she was a nun who was quite nervous . . . "What kinds of exercises did you undertake with her?" Julius didn't like her interruptions but he wanted to believe that it was due to her affiliation with geniuses. "The young man will explain to me what kinds of exercises he had undertaken with his previous piano teacher." That phrase was a long one and she kept on with the thing about undertaking and even pronounced it a certain way; moreover, it wouldn't be long before she dislocated her lower jaw and he began to wonder what he would do if that happened way in the back part of that . . . house, building, apartment block, rooms? He definitely had to ask his mom about the place where the academy was located. The poor guy had to respond quickly because Frau Proserpina would become impatient again. What should he say to her? He never undertook anything that was called sol-fa with the nun, she would transcribe the notes with their tails, and the cleft was a little harp, or a young girl, and then she would draw the notes that looked like little Peruvian or North American soldiers. Then they played "My Bonnie Lies over the Ocean" because it was easy for Julius . . . Grinning, that's exactly what he tried to describe to her on the first day of class, and he tried to make friends with the old woman and see if she would cry as she talked about her grandfather . . . "I understand," Frau Proserpina interrupted again.

If these interruptions were going to continue, she would become an old ugly hag and that will be the end of it. But there was the matter of the affiliation of geniuses . . . "It is my understanding that the young man and the previous young lady did not undertake any type of lessons that could be worth considering serious, hence the situation calls for you to begin all over again, starting with the first page." She finished at exactly the same moment that her jaw was about to fly apart. Julius didn't doubt for a moment that she was Beethoven's granddaughter. But now he would have to meditate about how nasty she was. He had always imagined that people who suffered, who were sick, who had headaches, or who had lost their minds were the kindest of all. He thought about Juan Lucas, he would never . . . Mommy wouldn't like . . . "The mission of the good disciple is not to let his mind wander," Frau Proserpina said, straightening up and murmuring something about fall and winter while she went over to the chair and picked up one of the shawls. She put it around herself. That was the first of many that she would wrap around herself.

And today, three weeks later, Frau Proserpina was wearing several shawls over her shoulders and she griped about the winter that was going to be so terrible. Julius looked over at the torn chair and noted that the same number of shawls were hanging over the back of the chair on the first day of his lessons. "Let's see," Beethoven's granddaughter said, and he put his hands over the keys and plunged into that dull exercise that was beginning to make him hate to play the piano. Frau Proserpina's pianos only smelled of dampness; besides, she showed no affection, she never smiled at him, nor did she control herself when he made a mistake. As a result, if they were to continue in this fashion poor Julius' talent was going to dissipate and the one person who was going to be pleased about it was Juan Lucas. "No way we're having artists in this family," he said one day. "No artists here, they don't earn their keep and they drain you if you have to support their studies all their lives. Undoubtedly, Julius is an intelligent type, much more than Santiago or Bobby, and some day he could easily take over the family business." Susan didn't deny it, for she was in complete agreement with what he was saying, but it's cute for the youngest child to play the piano or to be a painter. You dress him up elegantly, for he makes the house so charming, Look, Juan, isn't he cute sitting at the piano. Sure, little by little he'll play less and less, but for now he's really cute, you can't deny it, darling. Darling was also in agreement with her, that's exactly why he had sent Julius to study under a real teacher; in fact, he even believes that she is the granddaughter of a genius: just wait until she dispatches a couple of tongue-lashings, wait until he smiles at her and she sends him to the devil, then you'll see how soon he gives up these foolish piano lessons. He won't make it through the winter, woman . . . And after that he'll take up golf, athletics, and find more adventuresome friends . . . he's only a step away from dropping all these queer activities. Susan was completely in agreement, but not so fast, darling, and she began to explain everything all over again. But let's go more slowly, not so brusquely, when she remembered that her cousin Susana had told her that Frau Proserpina's only defect was that she would knock her students up the side of the head.

But Aunt Susana was wrong. Frau Proserpina didn't hit her students in the head, she whacked them with a tremendous ruler right on the wrists, and it was at precisely those moments when she came out with the famous goose step or her iron-clad discipline or God knows what. The truth is she even managed to regain her German accent that she had almost lost after so many years in Peru. "Raise your wrist!" she screamed on some occasions, and this was one of them: "Raise your wrist!" she yelled and, whack! Julius received a tremendous blow on the skinny little wristbone. "Screw your mother, Sánchez Concha," Julius, now furious, projected in his mind which he almost said out loud, but it wasn't precisely Sánchez Concha who had sent electric shocks up his arm with such sharp blows but rather Frau Proserpina, and why was Julius to blame if the nun with the fragrant piano had never told him to play with his wrists raised or other such stupid things? What does it matter if your wrists are raised or lowered so long as you play with feeling? . . . Whack! Another blow. And then: "Raise your wrists!" In that position he'd never play with feeling or anything. At the rate things were going, soon he wouldn't have one drop of feeling left. For the moment he wanted to tell her to leave me alone, Señorita, but something inside would still forgive her: perhaps it was the desire to find out what else went on in that . . . was it a house? a building? an apartment? rooms? Or perhaps it was the pretty schoolgirl, did she live there? How strange! Or perhaps it was because of the old man who undoubtedly is a real intellectual, or perhaps the court clerk as well, and the guy who fixes the old typewriters, they were like cathedrals with towers and bells that surely aren't good for anything, and who was working under a single dim light bulb hanging from way up high . . . Whack! another one. "Raise your wrists!" That one penetrated right to his soul and it hurt so much he believed Frau Proserpina's pianos smelled of cat urine and the four miserable benches at the back of the room were filthy. She had said only her best disciples gave recitals and lots of people would come. "I've got to continue. Some day there'll be a recital and for sure everyone who lives in this . . . house? building? rooms? will come . . ." Whack! "Raise your wrists!" And he raised his two wrists high in the air while she went for another shawl: "It's going to be a nasty winter," she announced. Her sad tone of voice gave Julius hope and he began to lower his wrists affectionately when he heard Frau Proserpina add something about snow: "It's going to snow a lot," she said exactly, and Julius lifted ipso facto both wrists and did his best to play the exercise correctly: "It never snows in Lima, Señorita." Distracted in trying to tell her that it never snows in Lima, he made a mistake, and starting over, he lowered his wrists and, whack! another one. "When I finish this class I'll tell Carlos and he'll break out laughing, saying for sure you really got it today. But I want to continue coming because someday there will be a recital and for sure everyone who lives here will come: the old bald wise man, the ill-humored woman who's always half-dressed, the court clerk, the schoolgirls, the pretty one the pretty one the pretty one."

"We have managed to undertake very little in three weeks," Frau Proserpina told him upon finishing his lesson. "You were recommended for having tremendous talent. Where do you hide that talent?" "Screw your mother, Sánchez Concha," thought Julius. Once again he felt like he had to take aim at a different target. Frau Proserpina stood up and went to the tattered chair for another shawl. "The way things are going, this winter is going to be nasty, and the snow . . ." Despite what he could have said, Julius was about to say good-bye but limited himself to promise to work harder on his exercises for next Wednesday. "Please be prompt," Frau Proserpina told him, but he had already stepped down from the raised platform where the pianos were illuminated. "A student leaves and another one enters. You leave and another comes. Please be on time so we can stay on schedule. Schedules are made to be followed." It was hard for Julius, as he approached the door of the big auditorium, to promise that he would be on time for the next class while his mind thought about things that were more interesting and at least as mysterious as Beethoven's granddaughter herself. As usual, Frau Proserpina remained seated while she waited for her next student who should arrive as Julius was leaving: schedules are made to be followed. Halfway down the corridor, Julius realized that he had forgotten his music book and went back to get it. He entered silently and saw that it was totally dark inside. "What should I do?" he thought. "Another student has to arrive and Frau Proserpina isn't here, how strange." He was thinking when the wooden floor creaked under his foot and the lights came on, immediately illuminating the pianos and providing some light at that end of the ancient auditorium: Beethoven's granddaughter was knitting a shawl. "I forgot my music book," Julius explained and Frau Proserpina, who had stood up quickly as if taken by surprise by something, threw down the skein of wool, grabbed the music book and, trembling, extended it to him without moving one step so he would have to approach her to get it. "Things are not to be forgotten, especially a music book. Leave immediately because another student will be arriving on time." Julius took his music book and bolted out of the auditorium. Then he walked along slowly until he was halfway down the corridor and everything seemed so strange, the punctual student hadn't arrived because he would have to walk down this corridor and no one was coming . . . something made him return for a second time to the auditorium door. He peeked in and then took off running when he discovered that Beethoven's granddaughter had turned out the lights again. She was probably knitting shawls and he was ready for anything except the creaking floor again.

He walked slowly along the corridor that bordered the interior patio and led to the stairs. As he passed by the old man's window, the old man with the shining bald head, Julius looked in because he wanted to know once and for all what wise men were like. He was sitting down wearing his little glasses with soda pop bottle ends. Julius went by hardly making a sound, but the old man looked up at him over his glasses. He always looked up and smiled, but this time he tried to stand up which frightened Julius. Nilda had said never to trust anyone, and he stepped up his pace when he noticed that the old man motioned to him with his hand, the same as if he were saying good-bye, raising his arm feebly and barely moving it as he trembled. Julius didn't dare look back to see if he really had managed to get up and make it to the window. He ran to the stairs but he had to slow down because there wasn't any light there and the stairs were falling apart. When he got to the bottom he stopped in the dark passageway between the two patios and thought for a while: it was as if he had been dreaming up some Machiavellian plan in order to cross the patio without fear or anything and to find out once and for all what was happening behind each window with the light bulb hanging down from way up high. He must have counted, one, two, three, go! for he took off and before he could stop he was already in the middle of the next patio, thinking that everyone must have seen him run by and were probably looking at him with hatred from their windows. In one window to his right, the two schoolgirls were studying in semidarkness. Soon they'd be needing eyeglasses, poor things, they're going to ruin their eyes. And how they studied! He had already been there watching them for a short while and they didn't even notice him. He took advantage of the moment to examine the walls of the dwelling, they looked like they were made of cardboard, he went even closer and there was a large blanket hanging toward the back and behind it there was another room. Which one was the pretty schoolgirl's window? . . . Julius looked for it with more self-confidence now: that's not it, no, it's not that one, and that one belongs to the court . . . he moved closer to the plaque on the wall: COURT CLERK. The guy inside was totally surrounded by papers . . . Now, which one is the pretty schoolgirl's window? . . . He had already started to feel happy, naturally, for he was always right: the girl didn't live there but in a house that he began to imagine when, all of a sudden, he spotted a window in the corner of the patio that he had never seen before. The pretty girl was a schoolgirl who lived there and she smiled at him as she painted her fingernails in the dim light. Julius looked away and acted like he didn't notice and then looked toward the window where the very white woman who dressed in a spacious white gown was shutting the curtains defiantly. What do you want, brat? His only recourse was to take off toward the huge main door that was always open and where Carlos waited while he smoked calmly.

"Some really good-looking chicks walk along Arequipa Avenue," he told Julius, adding, "Let's go look for little Merceditas that's parked around the corner."

SÁNCHEZ CONCHA'S REIGN lasted no longer than a flower blossom. He still hadn't become accustomed to being the biggest and the strongest at school when one morning in the middle of the English class the door opened and the Mother Superior brought in a new boy who looked at everyone furiously. The Mother Superior began with the bit about the new little schoolmate: he is Peruvian but he has been living in Argentina. His father was ambassador there and now they have returned to Peru, and they sent their son to us. All of you are going to be good friends, you have to help him since he is getting started a little late, but he is very intelligent and will soon be up to full speed. You have to loan him your notebooks so he can catch up. Fernandito, you also are going to be a good friend of theirs, right? Fernando didn't say a word, he just looked at everyone furiously. They also had been watching him, sizing him up; in reality, he didn't seem like much of a threat because he was pretty short. The Mother Superior continued to give them last minute instructions on how they should treat their new classmate. He was a little behind and at a disadvantage. Good, now everyone knows him. She tried to pat his head with affection but Fernandito moved out of the way, it looked like he was adamantly trying to protect his hairdo. Finally, the Mother Superior said his name in full: Fernandito Ranchal y Ladrón de Guevara. Del Castillo laughed upon hearing such a long last name, but he realized right then and there he should stop the joking because Fernandito Ranchal y L de G, which is the way he signed his name on his notebooks, gave him a piercing stare. Del Castillo lowered his eyes and even started to scratch off an imaginary piece of dried glue from his desk with his fingernail.

Fernandito's desk was the last one in the first row, which was known as the bullies' row. The Mother Superior pointed his desk out to him before she left the classroom. Mother Mary Joan, the soccer nun, told him he could sit down. He started to walk slowly toward the back, looking furiously at the thirty-five students in the room. De los Heros noticed that he didn't look down at the floor as he walked, and he decided to stick his leg out and trip him royally. As Fernandito approached he still looked at everyone straight in their faces. He couldn't have seen that foot waiting for him. How in the hell did he see it? It was a question that even today de los Heros must be asking himself, for what happened was that he cried out painfully and pulled his leg back in, his shin burned like fire. On top of that he had to fake it when Mother Mary Joan turned around and asked what was going on? Nothing, Fernandito Ranchal y Ladrón de Guevara walked calmly and furiously toward his desk.

Sánchez Concha, who wasn't stupid, adopted an attitude of contemplation. Several others followed his lead, including Julius. It wasn't Fernandito's height that made them wonder about him but rather his ferocious-looking face. Also, it was his savage silence that baffled them. The time bomb almost went off one morning during recess a few weeks after Fernandito had arrived but, unfortunately, that incident didn't have the significance those in third grade wanted it to have, for it wasn't in any way a definitive incident. Fernando had just furiously bought a chocolate bar and he was removing the wrapper when Chubby Martinto approached him, the dummy. Chubby wasn't aware of anything. He wasn't even aware of the fact that Fernandito was in third grade and that he was always furious. He simply noticed that he was new at school and decided to attack him at the exact moment that the other was about to eat his candy. Fernandito would have never expected it, but all of a sudden he found himself with a sword pointing at his chest. He smiled furiously and Chubby answered with a laugh, satisfied. "A new one to challenge," he was probably thinking, but Fernandito kept on looking at him with so much insistence that poor Martinto began to debate between whether he was a happy child or the source of all evil in the world. Fernandito was furious but kept smiling so that even Chubby began to realize something wasn't going right in his world at that moment, realizing suddenly that everyone in third grade was watching at a distance and feigning disinterest. Chubby's joy evaporated and his clumsiness took on a sense of bewilderment. When Fernandito told him to give him the stick, he did so just the way a dog retrieves the ball and takes it back to its master who then throws it again. Martinto acted exactly the same way and even thought they were still playing the game because he smiled and said: you can keep the sword. I'll bring another one tomorrow and we'll have a duel. Fernandito continued to smile and became even more furious. Chubby thought that it must be his style. "Quite a guy, this new pirate," he must have thought and he turned around in order to look for another sword, when he felt a terrible swat that burned his rear end. "Take it," Fernandito told him, returning the stick to him calmly. Chubby just stood there displaying an impressive expression of stupidity. He rubbed his rear end feeling more pain than anger, took back the stick that didn't serve any function anymore as he discovered sadness one morning in June; and that was the end of Chubby Martinto as we knew him. From then on he would be clean when he got to school and he even started to get slimmer. One day someone said he saw Martinto go into the matinee alone, looking serious. He passed his exams that year with good grades and in future years he would be among the ten best students in his class.

Sánchez Concha did some calculating. Martinto had been a classmate some years back and, while having failed twice, it didn't stop him from growing up, for Martinto was old enough to be in third grade. As a result, he was one of the big guys but at the same time he wasn't . . . other students in third grade must have thought about those things, too. Moreover, Fernandito hadn't punched out anyone, nor had he been seen in action. Was there a way to destroy someone without ever going into action? There was the rub. Life around there had become complicated because of Fernandito. Before it was simple: meet you outside after school, I dare you, let's go, come and get it queer, and then a tremendous wrestling match and the matter was settled when you would say I give up and you were sad for a couple of days or for the rest of your life or, with a little luck, you would hear the other under you say let me go or I give up and you left boldly and felt that way for several days until Broken Mirror showed up to tell you that in the nearby town there was this new dude who could draw faster than you, and the whole thing repeated itself, with the same advantages and disadvantages. In the case of Fernandito, the situation was definitely more complicated.

Weeks went by and Fernandito continued to act serenely yet furiously. Each day he looked more mature, or older, and in worse humor. Even Morales showed respect for him. The Spanish teacher, who was really crass and had been seen with her boyfriend walking along Wilson Avenue, said Fernandito was exceptionally arrogant. This attitude gave Sánchez Concha goose bumps; he felt like he had become a common bully. "No problem," Sánchez Concha decided, "starting tomorrow I'm gonna shut my mouth, not going to talk to anyone, going to be real serious, and if anyone starts to bug me, I'll punch him out hard and then look him in the eye until he looks back at me stupidly and walks away sadly like Martinto." At home that afternoon, he stared at himself in the mirror and finally, after much effort, expression number twenty-seven seemed the most convenient to him for his new destiny. He practiced it a hundred and twenty-seven times and, the next morning, he practiced the same expression all the way from home to Immaculate Heart School. When Sánchez Concha arrived, Del Castillo said he should take on Fernandito. Sánchez Concha knitted his brow and slapped Del Castillo hard on the face. Immediately, he squinted even more to create the right psychological effect—Fernandito style—but Del Castillo was a real macho and even though Sánchez Concha had already punched him out three times, he jumped on top of him, initiating the typical wrestling match, surprised that Sánchez Concha continued to squint. Fortunately he had reacted quickly, because there was a moment in which Del Castillo was on top of him and had immobilized him and all. When the fight was over, Sánchez Concha was tempted to explain to Del Castillo that the awkward situation in which he had found himself was the result of poor use of a new technique and not a matter of an illogical loss of strength. "Don't think that just because you almost . . . ," he was telling him, but then he remembered Fernandito and became very serious. He didn't have to give excuses to anybody. To anybody? . . . Well, yes, to himself, because he had just screwed up his tactic of the single punch and then the matter of *your eyes were fixed on me with such force,* which is when Del Castillo should have looked down but instead he jumped on you and almost . . .

Another guy by the name Del Castillo, a Mulatto, thirty-five years old and official school photographer, had arrived that morning to take the annual school pictures. He had eaten breakfast early at the bar on the corner. Neighborhood buddies were there too: hey, let's start off the day with a shot of brandy, but Del Castillo, who was part artist and hence a night owl and a Bohemian decked out with a cravat and an application of emollient, responded in a virile tone that in no way could he stick around for barbershop talk, for that morning he was off to earn some money: I have to take pictures in a convent. Those pictures are serious business, and it's important to watch your breath. He was going to take pictures of thousands of little white kids who study in some incredible school run by North American nuns over in San Isidro. The shot of brandy will be for another day, never when you have to take pictures at a cloister. He abandoned his cohorts at the bar, cleared his throat from the previous night, spit on the morning sawdust, became serious, and started off for the school and some real business. And now the Mother Superior was introducing him like every year: Siñor Delcastilo, and everyone responded, Good Morning, Señor Del Castillo. Then the Mother Superior, speaking in English this time, said he has come to take your picture so you will have a keepsake, for some day when you show it to your grandchildren and say, Look, grandson, your grandfather was a child a thousand years ago. She became grandfatherly, at least she thought so, squinting and trembling, and she was showing you the picture that Del Castillo was going to take, as soon as the corpulent nun, yes Mother, yes Mother, as soon as the fat lady here finishes with her discourse and leaves me alone so I can earn my money. But the Mother Superior continued a while longer, telling the story of the grandson and grandfather. She loved to see the children laugh at her jokes. Even Sánchez Concha laughed for a moment, but that's when he saw Fernandito watching the scene with wrath; hence he adopted expression number twenty-seven. The pathetic part was that the following week when Del Castillo returned with the pictures, Sánchez Concha discovered that Fernandito had smiled for the pictures, a smile from ear to ear that no one had ever seen before, while he himself was sitting in the middle row taller than the rest, but with a face that suggested he was about to fart at any moment or that his stomach was hurting badly: life was complicated. Sánchez Concha quickly stuck the picture into his jacket pocket and turned around to see what was going on with the rest of the class. Nothing seemed to be happening but, in reality, something was happening: everyone was buying a picture of themselves to show to Mommy and to prove they hadn't asked for the money for nothing. Everyone except Fernandito, that is, bought a picture; he didn't even bother to look at it. Del Castillo the photographer went up to him and

Fernandito said flat out no in a voice that was drier that the deserts along the Peruvian coast. Del Castillo, who was the photographer of memories, had captured the child Fernandito who, in a few more years, would become completely vitiated and degenerate, taking his place far away from San Isidro, sitting at the bar along with those who knocked back their morning shots of brandy.

THE ARCHITECT HAD sent a cable: "Everything is ready for the move." Juan Lucas read it to Susan in their suite at the Ritz Hotel in Madrid. It had been a lightning-fast trip: first a short week in London, and they adored each other in a Hindu restaurant whose chef was a friend of Juan Lucas; then it was on to Madrid, where they took advantage of three bullfights by Briceño who was fabulous. "Everything is ready for the move," Juan Lucas repeated, and they decided to bring all this pleasure they were having to an end. The golfer picked up the telephone and asked the switchboard to call his travel agent. Yes, the first flight to Lima. All they had to do was to pack the pig-leather suitcases and cancel two or three engagements that were pending with friends in Madrid. It was going to be a nightmare having to move to a new house, but Juan Lucas was delighted with his new mansion and couldn't wait to inaugurate it with an enormous cocktail party. Susan was pleased with the idea of returning to Lima immediately because she had left the boys alone together in the suite at the Country Club and Bobby, above all, was capable of doing just about anything. "He might have even thrown Julius out and installed the Canadian girl in our bedroom," Juan Lucas told her, laughing out loud, picking up the telephone again to order some martinis that would be perfect at eight o'clock in the evening.

Bobby hadn't installed anybody in his parents' bedroom but, on the other hand, he had wrecked the station wagon in front of the new girl's house, the one who goes to Villa María, and he had left the Mercedes without brakes during one of his frequent fights with Peggy, the Canadian. They hadn't been getting along lately, and she didn't want to sneak out and go riding in his car. One afternoon they argued a long time, and when Bobby ran out of arguments he started the motor and took her, frightened, in the direction of the new girl's house, the one who goes to Villa María. He did spinouts with the car to the point of making Peggy cry out of fear, and she told him that she still loved him just at the precise moment the brakes gave out on the Mercedes. As a result, Carlos had to pick up the Señores at the airport in the Jaguar, but Juan

Lucas preferred to pay for him to take a taxi back to the hotel because it was too crowded for three people in that small car.

Susan kissed Julius and told him that she had missed him immensely. Susan was a good liar but also a good person, because as she finished telling him how much she had missed him she realized that she hadn't even thought about him and she didn't feel much of anything when she told him that she had missed him immensely. Then she pulled him toward her and kissed him with affection and told him again, I've missed you immensely, darling. Then she felt love and affection and, consequently, at ease with herself. Juan Lucas jokingly asked him if he had any gripes concerning his brother Bobby. Julius didn't have any and the golfer praised him saying that only fairies, prissies, and dummies complain about their brothers or their friends. "Only prissies are snitches," he added, charmed by the Spanish expressions he had retrieved to enrich his vocabulary. Carlos appeared at that moment bringing in the suitcases he had brought in the taxi, and Juan Lucas wanted to know how was it possible he would give Bobby the keys to the Mercedes, as if he hadn't had enough wrecking the station wagon. Carlos initiated an elaborate explanation: who can stop the boy when he wants to do something? He only had the keys to the station wagon, and the boy probably found the keys to the Mercedes in the suite, bla, bla, bla. Julius, who had been following the conversation with some interest, told Carlos to stop accusing Bobby because Uncle Juan called those who accused others queers and prissies. Juan Lucas cursed the hour that he had met Julius, and Carlos, who was quick-witted and knew something about strikes and the sort, debated among I'll-turn-in-my-resignation-to-the-Señor, cussing him out, let's go outside, and here you're in your territory but you still have to show some respect. The situation was tense and, fortunately, Carlos looked at Julius and felt respect for the child's stepfather and swallowed his bitterness. From now on, hence, he was only going to be the Señora's chauffeur and that's it. He doesn't have to take guff from anyone. He should just show some respect. He put the suitcases where Juan Lucas had told him to put them and went out to have a smoke where the atmosphere was not so tense. The bad thing was that Juan Lucas had already been giving Carlos, not Julius, a bad time. Perhaps you haven't turned out to be a little queer after all, but you act like a parrot, always repeating everything . . .

"Well, get going, call a bellboy to help take up this luggage . . . get a hurry on."

Three days later Julius was entertaining his third grade friends, telling them about their move. He wasn't studying or doing much of anything, and that evening was going to be their first one in the new mansion. Everything was in disarray and Susan occupied herself with lots of chores but, at a closer look, she never managed to do anything. At most, she supervised the movers and made sure they didn't break one of her pieces of new furniture or ruin one of her favorite paintings. But it wasn't necessary to show so much concern because the movers were true specialists. There just wasn't any reason to be so worried. Later the interior decorator came to the mansion but only to take care of the minor details, because for some time now Juan Lucas had been signing enough checks to make sure the mansion would be completely livable on the day they were to move in. The interior decorator was utterly queer but that didn't mean he didn't drool over Susan. And Susan was ecstatic because queers always love to talk. You can talk to them for hours and not feel like they want you for something else. In fact, when Julius arrived from school she advised him not to wander off because the decorator had already made eyes at him. The decorator was from a good family, one as elegant as Juan Lucas' family only with a bit more color because of this queer. And he wasn't one of those who follow the candy sellers around at the movie theaters. No sir! This guy was one of those types you find in any mansion in Monterrico or San Isidro who likes to play with children and, amid a joke here and there, he starts play-fighting and then wrestling and so on . . . But happily the person hired to create a sense of good taste in the mansion was an artist with professional integrity and when it was time to work he forgot all about everything else; in other words, the incident didn't go any further than a certain look he gave Julius, who didn't understand what the hell this peacock was up to, what with ordering everyone around, but little by little he started to understand, for as the weeks went by the mansion became more and more attractive and, any day now, this guy with such good taste would faint upon seeing the project finally finished. The interior decorator was in seventh heaven; sated with inspiration and shrieking nervously, his hair would become completely disheveled. Ah, it was a pleasure to work: "There's lots of money in Lima," he told Susan and Juan Lucas. "Yes, there's a lot of money in Lima but there are some strange Señoras, too . . . oh, what's the use of trying to explain it! It's hard to imagine how much gaudiness exists in this city. They hire you to decorate their homes and they're the ones who end up wanting to direct everything. So why did I study in Rome? Why? What was the purpose? Tell me! Tell me why! . . . so that a lady who has never been anywhere in the world forces you to decorate a stupidly designed pistachio cake? Horrible! Dreadful! Lima is for work and money but that's all. Really, it's Europe for everything else. Europe, it's true, there's nothing like Europe . . . but don't tell me about your last trip just yet . . . I'll simply die of envy because I still have a lot to do in the dining room. The curtains? Did they install them yet? Let me look. I'm coming. I'm coming. I'm coming. They need to be installed before deciding on where to hang the paintings. That's the way I work: everything has to be perfect." For Juan Lucas not only did everything have to be perfect but also the men had to be men, or at least not effeminate like this specimen of good taste. He offered him a whiskey so he would shut his mouth. Who gives a damn if he was one of your father's friends: there was no reason why he had to put up with so much queerness in this guy.

Celso and Daniel came back to work about that time. Arminda had returned beginning the first day and tried to help in whatever she could, although Juan Lucas didn't like such an ugly woman, dressed in black and black locks of hair hanging down in her face, wandering around the house. Susan had to send Carlos to the slums to fetch her two butlers. They waited until the last moment, taking advantage of their paid vacation in order to finish their own houses, built-with-my-own-hands style, on their own property. There were lots of effusive hugs and a big reunion in the servants' quarters of the new mansion. Susan even came to greet them and, of course, Julius parked himself there the minute Celso and Daniel arrived and stayed up with them until late that night. The service area was very modern and functional. There were service buttons all over the place and every minute Juan Lucas' voice could be heard over what seemed like a thousand speakers hidden in the walls. Carlos was the one who enjoyed the new system the most: to be able to hear the Señor's voice and then answer go to hell without anything happening was neat. Suddenly, for instance, Juan Lucas' voice ordered ice for a drink, and Carlos answered elatedly: Come and get it yourself. Of course, the person at the other end didn't hear anything but it was neat anyway. Arminda didn't like the new apparatus much, above all when Carlos would say those things in front of Julius. She lowered her face, expressing God only knows what among her locks of hair. Another thing she didn't like much was that the place was so modern. It's true everything was nice, white, new, and clean, but tables always have four legs and now, all of a sudden, the poor thing had to deal with a table that had only one leg in the middle. "One of these days it'll topple over while we're eating," she thought. She didn't dare cut meat on it or lean on it with her elbows: couldn't put pressure on it. Also, the chairs had very little space for a person's rear end and at any moment she would forget about it and probably fall off one side, and it would be a nasty fall because "at my age falls and bumps tend to be quite evil," she explained to Carlos, who was always respectfully mocking the Doña.

Julius interrogated Celso and Daniel at length about their activities during their vacation. Celso's uncle was still the mayor of Huarocondo, near Cuzco, and Celso was still the treasurer of the Social Club of the Friends of Huarocondo, located in the Lince neighborhood. He still used the same box which he preferred to keep stashed in his room because it was safer in the mansion. The topic that really captured Julius' attention was the one dealing with their houses in the slums. Someday they would take him to see them . . .

For now they had to deal with more urgent problems. Only four of them were left from the old mansion and while Arminda prepared food for the boys and themselves (Juan Lucas and Susan always ate out) for the moment, it was going to be necessary to hire a regular cook. Arminda had high blood pressure and Daniel said her work should be limited to washing clothes in the electric washer and to ironing. Anything more would be abusive. They'd have to talk to the Señora about it. Celso said the Señora would take care of the matter in due time, but Daniel insisted they had the right to talk to the Señora about the matter sooner. Daniel, of course, had heard some dangerous speeches in the slums. He wanted to talk to the Señora not just about Arminda but also about his right for an increase in salary because, according to his calculations (he had been working recently with square feet at his construction site), he had to sweep a larger area in the new house than in the old one. Julius listened to the whole conversation with trepidation. He could already see Daniel talking to his Mommy, unleashing those things on her. She'd get very nervous, tell Juan Lucas about it, and he was capable of firing the whole lot. But there were even more problems. They didn't have a gardener because Anatolio refused to abandon his flowers at the old mansion, and ever since Imelda graduated from her sewing classes and took off without saying good-bye to anyone or showing any feeling, they had been needing a servant to take care of the children's clothes too.

Fortunately there wasn't a row. Susan saw herself that some things were lacking and, in addition, she considered it normal to increase everyone's salary. However, it became a long process to select a cook and a girl to take care of the children's clothes. Many a sun had set before Susan could even begin to choose one of the candidates that her cousin Susana Lastarria, so useful in such matters, sent to her when she requested her help. By telephone, of course, for Susan would only get as close to her cousin as the telephone permitted. Any closer contact caused her profound lethargy. Susana Lastarria had reduced her life to this type of activity ever since her husband, as he devoted himself to a life of leisure more at the level of his investments with Juan Lucas, had begun to abandon her within the limits permitted by society in Lima. They continued to go to mass together, for instance, but he hardly ever took her to the movies, never anymore to the clubs that he liked to patronize, and absolutely never to cocktails where he thought that by going alone he would make a better impression. Poor Susana didn't even show up at the Golf Club anymore, and there had been several tremors and even some earthquakes since their last sexual relations. But it was better that way, for she had always felt some apprehension when she would do it with him. Frankly, it hadn't been worth so much perversity to end up with just two children. If she had known exactly the days in which God ordered her to conceive Pipo and Rafaelito, the little shits, she would have avoided what she had done in the past, that which she now despises and for which she feels shame but that kept reappearing obsessively in her dreams, in her moments of languor when Juan would slither toward her legs with a strange expression on his face, lingering to wallow in lewd and perverse sex acts, was that love? instead of finishing quickly to see if Pipo was on his way. And, later on, to see if Rafaelito was on his way too. She had nightmares. Aunt Susana, horrible, didn't want to think about it anymore, and for that reason she looked around for someone's household problem in which she could stick her nose. The servants were always committing some kind of stupidity. As usual, Victor, who was the only servant in the castle who had survived, had forgotten to dust some furniture: you always have to keep on top of him. Victor was becoming spoiled more and more as time went on. Pipo and Rafael's social life also occupied a lot of Aunt Susana's time. She was always worried about who their dates were and what time they would come home. She was always worried until she found something else to worry about. And now Susan had given her something to worry about. She would say that Susan was driving her crazy with all of her telephone calls, but she lit up like a Christmas tree every time Victor picked up the phone, answered it, and then went to inform her: it's your cousin Susan. Horrible and happy, Susana Lastarria would rush to the telephone.

And Susan continued to interview all of the girls her cousin was sending her, but not one of them seemed to win her over, until one day she realized she had been longing for Vilma and Nilda to return. She was a little surprised, but as she thought about it, she realized she really didn't have any experience in hiring servants, which is why she had looked around for a cook and a servant who were already known. But without realizing it, she had been waiting for Vilma and Nilda to appear among the servants that her cousin had recommended. She was wasting time. Sitting out on the small terrace where she would interview them, Susan decided to hire the first person who appeared that morning.

You could almost say that the first one who appeared that morning hired Susan. A robust, buxom Chola arrived and she entered the mansion talking in a voice that was too loud for her condition as a servant. In reality, the Chola always talked loud and she was accustomed to having her way. She was nice but she demanded to be right and for that there was nothing better than yelling. That's why that morning she entered the mansion yelling, even as she crossed through the garden she was yelling, and she was also starting to impress Celso with all of her yelling. She was already convincing him that she was right in everything, in her reason for looking for work, in being an excellent maid, and in whatever else occurred to her to yell about but, without knowing how, her voice became muffled, her mouth seemed stuffed with cotton balls, at least that's the way it seemed to her, the poor thing, and it's true that you almost couldn't hear her cross through the big living room. The Chola wasn't aware that Juan Lucas had installed a sound-proof ceiling and she believed that she was losing her mind; hence, she was always right and even yelled more in order to convince Celso once and for all about everything. But out on the terrace there wasn't any of Juan Lucas' soundproof ceiling and she ended up screaming even louder, more right than ever.

Susan felt like the French people were coming in search of María Antonieta, but just then and there Peruvian reality came back to her: It's our history. Juan Lucas had once said, with a sense of humor, "The Chola's got it together," upon seeing her round calves, her intimidating rear end that was much more round than her calves and, finally, her breasts which were like one big, enormous, round, bold breast. Her young, round face capped off her optimism. She was fully satisfied with herself. Susan abandoned her cultural humor to assume her duties of Señora and asked her name.

"Flora, at your service, Señora."

Susan, lovely, was surprised and tried to think of something to say but only came up with bon appetit which wouldn't work in order to get her out of this jam. She nodded slightly and prepared for the next question.

"Have you worked before as a cook?"

"The Señora is mistaken," Flora responded, inflating herself and insulting Susan merrily with her enormous bold chest. "The Señora is mistaken. My occupation is the children, to take care of their clothes and their rooms. My occupation is not the kitchen."

"Of course, of course. The thing is that I'm also waiting for a cook to come," Susan told her, becoming calm again upon seeing that the Chola contracted, satisfied with her explanation. "It's that we've just moved in and I need a servant and a cook. This house is brand new and we need servants."

"Young Celso here has already informed me. Your *chalet,* Señora, is beautiful, let me congratulate you. As soon as I have the pleasure of meeting the Señor I'll congratulate him too. Your *chalet* is beautiful, Señora. Your name, please?"

"Susan," she said, somewhere between lovely and frightened. She almost said at your service as well, but she imagined Juan Lucas bending over backward laughing when she would tell him, so she preferred to turn to Celso who followed the scene somewhat perplexed.

"Celso, bring me a cup of coffee, please." She probably wouldn't drink any, but the idea of hot coffee helped her confront Flora again so early that morning.

"Have you worked before? Do you have any experience?"

"The Señora will have noticed that I spoke of my occupation, but if the Señora distrusts me you can read in detail all of my recommendations. Here."

Flora, expanding, proudly opened her perfumed purse and removed calling cards with names of very important families in Lima. The cards say she acts properly and does her job.

"I have never been fired. I always leave jobs because I want to. Here, Señora, read the cards."

Susan found herself reading a series of boring calling cards, she had signed one herself for Nilda when she left. "Enough," she thought as she returned them to her . . .

"Read them, Señora . . . Take your time. You have every right."

Susan didn't know what to do. She didn't have any recourse but to read three calling cards under the shadow of the immense chest of Flora who waited resolutely for some commentary.

"Very good . . . I congratulate you. I've read enough. When Celso comes back, he'll take you to your room. I'd like you to stay with us starting today. The chauffeur can take you to get your things. You can get settled today and tomorrow . . ."

Susan was beginning to find the vocabulary and ideas that her cousin Susana used, even to the point that she thought the matter was settled when Flora, very boldly, started to inflate dangerously, placing her hands on her hips and converting herself into an enormous washtub, with her perfumed purse hanging from one arm like a round bow on one handle of the tub.

"The conditions of employment have not been discussed, Señora."

"The conditions of employment have not been discussed," Susan repeated, sitting in the shadow of Flora's oppressive, decisive chest. She vaguely thought that the conditions meant salary. Well, it was very good, of course, how foolish, she had forgotten the most important matter. But in any case the salary would be the end of the conversation: she would tell her the very good salary, the hot coffee would arrive, and Miss Decisive was staying on to work for them, imposing her shrieking yet cheerful terror in the new house. All she had to do was work hard and, don't worry, no one will hear her cleaning upstairs, just let her be happy in the kitchen and in the servants' quarters. The Chola is so chipper, Miss Decisive . . . no one will even be aware of her back in the service area . . . Susan was going to give her a good salary . . .

"I have three conditions and they are the following: a salary in accordance with my expectations, salubrious living conditions, and the same food as the family."

They were going to give her everything, absolutely everything, and Susan began to remember her youth and/or her afternoons playing golf and she wanted to stand up right then and tell her: Flora, enough. But she felt like it was impossible with the Chola's enormous round, bold chest towering over her. It all seemed so ludicrous but she had remained seated forever on the white layabout with a green pillow. Alone on a small terrace of the new mansion that humid morning with boiling coffee that never came, Susan had been conquered by Miss Decisive.

Three more girls came that morning but all of them wanted to work for the children and take care of their clothes. Celso told them that they didn't need anyone anymore: they already had someone. On the other hand, not one cook came, which allowed Susan to rest and recuperate from the encounter with Miss Decisive. She had mulled over the scene with her typical sense of humor and she thought the woman was wonderful. And she was elated with the nickname—Miss Decisive—that she had just invented for her. Juan Lucas was going to die laughing when she tells him that we've got a new one called Miss Decisive and she was going to appear in front of him expanding in size. She was going to greet him with the most absolute confidence that her chest and voice allowed, perhaps she'll shake hands with him and they were going to fall over from laughing when she leaves. Darling, you are going to enjoy

Miss Decisive . . . What else was she going to invent? . . . Now she was looking at him, holding a drink at the golf course and describing the woman's body, her voice, and the vanity of the round, happy, buxom woman.

Juan Lucas showed up about noon with the news of the new cook, who would be along soon. Friends at the golf course had recommended him that morning and he had even tried his food years ago at a friend's house: an excellent cook, you'll see, dear. From now on eating at home will be as pleasurable as eating out at the best restaurants. Susan got excited about the idea. Juan Lucas was very picky about his food and it seemed like finally they had found the person to satisfy him every day. Hence the problem of the servants was practically resolved. All they needed was a gardener, but Anatolio had promised to send his cousin. Susan communicated with Celso from the bar and ordered ice for the drinks. A few minutes later Celso came with the ice and with Abraham. Susan looked at Juan Lucas, Juan Lucas at Celso, and Celso, against his character, could barely hold back a laugh. And all of them just stared at Abraham who had just arrived at the mansion. Now he was approaching the bar with a large-handled briefcase that hung from his left arm. He was wearing a white turtleneck sweater, looking as if he had just come in from a morning of tennis. "Oh my God!" Susan said to herself, upon seeing the Mulatto complete with hair in enormous ringlets, sporting what looked like a permanent and several curls still maintaining the cockroach color from the last oxygenation. Abraham lightened his curls with oxygenated water and now he had them on display right in front of them. Susan and Juan Lucas could smell the mixture of hair tonic, perfume, and armpits that emanated from the new servant.

Juan Lucas fixed two gin and tonics, added ice, and began to stir the drinks with long silver spoons, squeezing slices of lemon against the sides of the glasses. Abraham cleared his throat queerishly and Susan let Juan Lucas talk first.

"Well, dear, this is the new cook."

Susan armed herself with patience and decided to behave like a true woman of the house.

"What are your conditions?" she asked, remembering Miss Decisive and placing her glass closer to her nose than her mouth in order to see if the aroma of the lemon and the gin exorcised Abraham's smelly presence.

But Abraham didn't understand one iota. "Conditions? What conditions?" he seemed to ask with his smiling, revolting eyes. The only condition he imposed was his happiness, which was the pleasure of working to serve Don Juan.

"I believe, Señora . . ."

"It's all done, dear," Juan Lucas intervened before the other could begin with some pleasant, queerlike chatter and bad breath besides.

"That's right," Abraham confirmed, ecstatic to be in total agreement with Don Juan Lucas.

"Stupendous. That's it, then. Go get your things and let's see if tomorrow you surprise us with a lunch that matches the caliber of your fame."

Abraham started quivering all over, fluttering as if an electric tremor ran up and down his body. Don Juan's flirtatious remarks left him ecstatic, and he postured like "Look at him walkin' down the street, ain't he neat," waiting to see if the handsome Señor offered him another. Juan Lucas almost lets loose with a nervous "Hey, there, your hairdo is pretty," but this was almost like descending to the coveted Sodom of Abraham, down to the poverty-stricken Gomorrah of the ugly Mulattos, cooks, queers, and those who yearn to imitate me.

"That's it, then," he interrupted in a definitive tone of voice, because he had just interpreted almost too well an obvious aspect of the cook's reality that compromised him. "That's all," he ordered, disgusted, because he felt like he was obligated to the guy now. And it was before lunch, in the middle of gin and tonics. "Hey, you can go now!"

Abraham started to quiver again but he straightened up immediately. He remained stiff and obedient, waiting for the Señor's orders, and lowered his eyes in the same way harsh words punish a child in school. He must have remained in that pose for about three seconds, then his usual stance stimulated him to quiver again, but he couldn't control it. There was something about the way he moved his arm, the right one, as if it were twitching . . . Susan decided to intervene, she idolized Juan Lucas and now with the new cook she could order his favorite dishes every day.

"For lunch tomorrow, why don't you prepare chicken in wine sauce for the Señor? We'll have the architect and his wife over for lunch. Count on ten people, just in case . . . The Señor just loves chicken in wine sauce."

But Abraham, let's don't forget, was a citizen of Sodom and Gomorrah, and he knew about the evil he could do, the queer was pure venom, and Juan Lucas had treated him harshly, and I just got here and the woman is already ordering me around, the cobra in Abraham came out.

"Ugh, Señora! You're going to tell me what the Señor likes! I know what he likes. I know the Señor's preferences. Tomorrow, if you like, I fix his favorite: baked goat . . . the Señor said it once at Señorita Arán-zazu's house . . . Ay! in fact he said it more than once at her place . . . Whenever I prepared goat at Señorita Aránzazu Marticorena's house, the Señor would always say no one could get his goat like I did . . . the nights I must have fixed goat for him at that Señorita's house!"

Juan Lucas poured himself another gin and Susan turned to laugh as she looked at the bottles on the bar so that upon seeing her Abraham would become encouraged and continue speaking about Juan Lucas' lovers in front of her.

"Well, fine, then, the butler here is going to take you to the kitchen so that you can check it out and get accustomed to the place."

"Nothing else, Don Juan?"

"Nothing. You may go. Take him out, Celso."

Abraham spun around nervously at the same moment that Julius and Bobby arrived from school to eat lunch. Both of them could see his strange male rear end and that he wore his pants nauseatingly tight, wanting to look like Juan Lucas. Abraham had disappeared. He looked like a frustrated down-and-out tennis player who practiced alone, using a broken racket to hit old balls up against adobe walls in the slums.

"Where did you find that queer?" Bobby asked.

"Ask Juan Lucas," Susan intervened, mockingly, now that her disgust had dissipated.

"Tomorrow is Saturday, right? Well, stay to have lunch with us, young man, and you'll see where this queer came from. We now have the best cook in Lima."

"She's a cook," Julius blurted out, either discovering homosexuality or simply thinking about Nilda.

"Darling," Susan exclaimed, looking fearfully at Juan Lucas.

"This character isn't going to live here, woman. He's only going to cook here . . . *Anyhow, do you think he would dare?*" he said in English.

And Julius, who was the best student in his English class, just stood there.

The next day, at lunchtime, Carlos ate with pleasure because now he had someone—Abraham—with whom he could pick fights and argue from time to time. If he can't take it, I'll crown 'im. Abraham cooked well because the chauffeur, a large Negro with that typical moustache, was a real temptation, living in the house and all. Arminda wasn't aware of those things. She simply rounded out the needs of the service person-nel of the mansion, and she never picked up on the nuances that enrich history. Lately, she only seemed to be aware of the presence of Julius and her daughter, the former sometimes during the day and the latter sometimes at night. But both of them were often with her at the same time, which would happen when she spent hour after hour up in the ironing room. The heat and the sweat would almost put her to sleep and images of both of them would appear together; nevertheless, she knew she was alone. Another strange thing that happened to her made her nervous, although she immediately forgot about it. Something was strange, but she didn't keep asking herself why her wishes were met before she could ask them. For instance, Julius might be going through the kitchen or the pantry and she would say Put your sweater on, but he would already be wearing a sweater or maybe he had just walked through there without it. Only her daughter never came back with the ice cream man, but that was because she never talked to anyone at length about it because there in the pantry she had never expressed the wish for her daughter to return; she did that only when she was alone in her room. Hence her daughter only came at night. On the other hand, Julius would be with her anytime, Put on your sweater, child, while he was already wearing one or it's that he had just been there without one. But the black locks of hair tumbled down over her face, interrupting her restlessness when she would ask why . . .

Miss Decisive also came down to eat lunch that Saturday and she unexpectedly ran into Abraham. She said hello as is customary, but only because the man—he's a man?—was an employee and had the same rights and obligations as the others. Carlos doted on Miss Decisive. She called him Don Carlos and made sure that he ate the same food as the Señores. The moustache would smile at her ironically, and he would entertain himself afterward with the inevitable toothpick from lunch and then stick it behind his ear for use in the evening. Daniel prepared the fruit dish and the silver finger bowls while Celso took out the exquisite platters of food that Abraham had prepared. Relying on their mountain culture mirth, the two of them made fun of the Creole queer who, in turn, scorned them with his tennis sweaters and oxygenated coiffure.

In the dining room, the architect in vogue and his wife, that is, the diminished Susan, relished the baked goat that Juan Lucas classified as unsurpassable. "I don't mean to praise him," he said, "but the queer is in great form."

"Señor," Celso interrupted, "the cook has asked if the goat is as tasty as it was at the Señorita Martínez' house."

"Marticorena," Susan corrected, smiling as she turned toward the architect in vogue to see if he still loved her like before. But the architect in vogue had just collected a fabulous sum of money from Juan Lucas, and while his wife was still diminished she was coming along and, to top it off, the other day he had bedded down with the Swede who, still in Lima, was saturated with sexual freedom. Even some ministers had gotten to know her. Susan turned to Celso and told him that Señor Juan Lucas thought the cook had gotten his goat perfectly.

"Tell him it's like always: very good!" Juan Lucas exclaimed as Celso was returning to the kitchen. "Succulent," he added, looking at the architect and forcing him to acquire a new dimension in his young elegance, which was to provide good food for your guests.

"In effect, Juan, I've never eaten it better."

"It's delicious, Susan," the diminished Susan said, who was coming along.

"It's great, Mom. I would have some more but I've got to take off. Does anyone need the Mercury?" Bobby threw down his napkin and shot out of the dining room.

"Don't have another wreck or you'll find yourself walking."

"I liked it better when Nilda would add onions," Julius blurted out, completely distracted because of the number of windows in the dining room.

Juan Lucas wanted to get mad but it wasn't worth losing one's temper over this little jerk, and the next morsel was, frankly, delicious, and now the wine and that very British cloth of his shirt cuffs as I raise my glass. Susan, still lovely, was jesting with the architect and his wife. In truth, their visits would be less frequent from now on. We'll only have our best friends over for dinner. Ah! Luis Martín Romero is going to flip over this queer's food . . . Celso came in to say that Anatolio had sent the new gardener and he needed a hose to water the lawn.

"Who is Anatolio?" Juan Lucas asked.

"The gardener at the old house," Julius explained.

"Celso," Susan intervened, "tell Carlos that as soon as he finishes lunch to take the gardener to buy a hose and anything else he needs."

"But how do we know he's going to stay? Have you hired him, dear?"

"No, darling, but Anatolio had promised that he would send his cousin. He says he's a good gardener and he needs the work. We'll see what happens. Anyway, we need him now."

"His name is Universo," Julius said, totally informed about the matter.

"What's his name?" Juan Lucas exclaimed. "Universo?"

"Yes."

"Ah! I've got to see this! What do you think of that name?"

The architect in vogue and his wife enjoyed the surprise and laughed at Juan Lucas' curiosity.

"Celso, tell Universo to come in."

"Darling . . ."

But while Celso was returning to the kitchen to fetch the gardener, Juan Lucas had lifted the glass of wine to his lips, and through the largest window of the dining room that overlooked the garden he could see the enormous green polo field beyond. The garden of the mansion extended onto the polo grounds and the eye could see for hundreds of yards through the trees to the far end. From there he returned to feel the elegance of his dining room and, son of a gun, those paintings from Cuzco fit right in. The luxury of the dining room enclosed him, its limits almost entrapping him. He put the glass down on the marble tabletop and, extending his tweed arms parallel to the silver tableware, he put the palms of his hands on the table in order to feel the freshness of the beautiful fall day: it wasn't too cold or too humid because the very British cloth of his shirt cuffs began right there and a second later Celso had decorated the table with a fruit dish full of color where his eyes took refuge for an instant: oranges, mangoes, and figs, all ready to bounce back immediately as if looking for the trees from whence they came and flying off toward the garden and gaining altitude beyond the grassy green polo field that some miniature men were crossing on beautiful horses . . . Susan's marvelous blond lock of hair came falling down closing off the green with gold, but something ugly caught his eye to one side.

"Universo," Celso announced.

Juan Lucas turned to look, and it was a little Indian from the Andes, about nineteen years old, but one never knows with Andean people. He entered humbly removing his hat and prostrating himself somewhat, and his straw hat covered a part of his leg where Juan Lucas had seen a blue patch over those khaki pants the Cholos always wear. Universo said good afternoon, but Juan Lucas couldn't remember having sent for a character called Universo in order to find out who in this world could possibly be called Universo. He looked toward the polo field and once again those horses in the background caught his attention, but then something else in the corner on the floor of the dining room also caught his eye. Julius was concerned about it, but for the first time it turned out to be less important than what he thought: Juan Lucas limited himself to a cutting stare at poor Universo's stupid ugly shoes, destroying him. His straw hat wasn't quite big enough to cover his old soccer shoes. "Fine, fine," he said, "go ahead and give him lunch." Celso led him away immediately and there wasn't any joking because when Juan Lucas remembered that the gardener was called Universo and it was funny enough to laugh about, Universo had already left the corner of the room. Now he was lifting the glass of wine to his lips once again. "Look at those horses out there," he told them. "It must be the afternoon match."

ON ANOTHER AFTERNOON it rained harder than usual in Lima and Morales said something about earthquakes. You see, there are always earthquakes when it rains so hard, and the Mother Superior said they had better suspend recess and remain calmly in their classrooms because the classrooms, well, the entire school for that matter, were earthquake-proof. The patio looked sad and dark from the enormous window of the third grade classroom. Carrottop was in charge of their class. She allowed them to play and talk because it was recess time, but they couldn't get up and move around too much because they were inside today. She was going to say that Morales would be bringing in the chocolates and other sweets to sell for the missions, just like they always do at recess time. About then Cano, who was sad and distracted, took three of the Pirate's candies, now squashed and gooey, from his jacket pocket. Carrottop became angry: How many times have I told you! She got furious and looked like she was going crazy. There are some people who just won't learn! Finally, she lost control of herself and ran halfway across the classroom, swishing the air with her habit on the way, in order to get to Cano and give him a good whack upside the head. She didn't give it to him with any bad intentions: it was the typical little whack given by a nun to a bad student, with an open hand and everything. But Cano would have preferred that she strike him on the head with a shovel instead of that false, gentle blow with her hand sliding down the side of his head, followed instantly by her wrinkling her nose upon discovering the grease on her hand. Ugh, it was grease, Cano's grease, from his greasy hair. Worse yet, all of them saw a pile of dandruff fall onto the desk. Cano tried to cover it with his hands, instead, everyone saw his ragged, filthy cuffs. She left, fortunately, and behind her the whole class had turned around to see what was going on; once a wave of looks had drowned him, he wanted to see the bungalows at the end of the beach, to see the classroom window and the patio. He had to get out of there so he could breathe and he managed to do it. And for the first time he made that strange, sad gesture. He looked the other way, dropping his chin to his chest next to one shoulder, rubbing his chin along the length of his shirt, and pulling his tie toward one shoulder.

On the day to give money to the missions, Cano surely made the same strange, sad gesture, which was especially noticeable at his age. He must have done it several times but Julius only saw him repeat it the time he was invited to his house. The matter of the missions was hard for Cano but Julius thought he was also dumb: why didn't he stay home sick if he didn't have any money to contribute? He should just play sick instead of going several days without buying any candy. Cano, in effect, had gone several days without buying any, keeping the money for the collection for the missions. He's dumb: he had gone to Immaculate Heart that long and he still didn't realize that a lot of money is needed for the missions and the priestly vocation and, for those reasons, they needed large bills, not just coins. Cano, why didn't it occur to you? It would have been better to get sick and not go that day. But he came anyway. And he even came thinking he was going to buy off Fernandito Ranchal, tell him I brought all of my money for the entire week, we're going to win, our row will give more than the others, we're going to win, we'll get the day off. The Mother Superior would promise a day off to the row that gives the most money. And, of course, Fernandito wanted to win and have his day off, he wasn't so bad, really, but not Cano nor anyone else was going to buy him off by saying I brought my week's allowance, I'll give it all to you, we'll win, Fernandito, we'll win.

They were clever but Cano didn't even realize it. They were clever because they held back the big money until the very end of the competition; they weren't going to give all their money at the beginning, they had to keep it until the end, just in case the row next to us wins the first round, or in case there's a tie and we have to break it. The first round, in reality, counted for very little. Mother Mary Joan kept the tally for each row. My, how little they had given so far! What is the Mother Superior going to say when she comes back? Mother Mary Joan wasn't very savvy, for she didn't know that our billfolds were stuffed with money. She was dumb. And Cano was too, because he became emotional when he heard that his row had won. They were winning because the other rows hadn't given much money yet. Then someone said, Here, we've got more, and Mother Mary Joan smiled. Cano was foolish to think that his row had won when they had just started to announce the end of the first round of donations; yes, he was foolish because he jumped up happily to hug Fernandito who, surprised and furious, turned and yelled: Get rid of your dandruff! Get a new uniform! Get your money ready because it'll be your fault if the others give more! Cano immediately made that strange, sad gesture again, but only Julius saw it days later when Cano invited him to his house. Of course, he had made that strange gesture before, it was so sad; and at his age, too. But not Julius nor anyone else was paying any attention to him at that moment. Fernandito had destroyed him with his glare and then turned again to follow the tally that Mother Mary Joan had initiated. He saw the smiling faces emerge from the losing rows as they stuck out their hands waving the first bills to appear in the competition: Ahhhhhhhhhhhhhhhhh! You were hiding it! It was the first time that Mother Mary Joan spoke to them in Spanish, hahahahahahahaha, everyone laughed exaggeratedly except Fernandito, who was furious. They laughed because Mother Mary Joan had spoken Spanish but she was supposed to speak only English. Mother Mary Joan was a likable person . . . Shhhhhh, don't yell, she's counting the money and if we've lost we'll give her more because she's so nice. The third row won! No, the first had won. No! no! no! And then the second row. No! no! And the fourth, and the fifth, all of them. No! no! no! Mother Mary Joan said, Calm down, calm down, everyone, let's go by rows, come up by rows, because all of them wanted to win, they only thought about winning and came up running, precipitously, running hard, they weren't thinking anymore, they weren't adding anymore, they opened up their billfolds next to the nun and she was pleased to see how sly they were, how they had kept the largest bills until the end . . . Shhhhhh, Mother Mary Joan is adding, by rows . . . sssssshhhhhhh . . . no! no! no! no! no! the fourth row couldn't have won. Yeeeeeeeeessss! Nooooooo! Yeeeeeesssss! Nooooooooooo! Mother Mary Joan said, There's still time, but only until the Mother Superior arrives. There's still time, and she took a handful of money and let a bunch of coins drop into a can, tacatacatacatacata, and once again the children swarmed around her with more bills, for no one was giving coins anymore, tacatacatacata-cataca, and now only bills, ones, fives, tens. How nice! Ah, another ten-dollar bill, and they loved Mother Mary Joan's accent: How nice! The third row was winning again. Nooooooo! Yeeeessssss! Nooooooooooo! Yeeeeeessssss! But the other rows still had hopes because they had some big bills left. Their mommies and daddies understood how important all this was, their children should be in good with the nuns, with the missions, so their dads had emptied their wallets for them but they hadn't emptied theirs yet. They were really sly, for they were holding back to the end. Fernandito was at the last desk of the first row in the bullies' corner. The first row just had to win, at least that's how he told it to Cano who was feeling sad now and stood at the front of the row. Cano began to feel bad because the other one was asking for his billfold. What do you mean? What billfold? Get out of here, jerk, get rid of your dandruff and get your money out. You've only given a few coins. And there was Cano trying to explain to him once again, trying to make him understand that he had already contributed a week's allowance that he normally uses for candy, a week's worth of his grandmother's money, but at that instant the Mother Superior came in and God only knows how, Cano, upon seeing her enter, remembered that Fernandito still hadn't contributed one red cent. It was the biggest moment of his life, he turned to him feeling both hatred and sympathy for his lack of money, but *there are blows in this life, I don't know.* He saw how Fernandito was counting furiously large denominations that he kept safeguarded in a handsome billfold bearing his gold initials, F.R.L.G. It was then he probably made that strange gesture again, the same one that Julius would see days later when Cano invited him to his house. He was probably just making that strange, sad gesture when he heard Fernandito calling the members of the first row over to him: "Cano hasn't given anything," he told them, and they started to chant: Cano! Cano! Cano! Cano! Just then the Mother Superior looked up at him and gave him the opportunity to close out the competition with a triumph. Let's see, Cano, you can be the hero, and everyone chimed in laughing, hahaahahahahahah, because the Mother Superior also spoke funny Spanish: if only the Spanish teacher could hear her. But everything was riding on Cano and he turned sadly to Fernandito, whose stare thrust Cano up against the Mother Superior. She was waiting for him with open arms, Cano looked at the class but he couldn't, then he looked at the nuns but he couldn't, all the while searching through his pockets as the Mother Superior became unhappy. He straightened his leg and stood on his toes in order to look for that secret pocket in his pants, that little pocket underneath his belt, there was the last little coin, worth three candies. He pulled it out and handed it over. He didn't see anything after that because he turned toward the blackboard in order not to look at the nuns who laughed and became upset, then they laughed and became upset again, go back to your seat, quickly now. The third row—Julius' row—had won, and they all screamed rahhhh! free day tomorrow, rahhhh! While Julius yelled and celebrated the triumph with his classmates, he didn't see Cano repeat that gesture in front of the blackboard before returning to his seat, just before running into Fernandito's furious expression and sitting down at his desk where he sunk his dandruff-covered head into his folded arms which were also sprinkled with dandruff and cried in silence for a while.

The first row continued to blame Cano for their loss, but he had hidden reality in his arms. He had trapped and crushed the truth between his arms, his face, his shoulders, and the top of the desk. No one turned to look at him anymore. Now everyone was involved in listening to the Mother Superior's speech in front of Mother Mary Joan's approving and smiling gaze. Of course, Mother Mary Joan said with her cheerful eyes, of course, of course, that's right, that's right, yes, yes, they deserve a prize, of course, of course, of course, of course. The fact is that the Mother Superior was taking them down the primrose path, they could see the end coming, and out of respect they didn't yell rahhh! just yet. They sensed that the reward was coming, for not only did the third row do well, the prize was on its way, but also everyone collaborated as best they could, their hearts were beating underneath the red initials of the school: the children in the missions will receive our contribution, only one row could be the winner, that's the way life is, but everyone did the best they could, their hearts pounded, the end of the speech was a prize for everyone, they could see it coming. For these reasons and because you have collaborated like never before with the missions and the priestly vocation, not only the third row . . . rahhh! but everyone . . . three hurrahs for the Mother Superior, all of the rows . . . hip! will have . . . rahhhh! the . . . hip! day . . . rahhh! off . . . hip! and Mother Mary Joan was yelling rahhh! as well, arms outstretched up high, an unforgettable soccer nun, always so friendly and happy.

Afterward the Mother Superior started to leave with the coin bags and boxes of bills, uuuuuuuuuugh, she almost dropped them because they were so heavy, and they were euphoric, for she jokingly acted like she couldn't carry them because of their weight. Mother Mary Joan joined the skit, offering to assist her. Together they left the classroom. "Quietly," the soccer nun told the class upon closing the door. "You can play but do it quietly," and they continued to talk animatedly, no school tomorrow, do you want to come to my house, etc.

That's when Julius turned to look toward the back of the room, over to the right, where Fernandito's voice could be heard. He saw him asking for his baseball glove from de los Heros. De los Heros didn't understand why, but it wasn't a matter of asking questions because Fernandito was becoming annoyed, and several others had turned around to see what was happening. He took the glove to his desk and everyone turned to watch. Everyone except Cano, whose shoulders had ceased to quiver but who continued with his face buried in his arms. Fernandito put the glove on and called out to him. "Cano," he said to him, and Cano was starting to look up when the glove, with a hand inside, pushed him back down into his sorrow. "It's not fair to hit from behind," poor Julius said without thinking. "Hit him from the front, then," someone else said. Fernandito stood up and the class grew silent. "Don't hit from behind," Julius repeated, also standing up, going over to him and looking more benevolent and justice-loving than Mighty Mouse in the latest issue of the comics. He was imagining page 13 of the comic book when wham! a baseball glove hit him in the face and stopped him in his tracks. Fernandito had taken the glove off and thrown it point-blank at him. He only saw it when it hit him, too late, although he tried to stand firm but it only caused him to receive a tremendous pounding on his nose and behind the impact of the punch were Fernandito's furious face and penetrating eyes, which worked on him psychologically. Mighty Mouse, page 13, lunged at that facial expression and pafff another jab, and behind those eyes Cano's sobbing shoulders and pafff another jab, blood on my hand and pafff another jab, my nose stings and pafff another jab, and Fernandito was getting tired of hitting him, Julius always repelling him, pafff another jab, Julius, macho, and pafff another jab, and a new attack and pafff another jab . . . The nun! The nun! What's going on? What's going on? And pafff another jab, just before they take him away: just so you won't forget.

Three days later Fernandito handed in a long sheet of paper on which he had written "I won't hit my classmates" one hundred and fifty times. Also, part of Mother Mary Joan's orders was to shake Julius' hand while he smiled furiously under her watchful eye. And though Julius' nose didn't hurt anymore, it did hurt him when Juan Lucas told him that he got his nose bent out of shape because he had stuck it exactly where he shouldn't have and Cano, without a doubt, was a fool. It hurt him to remember that scene and there was even a sad moment when, hiding in the bathroom, he flipped through the pages of the last issue of the comics to see if Mighty Mouse had ever found himself in a similar situation, or discover if he had ever run up against anything like hitting himself and hitting himself over and over again against a wall. Of course, the more one knocks himself against the wall the less it hurts, but the wall was always a wall and he had ended up without one single jab as they took him to the bathroom moaning with anger and dripping with blood. He tried to take on Mighty Mouse's image and the character didn't really do anything in life except jump over walls, he never ran into them. Obviously, the little animal of justice knew what he was doing, but what am I doing hiding sadly in this bathroom? . . . Julius felt a little embarrassed, the loneliness of the immense, elegant bathroom frightened him, so he abandoned it leaving behind porcelain jars with names in Latin that sat next to Susan's bathtub-pool. He couldn't sleep that night and, finally, when he did, there was the wall and then Fernandito. Then on the following day he started imagining things, imagining things he would have said, but one morning he heard someone say those exact words. The Spanish teacher, who was really crass and who had been seen walking along Wilson Avenue with her boyfriend, said that Julius was an introverted child, given to reflecting on things, and capable of . . . he didn't hear the rest, precisely because he was imagining things.

Cano also went around imagining things. At least that's the impression he gave Julius. What else could he be doing as he walked around the patio again, through the yard, around the patio, through the yard, along the school corridors, and even inside the immense white, cold bathrooms. And he was always carrying his little stick. He always walked around with this long thin stick. Maybe he used the same one every day or he would find a similar one each morning before he got to school. He looked like a forgotten god creating his own little revolution or one ruining the creation of the real God, for he would walk around touching everything he found along the way and give it a different name. That is exactly what Cano did. As curious as a cat, Julius had been observing him until one morning at recess time he decided to hide behind a tree because he had just discovered that Cano not only touched things, but also gave them names that didn't exactly correspond to what they were. It was as if he were reinventing the world. Of course, Cano wasn't a god, he wasn't crazy, nor was he an adult to seem so strange, but the truth is he didn't seem that far from being all of those things rolled into one. And Julius was a witness to it all. His curiosity got the best of him when he heard a murmur each time Cano, tic, touched something with the little stick. Now Julius was really curious. Perhaps he shouldn't stick his nose where it didn't belong, but he remembered that the phrase belonged to Juan Lucas and he immediately stuck his nose exactly where he shouldn't have: right behind a tree, where Cano couldn't see him. Here he comes. He touched the flowerpot several feet away from the bench and he called it doggy; he continued walking toward the tree but there was a faucet handle that came up out of the ground like a plant, tic, he touched it with his stick: cat. Then he went over to one of the Mother Superior's rosebushes, stopped to contemplate the numerous roses, began to touch each one, and called them Mommy this one and Mommy that one, and so on. Julius continued to watch the scene and remembered that Cano was an orphan. Then Cano contemplated a half-withered rose over to the right: grandmother. Then he touched the other roses: Mommy, Mommy, and Mommy. Finally, he started out toward the tree where Julius couldn't go on hiding because he'll surely come and touch it. But the bench was in between the roses and the tree. Cano looked at it a little while and, tic: house. Then there was a spider on top of the bench and he touched it with the stick, but then he immediately raised his foot to squash it before it could escape: Fernandito Ranchal y Ladrón de Guevara. After that only the tree was left. Julius mentally assumed Cano's angle of vision and from there he could see himself clearly behind the tree. He preferred to take off running but the stick was in his way, Cano was saying a pencil, and he just about poked his eye out with the stick as Julius started to walk away, whistling. Right then, he saw him make that strange, sad gesture for the second time. Cano touched him with the little stick: he called him Julius, who preferred simply to walk away as he whistled. "Julius, my grandmother said you could come over for a snack on Saturday." He immediately looked to one side, dropping his chin to his chest next to one shoulder, rubbing his chin along the length of his shirt, and pulling his tie toward one shoulder. Julius barely managed to say yes, and together they returned silently to fall into line because the bell had just rung signaling the end of recess.

At lunchtime that same day, Julius told Susan about the invitation. She had just gotten out of her bathtub-pool looking fresh and lovely. "What an ugly name, darling," was all she said, but Juan Lucas, who was relishing one of Fats Romero's recipes, prepared by our queer, couldn't contain himself.

"He must be the son of an old barber at the Club," he said. "The kid's worthy of your son, dear."

Julius and Cano went around imagining things everywhere, but each one did it by himself and in his own special way. Julius was surprised Cano hadn't said anything to him since being invited to go to his house on Saturday. Not a word. On the other hand, he was ready to establish a lasting friendship with that strange kid, but every time he looked at him in class or at recess, Cano would look away and repeat that same strange, sad gesture, until Julius suddenly felt something pulling at him inside his face and decided never to look at him again, for fear that such an ugly gesture, at his age, might be contagious. Nevertheless, Saturday was the day after tomorrow and he didn't know what to do. If they continue in this friendship of silence he was going to show up at Cano's house and what were they going to talk about since they practically didn't know each other? Things got worse for Julius when, at night, he dreamed he was crossing some immense field and had to walk until it got dark in order to get to a house he thought was his but, drawing near, it turned out to be Cano's house. And he had become Cano and was returning home after school. He barely woke up and began to reflect on it all so not one of the important details of the dream would be lost from his memory. Hence he discovered that the walk home every afternoon made him terribly weak. But having to touch everything with the little stick and give new names to every object he ran across helped him overcome his fear of having to cross those fields. He almost discovered that it was embarrassing to have to start out from home walking by himself while others left home in luxurious station wagons . . . he just about discovered that the rear fender of Julius' station wagon almost banged him in his butt and forced him to cross the street on the run . . . he might have discovered a thousand more things, but Miss Decisive entered his room shouting if he didn't get up and head for the bathroom in a hurry, he was going to be very late for school. He tried to make her shut up, he motioned to her with his hand, something like don't bother me, please, but Miss Decisive was right and shouted even louder, so Julius had no choice but to interrupt a series of vexing discoveries.

Tomorrow is Saturday, and Cano remained enveloped in silence as he walked from one side of the patio to the other, touching everything with his little stick as if he wanted to finish the arduous job of organizing the world anew all in one day. Julius tried to approach him twice and two times he was rejected by that sad, ugly gesture. A strange idea began to torment him: Cano probably regrets having invited me. Should I go? Maybe he doesn't want me to go and he's afraid to tell me. Julius spent the whole day Friday consumed by questions that tortured him and he watched Cano to see if he signaled to him not to go. But nothing happened. Cano continued caught up in his own world. Finally, by the end of the day, Julius had confidently decided not to worry about the matter anymore. He had been invited and no matter what happens, he was going, yes, he was going . . . he was thinking about all this when Cano passed by and Julius had not even noticed him approaching.

"Don't forget. I'll be waiting for you at four o'clock," he said as he ran by.

Julius was able to conjure up the appropriate words to respond to him by the time Cano had already started to traverse the first field after crossing a street full of cars and station wagons amid blowing horns signaling that mommies and/or chauffeurs were waiting impatiently. There was Carlos.

In his dream that night, Julius began the long walk toward Cano's house. He crossed the street next to the school and had to jump out of the way because a luxurious Mercury station wagon was speeding off and almost gouged him in the butt with a fender. Everyone was about to break out laughing. He was forced to leap onto the sidewalk and from there jump over a ditch. All in all, it was like a giant hop, skip, and a jump that ended with him standing in the field and his shoes heavily powdered with a thick layer of dust. Julius felt his eyes turn to one side and his chin push down hard against his chest and his tie pull toward the other shoulder. He felt sad and cold but habit forced him to continue on. It didn't seem so dangerous or lonely to return along the streets toward his house. Although the streets weren't completely finished, they were much less desolate than those fields where one would frequently run into a beggar or one of those child abductors. But now he was forced to use them. Grandmother had come to expect me to arrive home at a certain time. It was just bad luck because at first he would return home via the streets and just on that day when it occurred to him to take a shortcut through the fields, his grandmother decided to time him to see how long it took him to get home and now, if he lingered at all, she would become frightened and he might find her dead at home. He didn't have any alternative but to return home through the fields and those uninhabited lots. It was the only way to make sure grandmother wouldn't die and leave him alone in the world. On the other hand, if you are a good child and arrive home on time, your grandmother will live peacefully until you are grown up and become a pilot or a navy man, get married, and take me to live with you. Your wife will be very nice and I'll be able to see my first great-grandchild before I die in peace. Poor Julius, the grandmother's words touched him so deeply that he began to run like crazy in order to arrive on time and hopefully find her still alive. He was afraid he might get lost, but how was he going to get lost if he was Cano? . . . Since he had to hurry, he dropped the little stick. Fortunately he had taken this route a thousand times already and he had this part of the world well organized. Each object had its new name except for the excrement that was all over the place. For the life of him, he couldn't find any better word than shit. Juan Lucas and Susan must have arrived at that moment because he heard steps in the distance, Mommy's voice in the hallway, and he stopped being Cano when a comfortable and obscure presence began to invade the route to Cano's house, just as the rest of the dream began to vanish and, all of a sudden, he discovered he didn't even know where to go in order to get to Cano's house: fortunately I've got the address on a card in my nightstand and Carlos is going to take me this afternoon. Mommy's gone to bed, he didn't have to pee pee, and a yawn closed his eyes, after which it was something like being at the movies when they turned the lights down low and the movie doesn't quite start yet, nor is there any music until Del Castillo arrives, in first grade, to tell them Cano had invited him to his house. He was telling them about it and that kid Julius heard I had invited him and my grandmother, how embarrassing, well, he lives with his grandmother, he's an orphan, his grandmother is an old lady, she's really old, with white hair. She told me he was an orphan and she was the only person he has in the world. Don't say anymore, Grandma. We're poor. Don't say anymore, Grandma. His father was going to be the best lawyer in Lima, but he died young. God wished it that way: may His will be done. No more, Grandma, tomorrow he'll tell everyone at school and he's my only friend. No one is a fan of Sport Boys at school and they treat me as if I were a thug: take out your knife, they say to me. Grandma, no more, please, it embarrasses me and tomorrow he's going to betray me for sure. At teatime the grandmother served one of those small bottles of Coke. Del Castillo, please, here, take a glass, and she served us some in tiny little glasses. There was even a little left over, so she capped the bottle and put it away. The whole class laughed at him and he tried to laugh too, but it didn't come out the same as it did for the others. I don't know, sometimes I would like to hate my grandma but at other times I love her. Del Castillo transformed into Espejo in second grade, telling everyone that every Sunday Cano and his grandmother would walk to mass in the central park of Miraflores and walk back afterward. It was a long ways, and they would go back to a very old house made of mud and wood . . .

Julius awoke imagining an old large colonial house in Miraflores with high yellow walls, brown wood gratings, and some little red-tiled paths, shiny or slippery because they had just been scrubbed, maybe one or two tiles were missing, then a little further away two or three steps, a small terrace with wooden flower troughs, all painted green, and wilted geraniums on both sides of the double-door entrances with their metal gratings over the little windows through which one sticks his hand and opens the door from the inside. He thought he was going to see Cano's grandmother there too, but Miss Decisive discharged her second volley on that Saturday morning, forcing him to get up immediately. He remained sitting in bed for a moment while she opened the curtains and, looking important, returned to his bed in order to transform herself magically into a washtub and inflate her already large chest even more, which was more than enough to send Julius speeding off like a bullet to the small breakfast nook, which was like an intermission from the long series of bedrooms and bathrooms strung out along that unending corridor of the mansion. From there he went to the bathroom, where Miss Decisive would finally leave him alone, once he was well into taking his shower. "The colder the better," she would bellow at him, expanding her uniform with enough generated mass to let fly with more shouting, but always without becoming angry, it's true, because upon letting out a scream, Miss Decisive replaced her rage with her rights.

Juan Lucas proposed a game of golf for everyone that morning, but Julius disappeared as they were leaving. Happily, they didn't insist much on looking for him and ended up leaving without him because the cold shower had left him filled with many great projects for the day. Thanks to his dream, he had come to understand many things about Cano; but not everything, unfortunately, because Miss Decisive interrupted him, awakening him just when he was going to arrive at his house. Of course, at that point there was going to be a terrible mess: on the one hand, he was the one who was dreaming and, on the other, he was Cano in the dream; oh well, it doesn't matter. Julius was ready for any potential problems. It was still early and a sleeping pill, surely Mommy has some, would clear things up definitively. There were many things that needed clearing up: he needed to know exactly what Cano's house was like, what his grandmother was like, that way when I arrive I won't be afraid, and I'll know what to talk about and everyone will like me. Julius was thinking about all these things and many more while he searched among Susan's jars and bottles, reading attentively the instructions for each one of her medicines. He finally found one that assured long, profound, and restful sleep. Just what the doctor ordered, so he downed two pills hoping his dream would be really long and profound, above all, profound. Now he'll get to know Cano intimately. He went running to look for Miss Decisive and told her he was going to study in his room all morning and to call him only if there was something very urgent. That's the way Mommy said it and it always worked because they never woke her up during her long naps. Arminda was going to tell him it was Saturday and not to study too much but rather go outside and play in the garden. Apparently, one Julius disappeared upstairs and the other went in the direction of the garden to swim in the pool. Arminda shook her head slightly and forgot all about it. Julius forgot to take his shirt off, that is, he didn't make it in time to take it off because a feeling of drowsiness overtook him for the first time while he was looking for his pajamas underneath the pillow, the second time while he was taking off his pants, and finally, the third time when he started to unbutton his shirt. He was out cold.

He was still out cold when Miss Decisive pushed her chest through the doorway and announced with one loud shout they had been waiting hours for him to eat lunch. Since his parents weren't there today, he had to eat by himself, and early too. Half an hour later Miss Decisive again stuck her chest into the doorway, but this time she decided to peek inside the room and saw that Julius was not at his desk. What could have happened to the child? Perhaps the Señores took him without telling anyone. The Señores were so inconsiderate. She should say something to them. But she had seen the Señores leave without him and Julius had gone to the kitchen to say that he was going to study in his room. As a result, he couldn't have left with the Señores. Whatever the case, it's a lack of consideration on the part of the Señores to leave without telling them that they're taking the child with them. Where is Julius? Miss Decisive left bellowing at the top of her lungs because she didn't feel completely sure she was right in her last discussion with the Señores . . . What Señores? . . . What discussion? . . . Where is Juliuuuussss!

That scream woke him up; worse yet, he didn't have the chance to find out anything about Cano, nor anyone for that matter. On the other hand, he had a headache and a strong desire to go back to sleep, all of which made him doubt the success of his plan. "What rotten luck," poor Julius thought, and he was about to fall asleep again when another of Miss Decisive's screams forced him to get out of bed and go look for her.

Where had he been! He should have finished lunch hours ago! This can't go on any longer! He lacked consideration for his parents! No! For the servants, in fact! Yes! That's it! Julius tried to eat while barely opening his mouth because just now an open mouth meant possibly a tremendous yawn and he would be out cold once again right then and there. And maybe they wouldn't be able to wake him up until the evening. That means he would have stood up Cano. The last straw. Miss Decisive's presence, complying strictly with her responsibilities and demanding, as a result, that Julius finish everything right down to the last bite and respect her rights, which included a brief nap after lunch for herself, forced him to act with superhuman courage in order to finish the fruit and ask for a cup of coffee instead of dessert. Coffee? No way! Since when do you drink coffee at your age! Julius looked at Miss Decisive and told her that he didn't feel very well and he was going to rest for a while. "Please tell Carlos he has to take me to a friend's house at four o'clock," he added. "Wake me up at three." Fortunately Miss Decisive agreed.

They woke him up at three o'clock on the dot. One hour later, he left elegant and sleepy in the direction of Cano's house. On the way, his head began to nod out of drowsiness. He felt like his head was banging against the window of the station wagon door, and each time it got harder to hold his head up. Carlos got tired of telling him not to lean against the door, it might come open and you'll fall out on top of your noggin, but there was nothing he could do to stop him. He woke up when he heard, We're here, young man . . . He looked at Carlos terrified and threw away the little stick he had brought with him, touching thousands of things along the way while, in reality, he had come in a station wagon and not through fields nor putting names on anything with a little stick that he wasn't even holding in his hand. "That was a long, deep, restful dream," he thought as he got out of the Mercury. He was yawning again. Fortunately the doorbell which was enveloped in the humidity of the yellow cold wall shook him up a little. He looked carefully at it, rang it, convinced himself that the visit had begun, and he heard it ringing inside Cano's house. He shouldn't fall asleep leaning against the door because perhaps the grandmother will open it and think I'm dead and if she dies of fright, that would mess up Cano because he would be all alone in the world.

"Come in, sonny," the grandmother said, who had gray hair so white and such a sweet face that he began to adore her at exactly the moment she was capping the smallest bottle of Coke because there was still some left. He shook his head and again thought about his peaceful, deep sleep. Now what do I do? Yes Señora, no Señora, no Señora, no Señora, yes Señora. When did it happen, Señora? Did it hurt him much? Julius woke up with the explanation.

Cano had been waiting for him all day long; in fact, both of them had been waiting all day long. But the garden wasn't large enough. It was tiny and Cano said it was impossible to play soccer there. He said it would be better to play basketball. She asked him how and he explained: "It's easy. You get the bottom part of the old dirty clothes basket, climb the tree, and hang it from the highest branch. We can bet to see who gets the most baskets and we can play until it gets dark." He climbed the tree while she was watching, poor thing, and she was looking out for him too, but it was God's will . . . Yes Señora, yes Señora, yes Señora.

Cano had really done it to himself this time. He fell from the highest branch and they had to take him to a neighborhood clinic where they put a splint on his arm. Julius followed the grandmother through horrible hallways where all the tiled floors were cold and damp. He stumbled over a small, very ugly table and almost knocked over a flower vase with plastic flowers that Mommy had said were dumb and ugly. And they really were; in fact, everything in the house was very ugly. So was Cano in his old high bed. It went back to the time of Methuselah. He was just sitting there, wearing pajamas like those that Celso and Daniel use, smiling and saying I really screwed up. They had put a splint on his arm and wrapped it. He wasn't going to be able to take it off for at least two weeks.

Seemingly Julius had sat for hours in an old uncomfortable armchair whose springs had popped out, which is where the grandmother had left him when she went to prepare a snack for them. She would let them know when everything was ready: Put on your robe, child, both of you come to the dining room, then it's back to bed because the doctor has ordered lots of rest so you can go to school on Monday as usual. Julius looked around, even scrutinizing the corners of the room, for the little stick. He didn't see it anywhere. The grandmother returned bringing Donald Duck comic books for each one to read. Cano straightened his wrapped arm: "Ay!" he moaned. Be careful, child, the doctor said not to move it. We all have to suffer. He taught us how to suffer. He suffered more than anyone. He suffered for us . . . He was a crucifix that hung over the bed and induced chills. Everything in the room induced chills. The old armoire for his clothes, the stuffed chair and, above all, the immense iron bed. It looked like it had been made of iron pipes, cold water pipes at that. The clothes armoire was worse than the huge bed. They must have had to take it apart to get it into the bedroom. That piece of furniture induced a state of defeat, and Cano lived under the influence of that huge piece of furniture. How peacefully he read curled up under the light of the single light bulb also hanging from way up high. Julius barely managed to read a few lines of the Donald Duck comic, and then sleep came, long, profound, and peaceful . . .

The Last Supper was done in standard silver over a black background under another single light bulb that dangled from up high, almost touching the immense, dark dining room table. Julius felt a shiver run from his testicles to his head that, if it wasn't because I'm a child, would probably turn into cerebral hemorrhage. But he controlled his body. Then he felt better. Of course he felt better, and there came the grandmother with a huge bottle of Coke, the two-liter size: Del Castillo is a liar. He gave Cano a triumphant smile, the kind a friend would give, and Cano looked at his wrapped arm and at that moment the grandmother handed them two glasses, well, sure, they were small, but Julius bet they were going to drink more Coke than Del Castillo ever did. The grandmother filled their glasses, true, they were little glasses, and she capped the bottle: it's for the next time you come, sonny, and she took the bottle back to the kitchen. She returned with bread that probably had been stored in some cold dining room cabinet. She served bread with avocado that Julius wouldn't be able to stomach.

His drowsiness disappeared when Cano told him he was going to tell him his secret and about his plans, but Julius had to promise he wouldn't say anything to anyone. Julius swore before God, and in order to convince him he almost promised he wouldn't tell anyone that your house is so dirty and ugly, but right then he caught himself and didn't make the promise. Cano told him not to move for a few seconds and they listened in silence; in effect, the grandmother was in the kitchen, now it was time for her to say her rosary. Now they could shut the door and be alone for a little while. Cano went over to the armoire that had such an influence on him and opened the door. "Come here, get closer," he told him, and Julius went over to his side and saw him pointing at three large rocks.

"I can't lift them right now," he told him, "but within two weeks I'll be able to pick them up again."

"Why?"

"A kid in the neighborhood who doesn't go to our school told me that if I lift them every day for two months I'll be stronger than Fernandito."

"How do you know?"

"A kid in the neighborhood who doesn't go to our school told me."

Cano began to scratch his head and smiled confidently at Julius. Julius was thinking that around his house there had never been neighborhood kids. What would it be like to have neighborhood friends? Cano kept looking at him, smiling.

"But how do you know?"

"Because you lift them every day and each time you get stronger."

Julius thought about Fernandito and asked him again: how do you know? But Cano didn't catch the subtleness of his question. He didn't know how else to ask him. Besides, Cano told him to believe him: just wait and see what's going to happen in two months. He begged him, that's for sure, not to tell a soul. Julius swore once again before God, so that Cano wouldn't worry about it. Julius explained that he would have to be really dumb to tell everyone now because Fernandito would find out, and since there's still a lot of time to go before two months are up, he'd come and beat the shit out of you, Cano.

The grandmother opened the bedroom door and Cano quickly closed the door to the armoire. She noticed something strange going on but she didn't scold them because she could see that Julius was a decent little child. She told them that they could switch Donald Duck comic books now and that way they would get to read two books, adding that it was too bad they couldn't play on the patio a little while, but this child has to rest so he can go to school on Monday. Off to bed and don't move around. Grandmother's orders. Ever since he was a baby he had to learn to resign himself. He had given us the best example of what resignation means: who but He had been more resigned all of his life? . . . Yes Señora, yes Señora, yes Señora, yes Señora, welllllll . . . no Señora.

"WELL, HERE WE are at that German's place," Carlos told him. Julius looked at him wanting to say she's Beethoven's granddaughter, show more respect, but he preferred not to say anything because, as always, Carlos would look at him mockingly. Besides, this wasn't a modern apartment building but a large old colonial house. Susan had already explained it to him. She told him the old house had undoubtedly be-longed to some aristocratic family whose descendants were probably living today in San Isidro or Miraflores, or maybe Monterrico; unless, that is, they had become poor, in which case she wouldn't know what might have happened to them. But why explain those things to Carlos, he'd just laugh at me, and when I would tell him that Mommy told me about it, he'd laugh even harder. Julius picked up his music books, got out of the Mercedes, and took off running.

All of a sudden he came upon the dark entryway, but he crossed through it calmly because now he knew his way around. Of course, Mommy's right: they used to be great houses full of rooms that are now rented out as offices or sleeping rooms because everybody works in the center of Lima and it's convenient to have their offices there. Also, there are people who actually live there, the middle class, Julius, the middle lower class, sometimes really lower class, and the white woman wearing a large white gown is the widow of a state employee who every month goes to collect her pension . . . Pension, darling, that's what they pay widows whose spouses had worked for the state. They also live in those old large houses because they pay really low, controlled rent. Ask your uncle Juan Lucas about it: those people are a real problem. For instance, you buy one of those dilapidated houses that's about to fall down so you can put up a new building and you've got to send in the army to remove the renters. They don't want to lose out on that windfall of low rents; well, it's so cheap to live there. Julius walked calmly along the corridor of the second floor, looking down at the patio and thinking those schoolgirls are the ones who go to the public schools. "Ah!" Uncle Juan said, "those crass, vulgar girls, they make the best secretaries. About the pretty one who paints her fingernails, what should I tell you, boy? That one seems to me to be headed down the wrong road." Julius had stopped at a strategic point from which he could contemplate the pretty girl who was painting her fingernails. She was always sitting there, painting her fingernails underneath a window, and he had unconsciously begun to hurry to get to the academy so he could linger a few minutes there, contemplating her before his class started. Hiding, he watched her taking the wrong road. She seemed happy, though, smiling and painting her fingernails carefully, humming boleros. He had given Juan Lucas all the details and his only comment was that the girl likes what's forbidden. That can't be. It's a lie, Carlos. Nilda, Vilma, all of them hummed boleros. But why, then, didn't she get together with the two girls who were going to be good secretaries? Why? They were in the same school, you could tell from their school uniforms, they lived in the same apartments, but the secretaries studied all the time, whereas the other one was constantly taking the wrong road: she was always smiling, always painting her fingernails, and always humming boleros. She would look at her nails, blow on them, and turn to look toward the patio. Then Julius would quickly move to one side. His class would be starting in one minute and he wanted to contemplate her a little longer when all of a sudden the pretty girl bent down in order to dip the brush into the polish and, as she straightened up, waved at him with the hand that she was blowing on. Julius turned pale because he was sure she had never seen him up there, impossible, she had to have been waving at someone else, but the girl smiled straight at him and began to sing something to him or was it to the air? *It hurts you to know about me, my love, you hurt me so much* . . . It had been dedicated to him. Panic overcame him and he jumped back to one side and heard a short little snicker nearby.

He he he . . . He debated between trying to find out where that snickering was coming from and taking off running without understanding anything, but at that instant the funny laughter turned into words which came from the window of the wise old man with the bald head. "The girl, the girl," the old man said, and Julius dared at last to turn around and look at him. "The girl, the girl," he repeated with gleeful eyes, squinting happily behind his glasses. "It's been several days since the girl, the girl ha ha ha ha . . ." Julius didn't know what to think about the wise old man's glee, much less what to do when his happiness turned to coughing and he began to choke behind the window. The wise man was going to die happy, laughing between coughing spasms while he continued to talk about the girl. The girl. The girl. It wouldn't be long before he died with those words on his lips. Julius left him there, explaining once again he was going to be late for his piano class. "Frau Proserpina is going to be mad," he said as he left. All of a sudden the old man turned serious. He even looked out through the iron grating of the window in order to say something that Julius couldn't hear very well, something to the effect that Frau Proserpina wasn't capable of even giving herself the pleasure of getting mad.

That same afternoon Julius convinced himself that he had completely lost all feeling for playing the piano; only his curiosity about the boarding house would be strong enough for him to suffer more ruler whacks on his wrists. Frau Proserpina became more severe each time and didn't stop until she became insolent and ill-mannered. She repeated over and over that he was her worst pupil and if he didn't get noticeably better she was going to write a letter to his mother explaining that the classes had to be canceled because the student didn't have any talent. The whacks continued to be a regular part of the classes and the shawls as well. The matter of the shawls was frankly incredible. She almost couldn't move with the ones she had over her, but the back of the tattered chair was full of new ones. And the matter of her other students was strange. "They all arrive on time but you," Frau Proserpina would repeat, but Julius had his doubts. Of course he always arrived a little late because until today, when he discovered the girl had discovered him, he would stand there for a few more seconds watching her which is when he would lose a few minutes of class. Perhaps the punctual pupil prior to his class was on his way out at that moment, but why didn't he ever see him go by? That pupil had to use the same corridor, but he could have been so absorbed in the girl who was taking the wrong road that he didn't even realize when the other had left. But what about the student who is supposed to come after me? He hadn't ever seen him either. With so many ideas flying around inside his head, Julius wasn't able to think about the problem of his wrists or the new series of whacks with the appropriate raise your wrists that followed. Finally, one hard whack set him off and Julius, who was flying up and down the scales, decided right then and there he should get to know the wise old man, show the girl with the painted fingernails the right road, ask the white woman who wore the spacious white gown how much her pension was, change the light bulb for Juan Lucas' future secretaries, ask the man who fixes useless typewriters what he lives on, read a few documents belonging to the court clerk and, finally, don't hit me, you old fart bag, to find out about the murky secret surrounding the academy that belongs to Beethoven's granddaughter. "We haven't even finished with the exercises and we're already tired?" In effect, Julius had sighed out loud, but not for the reasons that Frau Proserpina had thought. It was due to the large number of decisions he made in a few seconds that had left him groggy. He almost asked for another whack from the old woman in order to see if it inspired him with even more courage to initiate so many adventures. "This situation is going from bad to worse," Frau Proserpina told him. "We can't undertake anything new until you learn these exercises." Julius was going to respond that he knew them and to let him try again when, only God knows why, she added: "This is not going anywhere." Inquisitively, she just looked at him. Disconcerted, Julius also just looked at her, hoping for some kind of explanation about her remark, but Frau Proserpina, as if coming out of a coma, reverted back to the same strident tone and told him that there wouldn't be any classes the day after tomorrow. "We have recitals that day. Stay home and practice your exercises. The recital is only for the best pupils." For Julius, who had been among the best pianists at Immaculate Heart, her statement was like a kick in the groin. He was deeply offended and took to heart the statement that was like a symbolic moral whack on his innermost soul. However, he didn't say a word but what he did do, though, was raise his wrists higher than ever and begin the exercise like during the initial days, and he overflowed with feeling. He was about to become the best pupil in the world when Frau Proserpina placed the clock on the keyboard. He almost knocked it off in his impressive demonstration. She told him the lesson had ended and the next pupil would be arriving in a matter of seconds. This was a new symbolic moral whack for Julius who stood up furious, grabbed his music books, and marched out almost without saying good-bye, murmuring crazy old bitch, it never snows in Lima as he went out the door. He stopped as soon as he felt free and rested a few minutes half-crouched against the wall of the corridor. There wasn't a trace of the punctual pupil and the symbolic moral whacks still hurt. It was easy to turn around and take a look into the doorway of the academy: strangely, Frau Proserpina had turned off the lights that illuminated both pianos. Julius looked into his soul. The punishment still hurt. It wasn't difficult to let out a slight cough, a small clearing of the throat, in order for Beethoven's granddaughter to throw down the skein of wool and jump to the light switch. But he had already taken off running.

He ran right into the wise old man's chuckling. "Impossible," he thought, upon seeing the old man still dying of laughter. "He should have choked by now." The old man didn't hear him approach his window and look in again. Moreover, he was laughing at something else now. "She's nasty, she's nasty," he was saying, and there was lots of ha ha ha, and soon the coughing with which his joy always ended would start: "Frau Proserpina, she's very nasty." Julius told him that she was Beethoven's granddaughter and the old man's eye lit up with delight, and once again he started to die of laughter. As he laughed, he didn't manage to say what he wanted to say, the laughter dominated him. Julius couldn't understand him: . . . ha ha ha, yes, yes, ha ha ha, sonny, ha ha ha the granddaughter ha ha ha of her grandfather ha ha ha Beethoven ha ha ha . . . Finally there was something that Julius could understand very clearly: "Who told you that?"

"My uncle Juan Lucas . . . He's married to my mom."

"Ah! Your father, yes, yes . . ."

Julius thought it was a good opportunity to continue the dialogue. The wise man had stopped laughing and looked at him seriously.

"The girl . . ."

He had stuck his foot in his mouth. As soon as he had mentioned the girl, the old man broke out laughing again. Julius had to wait patiently until he could stop.

"And in that window? The man who fixes typewriters?"

"We all have to work in life. Everyone has to work. Do you work too?"

"I'm in school."

"Are you studying to go to work?"

Julius thought about the man who fixed typewriters and about Juan Lucas. The old man wasn't as wise as he looked. His answers didn't amount to much.

"But who wants those typewriters? They're so old."

"Their owners want them. They don't have any money to buy new ones."

"And how does that man make money?"

"He works hard but makes very little."

"And you, Señor?

"Philatelist."

Julius thought that Philadelphia was in the United States and he looked at him stupidly.

"I'm a stamp collector. That's what philately is. I'm a philatelist. Look at my albums on the table over there."

"And the woman in the window downstairs?"

What could he have said to make the old man wave no, no, no, with his hand, and express disgust? Julius was completely baffled, just when his questioning was starting to get somewhere . . .

"I never go downstairs. I'm too old. I'm not interested, not interested . . ."

"She's the widow with the pension . . ."

"And who's told you all this?"

"Uncle Juan Lucas . . . No. My mom did."

"Do me a favor, sonny. A big favor. I can't go down the stairs anymore. It's hard for me to go up and down the stairs. Buy me a newspaper, will ya? We'll talk about that woman next time."

The old man turned around to go to his desk and began digging around in ashtrays until he found a coin. He returned to the window to give it to him. And Julius said he would be right back. He took off running and didn't stop until he ran into Carlos. He had looked all around as he ran. They were all in their windows, and she was there painting her fingernails, watching and smiling. He didn't smile or do anything except make a beeline to the main door. "Where are you going in such a hurry?" Carlos said, stopping him. Julius explained what he could about the old man, and Carlos said the wise man was a faggot. "What's that?" "He's queer, man," Carlos explained. But he couldn't keep the old man's money, he's so poor, and besides, why should he? Carlos, he's not queer, let me go, let me go. Carlos agreed only if he would do it fast while he watched him from the shadows. Julius crossed the street, purchased the afternoon edition of *The Daily Commerce*, and came running back. *It hurts you to know about me, my love, love, you hurt so much* . . . , but he didn't want to know the meaning of such perverse words and he continued up to the second floor. Carlos, on the other hand, stopped and turned around to look at the virgin flower, he was already calculating her age, thinking that in a couple of years she'd be ready for the picking, but the flower drooped, hiding her face when she saw him, grew silent, turned her back to him, and looked into her room. Carlos cursed the young girl and threw his head back. At least he could watch Julius from here.

"Thank you. Thank you. At my age, sonny, at my age there are things one just can't do . . . She's Beethoven's granddaughter, you say?"

"I don't like her," Julius blurted out, remembering that afternoon and all those symbolic moral whacks.

"We don't like her either, sonny. Here."

Julius' hand trembled as he received it. At first he decided not to look at it and he continued looking at the old man, but then his eyes started to water and he looked down at the coin: cold, bright, weightless, and it uncomfortably filled his whole hand. He already had the five cents, thanks, he didn't want it, thanks, he didn't wa . . . But the old man had opened his arms as if he were the Pope blessing the masses and the newspaper was fluttering in the air while he talked. "It's new, it's new," he repeated. "It shines like gold and it's worth a piece of candy." Julius decided that the old man was wise and that Carlos was nasty. He was always making fun of everyone. Well, no, Carlos wasn't nasty, he was only wrong. Why can't he come up here and see he wasn't queer but a wise man?

"I have to go. Carlos is waiting for me."

"Who is Carlos?"

Julius turned toward the entryway where Carlos was watching and waiting. "Carlos is waiting for me," he repeated and he started to leave, but he had one last question for him: who was the girl? But he was afraid to ask, the old man just might start laughing.

"Who is the girl taking the wrong road?"

"Is that what your father also told you?" Then the old man became sad. "Who is your father?"

"He's my uncle Juan Lucas. He's married to my mom."

"Who is he?" the old, bald-headed wise man repeated. But more than wanting to ask questions, he was thinking, looking down below at the young girl seated next to her window painting her nails, smiling. She was humming again.

"Who is she? Why is she . . . ?"

"Everything and everyone here end up taking the wrong road," the old man interrupted.

"Hey, let's go," Carlos yelled at the same time from down below. "You've talked long enough."

He started out toward the main door when he saw Julius coming down the stairs. *It hurts you to know about me, my love, love, you hurt so much. The flowers that in heaven believed you came falling down, defeated by humility.*

He tried to give an explanation to him, beginning with the stamp collection, but Carlos interrupted him.

"Philatelist or lunatic?" he asked, starting the motor.

Julius became silent: Carlos is impossible. He looked at his moustache and discovered that some moustache hairs are styled so as to take life as a joke. Julius put his hand over his mouth, right there where he didn't have any moustache hair; he wouldn't have any for some years to come. He looked out the window of the Mercedes and, in the darkness, in that old, ugly part of Lima, the old man had repeated: Here everything and everyone end up taking the wrong road.

"Everything and everyone," the old man thought simultaneously, "but the child is likable, floppy-eared just like the way they draw us Jews . . ." He had stood by the window, listening vaguely to the girl's humming, not even realizing that he liked it, but his hands turned cold as he grasped the bars over the window at a concentration camp and then had to let go. He went over to glue his last three stamps for the night and read the newspaper that years ago stopped being of any interest to him. Now it's just the child, Beethoven's granddaughter, and childhood days . . . *He's married to Mommy* . . . He heard the song clearly and for a moment looked at a radio like the typewriters in that window, but the song came from downstairs . . . *Who is the girl taking the wrong road?* . . . He went over to shut the window. He closed it but now he missed hearing the song, just imagine all those years, so many years. He opened the window, the first time the music in this country . . . His white hand stained with green and blue ink trembled a lot when he tried to paste the three remaining stamps; the girl interrupted him when she began to sing louder. He put the stamp to one side, just imagine, he even decided to sit down for a while, think without memories, yes, yes, a girl who sings and boy who comes . . .

HERE HE COMES. He heard him climbing the stairs slowly and, for the first time in many years, he was happy not to have any stamps left to paste that night. He was going to be awfully tired in the evening, in fact, extremely agitated after proving to the child that Frau Proserpina was bad and crazy. He was very nervous after telling him the truth. Yes, those were the child's steps in the corridor and he didn't hear him coming anymore because he had stopped to look at the schoolgirl. The old man went to the window. There was Julius. He still hadn't taken his

317

strategic position when the enemy-friend had already seen him. It was the same as the other day. He darted off, jumped back to one side, took a few steps and all he had to do was turn around and say hello to him.

"I don't have class today."

"What? Why did you come then?"

His explanation was too long to give and, besides, Julius, who had plans that couldn't be postponed, wasn't aware that the wise old bald man was also full of ideas that ran parallel to his. He hadn't forgotten about the recital. It was only for the best pupils and he was supposed to be at home practicing hard, but those symbolic moral whacks continued to burn, and there he had arrived to attend the recital, no matter what.

"I didn't have to come today," he explained, "but there's a recital for the superior students."

The old man began to understand what was going on. "Ah," he said, moving away from the window in the direction of the wall at the back where a calendar was hanging.

"Of course, of course . . . Now I remember. Today is the first Friday of the month. Every first Friday of the month there are recitals. Ah, yes . . . a recital, right? And you're not invited to the recital, ha ha ha, of course not . . . The great academy of Frau Proserpina! The great academy of the granddaughter of Beethoven! Who told your father that Frau Proserpina was Beethoven's granddaughter?"

"I don't know. Uncle Juan Lucas just knew it."

"Uncle Juan Lucas?"

"He's married to my mommy."

"True. Did you tell her that she is Beethoven's granddaughter? Did you say it to her, to Frau Proserpina herself?"

"No! Uncle Juan Lucas told me not to."

He's married to mommy . . . No. Maybe this crime can't be attributed to this wicked woman, but she was partially wicked in any case. The old wise man definitely had his own ideas about Frau Proserpina.

"The people who live here probably go to the recital."

"I don't know, sonny, I'm not sure about that . . . But you and I are going to attend the famous recital."

He asked Julius to wait. Then Julius saw him put on a scarf and come out through the door of his room. He thought he had time to go over to the railing and take a look down below at the girl, but the wise man's meek voice surprised him, calling to him at the other end of the corridor.

"Come," he said.

Julius barely noticed that the girl who sang boleros wasn't in her window, she's probably getting ready to attend the recital. He hurried to catch up with the old man at the corner of the corridor. Together they went to the right and walked toward the end of the other corridor, the academy, and Julius began to tremble as soon as he saw the door.

The recital had begun. There wasn't any doubt that one of the better pupils was playing because the piano sounded like one of Uncle Juan Lucas' records. For the first time in his life he understood the difference between "My Bonnie Lies over the Ocean" and what the students were playing who had undertaken many lessons with Beethoven's grand-daughter. When he got to the door Julius wanted to retreat, but the old man seemed determined to go in. He even took his hand in order to give him courage, or so as not to let him escape. "Look," he said, pushing the door slightly ajar, and Julius could see the four benches that were always at the back wall, it was dark, just the pianos were illuminated and the person who played much better than he did, even during his prime, was none other than Frau Proserpina herself.

"You are her only pupil!"

The old man's voice convinced him. Now he really wanted to leave but he couldn't. The old man, who squeezed Julius' hand even harder, was out of breath and trembled as if he were about to have a seizure.

"She doesn't have any pupils because she's old and nasty. Old and nasty! Old and nasty!

The old man lost his balance but managed to lean against one of the double doors that was still closed. "What luck," Julius sighed. "If he would have leaned against the other one he would have fallen flat on his face inside." The old man began to pant even more, and he didn't seem to care if he made any noise. As soon as he regained his balance, he pushed the door open a little wider as if to convince Julius even more of what he was witnessing. Julius took a closer look and it was horrible because at that very instant Frau Proserpina made a mistake and suddenly stopped playing.

"It's intermission time," the old man told him. "Now she's going to announce a brief interlude so that the audience can get refreshments at the bar before the second part of the concert."

Frau Proserpina walked over to the edge of the raised platform and made an irascible gesture to the audience. Julius pulled his head back immediately, but the old man told him to look again, and he had no choice but to watch: she picked up a skein of wool, sat down, and began knitting during the intermission.

He had seen enough, but the old man couldn't hold back his anger.

He insisted that Julius had to see the whole show right to the end because Frau Proserpina would now return to the edge of the platform and announce the second part of the program.

"She's been doing this for years."

Julius pleaded with the old man to take him out, but the old man was caught up in his own anger.

"Yes! Yes! But first I want you to understand why. Fully understand why that woman isn't going to teach you anything! She's wicked! Crazy and wicked! You are her only pupil and she wants to take it out on you. Who sent you here? I imagine it's the guy married to your mother. Well, everything's finished here! Here everyone's taken the wrong road. Frau Proserpina is a nobody! She was a great teacher but now she's a nobody! And there's no reason for you to be a victim! A victim like me! I sublet that miserable, dumpy room where I live and now they want to kick me out. They're raising the rent and I can't pay more . . . she wants to maintain . . . at our expense . . . she wants to maintain . . . of course, you must be a rich boy . . . that's why she treats you that way . . . she wants to believe you are simply one more pupil among dozens but, frankly, you are the only pupil she has in the world . . . and me, with my rent I also have to maintain . . . maintain . . . I have to maintain . . .

The old man stopped shouting and Julius realized that he wasn't squeezing his hand anymore, but the old man was still trembling and Julius saw that his anger had dissipated. He was sobbing now and he tried to leave, but it was too late. She was already at the door.

"Evil-tongued Jew!" Frau Proserpina shrieked as she opened the other door behind which they had been spying on her.

But the old man was crying now. She really hadn't understood what was going on until she noticed that someone else, who was much smaller, was hiding behind the door. Frau Proserpina leaned through the doorway and discovered Julius.

"Evil-tongued Jew!"

"No! No! No!," implored the old man, weeping, and his anger subsided. He was raising his arm as if trying to stop the scene; it was as if he had never wanted this to happen.

"You're going to pay for this, you old evil-tongued Jew! You devil!"

"No! No! I didn't know . . ."

"You have rent to pay! You'll pay whatever I demand from you!"

"All right! All right! I didn't realize! The child is leaving . . ."

"You are going to sleep in the streets tonight, you evil-tongued Jew!"

But the old man wasn't listening anymore. He had turned around and, sobbing, looked at Julius who was disappearing for the last time for both of them. He hadn't realized, it was the enthusiasm of the other day, the happiness, the anger afterward, the misery . . . the old man tried to say it all and so did I . . . but Julius had already gone to the right, he was no longer in the corridor and neither he nor she would ever see him again . . . Frau Proserpina walked over to where he was standing and, disconcerted, looked toward the darkness of the empty corridor.

"There will be no more academy for you!" she yelled, so that Julius would understand his lack of talent forced her to cancel his lessons.

A woman turned on the light in her room and went to the window that looked out onto the corridor next to the academy. She was going to hang out a bed sheet when she encountered the two of them standing there. The light that emanated from her window allowed her to see them clearly. How old Frau Proserpina looked, always so stiff like a German soldier. And the old doddering Jew? What are they doing here together without fighting? For once they're not fighting. They're the ones who were yelling before . . . The woman hid when she saw the old man approach. He was nodding no with his head. He didn't have any stamps for that evening . . .

"No one is ever thrown out into the street during the winter," Frau Proserpina told him. "We'll talk about it when it stops snowing."

Then she turned around and went back into the auditorium. She closed the door behind her to prevent the great academy from getting cold. As she walked toward the chair with the shawls draping over it, she suddenly heard everyone's applause.

IT WAS GETTING dark when Carlos began to honk the horn in front of the mansion's large exterior door. He was thinking about all the money they had spent on such a huge place and they hadn't even given any thought to spending just a little more on an automatic garage door opener. He tried mentioning it to Julius, but the kid was really downcast: better leave well enough alone. He kept honking the horn without any response. "How do they recognize it's not the Señor's car," he wondered. "If it was his car, then the bloody Indians would for sure come running out to the street. Of course, Don Juan doesn't spend any money on automatic doors because he's got two humble servants to open the door automatically. That Jaguar guy knows it all, he sure knows how to live." Finally, Celso opened the door and as the Mercedes drove in Julius was startled by an incredible automobile. Carlos parked the car and contemplated the museum piece that they had brought to the mansion.

It was a very old black La Salle but it looked brand new. They looked at it as if it shouldn't exist except in the movies. Julius ran to look inside. Yes, it was just like in the gangster movies: there was the window separating the driver from the back seat; in that way the chauffeur wouldn't know what the Señores were planning in the back or who was the owner of such an incredible limousine. Celso was going to say it belonged to one of the Señor's friends who had just arrived, but Carlos interrupted him.

"And did they assassinate the family?" he asked.

"Yes, of course, it looks like a bandit's car," Universo, the gardener, said appearing on the scene.

"What do you mean bandit? What bandit are you talking about? *Gáster,* man! Get smart!"

The door of the La Salle opened. A large Negro chauffeur, wearing a much fancier uniform than what Carlos tends to wear, appeared from inside. Carlos almost went back for his cap but the large Negro was already taking his off, hence they would talk for a long while after the child and the Indians had left. For them it was a pleasure to talk together: both of them paid homage to the same black Jesus Christ, were in the same profession, and black is beautiful! Both chauffeurs smiled with pleasure.

In elegant fashion, Daniel opened the door of the mansion and Julius greeted him by asking who had come. Daniel still didn't know, some strange person whose name he didn't even know, only that Don Juan Lucas had told them that a friend was coming over that afternoon. Julius asked about Miss Decisive at the same time her boisterous voice reverberated throughout that area of the mansion. Aware of his arrival, she came to yell at him for getting his uniform dirty, just like she did every day, and because it was time to do his homework. She directed her comments at Julius from the other end of that area of the mansion but he saw that she stopped suddenly, and Miss Decisive began to walk more slowly. It wasn't just the effect of Juan Lucas' soundproof ceiling, there was something else, for she could barely be heard, *the one who was always laughing and who boasted of breaking hearts . . .* Julius approached Miss Decisive who grew silent after murmuring a languid good afternoon, just before riveting her gaze to the ground.

"Good afternoon, better yet, good evening, because all the lights are on."

And poor Julius, who was still imagining the girl who wasn't taking the wrong road anymore so he could say good-bye, I'm leaving forever, was almost frightened to death.

"Good evening," said the evil voice of the man in black with a black hat, seated at a stool in the winter bar of the mansion.

"Excuse me, Señor. I wasn't paying attention," Julius smiled, approaching Juan Lucas' gangster friend and shaking his hand. "Good evening, Señor," he repeated smilingly.

But young boys' smiles made them look like women, and this one still had a quivering queer's voice. What kind of kids did Juan Lucas have? Whatever the case, Al Capone only gave him a strong handshake and Julius' smile ended up looking at the same eyes that had just decimated Miss Decisive. Julius didn't know what to do, and Al Capone continued sitting on the stool without showing any interest in the books that he had with him. Anyone else would have asked: And where do you go to school? And those books, what are they about? Then he would have been able to explain he was coming from his last piano class and perhaps, if he had been a friendly person, he would have even told him about what had happened and about the girl who wasn't taking the wrong road as Juan Lucas believed, and they could be friends openly, but never with Capone. He hadn't even taken off his hat, and there was that attitude of sticking out his chest as if he were constantly receiving medals. And that terrible look on his face underneath the brim of his hat: besides, no one wore hats in Lima anymore, nor those square suits of the thirties that men used to wear, nor so many gold chains on their vests.

"Your parents are about to arrive," he said, looking at him in that malicious way, which seemed so strange, for Julius had seen that expression somewhere else. But where? Who?

He was going to ask him if he would rather wait in the living room, but Al Capone pierced him with his eyes. Yes, he had seen that look before.

"They're waiting for you, young man."

He stuck out his chest further and found another victim: it was Miss Decisive who was just recovering her roundness and who again was reduced by so much power.

"Hurry up, Julius. I have to clean your uniform and it's time for you to do your homework."

Even Miss Decisive's voice trembled but as soon as she finished talking she made a supreme effort, turned around so she wouldn't have that look piercing her and marched off, swelling in size as she went, recuperating her splendor as she left that part of the mansion. She was once again Miss Decisive by the time she reached the pantry, overflowing with rights and corresponding duties, intimidating everyone with her

huge bold chest and letting Arminda know she had returned. She announced her arrival to Arminda sitting there and to Carlos who was
heating up water for tea with the other chauffeur. "Damn, ol' Big
Breasts there isn't all that bad," the La Salle driver pronounced in a low
voice, removing his cap, bowing, and putting it back on. But Miss Decisive had already turned her back to him and the phrase reached Julius
beside Arminda: Sorry, Señora, with all due respect. When she heard
something about sorry, Arminda looked up because perhaps it was her
daughter who had come back.

The one who had come back was Juan Lucas. Susan was at his side,
but they weren't riding a buckboard or a stagecoach, like the idiot Universo had said. He had opened the large outside door, and what did he
know about the past? In reality, they had arrived in a carriage. They
were in a hurry because Fernando had probably been waiting for them.
It had taken them a long time to pick up the carriage. Julius was changing his uniform when he heard the clippity-clop of horses outside on the
front patio. What the hell was that? He ran to the window and saw his
old carriage, now newly refurbished and, of course, he had never seen
it hitched up to horses. He flew down the stairs. Susan and Juan Lucas
were just getting out. "Don't shut the outer gate!" the golfer yelled at
poor Universo who was dumbfounded with the arrival of the royal
family. "Don't close that door yet because they're coming to get the
horses and bring my car!" Celso went out to meet them and informed
them a man was waiting inside. They had barely opened the door when
Julius came running out. He didn't stop until he was sitting inside the
carriage and firing at the Indians, just like he used to do when he was
four years old. If only Cinthia could see it, and Nilda, Vilma, and Anatolio too. He stopped firing after the cloudy mist of emotion lifted and
his present age appeared when the game without so many of its players
turned sad. "Mommy," he called out. Susan, who was going into the
mansion, sensed something was up when she saw the prince's sad face
in the carriage window. Lovely, she went over to him, telling him he
should get down, for that period in his life with the Indians was over.
It's just a decoration now, it's your daddy's whim; frankly, this whole
thing is kind of silly, darling. The coach driver didn't even know how to
drive it. But you know your daddy: he was flat out determined to bring
the carriage home himself. But then on the way home he got angry
because they whistled at him and yelled queer . . . And the adventure
didn't end there, darling: Daddy insists that the axle was squeaking but
it was obvious they were throwing rocks at us in Lince. Come, darling.
Daddy has a friend inside. My God! Look! I hope he's not as strange as

his car. Why don't you take a picture with all these crazy vehicles on the patio? Come, let's go inside.

"Perfect," Julius thought, upon seeing the midget Capone, dressed in mourning, enveloped by Juan Lucas' lively checkered tweed jacket; they were giving each other a hug. It had been years since they had seen each other.

"Married and settled down," Capone shouted, raising his short, strong arm, swiveling around like a bullfighter giving thanks to the audience and demonstrating his admiration for that part of the mansion. "Long live luxury and the guy who invented it!"

"I knew you had returned from Buenos Aires, but I thought you were in Trujillo."

"I arrived this morning! A short period at the hacienda to put things in order, and then back to Lima to see my friends!"

"Man, I believe you. And how's it going in Trujillo?"

"Well, just imagine . . . Six years as ambassador. Six years without returning home . . . but I have good people up there. I'll tell you about it . . . A few weeks of hard work was all that was needed."

"I'm glad to hear it, now let's see what we're going to have to drink."

"Real nice," Julius continued thinking, noticing that the giant on the bar stool had shrunk when he got down and stood up. Sure, he had short legs, but that look . . . Susan, on the other hand, observed the emotion of the two buddies, laughing to herself at Capone, but ready to provide a kind smile as soon as they acknowledged their presence.

"Darling, we're here . . ."

"Congratulations," Capone exclaimed, enormous torso and short legs.

Susan consulted her dictionary: naturally, congratulations, because Fernando was already an ambassador when Juan and I got married.

"Thank you," she said, approaching them.

"Well, now you've met her."

"Señora, it's a pleasure."

"Susan, please."

"My pleasure, Susan! Let me congratulate you in person. At that time I remember having sent it in writing."

At last Capone took off his hat. The guy had his whims, and with good reason because being totally bald didn't go well with the gangster look nor his elegant, old-time getup. Susan didn't stare but she did calculate the damage that his baldness did to his image. One could tell she was calculating it. Capone noticed it more than anyone else and God only knows why, probably because it's always children who make fun in such cases or because they're never bald, but why did he give such a terrible look to Julius? He cut him off, be careful about laughing and all, there was no reason to laugh, because Julius just stood there, waiting to join the group and thinking this is real nice, perfect.

"Well, fine . . . let's see about that drink," Juan Lucas said.

"After six years: a toast!"

"Fernando was my classmate and has been a friend ever since we were in school together."

"And before that if it had been possible!" Capone exclaimed. A little chain on his vest clinked.

"I think I spent every vacation at your hacienda in Trujillo."

"God was born in Trujillo, according to those popular Peruvian lyrics."

"I think we should go to the bar."

"Well, Susan, I want you to know that when I left him years ago, he was single and swore he'd stay that way."

Julius stood outside the circle of adults and could have easily left, but he was bothered by those looks that Capone kept giving him: he had seen them somewhere before. Capone went up to the bar with Susan and Juan Lucas and, while she wasn't paying attention, he jumped up and sat down ponderously on a bar stool. Capone recuperated his splendor and, upon feeling like a big shot once again, he let fly one of those classic flirtatious remarks at poor Susan, riveting his gaze on her at the precise moment she was going to adore him. Susan became a little embarrassed as Capone included some double meaning in his words and in the way he looked at her, it was a flirtatious remark, true, but also an indication of his excellent past with women: there have been lots of destructive looks in my life, love affairs, the expertise required to become involved with any woman, even the women of his friends, even in the case of someone like Juan Lucas, but never in the case of a friend, no, not Juan Lucas, I'm a gentleman and I can do anything I want except what I don't want to do . . . Susan let her lock of hair come tumbling down in order to hide the smile produced by the knowledge that she was going to have an interesting game with Fernando, frankly, all of Juan Lucas' friends were darlings in their own way and this one, well, this one was somewhere in between the sublime and the ridiculous.

"Hey, Fernando, it seems to me you've got some relatives who were viceroys and were related to Susan's family on her mother's side. Let's see if you two can figure it out . . . it seems to me that you've got a common surname back there somewhere."

"Mommy," Julius intervened.

"Hi, darling . . . Have you said hello to this gentleman?"

"Yes, Mommy," Julius responded, making sure he did not look at him so as to evade his evil eye.

"He was the first member of the family I met today."

For sure he was looking at him like that again, but Julius didn't dare look to find out. He didn't pay any attention to him and began to tell Susan about the incident at Frau Proserpina's academy. Knowing Juan Lucas was going to interrupt him, he tried to make it brief.

"Mommy, I don't want to take piano lessons anymore."

"Good news," Juan Lucas blurted out. "That's the end of the piano stuff. This one was headed toward becoming an artist," he added, looking at Capone.

"How noble!" exclaimed the bar stool giant, but then regretting it somewhat, art isn't a very manly thing. Just in case, he repeated the look that accompanied his previous flirtatious remark with the same intention, and Susan's lock of hair tumbled down once again. "Hasn't changed a bit," Juan Lucas mused, looking at his friend.

"Sure it's a noble thing, but not in this house. Sure, all children take piano lessons but this kid is getting older. He's going to be twelve soon."

"Eleven," Susan amended.

"Ten," Julius corrected, knowing that Capone was gunning him down with that look of don't contradict your elders, sonny, respect the authority of the patriarchy and all of that stuff. But he wasn't going to give him the satisfaction; good, he didn't look back at him.

"Darling, we'll talk about this another day. We really don't need to talk about it now."

Julius knew that the matter of the piano lessons was finished forever. No more piano lessons, no more girls taking the right road, no more Frau Proserpina. He watched Juan Lucas pour whiskey into large rock crystal glasses. Who was Juan Lucas? And he looked at Susan: who was Juan Lucas? Who are you, Uncle Juan Lucas?

"Uncle, the story about the girl taking the wrong road isn't true. I saw her studying her lessons with two other schoolgirls."

"Really?" Juan Lucas asked, pressing the intercom button.

"Julius never lies," Susan said, hopping onto a bar stool next to Capone.

"Uncle, isn't it true that Frau Proserpina isn't Beethoven's granddaughter?"

"Listen, bring some ice to the winter bar," Juan Lucas said, bending over slightly in order to talk into the intercom. He straightened up immediately and looked at Julius: "Hey, go to the kitchen and tell them to hurry up with the ice."

"What's this about Beethoven's granddaughter?" Capone asked as Julius was leaving.

"One of Juan Lucas' little stories, and poor Julius . . ."

Everyone in the kitchen was absorbed by the conversation, for Juan Lucas had forgotten to turn off the intercom. Now they were laughing their heads off in the winter bar.

"Incredible," Susan was saying. "It can't be."

"This guy?" Juan Lucas insisted, pointing at Capone with a long finger. "He's capable of anything. You'd have to be there to believe it. Oh, the summers I spent on that hacienda!"

"But you mean you actually shot real bullets?" Susan asked, noticing that Capone was turning serious.

"You always have to have a target to shoot at," he said solemnly.

"Of course he didn't hit them, woman. Don't be naive. But he made them dance. He would call the peons over . . ."

"Were they Indians?"

"Cholos, people from the Andes, you know, whatever! The incredible thing was to see them jump so high into the air. "I'm going to fill your feet full of holes," he would yell at them. And then, pum! pum! pum! Then another: pum! And they jumped all over the place. "No! No! No! Master Fernando," the workers would yell at him.

"Oh! Noooooo!"

"Well, looooook, you see . . . they didn't get hit, but . . ."

"You didn't hit them because it wasn't necessary."

"Take the ice to them," Carlos interrupted, turning to Celso.

"I'll take it," Arminda said, but Celso was still standing there.

"Just leave it there," Daniel said. "I'll take it."

"Give it to me," Julius said. "I'll take it."

But at that moment he could place the guy's expression that had intrigued him so much.

"Parents pass it on to sons!" Capone ejaculated: "Fernando Ranchal y Ladrón de Guevara!"

"Poor Cano," Julius murmured.

THE SPANISH TEACHER, who was really crass and vulgar and who had been seen walking down Wilson Avenue with her boyfriend, assigned an essay about some event or character that had impressed them during the last few months. They could write, for example, about the visit of the Cardinal to the school, or about the Mother Superior's birthday party. They weren't allowed to write about that most recent crime in the papers. No, not about that either. And it was completely forbidden to write about the lives of movie stars. Who tells you about those filthy things? Ugh! Be quiet! They could write about Saint Rosa of Lima, or about the Negro saint because there's democracy in heaven. Nevertheless, it was better to write on a more contemporary topic. They could write about their best friend at school.

"Or possibly about your worst enemy," Julius thought, and the next day he was the first one to turn in his essay. The young teacher, who had been seen with her boyfriend on Wilson Avenue, told him to wait a moment because Espejo was making noise and she had to take care of disciplinary matters first. Apparently, Espejo had looked down the neckline of her blue taffeta dress and he was telling Del Castillo about it who, in turn, looked at de los Heros, touching his chest and pointing to the teacher. A second later they all were touching their chests and pointing at the teacher. Julius was standing next to her; since he wasn't dumb, he understood and took a look while the teacher was sitting down. He did it out of obligation more than anything else, but all of a sudden he realized that the teacher's hair was reddish in color, and he imagined her hugging her boyfriend along Wilson Avenue, and he felt weak inside when his eyes followed her brown body as it descended down to the rounded lighter parts, until he got lost in a shiver that began in his testicles and, if I hadn't been a boy, it might have turned into a cerebral hemorrhage.

"Sit down, Julius," the teacher said, buttoning her pink sweater and discovering simultaneously Fernandito Ranchal's look. She missed a button. Sitting at the back, Fernandito continued to watch her. He had become the devil, and he continued to look at her as if he had just seen much more than the others. You're an insolent little twit, if my boyfriend gets a hold of you, I've got a date at six with Lolo, Lolín, Lololo . . .

But before the six o'clock date, it was Julius' turn and he had been getting ready for it since yesterday. Last night everyone in the kitchen had intervened in the writing of his essay. Julius was really smart: he sat next to Miss Decisive who was drinking her tea, and he asked her about the Señor who had come that time when they had brought the carriage back, the one dressed in black, the one with the black limo, don't you remember, Deci . . . Miss Decisive remembered and that was the beginning of a long talk in which they took turns giving opinions about the strange character. The bad part was that little by little that strange character was losing what mystery there was about him while at the same time he was becoming ridiculous in proportion to the details they added. Carlos and Abraham also added theirs to the story, and Celso added his two cents worth: he said when they were about to go to the dining room, Señor Ranchal tripped as he got down from the bar stool and found himself grabbing the Señora for support. The Señora had to laugh, although she tried to hold it back because it seemed like Señor Ranchal had become annoyed; in fact, Señor Ranchal got very serious and he let her know he was annoyed when he riveted his eyes on her. Frankly, Señor Ranchal has a somewhat ugly, furious look about him. Señora Susan had to stop laughing, so she let all of her hair come tumbling down over her face, as she was probably hiding her smile underneath. And Daniel, who had served the meal, had something else to add: before sitting down at the table Señor Ranchal looked at the legs of the chairs; in fact, twice he looked at the legs of the chair, probably hoping the servants would bring a bar stool for him. Then Arminda intervened, but it was only to make them aware of her poor health. Miss Decisive decided the time had arrived for Arminda to retire. She just couldn't continue that way anymore. Lately she was getting everything confused and when they thought she was laughing at Carlos' joke, she blurted out for them to lower their voices, she didn't want the man dressed in black to hear them. Immediately, Julius decided that the title of his essay would be: "The Man Dressed in Black."

He arrived at school and ran to look for Cano: all he had to do was convince him not to tangle with Fernandito. "I'm going to hit him, I'm going to hit him," was the optimistic response of the other, and in vain he tried to explain to him no matter how many times he had lifted those stones, Fernandito was going to beat the shit out of him. "I'm going to hit him, I'm going to hit him," Cano insisted, and Julius could not make him understand that he was the one who was going to get him, he was going to devastate him with his essay entitled "The Man Dressed in Black." Cano wasn't very bright. He didn't understand anything about psychological punishment and all that stuff but, over and over again, Julius tried to explain his plan to him. He even tried reading a page of the essay to him, but in no way did Cano understand. Finally the main school bell rang, followed by Carrottop's bell, and Julius ran to get into line because he wanted to speed up things and read "The Man Dressed in Black" to the class.

Black was the Señor and so was the little master, because if Fernan-

330

dito took a while to understand the first allusions in Julius' text, little by little several started to sound familiar to him and, by the second page, Fernandito was suffering badly, all alone, thinking that the character Julius described in his story was very much like his father. Of course, Julius couldn't know, how was he going to know his father? But how to deal with the fact that the entire class was laughing at his father. It was incredible! The Señor even dressed exactly like his father: all in black. And now everyone was breaking out laughing again at his father because he had just tried to climb up on a bar stool three times and failed, and because he had looked over at a little kid who was staring at him scoffingly in order to pierce him with his Al Capone look, he lost his balance and slipped off the stool, and there he was trying to climb up again, but one of the delicate chains of fake gold that hung from his vest, Fernandito gave a sigh of relief because his father's chains were made of the finest gold there was but immediately became embittered, because in any case they were chains and one got caught on a doorknob as he went into the dining room and he wanted to go in to eat but couldn't.

"Read more slowly and don't raise your voice," the teacher intervened, adding that there were serious syntactical errors, more than likely orthographical errors as well, and of course his pronunciation and accentuation weren't perfect either.

"And since he couldn't reach the table because he was so short, the butler had to bring in a bunch of pillows, and the cook who knew he was accustomed to staring like that served him a mackerel and placed the mackerel's eyes in such a way that the Señor discovered the mackerel staring and staring at him. And since the fish looked at the Señor dressed in black and then the Señor in black looked back at it, the man in black was rigid throughout the whole meal. Everyone finished eating, but the Señor in black continued staring at the mackerel and the mackerel continued to stare back at him. No one could believe it when a laundress named Arminda told them not to laugh at the Señor in black because he was in the kitchen now. It's true, because the butler had to clear the table that night and the Señor in black continued staring at the mackerel and the mackerel began to rot. The butler had to take it to the garbage in the kitchen, and the Señor in black wanted the mackerel to lower its eyes, and because he was obstinate, he followed it to the kitchen, and the butler threw it into the garbage, and the Señor followed it inside the garbage to look for it, and since he was so small the butler didn't see him and he put the lid on the garbage, and the next day the garbage truck took him away."

"Don't say the garbage, Julius, one says garbage can. You read badly and too fast. Many times the subject could be replaced with a pronoun that would serve precisely . . . de los Heros, what's the purpose of the pronoun?"

"To replace the noun and avoid repetition."

"I said de los Heros, not you Palacios. Your topic is interesting, Julius, but who helped you write it?"

"My mother corrected it a bit and we all wrote it together."

"The essay is supposed to be personal, Julius."

But he didn't care one bit if the essay was personal or collective. The important thing was that Fernandito Ranchal was reduced to a pile of shit at the back of the room. Fernandito was a pile of s-h-i-t and, of course, Julius wasn't too far offtrack from his original idea, but he was terrified to present Fernandito's father exactly the way he was, with short legs and having to look for bar stools in all the bars he frequented. But dumb Cano hadn't picked up on anything. He laughed like the others, made fun of the Señor in black like the others, but his ridicule lacked that delicious double meaning it had for Julius. Julius was returning to his seat when he saw Cano raising his arms and flexing his muscles and showing his biceps, still ready to fight. His triumph came to an end when he saw him.

Cano was so dumb! What had he not tried to do in order to convince him that revenge had been consummated! But he kept insisting: "I'm going to hit him. I'm going to hit him." It's true that after lifting those rocks over and over he had acquired a great deal of self-confidence. But his self-confidence sounded as false as a wooden nickle; it made him look stupid as well. There was little or nothing Julius could do to stop him. The time period that he had set to acquire his new strength had been up for over a month, and Cano had become very impatient. Julius managed to convince him to postpone the matter, and now he was hopeful he would be happy with the essay, but it didn't work: "I'm going to hit him. I'm going to hit him." And soon too. Soon because the end of the school year was coming and he had to keep his promise.

It took place at the back of the patio area, next to the Mother Superior's roses. Fortunately, there was no one back there when Cano saw Fernandito walking by in a state of fury. He ran to find Julius. "Come and watch," he said, and they went off together looking for the enemy. The confidence with which Cano walked, as well as the news of the appearance of Mary the Virgin in Fátima, encouraged Julius. At first he felt like "why not," and, then, even something like "of course, man," when he noticed that Cano was quite a bit taller than Fernandito. But no sooner did they get to the roses than Julius lost all of his enthusiasm. And it got worse when he noticed that Cano, just before challenging Fernandito, repeated once again that strange, sad gesture: "I'm going to hit you, eh, . . . I'm going to hit you . . ." Fernandito smiled, shook hands with him, and it seemed as if he were going to say, "Hi, friend." Cano stood there waiting, but suddenly it seemed like he was waiting for the other to get tired of twirling him around in circles. Somehow Cano didn't fall down, for Fernandito was the axis around which he flew and he decided to continue a bit more before letting Cano go: running and running, gyrating and running, trying not to fall but he was going to fly as soon as the other let him go. Then Fernandito opened his hand, let him go, and watched Cano fly into the rosebushes and crash into the barbed-wire fence at the back. "Do you want more?" Cano didn't answer him because the crack-up left him dazed and back in his neighborhood where his friend was telling him to develop physically by lifting some rocks, it's really like lifting weights . . .

Final exams weren't long in coming, and they had to rehearse for the awards, too. This year, however, Julius spent a lot of time on his piano lessons and reading Mark Twain and Charles Dickens. That's why, perhaps, he wasn't going to receive any medals as in previous years. In any event he wasn't so concerned about getting prizes. And Susan was pleased because she wouldn't have to go. And what did he care? It wasn't the same as before, like the time when he played "My Bonnie Lies over the Ocean" and Mother Mary Agnes sat next to him. Moreover, it seemed like the nuns knew he was going to Markham next year and they didn't pay much attention to him anymore, or it was something he thought he felt: the truth is he wasn't happy about attending the ceremony. It would have been better not to attend because three moments had made him really sad. First, when a little kid with big ears played "My Bonnie Lies over the Ocean"; second, when the Mother Superior read her good-bye speech to the older students who were transferring to Saint Mary's; and, third, when they called Fernandito Ranchal to receive the medal for best soccer player of the school and, while he went up to receive it furiously, Cano was making that strange, sad gesture.

HOMECOMING

I

Juan Lucas' noiseproof ceiling wasn't enough to silence the scene that Bobby created a few days after Julius' tenth birthday. The first night, for it all began one night at seven o'clock in the evening, he didn't need liquor to sustain his firm and imposing anger. Bobby couldn't express himself very well and Julius, at first, was unable to get a clear idea of what the hell was going on. Finally, he perceived something that even made him happy: his brother's raging fury sabotaged Juan Lucas' plans for the following summer weeks. Julius was excited about going swimming with Mommy every day at Herradura Beach, and all of a sudden Juan Lucas comes up with the idea to move to Ancón for four or five weeks in order to inaugurate a new building that he had built in partnership with Juan Lastarria. Julius pleaded against it and Juan Lucas wouldn't even pay any attention to him. Wasn't it enough that he was forcing him to play miniature golf every morning? Juan Lucas had put in a miniature golf course at the mansion. He liked that sport, right down to its small size; in the evenings at sundown, having a drink, he loved to contemplate the way the nocturnal shadows would descend over the grassy polo field while he sat at the summer bar, all of which extended his yard into the depths of the night, and the way the entertaining miniature golf course, which was red with petite white houses, tunnels, tiny bridges, and dwarfish mountains, turned dark also, following, in turn, the darkening hues of the colors. He saw greens, whites, and reds do battle with the darker colors. That night Juan Lucas added a new dimension to his pleasures. It almost happened unintentionally. He put his glass of whiskey to his nose (the aroma, while the colors rivaled each other, was also a newly added dimension), but this time he continued raising the glass until the rock crystal covered his vision, enhancing it with an incredible spectrum as it rotated in his hand trapping a new perspective that was getting away, rotating the glass again, a car-ousel of visions by just raising the glass a bit, always rotating, and he added the fugitive yet trapped gold of the whiskey, ah . . . that's what he was seeing when Bobby's first furious scream, coming from some other part of the mansion, shattered his vision through the kaleido-scope, his miniature golf course, his yard, and the evening: his crystal glass of whiskey in the summer bar of his new mansion.

Juan Lucas found himself acting a little ridiculous, so sensitive, com-bining colors, inventing kaleidoscopes, and searching for the colors and deciding on the new cloth he was thinking of ordering from London. He was totally caught up in another world, but in this life it's necessary to be in this world; that's why Bobby's cursing at the top of his lungs had caught him by surprise, forcing him to turn around briskly, if only to discover the view toward the interior of the mansion which was, in its own way, as alluring as the view outside. He almost held the glass up in between him and the view, but Bobby was approaching from somewhere, adding a thousand swear words to his cursing, some of which Juan Lucas himself failed to recognize.

And not even his soundproof ceiling was enough to impose silence on the scene that Bobby had started that night. Someone, probably in the United States, thought that the problem of noise in the home had been resolved, but why? as they say in Lima, with Bobby going from room to room proving the opposite with so much cussing. Julius came to see what was going on but had to take off running because his brother was ready to punch out anyone who got in his way. Julius, with such an innocent, dumb-looking face, was a perfect target. Bobby didn't stop, he ran from one room to another; in one Susan saw him and he didn't hear her say: Darling! Darling! Darling! and in another Juan Lucas saw him and he didn't hear him say: Hey, kid, what's wrong? And on the stairs to the servants' quarters, Daniel saw him go by and he ran to tell Celso. Seconds later, upstairs in the corridor, Miss Deci-sive ran into Bobby who was still yelling like a crazy man. She wanted to yell back, but she quickly understood that his screaming was not directed at her and consequently did not infringe on any of her rights, although she did have to carry out certain responsibilities: she ran to tell the Señora who, at that instant, ran to look for Juan Lucas: Darling! Darling! All of a sudden she saw herself in a robe with a towel around her head, spun around, and darted back to the bathroom because she couldn't stand for Juan Lucas to see her unmade.

Bobby was arrogant: there was no way in the world that he would confess to them what the problem was, although Juan Lucas had already suspected something. Julius didn't understand anything at the moment. Evidently something was going on, because Juan Lucas already had three whiskeys instead of two and he still didn't understand anything. On the other hand, the kaleidoscope dreamer already had some ideas about the matter. He thought it would be best to give the adolescent a few whiskeys in order to channel his rage toward sorrow and, a while later, having gulped down three good-sized whiskeys, he would begin to tell his story, ragingly at first, then ferociously, about the diabolical things that had occurred to him with some girl.

The golfer's plans fell through and the ice in his whiskey melted because amid his crazy antics Bobby ran into his room and shut himself up in there for about an hour tearing his heart out after destroying just about everything that was in sight. "My Mark Twain," Julius thought. Juan Lucas had sent him upstairs to look for Susan. But she wasn't ready to go down yet. Still, Bobby's problem terrified her, that's what she said, although Julius didn't notice any expression in her face that looked anything like what he had seen in a horror movie the other day. The two of them stood at Bobby's door, Susan begging him to open up and telling him please don't torture me. Then she said in English she was going to go crazy out of grief. She said it with such feeling that Julius immediately turned to adore her. Of course he adored her, but it was because of how beautiful she looked every time she came out of her bathtub-pool, which is probably why she took three baths a day. Even now, the more she insisted on suffering the lovelier she became, even to the point of bending over and begging him through the keyhole to open the door that, being a supermodern type, didn't even have a keyhole. As she continued to beseech him, discovering her mistake and theatrical insistence, she dropped the towel that swirled around her head and all of her hair came tumbling down over her face. She stood up immediately, threw her hair back with both hands, and began to plead with him again: Open up, darling, *please!* Please open up, darling, while asking Julius to get her dress, it's on top of my bed, because she wanted to keep begging Bobby a little longer, after which she would run down to have a drink with Juan Lucas.

"Make way, bather," Juan Lucas said, looking appetizingly at the low neckline of the robe that covered Susan's unrestrained and refreshed body. He had just come upstairs, accompanied by Celso, who was bringing a bottle of whiskey, two crystal kaleidoscope-type glasses, and a new provision of ice, all neatly placed on a silver serving tray. Upon discovering him at her side, she made a sensual gesture of feminine frailty, not because she had no luck with Bobby but because of her robe.

I must look horrible, but she knew how to make herself look enchanting and all she had to do was throw her head slightly to the back, while at the same time running her hands through her hair until she reached the back of her head . . . Flirting, she had only played with her hair for an instant, you couldn't accuse her of doing anything else, but Juan Lucas had seen the outline of those breasts that, although no longer young like some twenty years ago, nevertheless continued to present themselves with that same disquieting curiosity of the first time which all of a sudden is now. "Take over, darling," Susan told him, smiling. While she walked away, Juan Lucas thought about taking a look at her through one of the crystal glasses, for his desire impelled him to enrich that vision, but Julius appeared with a dress at the end of the corridor and, in any case, the reason he had come upstairs was to take care of Bobby.

"C'mon, young man," he told him from behind the door, taking advantage of a moment of silence, but Bobby didn't pay any attention to him. He continued to scream: leave me alone, and something else about he wasn't going to stop until he took revenge and until . . . Juan Lucas didn't hear the rest because Bobby continued to break things inside and to throw himself against the walls. Repeatedly, the noise of a chair being thrown against a door or a window obliterated his words. "What are you saying?" he asked, maybe he would answer him, but he couldn't hear this time either because Julius had approached with an important message from Mommy: there was a chair that belonged to Alphonse XIII in that room and she begs him not to break it. It had taken a lot of work to get it. Julius tried to communicate the message but they interrupted him, first with the noise that Bobby made as he tore a book to shreds at the moment when he was going to talk, oh my poor Mark Twain books, and second with Juan Lucas: "Hey, why don't you get out of here, I'm the only one who can take care of this."

"Now listen, young man . . ."

"Go to hell, all of you!"

"Leave us alone, please," Juan Lucas said to Celso, who had been witnessing everything, serving tray in hand and respectful.

"There's no one here but me . . ."

"Go to hell, all of you!"

"Hey, what's this?"

"Would you please go to hell!"

"This is for men only . . ."

"You're not my father!"

"Hey, Bobby, take it easy . . ."

"Pimp! Bastard!"

Now you've heard something that no one has said to Juan Lucas in thirty years. The golfer was baffled and for once he didn't know what to do. Well, yes, he knew but later on: there was nothing else that could be done that evening. And he shouldn't even try to intervene unless Bobby asks for his help; after all, let things come as they may and they'll happen naturally. Of course, he could always help things along. "Julius," he yelled. When he saw him come out of his bedroom, he told him in a low voice that neither he nor Susan was going to dine at home that night but, just in case, tell Celso to leave some bottles of whiskey upstairs, make sure they place them in strategic places, understood? . . . Good. Just tell the butlers to leave some bottles out in the open so that your brother will find them. What? All of them? Don't be stupid, young man. The idea is that he should see some everywhere and fall into the trap. What? Temptation? . . . Call it whatever you like, the important thing is that he see them. After that, half a bottle will do the trick. Perhaps by the time we return he'll be ready to talk.

Twenty-four hours later, hunger forced Bobby to open his door just when everyone had given up worrying about him. He walked sadly down the corridor and his anger had dissipated now that he had broken everything that he could find in his room. He even realized it himself when he unconsciously responded affirmatively to Susan's sweet question that morning: "Darling, darling, did you break Alphonse XIII's chair?" He answered yes, looking at his watch. It was about eleven o'clock in the morning and he began to feel hunger pangs. He wasn't strong enough to get mad anymore. He thought he shouldn't have answered his mother's question, but immediately began to feel something like an immense but weak who gives a shit? then a feeling of relief, a strange sensation as if he had fog in his brain. Why didn't he feel sorry? What was going on here? Had all of this really happened?

Around noon Celso went to offer him something to eat, and he felt like he could say come in Celso, let's talk a while, but all that had happened last night and the history of his life forced him to say go to hell with tears in his eyes. At two o'clock in the afternoon he knew that they were eating lunch downstairs and Juan Lucas was probably cussing him out and all the possibilities of going to look for him had been lost, precisely last night. The hunger hit him and it hit hard. With that type of hunger it wasn't necessary to talk about anger, it was impossible to create another scene and be the center of things. Don't forget about me, sons of bitches! Fog again, and then hunger. Had all of this really happened? . . . He looked at his watch, six o'clock, and he almost congratulated himself for having valiantly staved off the four hours that he had promised to hold out. He felt a new surge of fury and let it fly, but no one heard him: it was small in comparison, unimportant, gone in three screams that were more like sobs and several sons of bitches pronounced in a low voice with his nose and mouth pressed against his pillow. He noticed his anger had abated and looked at his watch to see how long it had lasted: only five minutes. No one was even aware of it. All of a sudden there was fog again and, worse yet, hunger pains, even shivers: I'll go down at seven o'clock.

At seven o'clock all the broken things that were strewn around his bedroom expelled him. It seemed as if they had accused and harassed him for hours: you should be ashamed of yourself. That explains the remorse he showed on his face as he went down the corridor. He felt a little rage when he saw Julius' peaceful room, but he didn't trust those rages that come and go without anyone hearing them. Susan's bathroom, however, produced an outrage that could last for a long time, it was worth examining . . . it lasted. And then he saw a bottle of whiskey, the first of a fine collection of bottles that Juan Lucas ordered someone to distribute strategically throughout the mansion, all of which had been waiting for him since the night before. He opened a bottle, smelled it, and tried it. The fire of whiskey left him helpless but soon it spread throughout his body, quickly warming his legs. He took another swig, it was controlled fire and suddenly he felt a new force that rose up from his feet and through his stomach: renewed strength! This rage was going to last . . . Bobby returned to his room with the bottle.

And Juan Lucas' noiseproof ceiling wasn't enough to silence the scene with which Bobby initiated the second chapter of his furious adventures in the mansion that night. Julius was the first person to hear his wailing. He was watching the program called "Questions and Answers" on television when he heard a shriek that, unlike "Correct! Good response!" from the master of ceremonies, made him jump out of his seat. "My Mark Twain," he thought, and took off running toward the stairs, but he only made it halfway because the staggering rage with which Bobby came down the stairs had the makings of a head-on collision. "Get out of the way, son of a bitch! You little shit, do you want me to kill you!" Julius took off yelling Deci! Deci! I hope someone comes to let them know Bobby has gone crazy. It wasn't long before everyone found out: Susan and Juan Lucas found out first. They were peacefully contemplating the triumph of night over the polo field and the miniature golf course when a yell calling to them crossed through the summer bar. "He opened his door?" Juan Lucas asked, thinking it was the right moment to go looking for him, but he realized immediately that Bobby's screaming was coming toward them, so it was better to wait for him there. "Let's sit down," he said, taking Susan toward the rocking sofa out on the terrace. He left a small space between them, as if he were foretelling exactly what was going to happen. Bobby barged in, saw them, and his screaming immediately became unintelligible until it turned into pure sobbing. He threw himself upon the sofa, disappearing into the open space they had left between them for him. He wanted to drown his crying, be less noisy, for he was going to be seventeen years old and he already knew what a good fuck was.

Daniel, Celso, Miss Decisive, Julius, and Universo, the latter of whom had been watering outside somewhere, all appeared together when Juan Lucas made his way over to the bar counter to serve three drinks. Then he made one movement with his hand and they all disappeared automatically. But they hung around close by, listening . . . there was only sobbing at first and Susan's voice, darling, oh no! darling, nothing's wrong, and Juan Lucas seated once again waiting for the young man to start talking . . . No! It wasn't the new girl from Villa María, she's an idiot! Yes! Yes! Yes! It's Peggy! It's Peggy! . . . Susan looked at Juan Lucas and she saw him gesture in displeasure when Bobby started all over again. She was disconcerted and continued to look at Juan Lucas, as if to ask him if it was all right to die of sorrow or if it was better not to pay any attention to a jilted seventeen-year-old. The golfer, in an interior monologue, decided to buy a car for Bobby that no other youngster in Lima would have. Well, he'd have to think about it a bit more, see how things turn out, in any case it was better not to say anything right now. What had to be done now was let the kid pour out his problems, cry out his drunkenness, and then off to bed; better yet a sedative, time, and another girl were the only answer. Bobby wasn't dumb, he'd recover quickly . . . But the story got complicated. It turns out Bobby was never interested in the new girl at Villa María, he never did like her, she liked him. He was only interested in Peggy . . . Juan Lucas almost asked him why he was acting the role of the great Don Juan, but Bobby was too involved in the story and he was merely crying out the whole affair. No, he had never cheated on her, but she, yes! no! yes! no! She flir, she flirts, she flirted with him. No, she didn't flirt with anyone yeeeeeesaha-ah-ah-ah. He, ah, he's in Santa María, ah, aha, ah . . . "This will take a while and there goes my work," Juan Lucas thought. "Now I understand the situation: it's a problem of pride. A Markham student lets his girl be taken by a student from Santa María and the whole thing ends up in a schoolboy fight." He grasped Bobby's head and made him look at him: "You were unlucky and that's all there is to it," he told him, but then he noticed blood stains on his hands and made him show him what had happened: nothing, he probably fell with the bottle in his hand, it was just a small cut, it wasn't serious. But Bobby, upon noticing they had discovered his bloody hand, felt rage returning: "I'll kill him! I'll kill him! Carlos, the station wagon!" He was yelling when Susan looked at his eyes and she threw herself on him, smattering him with kisses. How did your eyes tell me that? Oh, my God! so that's what it is to be a mother, I'm a happy mother because of him. "Leave him alone, Juan Lucas! leave him alone. Now it's my turn! Pipo Lastarria stole his girl from him! Darling! . . ."

Julius had begun to have fights with Rafaelito Lastarria, but who knows why when the other brother, Pipo, was probably just beginning to go to dances at the Casino in Ancón and bribing the photographers to take pictures of him with the Señora Marquis' daughter. He quit being so concerned about revenge for Bobby and it was probably a bad idea, for once that solidarity with Bobby ended, another idea came to him and he even felt a muffled hurrah! that fortunately didn't amount to anything, because it would have been a sin. As it turned out, Juan Lucas wanted to take all of them to Ancón for a short vacation in order to take advantage of the inauguration of a new apartment building he had built with Juan Lastarria. And Juan Lastarria was going to be there, too. Another hurrah! Julius thought, but he didn't say it, hence it wasn't a sin: for sure Uncle Juan Lucas won't take us to Ancón now, Peggy will be there with Pipo. Uncle Juan Lucas isn't taking us to Ancón: hurrah!

The next day at lunchtime, Julius was still thinking that his desire not to feel a big hurrah implied a situation similar to making amends and, consequently, he was free of guilt and decided to forget about it when, all of a sudden, Juan Lucas formally announced there were no plans to go to Ancón. Why go? It's too crowded right now, etc. Julius avoided making amends and said hurrah to himself without moving his lips, promising never to do it again. He swore he would never do it again when he saw Bobby enter the room with his head down suffering from a headache and a heartache. "Don't worry, Bobby," he said to himself, looking at Bobby who didn't see him. "One afternoon you and I are going to Ancón in the station wagon, we'll look for the Lastarrias, and we'll punch out both of them. Hey, what have they done to me that's so bad? I had better make amends, say I'll never do it again, and not think about it because the tears will start flowing, and for sure Juan Lucas will say 'And what's wrong with you?' See, Bobby, how you don't find out about anything, but with Cinthia we found out about everything."

Susan would have preferred not to go out that night. It wasn't due so much to her slightly red eyes or because you have realized how much Julius has grown up, nor how he's not so floppy-eared anymore, nor because Santiaguito hasn't written a line in years, I'll tell Juan Lucas to bring him home for vacation, but rather she had just found out that whenever Bobby asked for money he also would have liked to have kissed her and he has bedded down with twenty-seven prostitutes since his fourteenth birthday; also in Ica, Nana Portobello, a dancer who had swum in Abdul's swimming pool when he was still Abdul of Egypt, charged him a full month's allowance and infected him with gonorrhea that cost Juan Lucas a mint to cure. Susan was beginning to find out about these incredible things, she had found out about everything by the time she was eighteen years old, but these things? She didn't kiss or hug him anymore and now, instead, she would laugh when he explained that you are a corporal after one venereal disease, a sergeant after two, who knows what you could become after that . . . "Even President of the Republic," Susan interrupted, and Bobby laughed freely, no Mom, just marshal, and he tried to keep smiling, but it was for that reason that he didn't kiss Peggy for the longest time and she, I should have told her, she began, she began to flir, to flirt . . . Susan kissed him, and why didn't he kiss Peggy? No, it wasn't contagious that way, not with just kissing, but there was something else: respect . . . That's fine, darling, don't worry, I'm going to ask Daddy to bring Santiaguito home to spend Christmas vacation with us. Bobby looked at her, feeling ashamed at certain moments and then feeling comfortable with her at other times. She also told him stories about his father, she always loved him. No, he wasn't like Juan Lucas, you must remember, of course, you were very small then, but his eyes, his smiling ironic look is unforgettable . . . What? No . . . No . . . Juan Lucas wouldn't be here if he . . . No, darling . . .

"Yes, darling! I'm coming!" she responded, hearing Juan Lucas' voice. But she would have preferred not to go out. And Julius would have preferred she not go out. Juan Lucas was to blame, but not for her having to go out, that was something else. For the first time he saw clearly that Juan Lucas was to blame. He always believed he was right and he always was right because he was the tallest and he spoke so well. But he couldn't go through life being wrong unless he reaches the stature of Juan Lucas. He wasn't even interested in having the same voice because with that voice you are always right while you talk and afterward you're not. This time Julius was right. He remembered perfectly asking "All of them?" protesting, when Juan Lucas ordered the bottles to be put out in strategic places for Bobby. Dummy, he said, or something like that when Julius protested. And who was the dummy now? Who had gone to the Pratollinis for cocktails? Who had taken Mommy out? She was the only one who could bring any sense to Bobby. And above all, who forgot to tell someone to put the strategic bottles away? Who, eh? You, Juan Lucas, You, Juan Lucas.

Susan went to the pantry to inform everyone she was going out with Señor Juan Lucas and they would be returning late, so they wouldn't be eating dinner there. Abraham took an insolent drag on his cigarette, that's their problem if they don't know what they're missing. Out there she could even lose Don Juan tonight, he's so well preserved and all. Susan didn't perceive his insolence and gave a few more orders: Bobby's going to eat dinner in his room. Let him go out if he wants to, don't worry about him. Arminda finally raised her head after Susan had already left the pantry area. Until then, she hadn't opened her mouth even once to comment about young Bobby. It seemed like she hadn't been aware of anything, despite his being all they talked about around there. And as soon as Susan left they began to chatter again—Carlos with his ironic comments; Celso and Daniel with theirs but always respectful; Abraham with the same old song: Am I not right? Am I not right? Women never pay; and Miss Decisive repeating over and over: It happens to the best of families. She repeated it again and Julius looked at her, remembering all of a sudden the bottles that no one had put away, and Bobby could get drunk again. He was going to say something, but right then Arminda stood up and said, "Santiaguito is going to try to rape Vilma," walking slowly toward a pile of shirts she had to iron that night.

"Loony," Carlos said, tapping his head three times with his knuckles as she left. The Doña is a lost cause, she gets everything mixed up, she confuses everything. Abraham put out his cigarette and returned to the kitchen. Celso and Daniel fixed the table for Julius' dinner. Carlos, on the other hand, was finished for the day, all he had to do was put the cars away and leave. The group dispersed when Miss Decisive went upstairs to fix the beds for the evening. Julius followed her and wanted to watch television for a while before dinner. "There's a bottle missing from this table," Julius thought while he walked down the corridor leading to the bedrooms and bathrooms. He immediately looked toward Bobby's room. The door was closed and he heard music.

"Young Peggy is not in Lima . . . Yes, she's in Ancón." He already knew where she was, he simply called to dial the number, but more than anything else the operator had told him that in ten minutes they'd have her number in Ancón. Bobby started playing that record again, the one she had given him. He had it in three different versions, but he liked that one the best because it was the saddest. He drank another swig directly from the bottle and lunged at the telephone when it rang. She wasn't there either, she had gone to a party at the Casino. He threw down the telephone, kicked the record player like a soccer ball, and took off toward the station wagon. Julius heard him leave: Juan Lucas was wrong. Celso opened the outside door of the mansion and had to jump aside or Bobby would have run over him.

An hour later, Julius was eating silently and worried that Bobby could kill himself on the highway: Juan Lucas was dead wrong. In the kitchen, Celso told how Bobby had sped away from the mansion, driving with one hand and drinking from the bottle with the other. Miss Decisive decided to call the Señores and it took a long time to find the Pratollini phone number in the telephone book. When she was finally able to get through, the Señores had already left and they didn't know where they were going next. The only solution was to wait; Carlos wasn't there and there wasn't anyone who could drive the Mercedes to Ancón in search of young Bobby. Miss Decisive blurted out again it happens in the best of families and she immediately ordered Julius off to bed.

But an hour later he still couldn't go to sleep. It was impossible to sleep with everything rushing around in his head. First he imagined that the summer would come to a happy and peaceful end by going to Herradura Beach every day with Susan. They'd leave very early, just as soon as he finished his morning session of miniature golf, then she would leave to have lunch with Juan Lucas at the Golf Club. No, they wouldn't go to Ancón, but this time he didn't feel the hurrah! rise to his lips; to the contrary, the name Ancón, its beaches, its buildings, its docks fertilized his imagination and now he saw himself walking calmly toward the Casino in order to beat the shit out of Rafaelito Lastarria. Of course, there was the problem of his age. Lastarria must be going on fourteen and it was going to be difficult to punch out someone that old. In any case, the cause was justified because they had taken Peggy away from Bobby, even though it was strange for Bobby to cry so much over a girl who lives so far away when, curiously, a pretty girl lived right across the street from their new house. Without a doubt, life was complicated. Perhaps because the girl who was or wasn't taking the wrong road also lived far away. Something like that had to be involved in Bobby's sob story . . . nevertheless, if the situation didn't work out right, for instance, if Rafaelito Lastarria has grown a lot since the last time I've seen him, then Bobby can punch out Pipo first and then help me . . . no, not that way either, Bobby is older than Rafaelito, there's no solution to the matter . . . Julius turned over in his bed and laid his head on the other extreme of his pillow, it was colder and more than likely it was going to give him new ideas: everyone is dancing in the Casino, Bobby and I walk in, they take off running, and we pound the shit out of them. How did Carlos say it? Flatten their noses? . . . Julius turned over again, nervous, uneasy this time, as he tried to remember Carlos' invincible words that had erased the scene in which Bobby and he were cleaning up on the Lastarria brothers. The pillow was hot on that side, he closed his eyes, but he continued to imagine the night table with Cinthia's picture, smiling and talkative. He covered himself with the blanket, disappearing into total darkness around him, but the fuzz on the blanket made his nose itch, so he threw off the sheet and the blanket, it was almost like a punch right in Rafaelito's face. He turned over but the pillow was hot again, he had just laid his head there, hot, in the middle of the pillow once again, so he reached over to the night table and turned on the light. There was Cinthia, smiling and talkative again. Slowly he drew her picture close to his face, clutching it with both hands and asking her, she would be fifteen, if she would like to dance at the Casino in Ancón, you would? . . . But the silver picture frame made his hands cold and, in any case, nothing could be done: Bobby's fight was going to be somewhere else and he was trying to imagine what it would be like to enter the Casino, but he couldn't because the lamp lit up every part of his room and Ancón was at the other end of a long highway . . . He turned off the light, no dreaming this time . . . why dream when as soon as he initiated a trip to Ancón, a wrinkle in the sheet stopped him.

Miss Decisive's screaming woke him up in the middle of the night. Earth tremors, earthquakes, and the Lord of Miracles came to mind, but nothing was moving in the mansion and, when he jumped out of bed, he knew it wasn't a life-or-death situation. It had to be something else, but he didn't find out what it was until the next morning, because when he left his room headed for the servants' quarters he ran into Bobby in the corridor. He was raving mad, yelling, and running around completely crazy or drunk. Miss Decisive ran behind him in a nightgown throwing things at him. Every time she caught up to him she hit him again. Celso and Daniel managed to contain her and, using force, they took her back to her area, while Bobby threatened to rip Julius apart if he continued looking at him like that or if he said anything to Mom in the morning.

But what was he going to say, if they had already been arguing for hours and hadn't come to any clear conclusion? Carlos, who was in the pantry, was also a little bewildered, although his confusion didn't last as long as the consternation Julius felt. It turned out that the next morning he found the Doña eating breakfast. "Good morning, Señora," he was going to say to her, but she surprised him repeating the bit about Santiago raping Vilma, at the exact same moment Miss Decisive came in yelling that young Bobby deserved what he got, scratched face and all. Carlos felt a chill run down his spine; worse yet, it came together by an unexplainable frozen strand with another chill he once felt in the kitchen of the old mansion, along that same strand he returned shaken to the new pantry. There was even a moment in which he believed that the real chill was back there at the old place and the one he felt now became some sort of prophesy surrounded by the new decorations in the modern pantry and all. Time almost became distorted for the man in uniform and cap, and he almost grasped a new dimension of the profound, but no way, forget it, for God helps him who helps himself: he immediately asked for an invigorating hot tea while he went to get Merceditas out of the garage, to hell with their problems . . . still, Carlos was a little concerned. Fortunately, as he got into the Mercedes he saw his perfect moustache in the rearview mirror, that moustache with so many stories to tell, be patient Hortensia, be firm Ramón, everything in its proper moment: Santiaguito and Vilma there, Bobby and Big Breasts here, and the Doña is totally out of it.

Bobby's odyssey had been a long one. It took him hours to explain it coherently. He remembered how it all began, but no way was he going to explain how long he looked for her and found her dancing cheek to cheek and with Pipo Lastarria. First he told him to go to hell and begged her, but then he quickly discovered she was telling him off and he had to confront his cousin. He remembered kicking and punching but now nothing was very clear. Then he remembered the blood from both of them. He remembered they threw them out of the Casino. Some people felt sorry for him, others swore at him. Then it was a dark night as he advanced along streets that were never long enough as thousands of ideas stimulated the station wagon onward, curve after curve, many times over cement posts like the ones on sidewalks in front of houses, on the edge of death. One eye was hurting him when he entered the whorehouse . . . So Pipo Lastarria had shut that eye for him . . . Yes, one eye was hurting him when he entered the whorehouse and he desperately wanted them to take notice. He looked for money and didn't find any, he yelled out his name, then his surname, and nobody paid any attention to him. Once again, no money. Then he thought about

Miss Decisive: Mom wasn't home and everyone knows—Mom, Juan Lucas, Carlos—that I'm a cuckold. No! No! No! Afterward, everything began to happen like he envisioned it because he drove like a maniac in order to kill himself but the station wagon just wouldn't crash. When he got home he made a lot of noise but he didn't want them to hear him. And no one did. Yes, he had that swollen eye, but there was no way in heaven he was going to tell them who did it, even though he regretted having accused Miss Decisive of giving him both black eyes.

As he listened to Bobby's lengthy description, Juan Lucas had his doubts but was ready to believe both of them, even though they contradicted each other. Miss Decisive yelled that when young Bobby tried to "waylay" her, one eye was already battered and bruised and his shirt was torn. Bobby totally denied it, but all of a sudden he began to feel ashamed that a woman could have beaten him up so badly. Then he changed his story, saying that maybe he had made a mistake, and now he remembers he had fought in a whorehouse and had broken a Negro's nose and the Negro managed to connect with a pair of punches, one in each eye, because he was drunk, of course, having downed two bottles that he had found upstairs. "Lies," Miss Decisive yelled, claiming one of his black eyes as her doing. "It wasn't any fun, Señor, there's nothing more disagreeable for a poor but honest woman. It wasn't out of pleasure but my honor demanded that I defend myself." Juan Lucas sighed and ordered ice for a gin and tonic. "Take it easy, take it easy," he said. "We can handle this without any problems, what do you think, dear?" Susan almost raised her hand in order to answer: how frightening! She had been taken by surprise and thought her children had such poor taste. At this rate, we'll have to hire a midget when Julius begins to . . . What did she think? She thought that Deci was a good, efficient woman, and fortunately nothing had happened . . .

"Almost nothing happened," Miss Decisive corrected. . . . Yes, almost. She would have to be paid for the pajamas that had been ripped and, above all, she felt Bobby should apologize and promise them he'll never drink whiskey again . . . at least the way he did that night. Those were her feelings and, no sooner had she finished, lovely, smiling, and frightened, she turned toward Miss Decisive to see if she was in agreement with her decisions.

Absolutely. Miss Decisive felt that the matter could be forgotten and that young Bobby had acted that way because of a feeling of rejection. We know that the feeling of rejection is an evil feeling, and mixed with liquor it could become an infuriating rejection. However, she continued, that form of evil, consequently, was not the result of young Bobby's wickedness but the liquor along with the rejection that became the attenuating circumstances of the assault. They had respected her rights in that mansion and the black stain could be erased by acting decently in the future; also, the feeling of rejection is human and the situa . . .

"Bobby, apologize to this Señorita," Juan Lucas ordered.

Bobby told her that he had been drunk and said he was sorry. Miss Decisive was going to start all over again about rejection, but Juan Lucas interrupted her saying that the matter was closed, she should harbor no rancor and, just when she tried to say something else, he asked her to bring chipped ice from the pantry for a special beverage for young Bobby. Let's see if we can get rid of that miserable face because looking like that they won't let him into the Golf Club. Bobby smiled, Susan smiled, and Julius was dying for Miss Decisive to leave so he could ask the meaning of the word rejection. "I'm going for the ice now," she said, finally. Susan and Juan Lucas were about to break out laughing at her trembling chest when she said rejection, but she was always the one who concluded these situations: "Don't worry, Señores, this happens to the best of families," she said before she left.

She was overjoyed when she went to the kitchen with all the good news. They had fully satisfied her demands and she was pleased to be able to tell the others about the results of their meeting. "A Negro?" Carlos interrupted when she got to the part about the fight in the whorehouse. "And since when are the Lastarrias Negroes? The one who punched him out was his cousin Lastarria, the one he's calling . . . Negro? Ha ha ha. I would like to see him face a real darky: they'd chew 'im up and spit 'im out."

In the summer bar all it took were three witty remarks from Juan Lucas for Bobby to look him in the face and smile. There were glasses for everyone, and it wouldn't be long before the drinks were ready, as soon as Miss Decisive remembered to bring the ice. But Bobby said he wasn't in that much of a hurry. First, he was going to take an Alka-Seltzer, then he'd come right back. Juan Lucas took advantage of his short absence to use the intercom: please gather up the whiskey bottles and put them away, thank you. When he raised up to continue with his good humor, he encountered Julius' accusing look.

A BIG FAT DROP of sweat scurried down Arminda's long, black hair dampening a spot next to a button of the marble-colored silk shirt. Arminda saw the drop, but at the end of the ironing board, next to her, she had the glass of water for wetting the cloth, so it could be ironed perfectly once again. She introduced four fingers into the water about halfway down and continued to sprinkle because the drop wasn't wet enough . . . Now it was just right. Her fingers remained wet and she dried them on her face because it was so hot, but even when she lowered her hand her fingers remained wet and, like always, she dried them on her black dress. She still hadn't noticed that her dress was hot and humid like the shirt she was ironing, hot and humid. Of course, it was the water and the burning hot iron on which she leaned in order to continue ironing . . .

She was, as always, alone in the ironing room at that hour. Juan Lucas had walked down that corridor and by that room once when the architect in vogue insisted on showing him the servants' quarters first and then that other part; the three rooms along a corridor that ended with a door whose beauty proclaimed the luxury of the family part of the mansion on the other side. The corridor and the three rooms were white: one was the ironing room, next came the sewing room and the third could be for a part-time nurse or charity nun if, for instance, some day the kids had to have their tonsils removed and they needed home care, or for some such reason. But the kids were operated on in the hospital and no one was ever sick at home. The second room was never used either because Miss Decisive always sewed in her own room.

Arminda was in the pantry when Daniel said good-bye. He had some time off coming to him. Celso wasn't around either, but she had seen him headed for the small interior patio where, after placing all of the silverware on the tiled floor, he would polish it for hours and finish late in the evening. Today was Universo's day off, and Julius had gone to a dental appointment in the Mercedes with Carlos and Miss Decisive. The Señor, Señora, and Bobby had gone to eat lunch at the Golf Club and wouldn't return before seven that evening. "Good-bye, Señora. See you this evening," Abraham said. Without understanding why, Arminda felt more at peace with herself seeing the empty kitchen area and no one upstairs either. She always went upstairs to iron at that hour, but today it seemed like the first time ever. She couldn't explain her feeling in wanting to see everyone leave the mansion, nor her desire to go upstairs to work knowing she was alone.

She stopped for a moment on the landing of the stairs and listened: not a sound. She imagined them leaving once again and remembered that Celso is outside rubbing and rubbing on that teapot. Upstairs she detoured a little in order to listen to make sure Miss Decisive wasn't in her room, but then she remembered and walked on calmly. All of the bedrooms were empty, the service bathroom door was open, only silence emerged from it. Then three steps up the white corridor, the door at the other end was closed, the family was at the golf course anyway, and Julius was at the dentist. She became frightened because summer was just about over, but when she looked around she calmed down: "Victoria Santa Paciencia, the seamstress, hasn't even come yet to make the children's school uniforms." She backed up to look, but there wasn't anyone in that other white room either, no furniture, the one they sometimes call the infirmary.

She was happy to see the bundle with the Señor's shirts on the white table. She went to pick it up and open it, the sun blinded her as always, and once she thought about asking them to put up curtains over that window, but afterward she solved the problem by putting up newspapers while she worked, now she was too tired to put them back up, so it would be enough to turn her back to the window while she ironed. The water was there, as always, at one end of the ironing board. She blinked to remind herself that she had filled the container yesterday, but she never remembered that she had ever filled it. She blinked again: it didn't bother her to lose that little bit of information forever. Let's see, water's there. She plugs in the iron, turns around because the wall plug is next to the window, sun hits her again, blinds her completely, she bends down to plug it in and, crouching, discovers she has no body. She fainted momentarily, then her body returned, filled with nausea, a spark flew out when she plugged it in, she always prayed, let go of the plug, no more sparks, she stood up with her eyes closed, visions of sparks in the darkness, saw her coming, yes, yes, behind the trees, behind the houses, behind the sparks, yes, she saw her coming. Why didn't she know about this before so as not to open her eyes? And she opened them just as she appeared over there behind the houses and the trees, she looked at the sun as much as possible and closed her eyes again . . . she looked at the sun as much as possible and closed her eyes . . . Arminda believes in miracles with all of her heart and that had to be a sign.

Facing a lot of ironing, she returned to the ironing board and flattened out the first shirt. She had to be very careful around the Señor's embroidered initials. Her hands were clean and she began ironing to feel in her body the heat radiating from the electric iron. It felt good, combining itself with the heat from the sun that shone through the window and almost seemed to flicker intermittently on the windowpane, now that she had found a place in front of the window so as to look out from time to time, opening and closing her eyes from time to time . . .

Now fat drops of sweat were trickling down Arminda's long, black hair, dampening the white silk shirt; she saw them but no problem, she would dry her hand on her black dress and press down on the iron again. She began to get tired, the sun had started to set, and now she looked at it more intensely but it was always the same: nothing. She sprinkled water on the shirt sleeve and let the sun blind her. Then she saw her appear and disappear. She was coming but the container of water had enveloped her, maybe a brief moment of her past, a minute ago, it had fallen off the ironing board. She was going to ask herself about those drops on the shirt which forced her to reach down and pick up the container, then she smiled as she saw her coming. Regretful and ashamed, she came hiding behind the container. How she ran! But now she ran to save her and ordered her to get down from that cart. Dora! My daughter! Obedient and submissive, she jumped down from the cart and the D'Onofrio ice cream man disappeared from her smile; in the background Vilma, Julius, Nilda, Señor Santiago, Señora Susan, young Cinthia, and Celso congratulated her. Then she couldn't see Celso anymore and she tried to trap him in her vision, and Daniel started to disappear too, and she tried to stop him. All of them started to jump around, they were escaping, they were disappearing, then they reappeared right in front of her. Suddenly Julius disappeared, and then they all disappeared, everyone except her daughter. She calmed down, smiled, and thought that everyone had disappeared so the two of them could be alone together and talk for awhile.

Celso ran to open the outside door when he heard the horn of the Mercedes. "I've got a wounded person here," Carlos said, looking jokingly at Julius who was returning in pain and furious because the dentist had hit a nerve a thousand times with that stupid drill . . . He parked Merceditas to one side of the big patio behind the carriage that already had a broken wheel because Bobby crushed it with the car when he returned home drunk the other day. Miss Decisive was the first one to get out of the car, offering to fix tea for everyone except Julius, "I'm going to fix a bag of ice for you," she said. The four of them entered through the service entrance and headed for the pantry. Once they were in the corridor they smelled something burning: "Arminda!" Miss Decisive yelled, and they ran upstairs together.

She was flat out on the floor next to the container of water with the ironing board laying across one leg. The iron was next to her, on the floor, partially enveloped in a shirt that was full of scorched holes. They thought she was suffering from vertigo but immediately realized she was dead. Carlos removed his hat, Celso began to cry out of fright, and Miss Decisive searched for the right words to say, but it wasn't the moment for them. And the telephone occurred to all of them at the same time. Then they asked each other whom do they call in these cases. Julius, almost asking them for permission, suggested they look in Susan's little directory next to the telephone by her bed. Carlos told them to run and get it, I'll stay with Celso, and we'll put her on the table. Julius and Miss Decisive hurried down the corridor to Susan's bedroom. Should they call the golf course first? No, try the family doctor first. They had the telephone numbers, but who do we call first? Anyone! They called the family doctor and he was at the Golf Club. They called the Golf Club and no one was there—not the doctor, not Juan Lucas, not Susan, no one. They could call Aunt Susana but she was in Ancón. Try her, she was always coming back to Lima. Julius dialed his Aunt Susana's number and, yes, she was in Lima but she had gone to confession. A servant had answered the phone: no, there wasn't anyone else at the house. Julius hung up and Miss Decisive yelled at him for not leaving a message. He picked up the phone to call again, but at that moment they heard the Jaguar honking outside, along with the station wagon, honk, honk, and Bobby demanding that they open up immediately. "That boy doesn't know what he's doing," Miss Decisive said, swearing at him as she ran downstairs.

And as the cars were entering the patio area, Miss Decisive came out on the run screaming, interrupting Celso's terrified version and creating greater confusion, telling them finally that they had found Arminda dead in the ironing room. "The doctor must be on his way home about now," Juan Lucas said, getting out of the Jaguar while Susan, frozen in her seat, rested her elbows on her knees and hid her face in the palms of her hands. She flinched when she remembered Arminda ironing Santiago's shirts, shortly after her marriage . . .

There were some necessary steps to take and Juan Lucas handled it all very well. True, it was a little tiring. Silence reigned supreme, everyone walked around on their tiptoes, and they spoke only when it was necessary, always in a low voice. Juan Lucas proposed to take her to her room, but Miss Decisive said she had always worked in the ironing room and they should let her rest there. Susan agreed by nodding her head, and Miss Decisive fought back her fear by breaking into a sonorous and contagious sobbing. Celso cried also and Carlos pulled on his moustache in order to hold back the tears. "We have to let Universo and Daniel know about it," Susan said, and Carlos went over to her and said, I'll go, Señora, putting on and taking off his cap, letting the first tears flow as he ran to the car. After taking the doctor to the door to leave, Juan Lucas returned. Walking along that corridor, he remembered when the architect had shown it to him during the construction. He had never been back there since. "Bobby, Julius," he called out. "Why don't you go up to your rooms for a while?" But neither Bobby nor Julius wanted to leave the room where Arminda was resting, and he didn't insist on it because he was already thinking about something else: now that he had seen this part of the mansion again he started to do some mental remodeling; for instance, it wouldn't be a bad idea to move the sewing room to the first room, we can leave the ironing room empty, and we have an ideal area for installing an elevator. He stopped at the ironing room to show his respect briefly but left disgustedly when he saw Abraham show up whimpering and kneeling down in front of the table: She was so nice! She was so nice! Excuse me, Don Juan. But Juan Lucas had already left.

"*Poor thing*," Susan said, but she cursed having learned English and felt horribly sad. They ate in silence and, more than once, Juan Lucas had wiped his lips with his napkin in a nervous gesture. Bobby insulted Arminda in silence, it was her fault that he couldn't go out and get drunk tonight, but then he changed his attitude almost immediately, feeling sadness on the one hand and then anger on the other because when his sadness evaporated and he wanted to cry, it was always Peggy's fault. Julius began to sob and Juan Lucas patted his lips nervously with his napkin. Then Julius started to weep as he looked at him, and he put his napkin on his lap, and I'm sure there was a moment then when they all felt sad, thought about Arminda, and perceived her presence as she rested upstairs, dead.

Bobby didn't go out that night. Nor the next night either. He behaved well and kept his promise to spend at least five hours at the wake in the small chapel. It's true that he went less and less but he did manage to complete the five hours, always feeling moments of sadness, and if it had been difficult to be there, it was because of Peggy, not Arminda. The desire to go out was tearing him up: he wanted to get drunk and imagine they were making up and, when the nausea would hit, take off to a whorehouse, fornicate until he would cry or whatever, now it's just get to that whorehouse where he thought he had seen a familiar face. Tonight he'll go, but he shouldn't think about those things during a funeral.

Juan Lucas had taken charge at the beginning, then gave precise orders to Carlos, Celso, and Daniel who then transmitted them at the proper moment to the elegant Negroes who worked for the funeral home. "It'll be a first-class funeral," Miss Decisive thought, satisfied. "The Señores are the right kind of Señores. The Señor has acted appropriately: first-class laundress, first-class funeral." Somehow that phrase didn't ring true and she decided to stop thinking about it and simply help in whatever was necessary. But Juan Lucas' instructions, transmitted mainly through Carlos, were enough. The best thing they could do was accompany Julius, who was very nervous despite the sedatives the Señora shouldn't have given him in such large quantities. Julius closely followed the removal of the casket and he cried at moments; now, however, he had dominated his sadness and something occurred to him. Bobby had already figured it out, because he had seen Julius asking the whole time which door were they going to use to take out the casket. Last night, however, he had asked very few questions in relation to what he usually . . .

And the reason was that he still hadn't formulated any questions. Kneeling in the chapel, he spent a long time thinking about his father's funeral and about Cinthia. He asked his Mommy why they took Bertha out through the servants' door, or the side door as it was called. What did Cinthia think about Bertha's funeral, that is, the little box, the comb, the brush? . . . Cinthia too had died . . . Then he cried and they came to get him, but wherever they took him—to the bathroom where Susan gave him a sedative, or to his room and to bed—he continued to think about Cinthia: she would have thought of something for Arminda . . .

That morning he asked over and over again how they were going to take out the casket. He was pleased when he heard Celso repeat the instructions that Juan Lucas had given him. He seemed to be so relaxed about everything that they forgot about him until Miss Decisive went looking for him because she began to notice he looked quite nervous again. The elegant Negroes from the funeral home had just picked up the casket and were preparing to take it toward the service stairs. While everyone's head was lowered, Julius left ahead of them, ran down the stairs and locked the corridor door leading to the service entrance behind him. After going out that door, he crossed through the patio and ran inside again through the terrace of the summer bar. Juan Lucas saw him go by and stood up, thinking they had started to leave. He walked slowly toward the main part of the mansion because Susan hadn't come down yet and he preferred to wait for her there. In the meantime, Julius returned to the corridor and waited in front of the door. The casket was already coming downstairs and, as they drew near, he tried to open the door but it was locked. He pointed to the corridor but in the other direction. "You can also go out this way," he said, and the elegant Negroes of the funeral home obeyed because it made sense, they all thought it was the logical thing to do since someone had absent-mindedly locked the door. They proceeded forward and Julius opened more and more doors for them, until they appeared in the immense hall where Juan Lucas was waiting for Susan to come downstairs. Julius pointed to the large front door, in the background, past all those immense rooms: it was straight ahead. Juan Lucas stepped out of the way, too late to protest, asking who had altered his instructions: by then everyone was passing in front of him and Susan. She joined the procession. Julius stayed back so he could see the two limousines, one was large and black, and from back there he could observe Arminda's funeral procession as it left through the front door of the mansion.

VICTORIA SANTA PACIENCIA tried to explain to them how difficult it was to find the house, she wasn't used to coming around to these new neighborhoods, they were so beautiful, so modern. She tried to explain what she thought of such a marvelous house, the refined taste and all, but every time she opened her mouth to say something, Bobby would interrupt her, bored, and tell her to hurry up. On the other hand, Julius wanted to *watch* her talk more, he loved to watch her mouth open and close, yakety-yak, a thousand times without letting one single straight pin fall out from between her lips while she unstitched and marked the school clothes to let them out. She would place the piece of chalk behind one ear and, no matter how much she bent over to the floor, it never fell: Victoria was a true artist. Moreover, she venerated her nickname, Santa Paciencia, because Bobby treated her badly and she never flinched once but just continued smiling with her mouth full of pins. And she didn't drop one of them either, not even when she was bent over, almost looking at the floor and asking Julius if he was happy about changing schools: do you like your new school uniform? "Hurry up, damn it!" Bobby yelled, and pins went flying all over the floor. Victoria, who got up in order to draw the lapel on the cloth for the jacket, had turned pale and tears were welling up in her eyes. Bobby wanted to apologize, but Peggy was to blame and he repeated it again: Hurry up, damn it! She tried to fix it as fast as she could. They were waiting for him, he was running late, it was an important date. Victoria told him I'm just about finished with you, Bobby, I just have to mark the buttonholes, but her nervous condition prevented her from going any faster and she got mixed up. Now she didn't know behind which ear she had put her piece of chalk; also, when she put her hand to her mouth to get another pin, they had simply disappeared. "You're done, Bobby," she blurted out against her better judgment because she liked to do things with precision, but she'd find a way to do the buttonholes later.

Bobby hightailed it out of there and didn't return until late that night. He was angry when he arrived but his anger was both happy and forced, joyful and furious. He had satisfied his self-esteem, yet he felt the same sadness deep down inside. And what he did that night in front of his parents, he repeated in class at school several times the following week: as if he weren't aware of it, he would let his wallet drop to the ground and along with it a picture of a girl. "New girlfriend?" Juan Lucas asked him. Naturally his classmates asked him the same thing: your new chick? Carlos, on the other hand, explained it handily as he smiled in the kitchen: one grief cures another. But everyone noticed that it was a matter of different types of cures. Maruja didn't have anything like Peggy's little turned-up nose and casual curves that she displayed one day at a tea/style show/bingo benefit, organized by the lady society members of the Unnamed Slum Project Committee, held in the banquet rooms of the Crillón Hotel. Peggy wore three styles belonging to the Louvre Museum Boutique (owned by none other than Mireille Monaco and Papotita Castro y Castro). Pier Paolo Cajahauringa had done up her hair. He also undid it because once the style show was over she asked him to let her hair down, to comb it out a bit, and leave it that way, loose and lank the way she liked it, for tomorrow she was going to play tennis or ride horses, she still wasn't sure. Maruja had also been in the style show, but that was a year ago when, representing the young people of Huaral, she barely got second place in the competition entitled "Miss Beaches of Peru." She was annoyed when they gave the crown to the other one and she even declared that the reason she had lost was because Miss Beaches of Peru had used a gold bikini. Fortunately, she didn't get too upset, and when it was time to take pictures and make statements to the press, she said the winner had won because she deserved to win. Later they took her to Herradura beach and she posed on a rock, looking out at the ocean, and declared that out of all the musicians in the world her favorite was Beethoven and that she aspired to be a model on TV. Yes, she was interested in acting in Peruvian movies but to do that she needed to study drama. She lied that she

356

still didn't know what love was, but stated that she was romantically inclined and somewhat passionate. After the commotion of the competition died down, Maruja went to live with her godmother who didn't live very far from a television station. Months went by and Maruja began to lose hope because the station was packed with girls as lovely as she was. It was like that until one day her godmother accused her of being lazy, of not wanting to work, and spending all that time hanging around those places and still not even one worthwhile young man! The truth was that there had only been one, a good-looking Argentine, but he also wanted to be a model. Happily Maruja didn't cry; happily because if Bobby had seen her with those swollen eyes he probably wouldn't have hit the brakes nor gone around the block seven times, screeching at the corners, the first time he saw her. In fact, he saw everything but her eyes, and was already imagining her on some solitary beach to the south. Each time he went around the block and imagined her naked, he floored it and took off again toward the corner. Then he would go around the block and pass by again. He seemed to be staring at her but hardly daring to look. When Maruja barely waved at him from underneath her purse and gave him a little smile, he hit the brakes for the last time.

He bought her a gold bikini and a gold watch; stretched out on a lonely beach to the south, he listened to her talk beside him. He tried to like her because she was older, a real hunk of meat, and if he liked her he didn't have to like Peggy anymore. Perhaps his wounded pride would heal forever. He did everything possible to like her; he listened to her gab, he paid attention to her when she talked about her personal life, even about the School for Señoritas Number 27, District of Huaura. One day he even imagined going to her godmother's house and the three of them would be drinking tea and he'd be feeling very emotional. That could be love. After all, she's poor but virtuous. But then he imagined Juan Lucas asking for her hand in marriage and, all of a sudden, found himself listening attentively to his words, the ones he used when he talked into her ear. Santiago would have already taken her to bed, that tasteless wench! Screw her if you can't like her but . . . and Peggy? Dummy, don't you see the piece of meat you're missing out on? . . . So he flung himself on her, trying to rip off her gold bikini, taking advantage of the moment when she was saying that her temperament was romantically inclined and somewhat passionate. He put his mouth over hers and when he pulled away slightly searching for a better position and to take a breath, the insult came with such force that he had no alternative but to continue, falling on her again in order to seal the words cock teaser on her lips.

In two weeks time Maruja had him all confused; nevertheless, Bobby had just turned seventeen and every time he let the picture fall out so someone would pick it up, he wouldn't say he had a new girlfriend but only that he was going out with a really hot number; then he would get that yearning to see her again. One afternoon when he couldn't find her anywhere (he had forgotten she had an appointment at the television station; he had falsified a name card signing Juan Lucas' name with a recommendation to the owner of the station), Bobby didn't have any choice but to continue his crazy wanderings in the station wagon until he ended up at a whorehouse in La Victoria. What a delusion: she was expensive and there was no comparison to Maruja. Moreover, he looked for the face that he had recognized the time before but didn't see her, another small matter that at times made him think: he almost didn't pay any attention to that face the first time he saw her, only when the woman hid herself and he wondered who could it be? And now he was thinking the same thing, but the hell with it! I have a date with Maruja at ten o'clock and it's almost time to pick her up. He drove straight to her house and announced his arrival with a tremendous screeching of the brakes, followed immediately by three blasts of the first horn, which boomed out "March Over the River Kwai," and three blasts of the second horn, ding-dong, ding-dong, ding-dong. Maruja came out rapidly and approached the station wagon looking like she was ready for a beauty competition. She got in smiling: they had promised her a tryout at the station within a month. While it was only a tryout, something was something. Bobby celebrated the news by blowing both horns at the same time and took a direct route to lover's lane where, fifteen minutes later, he converted the seats of the station wagon into an impressive double bed, complete with pillows and all. Maruja let him kiss her, she let him open her blouse a little bit and, when he went for more, she said stop and pulled away from him.

And she kept pulling away from him for a long time. Bobby became infuriated, he started ranting and raving, he yelled, he screamed, he called her a prick teaser! But she continued to pull away from him every night. Finally one day she explained to him the situation: he would get nothing until she finished school, nothing afterward either, and when he gets a job on one of his father's ranches, still nothing. And nothing later on, even when he comes to her house to ask for her hand in marriage and they become engaged, still nothing, nothing until they are married like God commands. Again Bobby screamed, You low-class bitch, and left in a fury. Then he began to woo a girl from Villa María. But a week later he was back and Maruja welcomed him with kindness and smiles. She smattered him with kisses and, sitting beside him and caressing his hair, she let him take her to lover's lane again, where Bobby once more prepared the double bed and threw himself on her, promising an immediate wedding just at the moment she pulled away.

At Markham School he was thrown out of class three times in a row for telling the Spanish teacher to go to hell; they even threatened to expel him from school if he continued to act in such a deplorable fashion. But he insisted on acting that way; for instance, one day he made Julius fight a guy who was bigger than he was and, when he saw that Julius was winning, he gave him a rap on the head with his knuckles and told him to go to hell. Nothing went right for him and Maruja kept pulling away from him every night. The only positive thing in his life was that he didn't think about Peggy anymore, but maybe it had been better when he thought about Peggy; moreover, who said that he didn't think about Peggy anymore? That same afternoon he ended up driving around the Gutiérrez oval and, when he least expected it, another station wagon honked at him and he heard "March Over the River Kwai." Pipo Lastarria went by and Peggy was sitting next to him, prettier than ever. Provoked, he floored it but another car cut him off and he lost the love birds on the following curve . . . What would happen if he were to go to confession, maybe his luck would change, talk to someone, go to confession. No! No way! . . . Of course! That was it! Write a letter to Santiago, tell him everything, and ask his advice. Inspired, he accelerated again, this time in the direction of the mansion.

It had been years since he had seen his brother and centuries since he had received a letter from Santiago. What was Santiago like? He only knew him through the brief letters that he sent Juan Lucas from time to time and the pictures he would send every time he bought a new car. But he admired Santiago, he had always admired Santiago, he's a great guy, the year he studied agronomy in Lima was one constant game of musical chairs, except it was with girls. I'll bet a girl never dumped him. He'll probably crap in his pants laughing if I tell him everything I'm feeling right now, maybe he'll tell me to go to hell or go cry on Mom's lap. Bobby spent hours trying to write the letter to his brother, and he was already tired of sitting there, just looking at the blank sheet of paper and the pen on the table. Every time he picked it up he had to put it right back down. All he had written was "Dear Santiago." He picked up the pen again and added the colon and once again he didn't know how in the hell to begin . . . Santiago: if you don't like my letter don't read it, but how's he going to find out he doesn't like it if he doesn't read it? Santiago: I'm destroyed. Peggy has jilted me. I'm going out with a hot number but she's cheap and I really don't love her. But something strange is happening because ever since she wouldn't go to bed with me, I've fallen head over heels for her! Almost as much as with Peggy. Nothing turns out right for me. Her name is Maruja and she wants me to marry her. I don't understand what's happening. If you like a woman you marry her (of course I still have to finish high school and study a bit and then go to work). I like Maruja and I'd like to marry her, but I think after I marry her I won't want to marry her . . . Do you understand? I don't either. How can I explain it? Wait . . . I think I know: I get married to Maruja (because I want to marry her), and the day of our marriage Juan Lucas shows up and shits in his pants laughing and Mommy says darling to Maruja and the whole thing goes up in smoke. Or this: Juan Lucas rejects the Pisco they offer him at Maruja's house (another problem is their house; I imagine their house in Huaral is worse than the godmother's house). I feel bitter about it, but when I really get bitter I drink Pisco or whatever it is (better yet, Chilcanito), and then I don't get upset with Juan Lucas. Shit! I know: all of a sudden I'm realizing they're laughing at me. Then I really get bitter and begin to pulverize Juan Lucas, or you (if you're at the wedding, I imagine you'll come home when I get married), and everyone else who has made fun of me . . . You more than anyone; yes, you, you'll make fun of me more than anyone else. I hope when you return to Lima you'll fall in love with another Maruja type and she also closes her legs on you. And (unlike me) you'll marry her, vulgar bitch, and I promise I'll go to your wedding and I'll make fun of you and I'll die laughing just looking at Maruja's wedding dress . . .

Bobby jumped when he realized he was still looking at a blank sheet of paper. "Dear Santiago:" was the only thing he had written. He picked up the pen and was going to write something, but at that moment his brother's answer came back via telepathy: "The problem you have with Peggy is called being cuckolded, that's the real reason. The only remedy (works every time, guaranteed): fall in love with her best friend. The situation with Maruja, you idiot, has a name and you know it very well: cuntitis." Bobby took notes, word for word, on the same sheet of paper on which he had written "Dear Santiago:" He read it and reread it and became convinced that what was written on the sheet of paper was right, perhaps out of respect for the written word or to see some form of evidence.

He immediately took out another sheet of paper and wrote "My Dear Santiago:" because he still wanted to correspond with him. This time it was a lot easier to write; in reality, he had very little to tell him, for he would already know about the problem with Peggy, a case of bad luck, that skinny bitch was getting on my nerves anyway, and it's better that it happened this way, much better because if I had left her, her friends would have sided with her. "On the other hand, there are some others who got mad at her and who can't stand our cousin. But if you haven't heard, I pulverized him at the Casino in Ancón. I've been dating for quite a while one of the girls who got mad. But I've decided to punish her a little and take a vacation . . . with feminine company, naturally. Would you tell me what you think about the hot number whose pants I've been getting into? Suddenly, Maruja pulled away and Bobby tried to finish the letter quickly. He hastily stuck a picture of the chick into the envelope because he didn't even want to look at her.

It wasn't long before a package from the United States addressed to Bobby arrived with writing on one corner: "Personal. Do Not Forward." Bobby grabbed the package and took off running upstairs to his room. Full of emotion, he tore it open and spilled the contents all over his bed. What a response! You're something else, Santiago! The short note said not to show it to either Juan Lucas or Mommy. He's right! He ran over to lock the door and returned to immerse himself in a detailed and meticulous contemplation of each and every picture. He had sent enough to spend quite a while at it. The guy's something else! Look at this! And this! And all the pictures were great because they summed up perfectly that period of his brother's life that interested him so much. There were pictures of cars with unbelievable colors and women with enormous breasts standing next to them. They were Maruja types, all gringas, in abundance, elastic and delicious. In one picture, you could see Santiago and Lester Lang IV carrying nude stripteasers down a corridor, or dancing with them in a topless bar where they had taken off their clothes, or leaving a building at the university with beautiful girls in tow, or kissing a Peggy type, and another, and another, and a sister look-alike of another Peggy . . . If only Peggy had a sister! No doubt about it, Santiago was right. Bobby hid the pictures in his desk and with renewed optimism ran to look for the telephone number of Peggy's friend. He wrote it down in his little address book and took off to go looking for Maruja to tell her to get screwed; of course, it wasn't going to be easy because she always aroused . . . Bobby hesitated, but at that moment he believed he had recognized the face of the woman whom he had seen at the whorehouse. "Ah, yes," he blurted out and made a beeline for the station wagon.

SUSANA LASTARRIA HAD been living in a world of trepidation ever since she found out that Pipo had taken Bobby's girlfriend away from him. No way was she going to tolerate such a thing! She put Pipo on the carpet and started to yell at him, but at that moment Juan Lastarria came in and made her shut up by yelling even louder. Susana, horrible, made her declaration: Something like this is intolerable among cousins, what will everyone think? Well, I'll tell you: everyone will think we're not a united family. Juan decided to let her talk, but he let Pipo leave the room. Lastarria had learned a long time ago that no one could silence his wife for more than one minute; hence the solution was always to let her say whatever she wanted and depart whenever she started to talk stupidly. That was the solution to the problem. She would continue talking after they had stopped listening to her. Finally, when she realized they had vanished, she would run to the telephone to call her sister Chela who also had been left alone. As soon as one of them would call, the other would answer.

And it was during one of those calls that Chela advised her to write a letter to Susan, that is, if she wasn't brave enough to call her. Her sister's suggestion seemed like an excellent idea, all she had to do was consult with her confessor; hence she hastened to tell Father Paul about the situation. As always, he listened with saintly patience and a smile on his lips. Father Paul managed to allay her fears, telling her it was simply a part of the world of adolescents and, more than likely, her cousin Susan would see it that way as well. She could send the letter if she felt like it, but he personally thought it would be easier to call her and talk about it on the phone. Susana, horrible, insisted on saying a letter seemed more appropriate for such cases. Father Paul wasn't about to refute her; in effect, a letter just might be the best solution; in effect, it was because Señora Lastarria would have something to occupy herself, for she would surely spend hours writing that letter to her cousin. Yes, definitely, a letter.

The next morning Susana Lastarria began writing the letter. It took her the whole day. Juan arrived just as she was finishing it. She asked him to sign it, right above his name, but Juan had just had a few drinks with Juan Lucas at the Golf Club, and the two of them had even been laughing once again about the brawl at the Casino in Ancón and about Bobby's drinking binges ever since he had lost Peggy; moreover, Peggy was a girl with experience because her parents had been ambassadors in other countries before coming to Peru, and to switch boyfriends at her age seemed perfectly normal. Precisely that afternoon when she came over to their table, she said hello to Juan Lucas with the same affection as before. The youngster is adorable. The situation couldn't have pleased Lastarria more, especially now that Juan Lucas commented on the situation splitting his sides with laughter and then inviting him to meet his "future in-laws," ha ha ha ha, who are having a drink together on the Club terrace. Juan Lastarria was delighted with the honorable ambassadors, of course Peggy and Pipo's relationship wasn't discussed at all, trivialities, adolescence, one would have to be goofy to be thinking about engagements and weddings, which was the reason Lastarria stopped thinking about engagements and weddings and bid farewell to the honorable Canadian ambassadors. He returned home, pleased, and on his way he thought about how great life is with children like his, that's the way he wanted life to be: the children always surpassing their parents. And now he was starting to see the end result. It had been a lot of work and sacrifice, especially sacrifice, the living symbol of which was standing next to him at his desk, begging him to sign the letter.

"Have you gone to confession yet?" he asked, trying to avoid Susana's inevitable insistence.

"No. I didn't have time today. Sometimes Victor has really bad days. I'm going to have to get rid of that butler. There are days when he does everything wrong . . ."

"Well, there's still time to go to confession . . ."

"Ay, Juan! How many times do I have to tell you that Father Paul gives confession only until six o'clock in the afternoon?"

"Fine, fine, you can go to confession tomorrow . . ."

"You have to sign here . . ."

"Look, Susana, that incident has been talked to death, understood, and forgotten. Precisely this afternoon Juan Lucas and I were laughing about the incident. Incidently, I just met your . . . my future in-laws . . . I'm only joking, of course, we were just kidding."

"And what did you think of the ambassadors?"

"And what do you think you are going to seem like to them?" Lastarria thought to himself. The thought gave him the willpower to take her by the hand in which she was holding the letter, and gently brush it aside as he stood up.

"I'm going out," he told her, pushing her hand aside and bumping her slightly.

"You have to sign."

"I don't have to sign. And do you know why? Because this is a matter involving adolescents and that's the way it should remain; besides, it happened in February or March and this is September already. Do you need more reasons?"

" . . . JUAN WOULD HAVE loved to sign it, too. Please forgive him, but he just called to tell me he has lots of work to do and won't be home until late. I can't wait because the chauffeur has to leave and I want to send it to you this afternoon. I'm sorry for not having sent it sooner, but it has been such a painful incident . . ."

"Incredible," Susan said, interrupting herself as she read the letter.

"She's hysterical," Juan Lucas added.

"Celso, has my cousin Susana's chauffeur left yet?"

"Don't tell me you're going to answer her?"

"No, darling . . . I just wanted him to tell her I read the letter and, please, to forget about the whole thing; that way I don't have to call her on the phone."

"Give her a call? Forget it. She's off her rocker!"

"*Poor thing!* Juan doesn't give her the time of day anymore."

"And even if Juan did give her the time of day, no one would give it to Juan," Juan Lucas blurted out, imitating Susan's feeling of compassion.

"That's fine, Celso. Tell the chauffeur he can go now."

"Very well, Señora."

"But this happened centuries ago! . . ."

"Call and tell her Bobby is going out with Peggy's most intimate girlfriend."

"Talking about Bobby, darling, I'm pleased he's her boyfriend . . . I can never remember her name . . . everything's fine, darling, but he's been drinking a lot lately and every day he comes home later and later . . ."

"That's your problem, woman. Don't get me involved in those things. Moreover, it's only natural at his age . . ."

"But he's so temperamental and easily becomes very violent. And his grades are getting worse every month; this is his last year of high school and it would be a shame for him to fail."

"Well, what does one do in these cases? Do you want to send him to the United States?"

"I don't think it's the right time, darling . . ."

"The only thing I can do is cut off his allowance."

CUTTING OFF HIS allowance had dire consequences. Bobby began to steal money out of Susan's purse every afternoon until she finally realized why she never had one cent in her purse and decided to hide the money in the mansion safe. But Bobby didn't give up and he spent several days trying to figure out the combination. Impossible, he couldn't get it: he kept trying different sets of numbers, but he could never come up with the right combination. And he needed money tonight more than any other night: first, he had to take Rosemary to the movies; then he had to hightail it to the whorehouse because, according to the madame, Sonia was coming back today. When he had arrived looking for that familiar face, the madame told him, some days back, that in effect the girl did work there but she was on vacation somewhere down south, and when she returned she'd have her all ready for him. In the meantime, he could amuse himself with the other girls if he liked, she said there were even better ones than her. The bit about better ones seemed a little exaggerated to Bobby, but it wasn't a lie either because from time to time you could find a good whore at Nanette's place. Of course, it turned out to be a little expensive, but there wasn't any better solution than to continue spending money there while he forgot about Maruja. He had to forget about her at any cost, and in reality he was achieving his goal until the money ran out . . . And wouldn't you know, it ran out just when Sonia was getting back! Just when Mom becomes tightfisted! Now she hides everything in that shitty safe! He banged on it but, of course, it still didn't open, yet the result was positive: another safe just opened up in his imagination. Bobby took off in the direction of the servants' quarters and Celso's room.

An hour later, Celso showed up in the summer bar where, taking advantage of the springtime sun, Juan Lucas, Susan, and Luis Martín Romero were discussing bullfighting and cussing out the promoter because he wasn't going to bring Briceño this year either, the one who continued to make Spain delirious and who, according to some people, was becoming a better bullfighter every day, he had a real classic style. "I'm going to have to become involved in the matter," Juan Lucas was threatening when Celso's voice interrupted him.

"Someone has stolen a box from my room. It contains fifty-seven dollars and sixty-nine cents that belongs to the Social Club of the Friends of Huarocondo."

"What?" Susan asked, surprised.

"As treasurer, I am the custodian of a box of money belonging to the Social Club of the Friends of Huarocondo."

Susan remembered the box he was talking about, Julius had mentioned it frequently: a Field Crackers box filled with dirty money.

"We'll have to do something about it, Celso."

"It has to show up somewhere. Maybe we could use that money to bribe the promoter to bring Briceño," Fats Romero intervened jokingly, but Celso's tear-filled eyes seemed to say screw your whoring mother, buddy. You lebidinous fat slob, you only know how to eat, drink, and laugh . . .

"I have a suspicion," Celso dared to say, stepping forward.

"Well, let's see here, son, what's going on?" Juan Lucas asked, remembering that Celso had been working for the family for the last fifteen years.

"I have a suspicion," Celso repeated, forcing Fats Romero to take a drink.

"It has to be the workmen. They're the only ones who have been around there."

"What workmen?" Susan asked.

"The ones who are installing the elevator, woman . . ."

"Ah, yes . . ."

"Look, son, go down to the police station and bring back a policeman."

"I have a suspicion," Celso insisted, taking another step forward.

"For that exact reason. The police will come and take care of the matter. Tell the chief of police it happened here at my house . . ."

"Tell him it's a matter of petty larceny," Fats Romero intervened, drink in hand and laughing. Juan Lucas enjoyed the bullfighting critic's joke, Susan too, but Celso didn't think it was funny at all. He almost took another step forward . . . And God only knows why he took three backward, turned around, and left.

He announced the theft to the staff in the kitchen and Miss Decisive swelled with a sense of honesty, saying she was prepared to be x-rayed.

No one understood what she said, but Carlos added they had no right to accuse the laborers when everyone knows who the little thief was.

"You're right, Don Carlos," intervened Abraham, who was becoming more queer every day and always said Carlos was right.

"Tell the Señores Bobby did it," Carlos said. Hasn't he been stealing from his mother as well?

"Don Carlos is absolutely right . . ."

Miss Decisive agreed with Carlos' arguments and was convinced that Bobby was the culprit, but she preferred to arrive at the same conclusion in a more democratic way. She said it was absolutely unnecessary to call the police, they could carry out the investigation themselves without the intervention of people who are not involved in the theft. The first thing to do was to talk to the laborers and the foreman who were installing the elevator and prove their innocence; once that was done, they would all go to the Señores to tell them their son was the culprit.

"I can't cook with so many laborers hanging around!"

"Don't be so self-centered," Miss Decisive said accusingly.

"And who are you . . . ?"

"All right, all right," Carlos intervened. "We can take care of it, but I think the best and quickest thing to do is for Celso to go to the Señores and tell them straight out that it was young Bobby."

"I'll go with you if you want," Miss Decisive said.

"No. I'll do it alone."

Celso returned to the summer bar where Juan Lucas, Susan, and Luis Martín continued to talk about bullfighting.

"I have a suspicion," Celso said, taking three steps forward.

"Celso, it was Bobby, right?" Susan asked.

"Yes, Señora."

"Take this," Juan Lucas intervened, handing him a check. "How should I fill it out? In your name, another name, or the name of that club?"

Meanwhile, Bobby was enjoying himself at the picture show and, from time to time, he would turn to look at Rosemary. The only thing left to do afterward was to go to Nanette's and find Sonia: she had to be the one despite the fact that she used an alias. Sonia had to be her working name. He squeezed Rosemary's hand and she turned to him, smiling: "Bobby," she whispered in his ear, "I'm proud to be your girlfriend." "Me too," he told her, moving closer to kiss her on the forehead. Yes, he liked her as much or more than Peggy and everything was working out exactly the way he had hoped it would, because she had been Peggy's best friend and now she was her worst enemy. But there was nothing better than finding out that Pipo Lastarria had courted her before Peggy, had asked her to be his girlfriend, and had been turned down. Now Pipo was courting Peggy just to get even; in fact, I'm the one who took Rosemary away from him. Bobby remembered, of course, that Pipo had taken Peggy away from him, but Rosemary was next to him now, he kissed her again, and tonight I'm going to Nanette's. The robbery he had pulled off in the afternoon would provide enough money for several visits with Sonia. Then he would begin to behave properly, they would start giving him his allowance again, and by the end of the year everything would be back to normal.

But at Nanette's they told him Sonia hadn't returned yet and probably wouldn't until summertime. Apparently, she had been detained in the south. Bobby cursed for a while, but the bad company he was with convinced him that Sonia wasn't the best one and with all that money he could have several nights in ecstasy. However, upon returning to the mansion that night, he realized his grades had dropped to the point that he might fail and he wasn't going to hang around Nanette's as much because there were only two months—October and November—until final exam time: "I'll go back in the summer when Sonia returns."

The next day he confessed he had stolen the money from the cracker box. Juan Lucas said everyone already knew about it and the money had to be returned immediately. Bobby alleged he had spent it in order to pay off a debt. How can he live without an allowance? What was he going to live on? Juan Lucas said he would get his next allowance when he passed his final exams. Who cares? he responded, remembering he still had thirty-seven dollars left for the next couple of months and he probably wouldn't spend it because he was going to hole up and study. Juan Lucas didn't appreciate that response, so he had the brilliant idea of telling him it would be even better not to give him an allowance until he passed university entrance exams to wherever the hell he was going to apply. Bobby didn't like that one bit, even less when he remembered Sonia would be returning to work at Nanette's next summer. He couldn't tolerate Juan Lucas making things worse for him and so began to snicker as if to say there's always some recourse when pam! he was struck with another idea. How dumb! Why didn't he think of it sooner: Julius' piggy bank. He's had it for years and everyone's been sticking money into it, coins and bills, how stupid of me! . . . he's had it since he was born . . . one thousand and one nights with Sonia, paid for by none other than Julius . . . Bobby chuckled out loud and Juan Lucas was just about to call him an asshole, but he didn't want to stick his nose into matters involving Susan's children . . . but he would have to stick his nose into things at the bullfighting commission.

" . . . AND THAT'S THE reason why she can't go to bullfights," Juan Lastarria explained to the architect in vogue, as he looked embarrassedly at Susana who had dressed up in the typical garb venerating the Lord of Miracles. The two of them had been drinking in the bar of the castle when all of a sudden Susana appeared wearing the tunic of the cult of the Lord of Miracles, and he didn't have any choice but to introduce her to him.

"Are you going to confession?"

"I'm coming from confession."

"Good. Send Victor in with some more ice."

"It's starting to get hot these days," the architect said, grinning as Susana left the room.

"Ah, but that's what adds exuberance to the bullfighting season," Lastarria exclaimed, raising himself slightly behind the bar.

"Do you like bullfighting?"

"I'm a fan like Juan Lucas; in reality, he's the one who taught me to appreciate the October bullfights, the traditions, the parties, the . . . the . . ."

The architect almost asks him: And if there's a fair in March, are you still a bullfighting fan?

"Juan Lucas knows a lot about it," he said instead.

"You learn a lot when you're around him . . ."

"No doubt about it . . ."

Juan Lastarria felt like any time now he was going to throw his whiskey in the architect's face.

"And you're not a bullfighting fan, are you?" he asked instead.

"I've gone a couple of times, but I'm not that enthused about it."

"And what sport do you like?"

"Surfing."

Juan Lastarria stuck out his chest again. "I don't have to put up with this," he thought. "Formalities." Fortunately Victor was coming with the ice and he took advantage of another slight stretch to reach for the little silver bucket.

"The Señora said to tell you not to drink too much, Señor. She says you end up tossing and turning in bed all night long."

"Tell the Señora to . . . Cheers, friend!"

"I guess Juan Lucas is really upset about Briceño not coming this year either."

"I've heard he's going to sniff things out at the bullfighting commission. If Briceño happens to come, I might give it another try; if he's as great as Juan Lucas says he is, I might even become an aficionado again . . ."

"I doubt it. It's something that's in the blood; you take to it the first time you see it or you don't . . . it's in the blood . . . another whiskey, friend?"

"Have you seen Briceño fight?"

"Yes. Ice?"

"Thanks. In Madrid?"

"In Lima . . . but only on film."

"Ah . . ."

"With some friends at Juan Lucas' house. We watched a few reels he took during his last trip to Madrid. Very good movies, with comments by Luis Martín Romero. Do you know him?"

"The bullfighting critic?"

"You've got to meet him. When he's in a good mood, he's great. Pipo, come here . . . He's one of our little devils."

"What's up, Dad?"

"Say hello to the architect. He designed your uncle Juan Lucas' house and now he's drawing, oops, designing ours."

"Is he the oldest?"

"The family Don Juan. Are you going out, son?"

"If you can talk Mom into it . . ."

"Here's some money."

"See you later, Dad."

"Peggy's boyfriend . . . You know her, the daughter of the Canadian ambassador . . . He's a serious, studious kid. Do you have any children?"

"One."

"It's hard to believe how fast time goes by. Anyone would say it was just yesterday you were dancing with Susan at that party . . ."

"You have a gorgeous bar, Juan."

"You were still a bachelor, just got your degree . . ."

"Juan! Juan! Pipo has gone out again and it's nighttime. He's got to get up early for school tomorrow. Who gave him permi . . . ?"

"I did."

"Señora, please join us. Would you do us the honor of having a drink with us?"

"I don't drink, young man . . . Pipo . . ."

"Just join us, then, Señora. Your husband and I have been discussing the plans for your new house. I imagine you are interested in knowing what it's going to look like."

"Yes I am. But what is one to do but put one's trust in God? Where am I going to get the strength to clean a larger house than this one? . . . And with such undependable servants. Perhaps you could convince my husband to build a smaller house. How I've tried! But he's like a child and his dream is to have a house even bigger than my cousin-in-law Juan Lucas."

"That's precisely what we've been talking about, Señora. It's impossible for the house to be bigger: it can have more rooms if you wish, but the perspective would always make it appear smaller. Don't you see Juan Lucas' house was built with an eye to take advantage of the polo field behind it? That's what makes it look so big, much larger than it really is. Don't worry, Señora, your house will be smaller. I think I managed to convince your husband of that detail this afternoon."

"You don't know how much I appreciate it, sir . . . Juan, Pipo has to go to school tomorrow, didn't you think about that?"

"Well, Juan. I'm at your service. Just give me the word when you want to start work. I must be leaving now."

"Yes, of course. I'll take you to the door. I'm leaving too."

"Juan. With your cold?"

"Let's go."

"Good-bye, Señora. Good night."

"How time flies; it seems like yesterday when you left Juan Lucas' house three sheets to . . ."

A sneeze interrupted the incisive phrase that Lastarria wanted to say in order to end their conversation. Better not say anymore, just get him to the door, for Susana might launch into another long tiresome speech about the flu and how dangerous it will be to go out tonight. Lastarria nudged the architect in vogue forward when he heard in the background something about you're not so young anymore . . .

"Good night, Juan," the architect said, perhaps sarcastically.

They shook hands and smiled. Basically both were satisfied: Juan Lastarria was going to build a house with the architect in vogue and the architect in vogue was going to charge him a fortune for a half-castle, half-functional house.

Lastarria went back to the bar to tell Susana he didn't have the flu and he was going out, but when he got there she had already disappeared down some dark corridor of the castle, and so he decided to have a drink as if he were celebrating her departure. "Fortunately, she's gone," he thought, as he felt an uncontrollable sneezing fit coming on full force that he barely managed to muffle with his handkerchief. But right then he noticed he hadn't pulled out his handkerchief for colds but the one for the Club, and in a flash he pulled out the ordinary one, sneezed in it, but imagined all of a sudden Juan Lucas sneezing into his handkerchief with his initials on it, the silk cloth barely rubbing against the more sensitive edges of his nose. Lastarria switched them again, taking out the silk one, but by then he didn't need it anymore. "Next time," he was thinking, "no one saw me this time," when abruptly another sneezing streak hit him and he was going for the finer one, but Lastarria played a trick on himself: just before sneezing he switched back to the ordinary handkerchief and sneezed, trying to hide it from his thoughts and from his view, alone in a corner of that bar. Alone he was discovering how ridiculous he was, when another sneeze precipitated an unexpected, detestable voice that came from a room nearby where Susana, probably horrible and sitting in the dark, had been listening the whole time and now articulated her little phrase charged with pity and double meaning: "May God bless you." Juan Lastarria threw down the flu handkerchief and decided to go public with his lover that same night.

BOBBY'S GRADES WENT up noticeably in early November, and Juan liked Susan's suggestion to take him with them to the remaining bullfights of the season, the ones that would have been much better if that queer promoter had contracted Briceño. One afternoon near the end of the month, Fats Luis Martín Romero called Juan Lucas on the telephone to announce Briceño was going to make his debut on the Hispanic American circuit and he was going to perform on two consecutive Sundays in Quito. Juan Lucas told him not to hang up and, using another telephone, called Susan to see if she would be interested in spending a couple of weeks in Ecuador. "This will be the bullfight of the century," he added, because he woke her up in the middle of her nap and Susan didn't make any decisions before drinking her cold Coke that she always drank upon waking from her nap. Susan yawned loudly as she said yes and hung up ordering her cold Coke via the intercom. Juan

Lucas, who was in the middle of a meeting, also hung up as soon as he heard the affirmative response and quickly picked up the other phone in order to tell Fats Romero he was invited to see Briceño's fights in Quito: we'll take care of the details tonight, Luis, yes, bye . . . Excuse me, Señores, where were we . . . ?

The trip was a perfect disaster. As it turned out, Briceño had not recuperated sufficiently after having been gouged by a bull three weeks earlier in the third fight of the afternoon in Logroño, Spain. The worst part was how badly Romero reacted to the altitude in Quito; instead of taking it easy, he ate and drank like never before, and the fat guy almost died on them; hence they had to return urgently, and just when there was hope Briceño would get better and participate in the second bull-fight that had been planned for Quito.

It was in Quito and precisely one evening when Fats was about to keel over from pain at the reception desk at the hotel that a bellboy approached with an urgent cable from Bobby. Susan panicked but opened it in a matter of seconds, began to smile, and by the end of the message began to laugh so hard she had to apologize to Fats Romero who continued to complain pitifully. She handed the piece of paper to Juan Lucas and he also began to laugh as he read it, ending with three loud belly laughs, ha ha ha, that muffled the fat guy's pain.

"What happened?" Romero asked them, bitter because of so much laughing.

"Bobby is asking if he can have his graduation party at the house."

"Frankly, I don't see why that's so funny."

"Read the message . . ."

"No thanks . . . Ay . . ."

"Here, read it, you fat complainer."

Fats Romero felt insulted with the bit about being a complainer and he took the piece of paper in order to read it and make sure he didn't find it funny at all. In effect, it wasn't funny. What's so original about their son asking permission to have a party at their house? And money for an orchid for his date? And this? He had listed his grades in order to prove to them they had gotten better in November . . . So what's so funny? He was going to give it back to them, but Susan insisted he read the last part, the end, darling. Fats read it unwillingly and smiled while she told them that knowing the woman might make it funny, ay! he complained, and Juan Lucas didn't like people who complained, not even in the case of Luis Martín, and took the piece of paper in order to read out loud Miss Decisive's words, who was testifying to the truth of the grades: "This is an exact copy of the original that is at the disposition of the Señores at Bobby's school, Markham it's called," which was followed by some scrawling under which she had written "Signed and Initialed." Juan Lucas chuckled loudly, ha ha ha, and told Fats to stop complaining because they were leaving for Lima: "Now we've got to get ready for this party," he added jokingly.

Back in Lima and feeling better, Luis Martín Romero found out Briceño wasn't going to be able to make his debut at other Hispanic American bullfights. In reality, he was happy to hear about it, for Juan Lucas would have more time to sniff around the bullfighting commission and perhaps it would be he who for the first time would bring that magnificent bullfighter to bullrings in the New World and, in that way, reserve a spot for Juan Lucas in the history of bullfighting and all.

Bobby had been anxiously awaiting an answer and, upon arriving home from school one afternoon, he was greatly surprised to find Susan and Juan Lucas back home ahead of time. "Yes or no?" he asked them, smiling and noticing they welcomed him in similar fashion. Susan kissed him: Aren't you going to ask us how we liked it? So he asked them how it went and she said they had purchased a marvelous painting from the Quito school. Bobby confessed an electrician had already come to figure out the lighting for the party. He saw Susan and Juan Lucas smile and took advantage of the moment to talk about the orchid, because he didn't have one cent to buy one. And it was important to order one now, for time was running out, all the schools have their gradua . . . But Juan Lucas interrupted him saying that in Lima geraniums were called orchids and that you're not going to order anything! Bobby felt like Peggy had just jilted him, Maruja had just pulled away again, and Sonia hadn't returned yet when, fortunately, Juan Lucas picked up on his reaction. "Let me finish," he said, and he began to explain. As it turns out, he also knew something about orchids or, in any case, he had orchids and they didn't know about it. He had millions of orchids and they were going to waste; moreover, they grew wild, the real ones, like God would have it, not those scrawny orchids one buys in Lima. It's always necessary to choose the best from the good ones, and to do that you have to get orchids from his plantation in Tingo María. Susan asked him to go slower, please, I don't understand anything you're saying, but Bobby understood him to say he had a plantation in the middle of the jungle. It was an experimental project, rather, with linguists studying Indian dialects of the savages in the jungle and all, and it even seemed like some Jehovah's Witnesses had arrived there recently . . .

"And who is in charge of that, darling? Why hadn't you told me anything?"

"We'll go see it one of these days. We're building a small airport for our plane. A pair of Yugoslavians . . . immigrants . . . are working for me out there. They're going to bring back an orchid for Bobby that will knock your socks off."

AT SIX O'CLOCK in the afternoon, the head electrician announced everything was ready for the final test and Miss Decisive, in a state of frenzy, ran to turn on the lights that would illuminate the extraordinary graduation party. She flipped a switch and all of a sudden everything went chuc! and sparks flew out from the outlets all over the mansion. It went dark and the place smelled like smoke. The head electrician smiled and announced it was a matter of a minor electrical problem, but Bobby showed up screaming he was an idiot and because of him his party was ruined. The electrician's son came to his father's defense and was talking defiantly to Bobby when, fortunately, Miss Decisive intervened apologizing for the young man of the house and explaining he was really nervous because he had taken several sedatives. Bobby left screaming that he wanted lights in five minutes and he was ready to take on the boss's son wherever and whenever he wanted. At about six-thirty, the orchestra's truck arrived with the piano and the organ. From a window on the second floor, Julius watched them take the piano inside the mansion and went running downstairs to see if it was exactly like Mother Mary Agnes' piano. No sooner had they put it in a corner of the terrace for the orchestra than he pulled up a stool and started to play the exercises he had never managed to play very well for Frau Proserpina. He played perfectly and even dared to add a little feeling toward the end, but he didn't manage to finish because suddenly Bobby showed up yelling at him to close the piano right then or he was going to smash his face in with one single blow. Julius left quickly but turned around to look at it as soon as he was beyond his brother's reach.

"It's just a plain piano, nothing more," he said.

"What the hell do you know, shithead?"

"The good pianos don't smell like cat pee, ha ha . . ."

At that moment he took off and Bobby just about ran after him, but the electrician's son was in his way, chewing gum and tapping a foot to the beat of his battle anthem. Bobby decided once again to screw Sonia with the money from Julius' piggy bank, turned around and went back the way he came out, thinking he'll meet the electrician's son whenever and wherever he wants. "These guys too," he said to himself, passing by the three movers who were bringing in the organ for the orchestra. At that moment the telephone rang. Bobby ran to answer it, it might be a classmate who needs to know something.

"Is this Julius?"

"No. It's Bobby."

"Son, I'm calling to congratulate you on your graduation party . . ."

"Thanks."

"I imagine there will be chaperones, right? . . ."

"A bunch."

"Is your mom there? . . ."

"No one's here . . ."

"I want to congratulate her because everything must be stupendous . . ."

"No one's here."

"I hope everything turns out as nice as our . . ."

"Yes."

"And who are the chaperones, son?"

"I don't know."

"Your mom isn't home, right?"

"There's no one here!"

Susan turned around to look when she heard Bobby throw down the receiver and blurt out furiously: That old bitch! She had been listening inattentively to the conversation while she sat reading a magazine.

"Your Aunt Susana, darling?"

"If she comes around here I'll kick her out on her butt!"

"I don't think she'll come, darling . . ."

Wearing their uniforms, Celso and Daniel were in the kitchen drinking their tea while the waiters from Murillo's Wedding, Banquet, and Reception Caterers finished fixing the last tables outside and began to prepare the cocktails for later. Abraham snickered skeptically in front of the trays with the appetizers that were to go along with the drinks, and Carlos said jokingly, The ones your competitors make aren't half-bad, are they?

"Have you tried them, Don Carlos?"

"The only thing left to try is one of these," the chauffeur responded, picking up a filled oyster shell from one of the larger serving trays.

"Take it easy. There'll be hell to pay if there isn't enough later . . ."

But Carlos picked up another one anyway, and Abraham didn't have any choice but to look away in front of such masculine authority: "You're so bad Don Carlos," he told him.

Meanwhile, Bobby had just finished cutting himself as he shaved in one of the bathrooms. When he saw the blood he remembered the orchid still hadn't arrived. He threw down the razor and ran downstairs to tell Juan Lucas it was his fault there wouldn't be any graduation party. On the way, he ran into Susan who was going upstairs to change and he asked her where Juan Lucas was, it was going to be his fault there wouldn't be any graduation party. Susan told him Daddy was playing pool in the green room with Luis Martín Romero and the new director of the bullfighting commission.

"Where's my orchid?" he yelled, barging into the pool room.

"In Tingo María," Fats blurted out, driving the billiard stick into the ground like a spear and opening his enormous mouth while a whale-sized, Spanish-sounding belly laugh rose from inside his stomach.

"Ah, damn it," Juan Lucas exclaimed. "It hasn't arrived yet?"

"You told me that plane arrives every morning."

"Sometimes it arrives late, buddy . . ."

"And what if it crashed?"

"Wait, wait," Romero intervened. "Bring me a telephone, boy. I'm going to call the newspaper. If there's been an accident, they'll know about it before anyone else . . . Damn it! That's all we need!"

"Wait," Juan Lucas intervened. "Quick, let's call the airport . . ."

But at that moment Julius came in: Uncle Juan, two men are here looking for you. They have a little box. When he brought them in, one was completely hoarse but said, "Don Juan's orchid." That's as far as it went because at that same moment there was another chuc! and once again sparks flew out of the wall sockets throughout the entire mansion. By then it had gotten dark outside and the whole place was dark.

"Those electricians!" Juan Lucas swore.

"Curse 'em . . . now I can't find my whiskey," Fats complained.

One hour later Bobby had his tuxedo on and was leaving the mansion in the Jaguar toward Rosemary's house. She still wasn't ready because it so happened that today the beauty parlor had done an appalling job on her hair. As Bobby was leaving the mansion, he saw two taxis pull up, but he didn't wait to see who had arrived. It was the orchestra—the musicians, the director, and the crooner as well. The group was called Rhythms of Youth, its director was Benny Lobo, and his crooner was Andy Latino who protected his throat a lot, that's why he always wore a scarf between songs. They were eleven in all: Lobo, Latino, and nine professors, that is, nine magicians of rhythm. Lobo was white, while Latino was whitened anyway by the night, the rum, the smoke, the wee hours of the night, and the neon signs. The professors went from light-skinned Mulattoes, who were even good-looking, to dark Negroes. Several could have been elegant Negroes from the funeral home, almost all of them could have been chauffeurs, and some of them, the more appealing ones, even barmen in dark places for dancing. But the nine professors were artists and that's exactly what they proved as soon as they got to the interior patio where the greased-down waiters of Murillo's Wedding, Banquet, and Reception Caterers, running a little late now because of the second blackout, finished getting ready. The nine musicians were artists and Carlos, like a vexed turtle, pulled back inside his shell as soon as he saw the nine chauffeurs who were more successful than him. The nine professors didn't notice Carlos. Arriving in a state of ebullience, they didn't even notice him, probably because the appetizers meant drinks, and drinks meant music, and in the world of rhythm, you don't ever notice sad Negroes. Abraham, on the other hand, welcomed them with a giggle of ecstasy. He sat down on a little bench among the musicians, lit an American cigarette, wanted to die in vice, and sat there watching amid the cigarette smoke how the nine darkies were taking off their jackets, showing off their loose-fitting red-and-white polka-dotted silk shirts, which, buttonless, were open over their nocturnal chests and tied in a knot over their belly buttons. Lower down, their white pants billowed out down to the knees and narrowed at their ankles, complete with protruding trouser flies loaded for the whorehouses. Celso and Daniel didn't know whether to remain silent, ask for an autograph, or just smile like ignorant Indians. They decided on silence when they saw Miss Decisive go by looking serious, saying good evening and showing professional respect for the musicians who, on the other hand, answered back insolently, one of them shaking his maracas to the movement of that one enormous rhythmic breast, and the others responding to the rhythm with a little Caribbean shoulder-shaking that ended with one strong stomp on the final maraca rattle, upon which Miss Decisive disappeared. Andy Latino cleared his throat, tuned his voice, and asked for a few early drinks in order to oil up the machine. Abraham jumped up and ran off to get what they wanted. They all drank except orchestra leader Lobo who had to sign the contracts.

Julius was combing his hair when he heard the rhythm of a popular song. He threw down the comb and flew over to the window which was right over the orchestra. He opened it, looked out, and discovered there wasn't a soul on the dance floor, nor anyone at the tables on the patio. Just the orchestra was down below in the corner. Now they weren't even playing, they just talked among themselves, smiling, fiddling around with their instruments, or listening to some instructions from orchestra leader Lobo. Julius closed the window and returned to the bathroom in order to continue combing his hair very carefully, because Miss Decisive had told him he had to look very elegant. Bobby, on the other hand, had threatened to smash his stupid face if he even dared to take a peek at the party: "It isn't for little snots like you," he added violently. Well, who cares? He could watch the whole thing from his window upstairs; moreover, Bobby wasn't even going to remember his threat once he's out on the patio. Julius finished combing his hair and put on his bow tie, but it was true that Juan Lucas had taught him to tie his own tie and had said those clip-ons were so crass: you don't want anything that's ratty looking, you either do it right or not at all. He took off the bow tie and went back to his room to look for a regular tie. He found one he liked, but Uncle Juan Lucas will probably tell me it looks tacky with that suit. He looked in the mirror and it seemed fine to him, perfect. Now he'll probably say something else: When are you going to learn how to match your clothes, young man? I already learned, do you like it, Mommy? Susan, smiling in the picture over the dresser, answered affirmatively. Then Julius turned around to look at Cinthia's picture, smiling and talkative, on the night table, yes it's fine . . . but all of a sudden Cinthia decided to talk about something else and Julius looked away suddenly because he didn't want to get sad: I can't, Cinthia . . . Then all of a sudden he heard the rhythm of another popular song and flew over to open the window, but when he looked out the last dissonant chords were fading away and then cut short with a final, brisk blast of a trumpet. He closed the window and turned to look at Cinthia's picture. He just stood there, looking at her. For the third time the musicians started playing another popular song, but they were probably just practicing and Julius didn't go to the window this time. He stood there listening to Cinthia and to the musicians getting ready to play down below. He shouldn't get so sad or nervous whenever there's a party . . . instead he should go downstairs even though no one has arrived yet, entertain himself by watching or listening to them practice . . . They've been practicing with several songs . . . Cinthia. Julius started to leave, he forced himself to leave, and he flew down the stairs toward the patio, worried. He thought he would talk with the musicians while they were practicing, but once out on the patio he found it full of couples dancing while the musicians played standing up, swinging to the rhythm of the music, almost dancing themselves, sweating up a storm because of the energy they put into it.

"Julius, where have you been? . . . Come here!" Miss Decisive yelled at him, calling him over to the corner where the servants could secretly observe the party.

Partially hidden, the group was excited; they acted like it was their party, laughing and even following the rhythm with their feet, Look at young Bobby! They relished every minute of it. And with good reason. With very good reason, because Bobby had brought a beautiful gringa to the dance.

"Bobby's little girl," Universo commented, apologizing to Carlos for having stepped on his foot with his large, floppy, mud-caked soccer shoe.

"The Canadian was better," Carlos explained. "She was fuller, this one's got matchstick legs that are gonna break."

"What?" Julius interrupted.

"Her matchsticks, her legs."

"Ha ha, her matchsticks . . . Fantastic, Carlos renames everything . . . 'like Cano' . . ."

He didn't say it to him, nor did he even finish thinking about it because there's no reason to get sad at a party, getting sad at a party brings up Cinthia again . . .

"Ha ha, matchsticks . . . Carlos gives a different name to everything . . . 'Like Cano would do, Cinthia . . . ,' Which one do you like the best, Deci?"

"All things considered, Bobby's date is very beautiful."

"And you, Carlos?"

"They're all knockouts, but I would have them all gain a few pounds . . . Rosa María isn't too bad . . ."

"Rosemary," Julius corrected.

"Bobby's girl!" Celso exclaimed.

"Bobby's girl!" Daniel exclaimed.

"Bobby's girl, naturally, Rosmarí's her name," Universo exclaimed.

But Carlos interrupted telling him to quiet down because the orchestra had stopped playing and all their jabbering could be heard out on the patio. "Turn off the lights," Miss Decisive said. It wasn't a bad idea because that way, in the dark next to the window behind the orchestra, they could watch everything without anyone on the patio noticing them.

An hour later, orchestra leader Lobo ordered low, mellow organ music while everyone ate dinner. "Go on and eat with your parents," Miss Decisive told Julius. Julius abandoned the hideaway and went by the tables toward Susan, Juan Lucas, Luis Martín Romero, the chaperones, who turned out to be decent people, and the two tall white guys who had arrived hours earlier with Bobby's orchid. "Darling," Susan exclaimed, as she saw him approach. "Have you eaten yet?" As he was saying no, somebody nearby must have heard him because all of a sudden a waiter from Murillo's Caterers appeared bringing him a glass of Coke and the first dish of the banquet.

As each dish was being served, orchestra leader Lobo played even more mellow music; hence those who were really in love or who that night might ask their dates to go steady with them would get up slowly from the tables, silently extend their arms to their dates, the girls would smile, get up, follow them, and take their hands, or they would follow behind, reaching out to hold hands and, without going too far from their tables, draw close to each other, magnetized, eyes closed with a serious look on their faces, taking a step from time to time and to one side with the rhythm of the music. The bad dancers, the ones with two left feet or the timid ones, also took advantage of the slow music and danced horribly without even getting close to their partners. Even the class dunces and those who should have stayed home took advantage and, after traumatic efforts, matched up with the ugly ones and those who would have preferred to stay home. They wasted opportunities, of course, to sway to the rhythm of coffee-in-a-foggy-tropical-seaport that Andy Latino had added to his repertoire of love songs.

The best part began after dessert. The nine professors were there again undulating like crazy, and the orchestra leader directed them as he played the piano and the organ in lithesome fashion. Andy Latino no longer sang. Lost among the professors, he inspired them with short Cuban refrains and, from time to time, he approached the microphone in order to sing one. The dancers with two left feet were screwed. Several girls got bored because the timid ones didn't have any idea how to dance to that music. On the other hand, the experts danced apart from their partners when they felt like it or intimately, slow, glued together if they wanted, but always following the rhythm. There was a little of everything: Caribbean rhythms, rock, cha-cha-chas, etc. When they started playing a potpourri of dances, everyone let loose; they danced, jumped into the air, made trains, and ran among the tables. It was quite a sight.

Of course it was. And there's that lovely, happy, likeable girl: the one with the blue dress covered with the fine sheer net; the one with the curvy skirt; the one who embraced her own naked shoulders as if she were cold but communicated pure happiness. Here she comes! Here she comes! She passed by in front of them in the line of dancers and she waved incessantly and smiled happily. She waved to the chaperones, to Juan Lucas, to Susan, to the blond giants, to the photographers who followed her around because she would get lost again dancing, jumping, singing . . . Julius took advantage of the noise to ask Susan who the blond giants were. They were Juan Lucas' partners in Tingo María, Atilio and Esteban, from Yugosla . . . but here she comes again, she's really appealing, everyone wanted to get a look at her face but they couldn't because she laughed, jumped, spun around and all her blond hair came down over her face. The sheer net enveloped her, the photographers blinded her, she was going around again, and she disappeared saying she'd be back, motioning to Julius to join the chorus, hook up to the train, come on, kid! and the train took her toward the back of the patio. He couldn't see her. Where is she? Atilio and Esteban were dying of laughter, Julius got cold feet. No! No! He didn't want to join in, and here she comes again, looking at him, and while she invited him to join in she almost broke loose from the line, spinning, passing by faster each time. She was lovely and didn't care if they stepped on her sheer net, pieces were falling all over the ground everywhere, what did she care, she continued to enjoy herself, swirling around, changing the pace every time the professors changed rhythms. And now they were playing a swinging piece: *Dance! Dance! Dance! That popular dance!* everyone noticed how vivacious she was, her little hands on her hips, dancing to an exotic Latin American beat, and jumping like crazy. She didn't even know who her partner was anymore, anyone who happened to be in front of her, she danced with everyone, and passing in front of the Yugoslavians, called them out to dance, but they told Julius to take their places. Julius was ready to go but just then Bobby went racing by, flying, arm in arm with Rosemary, while everyone else was twirling to the rhythm of the song, hooking together, then letting go, changing partners, linking up again with whoever was next to them, and the pretty girl disappeared again, they had taken her by the arm, spinning her toward the back of the patio, the song was coming to an end. Julius looked desperately for her among the couples and Susan looked at the orchestra: she didn't want them to stop. Then she looked out among the couples and saw her jumping at the back of the patio, then she was gone. Once again orchestra leader Lobo changed the rhythm and Susan smiled at the musicians, "Roll Out the Barrel" was next. "Polka," the Yugoslavs yelled. The couples rushed along with little skips from one extreme of the patio to the other, and the vivacious young girl was back again, she had really let go this time. "Come on," she yelled to them and at everyone, and again she left, jumping toward the back, disappearing. "Polka," yelled Atilio and Esteban. "They dance it in every form you can imagine," Juan Lucas commented, ebullient. "Young people!" Luis Martín Romero exclaimed. "Polka! Young people! Polka!" Once again the lively young girl appeared in full swing: "A doll!" Juan Lucas said. "Bold," Romero yelled. "Untiring," a chaperone added. "Here she comes again," Atilio announced. Come on! Join us! Don't be afraid! she yelled, almost running into them. "Señora, dance!" she yelled to Susan, with laughing, joyful eyes. "Yes, honey. Yes, darling," Susan said to her, smiling as tears welled up in her eyes. "Señora, dance! Señora, dance!" she yelled while they spun her away, jumping, dancing, swirling, lovely, toward the back of the patio where Julius continued to look for her . . .

"Luis Martín," Juan Lucas said, "take care of the guests for a moment."

"What's wrong with Susan?"

"I don't know. Slightly indisposed . . ."

Juan Lucas entered the door through which Susan had disappeared. There she was, at the back of the first room, smiling and putting away her handkerchief.

"It's nothing, darling."

"Susan . . ."

"You have to take care of the guests."

Juan Lucas tried to kiss her but she didn't respond to him.

"Susan . . ."

"Darling," she said to him with a kiss, "let's go back to the patio."

Now Julius was the one who had disappeared. Fortunately the guests weren't aware of anything. Atilio and Esteban, the latter of whom was very hoarse, continued commenting on the virtues of the polka with the chaperones. The orchestra had stopped playing and the exhausted couples rested at their tables. One could see some holding hands above the tables and could imagine others holding hands underneath the tables. Andy Latino and the nine professors slowly drank their glasses of beer that Abraham had just brought out to them, while orchestra leader Lobo sat once again at the organ and played a slow, mellow song, and the photographers went around taking pictures of each couple.

It would be a while before the music had completely ended. At first Julius thought he would be able to go to sleep. He didn't want any more partying. He was happy at first but afterward something always happens. He thought the organ music meant the end of the party and, since it was so slow, he would be able to go to sleep. However, suddenly down below orchestra leader Lobo initiated a fast rhythm and little by little the other instruments started to join in, and now the trumpet, "*Time to dance the merengue!*" Andy Latino yelled, and Julius fell out of his bed. He thought about getting dressed again and going downstairs, but no, not now; not even open the window and look for her either. He looked at Cinthia's picture, they don't remember you, Cinthia, only Mommy knew it, I saw it in her smile tonight, I was five years old the last time I saw her smile that way, when you didn't come back from Boston, Cinthia. Your classmates were downstairs tonight, for sure many of them would have been your friends from school, from your class, Mommy noticed, she saw you, no, Cinthia, she didn't see you but she remembered you in her smile, but I saw you, it frightened me, that's why parties are sad, that's why they're always held at night. They don't remember you, Cinthia, that girl frightened me. Once Mommy found me talking to you and everyone said you were in heaven. Once Mommy found me praying to you: *No! No! No! Julius! No, darling! No, honey! No, sweetie!* I went to confession, I didn't pray to you anymore but I still talk to you, weren't we talking to each other before the party? You wanted to talk but I didn't, and I've always talked to you, that's why Mommy cried and I didn't, but I wasn't frightened. Mommy's right: *Julius, no, my love! you can't! you shouldn't! it will be bad for you, my love! Cinthia is . . . it's bad for you!* That was a long time ago, Cinthia, but I've continued to talk to you in the mornings and at night, talking to your picture, to you at night, you know everything when I look at you as I go to bed. In the mornings, you know everything when I look at you as I wake up, Cinthia. Mommy's right, that's why I was afraid, one day a year they remember you and they cry, that's the way people are. But I told you about Cano, Bobby, and Mommy, and today I became frightened, you have to pardon me, Cinthia. It's only your picture, you have to excuse me, Cinthia: I'm going to put you on the dresser, further away from my bed, I always think in my bed. I'm going to put you further away from my bed, on the dresser, Cinthia. I apologize, don't you see? I've been talking to you for hours, that's why tonight I became afraid and maybe it's not good to become frightened this way: my hands tremble and my stomach hurts, always at four in the afternoon, sorry, Cinthia, you are . . . it was the way Mommy smiled tonight, I'm sorry, I'm going to put you on the dresser, I'm going to be eleven years old, on top of the dresser, one day I'm going to have to go to a party and I don't want to become frightened. I've already told you about my dream, Cinthia, the other night, please understand, it was Bobby's party and I was like a little boy, before Boston, but I had talked to you before that night, tonight, until you were fifteen years old and I went looking for you, I ran to see you with your friends but you weren't there. Where is she? I asked, but they didn't remember you, Cinthia. I've already told you that, don't cry, don't you see? This isn't good, it only makes you suffer and that's all. And it frightens me, it's not worth it: me, a little kid, and I can't find you. And Bobby wants to kick me out of the party because I'm bothering everyone. It's true, I was bothering everyone, you didn't see the dream, Cinthia: I went from table to table asking, bugging everyone and, all of a sudden, one of them was you, and another, and another, probably because Mommy said one day everyone looks the same at fifteen, but today Mommy was wrong. Poor Mommy. But then I believed her and that one was you, and the other one was you, and you were the one whom I thought was Cinthia: Mommy, why did you say they were all alike? It was difficult, very difficult, the party was ending and I couldn't find you, Cinthia, I got drowsy, not many were left, they were all leaving. I was still running around and getting tired of looking for you all night long, Cinthia. Finally at the end you smiled at me, I've already told you about it, only now does it seem easy, finally your smile took me beyond her to a table, your smile, Cinthia, I've already told you about it, the morning sun woke me up at your side, as always, looking at you, don't you see, you know everything when I look at you in the morning . . .

"Julius!"

Startled, Julius heard Susan's voice. He even thought there was a reason for calling out it's the last time I'll do it, Mommy, but when he turned over he discovered it was Bobby.

"Is the party over?"

"Do you hear any more music?"

"Yeah, yeah, you're right, how dumb . . ."

"I've come to make a deal with you."

" . . ."

"If you give me the money from your piggy bank, I'll tell you who I'm going to screw tonight."

Julius remembered that Juan Lucas had told Bobby not one cent until summer's over and he almost handed him the piggy bank, ha ha, what can Juan Lucas do about this? But the fact that his brother shows up at four o'clock in the morning, smelling of liquor and asking for all of his money worried him.

"The summer is just beginning," he told him. "You won't be able to pay me back."

"Hurry up, idiot. Yes or no."

"No!" Julius yelled, hurling himself on top of his little piggy bank made by the International Bank of Peru.

Bobby had already grabbed it and the jerk was on his way out . . .

"Mommy has the key in the safe . . ."

Bobby knew very well how those piggy banks worked, but it's more difficult than trying to open the International Bank vaults. He also had one once, now it's empty unfortunately, and soon they were going to close the whorehouse.

"Shit," he yelled, throwing down the piggy bank. "You don't get to know who I'm going to screw tonight!" he added, taking off furiously. Sonia should have returned to Nanette's by now . . .

But Julius didn't know anything about that. *If you give me the money from your piggy bank, I'll tell you who I'm going to screw tonight.* He turned to Cinthia. What is he going to do? What does he want? *The person I'm going to screw tonight . . .* I'm sorry, Cinthia, you're going over to the dresser. Mommy's right, I'll put you over on the dresser. Julius picked up Cinthia's picture and put it on the dresser, next to Susan's. *Screw?* Screw? Screw on a nut, I'm sorry, Cinthia, screw, don't you see, I have to put you over here, I'm going to turn out the light now, Cinthia. I'll say good-bye, Mommy's right. Screw? Don't you see? You know everything when I look at you before I go to bed . . .

Julius had finally made all his decisions. He was undaunted. He went to sleep with a knot in his throat just when the sun was coming up, but he slept with his back to the dresser. Not long afterward, the sun's rays almost woke him up because Miss Decisive, what with last night's party, had forgotten to go upstairs to close the drapes in his room as she usually did. Julius felt a ray of light hit his closed eyes, but at that moment Cinthia, smiling, called him from a table at the other side of the patio. Excuse me, Mommy! Excuse me! Susan didn't manage to stop him and Julius, panting, could barely make his way through the couples that now, all of a sudden, were leaving his bedroom, creating an open space between him and the table, between his bed and the dresser . . . you know everything when I wake up and look at you in the morning.

II

And that was, if I remember well, the last time I sobbed like a child. In some ways, it was already contaminated by something confusing and bitter.

— FEDERICO CHIESA, *TEMPO DI MARZO*

. . . we heard Maurice O'Sullivan's voice saying that a significant part of him also died that night: an integral and profound part of his life: his childhood.

— DYLAN THOMAS, *TWENTY YEARS A-GROWING*

"PROMISES HAVE TO BE KEPT," Juan Lucas said, showing the telegram to Susan. What? You mean you don't remember that he promised them to bring him home for Christmas? Susan, smiling, read the telegram: "Arrive 24th. Three in the afternoon Lima time. Flight 204. New York–Lima. Lester Lang is coming with me." Bobby was really happy Santiago would be arriving within a few hours.

They ate lunch on the run and then climbed into the station wagon. Juan Lucas told Carlos to drive, so he could drop them off at the main door of the airport and then look for a place to park. Everyone was happy when they got to the airport. "There it is," Bobby said pointing to a descending airliner. Julius looked at his watch: yes, that had to be it. "Do you remember your brother?" Susan asked, taking him by the arm as they entered the terminal.

Sure, sure, he remembered. Everyone remembered Santiago; even Carlos. He had parked the car in a matter of seconds and ran to see young Santiago's plane land. He was standing next to them on the observation deck pronouncing Santiago's name until, finally, they saw him appear from behind two stewardesses who opened the door of the plane. Bobby raised his arm to wave at him, but at that moment Santiago hugged a stewardess and kissed her for the longest time. After he had finished, Bobby was about to wave again but then another young man, even more blond than Santiago, appeared and hugged the other stewardess and kissed her for the longest time too. "Lester's son," Juan Lucas commented, delighted. "They're not letting the other passengers get by," Julius intervened, ruining everything. At least it seemed that way as he saw the way Juan Lucas looked at him. Finally, the travelers looked up at the observation deck. Santiago identified them immediately among the crowd waiting for family and friends. "There they are," pointing them out to Lester. "Yes, yes, that's them." Then Lester Lang IV removed a large, imaginary Texan hat and began some long and protracted waving back and forth, forming and breaking 180-degree arcs in a type of greeting that looked like an expression of friendship, we're among friends . . . "Yes sir, that's Lester's son," Juan Lucas commented, laughing.

Santiago's excess baggage cost them a bundle. He lunged at the family, followed closely by Lester Lang IV. Susan jokingly braced herself in order to confront her son's emotion, but she couldn't prevent him from quickly disarming her. "Clinch, gotcha!" yelled Santiago, and did whatever he wanted with her: he kissed her, stood back and looked at her, admired her, hugged her again, kissed her, and completely disarranged her hair. "Darling! Darling! Darling!" cried Susan, defenseless, but they twirled around twice more, hugging each other. "Mastodon!" she exclaimed, freeing herself from Santiago's joyful fury, who then pounced on Bobby, who was bewildered by it all and quickly disarmed him. Juan Lucas guffawed. The next one was Julius: "Dumbo," he exclaimed, giving him a soft elbow in the side and a swift pull on his two ears. Then he hugged Juan Lucas after which he saw Carlos standing in the back and took advantage of the happy moment to give him a hug as well. "This is Lester," he said, introducing Lang III's son, but he had already said hello to everyone.

Once they were back home, Julius felt it was his obligation to show the new house to Santiago and his friend, but both of them breezed by every room as if they had been living there all their lives. Susan disappeared because she was sleepy and needed to take a nap. Juan Lucas also said, Well, fellas, we'll see you tonight; we'll have dinner together here at home. Santiago and Lester sat in the summer bar, drank a cognac, and decided they should probably take a shower and rest a while. That's when Celso, Daniel, and Miss Decisive came in. Santiago explained to Lester in English who they were and why they were so ugly, but he greeted them in Spanish with affection and even commented a bit about years past, especially with the butlers. "And that guy?" he asked suddenly upon observing Abraham, about whom no one had said a word, when he nervously crossed the patio and looked at them out of the corner of his eye. "He's the cook," Julius explained to him, "but I don't know what he's doing here now; he always leaves after lunch and comes back later to cook dinner."

Lester and Santiago were still stroking their cognacs when Bobby came in and served himself one right in front of Julius' critical look. "What are you looking at?" he told him, and Julius almost answered him saying with one little glass you always get drunk, but he preferred not to become the tattletale in front of these travelers who, for the time being, seemed likeable enough, although his brother had a strange look about him.

"What kind of cars do we have these days?" Santiago asked out of the blue.

"A station wagon and a Mercedes, apart from Juan Lucas' Jaguar."

"You've got the station wagon?"

"Yes."

"Then Mom has the Mercedes. So what's for us?"

Bobby was going to explain the Mercedes isn't used all the time because Susan usually went with Juan Lucas when Santiago abruptly changed the topic.

"Where's the pool?"

"*The swimming pool*," Lester said, who was always consulting a book that gives instructions on how to travel in Latin America and be liked by the natives, a bestseller, according to the book cover.

"Don't worry," Santiago told him in English, "everyone you'll be meeting speaks English. You don't need your little book for anything. Better yet, you could stick it up your ass . . ."

"Culo, *ass*," Lang exclaimed. He knew that one without having to look it up in the book.

"Where's the pool?" Santiago asked once again.

"Over there," Bobby explained, pointing it out. "It's right under your window."

"Yes, I like Lima a lot," Lang was pronouncing horribly in Spanish from his little book.

"Is it deep?"

"Yes, why?"

"Nothing . . . C'mon, let's go see it."

"I like Lima a lot, Señou*reta* . . ."

"Señorita," Julius corrected happily, turning to see if Santiago approved of his intervention.

Indeed, there was something strange about the way he looked. He observed him when he stood up and started walking toward the swimming pool. Everyone followed him out. Bobby, who was in front, turned around abruptly:

"Why are you following us around, you little snot-nosed shit?" he yelled at Julius. "You can come with us if you give me your piggy bank!"

"No!"

"Well, go to hell and you'll never know who . . ."

"What's the matter?" Santiago intervened, stopping in his tracks.

"*What's the matter?*" Lang also knew that one in Spanish.

"He always follows you around everywhere you go!"

"When have I ever followed you around?"

"Aw, leave Dumbo alone."

Julius felt relieved when he saw Santiago turn around and grin, as if he were going to intervene on his behalf, but he understood right there he wasn't defending him, nor condoning his actions, nor anything. Nothing. Once again he noticed something strange about the look on his face, something that made him remember that instant at the airport, a brief moment in which he saw that same expression of emptiness reflected in his eyes . . . Yes, yes, he also saw it when he greeted Celso and Daniel . . . They continued walking toward the pool.

"It's deep enough," Santiago said when he saw it, and both of them looked up at the bedroom window on the second floor where they were going to sleep.

"Let's go upstairs!" Santiago blurted out suddenly. "*Upstairs!*" he translated for his friend, pointing to the bedroom window.

Bobby followed them inside. They didn't even realize that Julius had remained at the pool. His face reflected the anguish of an afflicted guest, awaiting anxiously the important social outcome of cramps in the middle of dinner: he had just remembered another instant when Santiago looked so strangely and he was about to define it. In any case, he had managed to capture one more detail: his smile, yes, that smile had something to do with the problem.

The bedroom window was open and Julius, still standing next to the edge of the pool, could barely make out the conversation among his brothers and the visitor upstairs. First Bobby was telling them no, it was impossible, but then his voice became inaudible. On the other hand, Lester and Santiago could be heard arguing in English. They were looking for their bathing suits, where in the hell would they be in all these suitcases. Then they said it didn't matter, take off your pants or, if you want, go fully dressed. Julius also heard some giggling but then a brief silence allowed him to concentrate on the strangeness of his brother's gaze. Then voices once again, a lot closer this time, and when he looked up to see why they seemed so close . . . Go! they yelled from above: Santiago and Lester flew out the window one behind the other and intently penetrated the water. They reappeared calmly and swam over to the edge of the pool to get out; they were wearing their underwear. Once they were out of the pool, they just stood there with their hands on their hips and simply stared at the water, satisfied. Bobby was impressed and looked at them from the bedroom window, while Julius looked at them from the other side of the pool: they were Tarzan types, real athletes, every muscle stood out as they breathed deeply. They turned to look up at the window in order to measure the extent of the danger, and Lester smiled as if to say it was a notable feat. Santiago also smiled and that's when Julius was able to observe that his joy disappeared from his smile, and then as he looked up beyond the second floor the weak smile faded altogether, escaping through a spark that was snuffed out in his eyes, through a large ephemeral soap bubble that disappeared and then splattered his look with emptiness, leaving it lost in another window, the one up above, on the third floor that doesn't exist in the mansion: perhaps for that reason also there was the anguished expression on his lips, still stretched and bent but totally deprived of joy.

"Let's rest," Santiago said to his friend, interrupting Julius' rigorous observation. "Christmas dinner with the old folks tonight, then we'll go out. A couple of hours of sleep right now wouldn't do us any harm. Are there any weights?" he asked abruptly, looking at Julius.

Julius was going to say no, and even thought about telling them Cano's story, but he realized it would be in vain because Santiago had already lost interest in his response.

"Dumbo!" he shouted all of a sudden, smiling, approaching him to pull on his ears affectionately, but at that moment he saw a different Julius standing there. "Let's get some shut-eye," he said, with the spark missing from his eyes.

THAT AFTERNOON Miss Decisive was a little upset and, as always, Julius was the one who had to make it worse. Fortunately, he was learning not to take her very seriously and, he would tell her, like Carlos, not to blow her cool, it was bad for her blood pressure; that's why now, seated at the table in the dining room, waiting for the newly arrived guests in order to begin the Christmas dinner, he smiled as he laughed at Juan Lucas' curiosity, while he remembered Miss Deci's objections: "Above all, it's an uninhibited state, call it American or whatever you like, it's an informal, primitive education that produces what we have today and it's a total lack of respectiveness. They don't respect Christmas here; tonight is Christmas Eve and there isn't one single Christmas tree in this house." Julius intervened to tell her that he thought his mommy was right: "Mommy says you can't put up Christmas trees decorated with little balls of cotton in order to make it look like snow when here we are sizzling from the heat. It's fine in Germany or in the United States, not in Peru." But Miss Decisive only agreed. "What I don't like is that the Señora doesn't state it outright and, instead of Christmas trees, she should set up nativity scenes. And don't go telling me they're also from the United States . . . Your brother and his friend Lester have been sleeping for two hours and they won't let me go in and fix their suitcases; they've probably thrown their clothes all over the room . . . Don't try to tell me that young Lester brought nativity scenes with him." "Deci," Julius explained, "Christmas is awfully sad, I don't know why it's so sad. I've thought about it and it must be that way because we don't have Cinthia. Before we had a tree and a nativity scene. Ever since Cinthia died I don't think Mommy has wanted any more of that." Miss Decisive became mute, but her silence didn't last very long; she said she respected bereavements, but one's feelings were inside one's self and they didn't have anything to do with Christmas trees that were outside one's self. "To each one their sadness," she added, "but to everyone, happiness." She was pensive and proud of her proverb, even to the point that she wasn't in a bad mood anymore after having said something so profound. She remained seated, looked at Julius, and lowered her head from time to time as if she were trying to get to the very essence of his words.

"When are the travelers coming down?" Juan Lucas asked, a little impatient.

"I don't know, darling."

"Celso, bring in a bottle of champagne."

"Yes, sir."

Julius remembered Celso as he entered the kitchen while he and Miss Decisive disputed, one-on-one, the matter of Christmas. Pleased, he came in saying that the Señor and the Señora had been very generous with the indemnity they had given everyone for Christmas. "Each thing with its proper name," Miss Decisive interrupted. "That's not an indemnification but a Christmas bonification, no, that's not it either, ah yes, it's a bonus," she corrected herself quickly. Julius smiled when he remembered the scene, and Juan Lucas was going to ask him, may we have the honor of knowing why you are laughing, young man? But at that moment Susan, lovely, who was sitting at the end of the table, raised her eyes looking above the candelabra with twelve flickering candles and, pushing back her blond lock of hair, smiled and her expression of tenderness announced with affection the entrance of the travelers into the dining room.

"The sleepyheads," she said, touching the base of the candelabra with a finger.

"Carajo," Lang IV thought of saying upon discovering Susan's figure, half-hidden now by the candelabra; fortunately he remembered on the plane Santiago had told him he'd let him know when he can use that word. The gringo could barely hold back saying son of a bitch, but the expression on his face revealed the impact Susan had produced when he saw her behind the flickering candles, enclosed by huge windows, looking out upon imaginary tropical gardens well to the south of the Rio Grande, and between walls on which hung obscure paintings probably of strange saints, like the great work of the Cuzco School that his father took back with him once from Lima. The son of the investor wasn't stupid. He waited for Santiago to kiss his mother and, behind him, he approached her with a gift saying, "For you, Señora, with affection from my parents," and before Susan could thank him, he pulled out another gift that he indicated was from him and he handed it to her saying, "There aren't words," in English, of course.

Juan Lucas' cork popped a lot better than the thousands that explode night after night in bars around the world. Celso brought out the serving tray with the champagne glasses. Two minutes later everyone was drinking and toasting, without ever saying why or to whom they were toasting: "Cheers!" they repeated, and that's all.

"So affectionate! *So sweet!*" Susan exclaimed suddenly, shaking her head in order to toss back a lock of hair, because both of her hands were involved with opening the card and the little box.

"So affectionate!" she repeated, reading the card. "Lester sends with their son the golden key to their new house in Boston, the house is ours whenever we want, it will always be at our disposal . . . *So sweet!*"

They toasted again, this time probably for the key and the investments in gold. Juan Lucas, who never let himself be topped by anyone, also produced a key.

"Young men, this is a Swedish key! It unlocks the door and starts a Volvo sports car that's waiting for you outside!"

Santiago translated it to English for Lester, and Lester accelerated with one foot under the table, and took off in any direction with a zooooooooooom of automobilistic joy.

"Thanks, Juan Lucas!" Santiago exclaimed, pleased, but at that instant Julius noted that his gaze turned toward the large window, and it seemed to be looking off into the night at the polo grounds for a sports car that was beyond the Volvo.

They began to exchange gifts. Juan Lucas announced that as soon as Santiago and Lester returned to the United States, in early January, the Volvo would be locked up in the garage, awaiting the results of Bobby's entrance exams. "If you pass, it's yours," he added, handing him a thick wad of bills: "And this is to enjoy yourself until New Year's Day. One week of pleasure is enough: on January second, you need to hole up and start studying." Bobby looked at Julius, as if to say you'll never find out who I'm going to screw, and Julius decided to ask Carlos what the other meaning of the word screw meant. That was that for the time being. Susan had just asked Celso to bring out the presents for young Julius, and the butler came back in with a brand new racing bicycle that Juan Lucas had recommended, especially since the kid didn't even play miniature golf anymore. "He's getting skinnier every day," he said, "really ungainly, his clothes don't fit like his brothers' fit them." Julius went over to inspect the bicycle. It had everything, even special gears, or at least that's what the manual hanging from the handlebars indicated. The little lever was to change gears: some to go faster down hills, some to go slower up hills, others to go along easily on the flat stretches with the normal gears, and, finally, one gear in order to ride along like the rest of the world on a bicycle. Once he finished the inspection, Julius turned to Susan and looked at her as if to say: And where's the other present? Fortunately, Susan was paying attention, because with so much joy, accompanied by champagne, candelabras, kisses, gifts, and the servants spying through the door that was slightly ajar, she began to feel sad.

"Darling, I haven't forgotten," she said. "I haven't forgotten, but at the bookstore they showed me the latest catalog and very soon a beautiful edition covered with green leather of the complete works is coming out in the United States. I'm sorry, Darling, it'll take one or two months to arrive, but I've kept my promise. Won't you like having your Mark Twain collection covered in green leather?"

Julius almost told her it would be better in blue steel so that Bobby won't be able to tear them up again, but it's true that during Christmas, as in the Second World War, the soldiers stopped fighting for Christmas. In addition, Susan announced she had another little present for him in the event he wanted to entertain himself while waiting for Mark Twain to arrive. Julius took the package thinking the little guitar had nothing to do with Mark Twain and it was probably something that occurred to Susan at the last moment. He guessed correctly because Susan, in effect, walking around like a millionaire completely lost in a toy store the other day and thinking perhaps she had to buy some toys to send to the poor people at the racetrack, saw the violin in the display window and it seemed to her it would be cute for Julius, at five and floppy-eared, to play the violin. Julius finished unwrapping the little guitar and discovered that it was a violin. "Fortunately, it's a violin without a teacher," he thought, looking at Juan Lucas, who had just ordered the turkey to be served and then turned to Julius: "Tomorrow, get on your bicycle and head for the street. Get some exercise," he said.

BUT WITH ALL the money he had to spend in one week, Bobby didn't go looking for Sonia. He would leave that matter for a later date, because the whorehouse was a stage in Santiago's life that he had transcended, and if he wanted to hang around with his brother there was no alternative but to stick with him on his vacation adventures and spend all the money Juan Lucas had given him for Christmas on Santiago and Lester. He never thought his brother would let him tag along without complaining; on the contrary, he thought the visitors were going to tell him at some moment to buzz off, mainly because they were older and he still hadn't turned eighteen. Bobby was afraid that precise moment was about to come right after Christmas dinner when the three of them went outside to the outer patio of the mansion to begin breaking in the spectacular Volvo that was parked behind the carriage. Santiago smiled when he saw the car for the first time. "Not bad," he said, but as he moved closer his smile began to dissipate, and both Lester and he got into the car and closed the doors as if it had always been their car. Bobby just stood there, watched them, and thought as soon as they left he would get in the station wagon and haul ass to Nanette's place.

"Aren't you getting in?" Santiago asked him all of a sudden, opening the car door.

Bobby got in quickly and he sat in the narrow rear seat, hoping someone would come out to open the garage door. "Blow the horn," he said, but Santiago acted like he didn't hear him. He was thinking: what in the hell does one do in Lima these days? How does one act who has been out of the country for so long? What do you do in those cases? Do I have any friends left? Whom can I call? Which girl did I like? Who can I screw? Is there someone for Lester? Which beach do we go to? Ancón? Herradura? Las Gaviotas? El Waikiki? Well, he would take care of all that little by little, right now it was more important to find a bar, for it was already past one o'clock in the morning.

"Is there any place to go and dance?" he asked Bobby.

"Well, it depends . . ."

"Does Freddy Solo's still exist?"

"Yes."

"Open the door," Santiago told Abraham, who was leaving the mansion at that moment and walked by the Volvo looking out the corner of his eye.

The three of them got out of the car without seeing a scrubby man with a filthy sailor's cap offering to clean their car or at least let him watch it for them. The man greeted them and they went out of their way to ignore him. They crossed the wide sidewalk and went up to the door of Freddy Solo's Bar. A waiter approached them to escort them to a table, but Santiago motioned to him they were going to the bar. "The telephone?" he asked, and the waiter said the bartender would pass it to him over the counter. The bartender recognized Santiago and greeted him warmly. "The people over there are leaving soon," he told him, and the three of them walked over to some recently vacated bar stools. Freddy Solo's was full up. It was Christmastime, of course, and there was a lot of drinking going on. No one seemed to notice Santiago had returned, although there were several people there who knew him and knew he was the heir to one of those great fortunes. The bartender placed the telephone in front of him, here you are, Señor Santiago. Bobby decided to be twenty years old. He also ordered a whiskey, yeah, that brand. Santiago talked on the telephone. He dialed one number after another. "No one's home," he commented to Lester between calls. "Everyone goes to Ancón this time of year." Bobby took advantage of the fact that Lester didn't know what the hell Ancón was and explained it to him, but halfway through his explanation he realized the gringo wasn't following him, even less so when he tried to tell him it was the Acapulco of Lima, the Peruvian Riviera . . . Bobby was definitely confusing the guy, because Lang IV had already been to Acapulco; in fact, he had bedded down with a harem of girls in Acapulco, and the last time he had gone he got bored there. "No one's around," Santiago said, pushing the telephone to one side and drawing his drink closer to him. Amid the smoke, he turned around to see who was there. In reality, few people were dancing and the noise and laughter were coming from the bar and nearby tables. The place was replete with drunks: some were dull, boring types who were sitting down and others were congenial, irritating types. "There's that immortal idiot, Mr. Mouse Turd Siles." "Little Santiago! It's been years!" Mouse yelled when he saw him. Santiago looked at him without seeing him and Mouse coughed into his hand and returned to his engaging conversation with the same girl who had been putting up with him for the last few hours. Lester remained silent. If he looked at anything, it was the music. But he was aware of everything that was going on there because it was internationally the same as anywhere else. Bobby, on the other hand, had to follow his brother's every move in order to learn the details. Santiago lit a cigarette. Lester was already smoking. Bobby lit another cigarette. Lester and Santiago barely touched theirs, but Bobby puffed away on his. He had finished his whiskey and then he noticed their glasses were still full, for they barely took sips, only from time to time, mainly to make the ice jingle. Mouse Siles spilled his glass of whiskey and while he was bending over to pick it up, the girl with whom he had been talking so elatedly disappeared. At that instant, Santiago heard Tonelada Samamé's brandy-saturated laugh. Amid the smoke, it sounded the same as it did years ago, perhaps now with a stronger overlay of tobacco. He laughed again, louder this time because he was right behind them, yelling at him: Where have you been? Don't tell me you've been studying all this time. "You're still alive?" Santiago asked him, turning around with a smile and a hello. He introduced him to Lester. "This is the new one?" Tonelada asked, sluggishly, slapping Bobby on the shoulder and with the other arm pulling Piba Portal over to him, the one who didn't screw in Santiago's time but did now. "Two whiskeys," Tonelada yelled, and before the bartender could ask him about the bill for the previous one he told him, "Those go on Mouse's tab, these on this new guy's tab." Bobby felt him put his hand on his shoulder and he turned to look at Santiago, but Santiago didn't pay any attention to him and continued talking calmly to Piba. Tonelada pulled his hand from Bobby's shoulder when he saw the two whiskeys arrive.

"And give one to . . . what's your name?"

"Roberto."

"Give one to Roberto over here."

Bobby turned to look at his brother again, but now Santiago was talking to another guy who had joined the group. Meanwhile, Piba struck up a conversation with Lester in English. Lester was delighted. Piba, apart from the fact that you could screw her, was extremely appealing. She could tell you a thousand stories. And Tonelada two thousand. Two thousand, all in English, all in English, thanks to a total of forty-five words, the only ones he's retained from a good education, stories soaked in whiskey, smothered in belly laughs, adorned with moments of silence with the necessary gestures of his lively hands, whose palms he looked at repeatedly, ah! if Versailles could only talk. Amid all of this Tonelada was constructing perfect English, at least whatever was necessary for the moment; he blurted out three idiomatic expressions that fit the situation, then something of what he wanted to say, and the rest of the story was communicated with his hands, a few monosyllables pronounced in a perfect international tone and, reaching the end of the story, he underscored the denouement with the exact word, finishing it off with the standard, contagious roar, because if the story didn't end in general laughter, it wasn't worth telling.

Lester was having a great time with Piba and Tonelada. Peruvian nightlife. Lima nightlife style and all the big laughs. Translated into English, as well. Lang IV was enjoying it. He took a sip of whiskey and asked for another while Tonelada gulped his down, spitting the ice cubes back into the glass in order to shake them and quickly order *one more.*

He turned his back on Bobby, but then turned around to say he was sorry and to explain that what he really wanted to do was turn his back on Mouse, who had just come over to him, insisting on jostling shoulders and talking to him even if it was behind his ear, until finally Tonelada stepped backward in order to step on him. He stood that way for a time while Mouse attached himself to Bobby. Meanwhile, he continued laughing out loud with Lester and Piba.

"The girl's nostalgic," he commented sarcastically.

"Why nostalgic?" Lester asked.

"I'm always like this at Christmastime . . . it must be because of the child Jesus . . ."

Piba shouldn't have said that because in truth she did get nostalgic. Fortunately, Tonelada intervened, he cared about her a lot, "Damn," he exclaimed, looking down at his hands. Piba had talked about the child Jesus in other years too, and the Christmas season had given rise to the beginning of a drunken binge of the type that even corrupts God . . . She was, nevertheless, a great companion . . .

"There isn't any nostalgia like hers," Tonelada explained to Lester. "What happens is that there's always something left over."

Lang didn't understand the idea of leftovers and he asked Piba to translate the exact word, one that was absent from Tonelada's English vocabulary, too complicated, perhaps, for this environment. Piba translated it and Tonelada was able to continue his explanation: something had stayed with her, something from her schooling with the nuns. Three years running I've been trying to get her to go to bed on Christmas Eve . . . with someone she likes, of course, and it's always the same, not on Christmas. They all let fly with raucous laughter. Bobby peeked through from behind Tonelada and participated with a smile.

"Ah ha!" Mouse Siles squeaked suddenly. Tonelada thought that maybe he had stepped on his foot too hard, but he discovered that the mouse had pulled his foot away and was moving through the crowd in order to hug a large, recently arrived man whom everyone, especially

Mouse, recognized: "Viceroy! Viceroy!" yelled Mouse. Viceroy, between hugging him and pushing him to one side, made his way through
the group to the bar, taking a position close to Santiago, who said:
"Viceroy!" Both of them got down from their stools and went over to
each other for the tremendous embrace. "I'm falling over from a jag,
I've been drinking for three days now," Viceroy announced, looking
over the crowd at Freddy Solo's, just in case someone might want to
take the opportunity to punch him out while he's drunk. But through
the smoke no one jumped him and Ray Charles continued to sing serenely for the couples that were dancing and for the drunks who at
Christmastime tottered toward nostalgia. Santiago brought Viceroy
over to the group in order to introduce him to his friend. Lester Lang
IV stood up ipso facto to show him that in the United States there's a
popular tradition kept alive by John Wayne in the movies that consists
of a confrontation among giants in a bar up there in the north who
proceed to destroy the luxurious decor during several hours of fighting.
This was for the purpose of conquering the West and now for maintaining the image of the ugly American; here, it's for the idea of I'm proud
to be a Peruvian and I'm happy. Tonelada, who was half hidden,
laughed heartily when he saw the Peruvian squeezing the shit out of
Lester's hand, but in a friendly manner. One had to understand Viceroy
was about thirty years old and Lester, who was huskier, wasn't even
twenty-one yet. Lester himself realized the same thing and, fortunately,
let go at the opportune moment. Viceroy smiled, delighted, but as he
looked at Piba he heard Tonelada's belly laugh again from a few moments earlier. He turned around to look for him, and quickly too, because Tonelada had taken advantage of one of those moments when
Viceroy turned to look for him, this was months ago, when he was on
a jag like now, and nailed him with a butt of his head, then a swift
punch and even a kick in the balls; the bad part was, after all that,
Viceroy acted as if nothing had happened, he seemed unscathed and
worse yet, he sent Tonelada flying across the room and gave him such a
beating that for over a month not one woman in Lima would pay any
attention to him. Listen to him, yes, because he was always congenial,
the most pleasant and disoriented character there is in Lima, but nothing more until your eyeballs return to their sockets, Tone. "But at least
I've got personal charm," the parasite protested, but no response.
"Then I'm leaving," he announced, feeling he had been found out.
"Sorry, Piba. I'm leaving you here with friends. I'm leaving this darling
Lester with you. Viceroy is going to punch me out any moment now.
Every time he gets drunk he beats me up." He left for the door, despite

the shouting from the bar for him to come back. "Sure, sure," he said, from behind the drapes covering the entrance to the bar. "Yeah, yeah, Germán," he repeated, pointing to Mouse and referring to the bill for the whiskeys. Santiago, smiling, had watched the whole scene: Tonelada was incredible; he had been his idol at school, and Santiago was still young when Tonelada was the top swimmer of the school. He was his idol in high school, a dolphin, interschool champ, king of the parties. He tried to figure out why he had ended up that way, until it occurred to him that it was his affability that had brought him down . . . He was going to think about the matter, but at that moment his eyes darkened, as if all of a sudden he had begun to look far beyond his memories, as if they had seen a place where feelings dissolved into obscurity.

"Tonelada's gone, right?" Viceroy asked.

"I think so," Santiago said.

"Well, Mouse, talk to me about something."

Mouse Siles, already balding somewhat and a little gray-haired, turned his back on Bobby and, delighted, approached Viceroy. He immediately began to eulogize Viceroy's capacity to drink, but Viceroy overheard Piba's voice telling Lester and Santiago about her friend's latest escapades, mentioning the name Tonelada repeatedly. In the midst of his drunken stupor, he confused places and events, then he remembered, and again he found himself discovered one night recently, a long time ago, or recently, in any bar in Lima, in Buenos Aires, or was it Santiago, kissing a millionaire, a car for a week on a honeymoon, kissing that queer of a shit and all of a sudden tonight, that night here, in Buenos Aires, or was it Santiago, so many nights and all of a sudden Tonelada's laugh looking at him, finding him out, he who no one has ever hit.

"Where's Tonelada?"

"He left," Piba said. "But what do you want looking so mean?"

"If the gringo tries to take Piba with him tonight I'll kill him," he thought, ordering drinks: "Piba, what are you drinking?"

"Pay, Bobby," Santiago said, "we're going now."

"We're leaving?"

"Yeah, we're leaving . . . *Let's go*, Lester. Pay, Bobby, I still don't have any money. I'll pay you back later . . . Viceroy is dying to deck someone and with her next to Lester it won't be long before he picks a fight with him," he added in a low voice.

"Let's go," Bobby said, asking for the bill.

"Let's see what we can find elsewhere," Santiago translated for his friend when he asked why were they paying the bill. Lester was doing just fine with Piba, and he even had figured out how to resolve her Christmas prejudice, but Santiago convinced him that there were better places and the evening was going fast.

Moments later, Santiago, Bobby, and Lester were having a drink in the Saratoga Bar. Bobby was falling asleep: he was disillusioned with his brother. Several hours had gone by and, discounting the scene at the swimming pool, he didn't see anything in him or his friend that looked remotely like the pictures he had sent him some weeks back. He thought about telling them he was going home because he was tired, but at that moment Tonelada's laugh resounded throughout the bar.

"You didn't bring Viceroy with you, did you?" he asked sluggishly.

Santiago smiled. Lester was going to order a fourth whiskey, but Tonelada said no: "Later, friend. There are many apartments with the lights still on in this city . . . Not all of them sleep by the warmth of the Christmas trees and there are girls . . . *girls*," he translated for Lester.

"*Yes, girls!*"

Tonelada stuck his hand into his pants pocket and took out a five dollar bill: "The last one," he said, "but a better life is waiting for us."

"Take this and get a taxi," he added, handing it to Bobby.

"Pay for one of your own, at least," Bobby told him, rejecting it.

"Family spirit," Tonelada commented, and let out a huge belly laugh while Bobby stood up, looking at his brother.

"Go home, Bobby. We'll see you tomorrow," Santiago told him, watching him leave angrily. "Are there weights at home?" he asked suddenly, but Bobby didn't hear him.

Santiago and Lester woke up two times the next day, the first at about one in the afternoon, flat out in strange beds next to the girls Tonelada had taken them to see the night before. Santiago was the first one to crack an eye. He got up and went looking for the other bedroom to wake up his friend. Fortunately, he hadn't drunk much. He felt a little tired but that was all. Lester also didn't look bad for worse, it was due to that smile on his face welcoming Santiago when he entered the room. He jumped out of bed and the first thing he wanted to do was take a cold shower and drink a glass of orange juice. Santiago told him to forget about that for the time being: he'd find everything he wanted at home. Right now the important thing for them to do was leave before the girls woke up and began to ask them to stay a little longer or to take them to the beach or whatever. And something like that was going to happen if they didn't hurry up, because Lester's girl, somewhere between sleeping and smiling, had just begun to stretch with a little sigh and all, just enough for the gringo to jump headfirst back into warm waters. But too much could be excessive, last night and this morning were enough, it was necessary to keep fit. Santiago returned to the other bedroom while Lester got dressed. The two of them dressed hurriedly and said good-bye to their respective partners with a tap on their rear end and a promise to return soon.

The second time they woke up was at four o'clock in the afternoon at the mansion, where, of course, there were showers and orange juice. Later they went downstairs and Santiago asked Bobby again if there were any weights. Juan Lucas, who was also there, told him that between a pair of loafers like Julius and Bobby there was never any need for weights in the mansion. Today, moreover, was a holiday, but tomorrow he would see to it himself that a complete set of weights was delivered to the house.

ONCE THE SET of weights had arrived, the Christmas visitors' lives became more normal. They got up late every day, put on their bathing suits, went down to the garden, and for hours lifted all kinds and sizes of weights. There were weights for the forearms, for rounding out the shoulders, for the chest, dorsal muscles, biceps, triceps, gluteals, thighs, calves, etc. They spent hours at it, and Bobby watched them angrily, waiting for them to finish so they could decide finally which beach to go to that morning. One day they got Bobby involved in lifting weights, but he knew from the mirror in his room that weights were absolutely unnecessary unless he wanted to become a Tarzan like them. "No way," he thought, "too much slavery." All one had to do was look at them pumping away, bathed in sweat, dressed in plastic to make them sweat even more and eliminate the least bit of excess fat. It was fat, moreover, that only they noticed, the product of three or four days that, due to the trip and Christmas, had prevented them from their morning and afternoon workouts. In fact, they seemed queer, worrying about one millimeter more or less of thorax than last month: such big guys, it was something to see how they took care of themselves!

And then those long showers! And all those glasses of grapefruit juice! And the exact number of vitamins! And counting calories! And the North American breakfasts! Rest and digestion! . . . "Queers, they're just queers!" Bobby thought. Fortunately they had already screwed several girls whom Tonelada had found for them; fortunately too because they had looked at themselves in the mirror so much that he got worried. They touched themselves as well, but they were fanatical about it, let's see how you're doing, is it hard? Let's measure those biceps. Do you want me to measure them? Bobby started to doubt them, but he calmed down knowing they were screwing several of Tonelada's girls. The matter was technical, cold physical fitness. Exactly! Of course! That's it: physical fitness. Fortunately that's all it was!

And it was fortunate as well that after their rest every day they didn't worry anymore about their bodies. At least that's what Bobby thought. The kid was a little dense because the concern for their physique continued later at the beach as well: Waikiki, Herradura, Ancón. Once the rest period was over, they would decide which beach to invade that morning and then take off in the Volvo. Bobby would go with them. Those times were the best for him: Santiago and Lester were friendly and they didn't treat him like a baby or anything. In fact, they would introduce him to girls and they would talk to him even though they were a little older; moreover, when he would bring Rosemary along, they greeted her in a friendly way and were really nice to her. They would meet at the seawall and walk down to the beach together where other girls were waiting to meet them: Hey, girls, how's it going? and stretch out in the sand, conscious of other groups of girls over there who would have preferred they sit with them. But Lester and Santiago had their preferences; they had already chosen their girls and hence they were already partially paired off. Lester's girl was called Delfinita. Her eyes, like her name, matched the sea. The beach made her attractive.

Those were the times! That's where his brother and the gringo were real experts. It was something to see them lure the girls over to them, for the whole beach had fallen in love with them! And they would simply stretch out on the sand, hiding their gaze behind those big dark glasses, seemingly indifferent, self-confident, and all of a sudden determined, agile, jumping up energetically, running a race to the ocean, a dive and pam! they would fly into the breaking wave. They would reappear among the waves, wanting to swim out beyond the breakwater! going farther and farther out until they disappeared, at which time the girls would start to get worried.

Other times it was water skiing. Somersault after somersault while Bobby drove the speedboat, obeying their instructions: Get closer! Get closer! They would yell at him from behind, and Rosemary was frightened to death because the boat would pass dangerously close to the beach and any one of those waves could capsize it. What the hell! The important thing was to make sure everyone on the beach could see it was them out there who were acting so crazily. Santiago and Lester, what a pair!

Then came lunch in swimming trunks. It was less interesting then because Santiago and Lester began once again to worry about their bodies. Even though they ordered drinks, usually vodka tonics, they barely touched them. On the other hand, Bobby would always drink one more than he should have which triggered arguments with Rosemary, who could be a little overbearing at times. "Girlfriends are always like that," he thought. "My next one won't be a girlfriend, I'll do it like Santiago and Lester, why, of course, just like them." They kissed their girls, they laughed with their girls, but no promises, nothing like I'm going to miss you when I return to the United States, or nothing like I'm going to write you when I get back. On the other hand, Rosemary repeated over and over the bit about the importance of getting into the university, that it was time to start studying, that New Year's Day is over and the rest of his friends who graduated are madly preparing for entrance exams. Bobby tried to calm her down, over and over he explained to her Juan Lucas would take care of the matter, the whole thing was a question of pull, influence, but Rosemary kept insisting that he not drink another vodka and that he start studying right now. She definitely was starting to rub the wrong way.

Fortunately she didn't pester him in front of them; in fact, Rosemary did just fine when they were together, but she took advantage of those moments when the others would go to shower off. She drove him nuts while they rinsed off in order to return to the table sans that sticky feeling from the saltwater. Ah, that was clever! Somehow their towels would always fall into the shower and get sopping wet and, as they returned to their table in the dining room on the beach, they came in wringing them out, walking among the tables, straining their muscles to wring out their towels, muscles sticking out from the brute force they applied to the towels as they twisted them. "That's a good tactic," Bobby thought, watching them approach the table. "Everyone's watching them, admiring them, that's a good one." He began to understand that everything his brother and Lester did was based on strategy.

Basically, everything the two university campusites did was engineered for a purpose. But they were slaves to their schemes. Bobby began to take notice of it during their last days in Lima. Then he realized the package with all the pictures and orgies was a period that belonged to the past, and he thought perhaps his brother had sent it to him for the purpose of cutting himself off from all that mayhem; then he could totally dedicate himself to his physique and the art of tactics. Well, sure, that was the reason. He probably would end up like that some day in a few years, more likely several years. These guys got ahead of the game.

On the other hand, he still had a lot of time, lots of time, forever . . . to screw Sonia and a thousand more like her. Yes, yes, as soon as they returned to the United States he would go to visit Sonia. The bad part was while they were in Lima he was spending all the money Juan Lucas had given him for Christmas. When he thought about tactics and money, Juan Lucas came to mind. He, of course, was the king of tactics, but in the case of Juan Lucas the process itself had become part of the pleasure. In addition, he knew how to stand firm on things: control, tactics and pleasure had produced a man who at his age was twenty years younger. Shit, that's difficult! He had always thought that with money everything was within reach—women, orgies, and more women and, as it turns out, all that stuff that ages you—and one has to plan his pleasures . . . what a bunch of bullshit! Bobby ordered another vodka tonic and, fortunately, Rosemary didn't say anything because he would have told her to go to hell in front of Santiago and Lester who, at that moment, had finished squeezing their towels and had sat down to calculate lunch.

Happily they calculated less in the evenings; in fact, with Tonelada Samamé next to them there was no way they could calculate things. And that's why on New Year's Eve, when they had ended up blind drunk in a bar and were on their way back from a party in Ancón, they even ran off the highway in the Volvo with Tonelada in the back telling jokes with three women on top of him, while Santiago, Lester, and Bobby sat up front. They lost all sense of calculation and began to race dangerously with another car full of friends who were also returning to Lima from Ancón. Amid the laughter, Santiago barely managed to keep the steering wheel straight. The girls were yelling hysterically, We're gonna be killed! We're gonna be killed! but no one that night believed in death, especially Tonelada who initiated a long series of jokes about death, half in English and half in Spanish so the gringo could enjoy them too. At one moment, finally, Santiago realized the car was going off to one side, but just when Tonelada told the punch line of another joke and Santiago, who had daringly run red lights in the United States, felt a strange sensation of whatever it was and decided he preferred their laughter over danger and abandoned himself to his desire to veer off the road with all those people who were laughing in the car. The Volvo shot ahead like a bullet precisely when his friends' Chevrolet was flying by them. Their car stopped some six hundred feet up the road. They all jumped out and went running over to the nearby sand dunes lining the highway. "What happened? What happened?" they were yelling as they approached them in the dark, they had to be alive . . . The Volvo was still in one piece . . . that's quite a car! It had flown through the air, bounced several times on the sand, and ended up completely bogged down in it. The girls were crying and screaming hysterically. The ones who came in the Chevrolet heard them as they approached the Volvo, but when they got to them, the men had begun to laugh again, and Tonelada was inquiring if anybody was hurt and then asked if anyone there was Saint Peter. There was silence and confusion before Tonelada spoke again: "If no one is hurt and no one is Saint Peter, then nothing's happened! *Saint Peter!*" he translated for Lang, and the gringo began to laugh once more, while Santiago looked at Bobby out of the corner of his eye. But a second before he began to feel the sensation like he was his brother and he loved him dearly, he returned to that desire to fly again, with them all laughing, and he let the feeling dominate him again.

"Well," he said, opening the door, "tomorrow we'll get a tow truck to dig out the car . . . Let's get a ride back in the Chevy. Let's go, everyone!"

That was the best evening Bobby had ever experienced. The most expensive, too. That night he spent every last cent of his money, but who gives a damn! With Santiago next to him, he wasn't worried about a thing; only a little kid would go around worried about spending all of his money in one place. As soon as he started at the university he would ask for a checkbook like his brother. For now, stay with him, accept his invitations until he leaves, there's always Julius' piggy bank afterward, three or four sessions with Sonia, and then start studying: that's the plan! Santiago and Lester would be returning soon; since they had to be back in early January, there was very little time left. But at least tonight, at that bar, no one talked about trips to the United States but about other trips, yes, trips to glory! Trips to glory with Gloria!

Come to glory with Gloria
Cha Cha Cha
Come to glory with Gloria
Cha Cha Cha

The essence of the evening was in the refrain that the orchestra had just begun to play while the master of ceremonies announced the second show of the evening to those who were on a New Year's Eve binge and tried to awaken those who were either plastered or tipsy: the magnificent Gloria Symphony! and her in-ter-na-tion-ally famous Glooorioooo-sa Symphony Variety Show! There was some applause, but no one came out onstage and the orchestra had to start all over again with

Come to glory with Gloria
Cha Cha Cha
Come to glory with Gloria
Cha Cha Cha

No one came out because Tonelada had just gotten to the punch line of another joke, and poor Gloria Symphony, because the joke was excellent, she had just had seventeen whiskeys, and the judge had given custody of her son to the father, because on New Year's Eve last year she had shacked up, like any other night in Miami or Cali, with a gringo like the one over there in front of us, because she was good-looking and moved her rear end marvelously under Batista's regime, another seventeen whiskeys and Tonelada's joke, and a million other things, Gloria Symphony burst out laughing with such vehemence that her tears just about destroyed her makeup, and no matter how much they repeated the refrain to announce her debut, Come to glory with Gloria, she couldn't get up. The show girls pulled at her but nothing, the laughter fanned out through thousands of bars in her life, New Year's Eve was always the same, ha ha ha ha ha ha ha ha ha-aaaah . . . but Santiago reacted with indifference to the dramatic orgy of just another dancer.

Tonelada, on the other hand, went over to help her. "I'll be right back, honey," he said to the chorus girl who was admiring him as he stood up and went to help Gloria Symphony get to the stage amid applause and shouting from envious barflies who couldn't tolerate the idea that Tonelada was the one to take the dancing woman back to work. There was even more protest when he left her with the orchestra.

"He's as irritating as ever!" somebody said nearby.

"Yes," Tonelada responded, stopping for an instant and looking over to one side where someone had made the remark, "as a little kid I also had soldiers made of lead, but I didn't play with them, I ate them."

Tonelada's table let fly with laughter and a round of applause, while Bobby translated the rogue's witty response and Santiago and his friends spent money and let themselves be loved by the show girls. Tonelada came back and asked them to make room for him next to his damsel. "With you I'll have a new life, we'll be together until the end of the world," he said as he sat down next to her and she showered him with laughter and kisses. The maiden, the one for frolicking who promised a new life, was going to stay in Lima for a month. Tonelada had already looked her over: "She's mine," he thought. He had to treat her right, make her sentimental. Turning his back to the others, he cornered her, she became his date, face to face. "And you, how did you happen to get involved in this shameful business?" he asked her, adding whiskey to her glass and explaining to her it was important for him in his heart to know why.

"Girls, our number is next," the one with Lester exclaimed.

The girls had to change for the next set, they had to hurry, Ugh!, as they got up quickly and promised to return shortly. They headed toward the dressing rooms and, as they gyrated, those at the table, half-drunk by then, found themselves face-to-face with a row of rippling rear ends that rubbed up raucously against the side of the table and their glasses as they were leaving. "Carajo," exclaimed Lang IV, looking instantly at Santiago who then smiled at him as if to say yes, this is the time to use that word. "Wow, you're so scantily clad!" Tonelada yelled at them as they were leaving. Some of them turned around to blow him a kiss, but he was already absorbed with Gloria Symphony's movements, who was walking among the tables as she sang:

Come to glory with Gloria
Cha Cha Cha
Come to glory with Gloria
Cha Cha Cha

Cha Cha Cha is what she would whisper in the ears of the men whose wives were sitting next to them. "Good-looking whore," the women thought, smiling, friendly, and offended, as they squirmed in their chairs. They were uncomfortable because at first they felt superior, then all of a sudden they felt inferior. *Cha Cha Cha* pulled herself away from one husband and headed in the direction of another table, allowing his wife to readjust herself in her chair. But *Cha Cha Cha* was Gloria Symphony at another table, and at another, and another, disappearing finally toward the back until she got to where Tonelada was and yelled at her: "Get it on, honey!"

Come to glory with Gloria
Cha Cha Cha
Come to glory with Gloria

And while she was singing *Cha Cha Cha* and returning to the stage, she peeled off feathers, sheer nets, silks, and taffeta until there was nothing left but a thin strand on top and, on the bottom, a very tiny bright shell covered with silver sequins.

"That little glittering shell has caused her a lot of problems with the mayor's committee on morality," Tonelada commented.

"Absolutely barbaric," Santiago said, smiling.

"Those ladies over there who criticize these girls are members of . . ."

But Tonelada interrupted his lively clarification of who they were because at that instant the orchestra stopped playing and a Black bongo player jumped to his designated spot, practically mounting the bongo drum, and caressed it like a monkey with an enormous banana, announcing the mystery and danger of Haitian witch doctors with three deep, sonorous beats: pum, pum, pum! His drumbeats produced terrible consequences for Gloria Symphony's famous abdomen that twisted, shrank, gyrated, and shriveled up with each cruel beat; just a little bit the first time, a little more with the second one, then more with the third, and the whole area folded into itself around her navel and down below the bright shell flipped into a horizontal position and was being sucked toward her navel from the tension. A fourth beat almost destroyed her, she began to pull on her hair, now completely disheveled due to the pain. Her suffering was horrible, her face a death mask, she was dying, and she would have died but the bongo player knew how to pull her out of it after looking to the side behind the curtain at the naked chorus girls who waited in hiding for their turn, and after looking at Tonelada who was approaching the dance floor. The taboo drummer yelled UNO! and began to save the life of the trapped white woman with a series of rapid-fire, life-renewing drumbeats. It was as if he had eased her birth pangs, replacing them through a thousand continuous tiny lean beats with a crazy tickling sensation that ran like scurrying ants through the sequins adorning the shell. Gloria Symphony went into a frenzy, even the bongo player almost lost control, but at last she was free and right in front of all those ladies she expelled thousands of Haitian witch doctors from her navel, right there in the middle of Lima, and the immoral ones, the most wicked ones, began to bedevil the husbands, vexing them in their seats, making them sweat, almost making them follow with their necks her captivating movements, anticipating everything down to the whipping motion of the bongo player's arms, consumed by his uncontrolled beat that had already penetrated the black secret of nocturnal life. And now, emaciated, disillusioned, incredulous, and professional, they became a continuous undefined beat that sought to bring her back into the world that was paying her to contort herself that way. But she didn't stop there, and he had to beat his drum to a new rhythm: hers. This time, however, she tortured herself disgustingly: the more lurid it got, the more scandalous it became; the more scandalous it got, the more they paid her; and the more they paid her, the more money she had to pay for a decent school run by priests for her son; she wanted to sweat out a law career for her son, but they didn't let her stop, there were catcalls, a new burst of taboo drumbeats, first with his elbow, then with his hand, hands and elbows, elbow and elbow, two elbow beats, the bongo player knew them all, he had trapped her in his rhythm, bringing her around: tun-tun . . . tun-tun . . . tun-tun tun-tun tun-tun tun-tun tun-tun tun-tun tun-tun tun-tun tun-tun, tun-tun-tac tun-tun-tac tun-tun-tac, tun-tun tun-tun tun-tun tun-tun, tun-tun-tac-tac, tac-tac tac-tac, tac-tactac-tac-tun tun tun, and Gloria Symphony fell dead, she died amid the applause, soaked in sweat, and amid Tonelada's horselaugh as he stood there, applauding with the others the drummer's performance who dismounted from his enormous banana and went over to lift her up and, together, acknowledge the applause and the insolent shouting of loaded and looped spectators. Some of the wives thought that was the end of it because they hadn't seen the others who were waiting, for as soon as the bongo player and the sinner left the stage, the girls for the next number came out brazenly and the husbands, because it was New Year's and because they were drunk, ordered more bottles of whiskey; by then there was no way to stop them: they wanted to drink more and more, they wanted to see the whole show, every bit of the glorious Symphony, right down to the last naked fanny. Gloria Symphony had already gone, leaving in place the full complement of the diabolic sorority of the wanton navel.

Undoubtedly, it had to be the best night ever for Bobby and now, he woke up with the image of the announcer appearing before his eyes yelling "A glorious finale with all the girls!" and then the image of Tonelada offering them drinks that he had helped prepare and ordering, at the same time, dozens of taxis to take all of them to his apartment. Bobby saw that his alarm clock on the night table was showing four o'clock in the afternoon and he smiled as he remembered Santiago and Lester throwing their calculations and tactics out the window in order to surrender to wantonness, noise, and partying, and Tonelada yelling "Orgy time!" as he opened new bottles of booze. That's when everything went wrong for Bobby; the malaise brought on by a horrible hangover was enough to tell him he was quite awake and it was useless to try to go back to sleep. He put on his robe and went downstairs slowly, where he ordered four Alka-Seltzers and four cold Cokes to be taken to the poolside. He wanted everything put on a serving tray, everything put all together next to the edge of the pool while he floated around, reviving himself, hoping to find in the cold water the necessary sedative for his afflicted head and fatigued body. He got angry when he ran into Santiago and Lester, who were casually reading magazines with a cheerful smile under their huge dark glasses, stretched out in two lawn chairs, not showing any indication of a hangover. There wasn't any doubt in his mind that they had participated fully in the orgy, but they had calculated everything, avoiding excesses; they had gotten up a bit later than usual today, nixed doing weights because it was New Year's Day, but that was all. Bobby dove into the water and he felt better. "Bah!" he smiled, I've got a lot of time on my hands and, in any case, I'm better off than Tonelada because he doesn't have a pool at his apartment. He swam leisurely.

Bobby would never experience another night like that again in his life. Everything had returned to normal, the weights, the beach, the Casino in Ancón, the obscure dancing spots. Once or twice he had hoped they could repeat that night, above all when he saw Tonelada appear in the Saratoga Bar or at Freddy Solo's, but nothing was happening: just laughter, whiskeys, and decent girls. No one ever talked about the girls they had New Year's Eve or Gloria Symphony and Company. Nevertheless Bobby had made plans: as soon as he got into the university and they turned the Volvo over to him, he would go looking for Tonelada. He knew where to find him, and the rogue had even invited him for drinks sometime. It was just a matter of two or three months of quarantine to get ready for exams, but no need to worry about that right now, he still had two or three more days with Santiago and Lester.

Those two or three days turned into a few weeks. There was a lot of talk about the United States and what life was like there, but they kept postponing their return. Classes had begun at the university, but they didn't budge an inch. Miss Decisive mentioned it to Julius: "Those young men are lazy," she told him. "It's the Señores' responsibility as parents of one of them and as intimate friends that they say they are of the parents of the other, it's their responsibility to tell them it's time to return to his friend's country." Julius took the matter very seriously and went around giving Juan Lucas and Susan funny looks whenever the visitors would show up in the dining room or the summer bar, two great places for family reunions. But neither Juan Lucas nor Susan said a word; on the contrary, they didn't get involved at all: they were pleased that the two of them had stayed on. "The advantages of being the oldest," thought Bobby. As far as Julius was concerned, he remembered that he started school a year late and, in addition, went straight to preparatory school, which prevented him from going to kindergarten that, according to a book he had just finished reading, was the most wonderful period in every child's life . . . Deci was right: Susan and Juan were not meeting their responsibilities.

The truth was that the Christmas visitors were staying on and Bobby had no choice but to abandon them and go into seclusion in order to study. Based on Susana's telephone recommendations, different tutors came to teach their son every subject possible. They were doing a superb job getting her son, Pipo, ready for the exam and promised he would score highly and become the top student. With all her praying, it just couldn't be any other way. Susan should do the same: pray, pray, pray, but Susan couldn't think about anything but hanging up on her, and she did finally. But dozens of tutors came to teach any and everything. Bobby confined himself to his room and became the most pitied person in the mansion. Everyone felt sorry for him when they saw him go down to the dining room in the evenings, dead tired but still having to finish several trigonometry problems before going to bed. Meanwhile, the visitors remained in Lima and no one had even asked them if their extended stay was going to affect their studies in the United States. One day Santiago explained that once they were back it would be easy to pick up the classes they had missed; what he didn't explain was why they were staying longer and longer in Lima. Susan, however, had already suspected something. One afternoon she had gone to Welch Jewelers in order to buy a watch for Julius, for he was going to turn eleven, and the manager told her her son had just been in with a North American friend and they had purchased a beautiful platinum ring.

But Susan didn't dare poke around in the affairs of the mastodons, and she never found out the rest of the story; she didn't even find out that it was Lester who had bought the ring for a girl. She did sense, however, a feeling of tension around the house and mistakenly attributed it to a series of arguments between Bobby and Julius: something about a piggy bank, but she didn't even realize it had been the same argument every night. Finally, Julius asked her one day if she still had the key to the piggy bank safely stored in the safe. He left feeling reassured when she said yes. The next day Bobby asked Juan Lucas for money, but he had just lost a golf tournament by one stroke and said he wouldn't get a cent until he was accepted into the university. Bobby tried to get some money out of Santiago, but he only smiled and repeated what Juan Lucas had said. Then he tried Lester and Lester told him in English to go to hell. His yelling could be heard all over the first floor of the mansion. Juan Lucas wasn't around, but Susan heard the furious explosion of their visitor: how strange of him because he had been so easygoing and seemed incapable of such behavior. Susan remembered the story involving the ring, but since she didn't dare poke around in the affairs of the mastodons, she never found out the rest of the story.

At least not at the time she didn't; however, she noted the tension was growing. The arguments between Bobby and Julius started up again and with greater intensity than before. He was turning eleven and was about to finish grade school, but Julius had been acting twice his age lately. He went around cussing here and there to the point that Susan felt obliged to tell Carlos not to teach him any more words, even though he would probably keep asking him over and over again what this and that meant. But Julius would say who gives a shit! He already knew what screw meant and he felt like he was on par with his brother. Bobby was something else: he was becoming more violent every day, poor thing, all that studying was going to drive him crazy. For the moment he had cussed out the chemistry tutor whom his aunt Susana had recommended. But that didn't eliminate the tension. That afternoon Lester came in acting very nervous and his shirt had been torn to shreds; fortunately they hadn't beat his face in or anything like that. He had survived the ordeal but they had to give him a sedative because he was running from one room to the other like a crazy man, yelling *Finished! Finished! Finished! Never more! The end! Finished!* Everybody knew what he was saying but no one understood why. "The end of what?" Julius asked himself. "The end of what?" He soon found out it was the end of their stay in Lima and, while Lester downed a sedative, Santiago called the airline company on the telephone. They were leaving tomorrow night.

Two hours later, Lester, who was still feeling the effects of the sedative, explained to Susan and Juan Lucas it was time to return and his visit to Lima had been absolutely fantastic. Susan preferred not to ask about the torn shirt, although it wasn't difficult to surmise the famous ring had something to do with the affair. Santiago told them they were going out that evening to have a few drinks with some friends to say good-bye. Everyone thought it was a splendid idea. What was remaining to be seen was whether Juan Lucas would accept Bobby's proposal. What was it? It was very simple and made sense: Bobby wanted to go out with them. He needed a change of environment, he had been holed up for weeks now, one night out wouldn't hurt anything, what better opportunity than his brother's good-bye party? Santiago smiled as if to say if you want to come, fine, it's all the same to me, I'm not going to cry just because I'm going away for a year or two. Bobby kept insisting and Juan Lucas, who had just gotten revenge against the golfer who had beaten him last year, said he could go out but just for one night. "Now you're happy," Santiago thought, looking at his brother, not expecting his reaction. Bobby didn't smile or show any enthusiasm, but preferred to wait for the evening in order to smile. He also had his tactics, too, for Bobby caught on quickly.

"No, I'm NOT going with you guys, I've got the station wagon."

"What do you mean, you're not going with us?" Santiago asked.

Lester didn't understand the two brothers' conversation. Bobby explained to him in English, "I'm sorry," he told him, "but I've got a woman waiting for me; she's been waiting all this time and this is the only opportunity I have to see her." Santiago was curious.

"What do you mean you've got the station wagon?"

"It's simple: I told Juan Lucas you guys would probably come back late and I didn't want to; the obvious thing to do was to let me use the station wagon and I could come home sooner if necessary and get up early to study."

"Good idea . . ."

"He also gave me some money; not a lot, but it's enough for tonight."

"Fine," Santiago said, "See you later . . ."

"Later . . ."

While Santiago gave him a shallow smile, Bobby smiled back with that same lifeless look. Their smiles widened when each one of them turned around to get into their respective cars, looking at each other for an instant with that hollow gaze while they turned around, a second was all it took for them to seal an eternal pact of indifference: the two of them were the inheritors of an immense fortune.

And while Bobby took off to screw Sonia once and for all and to reassure himself that it was her, Santiago and Lester parked casually in front of Freddy Solo's Bar, where they had agreed to meet some friends. But not Tonelada. No way. At least not while Lester was still in Lima.

"But I'm so charming," the rogue claimed, leaning against the bar at Freddy Solo's, surrounded by women who were splitting from laughter over the stories that he had invented.

"Why do they want to get rid of me? Am I not charming?"

"You're alluring," one of them said.

"Yeah, but don't come too close to me," the other said.

"Poor Tone!" Piba exclaimed. "No one pays any attention to him!"

"Until your eyes return to their sockets!"

"There's Santiago with Lester," Piba announced all of a sudden, watching them come in and go over to the bar.

"I'm out of here! That gringo punches like Viceroy . . . they've got them well trained up there in Texas. This isn't for me, Señoritas . . . it's time for the gentleman to mosey on."

"Don't be silly!" Piba exclaimed. "They're already quietly sitting down over there with their friends; moreover he saw you, so there's nothing to worry about . . ."

Nothing to worry about because Santiago grabbed him as soon as he opened the door and saw the other one sitting over in front; nothing to worry about because Lester still had three sedatives in his body that he had taken that afternoon; nothing to worry about because it was their last night in Lima and he wasn't going to spend it fighting. Santiago greeted Tonelada with a smile while he examined Lester out of the corner of his eye: he seemed unflappable, and he had just ordered several whiskeys and talked as he smiled with their friends who had already arrived.

Their friends kept arriving and more requests for whiskey was the order of the day. As usual, Santiago didn't drink much; Lester, on the other hand, knocked them back one after another as never before. He was ready to start another fight like that afternoon, especially if Tonelada stayed there, sitting in front of them at the other side of the U-shaped bar, and with all that laughter too. To top it off, there's the problem of the language: Lester didn't understand one iota about what was being said there, and he probably thought that the rogue was laughing at him, who knows? what with everything he had told him . . . nevertheless, the booze didn't excite the North American traveler; it just made him sad, and he talked less and less with their friends, practically limiting himself to ordering and offering more whiskey, while his sadness became more and more pitiful . . .

"*Incredible!*" he exclaimed, all of a sudden, as his head fell forward.

"What?" Santiago asked him.

"*Incredible!*" he repeated, burying his head even further.

He only raised his head in order to pick up his glass and order more. He repeated *incredible* once again about half an hour later. Santiago interrupted his conversation with the person next to him, but when he looked over at him, Lester had buried his head even further, falling into a dark pit that he had created, drink after drink, between the bar counter and himself. He still hadn't fallen off the bar stool. He was sliding down little by little, then a memory, another whiskey, try to create an even larger dark pit for himself, but the colors of the counter, his shirt, and his tie, kept filtering through his blindness, preventing him from collapsing into darkness. He wanted to close off his sad world, enter it, envelope himself in it, spend some time inside it, alone, but the music in the bar and some stupid laughter slammed into his world and he still hadn't sufficiently emptied it of his lifeless gaze. He still ran into them as he slipped on the steps of his binge, they kept filtering into his world among his deafening whiskeys, preventing him from silencing his obscurity and disappearing once and for all into the black pit of his memories. He would have brought it about, Lester was about to fall, when a sudden push knocked him off without recourse into a terribly bitter state of despair . . . when he turned around spinning to get up to one side feeling nauseated, defying the laws of gravity and in a second losing his newly created environment, to the point that his obscure world broke apart and filled up with a thousand gyrating, flashing lights, leaving only a few black spots where he could rest between two dizzy moments. But, little by little, coming to grips with himself, and tricking one by one each of the thousand little colors, Lester managed to invoke a burst of enormous energy that allowed him to get up in a bolt and avoid in that way another pirouette on the frantic merry-go-round, perceiving that the stool was in a vertical position now and taking advantage of the moment to grab his glass with both hands, holding it tight until, finally, the bartender relaxed at his post, moving only when it was necessary to serve the customers . . .

"Whiskey," he ordered.

He thought he could let go of his axis and a feeling of vomit dammed up inside him, so he grabbed onto the glass again and stood there clutching it until he descried Tonelada at a distance behind the bartender; his whole body went into contraction in order to pulverize him with a certain look, and then he felt like he had managed to control himself for a brief moment, and he meditated, looked savagely at Tonelada, insulted him with his eyes to the point finally that his throat was free of a bitter saliva, and he began to let go of the glass again, little by little, while a feeling of nausea dissipated itself and the rogue, over there in front of him, lowered his eyes.

And his voice. Tonelada lowered his voice a bit when he noticed that Lester was staring at him with hatred. He slowly finished telling his story as best he could, a little nervous, calculating. Lester orders another whiskey, Santiago intervenes, he insists, they give it to him . . . Tonelada initiates another story, this time more slowly, because he didn't know how Lester was going to react with another whiskey, and the girls had to rub up against him in order to hear the details. It was a fabulous story: How? How? they asked him. Louder! I can't hear you! . . . And they stuck a bowling pin up his ass! Tonelada concluded, raising his voice and guffawing while Lester, right in front of him, positioned his glass exactly on top of the ashtray, inclining his head a little bit, hanging it forward as if he were going to touch his navel with his nose, but the elegant, fresh leather padding of the bar counter stopped him. This time nothing filtered into his world. He bundled himself in darkness . . .

"Ah no! No, I don't believe it!" Piba exclaimed. "Put it away right now!"

"You see! . . . What did I tell you? My little friend has her heart . . ."

"Tonelada: put it away or I'm leaving . . . How can you be such a coward!"

But Tonelada insisted upon dancing his little finger elatedly in front of the girls' eyes, he waved his little finger back and forth in front of their noses, for it was embellished with a platinum ring that he had taken out of his pocket. Piba saw him hide it when Lester came in. She really got mad.

"How can you be so cynical?"

"Don't you see? . . . Didn't I tell you? . . . The more they drink the more righteous they become."

But his face was hurting him and he didn't have any desire to respect morality tonight. To hell with that! He wanted to tell jokes, make fun of everything . . . anything. And they knew Piba, with her problems, she's my friend . . . what more can you ask for than an affair on Christmas Eve? . . . do you want me to tell you a little secret? . . . nothing happened this Christmas Eve either . . . She wasn't with anyone . . ."

"Revolting!"

The others weren't even aware of the row over the ring but Piba, having already imbibed several whiskeys, had seized upon a sense of morality that had occurred to her unexpectedly and her eyes filled with tears. Tonelada tried to embrace her but she slipped out from under his arm.

"Revolting! Revolting!" Piba knew the whole story involving the ring.

"Your group is a little too noisy . . . Please, Señorita . . ."

Ugh! Why did she get started on this? Piba gulped down her drink and screamed out her accusation: no one would ever see her with Tonelada again! . . . they would never see her with him again! . . . there's a limit to everything! . . . Delfinita had become Saint Ursula! . . . prettier, nicer wasn't possible! . . . she was her cousin as well! . . . and this revolting bastard! . . . this revolting person finds out that her father is going to distribute some Argentine films! . . . they are going to inaugurate a new movie theater for his films! . . . they are going to bring in famous artists for the inauguration! . . . there's going to be parties! . . . cocktails, of course! . . . revolting!"

"Señorita Piba . . ."

"This revolting dolt still doesn't have one movie star on his list! . . . and how much money could that mean? . . . No wonder you disappeared, you revolting! . . . you didn't want to be seen with my cousin! . . . not even with me! . . . she got him invitations to everything! Take your arm off of me! Don't touch me you filthy bastard! . . . You know who that ring belongs to! You don't know? You don't know? No one comes to mind? Let go of me, you scoundrel! You crook!"

"I only stole her heart," Tonelada intervened, trying to save himself with the other girls' laughter, but the others had become a little concerned, despite the music that could be heard throughout the bar.

"Con artist! When are you going to jilt Delfinita? Tell me! When? Tell me, thief!"

"Señorita . . ."

"Tell him! Tell him! He's a crook! A scoundrel!"

"As soon as she gets drunk she starts to offend me."

Piba began crying because she really loved Tonelada. "She's loonier than a loon," Santiago thought, who had been watching the scene with a smile, seeing that all of a sudden Piba cried on Tonelada's shoulder, kissing him on his swollen eyes, his split eyebrows, and his cut lips. "Scoundrel! scoundrel!" she yelled at him, burying her face into his chest.

"A round of whiskeys," Tonelada ordered, pulling out a wad of money rolled up under his finger with the ring and handing it to the bartender before he could ask who is paying.

Lester felt an arm around his back and he shrugged his shoulders so they would let go of him and leave him be. He thought it might be Santiago and he tried to pull himself together, but the weight of his head pulled him down and he ended up once again leaning his head against the soft rim of the bar counter.

"An Alka-Seltzer," Santiago ordered.

"No Alka-Seltzer," Lester murmured, trying to explain that it had been the sedatives and asking them to leave him alone for a little while longer.

"What shall we do?" Santiago asked his friends, "I really don't want to take him home like this."

"Hey!" Bobby blurted out suddenly. No one had seen him arrive. He was displaying a face of pure satisfaction. "What's wrong with Lester?" he asked.

"You've got to help me get him out of here; he's like a corpse. It would be best for him to sleep it off somewhere for a while before we take him home."

"In the station wagon. The seat converts into a bed."

"Good idea . . . Let's wait a little longer and if he doesn't come around, you can help me."

It wasn't necessary. He pulled himself together on his own, little by little, very slowly. In addition, he hadn't been sleeping. Down there below, in his obscure world, Lester had not stopped fighting against the nauseating vertigo that accompanied his spinning and never-ending arrival at Delfina's house. He arrived and gave her the ring a bunch of times; a bunch of times he arrived at her house and would spend the afternoon with her, holding her hand and feeling the cold ring on her finger, while her father, on some afternoons, would talk to him about future contracts for distributing North American movies and he seriously thought about the possibilities of putting him in contact with his father. Then came the afternoon of the cockfights at Delfina's ranch and his mocking smile of how easy it was for Peruvian girls to say *I love you,* especially to him for he had never heard anything more than *I like you!* How easy it was for her during the cockfights to say how much I love you, *I love you,* she translated for him in case he didn't understand, for he had never heard anyone say more than I like you and who until that afternoon, an afternoon after the cockfight, he had never felt anything more than *I like you* and all of a sudden he found himself saying *I love you,* when Delfinita appears with a gift, two silver cocks, and he felt like he loved her and he told her so and he started to love her like crazy . . . "*Stupid idiot, stupid idiot,*" Santiago heard him blurt out, turning to see him slowly incorporate himself and how he fell onto the edge of the bar . . . and then he clearly saw the other afternoons on the beach at Ancón, at a party one night, everything had just happened, last night's party . . . "*Stupid idiot,*" he blurted out trying to straighten up just as he realized, just remembering now that only he had said *I love you* last night, and in an instant he danced the whole night through with Delfinita, dance after dance, while he straightened up realizing that it was an evening in which she never told him . . . He invited her to dance again, he turned to say good night at the end of the dance, "*Stu-*

pid idiot," he blurted out once again, straightening up a little more when he noticed that she was acting strange and seemed nervous, similar to this afternoon when he rang her doorbell and she opened the door of the garden herself, she looked strange and seemed nervous; then he noticed why the butler was absent, and she wasn't wearing the ring either, "*Stupid idiot! Stupid idiot! . . .*" Only then did he begin to understand what had happened this afternoon . . . "*Stupid idiot!*" He felt the rage of the afternoon in his body and through her the entire afternoon filtered into his black world, making him straighten up a little more, but he bent over again in order to enter into her garden where Delfina received him in order not to tell you that I love you but only I like you, and adding but . . . "*Stupid stupid idiot!*" he had told her I love you, noting she seemed strange and nervous, and just then Tonelada appeared at the corner of the garden, smiling, cocky, a coward in English, backing up, explaining, moving away from him, bending down, I lost my locket in the grass, but it was to pick up a stick and Lester pounced on him, managing finally to lean against the bar with both hands . . . He ground his teeth, punch after punch, with his teeth grinding away furiously, straightening up, the same as in the garden when a feeling of fatigue stimulated him to leave, getting up tense, and looking at Tonelada a little longer, prostrated on the ground, his face destroyed, there in front of him.

Moments later Lester slept peacefully in the bed of the Mercury, parked in front of Freddy Solo's Bar. A little further away, Santiago and Bobby were in the Volvo waiting for time to pass, half-asleep, nodding sometimes but trying constantly to find some topic of conversation that would prevent them from going to sleep. At about five o'clock in the morning they saw Tonelada leave, tottering and doing everything possible to keep Piba from falling flat on her face. Finally they got into a taxi and disappeared. Santiago took advantage of the moment to explain to his brother what had happened between his friend and the rogue. Bobby didn't say anything in response. There was a brief moment when Bobby was tempted to tell Santiago about his happy adventure at Nanette's, but he was afraid that he would belittle him for still getting involved with whores, so he kept quiet.

"Let's go for a ride," Santiago said, starting the motor of the Volvo.

"Not too long . . . it's starting to get light out."

"What else can I do if Lester isn't coming around?"

They returned at seven o'clock in the morning to wake him up. It wasn't difficult. One thing for sure, the poor guy felt horrible and he didn't stop complaining about it until he became convinced he had already slept several hours and at home they would fix him a good breakfast so he could go back to bed and sleep some more. Santiago got into the station wagon and told Bobby to drive the Volvo.

It was almost eight o'clock by the time they reached the mansion, blowing their horns at the gate. Universo, who was always there early watering, opened the exterior door immediately, and Bobby and Santiago had to steer with care in order to keep from hitting Julius who was coming out from one side on his bicycle. Because they turned to look at Julius, neither looked to the right and they almost mowed down a horrible-looking woman who signified for Lester, as he stared out the window, an extension of the ghastly malaise that inhibited him from going back to sleep.

THE WOMAN, ON the other hand, smiled at them and it was only afterward, when the station wagon had pulled up inside, that she became a little confused, thinking that the young blond man couldn't be one of the children. Bobby pulled up in the Volvo behind them, but she couldn't see very well because Universo confused her even more when he prevented her from entering the grounds. They stood outside arguing for quite a while. Universo wanted to know who Nilda was and Nilda wanted to know who Universo was. Both of them felt they had the right to question the other. Nilda had always considered herself the family cook and she didn't see any difference between the old mansion and the new one; the only problem was that all of her declarations were based on the old mansion and in Universo's case, who had never been the gardener there, the only mansion that existed for him was the new one. As a result, the one wasn't the gardener and the other wasn't the cook. Nilda became very insolent and she told him she hadn't come to visit him but young Julius; however, her declaration only served to complicate matters because, according to Universo, Julius had just left right in front of their eyes and, consequently, she didn't know who Julius was nor did he know who she was. Nilda yelled at him with a mouth full of gold and Universo answered back in like fashion with a mouth full of cavities and one or two gold teeth. They were fierce with each other: the carriage, according to Nilda, was very old and, according to Universo, it was brand new; they couldn't agree on anything and the worst part was that they were attacking each other personally, being offensive and showing lack of respect for each other. Each time they got further and further away from the original point until they ended up arguing about who had been disrespectful first. Universo accused her of saying Indians were stubborn, just like mules, and Nilda, after yelling at him that it wasn't true, counterattacked by declaring he had first called her an intruder and had accused her of trying to get into the mansion, probably to steal. They were close to fisticuffs from so much yelling and insults when Carlos, very pleased with himself, arrived to go to work and greeted Nilda as if she had never been gone. Nilda leaped up to embrace him and, at the same time, to make the dumb Andean realize that she was practically a member of the family. Then she accused Universo, and Carlos, smiling, asked him who appointed him sentinel. "You stick to your hose and those Indian songs," he told him, completely winning over Nilda who fell into his arms again, this time to tell him that her child had died of typhoid, or whatever it's called, in Madre de Dios province.

Carlos invited her into the kitchen, where he filled her in on everything that had happened since her departure. Celso and Daniel came in to say hello and they invited her for breakfast, while she talked about her life during the last few months. She talked nonstop, intermingling every story with the one about the death of her son; she would no sooner mention him than she would start crying out loud. She had them completely confused with so much calamity. Everything had gone wrong for her since she had left the family. No one wanted to hire her with a sick child and, finally, she decided to return home. But it wasn't any better there either, her child got worse, the climate, the water, who knows what had messed up his little tummy. After a week there, the boy began to cry: first at night and then during the day, until the poor creature ended up crying all day and all night long, poor thing, he didn't know how to say what was the matter, she's sure the doctor killed him with some bitter medicines that he had prescribed. Nilda began to cry once more and no one there knew what to do.

That's the way Miss Decisive found them when she came in asking if Julius had returned yet. All it took for Nilda's sobbing to become a wide, happy smile was to hear Julius' name. Celso introduced her as the old cook and the other as the new servant. Miss Decisive puffed up as she approached Nilda bruskly preventing her from getting up to say hello. They greeted each other in a strange way. Nilda said something and Miss Decisive responded with two even more complicated formalities which forced the other to drop her gaze as a way of recognizing the other's greater height, volume, and primary school certificate. Miss Decisive immediately asked if they had served breakfast to the Señora. Celso and Daniel said yes, of course they did, but since she was always right, she yelled at them asking them why were they not offering her another cup of tea. Nilda appreciated her kindness and began to tell her a thousand things about Julius. The butlers were fascinated, so they served up more tea and offered more bread. They also had their stories, memories, and their own versions to boot. Nilda let them interrupt her, she listened to them patiently, but she always provided the final and correct version of each story. Meanwhile, Miss Decisive ate her breakfast in silence, listening with envy to the stories about a time that was completely alien to her and which prevented her from giving an opinion and showing that she was right. And the other ones really got into it, too! And Carlos intervened, adding anecdotes they didn't know about because they had occurred outside the mansion, during those many occasions when he would take Julius to school, to a birthday party, or to a friend's house. Little by little the stories became intermingled and got longer. Their memories were abundant and emotional. Nilda talked and listened with big round eyes. Cinthia's name sparked one story she remembered and she just about dropped her cup when she started to cry: "Little Cinthia, little Cinthia," she sighed. But that memory triggered other stories about Julius' first meals in the little dining room that was decorated with famous animals, and Nilda picked up her cup and smiled happily until, God only knows why, the story about Bertha combing Cinthia was told, and the poor girl just about threw the cup down in order to prevent the sobs inside her from popping her eyes out or killing her like a swift blow to the back of the head. Carlos understood the way Nilda felt and decided to tell stories only involving Julius. Celso offered more tea and everyone there became chipper again. Everyone accepted another cup of tea except Miss Decisive, because she had gotten tired of not being able to participate in the conversation. "The past always seems better than the present," she blurted out all of a sudden, but it wasn't very successful because, instead of admiring her for her education, they agreed conveniently to continue with even greater enthusiasm their evocations of the past that they, in effect, thought were better. Like a chatterbox, Nilda dominated the conversation, continuing to repeat again and again the same story about Julius' childhood, he had always been a good boy, he had always behaved properly with his brothers, to think he was becoming a young man, to think he was about to turn eleven, she would always remember his birthdays, she had never forgotten, he'll turn eleven next week, ah! . . . she was there when he was born, she was the one who straightened out his ears . . . in a week he'd be eleven years old, but in a week she would be working and wouldn't be able to come, she had finally found work in Lima, now it was much easier, now that her son had died, that's the way people are . . . And while she cried once again, she opened a ragged cloth bag from which she took out a little brown paper bag; she had some little chickens and she was bringing six eggs her little chickens had laid for Julius' birthday in the name of her son . . . And she began to bawl like crazy, while everyone began to offer her more tea, more bread, more butter, Miss Decisive's animosity toward her disappeared and she ran out to get some marmalade, the same brand that the Señora eats, little Julius should be back any moment now, he's been going out bike riding every morning before breakfast, the Señor makes him do it. Little Julius should be back at any moment . . .

BUT JULIUS DIDN'T return. Sitting in the back seat of the station wagon with Bobby next to him, Julius made an effort to contain his anger, that infuriating, violent timidness that had welled up inside him upon re- membering Nilda this morning, as she took out the bag of eggs that she had brought for his birthday. It was that same uncontrollable shyness that stopped him from entering the kitchen when he had returned se- renely and encountered that horrible woman Nilda waiting for him to return. He couldn't go in. He simply couldn't go in and, now, while returning from the airport, the unexpected scene that had occurred that morning kept repeating itself in his mind. He was beside himself, his hands trembled, reducing everything else to singular unimportance that didn't have anything to do with that instant when he saw her sitting there, crying, erasing any feeling of sorrow that he normally would have felt with Santiago's new departure. Everyone was sad as they returned home, at least they were all silent and submerged in their own thoughts. Susan, lovely, silent, inattentive or sad, accepted Juan Lucas' proposal: Let's drop the kids off at home and go out for dinner. Juan Lucas stopped the station wagon at a traffic light; he hated stop lights because he never knew what to say while they waited for the light to change, because he didn't have anything to say while the light changed to green; in reality, the airport scene filtered through his impatient emptiness: Good-bye, kid, good luck, write us. All of a sudden he felt sad, loving him as if he were his son, coughing abruptly so as not to feel sadness in his throat. Why don't we leave the kids at home and go out to eat? . . . green light. Susan agreed with anything, yes, darling, good idea. She stuck her arm out the window of the speeding station wagon, stretching it out in order to feel the warm breeze of the summer night. She looked at her hand out there and, between her fingers that expanded out into a fan, she could see the lights of the houses rushing by. Suddenly she pulled her arm inside, preventing it from rising in the air like an airplane, yes, darling, good idea. She turned around to the back to tell Bobby, apologetically, that it would be better if he didn't go with them because she and Juan Lucas would be returning late that evening and he had to get up early to study. She finished talking to Bobby and discovered Julius, and what kind of an excuse would she give him? Turning around calmly as she saw he was completely distracted, like at the airport, and remembering he had hardly said good-bye to Santiago or Lester, she didn't pursue the matter because she was distracted by the lights of the houses in San Isidro, one after another, looking upward the buildings hid the sky but then an open lot, a missing house darkened that spot in the night, a falling star that disappeared instantly, like her hand a few moments ago embraced by the warm wind like the airplane that just left, yes darling, where are you taking me? Juan Lucas coughed in order to avoid getting choked up and stopped happily at the next red light, thinking about Lester: tell your father we're expecting them to come in October, I'll have Briceño here, the bullfighter of the century! In October! Don't forget to tell him, good-bye kid, good luck. See you soon! Ha ha! He turned to Susan: I know where I'm taking you, dear. It's going to be something special! Susan asked him where, darling? but the green light was a signal to start going, make the motor roar, and not have to answer her, keep quiet, ha ha, let her look at me with that pretty look of curiosity. Susan closed the window, she wanted to put her arm out again but she closed the window as she turned to look at Julius in order to forget about airplanes and remember that she didn't have anything to say to him. Julius turned away and found himself entering the kitchen, stopping suddenly when he saw Nilda, stepping backward and retreating when he saw her crying as she put the eggs on the table. No one had seen him enter the mansion, no one saw him collide with the invincible, sudden shyness, no one saw him see her looking horrible, crying, yelling, my dead son! no one saw him leave, jump backward, become upset, and hide behind the door in order to listen . . .

"Have some marmalade, Señora Nilda. English marmalade . . . Have some, Señora . . . little Julius will be back shortly, he rides his bicycle for a while before breakfast, orders from Don Juan Lucas . . ."

"Thank you, Señorita, don't you want some too? I hope little Julius comes soon, I always remember his birthday, he's going to be eleven, a young man, do you remember when he would play like he was shooting from the carriage? . . . Do you remember when he used to play with Vilma? . . . excuse me, I didn't want to talk about her, it's better not to . . ."

Julius quickly opened the car window, stuck his head out, but even out there, in the dark warm air, Vilma was still a whore, and worse yet a low-class whore, like Nilda had said that morning, even low-class, that was the bad part, the worst part. He closed the window and remained calm and quiet, as if nothing had happened. He's Susan's son, and she was married to Juan Lucas; he's Bobby's brother, returning from saying good-bye to his brother Santiago who studies in the United States and who had just left with his friend Lester; he's returning from saying good-bye to them and now speeding along Javier Prado Avenue in the Mercury station wagon. Look at me, nothing's happening, absolutely nothing. Only that Vilma is a worse whore now than when he had just opened the window, much worse than this morning: this morning when he felt for the first time that a huge balloon, expanding to a frightening enormous size, kept getting bigger as it followed him out of the kitchen . . .

"I ran into her on the street, all dressed up, boy, young Vilma was as beautiful as ever . . . and very arrogant . . . I was friendly . . . of course, I didn't even know . . . although so much perfume, Vilma seemed different, something made me suspicious, even the way she walked . . . I was friendly with her and she acted snooty from the beginning . . . And she talked dirty, she was crass, she became insolent and aggressive, mocking the fact that one is poor yet honest . . . and just like nothing, she blurts out that she's a call girl in a whorehouse in La Victoria . . . "

Perhaps if I had reacted . . . What for? From the moment she mentioned her name, from the moment she lowered her head, I knew it, *I'll tell who I'm going to screw tonight* . . . Julius controlled his rage, restrained his arms that were about to let loose a thousand punches at Bobby, seated detestably next to the other window of the car. He didn't realize it, nor did anyone in the front seat, neither Susan nor Juan Lucas, both of whom were immersed in their own little worlds. Julius took advantage of that quiet moment to stay calm: he's Susan's son, and she was married to Juan Lucas; he's Bobby's brother, returning from saying good-bye to his brother Santiago; and now he's arriving home at last . . . But as soon as he had calmly finished summarizing his existence, he added one last final effort: I'm alive, my name is Julius, I haven't punched out Bobby, absolutely nothing has happened, as soon as he remembered he was an eleven-year-old boy who was finishing primary school this year and was returning coolly from the airport and nothing else, Vilma was even a bigger whore, as if the enormous, monstrous balloon had kept getting bigger to the point of consuming the mansion and then chasing it along the streets of San Isidro, into Miraflores, through Lima, and out into the whole world, as if he had to continue to try to escape from it, if he continued opening windows and finding it there outside, even bigger yet, much bigger than this morning when he left the kitchen and ran to hide in a bathroom where Vilma swelled into even a bigger whore, while the balloon squashed him against the walls, against the cold water faucet of the shower, where Vilma was a bloated whore, and then escaping to the swimming pool, diving in to swim as fast as he could, don't look with his head underwater, not hearing anything, not seeing anything, kicking with his legs, arms, and feet like crazy until he became exhausted and stopped for an instant to breathe, but no matter what, Vilma was still a huge whore.

But much less so now because here and now, with the window closed, despite that he was calm, his name was Julius and he was returning from the airport with his mother who is lovely and I adore her, Vilma was a gigantic slut and he didn't have any option but to choose Susan from among the three of them, lurch toward her, hold on to her, hug her neck, and cry out loud: help me! . . . get this off of me! . . . it's like a balloon . . . huge! . . . it's heavy! . . . it's smothering me! . . . it's squeezing me! . . . it hurts! . . . take them away: Vilma! Nilda! Cinthia! . . . But no. No, because Julius won the struggle and the station wagon arrived at the mansion as usual. Absolutely nothing had happened.

It was totally unexplainable, incomprehensible, and indescribable how Julius managed to win the struggle of that moment and arrive home as usual, completely Susan's son, one hundred percent, returning from the airport. He had learned, of course, not to create an uproar in front of Juan Lucas, especially when he has decided to go in and have a drink while Susan changes to go out. No way: Juan Lucas' life always had to be the way he had just decided it should be, so that he could continue to stay so young and healthy. But the moment in which Julius had won the battle it looked more like a situation in which, for example, a man who has decided to cut his veins and hands with the letter opener turns to you and says, "Hold this for a few minutes, I'll be right back for it." It also seemed a lot like the other situation in which a character flees, and suddenly he realizes he's running away and he doesn't know why, after which he begins to feel stronger, and then stronger still, until he stops running, turns around, looks, takes a first step forward, and surprises his pursuer, so that many times the one fleeing loses the most precious seconds, the ones that would have enabled him to make his unexplainable escape.

He ran upstairs to his bedroom. He slammed the door shut in the intimidating whore's face, poor Vilma, almost killing her. Immediately, he searched the whole room to make sure no one was there with him. He breathed deeply, among other things, and opened and closed his eyes, and determined that the enormous and frightening balloon was still outside. And he was totally taken aback by the way he insolently and surprisingly slammed the door.

Susan also went upstairs. But, while she was changing clothes in order to make herself lovelier than ever and preparing to say to Juan Lucas take me to Europe tomorrow, she was disconcerted by the abrupt kiss that he had given her a few moments earlier upon entering the mansion. Poor Susan thought and thought about it, she was distracted as she thought about it, she used the wrong perfume, off in the distance she felt as if she had been left with something, as if Julius had left her something, saying: "Hold it a little while, please, I'll be right back for it." Yes, yes, she knew what she wanted; she wanted desperately to go into his room and give him a big kiss because he's probably sad his brother has left, one never knows with little children. Susan was leaving, she was going to look for him, tragedy! she used the wrong perfume. "And now what am I supposed to do?" she said to herself, bathed in that scent that Juan Lucas detests after six o'clock in the afternoon.

He was stretched out on his bed, the room was dark, and the door was closed all the way. Julius wasn't aware of the danger that had just threatened him. He breathed deep again, searching for tranquility in a moment of necessary relief, now that the battle against the moment had ended. It didn't even occur to him that Susan had almost gone in to look for him and return his kiss, thus ruining his lonely battle.

THAT NIGHT EVERYONE at the mansion was talking: Celso, Daniel, Miss Decisive, Abraham, Marina (the new laundress for Juan Lucas' shirts), Carlos, and Universo. They talked in the kitchen about young Santiago and his friend and the repercussions they could have on Julius who, according to Miss Decisive, had decided to stay in his room and not eat anything until tomorrow. Bobby too, eating dinner alone in the big dining room of the mansion, ended up conversing at length with his instincts: I'm going to sleep tonight, and starting tomorrow it's study straight through until the exam. Meanwhile, as the Jaguar sped along, Susan, without a drop of that perfume Juan Lucas can't stand at night, managed to convince him with ease.

"Whenever you say, dear . . . London first? Do you prefer Madrid?"

"London first, darling," Susan responded, moving closer to him, sacrificing the delicious warm night wind on her extended arm, just like an airplane that takes off for Europe and had allowed her to say so convincingly, Darling, why don't we go to Europe?

Julius was also finishing a long dialogue he had conjured up in the darkness of his bedroom that he, stretched out in his bed, could have done nothing to avoid.

"Mommy, please give me the key to my piggy bank."

"Sure, darling, here."

As soon as Susan handed him the key, Julius took off running because the moment was beginning to resemble that other one in which he lost the battle and because Bobby would soon arrive behaving innocently . . .

"Julius . . . I'm sorry: it was a lie."

"Thanks, Bobby . . . "

"Julius, I'm sorry: it wasn't true."

"I already knew it, Bobby. Thanks . . . "

"Julius . . . "

"Bah! . . . "

"If you give me the key I'll tell you who I'm going to screw tonight!"

"Take the key. Take the piggy bank . . . "

"Here, Julius, take it back: it was only a joke . . . "

"Bah! . . . "

"Julius, I'm sorry."

"Thanks, Bobby . . . But it turned out to be true."

"Let's shake hands, Julius . . . "

"Bah! . . . "

"If you give me the piggy bank . . . "

"I'll give you the key and the piggy bank on the condition that you never tell me . . . "

"I'm sorry, Julius, it was a joke . . . I didn't want to . . . "

"Bah!"

He couldn't continue that way anymore. He was going to die of sadness all by himself. Right then Julius accepted all the conversations he had refused to have because he was intent on selecting only those that were convenient to Bobby or to him. It was as if he had won the battle over the moment, but now it was forever. In an instant, he returned to the first time that Bobby had said to him:

"If you give me your piggy bank, I'll tell you who I'm going to screw."

Right then he ran to Carlos in order to ask him:

"What does screw mean?"

And he even dared to approach the kitchen where Nilda was finishing her story about Vilma. He tried to kid himself, putting Rafaelito Lastarria's face in place of Bobby's, but that was the last time he tried it: he reacted courageously and switched his cousin's face back to the satisfied expression that Bobby had on his face as they returned in the station wagon from the airport. At last he could breathe easy. But in between the enormous relief that he felt and the drowsiness that would come after some hours, there remained a vast, deep, dark void . . . And Julius had no choice but to fill it by sobbing quietly for a long time and, of course, asking a lot of questions.